CHUNG KUO
BOOK ONE
THE MIDDLE KINGDOM

"Tell me, Soren. If you could have one thing — just one single thing — what would it be?"

Berdichev stared across the darkened green a while, then turned and looked back at him, his eyes hidden behind the lenses of his glasses. "No more Han."

Lehmann laughed. "That's quite some wish, Soren."

Wyatt turned to him. "And you, Pietr? The truth this time. No flippancy."

Lehmann leaned back, staring up at the dome's vast curve above them. "That there," he said, lifting his arm slowly and pointing. "That false image of the sky above us. I'd like to make that real. Just that. To have an open sky above our heads. That and the sight of the stars. Not a grand illusion, manufactured for the few, but the reality of it — for everyone."

Berdichev looked up solemnly, nodding. "And you, Edmund? What's the one thing you'd have?"

Wyatt looked across at Berdichev, then at Lehmann. "What would I want?"

He lifted his untouched bowl and held it cupped between his hands. Then, slowly, deliberately, he turned it upside down, letting the contents spill out across the table's top.

"Hey!" said Berdichev, moving backwards sharply. Both he and Lehmann stared at Wyatt, astonished by the sudden hardness in his face, the uncharacteristic violence of the gesture.

"Change," Wyatt said defiantly. "That's what I want. Change. That above everything. Even life."

About the Author

Born in Battersea, South London, in 1954, David Wingrove was educated at Battersea Grammar School. He left school for a career in banking in 1972 and became one of the youngest ever Associates of the Institute of Bankers. Successful but deeply dissatisfied, he left the bank in 1979 and returned to education, obtaining in 1982 a First Class Honours degree in English and American literature from the University of Kent. He then began work on a three-year doctorate, but after successfully completing the Masters degree section of this work found himself bogged down in various projects, including writing several volumes of SF criticism, the care of three young daughters, and writing a novel called A SPRING DAY AT THE EDGE OF THE WORLD (later re-named CHUNG KUO) – all of which led to him abandoning the doctorate in 1986. That year also saw publication of the weighty and authoritative TRILLION YEAR SPREE: THE HISTORY OF SCIENCE FICTION, which he co-authored with Brian Aldiss – a volume which won the prestigious Hugo Award for that year's best non-fiction work in the SF genre. Despite writing for more than fourteen years, CHUNG KUO: THE MIDDLE KINGDOM is, surprisingly, his first novel. He presently lives in Stoke Newington in North London.

DAVID WINGROVE

CHUNG KUO

BOOK ONE

THE MIDDLE KINGDOM

NEW ENGLISH LIBRARY
Hodder and Stoughton

For Susan

"In the window full of sunlight
Concentrates her golden shadow
Fold on fold, until it glows as
Mellow as the glory roses"

Copyright © David Wingrove 1989

First published in Great Britain in
1989 by New English Library
hardbacks

First NEL Open Market
paperback edition 1990

British Library C.I.P.

Wingrove, David
    Chung Kuo: the middle
    kingdom.
    I. Title
    823'.914[F]

    ISBN 0-450-51610-5

Printed and bound in Great Britain
for Hodder and Stoughton
Paperbacks, a division of Hodder
and Stoughton Limited, Mill Road,
Dunton Green, Sevenoaks, Kent
TN13 2YA. (Editorial Office:
47 Bedford Square, London
WC1B 3DP) by Richard Clay
Limited, Bungay, Suffolk. Photoset
by Rowland Phototypesetting
Limited, Bury St Edmunds, Suffolk.

INTRODUCTION

Chung Kuo. The words mean "Middle Kingdom" and, since 221 BC, when the First Emperor, Ch'in Shih Huang Ti, unified the seven Warring States, it is what the "black-haired people", the Han, or Chinese, have called their great country. The Middle Kingdom – for them it was the whole world; a world bounded by great mountain chains to the north and west, by the sea to east and south. Beyond was only desert and barbarism. So it was for two thousand years and through sixteen great dynasties. Chung Kuo *was* the Middle Kingdom, the very centre of the human world, and its Emperor the "Son of Heaven", the "One Man". But in the eighteenth century that world was invaded by the young and aggressive Western powers with their superior weaponry and their unshakeable belief in Progress. It was, to the surprise of the Han, an unequal contest and China's myth of supreme strength and self-sufficiency was shattered. By the early twentieth century China – *Chung Kuo* – was the sick old man of the East: "a carefully preserved mummy in a hermetically sealed coffin" as Karl Marx called it. But from the disastrous ravages of that century grew a giant of a nation, capable of competing with the West and with its own Eastern rivals, Japan and Korea, from a position of incomparable strength. The twenty-first century, "the Pacific century" as it was known even before it began, saw China become once more a world unto itself, but this time its only boundary was space.

"History in China is like an old man's memory. The distant past is often more vivid than the present, and its stories are polished, exaggerated and distorted by many tellings. The Chinese have always looked to their ancestors for their sense of direction and of duty in life. They have had no epics and few creation stories, only history, full of moral examples to be drawn on and evaluated afresh in every generation. For history to the Chinese is not an objective account of the past. It is an endless morality tale in which the characters must be explicit villains and heroes, their virtues and vices made constantly relevant to the present day's concerns."

– Alasdair Clayre, *The Heart of the Dragon*

"Less than a day in paradise,
And a thousand years have passed among men.
While the pieces are still being laid on the board
All things have changed to emptiness.
The woodman takes the road home,
The haft of his axe has rotted in the wind:
Nothing is what it was but the stone bridge
Still spanning a rainbow cinnabar red."

– Meng Chiao, *The Stones Where the Haft Rotted*,
9th century AD

CONTENTS

PROLOGUE-WINTER 2190:

YIN/YANG

"Who built the ten-storeyed tower of jade?
Who foresaw it all in the beginning,
when the first signs appeared?"

Tien Wen ('Heavenly Questions') by
Ch'u Yuan, from the *Ch'u Tz'u*
('Songs Of The South'), 2nd century BC

YIN

In the days before the world began, the first *Ko Ming*
Emperor, Mao Tse Tung, stood on the hillside at
Wuch'ichen in Shensi Province and looked back at the
way he had come. The Long March, that epic journey of
twenty-five thousand *li* over eighteen mountain ranges and
through twelve provinces – each larger than a European
state – was over and, seeing the immensity of China
stretched out before him, Mao raised his arms and addressed
those few of his companions who had survived the year-
long trek.

"Since P'an Ku divided heaven from earth, and the Three
Sovereigns and the Five Emperors reigned, has there ever
been in history a long march like ours? In ten years all
China will be ours. We have come this far – is there
anything we cannot do?"

China. *Chung Kuo*, the Middle Kingdom. So it had been
for more than three thousand years, since the time of the
Chou, long before the First Empire.

So it had been. But now Chung Kuo was more. Not just
a kingdom, but the Earth itself. A world.

In his winter palace, in geostationary orbit 160,000 *li*
above the planet's surface, Li Shai Tung, *T'ang*, Son of
Heaven and Ruler of City Europe, stood on the wide
viewing circle, looking down past his feet at the blue-white
globe of Chung Kuo, thinking.

In the two hundred and fifty-six years that had passed
since Mao had stood on that hill in Shensi province, the
world had changed greatly. Then, it was claimed, the only

3

thing to be seen from space that gave evidence of Man's existence on the planet was the Great Wall of China. Untrue as it was, it said something of the Han ability to plan great projects – and not merely to plan them, but to carry them out. Now, as the twenty-second century entered its final decade, the very look of the world had changed. From space one saw the vast Cities – each almost a continent in itself; great sheets of glacial whiteness masking the old, forgotten shapes of nation states; the world one vast, encircling city: City Earth.

Li Shai Tung stroked his long white beard thoughtfully, then turned from the portal, drawing his embroidered silk *pau* about him. It was warm in the viewing room, yet there was always the illusion of cold, looking down through the darkness of space at the planet far below.

The City. It had been playing on his mind much more of late. Before, he had been too close to it – even up here. He had taken it for granted. Made assumptions he should never have made. But now it was time to face things: to see them in the long perspective.

Constructed more than a century before, the City had been meant to last ten thousand years. It was vast and spacious and its materials needed only refurbishing, never replacing. It was a new world built on top of the old; a giant stilt village perched over the dark, still lake of antiquity.

Thirty decks – three hundred levels – high, each of its hexagonal, hive-like stacks two *li* to a side, there had seemed space enough to hold any number of people. Let Mankind multiply, the Planners had said; there is room enough for all. So it had seemed, back then. Yet in the century that followed the population of Chung Kuo had grown like never before.

Thirty-four billion people at last count, Han and European – *Hung Mao* – combined. And more each year. So many more that in fifty years the City would be full, the storage houses emptied. Put simply, the City was an ever-widening mouth, an ever-larger stomach. It was a thing that ate and shat and grew.

4

Li Shai Tung sighed then made his way up the broad, shallow steps and into his private apartment. Dismissing the two attendants, he went across and pulled the doors closed, then turned and looked back into the room.

It was no good. He would have to bring the matter up in Council. The Seven would have to discuss population controls, like it or no. Or else? Well, at best he saw things stabilised: the City going on into the future; his sons and grandsons born to rule in peace. And at worst?

Uncharacteristically, Li Shai Tung put his hands to his face. He had been having dreams. Dreams in which he saw the Cities burning. Dreams in which old friends were dead – brutally murdered in their beds, their children's bodies torn and bloodied on the nursery floor.

In his dreams he saw the darkness bubble up into the bright-lit levels. Saw the whole vast edifice slide down into the mire of chaos. Saw it as clearly as he saw his hands, now, before his face.

Yet it was more than dreams. It was what would happen – unless they acted.

Li Shai Tung, T'ang, ruler of City Europe, one of the Seven, shuddered. Then, smoothing the front of his *pau*, he sat down at his desk to compose his speech for Council. And as he wrote he was thinking.

We didn't simply change the past, as others tried to do, we built over it, as if to erase it for all time. We tried to do what Mao, in his time, attempted with his Cultural Revolution. What the First Han Emperor, Ch'in Shih Huang Ti, tried to do, two thousand four hundred years ago, when he burned the books and built the Great Wall to keep the northern barbarians from the Middle Kingdom. We have not learned from history. We have preferred to ignore its counsel. But now history is catching up with us. The years ahead will show how wise a course we set. Or blame us for our folly.

He liked the shape of his thoughts and set them down. Then, when he was finished, he got up and went back down the steps to the viewing circle. Darkness was slowly encroaching on City Europe, drawing a stark, dividing line – a terminator – across its hollowed geometric shape, north to south.

No, he thought. We haven't learned. We have been unwise. And now our own Long March is fast approaching. The bright days of ease – of unopposed rule – lie in our past. Ahead lies only darkness.

The old man sighed again, then straightened, feeling the imaginary cold in his bones. Chung Kuo. Would it survive the coming times? Would a son of his look down, as he looked now, and see a world at peace? Or was Change come again, like a serpent, blighting all?

Li Shai Tung turned, then stopped, listening. It came again. An urgent pounding on the outer doors. He made his way through and stood before them.

"Who is it?"

"*Chieh Hsia!* Forgive me. It is I, Chung Hu-Yan."

Coming so hard upon his thoughts, the tone of panic in his Chancellor's voice alarmed him. He threw the doors open.

Chung Hu-Yan stood there, his head bowed low, his mauve sleeping gown pulled tightly about his tall, thin frame. His hair was unbraided and uncombed. It was clear he had come straight from his bed, not stopping to prepare himself.

"What is it, Chung?"

Chung fell to his knees. "It is Lin Yua, *Chieh Hsia*. It seems she has begun . . ."

"Begun?" Instinct made him control his voice, his face, his breathing, but, inside, his heart hammered and his stomach dropped away. Lin Yua, his first wife, was only six months into her pregnancy. How could she have begun? He took a sharp breath, willing himself to be calm.

"Quick, Chung. Take me to her at once."

The doctors looked up from the bedside as he entered, then bowed low and backed hastily away. But a glance at

6

the fear in their eyes told him at once more than he wanted to know.

He looked beyond them, to her bed. "Lin Yua!"

He ran across the room to her, then stopped, his fear transformed into an icy certainty.

"Gods . . ." he said softly, his voice breaking. "Kuan Yin preserve us!"

She lay there, her face pale as the harvest moon, her eyes closed, a blue tinge to her lips and cheeks. The sheets were rucked up beneath her naked legs, as if from some titanic struggle, their whiteness stained almost black with her blood. Her arms lay limply at her sides.

He threw himself down beside her, cradling her to him, sobbing uncontrollably, all thought of sovereign dignity gone from him. She was still warm. Horribly, deceptively warm. He turned her face and kissed it, time and again, as if kissing would bring the life back to it, then began to talk to her, his voice pleading with her.

"Lin Yua . . . Lin Yua . . . My little peach. My darling little one. Where are you, Lin Yua? The gods help us, where *are* you?"

He willed her eyes to open. To smile and say that this was all a game – a test to see how much he loved her. But it was no game. Her eyes stayed closed, their lids impenetrably white; her mouth devoid of breath. And then, at last, he knew.

Gently he lay her head against the pillow, then, with his fingers, combed her hair back lovingly from her brow. Shivering, he sat back from her, then looked up at his Chancellor, his voice hollow with disbelief.

"She's dead, Hu-Yan. My little peach is dead."

"*Chieh Hsia* . . ." The Chancellor's voice quivered with emotion. For once he did not know what to do, what to say. She had been such a strong woman. So filled with life. For her to die . . . No, it was an impossibility. He stared back at the T'ang, his own eyes filled with tears, and mutely shook his head.

There was movement behind him. He turned and looked.

7

It was a nurse. She held a tiny bundle. Something still and silent. He stared at her, appalled, and shook his head violently.

"No, Excellency," the woman began, bowing her head respectfully. "You misunderstand . . ."

Chung Hu-Yan glanced fearfully at the T'ang. Li Shai Tung had turned away; was staring down at his dead wife once again. Knowing he must do something, Chung turned and grabbed the woman's arm. Only then did he see that the child was alive within the blankets.

"It lives?" His whisper held a trace of disbelief.

"*He* lives, Excellency. It's a boy."

Chung Hu-Yan gave a short laugh of surprise. "Lin Yua gave birth to a boy?"

"Yes, Excellency. Four catties he weighs. Big for one born so early."

Chung Hu-Yan stared at the tiny child, then turned and looked back at the T'ang. Li Shai Tung had not noted the woman's entrance. Chung licked his lips, considering things, then decided.

"Go," he told the nurse. "And make sure the child is safe. Your life is forfeit if he dies. Understand me, woman?"

The woman swallowed fearfully, then bowed her head low. "I understand, Excellency. I'll take good care of him."

Chung turned back, then went and stood beside the T'ang.

"*Chieh Hsia?*" he said, kneeling, bowing his head.

Li Shai Tung looked up, his eyes bleak, unfocused, his face almost unrecognisable in its grief.

"*Chieh Hsia*, I . . ."

Abruptly, the T'ang stood and pushed roughly past his Chancellor, ignoring him, confronting instead the group of five doctors who were still waiting on the far side of the room.

"Why was I not summoned earlier?"

The most senior of them stepped forward, bowing. "It was felt, *Chieh Hsia* . . ."

"*Felt?*" The T'ang's bark of anger took the old man by

8

surprise. Pain and anger had transformed Li·Shai Tung. His face glowered. Then he leaned forward and took the man forcibly by the shoulder, throwing him backward.

He stood over him threateningly. "*How* did she die?"

The old man glanced up fearfully from where he lay, then scrambled to his knees again, lowering his head abjectly. "It was her age, *Chieh Hsia*," he gasped. "Forty-two is late to have a child. And then there are the conditions here. They make it dangerous even for a normal labour. Back on Chung Kuo . . .".

"You incompetent butchers! You murderers! You . . ."

Li Shai Tung's voice failed. He turned and looked back helplessly at his dead wife, his hands trembling, his lips parted in surprise. For a moment longer he stood there, lost in his pain, then, with a shudder, he turned back, his face suddenly set, controlled.

"Take them away from here, Chung Hu-Yan," he said coldly, his eyes filled with loathing. "Take them away and have them killed."

"*Chieh Hsia*?" The Chancellor stared at him, astonished. Grief had transformed his master.

The T'ang's voice rose in a roar. "You heard me, Master Chung! Take them away!"

The man at his feet began to plead. "*Chieh Hsia*! Surely we might be permitted . . ."

He glared at the old man, silencing him, then looked up again. Across from him the others, greybeards all, had fallen to their knees in supplication. Now, unexpectedly, Chung Hu-Yan joined them.

"*Chieh Hsia*, I beg you to listen. If you have these men killed, the lives of all their kin will be forfeit too. Let them choose an honourable death. Blame them for Lin Yua's death, yes, but let their families live."

Li Shai Tung gave a visible shudder. His voice was soft now, laced with pain. "But they killed my wife, Chung. They let Lin Yua die."

Chung touched his head to the floor. "I know, *Chieh Hsia*. And for that they will be only too glad to die. But

9

spare their families, I beg you, *Chieh Hsia*. You owe them that much. After all, they saved your son."

"My son?" The T'ang looked up, surprised.

"Yes, *Chieh Hsia*. You have a son. A second son. A strong, healthy child."

Li Shai Tung stood there, frowning fiercely, trying hard to take in this latest, unexpected piece of news. Then, very slowly, his face changed yet again, the pain pushing through his mask of control until it cracked and fell away and he stood there, sobbing bitterly, his teeth clenched in anguish, tears running down his face.

"Go," he said finally in a small voice, turning away from them in a gesture of dismissal. "Order it as you will, Chung. But go. I must be alone with her now."

YANG

It was dark where they sat, at the edge of the terrace overlooking the park. Behind them the other tables were empty now. Inside, at the back of the restaurant, a single lamp shone dimly. Nearby, four waiters stood in shadow against the wall, silent, in attendance. It was early morning. From the far side of the green came the sounds of youthful laughter; unforced, spontaneous. Above them the night sky seemed filled with stars; a million sharp-etched points of brilliance against the velvet blackness.

"It's beautiful," said Wyatt, looking down, then turning back to face the others. "You know, sometimes just the sight of it makes me want to cry. Don't you ever feel that?"

Lehmann laughed softly, almost sadly, and reached out to touch his friend's arm. "I know . . ."

Wyatt let his head tilt back again. He was drunk. They were all drunk, or they wouldn't be speaking like this. It was a kind of treason. The sort of thing a man whispered, or kept to himself. Yet it had to be said. Now. Tonight. Before they broke this intimacy and went their own directions once again.

He leaned forward, his right hand resting on the table, the fist clenched tightly. "And sometimes I feel stifled. Boxed in. There's an ache in me. Something unfulfilled. A *need*. And when I look up at the stars I get angry. I think of the waste, the stupidity of it. Trying to keep it all bottled up. What do they think we are? Machines?" He laughed; a painful laugh, surprised by it all. "Can't they *see* what

11

they're doing to us? Do you think they're blind to it?"

There was a murmur, of sympathy and agreement.

"They can see," said Berdichev, matter-of-factly, stubbing out his cigar, his glasses reflecting the distant image of the stars.

Wyatt looked at him. "Maybe. But sometimes I wonder. You see, it seems to me there's a whole dimension missing. From my life. From yours, Soren, and yours, Pietr. From *everyone's* life. Perhaps the very thing that makes us fully human." He leaned forward dangerously on his chair. "There's no place for growth any more – no more white spaces on the map."

Lehmann answered him drily. "Quite the contrary, Edmund. There's nothing but white."

There was laughter, then, for a short time, silence. The ceiling of the great dome moved imperceptibly, turning about the illusory axis of the north star.

It had been a good night. They had just returned from the Clay, the primitive, unlit region beneath the City's floor. Eight days they had been together in that ancient netherworld of rotting brick and savage half-men. Days that had marked each of them in their own way. Returning they had felt good, but now their mood had changed. When Wyatt next spoke there was real bitterness in his voice.

"They're killing us all. Slowly. Irreversibly. From the centre out. Their stasis is a kind of poison. It hollows the bones."

Lehmann shifted uneasily in his chair. Wyatt turned, then saw and fell silent. The Han waiter came out from the shadows close by them, holding a tray out before him.

"More *ch'a*, sirs?"

Berdichev turned sharply, his face dark with anger. "Have you been listening?"

"Sir?" The Han's face froze into a rictus of politeness, but Wyatt, watching, saw the fear in his eyes.

Berdichev climbed to his feet and faced him, leaning over him threateningly, almost a head taller than the Han.

"You heard me clearly, old hundred names. You were listening to our conversation, weren't you?"

The waiter lowered his head, stung by the bitterness in Berdichev's voice. "No, honoured sir. I heard nothing." His face remained as before, but now his hands trembled, making the bowls rattle on the tray.

Wyatt stood and took his friend's arm gently. "Soren, please . . ."

Berdichev stood there a moment longer, scowling at the man, his resentment like something palpable, flowing out across the space between them, then he turned away, glancing briefly at Wyatt.

Wyatt looked across at the waiter and nodded. "Fill the bowls. Then leave us. Put it all on my bill."

The Han bowed, his eyes flashing gratitude at Wyatt, then quickly filled the bowls.

"Fucking chinks!" Berdichev muttered, once the Han was out of earshot. He leaned forward and picked up his bowl. "You have to watch what you say, these days, Edmund. Even small Han have big ears."

Wyatt watched him a moment, then shrugged. "I don't know. They're not so bad."

Berdichev laughed scornfully. "Devious little shit-eaters they are." He stared out across the green, pulling his silk *pau* tighter about his neck. "I'd rather hand all my companies over to my bitterest rival than have a single one of them in a senior management position."

Lehmann sighed and reached out for his bowl. "I find them useful enough. In their own way."

"As servants, yes . . ." Berdichev laughed sourly, then finished his *ch'a* and set the bowl down heavily. He looked from one to the other of them as he spoke. "You know what they call us behind our backs? Big noses! The cheek of it! Big noses!"

Wyatt looked at Lehmann and both men laughed. He reached out and touched Berdichev's nose playfully. "Well, it's true in your case, Soren, isn't it?"

Berdichev drew his head back, then smiled, relenting.

"Maybe . . ." He sniffed and laughed, then grew serious again. "Maybe so. But I'll be damned if I'll have the little fuckers taking the piss out of me while they're drawing from my pocket!"

"But isn't that true of all men?" Wyatt insisted, feeling suddenly less drunk. "I mean . . . it's not just the Han. Our race – the *Hung Mao* – aren't most of us like that?"

"Speak for yourself," said Lehmann, leaning back, his whole manner poised, indifferent. "However, the Han rule this world of ours. And that changes things. It makes even the most vulgar little Han think he's a T'ang."

"Fucking true!" said Berdichev, wiping at his mouth. "They're arrogant bastards, one and all!"

Wyatt shrugged, unconvinced, then looked from one of his friends to the other. They were harder, stronger men than him. He recognised that. Yet there was something flawed in each of them – some lack of sympathy that marred their natures, fine as they were. He had noted it, down there in the Clay: had seen how they took for granted what he had found horrifying.

Imagination, he thought. It has to do with imagination. With putting yourself in someone else's place. Like the waiter, just then. Or like the woman I met, down there, in the awful squalor of the Clay.

He shivered and looked down at his untouched *ch'a*. He could still see her. Could see the room where they had kept her. Mary, her name had been. Mary . . .

The thought of it chilled his blood. She was still there. There, in the room where he had left her. And who knew which callous bastard would use her next; would choose to beat her senseless, as she had been beaten so often before.

He saw himself again. Watched as he lifted her face to the light and traced the bruise about her eye with his fingers. Gently, aware of how afraid she was of him. He had slept with her finally, more out of pity than from any sense of lust. Or was that fair? Wasn't curiosity part of what he'd felt? So small she'd been, her arms so thin, her breasts almost non-existent. And yet pretty, strangely pretty, for

14

all that. Her eyes, particularly, had held some special quality – the memory, perhaps, of something better than this she had fallen into.

He had been wrong to leave her there. And yet, what choice had he had? That was her place, this his. So it was fated in this world. And yet there must be something he could do.

"What are you thinking, Edmund?"

He looked up, meeting Lehmann's eyes. "I was thinking about the woman."

"The woman?" Berdichev glanced across at him, then laughed. "Which one? There were hundreds of the scrawny things!"

"And boys . . ."

"We won't forget the boys . . ."

He looked away, unable to join their laughter, angry with himself for feeling as he did. Then his anger took a sudden shape and he turned back, leaning across the table towards them.

"Tell me, Soren. If you could have one thing – just one single thing – what would it be?"

Berdichev stared across the darkened green a while, then turned and looked back at him, his eyes hidden behind the lenses of his glasses. "No more Han."

Lehmann laughed. "That's quite some wish, Soren."

Wyatt turned to him. "And you, Pietr? The truth this time. No flippancy."

Lehmann leaned back, staring up at the dome's vast curve above them. "That there," he said, lifting his arm slowly and pointing. "That false image of the sky above us. I'd like to make that real. Just that. To have an open sky above our heads. That and the sight of the stars. Not a grand illusion, manufactured for the few, but the reality of it – for everyone."

Berdichev looked up solemnly, nodding. "And you, Edmund? What's the one thing you'd have?"

Wyatt looked across at Berdichev, then at Lehmann. "What would I want?"

15

He lifted his untouched bowl and held it cupped between his hands. Then, slowly, deliberately, he turned it upside down, letting the contents spill out across the table's top.

"Hey!" said Berdichev, moving backwards sharply. Both he and Lehmann stared at Wyatt, astonished by the sudden hardness in his face, the uncharacteristic violence of the gesture.

"Change," Wyatt said defiantly. "That's what I want. Change. That above everything. Even life."

PART 1 - SPRING 2196:

A SPRING DAY AT THE EDGE OF THE WORLD

———— · ————

"A spring day at the edge of the world.
On the edge of the world once more the day slants.
The oriole cries, as though it were its own tears
Which damp even the topmost blossoms on the tree."

– Li Shang-yin, *Exile*, 9th century AD

CHAPTER·1

FIRE AND ICE

Flames danced in a glass. Beyond, in the glow of the naked fire, a man's face smiled tightly.

"Not long now," he said, coming closer to the fierce, wavering light. He had delicate, oriental features that were almost feminine; a small, well-shaped nose and wide, dark eyes that caught and held the fire's light. His jet black hair was fastened in a pigtail then coiled in a tight bun at the back of his head. He wore white, the colour of mourning – a simple one-piece that fitted his small frame loosely.

A warm night wind blew across the mountainside, making the fire flare up. The coals at its centre glowed intensely. Ash and embers whirled off. Then the wind died and the shadows settled.

"They've taken great pains, Kao Jyan."

The second man walked back from the darkness where he'd been standing and faced the other across the flames, his hands open, empty. He was a much bigger man, round-shouldered and heavily-muscled. His large, bony head was freshly shaven and his whites fitted him tightly. His name was Chen and he had the blunt, nondescript face of a thousand generations of Han peasants.

Jyan studied his partner momentarily. "They're powerful men," he said. "They've invested much in us. They expect much in return."

"I understand," Chen answered, looking down the moonlit valley towards the City. Then, unexpectedly, he laughed.

"What is it?" Jyan narrowed his eyes.

"See!" Chen pointed off to his right. "There! Up there where the mountains almost touch the clouds."

Jyan looked. Thin strands of wispy cloud lay across the moon's full circle, silvered by its intense light. Beyond, the sky was a rich blue-black. "So?"

Chen turned back to him, his eyes shining in the firelight. "It's beautiful, don't you think? How the moonlight has painted the mountain tops white."

Jyan shivered, then stared past the big man towards the distant peaks. "It's ice."

"What? Plastic, you mean?"

Jyan shook his head. "No. Not the stuff the City's made of. Real ice. Frozen water. Like the *ch'un tzu* put in their drinks."

Chen turned and looked again, his broad face wrinkling. Then he looked away sharply, as if the very thought disturbed him.

As it should, thought Jyan, aware of his own discomfort. The drugs he'd been given made all of this seem familiar – gave him false memories of such things as cold and clouds and moonlight – yet, beneath the surface calm of his mind, his body was still afraid.

There was a faint movement against his cheek, a sudden ruffling of his hair. At his feet the fire flared up again, fanned by the sudden gust. Wind, thought Jyan, finding it strange even to think the word. He bent down and lifted a log from the pile, turning it in his hand and feeling its weight. Then he turned it on its end and stared at the curious whorl of its grain. Strange. Everything so strange out here, outside the City. So unpredictable. All of it so crudely thrown together. So unexpected, for all that it seemed familiar.

Chen came and stood by him. "How long now?"

Jyan glanced at the dragon timer inset into the back of his hand. "Four minutes."

He watched Chen turn and – for what seemed like the hundredth time – look back at the City, his eyes widening, trying to take it in.

The City. It filled the great northern plain of Europe. From where they stood, on the foothills of the Alps, it stretched away northward a thousand five hundred *li* to meet the chill waters of the Baltic, while to the west the great wall of its outer edge towered over the Atlantic for the full three thousand *li* length of its coastline, from Cape St Vincent in the south to Kristiansund in the rugged north. To the south, beyond the huge mountain ranges of the Swiss Wilds, its march continued, ringing the Mediterranean like a giant bowl of porcelain. Only to the east had its growth been checked unnaturally, in a jagged line that ran from Danzig in the north to Odessa in the south. There the plantations began; a vast sea of greenness that swept into the heart of Asia.

"It's strange, isn't it? Being outside. It doesn't seem real."

Chen did not answer. Looking past him, Jyan saw how the dark, steep slopes of the valley framed a giant, flat-topped arrowhead of whiteness. It was like a vast wall – a dam two *li* in height – plugging the end of the valley. Its surface was a faintly opalescent pearl, lit from within. *Ch'eng*, it was. City and wall. The same word in his mother tongue for both. Not that he knew more than a smattering of his mother tongue.

He turned his head and looked at Chen again. Brave Chen. Unimaginative Chen. His blunt face rounded like a plate, his bull neck solid as the rocks surrounding them. Looking at him, Jyan put aside his earlier misgivings. Chen was *kwai*, after all – a trained knife – and *kwai* were utterly reliable. Jyan smiled to himself. Yes, Chen was all right. A good man to have at your back.

"You're ready?" he asked.

Chen looked back at him, his eyes firm, determined. "I know what I have to do."

"Good."

Jyan looked down into his glass. Small tongues of flame curled like snakes in the darkness of the wine; cast evanescent traces on the solid curve of transparency. He threw the glass down into the fire, then stared into the flames themselves, aware for the first time how evasive they were; how, when you tried to hold their image clear in mind, it slipped away, leaving only the vaguest of impressions. Not real at all, for all its apparent clarity. Perhaps that's how the gods see us, he thought; as mere traces, too brief for the eye to settle on.

There was a sharp crack as the glass split and shattered. Jyan shivered, then looked up, hearing the low drone of the approaching craft.

"They're here," said Chen, his face impassive.

Jyan looked across at the *kwai* and nodded. Then, buttoning their one-pieces at the neck, the two assassins made their way towards the ship.

* * *

"Your pass, sir?"

Pi Ch'ien, Third Secretary to Junior Minister Yang, glanced up at the camera, noting as he did the slow, smooth movement of the overhead trackers, the squat, hollowed tongues of their barrels jutting from the mouths of stylised dragons. Bowing low he took the card from his robe and inserted it into the security slot. Placing his face against the moulded pad in the wall, he held his left eye open against the camera lens. Then he stepped back, looking about him.

He had never been into one of the Imperial Solariums before. Even as District Magistrate, responsible for the lives of the twenty thousand people in his deck, he had lacked the status to enter such a place. Now, however, as Third Secretary to Yang Lai, he had been permitted to place his name on the list. But the list was a list, like all the others in this world – interminable. It would be many years and several more promotions before he would find himself inside for reasons of leisure.

The outer doors slid back and he made to go through.

An armed guard barred his way, indicating with his gun that Pi Ch'ien should go into the antechamber to his left. With a bow, Pi Ch'ien did as he was bid. Inside, in front of a vast, brightly-coloured tapestry that filled the whole of the back wall, an official sat at a desk. The man scanned the screen in front of him, then looked up, smiling.

"Good evening, Third Secretary Pi. I am First Steward Huong. Might I ask the purpose of your visit?"

Pi Ch'ien bent his head respectfully.

"Greetings, First Steward Huong. I have but a trivial message to deliver. For his serene excellency, Junior Minister Yang Lai. Ten thousand pardons for imposing on you like this, for it is a matter of the least urgency."

He looked up, holding out the almost translucent message card for the Steward's inspection. Both men knew it was immensely important.

"Forgive me, Third Secretary Pi, but might I have that?"

Again Pi Ch'ien lowered his head. "My deepest apologies, First Steward Huong. Nothing would please me more than to oblige you, but I am afraid that is not possible. I was instructed to place the message, unimportant as it is, only in the hands of the most illustrious Junior Minister himself."

Steward Huong stood, then came round his desk to stand beside Pi Ch'ien. "I understand, Third Secretary Pi. We are but our masters' hands, neh?" He smiled again, all courtesy now. "If you would be so kind as to permit me, I shall inform the Junior Minister."

Pi Ch'ien bowed, feeling a pang of disappointment. He was not to go inside, then?

"Please, follow me, Third Secretary," the Steward said, making the slightest bow, his head barely lowered as befitted their relative positions. "Junior Minister Yang is with the Minister himself and may not be disturbed at once. However, I will have a maid come and serve tea for you while you wait."

Pi Ch'ien bowed again, delighted by the courtesy he was being shown. He followed the official out and down a wide, high-ceilinged corridor on the walls of which hung a series of huge *shanshui* landscape paintings, depicting rugged peaks and pleasantly wooded valleys.

Where the corridor turned he had a brief glimpse of

another, more ornate passageway lined with bronze statues of gods and dragons, and, at its end a huge, brightly-lit chamber – the solarium itself. They walked on until they came to a small but plushly-decorated room, hung with colourful tapestries.

First Steward Huong turned to him and smiled, indicating that he should enter and take a seat. "Please be assured, I will keep you no longer than I must, Third Secretary. The maid, meanwhile, will see to all your needs." Then, with a bow, he was gone.

Almost at once a maid entered from a door to one side. She was wearing powder blue er-silks with a pattern of tiny yellow sunflowers. Smiling, she set down the tray she was carrying on a low table at Pi Ch'ien's side, then knelt and bowed low to him. Straightening up, she poured the *ch'a* and offered it to him, her eyes averted. He took the cup, studying her closely. She was a pretty little thing, her skin almost white, her dark, fine hair tied with silk ribbons of blue and yellow. He looked down at her feet and saw, with satisfaction, how petite she was.

"You would like something else, sir?"

He leaned forward and gently drew back the hair to reveal her neck. It was as he had thought. There was a small circular mark low down on the left hand side of the neck, close to the collar bone. A Capital G with a smaller S inside, the letters English, but the style – the brushwork of the design – pure Han. She was GenSyn. Artificial.

He hesitated, not knowing how long the Junior Minister would be, nor what etiquette prevailed here. Then he remembered the First Steward Huong's words. "The maid will see to all your needs." Screwing up his courage, he told the girl to close the door.

As she turned to face him again, he beckoned her back. Then, making her bow before him, he opened the front of his cloak and drew her head down into his naked lap.

"Here, girl. See to me."

* * *

24

The three men in the craft had been masked and silent; even so, Kao Jyan had recognised them as *Hung Mao* – whites – from the sour, milky scent of their sweat. It had surprised him. His own guesses had taken him in another direction. But even as the craft set down on the roof of the City he was adding this new fragment to what he already knew.

When the door hissed open he went through quickly, followed by Chen. The dome of the Imperial Solarium was directly ahead of them, no more than a *li* – five hundred metres – distant; a vast hemispherical blister, lit from within. Half a *li* further on was the maintenance shaft. The two assassins ran, side by side, in silence, knowing that if others hadn't done their work properly they were already as good as dead.

But it would be okay. Jyan sensed it. Every step he took made him more certain of it. He was beginning to see how things connected, could even begin to make guesses as to names and motives.

There were those who would pay well to know such things. Who would grant amnesties, perhaps, to those who were merely the tools of other men.

Coming closer to the dome Jyan slowed, looking about him. The moon was much lower now, over to the right of them. In its light it seemed as though they were running on the surface of a giant glacier.

"Circle left," he said softly to Chen. But it was unnecessary. Chen was already moving out around the dome towards the shaft. It was his job to secure it while Jyan was at work.

Jyan stopped, looking down at the dragon on his wrist. Timing was crucial now. He had four minutes to climb the outer wall, then three minutes a-piece after that to position and set each of the four charges. That left nine minutes to get into the shaft and away. If all went well it would be easy.

If all went well. Jyan took a deep breath, steeling himself. He knelt, then reached behind him. Four catches fastened the lightweight parcel. Gently his fingers released the catches and eased the cloth-wrapped package from his back. Carefully he laid it in his lap and, with delicate, practised movements, drew back the thin folds of cloth.

The four plate-sized hoops had been bound together tightly with a hair-fine wire. They were a dull bronze in colour, unmarked except in one place, where it seemed the finger-thick cords joined upon themselves, like snakes swallowing their tails. Quickly, carefully, he untied the wire knots and separated the hoops into two piles on his upper thighs. They were warm to the touch, as if alive. With the slightest shudder he pulled two of them up over his left arm, looping them gently over his shoulder, then did the same with the others, securing them about his right shoulder.

Taking a deep breath, he stood again. Chen was out of sight, behind the dome. Quickly Jyan ran the final distance to the dome's base and crouched there, breathing easily. From the pocket over his heart he took out the claws and clicked them open. Separating them, he eased them onto his hands, respecting the razor-sharpness of their tips. That done, he began to climb.

★ ★ ★

Lwo Kang, son of Lwo Chun-Yi and Minister of the Edict, sat back in his tall-backed chair and looked around the circle of men gathered about him. The folds of his salmon pink *pau* hung loosely about him and his olive flesh glistened damply in the dome's intense light. He had a strong, but somehow ugly face; his eyes too big, his nose too broad, his ears too pendulous. Yet when he smiled the faces of the dozen men seated about him returned his smile like mirrors. Just now, however, those men were silent and watchful, conscious that their lord was angry.

"You talk of accommodation, Shu San, but the Edict is quite clear on this. We are not here to interpret but to implement. We do as we are told, neh?"

To Lwo Kang's left, Shu San bowed his head abjectly.

26

For a moment all eyes were on him, sharing his moment of shame. Minister Lwo sniffed, then spoke again.

"Only this afternoon two of these businessmen – Lehmann and Berdichev – came to me. We talked of many things in the course of our audience, but finally they presented me with what they termed an 'ultimatum'." Lwo Kang looked sternly about the circle of his junior ministers. "They said that certain factions were growing impatient. *Hsien Sheng* Lehmann even had the impudence to claim that we have been subjecting them to unnecessary delays. He says that our officials have been over-zealous in their application of the Edict's terms."

There was an exchange of glances between the seated men. None had missed that the Minister had used the term *Hsien Sheng* for Lehmann – plain *Mister* Lehmann, not even the commonplace *Shih* or *Master* – when proper etiquette demanded the use of his full title, Under Secretary. It was a deliberate slight.

Lwo Kang laughed sharply, sourly, then shook his head in an angry gesture. "The impertinence of these men! Because they have money they think themselves above the laws of other men!" His face formed a sneer of disgust. "*Hsin fa ts'ai!*"

This time there was mild laughter from some quarters. Others, not understanding the term, looked about them for guidance, and formed their faces into smiles, as if half-committed to the joke.

Again Lwo Kang sniffed and sat back a little in his chair. "I'm sorry. I forgot. We are not all *ch'un tzu* here, are we?"

Lwo Kang looked about him. *Hsin fa ts'ai.* Social upstarts. *Ch'un tzu.* Gentlemen. These were *Kuan hua*, or Mandarin terms. But not all were bred to the tongue who sat about him. More than half the men here had come up through the levels; had schooled themselves in the five Confucian classics and climbed the ladder of the examination system. He did not despise them for that; quite the contrary, he prided himself on promoting men not through connection but because of their natural ability. However, it sometimes

27

made for awkwardnesses. He fixed his gaze on Shu San.

"We will say no more of this, Shu San. You know now how I feel. We will have no further talk of accommodation. Nor will I see these men again."

Shu San bowed his head, then met his lord's eyes, grateful for this second chance. He had come expecting less.

Lwo Kang smiled and looked away, his whole manner changing, relaxing. He had the reputation of being a scrupulously fair man, honest beyond reproach and incorruptible. But that was not to say he was liked. His appointment, three years earlier, had surprised some who saw family connection as a more important quality in a man than honesty or competence. Nonetheless, Lwo Kang had proved a good choice as Minister responsible for the implementation of the Edict.

While his subordinates talked among themselves, Lwo Kang sat back, contemplating what had happened earlier that day. It did not surprise him that there were those who wanted to subvert the Edict's guidelines. So it had ever been, for the full 114 years of the Edict's existence. What disturbed him more was the growing arrogance of those who felt they knew best – that they had the right to challenge the present order of things. These *Hung Mao* had no sense of place. No sense of *Li*. Of *propriety*.

The problem was one of race. Of culture. Though more than a century had passed since the foundation of Chung Kuo and the triumph of Han culture, for those of European stock – the *Hung Mao*, or "redheads" as they were commonly known – the ways of the Han were still unnatural; were at best surface refinements grafted on to a cruder and less stable temperament. Three thousand years of unbroken civilisation – that was the heritage of the Han. Against that these large-nosed foreigners could claim what? Six centuries of chaos and ill-discipline. Wars and further wars and, ultimately, collapse. Collapse on a scale that made their previous wars seem like oases of calm. No, they might seem like Han – might dress and talk and act like Han – but beneath it all they remained barbarians. The New

Confucianism was rooted only shallowly in the infertile soil of their natures. At core they were still the same selfish, materialistic, individualistic species they had ever been; motivated more by greed than duty.

Was it so surprising, then, that men like Lehmann and Berdichev failed to understand the necessity of the Edict?

Change, they wanted. Change, at any cost. And because the Edict of Technological Control was the Seven's chief means of preventing the cancer of change, it was the Edict they tried to undermine at every turn.

Lwo Kang leaned back, staring up at the roof of the dome high overhead. The two great arches of the solarium met in a huge circular tablet, halved by a snake-like S into black and white. *Yin* and *Yang*, he thought. Balance. These Westerners have never understood it; not properly – not in their bones. It still seems some kind of esoteric game to them, not life itself, as it is to us. Change – the empty-headed pursuit of the new – that was the real enemy of civilisation.

He sighed, then leaned to his right, listening, becoming at once the focus of their talk.

They are good men, he thought, looking along the line of faces. Han, every one of them. Men I could trust my life with.

Servants passed amongst them, dumb mutes who carried trays of *ch'a* and sweetmeats. GenSyn eunuchs, half-men in more senses than one. Yet even they were preferable to the likes of Lehmann and Berdichev.

Yang Lai was talking now, the tenor of his words strangely reflective of Lwo Kang's thoughts.

"It's a disease that's rife amongst the whole of this new generation. Things have changed, I tell you. They are not like their fathers, solid and dependable. No, they're ill-mannered brutes, every last one of them. And they think they can buy change."

Lwo Kang stretched his bull neck and nodded. "They lack respect," he said.

There was a murmur of agreement. Yang Lai bowed,

then answered him. "That's true, my lord. But then, they are not Han. They could never be *ch'un tzu*. They have no values. And look at the way they dress!"

Lwo Kang smiled, sitting back again. Though only in his late-thirties he was already slightly balding. He had inherited his father's looks – a thick-set body already going to fat at waist and upper chest – and, like his father, he had never found the time for exercise. He smiled, knowing how he looked to them. I am not a vain man, he thought; and in truth I'd be a liar to myself if I were. Yet I have their respect.

No, it was not by outward show that a man was to be judged, but by his innermost qualities; qualities that lay behind his every action.

His father, Lwo Chun-Yi, had been born a commoner; even so, he had proved himself worthy and had been appointed Minister to Li Shai Tung in the first years of his reign. Because of that, Lwo Kang had been educated to the highest level and had learned the rudiments of service in his earliest years. Now he in his turn was the T'ang's Minister. He looked about him again, satisfied. No, there was not one here who did not know him for their master.

"What these *Hung Mao* need is a lesson," he said, leaning forward to take a shrimp and snow pickle sweetmeat from the tray on the footstool next to him. He gulped it down, savouring the sweet, spicy *hoisin* sauce on his tongue, and belched appreciatively. "A lesson in manners."

* * *

Jyan clung to the outside of the dome like a small, dark insect. Three of the hoops were set. It remained only to place and arm the last charge.

Where he rested, one hand attaching him to the dome's taut skin, the slope was relatively gentle. He could look out over the capped summit of the dome and see the distant, moon-washed peaks. It was a beautiful night. Clear, like glass. Above him the stars shone like polished jewels against the blackness. So many stars. So vast the blackness.

He looked down. Concentrate, he told himself. You've no time for star-gazing. Even so, he took a final glimpse. Then, working quickly, he placed and fastened the hoop, taping it at four points. That done, he tugged gently but firmly at the joint.

Where he pulled at it, the hoop came apart, a thin thread joining tail to mouth. Like a snake's wire-thin tongue, he thought. Fully-extended, the thread was as long as his little finger. Already it was being coiled back into the body of the hoop. Eventually the ends would join up again and the hoop would send out a trigger signal. When all four were primed, they would form a single, destructive harmonic. And then.

Slowly, carefully, he backed away, edging back down the steepening wall of the dome. Like all else in the City its skin was made of the super-plastic, ice. Normal charges would scarcely have dented the steel-tough, fire-resistant skin, but these would eat right through it before they detonated.

He was balanced at the point where the dome wall fell sharply away when he stopped, hearing a noise beneath him. He turned his head slowly, scarcely daring to breath. Who in the gods' names . . . ?

The figure was directly underneath, staring up at him. As Jyan turned his face a brilliant beam of light shone directly into his eyes.

"You! What are you doing up there?"

Jyan looked away, momentarily blinded, then looked back in time to see Chen coming up behind the man.

The man turned quickly, sensing something behind him. As Chen struck out with his knife, the man raised the big torch he was carrying and deflected the blow.

Chen's knife went clattering across the roof.

For a moment the two faced each other warily, then Chen moved, circling the newcomer. He feinted, making the other back off, then dropped to his knees, searching for his knife in the shadows at the base of the dome.

The man looked at his torch, considering whether to use

it as a weapon and go for Chen. Then he turned and ran off to the right, where a faint patch of light revealed a second maintenance hatch.

"*Pien hua*!" swore Jyan under his breath. Loosening the claws, he dropped the last five metres and rolled. Crouched there, he looked about him.

He saw Chen at once, to his right, running after the stranger. But the man was already at the hatch and climbing down.

"Shit!" he said desperately, trying to ease the claws from his hands as quickly as he could. "Shit! Shit! Shit!" If the bastard got to an alarm they would both be done for.

He looked up in time to see Chen disappear down the hatch.

"Hurry, Chen!" he murmured anxiously, folding the claws and tucking them away in his pocket. He turned, looking back up the dome's steep slope, then glanced down at the dragon timer in his wrist. Six minutes. That was all that remained.

And if Chen failed?

He swallowed drily, then began to run towards the second shaft, his heart pounding in his chest. "Shit!" he kept saying. "Shit! Shit!"

He was only twenty *ch'i* from it when a figure lifted from the hatch and turned to face him.

"*Ai-ya*!" He pulled up sharply, gasping with fear, but it was Chen. The *kwai* looked up, the broad shape of his face and chest lit from beneath, his breath pluming up into the chill air.

"Where is he?" hissed Jyan anxiously, hurrying forward again. "Oh, gods! You didn't let him get away, did you?"

Chen reached down and pulled the man up by the hair. "He's dead," he said tonelessly, letting the corpse fall back. "There was no other way. He was trying to open a Security panel when I came on him. Now we'll have to find some-where to hide him."

Jyan shuddered, filled with relief. "Thank the gods." He

32

turned and glanced back at the dome. "Let's go, then. Before it blows."

"Yes," said Chen, a faintly ironic smile lighting his big, blunt face. "The rest should be easy. Like the bamboo before the blade."

* * *

The maid had gone. Pi Ch'ien sat alone in the room, his *ch'a* long finished, contemplating the fifteen hundred year old painting of Hsiao Wen Ti that hung on the wall above the door. It was Yen Li-pen's famous painting from the *Portraits of the Emperors*, with the Han Emperor attended by his Ministers.

Every schoolboy knew the story of Wen Ti, first of the great Emperors. It was he who, more than twenty three centuries before, had created the concept of Chung Kuo; who, through his thorough adoption of the Confucian virtues, had made of his vast but rag-tag land of warring nations a single State, governed by stern but just principles. Wen Ti it was who had first brought commoners into his government. He who had changed the harsh laws and customs of his predecessors so that no one in the Middle Kingdom would starve or suffer cruel injustice. Famine relief, pensions and the abolition of punishment by mutilation – all these were Wen Ti's doing. He had lowered taxes and done away with the vast expense of Imperial display. He had sought the just criticism of his Ministers and acted to better the lot of the Han. Under his rule Chung Kuo had thrived and its population grown.

Eighteen hundred years later, the Manchu Emperor, K'ang Hsi, had established his great empire on Wen Ti's principles, and, later still, when the Seven had thrown off the yoke of the tyrant, Tsao Ch'un, they too had adopted the principles of Wen Ti's reign, making him the First Ancestor of Chung Kuo. Now Wen Ti's painting hung everywhere in the City, in a thousand shapes and forms. This, however, was a particularly fine painting – a perfect reproduction of Yen Li-pen's original.

Pi Ch'ien got up and went over to the painting, remembering the time when his father had stood there with him
beneath another copy of the portrait and told him the story
of the finding of the handscroll.

For centuries the *Portraits of the Emperors* roll had been
housed in a museum in the ancient town of Boston, along
with much more that had rightly belonged to the Han.
When the American Empire had finally collapsed much had
been lost. Most of the old Han treasures had been destroyed
out of spite, but some had been hidden away. Years had
passed. Then, in the years when the Han were building
their City over the old land of America, skilled teams
had been sent across that continent to search for the old
treasures. Little was found of real value until, in an old,
crumbling building on the shoreline of what had once been
called California, they had found a simple cardboard box
containing the scroll. The handscroll was remarkably preserved considering its ill-use, but even so, four of the
original thirteen portraits had been lost. Fortunately, the
painting of Hsiao Wen Ti was one of those which had
emerged unscathed.

He turned away and went back to his seat. For a second
or two longer he contemplated the painting, delighted by
the profound simplicity of its brushwork, then leaned across
and picked up the handbell. He was. about to lift the tiny
wooden hammer to ring for more *ch'a* when the door
swung open and Yang Lai came hurriedly into the room.

Pi Ch'ien scrambled to his feet and bowed low.

"Well, Pi Ch'ien?" Yang Lai barked impatiently. "What
is it?"

His expression showed he was far from pleased by his
Third Secretary's intrusion.

Pi Ch'ien remained bowed, the card held out before him.
"I have an urgent message for you, Excellency. I was told
to bring it here at once."

"Give it here!" Yang Lai said irritably.

Pi Ch'ien edged forward and handed the card across.
Yang Lai stared at it a moment, then turned away. With

34

upturned eyes Pi Ch'ien watched him tap his personal code into the Instruct box and place his thumb against the Release.

There was a moment's silence from Yang Lai, then he gasped. When he turned to face Pi Ch'ien again, his face was ashen. For a moment his mouth worked silently, then, without another word, he turned and left the room, his silk cloak flapping as he ran.

Pi Ch'ien lifted his head, astonished. For a moment he stood there, rooted to the spot. Then he rushed across the room and poked his head out into the corridor.

The corridor was empty. There was no sign of Yang Lai.

He looked back into the room. There, on the floor, was the message card. He went across and picked it up, then turned it in his hand, studying it. Without Yang Lai's thumb on the Release pad the surface of the card was blank; even so, it might prove interesting to keep.

Pi Ch'ien hesitated, not certain what to do. Yang Lai had not formally dismissed him; but then, he had fulfilled his duty – had delivered the message. Surely, then, it was all right for him to go. He went to the door and looked out again. The corridor was still empty. Careful now, conscious of the watching cameras, he stepped outside and pulled the door shut behind him. Then, composing himself, trying to ignore the strong feeling of wrongness that was growing in him by the moment, he began to walk towards the entrance hall.

* * *

There was movement up ahead. Chen crouched in the narrow circle of the horizontal shaft, perfectly still, listening. Beside him, tensed, his breathing like the soft hiss of a machine, Jyan waited.

Chen turned, smiling reassuringly. In the dim overhead light Jyan's face seemed more gaunt than normal, his cheekbones more hollow. The roseate light made him seem almost demonic, his cold, black eyes reflecting back two

35

tiny points of redness. Chen wanted to laugh, looking at him. Such delicate features he had; such neat, small ears. He could imagine how Jyan's mother would have loved those ears – back when Jyan had yet had a mother.

He looked away, sobered by the thought. It's why we're here, he realised, waiting, knowing the noise, the movement would go away. If we had loved ones we would never have got involved in this. We're here because we have no one. Nothing to connect us to the world.

Chen kept his thoughts to himself; like a good *kwai* he cultivated the appearance of stupidity. Like all else, it was a weapon. He had been taught to let his enemies underestimate him; to always keep something back – something in reserve. And lastly, to make no friends.

Ahead it went silent again. He waited, making sure, then began to move up the access tunnel once more, his right hand feeling his way along the tunnel wall. And as he moved he could sense Jyan immediately behind him; silent, trusting.

★ ★ ★

Minister Lwo pulled himself up out of his chair and stretched his legs. It was almost time to call it an evening, but first he'd dip his body in the pool and cool off. His Junior Ministers had risen to their feet when he had stood. Now he signalled them to be seated again. "Please, gentlemen, don't break your talk for me."

He moved between them, acknowledging their bows, then down three steps and past a lacquered screen, into the other half of the dome. Here was a miniature pool, its chest-deep waters cool and refreshing after the heat of the solarium. Small shrubs and potted trees surrounded it on three sides, while from the ceiling above hung a long, elegant cage, housing a dozen songbirds.

As he stood there at the pool's edge two attendants hurried across to help him undress, then stood there, heads bowed respectfully, holding his clothes, as he eased himself into the water.

He had been there only moments when he heard the pad of feet behind him. It was Lao Jen.

"May I join you, Excellency?"

Lwo Kang smiled. "Of course. Come in, Jen."

Lao Jen had been with him longest and was his most trusted advisor. He was also a man with connections, hearing much that would otherwise have passed the Minister by. His sister had married into one of the more important of the Minor Families and fed him juicy titbits of Above gossip. These he passed on to Lwo Kang privately.

Lao Jen threw off his *pau* and came down the steps into the water. For a moment the two of them floated there, facing each other. Then Lwo Kang smiled.

"What news, Jen? You surely have some."

"Well," he began, speaking softly so that only the Minister could hear. "It seems that today's business with Lehmann is only a small part of things. Our friends the Dispersionists are hatching bigger, broader schemes. It seems they have formed a faction – a pressure group – in the House. It's said they have more than two hundred Representatives in their pocket."

Lwo Kang nodded. He had heard something similar. "Go on."

"More than that, Excellency. It seems they're going to push to reopen the starflight programme."

Lwo Kang laughed. Then he lowered his voice. "You're serious? The starflight programme?" He shook his head, surprised. "Why, that's been dead a century and more! What's the thinking behind that?"

Lao Jen ducked his head, then surfaced again, drawing his hand back through his hair. "It's the logical outcome of their policies. They are, after all, Dispersionists. They want breathing space. Want to be free of the City and its controls. Their policies make no sense unless there is somewhere to disperse to."

"I've always seen them otherwise, Jen. I've always thought their talk of breathing space was a political mask. A bargaining counter. And all this nonsense about opening

37

up the colony planets, too. No one in their right mind would want to live out there. Why, it would take ten thousand years to colonise the stars!" He grunted, then shook his head. "No, Jen, it's all a blind. Something to distract us from the real purpose of their movement."

"Which is what, Excellency?"

Lwo Kang smiled faintly, knowing Lao Jen was sounding him. "They are *Hung Mao* and they want to rule. They feel we Han have usurped their natural right to control the destiny of Chung Kuo, and they want to see us under. That's all there is to it. All this business of stars and planetary conquest is pure nonsense – the sort of puerile idiocy their minds ran to before we purged them of it."

Lao Jen laughed. "Your Excellency sees it clearly. Nevertheless, I . . . "

He stopped. Both men turned, standing up in the water. It came again. A loud hammering at the inner door of the solarium. Then there were raised voices.

Lwo Kang climbed up out of the water and without stopping to dry himself, took his *pau* from the attendant and pulled it on, tying the sash at the waist. He had taken only two steps forward when a security guard came down the steps towards him.

"Minister!" he said breathlessly, bowing low. "The alarm has been sounded. We must evacuate the dome!"

Lwo Kang turned, dumbstruck, and looked back at Lao Jen.

Lao Jen was standing on the second step, the water up to his shins. He was looking up. Above him the songbirds were screeching madly and fluttering about their cage.

Lwo Kang took a step back towards Lao Jen, then stopped. There was a small plop and a fizzing sound. Then another. He frowned, then looked up past the cage at the ceiling of the dome. There, directly above the pool, the smooth white skin of the dome was impossibly charred. There, only an arm's length from where the wire that held the cage was attached, was a small, expanding halo of darkness. Even as he watched, small gobbets of melted ice

38

dropped from that dark circle and fell hissing into the water.

"Gods!" he said softly, astonished. "What in heaven's name . . . ?"

Then he understood. Understood, at the same moment, that it was already too late. "Yang Lai," he said almost inaudibly, straightening up, seeing in his mind the back of his Junior Minister as he hurried from the dome. "Yes. It must have been Yang Lai . . ."

But the words were barely uttered when the air turned to flame.

* * *

The patrol craft was fifteen *li* out when its tail camera, set on automatic search-and-scan, trained itself on the first brief flicker from the dome. On a panel above the navigator's head a light began to flash. At once the pilot banked the craft steeply, turning towards the trace.

They were almost facing the dome when the whole of the horizon seemed to shimmer and catch fire.

The pilot swore. "What in *Chang-e*'s name is that?!"

"The mountains . . ." said the navigator softly, staring in amazement at the overhead screen. "Something's come down in the mountains!"

"No . . ." The pilot was staring forward through the windscreen. "It was much closer than that. Run the tape back."

He had barely said it when the sound of the explosion hit them, rocking the tiny craft.

"It's the dome!" said the pilot in the stillness that followed. "It's the fucking solarium!"

"It can't be."

The pilot laughed, shocked. "But it's not there! It's not fucking there!"

The navigator stared at him a moment, then looked back up at the screen. The image was frozen at the point where the camera had locked onto the irregular heat pattern.

He leaned forward and touched the display pad. Slowly, a frame at a time, the image changed.

"Gods! Look at that!"

Near the top of the softly glowing whiteness of the dome two eyes burned redly. Slowly they grew larger, darker, the crown of the dome softening, collapsing until the crumpled face of the solarium seemed to leer at the camera, a vivid gash of redness linking two of the four holes that were now visible. For a single frame it formed a death mask, the translucent flesh of the dome brilliantly underlit. Then, in the space of three frames, the whole thing blew apart.

In the first it was veined with tiny cracks – each fissure a searing, eye-scorching filament of fire, etched vividly against the swollen, golden flesh of the dome. As the tape moved on a frame, that golden light intensified, filling the bloated hemisphere to its limit. Light spilled like molten metal from the bloodied mouths that webbed the dome, eating into the surrounding darkness like an incandescent acid. Then, like a flowering wound, the whole thing opened up, the ragged flaps of ice thrown outward violently, flaming like the petals of a honey gold and red chrysanthemum, its bright intensity flecked with darkness.

He reached forward and pressed to hold the image. The screen burned, almost unbearably bright. He turned and stared at his colleague, seeing at once how the other's mouth was open, the inner flesh glistening brightly in the intense, reflected light, while in the polished darkness of his eyes two gold-red flowers blossomed.

"Gods . . . That's awful . . . terrible . . ."

The flat, Han face of the navigator turned and looked up at the screen. Yes, he thought. Awful. Terrible. And yet quite beautiful. Like a chrysanthemum, quite beautiful.

CHAPTER·2

THE SILKWORM
AND THE
MULBERRY LEAF

At the mouth of the narrow, low-ceilinged corridor they had been following, Chen stopped and placed his hand against Jyan's chest, looking out into the wide but crowded thoroughfare beyond.

Pan Chao Street teemed with life. Along both sides of the long, broad avenue ran balconies, four of them, stacked like seed trays one atop another, their low rails packed with people, the space between them criss-crossed with a vast unruly web of lines from which enormous quantities of washing hung, like giant, tattered veils, dripping endlessly onto the crowds below.

A hundred smaller corridors led into Pan Chao Street, the regular pattern of their dark, square mouths peppering the walls behind the balconies, like the openings to a giant hive.

Chen reached out and touched the smooth surface of the hexagonal, graffiti-proof plaque on the wall close by. "Level Eleven", it read; "South 3 Stack, Canton of Munich". Relieved, he looked back, ignoring the curious stares of passers-by. That much, at least, was right. But were they in the right place? Had they come out at the right end?

He glanced at Jyan, then nodded. "Come on. Let's find that lift."

41

It was a noisy, boisterous place. And it stank. The sharp, sour-sweet smell of spiced soymeats and overcooked vegetables was mixed inextricably with the sharper scent of human sweat and the damp, warm smell of the washing. Jyan looked at Chen, grimacing.

"It's worse than beneath the Net!"

Chen nodded. It was true. The air was a rich, unwholesome soup. After the freshness of the higher tunnels it made him feel like retching. Each breath seemed to coat the lungs.

Chen pushed out into the middle of the press, aware of Jyan at his back. Young children, naked, many of them streaked with dirt, ran here and there through the crowd, yelling. Some tugged at their clothes as they passed.

"*Ch'ian!*" one tiny, shaven-headed boy yelled, pulling at Chen's tunic, then putting his hand out aggressively. *Money!* He could have been no more than three at most. Chen glared at him and raised his hand threateningly, but the child only laughed and ran away, making a sign with his hand that was unmistakable. And you, thought Chen. And you.

People jostled this way and that, using their elbows and shoulders to force a way through the press. In the midst of it all a few of them simply stood and talked, making deals or just passing the time, oblivious of the noise, the crush, the rickshaws jostling to get by. Some turned and eyed the two men as they made their way through, but most ignored them, intent on their own business.

At the edge of things, small groups of women stood in doorways watching them, their arms folded over their breasts, their lips moving incessantly, chattering away in the pidgin dialect of these levels. Nearby, traders pushed their barrows through the crowd, crying out in the same strange, sing-song tongue as the watching women. Small MedFac screens were everywhere, on brackets fixed to walls and in shop fronts, on the sides of rickshaws or pushed along in handcarts, their constant murmur barely distinguishable above the general hubbub, while from every side countless PopVoc Squawks blared out, some

42

large as suitcases, others worn as ear-rings or elaborate bracelets. All added to the dull cacophony of sound.

Chen moved through it all slowly, purposefully, trying not to let it overwhelm him after the empty silence of the maintenance tunnels. His eyes searched for Security patrols, conscious all the while of Jyan at his side, matching him pace for pace. He allowed himself a brief, grim smile. It would be all right. He was sure it would be all right.

They were mostly Han here, but those *Hung Mao* about were almost indistinguishable in dress or speech. These were Chung Kuo's poor. Here, near the very bottom of the City, you could see the problem the City faced – could touch and smell and hear it. Here it hit you immediately, in the constant push and shove of the crowds that milled about these corridors. Chung Kuo was over-crowded. Wherever you turned there were people; people talking and laughing, pushing and arguing, bargaining and gambling, making love behind thin curtains or moving about quietly in cramped and crowded rooms, watching endless historical dramas while they tended to a clutch of bawling children.

Chen pushed on dourly, swallowing the sudden bitterness he felt. To those who lived a quieter, more ordered life in the levels high above, this would probably have seemed like hell. But Chen knew otherwise. The people of this level counted themselves lucky to be here, above the Net and not below. There was law here and a kind of order, despite the over-crowding. There was the guarantee of food and medical care. And though there was the constant problem of idleness – of too many hands and too few jobs – there was at least the chance of getting out, by luck or hard work; of climbing the levels to a better place than this. Below the Net there was nothing. Only chaos.

Below this level the City had been sealed. That seal was called the Net. Unlike a real net, however, there were no holes in it. It was a perfect, supposedly unbreachable barrier. The architects of City Earth had meant it as a quarantine measure: as a means of preventing the spread of

43

infestation and disease. From the beginning, however, the Seven had found another use for it.

They had been wise, that first Council of the Seven. They had known what some men were; had seen the darkness in their hearts and had realised that, unless they acted, the lowest levels of the City would soon become ungovernable. Their solution had been simple and effective. They had decided to use the Net as a dumping ground for that small anti-social element on whom the standard punishment of downgrading – of demoting a citizen to a lower level – had proved consistently unsuccessful. By that means they hoped to check the rot and keep the levels pure.

To a degree it had worked. As a dumping ground, the Net had served the Seven well. Below the Net there was no citizenship. Down there a man had no rights but those he fought for or earned in the service of other, more powerful men. There was no social welfare there, no healthcare, no magistrates to judge the rights or wrongs of a man's behaviour. Nor was there any legitimate means of returning from the Net. Exile was permanent, on pain of death. It was little wonder, then, that its threat kept the citizens of Pan Chao Street in check.

Chen knew. It was where they came from, he and Jyan. Where they had been born. Down there, below the Net.

And now they were returning.

At the mouth of one of the small alleyways that opened onto Pan Chao Street, a group of young men had gathered in a circle, hunched forward, watching excitedly as a dice rolled. There was a sudden upward movement of their heads; an abrupt, exaggerated movement of arms and hands and shoulders accompanied by a shrill yell from a dozen mouths, a shout of triumph and dismay, followed a moment later by the hurried exchange of money and the making of new bets. Then the young men hunched forward again, concentrating on the next roll.

As they passed the entrance, Jyan turned and stared at the group. He hesitated, then, catching their excitement, began to make his way across to them.

"Kao Jyan!" Chen hissed, reaching out to restrain him. "There's no time! We must get on!"

Jyan turned back, a momentary confusion in his face. His movements seemed strangely feverish and uncontrolled. His eyes had difficulty focusing. Chen knew at once what was wrong. The drug he had taken to tolerate the conditions outside the City was wearing off.

Too soon, Chen thought, his mind working furiously. You must have taken it too early. Before you were told to. And now the reaction's setting in. Too soon. Too bloody soon!

"Come on, Jyan," he said, leaning closer and talking into his face. "We've got to get to the lift!"

Jyan shivered and seemed to focus on him at last. Then he nodded and did as Chen said, moving on quickly through the crowd.

Where Pan Chao Street spilled out into the broad concourse of Main, Chen stopped and looked about him, keeping a grip on Jyan. The bell tower was close by and to his left, the distribution lift far to his right, barely visible, almost two *li* in the distance.

Shit! he thought. I was right. We've come out the wrong end!

He glanced at Jyan, angry now. He knew they had been in there too long. He had told him they had come too far along the shaft, but Jyan would not have it. "The next junction," Jyan had said when Chen had stopped beside the hatch: "Not this one. The next." Chen had known at the time that Jyan was wrong, but Jyan had been in charge and so he had done as he'd said. But now he wished he had over-ruled him. They had lost valuable time. Now they would have to backtrack – out in the open where they could be seen. Where Security could see them. And with Jyan going funny on him.

He leaned close to Jyan and shouted into his ear. "Just stay beside me. Hold onto my arm if necessary, but don't leave my side."

Jyan turned his head and looked back at him, his expression vacant for a moment. Then, as before, he seemed to come to and nodded. "Okay," he mouthed. "Let's go."

Main, the huge central concourse of Eleven, was a Babel of light and sound, a broad, bloated torrent of humanity that made Pan Chao Street seem a sluggish backwater. Along its length people crowded about the stalls, thick as blackfly on a stem, haggling for bargains, while high above them massive viewscreens hung in clusters from the ceiling, filling the overhead. On the huge, five-level walls to either side of the concourse a thousand flickering images formed and reformed in a nightmare collage. Worst of all, however, was the noise. As they stepped out into the crush the noise hit them like a wave, a huge swell of sound, painful in its intensity, almost unbearable.

Chen gritted his teeth, forcing his way through the thick press of people, holding on tightly to Jyan's arm and almost thrusting him through the crowd in front of him. He looked about him, for the first time really anxious, and saw how the long-time natives of Eleven seemed to ignore the clamour; seemed not to see the giant, dream-like faces that flickered into sudden existence and followed their every movement down the Main. They knew it was all a clever trick; knew from childhood how the screens responded to their presence. But to a stranger it was different. Nowhere in the City was quite like Eleven. Here, in the first level above the Net, life seemed in perpetual ferment; as if the knowledge of what lay sealed off just below their feet made them live their lives at a different level of intensity.

Jyan was turning his head from side to side as he moved through the crush, grimacing against the brute intensity of the noise, the awful flickering neon brightness of the screens. Then, abruptly, he turned and faced Chen, leaning into him, shouting into his face.

"I can't stand it, Chen! I can't hear myself think!"

Jyan's face was dreadful to see. His mouth had formed a jagged shape; his round and frightened eyes held a neon glimpse of madness. It was clear he was close to cracking up. Chen held his arms firmly, trying to reassure him through his touch, then leaned close, shouting back his answer. "Two minutes, Jyan, that's all! We're almost there!"

Jyan shuddered and looked up, away from Chen, his eyes wide. From one of the larger screens a huge face turned and focused on him. It was a classically beautiful oriental face, the eyes like almonds, the skin like satin, the hair fine and straight and dark. Meeting Jyan's eyes she smiled and, somewhere else, a computer matched the face she looked down into against its computer memory of all the faces in that sector of the City.

"You're a stranger here," she said, after barely a pause, the wire-thin stem of a speaker appendage snaking down to a point just above their heads. "Are you just visiting us, or have you business here?"

Jyan had frozen. Chen too had turned and was looking up at the screen. "Come on," he said tensely. "It's dangerous here."

As the seconds passed, and Jyan did not move, the computers spread their search, looking to match the face and find a name. It was good sales technique. This time, however, it came up with nothing. Fourteen near like-nesses, but nothing to match the retinal print of the man standing beneath its screen. In a Security post five levels up a warning message flashed up on a screen.

"Come on, Jyan!" Chen said urgently, tugging Jyan away; ignoring the curious looks of passers-by, pulling him along roughly now.

At the end of Main, only a quarter *li* away, the doors to one of the huge delivery lifts were opening. Chen increased his pace, glancing from side to side. As the doors slid slowly back, a number of Ministry of Distribution workers – *chi ch'i* – stepped out, their dark, uniformed figures dwarfed by the huge doors.

Nearer the lift the crowd thinned and the going grew easier. Chen slowed, then stopped and drew Jyan round to face him. The doors were almost fully open now. Already a number of the low-slung electric carts were spilling out into the Main, unloading the code-marked crates.

"You know what to do?" Chen asked, his hands gripping the collar of Jyan's jacket tightly. "You remember what we rehearsed?"

Jyan nodded, his eyes suddenly much clearer. "I'm all right," he shouted. "It was only . . ."

Chen put his hand to Jyan's mouth. "No time!" he yelled back. "Let's just do it!"

There were about thirty *chi ch'i* working the lift. All of them were wearing wraparounds – the bulky headpieces blinkering them from all distractions. Their close-shaven heads and the heavy, black, full-face masks gave them a sombre, distinctly mechanical appearance; an impression which their routine, repetitive movements enhanced. Chen walked towards them casually, aware of Jyan moving away from him, circling towards the lift from the other side.

There were two *pan chang* or supervisors. One of them stood only a few paces from where Chen had stopped, his back to the overhead screens, his headphones making him deaf to the surrounding noise. From time to time he would bark an order into his lip-mike and one of the *chi ch'i* would pause momentarily, listening, then respond with a brief nod.

Chen nodded to himself, satisfied. To all intents and purposes the *chi ch'i* could be discounted. Their awareness was limited to the colour-coded crates they were shifting from the lift: crates that stood out in simple, schematic shapes of red and green and blue against the intense blackness in their heads.

He looked across. Jyan was in position now, directly behind the second *pan chang*. At a signal from Chen, they would act.

Chen had made Jyan practise this endlessly; ripping the mike away quickly with his left hand, then chopping down against the victim's windpipe with his right. Now he would discover if Jyan had learned his lesson.

Chen brought his hand down sharply, then moved for-

48

ward, grabbing his man. Savagely he ripped the mike from the *pan chang's* lips and brought the heel of his right hand down hard against the man's throat. He felt the man go limp and let him fall, then looked across.

Jyan was still struggling with his man. He had ripped away the lip-mike, but had failed to finish things. Now he was holding the *pan chang* awkwardly, his right arm locked around the middle of his head, his left hand formed into a fist as he flailed frantically at the man's chest. But the *pan chang* was far from finished. With a shout he twisted out and pushed Jyan away, then turned to face him, one hand reaching up to pull his headphones off.

Chen started forward, then saw something flash in Jyan's hand. A moment later the *pan chang* staggered backward, clutching his chest. At the same time some of the *chi ch'i* straightened up and looked about blindly, as if suddenly aware that something was going on.

Chen ran for the lift. At the doorway he turned and looked back.

Jyan was kneeling over the *pan chang*, one foot pressing down into the dead man's shoulder as he tried to pull the long-handled knife from his chest.

"Jyan!" Chen screamed, his voice almost lost in the background noise. "Leave it!"

Jyan looked up sharply. Then, as if coming to himself again, he stood up and began to run towards the lift, skirting the unseeing *chi ch'i* and their carts. He had made only eight or nine paces when the first shot rang out.

Instinctively, Chen ducked. When he looked up again he couldn't see Jyan. He took a step forward, then stopped, backing up. There, a half *li* down the Main, were three Security guards. They were approaching in a widely-spaced line across the corridor, moving people out of their way brusquely, almost brutally as they walked towards the lift. Chen cursed beneath his breath and slammed his hand hard against the lift's control panel.

Slowly – very slowly – the doors began to slide shut.

"Jyan!" he screamed. "Jyan, where are you?"

49

A second shot rang out, ricocheting from the back of the lift. Out in the corridor there was chaos as people threw themselves down. Only the three Security men and the masked *chi ch'i* were standing now. As Chen watched, one of the electric carts trundled towards the narrowing gap. Angry with Jyan, Chen pulled out his gun and aimed it at the cart, then lowered it again.

It was Jyan. He was crouched over the cart, making as small a target of himself as possible.

There were two more shots, closely spaced. The second ricocheted, clipping a crate on its exit from the lift, and flew up into a nest of screens. There was a sharp popping and spluttering and a strong burning smell. Glass and wiring cascaded down amongst the unseeing *chi ch'i*.

With a painful slowness the cart edged between the doors. Seeing what was about to happen, Chen slammed his hand against the controls once, then again. The huge doors shuddered, made to open again, then slammed shut. But the delay had been enough. The cart was inside.

Jyan climbed down quickly and went to the panel.

"Hurry!" Chen's voice was low and urgent in the sudden silence. "They'll bring up burners for the locks!"

Jyan gave the slightest nod, then got to work. Pulling the panel open, he put his fingernails underneath the edges of the thin control plate and popped it out. Behind it was an array of smaller plates, like tiny squares of dark mirror. Only two of them were important. Gingerly, he eased them out, careful not to damage the delicate circuitry behind. At once a voice boomed out from an overhead speaker, warning him not to tamper. Ignoring it, Jyan felt in his pocket for the two replacement panels and carefully fitted them. Then he slipped the top plate back and closed the panel.

"Going down!"

Jyan hammered the manual over-ride and felt the huge lift shudder. For a moment there was a terrible groaning noise, as if the machine was going to grind itself to bits. Then came the sound of something very big and very solid breaking underneath them. With that the floor beneath the

50

lift floor gave way and the lift plunged a body's length before jerking to a halt. For a moment there was silence. Then, with a click and a more normal-sounding hum, it continued its descent.

Across from Jyan, Chen picked himself up. "We're through!" he said elatedly. "We've broken through the Net!"

Jyan turned. "That should keep them busy, eh, Chen?"

Alarms were sounding overhead, back where they had come from. Jyan could almost see what it was like up there. Right now they would be panicking, afraid of the sudden darkness, the blaring sirens; packing the lightless corridors that led to the transit lifts; screaming and fighting one another blindly; trying to get up and out, away from the breach, before the quarantine gates – the Seals – came down.

Jyan counted. At fifteen the lift juddered again. The sound was like a huge, multiple explosion, muffled and distant, yet powerful enough to shake the foundations of the City. "There!" he said, grinning at Chen. "The Seals! They've brought down the Seals!"

Chen stared back at Jyan blankly, the elation draining from him. He was sobered suddenly by the thought of what they had done. "That's it, then," he said softly. "We're safe." But he was remembering the feel of a small, dirty hand tugging at the sleeve of his one-piece as he walked down Pan Chao Street; the sight of a woman nursing her baby in a doorway; the faces of ordinary men and women going about their lives.

"We did it!" said Jyan, laughing now. "We fucking well did it!" But Chen just looked away, giving no answer.

* * *

Eight hours later and two hundred and fifty *li* to the north-west, two Security officers waited outside the huge doors of a First Level mansion. Here, at the very top of the City, there was space and silence. Here the only scent was that of pine from the crescent of miniature trees in the huge,

51

shallow bowl at one end of the long, empty corridor; the only sound the soft, shimmering fall of water from the ornamental fountain in their midst.

Major DeVore faced his ensign, his eyebrows raised. He had seen the look of surprise on the young officer's face when they had stepped from the lift.

"You'd like to live here, Haavikko?"

The ensign turned and looked back at the broad, empty corridor. The floor was richly carpeted, the high walls covered with huge, room-sized tapestries, the colouring subdued yet elegant. Bronze statues of dragons and ancient emperors rested on plinths spaced out the full length of the hallway. At the far end the doors of the lift were lacquered a midnight black. A solitary guard stood there, at attention, a *deng* 'lantern gun' strapped to his shoulder.

"They live well, sir."

DeVore smiled. He was a neat, compact-looking man, his jet black hair almost Han in its fineness, his shoulders broad, almost stocky. On the chest of his azurite-blue, full dress uniform he wore the embroidered patch of a third ranking military officer, the stylised leopard snatching a bird from the air. He was a full head shorter than his ensign and his build gave him the look of a fighter, yet his manners, like his face, seemed to speak of generations of breeding – of culture.

"Yes. They do." The smile remained on his face. "These are extremely rich men, Haavikko. They would swallow up minnows like us without a thought were the T'ang not behind us. It's a different life up here, with different rules. Rules of connection and influence. You understand?"

Haavikko frowned. "Sir?"

"What I mean is . . . I know these people, Haavikko. I know how they think and how they act. And I've known Under Secretary Lehmann's family now for almost twenty years. There are ways of dealing with them."

Haavikko puzzled at the words momentarily. "I still don't understand, sir. Do you mean you want to speak to him alone?"

"It would be best."

"But . . ." Haavikko hesitated a moment, then, seeing how his Major was watching him, bowed his head. "Sir."

"Good. I knew you'd understand." DeVore smiled again. "I've harsh words to say to our friend, the Under Secretary. It would be best if I said them to him alone. It is a question of face."

Haavikko nodded. That much he understood, orders or no. "Then I'll wait here, sir."

DeVore shook his head. "No, boy. I want you to be a witness, at the very least. You can wait out of earshot. That way you'll not be breaking orders, eh?"

Haavikko smiled, more at ease now that a compromise had been made.

Behind them the huge double doors to the first level apartment swung open. They turned, waiting to enter.

Inside, the unexpected. A tiny wood. A bridge across a running stream. A path leading upward through the trees. Beside the bridge two servants waited for them, Han, their shaven heads bowed fully to the waist. One led the way before them, the other followed, heads lowered, eyes averted out of courtesy. They crossed the bridge, the smell of damp earth and blossom rising to greet them. The path turned, twisted, then came out into a clearing.

On the far side of the clearing was the house. A big, two-storey mansion in the Han northern style, white-walled, its red tile roof steeply-pitched.

DeVore looked at his ensign. The boy was quiet, thoughtful. He had never seen the like of this. Not surprising. There were few men in the whole of Chung Kuo who could afford to live like this. Four, maybe five thousand at most outside the circle of the Families. This was what it was to be rich. Rich enough to buy a whole ten-level deck at the very top of the City and landscape it.

Pietr Lehmann was Under Secretary in the House of Representatives at Weimar. A big man. Fourth in the pecking order in that seat of World Government. A man to whom a thousand lesser men – giants in their own house-

53

holds – bowed their heads. A power broker, even if that power was said by some to be chimerical and the House itself a sop – a mask to brutal tyranny. DeVore smiled at the thought. Who, after all, would think the Seven brutal or tyrannous? They had no need to be. They had the House between them and the masses of Chung Kuo.

They went inside.

The entrance hall was bright, spacious. To the left was a flight of broad, wood-slatted steps; to the right a sunken pool surrounded by a low, wooden handrail. The small, dark shapes of fishes flitted in its depths.

Their guides bowed, retreated. For a moment they were left alone.

"I thought . . ." Haavikko began, then shook his head.

I know, DeVore mused; you thought he was *Hung Mao*. Yet all of this is Han. He smiled. Haavikko had seen too little of the world; had mixed only with soldiers. All this was new to him. The luxury of it. The imitation.

There was a bustle of sound to their right. A moment later a group of servants came into the entrance hall. They stopped a respectful distance from the two visitors and one of them stepped forward, a tall Han who wore on the chest of his pale green one-piece a large black pictogram and the number 1. He was House Steward, Lehmann's chief servant.

DeVore made no move to acknowledge the man. He neither bowed nor smiled. "Where is the Under Secretary?" he demanded. "I wish to see him."

The steward bowed, his eyes downcast. Behind him were lined up almost half of Lehmann's senior household staff, fifteen in all. They waited, unbowed, letting the steward act for them all.

"Excuse me, Major, but the master is out in the pagoda. He left explicit orders that he was not to be disturbed."

DeVore half turned and looked at his ensign, then turned back. "I've no time to wait, I'm afraid. I come on the T'ang's business. I'll tell your master that you did his bidding."

The steward nodded, but did not look up, keeping his head down as the Major and his ensign walked past him, out across the terrace and onto the broad back steps that led down to the gardens.

Lotus lay scattered on the lake, intensely green against the pale, clear water. Huge, cream slabs of rock edged the waterline, forming a perfect oval. To the left a pathway traced the curve of the lake, its flower-strewn canopy ending in a gently arching bridge. Beyond the bridge, amidst a formal garden of rock and shrub and flower, stood a three-tiered pagoda in the classic Palace style, its red-tiled roofs unornamented. Further round, to the right of the lake, was an orchard, the small, broad-crowned trees spreading to the water's edge. Plum and cherry were in blossom and the still air was heavy with their fragrance.

It was early morning. From the meadows beyond the pagoda came the harsh, clear cry of a peacock. Overhead, the light of a dozen tiny, artificial suns shone down from a sky of ice painted the pastel blue of summer days.

Standing on the topmost step, DeVore took it all in at a glance. He smiled, adjusting the tunic of his dress uniform, then turned to his ensign. "It's okay, Haavikko. I'll make my own way from here."

The young officer clicked his heels and bowed. DeVore knew the boy had been ordered by the General to stay close and observe all that passed; but these were his people; he would do it his way. Behind Haavikko the senior servants of the household looked on, not certain what to do. The Major had come upon them unannounced. They had had little chance to warn their master.

DeVore looked back past Haavikko, addressing them. "You! About your business now! Your master will summon you when he needs you!" Then he turned his back on them, dismissing them.

He looked out across the artificial lake. On the sheltered gallery of the pagoda, its wooden boards raised on stilts above the lake, stood three men dressed in silk *pau*. The soft murmur of their voices reached him across the water.

55

Seeing him, one of them raised a hand in greeting, then turned back to his fellows, as if making his excuses.

Lehmann met him halfway, on the path beside the lake.

"It's good to see you, Howard. To what do I owe this pleasure?"

DeVore bowed his head respectfully, then met the other's eyes. "I've come to investigate you, Pietr. The General wants answers."

Lehmann smiled and turned, taking the Major's arm and walking beside him. "Of course." Light, filtering through the overhanging vines, turned his face into a patchwork of shadows. "Soren Berdichev is here. And Edmund Wyatt. But they'll understand, I'm sure."

Again DeVore gave the slightest nod. "You know why I've come?"

Lehmann glanced his way, then looked forward again, towards the pagoda. "It's Lwo Kang's death, isn't it? I knew someone would come. As soon as I heard the news, I knew. Rumour flies fast up here. Idle tongues and hungry ears make trouble for us all." He sighed, then glanced at DeVore. "I understand there are those who are misconstruing words spoken in my audience with the Minister as a threat. Well, I assure you, Howard, nothing was further from my mind. In a strange way I liked Lwo Kang. Admired his stubbornness. Even so, I find myself . . . unsurprised. It was as I thought. As I *warned*. There are those for whom impatience has become a killing anger."

DeVore paused, turning towards the Under Secretary. "I understand. But there are things I must ask. Things you might find awkward."

Lehmann shrugged good-naturedly. "It's unavoidable. The Minister's death was a nasty business. Ask what you must. I won't be offended."

DeVore smiled and walked on, letting Lehmann take his arm again. They had come to the bridge. For a moment they paused, looking out across the lake. The peacock cried again.

"It is being said that you had most to gain from Lwo Kang's death. His refusal to accommodate you in the matter of new licenses. His recent investigations into the validity of certain patents. Most of all his rigid implementation of the Edict. That last, particularly, has harmed you and your faction more than most."

"My faction? You mean the Dispersionists?" Lehmann was quiet a moment, considering. "And by removing him I'd stand to gain?" He shook his head. "I know I've many enemies, Howard, but surely even they credit me with more subtlety than that?"

They walked on in silence. As they reached the pagoda, the two men on the terrace came across and stood at the top of the slatted steps.

"Soren! Edmund!" DeVore called out to them, mounting the narrow stairway in front of Lehmann. "How are you both?"

They exchanged greetings then went inside, into a large, hexagonal room. Black, lacquered walls were inset with porcelain in intricate and richly-coloured designs. The ceiling was a single huge mosaic, a double-helix of tiny, brightly-coloured pythons surrounded by a border of vivid blue-white stars. Four simple, backless stools with scrolled, python-headed feet stood on the polished block-tile floor, surrounding a low hexagonal table. On the table was a small green lacquered box.

Despite the heaviness, the formality of design, the room seemed bright and airy. Long, wide, slatted windows looked out onto the lake, the orchard and the surrounding meadows. The smell of blossom lingered in the air.

It was almost more Han than the Han, DeVore observed uneasily, taking a seat next to Lehmann. A rootless, unconscious mimicry. Or was it more than that? Was it Han culture that was the real virus in the bloodstream of these *Hung Mao*, undermining them, slowly assimilating them, "as a silkworm devours a mulberry leaf"? He smiled wryly to himself as the words of the ancient historian Ssu Ma Ch'ien came to mind. Ah yes, we know their history, their sayings. These things have usurped our own identity. Well, by such patience shall I, in turn, devour them. I'll be the silkworm delving in their midst.

"So how's the Security business?"

DeVore turned on his stool, meeting Edmund Wyatt's query with a smile.

"Busy. As ever in this wicked world."

Despite long years of acquaintanceship, Wyatt and he had never grown close. There had always been a sense of unspoken hostility beneath their surface politeness. It was no different now.

Wyatt was a slightly built man with an oddly heavy head. Someone had once commented that it was as if he had been grafted together from two very different men, and that impression, once noted, was hard to shake. At a glance his face revealed a strong, unequivocal character: aristocratic, his dark green eyes unflinching in their challenge, his chin firm, defiant. But looking down at the frame of the man it was noticeable at once how frail he seemed, how feminine. His hands were soft and thin and pale, the nails perfectly manicured. Slender *tiao tuo*, bracelets of gold and jade, hung bunched at both wrists. Such things made him seem a weak man, but he was far from that. His father's ruin might have destroyed a lesser man, but Wyatt had shown great courage and determination. He had gambled on his own talents and won: rebuilding his father's empire and regaining his place on First Level.

DeVore studied him a moment longer, knowing better than to underestimate the intelligence of the man, then gave the slightest bow.

"And you, Edmund – you're doing well, I see. There's talk your company will soon be quoted on the Index."

Wyatt's eyes showed a mild surprise. He was unaware how closely DeVore kept himself briefed on such things. "You follow the markets, then?"

"It makes sense to. Insurrection and business are close allies in these times. The Hang Seng is an indicator of much more than simple value – it's an index of power and ruthlessness, a club for like-minded men of similar ambitions."

He saw how Wyatt scrutinised him momentarily, trying to make out the meaning behind his words. The Hang Seng Index of Hong Kong's stock market was the biggest of the world's seven markets and the most important. But, like the House, it was often a front to other, less open activities.

DeVore turned slightly in his seat to face Berdichev, a warm smile lighting his features. "And how are you, Soren? I see far too little of you these days."

Soren Berdichev returned the smile bleakly, the heavy lenses of his small, rounded glasses glinting briefly as he bowed. He was a tall, thin-faced man with pinched lips and long, spatulate fingers; a severe, humourless creature whose steel grey eyes never settled for long. He was a hard man with few social graces, and because of that he made enemies easily, often without knowing that he did; yet he was also extremely powerful – not a man to be crossed.

"Things are well, Howard. Progressing, as they say."

DeVore smiled at Berdichev's understatement. SimFic, his company, was one of the success stories of the decade. It had been a small operation when he had bought it in '88, but by '91 it had been quoted on the Hang Seng 1000 Index, along with Chung Kuo's other leading companies. Since that time he had made great advances, leading the market in the production of HeadStims and Wraps. In five short years SimFic had achieved what had seemed impossible and revolutionised personal entertainment. Now they were one of the world's biggest companies and were quoted in the Top 100 on the Index.

For a while they exchanged pleasantries. Then, as if at a signal, Berdichev's features formed into a cold half-smile. "But forgive me, Howard. I'm sure you haven't come here to talk market." He turned away brusquely, and looked pointedly at Wyatt. "Come, Edmund, let's leave these two. I believe they have business to discuss."

Wyatt looked from Lehmann to DeVore, his whole manner suddenly alert, suspicious. "Business?"

There was a moment's awkwardness, then DeVore smiled and nodded. "I'm afraid so."

Wyatt set down his glass and got up slowly. Giving a small bow to Lehmann he made to follow Berdichev, then stopped and turned, looking back at Lehmann. "Are you sure?" he asked, his eyes revealing a deep concern for his friend.

Lehmann gave the slightest of nods, meeting Wyatt's eyes openly as if to say *trust me*. Only then did Wyatt turn and go.

DeVore waited a moment, listening to Wyatt's tread on the steps. Then, when it was silent again, he got up and went to the table, crouching down to open the small green box. Reaching up to his lapel, he removed the tiny device that had been monitoring their conversation and placed it carefully inside the box. Lehmann came and stood beside him, watching as he switched on the tape they had recorded three weeks before. There was the cry of a peacock, distant, as if from the meadows beyond the room, and then their voices began again, continuing from where they had left off. DeVore smiled and gently closed the lid, then he straightened up, letting out a breath.

"The simplest ways are always best," he said, and gave a short laugh. Then, more soberly, "That was unfortunate. What does Wyatt know?"

Lehmann met DeVore's eyes, smiling, then put an arm about his shoulders. "Nothing. He knows nothing at all."

Slowly, DeVore peeled off his gloves and laid them on the table.

"Good. Then let's speak openly."

* * *

The Stone Dragon was a big, low-ceilinged inn at the bottom of the City; a sprawl of interconnected rooms, ill-lit and ill-decorated; a place frequented only by the lowest of those who lived in the ten levels below the Net. A stale, sweet-sour stench permeated everything in its cramped and busy rooms, tainting all it touched. Machines lined the walls, most of them dark. Others, sparking, on the verge of malfunction, added their own sweet, burning scent to the heavy fug that filled the place. Voices called out constantly, clamouring for service, while shabbily-dressed waitresses, their make-up garishly exaggerated, made their way between the tables, taking orders.

The two men sat in the big room at the back of the inn, at a table set apart from the others against the far wall. They had come here directly, two hours back, unable to sleep, the enormity of what they had done playing on both their minds. To celebrate, Kao Jyan had ordered a large bottle of the Dragon's finest *Shen*, brought down from Above at an exorbitant price, but neither man had drunk much of the strong rice wine.

Jyan had been quiet for some while now, hunched over an untouched tumbler, brooding. Chen watched him for a time, then looked about him.

The men at nearby tables were mainly Han, but there were some *Hung Mao*. Most of them, Han and *Hung Mao* alike, were wide-eyed and sallow-faced, their scabbed arms and faces giving them away as addicts. Arfidis was cheap down here and widely available and for some it was the only way out of things. But it was also death, given time, and Chen had kept his own veins clear of it. At one of the tables further off three Han sat stiffly, talking in dialect, their voices low and urgent. One of them had lost an eye, another was badly scarred about the neck and shoulder. They represented the other half of the Stone Dragon's clientele, noticeable by the way they held themselves – somehow lither, more alert than those about them. These were the gang men and petty criminals who used this place for business. Chen stretched his neck, and leaned back against the wall. Nearby, a thick coil of smoke moved slowly in the faint orange light of an overhead panel, like the fine, dark strands of a young girl's hair.

"It's like death," he said, looking across at Jyan.

"What?" Jyan said lazily, looking up at Chen. "What did you say?"

Chen leaned forward and plucked a bug from beneath the table's edge, crushing it between his thumb and fore-finger. It was one of the ugly, white-shelled things that sometimes came up from the Clay. Blind things that worked by smell alone. He let its broken casing fall and wiped his hand on his one-piece, not caring if it stained. "This place. It's like death. This whole level of things. It stinks."

Jyan laughed. "Well, you'll be out of it soon enough, if that's what you want."

Chen looked at his partner strangely. "And you don't?" He shook his head, suddenly disgusted with himself. "You know, Jyan, I've spent my whole life under the Net. I've known nothing but this filth. It's time I got out. Time I found something cleaner, better than this."

"I know how you feel," Jyan answered, "but have you thought it through? Up there you're vulnerable. Above the Net there are Pass Laws and Judges, Taxes and Security patrols." He leaned across and spat neatly into the bowl by his feet. "I hate the thought of all that shit. It would stifle the likes of you and me. And anyway, we hurt a lot of people last night when the quarantine gates came down. Forget the assassination – someone finds out you were involved in *that* and you're dead."

Chen nodded. It had meant nothing at the time, but now that the drug had worn off he could think of little else. He kept seeing faces; the faces of people he had passed up there in Pan Chao Street. People who, only minutes later, would have been panicking, eyes streaming, half-choking as Se-curity pumped the deck full of sterilising gases. Children, too. Yes, a lot of them would have been just children.

He hadn't thought it through; hadn't seen it until it was done. All he'd thought about was the five thousand yuan he was being paid for the job: that and the chance of getting out. And if that meant breaking through the Net, then that's what he would do. But he hadn't thought it through. In that, at least, Jyan was right.

The Net. It had been built to safeguard the City, as a

quarantine measure to safeguard the Above from plague and other epidemics, and from infiltration by insects and vermin. And from us, thought Chen, a sour taste in his mouth. From vermin like us.

He looked across, seeing movement in the doorway, then looked sharply at Jyan. "Trouble . . ." he said quietly.

Jyan didn't turn. "Who is it?" he mouthed back.

Chen groomed an imaginary moustache.

"Shit!" said Jyan softly, then sat back, lifting his tumbler.

"What does he want?" Chen whispered, leaning forward so that the movements of his mouth were screened by Jyan from the three men in the doorway.

"I owe him money."

"How much?"

"A thousand yuan."

"A thousand!" Chen grimaced, then leaned back again, easing his knife from his boot and pinning it with his knee against the underside of the table. Then he looked across again. The biggest of the three was looking directly at them now, grinning with recognition at the sight of Jyan's back. The big man tilted his head slightly, muttering something to the other two, then began to come across.

Whiskers Lu was a monster of a man. Almost six *ch'i* in height, he wore his hair wild and uncombed and sported a ragged fur about his shoulders like some latterday chieftain from a historical romance. He derived his name from the huge, tangled bush of a moustache which covered much of his facial disfigurement. Standing above Jyan, his left eye stared out glassily from a mask of melted flesh, its rawness glossed and mottled like a crab's shell. The right eye was a narrow slit, like a sewn line in a doll's face. Beneath the chin and on the lower right-hand side of his face the mask seemed to end in a sunken line, the normal olive of his skin resuming.

Ten years back, so the story went, Whiskers Lu had tried to come to an arrangement with Chang Fen, one of the petty bosses of these levels. Chang Fen had met him, smiling, holding one hand out to welcome Lu, his other hand holding what looked like a glass of wine. Then, still smiling, he had thrown the contents of the glass into Lu's face. It was acid. But the man had not reckoned with Whiskers Lu's ferocity. Lu had held on tightly to the man's hand, roaring against the pain, and, drawing his big hunting knife, had plunged it into Chang Fen's throat before his lieutenants could come to his aid. Half-blinded he had fought his way out of there, then had gone back later with his brothers to finish the job.

Now Whiskers Lu was a boss in his own right; a big man, here beneath the Net. He stood there, towering over Kao Jyan, his lipless mouth grinning with cruel pleasure as he placed his hand on Jyan's shoulder, his single eye watching Chen warily.

"Kao Jyan . . . How are you, my friend?"

"I'm well," Jyan answered nervously, shrinking in his seat. "And you, Lu Ming-Shao?"

Whiskers Lu laughed gruffly, humourlessly. "I'm fine, Kao Jyan. I killed a man yesterday. He owed me money."

Jyan swallowed and met Chen's eyes. "And he couldn't pay you?"

Lu's grip tightened on Jyan's shoulder. "That's so, Kao Jyan. But that's not why I killed him. I killed him because he tried to hide from me."

"Then he was a foolish man, I'd say."

The big man's laughter was tinged this time with a faint amusement. His eye, however, was cold, calculating. It stared challengingly at Chen from within its glass-like mask.

Chen stared back at it, meeting its challenge, not letting himself be cowed. If it came to a fight, so be it. Whiskers Lu would be a hard man to kill, and the odds were that Lu and his two henchmen would get the better of Jyan and he. But he would not make it easy for them. They would know they had fought a *kwai*.

Whiskers Lu broke eye contact, looking down at Jyan, his thin lips smiling again.

"You owe me money, Kao Jyan."

Jyan was staring down at his tumbler. "I have a week yet, Lu Ming-Shao. Don't you remember?"

"Oh, I remember. But I want my money now. With interest. Twelve hundred yuan I want from you, Kao Jyan. And I want it now."

Almost unobtrusively, Whiskers Lu had slipped the knife from his belt and raised it to Jyan's neck. The huge, wide blade winked in the faint overhead light. The razor-sharp tip pricked the flesh beneath Jyan's chin, making him wince.

Chen let his hand slide slowly down his leg, his fingers closing about the handle of his knife. The next few moments would be crucial.

"Twelve hundred?" Jyan said tensely. "Surely, our agreement said . . ."

Jyan stopped, catching his breath. Whiskers Lu had increased the pressure of the knife against his flesh, drawing blood. A single bead trickled slowly down Jyan's neck and settled in the hollow above his chest. Jyan swallowed painfully.

"You want it now?"

"That's right, Kao Jyan. I've heard you've been borrowing elsewhere. Playing the field widely. Why's that, Kao Jyan? Were you planning to leave us?"

Jyan looked up, meeting Chen's eyes. Then, slowly, carefully, he reached up and moved the knife aside, turning to look up into Whiskers Lu's face.

"You mistake me, Lu Ming-Shao. I'm happy here. My friends are here. Good friends. Why should I want to leave?" Jyan smiled, then swept his hand over the table, indicating the empty chairs. "Look, you're a reasonable man, Lu Ming-Shao. Why don't we talk this through? Why don't you sit with us and share a glass of *Shen*?"

Whiskers Lu roared, then grabbed Jyan's hair, pulling his head back viciously, his knife held threateningly across Jyan's throat.

"None of your games, Kao Jyan! I'm an impatient man, just now. So tell me and have done with it. Do you have the money or not?"

Jyan's eyes bulged. Lu's reaction had startled him. His hand went to his pocket and scrabbled there, then threw three thick chips out onto the table. Each was for five hundred yuan.

Chen forced himself to relax, loosening his tight grip on the knife's handle. But he had seen how closely Lu's henchmen had been watching him and knew that they'd had orders to deal with him if it came to trouble. He smiled reassuringly at them, then watched as Whiskers Lu let go his grip on Jyan. The big man sheathed his knife, then leaned forward, scooping up the three ivory-coloured chips.

"Fifteen hundred, eh?" He grunted and half turned, grinning at his men. "Well, that'll do, wouldn't you say, Kao Jyan?"

"Twelve hundred," Jyan said, rubbing at his neck. "You said twelve hundred."

"Did I now?" Lu laughed, almost softly now, then nodded. "Maybe so, Kao Jyan. But you made me work for my money. So let's call it quits, eh, and I'll forget that you made me angry."

Chen narrowed his eyes, watching Jyan, willing him to let it drop. But Jyan was not through. He turned and looked up at Lu again, meeting his eye.

"I'm disappointed in you, Lu Ming-Shao. I thought you were a man of your word. To ask for your money a week early, that I understand. A man must protect what is his. And the extra two hundred, that too I understand. Money is not a dead thing. It lives and grows and must be fed. But this extra . . ." He shook his head. "Word will go out that Lu Ming-Shao is greedy. That he gives his word, then takes what is not his."

Whiskers Lu glowered at Jyan, his hand resting on his knife. "You'd dare to say that, Kao Jyan?"

Jyan shook his head. "Not I. But there are others in this room who've seen what passed between us. You can't silence them all, Lu Ming-Shao. And you know how it is. Rumour flies like a bird. Soon the whole Net would know.

And then what, eh? Who would come and borrow money from you then?"

Lu's chest rose and fell, his single eye boring angrily into Jyan's face. Then he turned sharply and barked at one of his henchmen. "Give him three hundred! Now!"

The man rummaged in the pouch at his belt then threw three slender chips down in front of Jyan.

Jyan smiled. "It was good to do business with you, Lu Ming-Shao. May you have many sons!"

But Whiskers Lu had turned away and was already halfway across the room, cursing beneath his breath.

When he was gone, Chen leaned forward angrily. "What the fuck are you playing at, Jyan? You almost had us killed!"

Jyan laughed. "He was angry, wasn't he?"

"Angry!" Chen shook his head, astonished. "And what's all this about you borrowing elsewhere? What have you been up to?"

Jyan didn't answer. He sat there, silent, watching Chen closely, a faint smile on his lips.

"What is it?"

Jyan's smile broadened. "I've been thinking."

"Thinking, eh?" Chen lifted his tumbler and sipped. The calculating gleam in Jyan's eyes filled him with apprehension.

Jyan leaned forward, lowering his voice to a whisper. "Yes, thinking. Making plans. Something that will make us both rich."

Chen drained his tumbler and set it down, then leaned back in his chair slowly, eyeing his partner. "I've enough now, Jyan. Why should I want more? I can get out now if I want."

Jyan sat back, his eyes filled with scorn. "Is that *all* you want? To get out of here? Is that as high as your ambitions climb?" Again he leaned forward, but this time his voice hissed out at Chen. "Well I want more than that! I want to be a king down here, in the Net. A big boss. Understand me, Chen? I don't want safety and order and all that shit,

I want power. Here, where I can exercise it. And that takes money."

Heads turned at nearby tables, curious but lethargic. Chen looked back at one of them, meeting the cold, dispassionate stare that was the tell-tale symptom of arfidis trance with a cold look of loathing. Then he laughed softly and looked back at Jyan.

"You're mad, Jyan. It takes more than money. You can't buy yourself a gang down here, you have to make one, *earn* one, like Whiskers Lu. You're not in that league, Jyan. His kind would have you for breakfast. Besides, you're talking of the kind of sums you and I couldn't dream of getting hold of."

Jyan shook his head. "You're wrong."

Chen looked down, irritated by Jyan's persistence. "Forget it, eh? Best take what you've got and get out. That is, if you've still got enough after paying Whiskers Lu back."

Jyan laughed scornfully. "That was nothing. Small change. But listen to me, Chen. Do you really think you *can* get out?"

Chen said nothing, but Jyan was watching him closely again.

"What if all you've saved isn't enough? What if the permits cost more than you can pay? What if you run into some greedy bastard official who wants a bit more squeeze than you've got? What then? What would you do?"

Chen smiled tightly. "I'd kill him." But he was thinking of Pan Chao Street and the quarantine gates. Thinking of the huge, continent-spanning City of three hundred levels that was there above the Net. He had hoped to get a foothold on that great social ladder – a place on the very lowest rung. But he would have to go higher than he'd planned. Up to Twenty-One, at least. And that would cost more. Much, much more. Maybe Jyan was right.

"You'd kill him!" Jyan laughed again and sat back, clearly disgusted with his partner. "And be back here again! A *kwai*. Just a *kwai* again! A hireling, not the man in charge. Is that really what you want?"

Chen sniffed, then shook his head.

Jyan leaned across the table again. "Don't you understand? We *can* be kings here! We *can*!" His voice dropped to a whisper. "You see, I know who hired us."

Chen met the other's eyes calmly. "So?"

Jyan laughed, incredulous. "You really don't see it, do you?"

Chen let his eyes fall. Of course he saw it. Saw at once what Jyan was getting at. Blackmail. Games of extreme risk. But he was interested, and he wanted Jyan to spell it out for him. Only when Jyan had finished did he look up, his face expressionless.

"You're greedy, Jyan. You know that?"

Jyan sat back, laughing, then waved a hand dismissively. "You weren't listening properly, Chen. The tape. It'll be my safeguard. If they try anything – anything at all – Security will get the tape."

Chen watched him a moment longer, then looked down, shrugging, knowing that nothing he said would stop Jyan from doing this.

"Partners, then?"

Jyan had extended his left hand. It lay on the table's surface beside the half empty bottle; a small, almost effete hand, but clever. An artisan's hand. Chen looked at it, wondering not for the first time who Jyan's father might have been, then placed his own on top of it. "Partners," he said, meeting Jyan's eyes. But already he was making plans of his own. Safeguards.

"I'll arrange a meeting, then."

Chen smiled tightly. "Yes," he said. "You do that."

★ ★ ★

Edmund Wyatt stopped beneath the stand of white mulberry trees at the far end of the meadow and looked back at the pagoda. "I don't trust him, Soren. I've never trusted him."

Berdichev looked sideways at him and shrugged. "I don't know why. He seems a good enough fellow."

69

"Seems!" Wyatt laughed ironically. "DeVore's a seeming fellow, all right. Part of his Security training, I guess. All clean and smart on the outside – but at core a pretty dirty sort, don't you think?"

Berdichev was quiet a moment. He walked on past Wyatt, then turned and leaned against one of the slender trunks, studying his friend. "I don't follow you, Edmund. He is what he is. Like all of us."

Wyatt bent down and picked up one of the broad, heart-shaped leaves, rubbing it between thumb and finger. "I mean . . . he works for them. For the Seven. However friendly he seems, you've always got to remember that. They pay him. He does their work. And as the Han say – *Chung ch'en pu shih erh chu* – You can't serve two masters."

"I don't know. Do you really think it's that simple?"

Wyatt nodded fiercely, staring away at the distant pagoda. "They own him. Own him absolutely."

He turned and saw that Berdichev was smiling. "What is it?"

"Just that you let it worry you too much, Edmund."

Wyatt smiled back at him. "Maybe. But I don't trust him. I'm sure he's up to something."

"Up to what?" Berdichev moved away from the tree and stood beside Wyatt, looking back across the meadow. "Look, I'll tell you why he's here. Lwo Kang was murdered. Last night. Just after eleventh bell."

Wyatt turned abruptly, shocked by the news. "Lwo Kang? Gods! Then it's a wonder we're not all in the cells!"

Berdichev looked away. "Maybe . . . And maybe not. After all, we're not unimportant men. It would not do to persecute us without clear proof of our guilt. It might . . . well, it might make us martyrs, eh?"

Wyatt narrowed his eyes. "Martyrs? I don't understand."

"Don't think the T'ang underestimates us. Nor the power of the Above. If he had all of us Dispersionists arrested, what then? What would the Above make of that? They'd say he was acting like a tyrant. He and all the Seven. It would make things very awkward, don't you see?"

70

"But Lwo Kang was a Minister! One of Li Shai Tung's own appointees!"

"It makes no difference. The T'ang will act properly, or not at all. It is the way of the Seven. Their weakness, if you like."

"Weakness?" Wyatt frowned, then turned back, looking across at the pagoda again. "No wonder DeVore is here. I'd say he's come to find a scapegoat. Wouldn't you?"

Berdichev smiled then reached out, putting his hand on his friend's shoulder. "You really think so, Edmund?" He shrugged, then squeezed Wyatt's shoulder gently. "Whatever else you might think about him, DeVore's *Hung Mao*, like us. He may work for the Han, but that doesn't mean he thinks like them. In any case, why should he be interested in anything but the truth?"

Wyatt stared at the pagoda intently for a time, as if pondering some mighty problem, then he shivered and touched his tongue to his teeth in a curiously innocent, child-like gesture. He turned, looking back at Berdichev. "Maybe you're right, Soren. Maybe he is what you say. But my feelings tell me otherwise. I don't trust him. And if he's here, I'd wager he's up to something." He paused, then turned, looking back at the pagoda. "In fact, I'd stake my life on it."

* * *

"Yang Lai is dead, then?"

DeVore turned from the window and looked back into the room. "Yes. The Junior Minister is dead."

Lehmann was silent a moment, then nodded. "I see. And the lieutenant in charge of the Security post?"

DeVore hesitated, then, in a quieter voice. "Dead too, I'm afraid. It was . . . unavoidable."

Lehmann met his eyes, understanding at once. "How?"

"By his own hand. The dishonour, you see. His family. It would have ruined them. Better to kill oneself and absolve them from the blame." He turned back to the window and looked out again, following the slow progress of the two men down below as they made their way back across the meadow to the pagoda.

"So we're clear."

DeVore gave a short laugh. "Not clear. Not yet."

"Then you think there's still a chance they'll find something?"

The Major's eyes met Lehmann's briefly, then looked away. "Remember how long this took us to plan, Pietr. We've been careful, and such care pays off. And anyway, we have the advantage of knowing all they do. There's not a move General Tolonen can make without me hearing of it."

He was quiet a moment, staring off across the meadow. It was true what he had said. He had spent years recruiting them; young men like himself who had come, not from First Level, from the privileged top deck of the City – the *supernal*, as they liked to term themselves – nor from the army families – the descendants of those North European mercenaries who had fought for the Seven against the tyrant Tsao Ch'un a century before – but ordinary young men without connection. Young men of ability, held back by a system modelled on the Manchu "banners" – an archaic and elitist organisational structure where connection counted for more than ability. Misfits and malcontents. Like himself.

Yes, he had become adept at spotting them; at recognising that look, there at the back of the eyes. He would check out their backgrounds and discover all he could about them. Would find, invariably, that they were loners, ill at ease socially and seething inside that others had it so easy when army life for them was unmitigatedly hard. Then, when he knew for certain that it was so, he would approach them. And every time it was the same; that instant opening; that moment of recognition, like to like, so liberating that it bound them to him with ties of gratitude and common feeling.

"Like you, I am a self-made man," he would say to them. "What I am I owe to no one but myself. No relative has bought my post; no uncle put in a word with my commanding officer." And as he said it, he'd think of all the insults, all the shit he'd had to put up with from his so-called superiors – men who weren't fit to polish his boots. He had suffered almost thirty years of that kind of crap to get where he was now, in a position of real power. He would tell his young men this and see in their eyes the reflection of his own dark indignation. And then he would ask them, "Join me. Be part of my secret brotherhood." And they would nod, or whisper yes. And they would be his: alone no longer.

So now he had his own organisation; men loyal to him before all others; who would neither hesitate to betray their T'ang nor lay down their lives if he asked it of them. Like the young officer who had been on duty the night of Lwo Kang's assassination. Like a hundred others, scattered about the City in key positions.

He looked back at Lehmann. "Are the trees real?" He pointed outward, indicating the stand of mulberries at the far end of the meadow.

Lehmann laughed. "Heaven, no. None of it's real."

DeVore nodded thoughtfully, then turned his face to look at Lehmann. "You're not afraid to use Wyatt?" His eyes, only centimetres from Lehmann's, were stern, questioning. There was the faintest hint of peppermint on his breath.

"If we must. After all, some things are more important than friendship."

DeVore held his eyes a moment longer then looked back at the figure of Wyatt down below. "I don't like him. You know that. But even if I did – if it threatened what we're doing . . . If for a moment . . ."

Lehmann touched his arm. "I know."

DeVore turned fully, facing him. He smiled, then reached up and held his shoulders firmly. "Good. We understand each other, Pietr. We've always understood each other."

Releasing him, DeVore checked his wrist-timer then

73

went to the middle of the room and stood there by the table, looking down at the box. "It's almost time to call the others back. But first, there's one last thing we need to talk about. Heng Yu."

Lehmann frowned. "What of him?"

"I have reason to believe he'll be Lwo Kang's replacement."

Lehmann laughed, astonished. "Then you know much more than any of us, Howard. How did you come by this news?"

"Oh, it isn't news. Not yet, anyway. But I think you'll find it reliable enough. Heng Chi-Po wants his nephew as the new Minister, and what Heng Chi-Po wants he's almost certain to get."

Lehmann was quiet, considering. He had heard how high the Heng family currently rode. Even so, it would use all of the Minister Heng's quite considerable influence to persuade Li Shai Tung to appoint his nephew, Heng Yu. And, as these things went, it would be a costly manoeuvre, with the paying-off of rivals, the bribery of advisors and the cost of the post itself. They would surely have to borrow. In the short term it would weaken the Hengs quite severely. They would find themselves beholden to a dozen other families. Yet in the longer term . . .

Lehmann laughed, surprised. "I'd always thought Heng Chi-Po crude and unimaginative. Not the kind to plan ahead. But this . . ."

DeVore shook his head. "Don't be mistaken, Pietr. This has nothing to do with planning. Heng Chi-Po is a corrupt man, as we know to our profit. But he's also a proud one. At some point Lwo Kang snubbed him. Did something to him that he couldn't forgive. This manoeuvring is his answer. His revenge, if you like."

"How do you know all this?"

DeVore looked across at him and smiled. "Who do you think bought Yang Lai? Who do you think told us where Lwo Kang would be?"

"But I thought it was because of Edmund . . ." Then

Lehmann laughed. "But of course. Why didn't you tell me?"

DeVore shrugged. "It didn't matter until now. But now you need to know who we are dealing with. What kind of men they are."

"Then it's certain."

"Almost. But there is nothing – *no one* – we cannot either buy or destroy. If it is Heng Yu, then all well and good, it will prove easy. But whoever it is, he'll remember what happened to Lwo Kang and be wary of us." He laughed softly. "No, they'll not deal lightly with us in future."

"And Li Shai Tung?"

DeVore spread his open hands, then turned away. There, then, lay the sticking point. Beyond this they were guessing. He, and the others of the Seven who ran the Earth, were subject to no laws, no controls but their own. Ultimately it would be up to them whether change would come; whether Man would try once more for the stars. DeVore's words, true as they were for other men, did not apply to the Seven. They could not be bought – for they owned half of everything there was – nor, it seemed, could they be destroyed. For more than a century they had ruled unchallenged.

"The T'ang is a man, whatever some might think."

Lehmann looked at DeVore curiously but held his tongue.

"He can be influenced," DeVore added after a moment. "And when he sees how the tide of events flows . . ."

"He'll cut our throats."

DeVore shook his head. "No. Not if we have the full weight of the Above behind us. Markets and House and all. Not if his Ministers are ours. He is but a single man, after all."

"He is Seven," said Lehmann, and for once he understood the full import of the term. Seven. It made for strength of government. Each a king, a T'ang, ruling a seventh of Chung Kuo, yet each an equal in Council, responsible to his fellow T'ang; in some important things

75

unable to act without their firm and full agreement. "And the Seven is against Change. It is a principle with them. The very cornerstone of their continued existence."

"And yet change they must. Or go under."

Lehmann opened his mouth, surprised to find where their talk had led them. Then he shook his head. "You don't mean . . ."

"You'll see," said DeVore, more softly than before. "This here is just a beginning. A display of our potential. For the Above to see." He laughed, looking away into some inner distance. "You'll see, Pietr. They'll come to us. Every last one of them. They'll see how things are – we'll open their eyes to it – and then they'll come to us."

"And then?"

"Then we'll see who's more powerful. The Seven, or the Above."

* * *

Heng Chi-Po leaned back in his chair and roared with laughter. He passed his jewel-ringed fingers across his shiny pate, then sniffed loudly, shifting his massive weight. "Excellent, Kou! Quite excellent! A good toast! Let's raise our glasses then." He paused, the smile on his face widening. "To Lwo Kang's successor!"

Six voices echoed the toast enthusiastically.

"Lwo Kang's successor!"

There were eight men in the spacious, top level office. Four were brothers to the Minister, three his nephews. Heng Yu, the subject of the toast, a slender man in his mid-twenties with a pencil moustache and a long but pleasant face, smiled broadly and bowed to his uncle. Kou, fourth son of Heng Chi-Po's father Tao, clapped an arm about Yu's shoulders, then spoke again.

"This is a good day, first brother."

Heng Chi-Po nodded his huge, rounded face, then laughed again. "Oh how sweet it was to learn of that weasel's death. How sweet! And to think the family will profit from it!"

There was laughter from all sides. Only the young man, Yu, seemed the least bit troubled. "He seemed a good man, uncle," he ventured. "Surely I would do well to be as he was."

The laughter died away. Chi-Po's brothers looked among themselves, but Heng Chi-Po was in too good a mood to let Yu's comments worry him. He looked at his nephew good-naturedly and shook his head in mock despair. Yet his voice, when he spoke, had an acid undertone. "Then you heard wrong, Yu. Lwo Kang was a worm. A liar and a hypocrite. He was a foolish, stubborn man with the manners of the Clayborn and the intelligence of a GenSyn whore. The world is a better place without him, I assure you. And you, dear nephew, will make twice the Minister he was."

Heng Yu bowed deeply, but there was a faint colour to his cheeks when he straightened, and his eyes did not meet his uncle's. Heng Chi-Po watched him closely, thinking, not for the first time, that it was unfortunate he could not promote one of his nearer relatives to the post. Yu, son of his long-dead younger brother, Fan, had been educated away from the family. He had picked up strange notions of life. Old-fashioned, Confucian ideals of goodness. Things that made a man weak when faced with the true nature of the world. Still, he was young. He could be re-educated. Shaped to serve the family better.

Kou, ever-watchful, saw how things were, and began an anecdote about a high level whore and a stranger from the Clay. Giving him a brief smile of thanks, Chi-Po pulled himself up out of his chair and turned away from the gathering, thoughtful, pulling at his beard. Under the big, wall-length map of City Europe he stopped, barely aware of the fine honeycomb grid that overlaid the old, familiar shapes of countries, thinking instead of the past. Of that moment in the T'ang's antechamber when Lwo Kang had humiliated him.

Shih wei su ts'an.

He could hear it even now. Could hear how Lwo Kang

77

had said it; see his face, only inches from his own, those coldly intelligent eyes staring at him scornfully, that soft, almost feminine mouth forming the hard shapes of the words. It was an old phrase. An ancient insult. *Impersonating the dead and eating the bread of idleness.* You are lazy and corrupt, it said. You reap the rewards of others' hard work. Chi-Po shuddered, remembering how the others there – Ministers like himself – had turned from him and left him there, as if agreeing with Lwo Kang. Not one had come to speak with him afterwards.

He looked down, speaking softly, for himself alone. "But now the ugly little pig's arse is dead!"

He had closed those cold eyes. Stopped up that soft mouth. And now his blood would inherit. And yet . . .

Heng Chi-Po closed his eyes, shivering, feeling a strange mixture of bitterness and triumph. Dead. But still the words sounded, loud, in his head. *Shih wei su ts'an.*

★ ★ ★

Big White brought them a tray of *ch'a*, then backed out, closing the door behind him.

Cho Hsiang leaned forward and poured from the porcelain bottle, filling Jyan's bowl first, then his own. When he was done he set the bottle down and looked up sharply at the hireling.

"Well? What is it, Kao Jyan?"

He watched Jyan take his bowl and sip, then nod his approval of the *ch'a*. There was a strange light in his eyes. Trouble. As he'd thought. But not of the kind he'd expected. What was Jyan up to?

"This is pleasant," said Jyan, sitting back. "Very pleasant. There's no better place in the Net than Big White's, wouldn't you say?"

Curbing his impatience, Cho Hsiang placed his hands on the table, palms down, and tilted his head slightly, studying Jyan. He was wary of him, not because he was in any physical danger – Big White frisked all his customers before he let them in – but because he knew Jyan for what he was.

A weasel. A devious little shit-eater with ambitions far above his level.

"No better place in the Net," he answered, saying nothing of the excellent Mu Chua's, where he and others from the Above usually spent their time here, nor of his loathing of the place and of the types, like Jyan, with whom he had to deal. "You'd best say what you want, Kao Jyan. I've business to attend to."

Jyan looked up at him, a sly, knowing expression in his eyes. "I'll not keep you long, *mister* contact man. What I have to say is simple and direct enough."

Cho Hsiang stiffened slightly, bristling at the insult Kao Jyan had offered him in using the anglicised form of *Hsien Sheng*, but his mind was already working on the question of what it was Jyan wanted. As yet he saw no danger in it for himself, even when Jyan leaned forward and said in a whisper, "I know who you work for, Cho Hsiang. I found it out."

Jyan leaned back, watching him hawkishly, the fingers of his right hand pulling at the fingers of the left. "That should be worth something, don't you think?"

Cho Hsiang sat back, his mind working quickly. Did he mean Hong Cao? If so, how had Jyan found out? Who, of Hsiang's contacts, had traced the connection back? Or was Jyan just guessing? Trying to squeeze him for a little extra? He looked at the hireling again, noting just how closely the other was watching him, then shrugged.

"I don't know what you mean. I am my own man. I'm not a filthy hireling."

He made the insult pointed, but Jyan just waved it aside. "You forget what you hired me for this time, mister contact man. It was way beyond your level. I knew at once you were working for someone else. And not just anyone. This one had power. Real power. Power to make deals with Security, to trade with other, powerful men. With money to oil the cogs and sweep away the traces. That's not your level, Cho Hsiang. Such people would not deign to sit at table with such as you and I."

Cho Hsiang was quiet a moment, thoughtful, then, "Give me a name."

Jyan laughed shortly, then leaned forward, his face now hard and humourless. "First I want a guarantee. Understand? I want to make certain that I'm safe. That they'll not be able to come for me and make sure of my silence."

He made to speak, but Jyan shook his head tersely. "No, Cho Hsiang. Listen. I've made a tape of all I know. It makes interesting listening. But tapes can go missing. So I've made a copy and secured it in a computer time-lock. Never mind where. But that time-lock needs to be re-set by me every two days. If it isn't, then the copy goes directly to Security.

Cho Hsiang took a deep breath. "I see. And what do you want in return for your silence?"

In answer, Jyan took the tape from the pocket of his one-piece and pushed it across the table to him. "I think they'll find a price that suits us both."

Smiling, Jyan re-filled his cup from the bottle, then, sitting back again, raised it in salute. "You said you wanted a name."

Cho Hsiang hesitated, his stomach tightening, then shook his head. He hadn't seen it at first, but now he saw it clearly. Jyan's talk of safeguards had brought it home to him. It was best he knew nothing. Or, if not nothing, then as little as possible. Such knowledge as Jyan had was dangerous.

"Suit yourself," said Jyan, laughing, seeing the apprehension in Cho Hsiang's face. When he spoke again his voice was harsh; no longer the voice of a hireling, but that of a superior. "Arrange a meeting. Tomorrow. Here, at Big White's."

Cho Hsiang leaned forward, angered by Jyan's sudden change of tone, then sat back, realising that things *had* changed. He picked up the tape and pocketed it, then got up from his chair and went to the door. "I'll see what I can do."

80

Jyan smiled again. "Oh, and Cho Hsiang . . . pay Big White for me on your way out."

★ ★ ★

Lehmann turned sharply, the low, urgent buzzing of the desk alarm sending his heart into his mouth. Four symbols had appeared on the screen of his personal comset, Han pictograms that spelt *Yen Ching* – Eye – the codeword for his Mid-Level contact, Hong Cao.

That it had appeared on his personal screen indicated its urgency. No computer line, however well protected, could be guaranteed discreet. For that reason, Hong Cao had been instructed to use the personal code only as a last resort.

Placing his right forefinger to the screen, Lehmann drew an oval, then dotted the centre of it. At once the message began to spill out onto the screen.

It was brief and to the point. Lehmann read it through once, then a second time. Satisfied he had it memorised, he pressed CLEAR and held the tab down for a minute – time enough to remove all memory of the transmission. Only then did he sit back, stunned by the import of the message.

"Shit!" he said softly, then leaned forward to tap in DeVore's personal contact code.

Someone knew. Someone had figured out how it all connected.

DeVore was out on patrol. Part of his face appeared on the screen, overlarge, the signal hazed, distorted. Lehmann realised at once that DeVore was staring down into a wrist set.

"Pietr! What is it?"

Lehmann swallowed. "Howard. Look, it's nothing really. Just that you . . . you left your gloves. Okay? I thought you might want to pick them up. And maybe have a drink."

DeVore's face moved back, coming into clearer focus. There was a moment's hesitation, then he nodded. "I'll be off duty in an hour. I'll come collect them then. Okay?"

"Fine." Lehmann cut contact at once.

The package from Hong Cao containing the tape and a sealed message card arrived a half bell later by special courier. Lehmann stared at it a moment, then put it unopened in the top drawer of his desk and locked it.

His first instinct had been right. They should have erased all traces that led back to them. Killed the killers. Killed the agents and the contact men. Killed everyone who knew. DeVore had argued against this, saying that to do so would only draw attention, but he, Lehmann had been right. And now they would have to do it anyway. If they still could.

When DeVore arrived they took the package straight through to Lehmann's Secure Room and listened to the tape through headphones. Afterwards they sat there looking at each other.

DeVore was first to speak. "He may have got it wrong, but he was close enough to do us damage. If Security investigate Berdichev at any depth they'll uncover the links with you. And then the whole structure comes crashing down."

"So what do you suggest?"

"We kill him."

"What about the copy tape?"

"Leave that to me." DeVore reached across and took the message card. He looked at it, then handed it to Lehmann.

Lehmann activated the card, read it, then handed it back across to DeVore.

"Good. This Kao Jyan wants a meeting. I'll see to that myself. Meanwhile I've something you can do."

Lehmann frowned. "What's that?"

"Yang Lai's alive. He tried to make contact with Wyatt. My men have found out where he is, but he'll only speak to you or Wyatt. It seems you're the only ones he trusts."

Lehmann felt his stomach flip over for the second time that morning. Yang Lai had been one of the Ministers of the Edict, Lwo Kang's chief officials. They had thought him with Lwo Kang when the Minister and all his principal men were killed.

"Then he wasn't in the dome when it went up?"

DeVore shook his head. "I only heard two hours back. All of the internal Security films were destroyed in the explosion, but the door tally survived. The body count for the solarium came out two short. It seems Junior Minister Yang is one."

"Then who's the other?"

DeVore shrugged. "We don't know yet. But Yang Lai might. Go see him. Do what you must."

Lehmann nodded. This time he would act on his instincts. "Okay. I'll deal with him."

DeVore stood up. "And don't worry, Pietr. We can handle this. You know we can." He glanced down at the tape and card, then back at Lehmann. "Destroy those. I'll see to the rest. Oh, and Pietr . . ."

"What?"

"My gloves . . ."

★ ★ ★

Jyan had spent two hours at Big White's after Cho Hsiang had gone. A meal of real pork and vegetables, a bottle of good wine and a long session with two of the house's filthiest girls – all on Cho Hsiang's bill – had put him in a good mood. It was all going his way at last. Things were happening for him. About time, he thought, turning the corner and entering the corridor that led to his apartment.

In the noise and crush of the corridor he almost missed it. Almost went straight in. But something – some sense he had developed over the years – stopped him. He drew his hand back from the palm-lock and bent down, examining it. There was no doubt about it. The lock had been tampered with.

He put his ear to the door. Nothing. At least, nothing unusual. He could hear a soft machine purr coming from within, but that was normal. Or almost normal . . .

He turned and looked back down the busy corridor,

ignoring the passers-by, trying to think. Had he left any of his machines on? Had he? He scratched at his neck nervously, unable to remember, then looked back at the marks on the lock, frowning. They looked new, but they might have been there some while. It might just have been kids.

It might have. But he'd best take no chances. Not in the circumstances.

He placed his palm flat against the lock, then, as the lock hissed open, drew back against the wall, away from the opening.

As the door slid back slowly, he looked into the room for some sign of an intruder. Then, drawing his knife with one swift movement, he stepped into the room.

The knife was knocked from his hand. He saw it flip through the air. Then a hand was clamped roughly about his mouth.

Jyan struggled to turn and face his assailant, one arm going up instinctively to ward off a blow, but the man was strong and had a tight grip on him.

Then, suddenly, he was falling backward.

He looked up, gasping. Kuan Yin, goddess of mercy! It was Chen!

Chen glared down at him angrily. "Where have you been?"

Two or three faces appeared in the doorway behind Chen. Jyan waved them away, then got up and moved past Chen to close the door. Getting his breath again, he turned to face the *kwai*, a faint smile returning to his lips. "I've been arranging things. Making deals."

He went to move past him again, but Chen caught his arm and sniffed at him. "You've been whoring, more like. I can smell the stink of them on you."

Jyan laughed. "A little pleasure after business, that's all." He moved into the room, then sat down heavily on the bed, facing Chen. "Anyway, what are you doing here?"

Chen sheathed his big hunting knife and crossed the room. There, in a corner recess, was an old-fashioned games machine. Turning his back on Jyan, he stared at the screen. "I thought I'd come and find out what was happening. You were gone a long time."

Jyan laughed, then pulled off his left slipper. "As I said, I was making deals. Working for both of us."

Chen toyed with the keys of the games machine a moment longer, then turned back. "And?"

Jyan smiled and kicked off the other slipper, then began to peel off his onepiece. "We've another meet. Tomorrow, at Big White's. We fix the price then."

Oblivious of the other man, Jyan stripped naked, then went over to the corner shower and fed five ten *fen* tokens into the meter beside it. Drawing back the curtain, he stepped inside and, as the lukewarm water began to run, started to soap himself down.

Chen watched Jyan's outline through the plastic a moment, then turned back to the machine.

It was an ancient thing that had three standard games programmed into it; *T'iao Chi, Hsiang Chi* and *Wei Chi.* He had set it up for a low level game of *Wei Chi,* and the nineteen by nineteen grid filled the screen. He was playing black and had made only twenty or so moves, but white was already in a strong position.

Chen looked about him once again. He had never been in Jyan's room before today – had, in truth, never been interested in Jyan's homelife – but now the situation was getting deep. It had seemed best to know how things stood.

Cheap tapestries hung on the walls. Standard works by Tung Yuan and Li Ch'eng; scenes of mountains and valleys, tall pine trees and gentle-flowing rivers. The sort of crap one saw everywhere in the Net. On the bedside table was a small shrine to Wen Ti, the evidence of burnt candles in the tray revealing a side of Jyan he would never have guessed. A small rug covered part of the bare ice floor at the end of the single bed, but otherwise the only furnishings were a pair of cheap fold-up chairs.

Some of the things there had surprised him. In a box under the bed he had found a recent generation SimFic HeadStim: a direct-input job that linked up to wires implanted in the brain. That alone must have cost Jyan at least five hundred yuan at current black market prices – maybe even the full thousand he had borrowed from Whiskers Lu – but unlike the two wraparounds he had, it was a useless item – a status symbol only – because Jyan, like most in the Net, hadn't had the operation.

A huge blue and gold er-silk eiderdown covered the bed. Underneath it, two bright red cotton blankets were spread out over the normal ice-cloth sheets of the bed – as if for a wedding night. For some reason it had reminded Chen of that moment on the mountainside when Jyan had pulled the wine bottle and the glasses from his sack. There was something dangerously impractical about that side of Jyan. Something hideously self-indulgent. It was a flaw in him. The kind of thing that could kill a man.

Chen cleared the board and switched off the machine, his sense of disenchantment coming to a head. All this – it was so ostentatious. So false. Jyan ached to be better than he was. Richer. More powerful. More cultured. Yet his attempts at mimicry were painful to observe. He was a cockroach imitating a turtle. And this latest scheme . . . Chen shuddered. It was doomed to failure. He knew that in his bones. You could not make deals with these people; could not be partner to them, only their hireling.

He looked about him one last time, watching the thinly-fleshed shape of Jyan bend and stretch behind the plastic curtaining. Then, his mind made up, he left quietly. It wasn't toys he wanted. He wanted something real. A new life. Better than this. More real than this. A child, maybe. A son.

He was tired of being *wang pen* – rootless, his origins forgotten. It was time he was connected. If not to the past, then to the future. He sighed, knowing he could do nothing about the past. But the future – that was unwritten . . .

As he walked back to his own apartment the thought went through his mind like a chant, filling his head, obsessing him – A child. A son. A child. A son – the words coursing through him like the sound of his feet as they pounded the bare ice flooring of the corridors. *A child. A son.*

Very well. He must be ready then. There was no other way.

★ ★ ★

Yang Lai knelt at Lehmann's feet, his head bowed low, his hands gripping the hem of Lehmann's *pau* tightly.

"You're a good man, Pietr Lehmann. A fine man. I've been so scared. So frightened that they would find me before you or Edmund came."

Lehmann looked about him. The room was filthy. It looked as if no one had tidied it in years. Had Yang Lai fallen this low, then? Had he no friends of higher rank to help him in his need? He drew the man to his feet and freed his hand, then reached across to lift his chin, making Yang Lai look at him.

"I'm glad you called, Yang Lai. Things are difficult. If Security had found you . . ."

Yang Lai averted his eyes. "I understand."

"How did you get out?"

The Han hesitated. "Does it matter?"

Lehmann noted the undertone of suspicion in Yang Lai's voice. The man had had time enough to work it out. Yet he wasn't certain. His trust in Wyatt had acted like a barrier against the truth. It had prevented him from piecing things together. Well, that was good. It meant things would be easier.

"I'm interested, that's all. But anyway . . ." He feigned indifference, changing tack at once, moving past Yang Lai as he spoke. "The Minister's assassination. It wasn't us, you see. Someone pre-empted us." He turned and looked back at the Han. "Do you understand me, Yang Lai? Do you see what I'm saying? Whoever it was, they almost killed you."

"No! No . . ." Yang Lai shook his head, confused. "That's not how it was. They . . . they warned me. Told me to get out of there."

Yang Lai shuddered violently and looked away. He was red-eyed and haggard from lack of sleep, and his clothes smelt. Even so, there was something in his manner that spoke of his former authority. He was a man accustomed to command.

For a moment Yang Lai seemed lost in thought. Then, like someone suddenly waking, he looked up at Lehmann again, a smile lighting his face. "Then Edmund had nothing to do with it?"

"Nothing." This time it was the truth.

For a moment Lehmann pondered the connection between Wyatt and the Han. Why did Yang Lai trust Edmund so explicitly? Was it only friendship? Or was it deeper than that? Were they lovers?

"Who warned you?" he asked, moving closer. "You have to tell me, Yang Lai. It's very important."

Yang Lai glanced up at him, meeting his eyes briefly. Then he looked down sharply, his shame like something physical. "A messenger came," he said softly. "My Third Secretary, Pi Ch'ien."

Pi Ch'ien. Lehmann caught his breath. Pi Ch'ien hadn't been on the list of names DeVore had given him. Which meant he was probably still alive. Lehmann turned away, pressing his left hand to his brow, trying to think. Then he turned back. "This Pi Ch'ien . . . where is he?"

Yang Lai shrugged. "I don't know. I assume he was killed." He looked away, his voice going very quiet. "I think I was the last to get out before the solarium went up."

Lehmann was still a moment, then, abruptly, he turned and made to go.

Yang Lai rushed after him and caught him at the door, holding tightly to his arm, his face pressed close to Lehmann's.

"What's happening? Please, Pietr, tell me what's happening!"

Lehmann turned back, taking Yang Lai's hands in his

own. "It's all okay, Yang Lai. It will all be all right. Trust me. Trust Edmund. But there are things we have to do. For all our sakes."

Yang Lai studied his face intently for a moment. Then he looked down, giving no sign of what he'd seen. "All right. Do what you must."

Outside, Lehmann paused and glanced across at the two men standing against the far side of the corridor. Behind him he heard the door slide shut and the doorlock click into place.

It would not help him. His men had the combination to the lock.

It's necessary, Lehmann told himself. All of this. All the killing and the lying and the double-dealing. All necessary.

He met the eyes of the taller man and nodded, then turned away, making his way quickly to the waiting transit lift.

Necessary. For all our sakes.

★　★　★

Cho Hsiang put the envelope on the table in front of Jyan, then leaned back, watching him carefully.

"What's this?" Jyan looked up guardedly.

"Open it and see. I'm only the messenger."

Cho Hsiang saw how suspicious Jyan was of the envelope. He had not seen anything like it before. It was all tape or mouth-work down here. No subtleties.

"You tear it open," he explained. "The message will be written on the sheet inside."

Jyan hesitated, then picked up the envelope and examined it. On one side of the whiteness was written his name. The other seemed to have been slit open diagonally, then sealed with something hot that had left the imprint of a double-helix. Seeing that, he laughed.

"I guessed right, then?"

Cho Hsiang said nothing, merely inclined his head towards the envelope.

Jyan tugged gently at the seal, trying to prise it open.

Then, more brutally, he tore at the silken paper. The seal gave suddenly and the message spilled out onto the table, coming to rest beside Cho Hsiang's hand. It was a single folded sheet. Gingerly, using only his fingertips, Cho Hsiang pushed it across to him.

On the paper was a figure. Jyan studied it a moment, then whistled softly.

"Will it do?"

There was the faintest trace of sarcasm in Cho Hsiang's voice.

Jyan had folded the paper. He unfolded it and stared at the figure again. Then he looked up over the paper at Cho Hsiang.

"Do you know what it says?"

Cho Hsiang shook his head slowly. "As I said, I'm only the messenger. But I know this. There'll be no haggling. Understand? You either take what's offered or you get nothing."

"Nothing . . ." Jyan laughed tensely. "That would be rather stupid of them, don't you think?"

Cho Hsiang leaned forward. "You heard me. Take it or leave it."

"And if I leave it? If I take what I know elsewhere?"

Cho Hsiang allowed himself a cold smile. "You're an imaginative man, Kao Jyan. Work it out for yourself."

Jyan looked down, unfolding the paper yet again. Cho Hsiang watched him, amused. They knew how to deal with such types up Above. Theirs was the way of ultimatum. Take it or leave it – it was all the same to them. Either way they would come out on top. He reached out and took his glass, draining it, then reached across and pressed the button on the wall that would summon Big White.

"I have to go now, Kao Jyan. What shall I say to my friends?"

Jyan looked up. From his face Cho Hsiang could see he was still undecided. He pressed him. "Well?"

There were sounds outside. The doorlock popped softly

90

and the door began to slide back. Jyan looked past Cho Hsiang, then back at him.

"Okay. We'll take it. And tell your man . . ."

He stopped, seeing Big White there.

"Yes?" Cho Hsiang stood up, letting Big White help him into his big mock-beaver coat.

"Tell him he'll have no more trouble. Okay?"

Cho Hsiang smiled tightly. "Good." He turned, as if to leave, then turned back. "I'll be seeing you then, Kao Jyan."

Jyan nodded, all the cockiness gone from him.

"Oh, and Jyan . . . See to the bill for me, eh?"

★ ★ ★

"What have we got?"

The technician tapped at the keys, running the recording back for analysis. Then he leaned back, letting DeVore read from the screen for himself.

51 words total. 14 repetitions. Total vocabulary 37 words.

"It's not enough."

The technician shook his head. "Maybe not for direct speech transposition. But we could generate new words from the sounds we have. There's a considerable range of tones here. The computer can create a gestalt – a whole speech analogue – from very little. We've more than enough here to do that. You write the script, the machine will get him to say it. And not even his mother would know it wasn't him saying it."

DeVore laughed. "Good. Then we'll move quickly on this." He took a hardfile from his jacket pocket and handed it to the technician. "Here's what I want our friend Jyan to say."

The technician hesitated fractionally, then nodded. "Okay. I'll get to work on it right away. Will tomorrow be too late? Mid-day?"

DeVore smiled and slapped the technician's back. "Tomorrow's fine. I'll collect it myself."

He went out, heading back down towards the Net. It

was early evening. In under four hours he was due to meet the General to make his report. There was time enough, meanwhile, to set things up.

In the Security lift, descending, he made contact with the two men he had left outside Big White's.

"How's our man?"

The answer came back into his earpiece. "He's still inside, sir."

"Good. If he comes out, follow at a distance. But don't make a move. Not yet. I want them both, remember."

He had barely closed contact when an urgent message came through on his wrist console. It was Lehmann again, his face taut with worry.

"What is it, Pietr?"

Lehmann hesitated, conscious that he was speaking on an open channel, then took the risk. "The missing body. I know who it is. It's Yang Lai's man, Pi Ch'ien."

"I see. So where is he?"

Lehmann laughed anxiously. "That's just it. I've been checking up. There's no trace of him. He hasn't been seen since the assassination."

"So he's in hiding?"

"It seems so."

"Right. Leave it to me." He paused. "All's well apart from that?"

Lehmann hesitated, then gave the coded answer. "It's a cloudless sky, Howard. I . . . Well, I'll see you sometime, yes?"

DeVore closed contact. So Yang Lai was dead. Good. That was one thing less to worry about.

The lift slowed, then came to a halt. For a moment DeVore stood there, his hand almost touching the Door Open pad, his skin, beneath the simple one-piece he was wearing, tingling from the decontamination procedure. Then, clear in mind what he had to do, he hit the pad and went outside, into the Net.

CHAPTER·3

A GAME OF
STATIC PATTERNS

Fifth bell was sounding when Major DeVore reported to General Tolonen in his office at the top of the vast fortress-like barracks that housed Security Central. The General stood as he came into the room and came round his desk to greet DeVore, a broad smile on his chiselled face.

"Good morning, Howard. How are things?"

DeVore bowed at waist and neck, then straightened up, meeting the old man's eyes. "Not good, sir. Our investigation of the Minister's death is proving more difficult than I thought."

The General looked at him a moment longer, then nodded. Briefly he rested a hand on the Major's arm, as if to reassure him, then turned and went back behind his desk. Ensconced in his chair again he leaned forward, motioning to DeVore to take a seat. "Still nothing, eh?"

DeVore gave the smallest hint of a bow then sat. "Not quite, sir."

Tolonen tilted his chin back, interested. "I see. What have you got?"

"Nothing certain. Only rumour. But it may prove a lead."

"Anything I should know about?"

DeVore took the tiny tape from his tunic pocket, wiped it on the cloth then handed it across the desk. Tolonen sat back and pushed the wafer-thin cassette into the input socket behind his left ear. For a minute or two he sat there, silent, his eyes making small, erratic movements in their sockets. Then, as if coming to again, he looked directly at his Major.

"Interesting, Howard. Very interesting." Tolonen squeezed the narrow slit of skin behind his ear and removed the tape. "But how reliable *is* this?"

DeVore tilted his head slightly, considering. "Normally I'd say it was highly reliable. But the circumstances of this case – particularly its political importance – make it more complex than usual. It would be unwise to take things at face value. For now I'm having the sources checked out. Playing ear. However . . ." He hesitated, then spoke again, studying the General more closely than before. "There is something else, sir. Something perhaps more important in the long run."

"Go on, Howard."

"Well, sir. I'm almost certain this involves Security. Maybe at Staff level."

Tolonen looked at him directly for some moments, then nodded soberly, his expression unchanged. "I agree. Though with great reluctance, I must say. The very thought of it makes me shudder."

DeVore bowed his head sympathetically. "Then . . ."

Tolonen stopped him with a look. "Let me outline the situation as I see it, Howard. Then we'll see how this new information fits with what we have."

DeVore sat straighter in his chair; his eyes watching the older man intently as he outlined the situation.

"First – what kind of weapon was used, and where and by whom was it manufactured?" Tolonen pulled broad, long fingers through neatly cut grey hair, his deeply blue eyes fixing DeVore. "We're working on the assumption that it was some kind of ice derivative. An ice-eater. Research into ice derivatives has been banned by the Edict, but we're not dealing with legitimate activity here. It's therefore possible that someone has come up with such a thing.

"Second – who knew Lwo Kang would be there at that

time? Most of those we might have suspected – Lwo's own Junior Ministers – died with him. Only Yang Lai is unaccounted for."

DeVore nodded. "No trace yet, sir. But we're still looking."

"Good. Now, third – who took the Security squad off duty? Are we safe in assuming it was the duty captain, or was someone higher up the chain of command behind the decision?" Tolonen paused and shook his head. "It seems almost inexplicable to me that the officer concerned acted independently. His record was without blemish and his suicide would seem to confirm it. But he was a frightened man, Howard. I believe he was acting under threat."

"I agree, sir. I knew the man as a cadet and I'd vouch that he would not have acted as he did without good reason. Our assumption is that his immediate family was threatened. We haven't yet located them – but whether that's because he placed them in hiding or whether they were taken we don't know. Even so, we mustn't rule out another motive. Gambling debts, perhaps. Or some kind of addiction. Women, maybe. Even the best men have their weaknesses. In any case, I have a squad investigating it."

"Good. Then, fourth – who were the actual assassins? As you know, our first idea was that it was done from the air – from a craft over-flying the dome. But now we've ruled that out."

"Sir?" DeVore tensed slightly, suddenly more alert.

"A search of the area surrounding the dome has brought a number of new items to light, chief amongst which is a corpse."

"A corpse?"

"Yes. We found the body crammed into a narrow feed tunnel, not far from a ventilation shaft that comes out close by the dome. A *Hung Mao*. Male. Aged thirty-five. He'd been stabbed twice with a large-bladed knife. Very expertly, so I'm told."

"Then we've got one of the assassins?"

Tolonen shrugged. "Well, I wouldn't rule that out, but it's more likely that the man simply stumbled onto things. His ID shows him to have been a maintenance engineer, cleared for First Level Security."

DeVore considered a moment. "It sounds the ideal profession for gaining access to the dome."

"My own first thought, Howard, but it doesn't check out with anything else. We can account for his movements up to the time he got into that ventilation tunnel. We've checked. He's on camera, climbing into the access hatch only twelve minutes before the dome went up. He made one check – timed and logged – halfway up the tunnel. That accounts for the first five minutes. That would leave him only seven minutes to climb the rest of the way, meet his partner, set the charges and get back down."

"Time enough. And anyway, what if his partner set the charges?"

"That's possible. But then, why would he be needed? And why killed? It doesn't fit. And anyway, we have something else."

DeVore blinked. "You've been busy, sir."

Tolonen laughed. "Yes, well, I did *try* to get you, Howard. Anyway, it's possible we have our men. Two low level sorts. They were involved in an incident with Security guards in one of the nearby stacks at Level 11. A CompCam unit noticed that one of the men had no ID match and had Security investigate. There was an exchange of shots and the two men got away."

DeVore was quiet a moment. "But you have them now?"

"No. Not yet. But listen to this, Howard. You'll never believe it. Do you know how they got out?"

DeVore shook his head.

"Well, our men thought they had them cornered in a Distribution lift. They'd called up a burner, ready to melt the doorlocks, but the two suspects did something to the lift. They over-rode its circuits, then rammed the whole thing through the floor and into the Net!"

DeVore whistled. "What happened?"

"The whole deck had to be sealed and cleaned out. A messy business. Thousands hurt. More than a hundred and fifty dead. We've had to put out a story about systems failure. But think about it, Howard. Our two friends must have had inside information. There aren't that many people who know those lifts go down another ten levels. Just as important, however, is the fact that they had a device that over-rode the circuitry." He paused. "It makes sense of other things, too. My guess is that they were dropped in. Picked up at one of the under-Net gates – perhaps near one of the agricultural processing stations – and landed on top of the City. They did the job, made their escape down the ventilation shaft – killing our maintenance man on the way – then emerged at Eleven."

DeVore nodded slowly. "It . . . makes a kind of sense."

"Good. I'm glad you think so. In which case there are a few other questions that need answers. Who were their contacts? Who gave them the information? Who trained them? Who physically landed them on the roof? This kind of operation would have needed a lot of planning. A substantial number of people would have been involved."

Again DeVore nodded, but this time there was an air of distraction about him.

The General leaned forward excitedly. "Just think, Howard. If we could get to just one of those involved – just one! – we could blast the whole thing open!" He laughed, then slammed his hands down firmly on the desktop. "And in order that we can do just that, I've been to see the T'ang."

"Sir?" DeVore seemed surprised by this new development.

"Yes, Howard. The T'ang has given me authority. The authority to cut through bureaucratic tape, to make deals, grant pardons, whatever's necessary, providing we get information on the people who were behind this." He smiled broadly. "So you see, Howard. What you brought me was of great interest. If Wyatt *was* involved, either as principal or as agent . . . Well, I want him. Understand? I want to know what his motive was, who his connections were."

"So you think it might be him?"

The General was silent for a time, then he shrugged. "I don't know. I thought . . . Well, you know what I thought. I listened to the tape of your conversation with Lehmann. He's an unpleasant specimen, but I agree with you. He's too bluff, too careless in what he says to have been behind this. As for Wyatt, I've met him more than once, and I liked him." Again he shrugged. "Still, do what you must. The T'ang wants answers, and he wants them fast."

★ ★ ★

When DeVore had gone, Tolonen summoned the ensign, Haavikko.

Axel Haavikko was a tall, broad-shouldered young man of nineteen years, his blond hair cut severely short. On his jacket he wore the insignia of the elite military school from which he had graduated only eight months previously, on his chest the embroidered sea horse patch of a ninth grade military officer. He marched briskly across the room and came to attention before the desk.

"Sir?"

The General smiled. "At ease, boy. Have you got the tape?"

"Yes, sir. But I thought . . ."

Tolonen raised an eyebrow. "I know. But I decided against it. Major DeVore doesn't need to know everything. He's tired. I could see it myself. He's taking on too much, trying to keep abreast of everything."

He leaned back in his chair, studying the young man; observing that he too was showing signs of strain. "We could all do with some rest, eh, Haavikko? A break from things. But the evil of this world goes on, whether we're there to deal with it or not." He smiled kindly. "Okay, let's see what we have."

The cadet bowed, then turned and went over to the viewer, placing the flimsy transparent card he was carrying onto the viewing surface. Immediately the wall-screen above his head lit up, showing two men pushing their way through a broad but crowded corridor. The tape sheet had been put together from segments of hundreds of individual tape sheets, then edited to make it seem as though a single camera had followed the suspects the whole length of the Main.

"These are the two men, sir. The one on the left was addressed as Jyan. The other is unnamed. There's no entry on either in Security Central Records."

The General sniffed. "Hold that a moment."

The image froze. A sign behind the first of the men read "Level 11, South 3 Stack, Canton of Munich", the English in blocked black figures above the blood red Mandarin pictograms. Crowds packed the Main. The second man – better built than the first; the tell-tale bulge of a knife at his waist – had turned to left profile, revealing a short, livid scar on his neck just below the ear.

"Interesting types, eh, Axel? From the Net. There's no doubt about it. If Security Central has nothing, then I'm certain these are our men. Can we tell where they appeared from?"

Axel tapped the controls. At once the picture changed – showed a smaller corridor; dimly lit, almost empty.

"Where's this?"

"Up five levels, sir. At Sixteen. It's a maintenance corridor, not used by the public. Watch."

As they watched, a hatch dropped down from the ceiling and two men lowered themselves into the corridor, one after the other. The two Han from the other shots.

"Where does that lead?"

"There's a long vertical shaft, about twenty *ch'i* back from that hatch. It comes out at Forty One. There we lose them."

"Any reason why?"

"Camera malfunction. Vandalism. It seems genuine. They've been having trouble with that section for weeks, apparently."

"Okay. So let's get back to Eleven. See what kind of men we're dealing with."

For the next ten minutes they watched in silence as the situation unfolded. They saw the fight. Saw Jyan draw and use his knife, then drive the loader into the lift. Then, less than a minute later, the screen went blank.

"That's all that survived, sir. When the quarantine seals came down most of the cameras blew. We've pieced this together from Central Records' copies."

Tolonen nodded, satisfied. "You've done a good job, Haavikko. It shouldn't be difficult to trace these two. We have arrangements with certain of the Triad bosses beneath the Net. They'll find them for us. It's only a question of time."

"Then we do nothing, sir?"

"Nothing until we hear from our contacts. But I want us to be ready, so I've arranged something. It'll mean that we'll have a squad down there, under the Net in Munich Canton, when news comes. It'll allow us to get to them at once. I've put Fest in charge. He has strict orders to take the men alive if possible. You and Hans Ebert will make up the squad."

Haavikko hesitated, then asked. "What are we to do down there?"

Tolonen laughed. "Until you're called on, nothing. You can treat it as a paid holiday. Ebert knows the place quite well, apparently. I'm sure he'll find something for you to do. But when the call comes, be there, and fast. All right?"

Haavikko bowed his head. "Anything else, sir?"

"Yes. One last thing. I want you to make a list."

"Sir?"

"I want you to compile a list of all those who might have planned this; anyone who might conceivably have been involved. Not just those with a clear motive, but anyone who might have had the right contacts."

"Anyone?"

The General nodded sternly. "Leave no one out, however absurd it might seem."

The cadet bowed deeply, then clicked his heels together. "Sir."

Alone again, Tolonen stood, then went to the window. Far below, the wide moat of the Security Fortress seemed filled with an inky blackness. In the early morning light the two watchtowers at the far end of the bridge threw long, thin shadows across the apron of the spaceport beyond.

He would not act. Not yet. For a while he would trust to instinct and let Wyatt be. See if Wyatt's name appeared on Haavikko's list. Wait for DeVore to gather something more substantial than the tattle of Above. Because deep down he didn't believe that Wyatt was involved.

He turned back to his desk, putting his fingers lightly to the intercom pad.

His secretary answered at once. "General?"

"Play me that tape again. Major DeVore and Under Secretary Lehmann. The part where Lehmann talks about suffocating and bad blood. A few lines, that's all."

"Yes, General."

He turned back to the window, looking down. As he watched a tiny figure emerged from the shadow and marched quickly but unhurriedly across the bridge. It was DeVore.

Major DeVore was a clever officer. A good man to have on your team. There was no fooling him; he saw things clearly. Saw through the appearance of things. And if *he* believed that Lehmann wasn't involved . . .

"The tape's ready, General."

"Good," he said, not looking round; continuing to watch the figure far below. "Let me hear it."

Lehmann's voice filled the room, urgent and passionate.

"We're suffocating, Howard! Can't they see that? Biting at the leash! Even so, violence . . . Well, that's a different matter. It hurts everyone and solves nothing. It only causes bad blood, and how can *that* help our cause? This . . . this act . . . All it does is set us back a few more years. It makes things more difficult, more . . ."

101

The voice cut out. After a moment the General sniffed, then nodded to himself. He had heard the words a dozen, maybe two dozen times now, and each time they had had the power to convince him of Lehmann's innocence. Lehmann's anger, his callousness, while they spoke against him as a man, were eloquent in his defence in this specific matter. It was not how a guilty man behaved. In any case, he was right. How *would* this serve him? Li Shai Tung would merely appoint another Minister. Another like Lwo Kang.

Down below, DeVore had reached the far end of the bridge. Two tiny figures broke from the shadow of the left-hand tower to challenge him, then fell back, seeing who it was. They melted back into the blackness and DeVore marched on alone, out onto the apron of the spaceport.

The General turned away. Perhaps DeVore was right. Perhaps Wyatt was their man. Even so, a nagging sense of wrongness persisted, unfocused, unresolved.

"I'm tired," he said softly to himself, sitting himself behind his desk again. "Yes, tiredness, that's all it is."

* * *

"Wait outside, at the junction. You know what he looks like?"

The Han nodded. "Like my brother."

"Good. Then get going."

The Han did as he was told, closing the door behind him, leaving DeVore alone in the room. DeVore looked around, for the first time allowing himself to relax. Not long now. Not long and it would all be done. This was the last of it. He looked at the sealed bag on the floor by the bed and smiled, then sat on the end of the bed next to the corpse's feet.

The *kwai*, Chen, had been hard to kill. Stubborn. He had fought so hard for life that they had had to club him to death, as if strangling the man hadn't been enough. His head was a bloodied pulp, his features almost unrecognisable.

102

The Han had enjoyed that. DeVore had had to drag him off.

Like animals, he thought, disgusted, promising himself he'd make the Han's death a particularly painful one.

For a while he sat there, head down, hands on knees, thinking things through. Then he looked up, looked about himself again. It was such a mean, shabby little place, and like all of this beneath the Net, it bred a type that matched its circumstances. This Kao Jyan, for instance; he had big dreams, but he was a little man. He didn't have the skill or imagination to carry off his scheme. All he had was a brash impudence; an inflated sense of self-importance. But then, what else could be expected? Living here, a man had no perspective. No way of judging what the truth of things really was.

He got up and crossed the room. Inset into the wall was an old-fashioned games machine. A ResTem Mark IV. He switched it on and set it up for *Wei Chi*; an eighth level game, the machine to start with black.

For a time he immersed himself in the game, enjoying the challenge. Then, when it was clear he had the advantage, he turned away.

The General was sharper than he'd thought he'd be. Much sharper. That business with the dead maintenance engineer. His discovery of Kao Jyan and the *kwai*. For a moment DeVore had thought their scheme undone. But the game was far from played out. He'd let the General find his missing pieces. One by one he'd give them to him. But not until he'd done with them.

He glanced at the machine again. It was a complex game, and he prided himself on a certain mastery of it. Strange, though, how much it spoke of the difference between East and West. At least, of the old West, hidden beneath the levels of the Han City, the layers of Han culture and Han history. The games of the West had been played on similar boards to those of the East, but the West played between the lines, not on the intersecting points. And the games of the West had been flexible, each individual piece given breath, allowed to move, as though each had an independent life. That was not so in *Wei Chi*. In *Wei Chi* once a piece was placed it remained, unless it was surrounded and its "breath" taken from it. It was a game of static patterns; patterns built patiently over hours or days – sometimes even months. A game where the point was not to eliminate but to enclose.

East and West – they were the inverse of each other. Forever alien. Yet one must ultimately triumph. For now it was the Han. But now was not forever.

He turned from the screen, smiling. "White wins, as ever."

It had always interested him; ever since he had learned how much the Han had banned or hidden. A whole separate culture. A long and complex history. Buried, as if it had never been. The story of the old West. Dead. Shrouded in white, the Han colour of death.

DeVore stretched and yawned. It was two days since he had last slept. He crossed the room and looked at his reflection in the mirror beside the shower unit. Not bad, he thought, but the drugs he had taken to keep himself alert had only a limited effect. Pure tiredness would catch up with him eventually. Still, they'd keep him on his feet long enough to see this through.

He looked down. His wrist console was flashing.

DeVore smiled at his reflection. "At last," he said. Then, straightening his tunic, he turned to face the door.

* * *

Jyan came laughing into his room. "Chen . . ." he began, then stopped, his eyes widening, the colour draining from his cheeks. "What the . . . ?"

He turned and made to run, but the second man, following him in, blocked the doorway, knife in hand.

He turned back slowly, facing the stranger.

"Close the door," DeVore said, looking past Jyan at the other. Then he turned to face Jyan again. "Come in, Kao Jyan. Make yourself at home."

Jyan swallowed and backed away to the left, his eyes going to the figure sprawled face down on the bed, the cover over its head. It was Chen. He could tell it from a dozen different signs – by the shape of the body, the clothes, by the black, studded straps about his wrists.

For a moment he said nothing, mesmerised by the sight of those two strong hands resting there, lifeless and pale, palms upward on the dark red sheet. Then he looked up again. The stranger was watching him, that same cruel half-smile on his lips.

"What do you want?" Jyan asked, his voice barely audible.

DeVore laughed, then turned to face the games machine, tapping in his next move. Jyan looked at the screen. The machine was set up for *Wei Chi*, the nineteen by nineteen grid densely cluttered with the small black and white stones. From the state of the game it looked as though the stranger had been waiting for some time.

DeVore turned back, giving Jyan a strangely intense look. Then he dropped his eyes and moved closer. "It's a fascinating game, don't you think, Kao Jyan? Black starts, and so the odds are in his favour – seven out of ten, they say – yet I, like you, prefer to play against the odds."

He stepped closer. Jyan backed against the wall, looking away.

"You have the envelope, Kao Jyan?"

Jyan turned his head, meeting the other's eyes. Only a hand's width separated them now. He could feel the other's breath upon his cheek. "The . . . envelope?"

"The offer we made you."

"Ah . . ." Jyan fumbled in the inside pocket of his one-piece, then drew out the crumpled envelope and handed it to him. The stranger didn't look at it, merely pocketed it, then handed back another.

"Go on. Open it. It's our new offer."

Jyan could see the body on the bed, the man waiting at the door, knife in hand, and wondered what it meant for him. Was he dead? He looked down at the sealed letter in his hand. It was identical to the one Cho Hsiang had given him.

His hands shaking, he opened the envelope and took out the folded sheet. This time there was nothing on it. The pure white sheet was empty.

DeVore smiled. "You understand, Kao Jyan?"

Jyan looked from one man to the other, trying to see a way out of this. "The tape . . ." he began, his voice trembling now. "What about the tape?"

The stranger turned away, ignoring his comment, as if it had no significance. "I'm sorry about your friend. It was unfortunate, but he was no part of this. The deal was with you, Kao Jyan."

Jyan found he was staring at the body again. The stranger saw where he was looking and smiled. "Go on. Look at him, if you want. He'll not mind you looking now." He went across to the bed and pulled the cover back. "Here . . ."

The stranger's voice held a tone of command that made Jyan start forward, then hesitate, a wave of nausea passing through him.

DeVore looked up from the body. "He was a hard man to kill, your friend. It took both of us to deal with him. Chu Heng here had to hold him down while I dressed him."

Jyan shuddered. A cord had been looped about Chen's bull neck four or five times then tightened until it had bitten into the flesh, drawing blood. But it was hard to judge whether that had been the cause of death or the heavy blows he'd suffered to the back of the head; blows that had broken his skull like a fragile piece of porcelain.

He swallowed drily then looked up, meeting the stranger's eyes. "Am I dead?"

DeVore laughed; not cruelly, but as if the naivety of the remark had genuinely amused him. "What do you think?"

"The tape . . ." he said again.

"You don't understand, do you, Kao Jyan?"

106

The Han in the doorway laughed, but shut up abruptly when DeVore looked at him.

Jyan's voice was almost a breath now. "Understand what?"

"The game. Its rules. Its different levels. You see, you were out of your depth. You had ambitions above your level. That's a dangerous thing for a little man like you. You were greedy."

Jyan shivered. It was what Chen had said.

"You've . . . how should I say it . . . inconvenienced us."

"Forget the whole thing. Please. I . . ."

DeVore shook his head. "I'm sorry," he said quietly, looking at Jyan with what seemed almost regret. "It's not possible."

"I'll say nothing. I swear I'll say nothing."

"You give your word, eh?" DeVore turned and picked up the bag on the floor by the bed. "Here. This is what your word means."

DeVore threw the bag at him. Jyan caught it and looked inside, then threw the bag down, horrified. It was Cho Hsiang's head.

"You understand, then? It's necessity. We have to sacrifice some pieces. For the sake of the game."

"The game . . . ?"

But there were no more explanations. The Han's knife flashed and dug deep into his back. Kao Jyan was dead before he hit the floor.

*　*　*

In Mu Chua's House of the Ninth Ecstasy it was the hour of leisure and the girls were sprawled out on the couches in the Room of the Green Lamps, talking and laughing amongst themselves. Mu Chua's House was a good house, a clean house, even though it was below the Net, and catered only for those who came here from Above on business. Feng Chung, biggest of the local Triad bosses and Mu Chua's one-time lover, gave them his protection.

His men guarded Mu Chua's doors and gave assistance when a customer grew troublesome. It was a good arrangement and Mu Chua had grown fat on it.

Mu – it meant mother in the old tongue, though she was no one's mother and had been sterilised at twelve – was in her fifties now; a strong, small woman with a fiery temper who had a genuine love for her trade and for the girls in her charge. "Here men forget their cares," was her motto and she had it written over the door in English and Mandarin, the pictograms sewn into every cushion, every curtain, every bedspread in the place. Even so, there were strict rules in her House. None of her girls could be hurt in any way. "If they want that," she had said to Feng Chung once, her eyes blazing with anger, "they can go down to the Clay. This is a good house. A loving house. How can my girls be loving if they are scared? How can they take the cares of men away unless they have no cares themselves?"

Mu Chua was still a most attractive woman and many who had come to sample younger flesh had found themselves ending the night in mother's arms. Thereafter there would be no other for them. They would return to her alone, remembering not only the warmth and enthusiasm of her embraces, but also those little tricks – special things she kept a secret, even from her girls – that only she could do.

Just now she stood in the arched doorway, looking in at her girls, pleased by what she saw. She had chosen well. There were real beauties here – like Crimson Lotus and Jade Melody – and girls of character, like Spring Willow and the tiny, delicate-looking Sweet Honey, known to all as "little *Mimi*", after the Mandarin for her adopted name. But there was more than that to her girls; she had trained them to be artisans, skilled at their craft of love-making. If such a thing were possible here in the Net, they had breeding. They were not common *men hu* – "the one standing in the door" but *shen nu* – "god girls". To Mu Chua it was an important distinction. Her girls might well be prostitutes, but they were not mere smoke-flowers. Her

House was a land of warmth and softness, a model for all other Houses, and she felt a great pride in having made it so.

Crimson Lotus and Sweet Honey had settled themselves at the far end of the room and were talking with another of the girls, Golden Heart. Mu Chua went across to them and settled herself on the floor between them, listening to their talk.

"I had a dream, Mother Chua," said Golden Heart, turning to her. She was Mu Chua's youngest girl, a sweet-faced thing of thirteen. "I was telling Crimson and little Mimi. In my dream it was New Year and I was eating cakes. *Nian-kao* – year cakes. Above me the clouds formed huge mountains in the sky, lit with the most extraordinary colours. I looked up, expecting something, and then, suddenly, a tiger appeared from out of the West and came and mated with me."

The other girls giggled, but Golden Heart carried on, her face earnest. "Afterwards I woke, but I was still in the dream, and beside me on the bed lay a pale grey snake, its skin almost white in places. At first it moved, yet when I reached out and touched it it was cold."

Mu Chua licked at her lips, disturbed. "That is a powerful dream, child. But what it means . . ." She shrugged and fell quiet, then changed the subject. It would not do to worry Golden Heart. "Listen. I have a special favour to ask of you girls. We are to have visitors. Three important men from the Above. Soldiers."

Crimson Lotus clapped her hands in delight. "How wonderful, Mother Chua! Soldiers! They keep themselves so fit, so trim!" She gave a low, seductive laugh and looked across at Sweet Honey. "If Mother Chua weren't here to look after us I'm sure I'd do it for nothing with a soldier!"

Mu Chua joined their laughter. "Yes. But these are not just any soldiers. These are the Great General's own men, his elite, and you will be paid three times your usual fee. You will entertain them in the Room of Heaven and you will do whatever they ask."

"Whatever they ask?" Sweet Honey raised an eyebrow.

Mu Chua smiled reassuringly at her. "Within the rules, of course. They have been told they are not to harm you in any way."

"And if they are not pleased?" asked Golden Heart, her face still clouded from the dream she'd had.

Mu Chua reached out and stroked her cheek tenderly. "They are men, child. Of course they will be pleased."

★ ★ ★

Ebert stopped at the curtained doorway and turned to face them. "Here we are, my friends. Mu Chua's. The finest beneath the Net."

Fest laughed, delighted, but at his side Haavikko looked uncertain. "What is this place?"

Fest clapped his shoulder and pointed up at the sign of the lotus and the fish above the doorway. "What does it look like, Axel? We're in Flower Streets and Willow Lanes here. In the land of warmth and softness. At home with the family of the green lamps." He saw comprehension dawn on Haavikko's face and laughed again. "Yes, Axel, it's a Sing-Song House. A brothel."

He tried to go forward, his arm still about Haavikko's shoulder, but the young ensign held back.

"No. I don't want to go in." Haavikko swallowed. A faint colour appeared in his cheeks. "It . . . it isn't my thing."

Ebert came back to him. "You're a man, aren't you, Haavikko? Well then, of course it's your thing."

Haavikko shook his head. "You go in. I'll wait for you."

Ebert looked at Fest and raised an eyebrow. Then he looked back at Haavikko. "That's impossible. I've booked us in for the night. We're staying here. This is our billet while we're down here. Understand?"

"You mean they do more than . . . ?"

Ebert nodded exaggeratedly, making Fest laugh once more, then he grew more serious. "Look, Haavikko, if you don't want to screw one of the girls you don't have to. But come inside, eh? Mu Chua will bring you a meal and show you to a room. You can watch a trivee or something while Fest and I enjoy ourselves."

Haavikko looked down, angered by the slightly mocking tone in Ebert's voice. "Isn't there somewhere else I could stay?"

Ebert huffed, losing his patience suddenly. "Oh for the gods' sake, Fest, order him inside! Don't you understand, Haavikko? We're a squad. We need to be together when the call comes. What's the fucking good if you're somewhere else?"

Haavikko looked to Fest, who smiled apologetically. "It's true, Axel. My orders are to keep us together at all times. Look, why don't you do what Hans has suggested? Come inside and take a room. Then, if you change your mind, you've not far to go."

"I've told you . . ."

"Yes, yes. I understand. Now come inside. I order you. All right?"

Inside Mu Chua greeted them expansively, then led them through to a large room at the back of the House where three girls were waiting. As they entered the girls knelt and bowed their heads, then looked up at them, smiling, expectant, as if waiting for them to make their choice. Axel stared at them, surprised. They were not at all what he had expected, nor was this place the gaudy den of harlotry he had so often seen in vid dramas.

"What is this room called?" he asked, surprising both Ebert and Fest by being the first to speak.

The girl on the far left looked briefly across at her companions, then looked up at Axel, smiling radiantly. "This is the Room of Heaven. Here a man may dream and live his dreams."

She was beautiful. Even for these tiny Han types she was quite exceptional, and Axel felt something stir in him despite himself. She wore a bright red satin *ch'i p'ao* patterned with tiny blue flowers and cranes and varicoloured butterflies, the long, one-piece dress wrapped concealingly

111

about her dainty figure. Her hair had been cut in a swallow-tail bang, the two wings swept down over a pale ivory brow that would have graced the daughter of a T'ang, a clasp of imitation pearls holding the dark flow of her black hair in a tight, unbraided queue. Her hands, small as a child's, were unadorned, the nails varnished but unpainted. She was so astonishing, so unexpected, that he could not help but stare at her, his lips parted, his eyes wide.

"What do they call you?"

She bowed her head again, a faint smile playing on her tiny, rosebud lips. "My name is Crimson Lotus."

"Well!" said Ebert, laughing. "I see Haavikko has made his choice."

Axel broke from the spell. "No. Not at all. I . . . I meant what I said. This . . ." He looked about him again, surprised anew by the tastefulness, the simple luxury of the room and its furnishings. "This isn't my thing."

He looked back down at the girl and saw, behind the surface smile, a faint hint of disappointment in her eyes and at the corners of her mouth. At once he felt upset that he had hurt her, even in so small a way, by his inadvertence. "I'm sorry . . ." he started to say, but Ebert spoke over him.

"Ladies, please forgive our friend. We thought we might change his mind by bringing him to your most excellent house, but it seems he's adamant." Ebert looked to Fest and smiled. "I should explain. My friend is *ya*, you understand? A yellow eel."

Haavikko frowned, not understanding. His knowledge of basic Mandarin included neither term. But the girls understood at once.

"My pardon, honourable sir," said Crimson Lotus, her face clear, her smile suddenly resplendent, showing her pearl-white perfect teeth. "If you will but wait a moment I shall call back Mother Chua. I am certain she could provide you with a boy."

Axel turned to face Ebert, furious. "What do you mean . . . ?"

Ebert roared with laughter, enjoying the confusion on the faces of the girls. Ignoring the edge in Axel's voice he reached out and touched his shoulder. "Only a joke, my friend. Only a joke."

The girls were looking from one to the other of the soldiers, their faces momentarily anxious. Then they too joined in with Ebert's laughter, their heads lowered, one hand raised to their mouths, their laughter like the faint, distant laughter of children.

Axel turned away from Ebert and looked at them again, letting his anger drain from him. Then he smiled and gave the slightest bow. No, he thought. Make nothing of it. It is Ebert's way. He cannot help it if he is ill-bred and ill-mannered. It comes from being who he is; heir to one of the biggest financial empires in Chung Kuo. He does not have to behave as Fest and I. We serve, but he only plays at being a servant. He, after all, is a master.

Yes, but watch yourself, Hans Ebert. One day you'll make one joke too many, speak out of place once too often, and then your riches will not help you. No, nor your connections.

The smallest of the girls rose with a bow and came towards them, head lowered. "Would the gentlemen like *ch'a*?"

Ebert answered for them. "Gods no! Bring us something stronger. Some wine. And something to eat, too. I'm ravenous!"

Embarrassed by Ebert's brash, proprietorial manner and awkward on his own account, Axel watched the others sit on cushions Crimson Lotus brought for them. "Will you not sit with us?" she asked him, coming much closer than she had before. The sweet delicacy of her scent was intoxicating and her dark eyes were like a lover's, sharing some secret understanding.

"I'd best not," he said, rather too stiffly. My sister . . . he had almost added. He looked down, suddenly embarrassed. Yes, that was why. He had promised his

113

sister. Had sworn on his honour that he would keep himself clean. Would not do as other men did.

He shuddered and met the girl's eyes again. "If you would send for Mu Chua. Perhaps she would find me a room. I'll eat there and take my rest."

Crimson Lotus smiled, unoffended, nothing behind her smile this time. Her disappointment had been momentary; now she was the perfect hostess once more, all personal thoughts banished. "If you will wait a moment, I shall summon her."

But Mu Chua had been watching everything. She appeared in the doorway at once, knowing what to do, what to say in this instance. She had been told beforehand that it might be so.

"Please follow me, *Shih* Haavikko. There is a room prepared. I will take you there."

Axel bowed, grateful, then looked across at Ebert and Fest. Fest met his eyes and gave the briefest nod, acknowledging his departure, but Ebert ignored him, concentrating on the young girl – she looked barely ten – who sat beside him now.

"What is the young girl's name?" Haavikko asked Mu Chua, keeping his voice low.

Mu Chua smiled. "That's Golden Heart. She's the baby of the house. A sweet young thing, don't you think?"

He stared at the girl a moment longer, then turned back to Mu Chua. "If you would take me to my room."

Mu Chua smiled, all understanding. "Of course."

* * *

Axel woke to find the room dark, a strange smell in the air. He sat up suddenly, alert, his training taking over, then remembered where he was and forced himself to relax. But still he felt on edge. Something was wrong. Something . . .

He heard it. Heard the second thread of breathing in the silent darkness. He felt to his left. Nothing. Then to his right. His hand met a soft warmth.

He swallowed, recognising the musky smell for what it

was. What had they done? Drugged him? And what else? He had seen too many covert operations not to feel vulnerable. What if Ebert had set this up? What if he'd had him drugged, then taped what he'd subsequently done? He shivered and slowly edged away from the girl – was it a girl? – who lay there next to him in the bed, then felt behind him for a lighting panel.

His hand met the slight indentation in the wall. At once a soft light lay across the centre of the bed, blurring into darkness.

Axel gasped and his eyes widened, horrified. "Kuan Yin preserve me!" he whispered.

The girl was *Hung Mao*. A tall, blonde-haired girl with full breasts and an athletic build. She lay there, undisturbed by the light, one hand up at her neck, the fingers laced into her long, thick hair, the other resting on her smoothly muscled stomach, the fingers pointing down to the rich growth of pubic hair.

Axel stared at her, horrified and yet fascinated, his eyes drawn to her ice white breasts, to the soft, down-covered swell of her sex. Then he looked at her face again and shuddered. So like her. So very like her. As if . . .

He turned away, swallowing, then looked back, his eyes drawn once more to those parts of her he'd never seen. Never dreamed he'd see.

It couldn't be. Surely it couldn't . . . ?

"Vesa . . ." he whispered, leaning closer. "Vesa . . ." It was his sister's name.

The head turned, the eyes opened. Astonishingly blue eyes, like his sister's. But different. Oh, so thankfully different. And yet . .

He pushed the thought back sharply. But it came again. Like Vesa. So very like his darling sister Vesa.

The girl smiled up at him and reached out for him, making a small sound of pleasure deep in her throat.

Instinctively he moved back slightly, tensed, but he was betrayed. Slowly his penis filled with blood until, engorged, it stood out stiffly. And when she reached for it

115

and took it he could do nothing but close his eyes, ashamed and yet grateful.

As he entered her he opened his eyes and looked at her again. "What's your name?"

She laughed softly, and for the briefest moment the movement of her body against his own slowed and became uncertain. "Don't you remember, Axel? I'm White Orchid. Your little flower." Then she laughed again, more raucously this time, her body pressing up against his, making him cry out with the pleasure of it. "And he said you were *ya* . . ."

★ ★ ★

"Shall I wake him?"

"No, Mother Chua. Let him sleep a little longer. The fight is not for another two hours yet. There's plenty of time. Did he enjoy himself?"

Mu Chua smiled but did not answer. Some things she would do for money. Others were against her code. Spying on her guests was one of them. She studied Ebert a moment, trying to establish what it was made him so different from the others who came here. Perhaps it was just the sheer rudeness of the man. His ready assumption that he could have anything, buy anything. She didn't like him, but then it wasn't her job to like all of her clients. As it was he had brought her something valuable – the two *Hung Mao* girls.

"Have you made your mind up yet?"

Ebert did not look at her. There was a faint smile on his lips. "I can choose anyone?"

"That was our deal."

"Then I'll take the girl. Golden Heart."

Mu Chua looked down. It was as she had expected. "She's untrained," she said, knowing it was hopeless but trying to persuade him even so.

"I know. That's partly why I chose her. I could train her myself. To my own ways."

Mu Chua shuddered, wondering what those ways would

116

be. For a moment she considered going back on the deal and returning the two *Hung Mao* girls, but she knew that it made no sense either to throw away such a certain attraction as the barbarian *shen nu* nor to make an enemy of Hans Ebert.

"Are you certain she's not too young?"

Ebert merely laughed.

"Then I'll draw up the contracts. It will be as agreed. The two girls for the one. And this evening's entertainment free."

"As we agreed," said Ebert, smiling to himself.

Mu Chua studied him again, wondering what game he was playing with his fellow officer. She had seen the way he bullied and insulted him. Why, then, had he been so insistent that she drug him and send the *Hung Mao* girl to him? There seemed no love lost between the two men, so what was Ebert's design?

She bowed and smiled, for once feeling the hollowness of her smile, then turned and went to bring the contract. But she was thinking of Golden Heart's dream. Ebert was the tiger come out of the West, and last night he had mated with her. Insatiably, so Golden Heart had said: wildly, his passion barely short of violence. And though there was no chance of Golden Heart conceiving, Mu Chua could not help but think of the image in the dream – the image of the grey-white snake. In most cases it was an auspicious symbol – sign that the dreamer would bear a boy child. But the snake in the dream had been cold and dead.

She shuddered. The first part of the dream had proved so right, how could the second not come about in time? And then, what misery for Golden Heart. Eat your year cakes now, thought Mu Chua as she took the contract from the drawer in her room and turned to go back. Celebrate now beneath the rainbow-coloured clouds, for soon Golden Heart will be broken. And I can do nothing. Nothing at all.

★ ★ ★

117

When he woke the second time he knew she would be there, beside him in the bed. He turned and looked at her, all shame, all horror purged from him, only love and a vague desire remaining. For a moment he was still, silent, watching her, a faint smile on his face. Then, as he watched, there was movement at the mouth of her sex. A dark and slender shape seemed to press up between the soft, pale lips of flesh. Slowly it emerged, stretching a thumbnail's length and more into the air, its blind snout moving purposively, as if sniffing the air. Axel stared at it, fascinated and horrified. It was alive – a living thing! He gave a small cry of shock and surprise and the thing vanished, as though it had never been, burrowing back down into the soft, moist folds of flesh.

His cry woke her. She sat up abruptly, her eyes as blue as a northern sea, heavy with sleep. "Axel . . . What is it?"

She focused on his face and seemed to come awake suddenly, seeing the horror there.

"Gods, what is it?" She got up and moved towards him, but he backed away, fending her off with his hands. She stopped still, her body tensed, and lowered her head a fraction, staring at him. "Tell me what it is, Axel. Please. Was it a bad dream?"

He pointed at her. "Something . . ."

It was all he could say, but it seemed she understood. She sat back on the bed, folding her hands in her lap. "Ah . . . I see."

She let out a deep breath. "What you saw . . ." She shrugged and looked up at him, strangely vulnerable. "We all have them." Her look was as much as to say, *Surely you knew about this? Surely you've heard?*

"I . . ." he swallowed. "I don't understand."

She stared at him a moment longer, then reached down into the folds of her sex and began to coax something gently from within. Axel watched, wide-eyed, as she lifted the thing with her fingers and placed it gently in the palm of her right hand, extending it towards him so that he could see it clearly.

118

"Look. It's all right. It won't hurt you. It's perfectly harmless."

It was an insect of some kind. Or so it first appeared. A dark, slender, worm-like shape half the length of a finger. It was smooth and perfectly black. Unsegmented. Unmarked. It seemed blind; devoid, in fact, of all sensory equipment. And yet it had reacted swiftly to his cry.

"What is it?" he asked, coming closer, unable to conceal a shudder.

"As I said, we all have them. All of the girls, that is. They keep us clean, you see. GenSyn developed them. They live off bacteria – special kinds of bacteria. Aids, herpes, venereal diseases of all kinds."

He wrinkled up his nose. "Gods," he said. "And it's been there all the time. While we were . . . ?"

"All the time. But it never gets in the way. It lives in a special sack in my womb. It only comes out when it senses I'm asleep or perfectly relaxed. It's a parasite, you see. A benevolent one." She smiled and petted the thing in her hand, then gently put it back.

There was a knock on the door. Axel looked about him.

"Here," said the girl, handing him a robe, but taking nothing for herself.

He wrapped the er–silk *pau* about him, then turned to face the door. "Come in!"

It was Mu Chua. "I heard a noise," she said. "Is everything all right?"

"Yes. Yes, it's fine." He glanced at the girl, who sat there on the bed, looking away from him, then turned back to face Mu Chua. "It was nothing. Really. Nothing at all."

Mu Chua met his eyes and held them just a moment longer than was natural, making him wonder what she was thinking as she looked at him; re-awakening, for the briefest moment, his fears of being taped and betrayed. But then she smiled – a warm, candid smile that held no subterfuge. "Good," she said. "Then dress and come through. I've prepared a breakfast for you."

Her smile warmed him, cleared away the shadows in his

head. "Thank you, Mother Chua. You run a good house. A very good house."

★   ★   ★

The Pit was a riot of noise and activity, its tiered benches packed to overflowing. On all sides men yelled and waved their arms frantically, placing bets, dark, faceless figures in the dim red light, while down below, in the intense white light of the combat circle, the two men crouched on their haunches, in the *wa shih* stance, facing each other silently.

Axel Haavikko, sitting on the front bench between Fest and Ebert, narrowed his eyes, studying the two combatants. They seemed an ill-matched pair; one *Hung Mao*, the other Han; one a giant, the other so compact and yet so perfectly formed he looked as though he had been made in a GenSyn vat. But there was a stillness, an undisguised sense of authority about the smaller man that impressed at once. He seemed immovable, as if grown about a central point of calm.

"The Han's name is Hwa. I'm told he's champion here," said Fest, leaning forward and speaking into his ear. "Seventeen bouts, he's had. Two more and it'll be a record."

Axel turned and yelled back at Fest. "And the other?"

Fest shrugged and indicated the small Han sat next to him. He leaned forward again, raising his voice. "My friend here says that no one knows much about him. He's a local boy, name of Karr, but he hasn't fought before. He's something of a mystery. But worth a bet, maybe. You'll get good odds."

Axel turned to look at the other combatant. Crouched, Karr was taller than most men. Seven *ch'i*, perhaps. Maybe more. Standing, he had been close to twice the size of Hwa; broad at the shoulder and heavily muscled, his oiled skin shining slickly in the brilliant whiteness. Such men were usually slow. They depended on sheer strength to win through. Yet Axel remembered how the crowd had gone quiet when the giant entered the arena and realised that Karr was something unusual, even by their standards.

120

For a moment he studied the tattoos on Karr's chest and arms. On each arm a pair of dragons – one green, one red, their long bodies thick and muscular – coiled about each other sinuously. Their heads were turned inward, face to face, wide, sharp-toothed mouths snarling, huge, golden eyes flashing. On his chest a great bird spread its wings, its powerful, regal head thrown back defiantly, its cruel beak open in a cry of triumph, a terror-stricken horse held fast in each of its steel-like talons.

Axel looked away, feeling suddenly quite awkward. His silks, his braided hair, his necklaces of silver and jade. Such refinements were an impertinence down here. There was no place for such subtleties. Here everything was bared.

It was warm in the Pit and unbearably stuffy, yet he shivered, thinking of what was to come.

"Look at him!" yelled Ebert, leaning close to join their conversation. "Meat! That's what he is! A huge sack of meat! It's a foregone conclusion, Haavikko! I'd not waste a single yuan on him! It'll be over in seconds!"

"You think so, Ebert?"

Ebert nodded exaggeratedly. "See our man here." He indicated Hwa. "I'm told he's a perfectionist. An artist. He practises eight hours a day, sometimes doing nothing but repeating one single movement." Ebert laughed and his blue eyes gleamed red in the dull light. "Such training pays off. They say he's so fast you daren't even blink while he's fighting!"

Axel shrugged. Maybe it was so. Certainly there was something different, something *obsessive* about the man that was quite chilling. His eyes, for instance, never moved. They stared ahead, as if in trance, boring into his opponent's face, unblinking, merciless in their focus. Whereas the other . . .

Even as he looked he saw Karr turn his head and look directly at him.

It was a fierce, insolent gaze, almost primitive in its intensity, and yet not wholly unintelligent. There was something about the man. Something he had seen at once.

121

Perhaps it was the casual, almost arrogant way he had looked about the tiers on entering, or the brief, almost dismissive bow he had greeted his opponent with. Whatever, it was enough to make Axel feel uneasy with Ebert's brusque dismissal of the man. On balance, however, he had to agree with Ebert; the small man looked like an adept – a perfect fighting machine. Height, weight and breadth were no concern to him. His strength was of another kind.

"Of course," continued Ebert, raising his voice so that it carried to the giant, "brute strength alone can never win. Intelligence and discipline will triumph every time. It's nature's law, my friends!"

Axel saw the giant's eyes flare, his muscles tense. He had heard and understood.

He leaned close to Ebert. "I'll wager a hundred yuan that the big man wins."

"Okay. I'll give you five to one."

"You're sure?"

Ebert laughed arrogantly. "Make it two fifty, and I'll give you ten to one!"

Axel met his eyes a moment, conscious of the challenge in them, then gave the barest nod.

Just then, however, the fight marshal stepped out into the combat circle and the crowd hushed expectantly.

Axel felt his stomach tighten, his heart begin to thud against his rib cage. This was it then. To the death.

The two men rose and approached the centre of the circle. There they knelt and bowed to each other – a full *k'o t'ou*, heads almost touching. Then they sat back on their haunches, waiting, while the marshal gave their names and read the rules.

The rules were short and simple. One. No weapons were permitted but their own bodies. Two. So long as the fight continued they were to keep within the combat circle. Three. Once begun the fight could not be called off. It ended only when one of them was dead.

Axel could feel the tension in his bones. All about him rose a buzz of excitement; an awful, illicit excitement that grew and grew as the moments passed and the two men faced each other at the circle's centre, waiting for the signal.

Then, suddenly, it began.

The small man flipped backwards like a tumbler, then stopped, perfectly, almost unnaturally still, half-crouched on his toes, his arms raised to shoulder level, forearms bent inward, his fingers splayed.

Karr had not moved. He was watching Hwa carefully, his eyes half-lidded. Then, very slowly, he eased back off his knees, drawing himself up to his full height, his weight balanced on the balls of his feet.

Hwa feinted to the left, then sprang at Karr, bounding forward then flipping his body up and sideways, one foot kicking out at the big man's groin.

There was a roar from the crowd. For a moment Karr was down. Then he was up again, his feet thudding against the canvas flooring, a hiss of pain escaping through his teeth. Hwa had missed target. His foot had struck Karr on the upper thigh. The skin there was a vivid red, darkening by the moment, and as Karr circled he rubbed at the spot tenderly, almost absent-mindedly.

"He's too slow!" Ebert hissed in his ear.

"Wait!" Axel answered. He had been watching Hwa's face, had seen the surprise there when the big man had bounced up again. Hwa had thought he had him. He really had.

Hwa crouched again, in the classic *ch'i ma shih*, the riding horse stance, moving side to side from the hips, like a snake. Then he moved his feet in a little dance. From the tiers on all sides came a loud, low shuddering as the crowd banged their feet in applause. A moment later Hwa attacked again.

This time he ran at Karr; a strange, weaving run that ended in a leap. At the same time he let out a bloodcurdling scream.

But Karr had moved.

At the instant Hwa leaped, Karr ducked, rolled and turned. It was a movement that was so quick and so

123

unexpected from such a big man that a huge gasp of surprise went up from the crowd. As Hwa turned to face him again, Karr was smiling.

Surprise turned to rage. Hwa attacked a third time; whirling his body about, thrusting and kicking, his arms and legs moving in a blur. But each blow was met and countered. For once Hwa's speed was matched. And when he withdrew he was breathing heavily, his face red from exertion.

The crowd roared its appreciation.

"It's luck!" yelled Ebert next to him. "You see if it isn't! The Han will have him soon enough!"

Axel made to answer, but at that moment Hwa launched himself again, flipping over once, twice, like an acrobat, then feinting to left, right, then left again. He was only an arm's length from Karr when the big man acted. But this time Karr moved a fraction too slowly. When Hwa kicked Karr was off-balance, striking at a place where Hwa had been but was no longer.

The crack of bone could be heard to the back of the tiers.

Karr groaned audibly and went down.

Hwa struck again at once, his foot kicking out once, twice, forcing the broken arm back at an impossible angle.

Axel gasped, feeling sick. Beside him Ebert gave a yell of triumph.

Hwa moved back, getting his breath, a look of satisfaction replacing the frown of concentration he had worn until that moment.

The Pit was tense, silent, waiting for him to end it. "*Shau,*" he said softly, looking at Karr. *Burn.*

Karr was down on one knee, his face a mask of pain. Slowly, very slowly, he got up, supporting his shattered arm with his left hand. For a moment he seemed to look inside himself. His breathing slowed and his face cleared. With a grimace of pure agony, he wrenched his arm back, the click of bone against bone the only sound in the whole arena. For a moment he swayed, then seemed to gain control of himself again and tucked the useless hand into the cloth belt at his waist, securing it.

"Come," he said, lifting his chin in challenge to the smaller man. "It isn't over yet."

The words were like a goad. Hwa exploded, twirling and somersaulting, kicking and punching in a furious rain of blows that went on for minutes. But Karr was up to the challenge. With his good arm and both legs he parried everything Hwa threw at him, weaving and ducking and turning with a speed and agility that surprised everyone. It seemed impossible for a man so big to move his weight so quickly, so subtly.

But Axel, watching, saw how much it cost him – saw, beneath the mask of outward calm, the agony as Karr flipped and jumped and rolled, avoiding the constant flood of blows. Saw it in his eyes, in the faintest movement at the corners of his mouth. Watched until it seemed impossible that Karr could take any more.

And then, just as Hwa was drawing off, Karr counterattacked for the first time.

Hwa moved back, his full weight resting momentarily – perhaps, for the only time during the contest – on his back foot, in *hou shih*, the monkey stance. And as he moved back, so Karr rolled forward, pushing up off the floor with his good left arm, his wrist straining and flexing, the whole weight of his huge frame thrust forward into Hwa.

He caught Hwa totally off-balance, his legs wrapping about the small man's neck, his huge weight driving him down into the canvas.

For an instant there was silence. Then, as the big man rolled over there was a groan of pain. Karr sat up, clutching his arm, his face rent with pain. But Hwa was dead. He lay there next to Karr, pale, unmoving, his back, his neck broken, the back of his skull crushed by the impact of his fall.

Axel let out a shivering breath. Beside him Ebert was suddenly very quiet. On all sides the Pit was in uproar.

"Magnificent!" Fest yelled into Axel's ear. "They were

giving odds of thirty-five to one! It's the biggest upset in five years, so my friend here says!" But Axel was barely listening. He was watching Karr, filled with admiration and respect for the big man.

"He was magnificent," Axel said softly, turning to look at Ebert.

"He was lucky!" For a second or two Ebert glowered back at him. Then he laughed dismissively and dug something out of his tunic pocket and handed it across to Haavikko.

"It's only money, eh?"

Axel looked down at the thick square of plastic in his hand. It was a secure-image holo-chip. A bearer credit for 2500 yuan. Axel looked up, surprised, then remembered the wager. Two fifty at ten to one. It was more than six months' salary, but Ebert had treated it as nothing. But then, why not? To him it was pocket money.

Ebert was leaning across him, yelling at Fest. "Hey! Let's go back to the dressing room and congratulate him, eh?"

For a moment longer Axel stared at Ebert, then he looked back at the big man. Karr was picking himself up from the floor painfully, no sign of triumph in his face.

Fest took Axel's arm and began to pull him away. "Let's go. Hans has had enough."

"Come on," said Ebert as they stood outside. "We'll buy the brute dinner. He can be our guest."

They stood in the corridor outside the dressing room, leaning against the wall, ignoring the comings and goings of the lesser fighters. There were bouts all afternoon – challengers for the new champion. But they had seen enough. Ebert had sent in his card a quarter bell ago, the invitation scribbled on the back. Now they waited.

"There's a problem with such mechanical virtuosity," Ebert said rather pompously. "It can so easily switch over into automatonism. A kind of unthinking, machine-like response. Totally inflexible and unable to adapt to approaches more subtle than its own. That's why Hwa lost. He was inflexible. Unable to change."

126

Fest laughed. "Sound stuff, Hans. But what you're really saying is that you knew the big man would win all the time!"

Ebert shook his head. "You know what I mean." There was a slight irritation in his voice. Then he relented and laughed. "Okay, I'm trying to rationalise it, but we were all surprised. Even Axel here. Even he thought his man was going to lose."

Haavikko smiled. "That's true. He was good, though, wasn't he?"

Fest nodded. "Impressive. Not the best I've seen, maybe, but strong. Brave, too."

Axel looked about him. "It's another world," he said. "Rawer, more basic than ours."

Ebert laughed, looking at him. "I do believe our young friend is in love with it all. Imagine, living down here, in the sweat and grime!" He laughed again, more viciously this time. "You'd soon be disillusioned."

"Maybe . . ."

He managed no more. Just then the door opened and the big man's manager came out. He had the same look about him. You're Karr's elder brother, Axel thought, looking at him.

"What do you want?"

Ebert smiled. "I watched your man. He fought well. I'd like to take him out to supper. My treat."

Axel saw how the man controlled himself; saw how he looked from one of them to the next, recognising them for what they were, Above aristocrats, and knew at once how it must be to live as this man did – wanting to stay clear of their kind, but at the same time needing them. Yes, he saw it all there in the man's face; all the dreadful compromises he had had to make just to live down here. It rent at Axel's soul; made him want to turn and leave.

"Okay," the man said after a moment's hesitation. "But Karr's not feeling well. The contest took a lot out of him. He needs rest . . ."

Ebert held the man's hands a moment. "It's all right,

friend. We'll not keep him. A celebration meal, and then . . ." He shrugged and smiled pleasantly, letting the man's hands go. "We have influence. Understand? We can arrange things for you. Make it easier . . ."

Axel narrowed his eyes. "What do you mean, Ebert?"

Ebert turned and looked at him sharply. "Shut up, Haavikko! Let *me* deal with this. I know what I'm doing."

Axel looked down. Do as you will, he thought.

Ebert had a reputation for being headstrong. For doing what others would never dare to do. But it was understandable. He had been born to rule. His father, Klaus Ebert, was head of Chung Kuo's second largest Company: a Company that had existed since the first days of the City; that provided all the body-servants for the Great Families – sweet, intelligent creatures, scarcely distinguishable from the human; that provided a range of taste-sculpted servants for the richest of the rich, and armies of mindless automatons for the Seven. A company that produced over a third of all the synthesised food eaten in the levels.

Hans Ebert was heir to GenSyn, second only to MedFac on the Hang Seng Index. Rumour was his father could buy the Net twice over. What, then, if he should haggle with the manager of a small-time fighter? Even so, Axel found himself annoyed. Hadn't Ebert *seen*? Hadn't he realised how fine, how powerful the man was?

"We'll go in, then?" Ebert said, his tone insistent, commanding. The manager lowered his head, then bowed to the waist, letting them pass.

So power is, thought Axel, moving past him. So power acts.

Karr was sitting at the far end of the room, his right arm strapped to his chest, a bowl of soup balanced in his left hand. He looked up at them sharply, annoyed at their intrusion.

"What do you want?"

Ebert smiled, ignoring the big man's hostility. "You fought well. We'd like to celebrate your success. To honour you."

Karr laughed. He set down the soup and stood up, then came across the room until he stood two paces from Ebert.

"You want to *honour* me?"

For the briefest moment Ebert seemed intimidated by the big man. Then he recovered, turning to smile at his fellows before looking back up at Karr. "Why not? It was a great victory."

"You think so?" Karr smiled, but his voice was sharp and cold. "You don't think it was the triumph of *meat* over *intelligence*, then?"

Ebert's mouth worked ineffectually for a moment. Then he took a step backwards. But as he did so, Karr spat on the floor between Ebert's feet.

"Fuck off! Understand? I don't *need* you."

Ebert's face turned ashen. For a moment he struggled to form words. Then he found his voice again. "How *dare* he!"

The words were high-pitched, almost strangled.

Fest held his arm tightly, whispering urgently in his ear. "Don't make trouble here, Hans. Please! They suffer us down here. But if we start anything we'll spark a riot."

"I'll kill him," Ebert said, under his breath.

Karr heard and smiled mockingly.

"He'd as like break both your arms," Fest said quietly.

Ebert sneered. "I think my father would have something to say about that, don't you?"

Fest pulled on Ebert's arm, drawing him back. "The less said about your father, the better, Hans. These fellows know only too well who manufactures the *Hei* they send in to crush any sign of an uprising. GenSyn and your father are about as popular here as Genghis Khan."

Karr was watching them hawkishly. At the mention of GenSyn his eyes narrowed. "So you're *Ebert's* son?"

Ebert threw off Fest's hand and took a step forward, his head raised arrogantly to face out the big man. "You understand what it means, then?"

Karr smiled tightly. "Oh, I know what it means *up there*. But you're not up there now, *Shih* Ebert. This isn't your

129

kingdom and you should mind your manners. Understand?"

Ebert went to speak again, but Karr lifted his good hand sharply to cut him off. His face was bitter. "Let me explain it simply for you. Today I killed a man I admired greatly. A man who taught me much about honour and necessity." He took a step closer to Ebert. "He was a *man*, Ebert. A *master*."

"You were lucky," said Ebert quietly, provocatively.

A faint smile played on Karr's lips briefly, but his eyes were cold and hard. "Yes. For once you're right. I *was* lucky. Hwa underestimated me. He thought as you think. And because of that he's dead."

"Is that a threat?"

Karr laughed, then shook his head. He was about to say something more, but at that moment there was a noise in the corridor outside. An instant later the door swung open. Two uniformed officers of the Special Security squad stood there, their standard issue *deng* rifles held against their chests. Behind them came the General.

Tolonen strode into the dressing room, then stopped, looking about him. Fest, Ebert and Haavikko had come sharply to attention. They stood there, heads bowed, awaiting orders, but the General ignored them a moment. He walked up to Karr and looked him up and down before turning his back on him.

"I'm sorry to have to break things up, but we've heard from our Triad contacts. I'd have notified you before but the matter's no longer urgent."

"Sir?" Fest straightened up, his face expressing his confusion. He had been told this was a matter of the utmost urgency and that he would be notified at once.

Tolonen turned his head and looked at Fest. "I'm sorry, lieutenant, I should explain. They're dead. Someone got to them before us. The *Kuei Chuan* Triad are sending a man to take us to the place. I've arranged to meet them here in an hour."

"Is it far?" Fest asked.

"I'm not sure. They don't use grid references down here. But it's a place called Ammersee."

Behind him, Karr laughed. "I know it well. It's quite a warren. You'll *need* a guide."

Tolonen turned and looked at the fighter again. He was a big man himself, but Karr was head and shoulders taller than him. "Who's this?" he asked Fest.

"His name is Karr, sir. He was the winner of the combat."

Tolonen stared at Karr, then nodded. "Yes. He doesn't look like a loser." Then he addressed the big man directly. "How far is this place?"

"Ten, maybe twelve *li*."

"And how long would it take us to get there?"

Karr shrugged. "By foot forty minutes. By rickshaw fifteen, maybe twenty."

"And you'll take us?"

Karr looked at Ebert. "I'm not sure I'd be welcome."

Tolonen looked from Karr to Ebert. "Oh? And why's that, Hans?"

Ebert lowered his head, not looking at Karr. "Just a small disagreement, sir. Nothing serious."

"Good," said the General. "That's settled then. The sooner we get there the better. I want to sort this out." He turned back to Karr. "I'm indebted, *Shih* Karr. I'll make sure you're well paid for your help."

Karr bowed, then turned to get his cloak.

* * *

DeVore met them in the corridor outside Kao Jyan's apartment. "I came as soon as I heard, sir."

"Well, Howard?" said Tolonen. "What have we got?"

"Three men, sir. Low level criminals. I've checked with our contacts. They weren't members of any of the local Triads. Two of them were *kwai*. Hired knives. The other – Kao Jyan, who owned the apartment – was a small time racketeer. Drugs, stolen goods, nothing big."

131

Tolonen nodded. "Nothing to connect them with anyone higher up?"

DeVore shook his head. "Not yet, sir. But we're still investigating. Kao Jyan was known to frequent a place known as Big White's. He'd do some of his business there, it seems. But the place was gutted yesterday. Victim of one of the local gang wars. Big White himself is dead, so that avenue's closed to us, too."

"It all seems too convenient. Too systematic."

DeVore gave a brief nod. "As if someone's tidying up after them."

"Yes," said Tolonen, touching his shoulder. "That's my thought exactly."

"In this case, sir, it seems genuine enough. Big White was playing off one Triad against another. It looks like he was a victim of his own greed."

"Hmm." Tolonen still seemed unhappy with the coincidence. "Dig deeper, eh, Howard? It might be genuine, but then it might not. Someone high's behind all of this. Someone high enough to pay off Triads as a matter of course."

DeVore bowed, obedient, then turned towards the guarded doorway. "Shall we go in, sir?"

Axel, watching from the doorway, saw the General move about the room; saw how he looked at everything, trying to fit it all into place. In the rickshaw coming over, Tolonen had turned to him, explaining.

"Sometimes, Axel, you need to see things for yourself. Sniff them out first hand. Sometimes it's the only way. You see things that another might have missed. Understand things. Bring things to light that would otherwise have remained hidden."

He saw now how the General went about that. How he looked from one thing to the next, his eyes sharp, alert for the hidden connections.

"This is odd, Howard. Very odd."

Tolonen was leaning over the corpse that lay face down on the bed, holding the surgeon's tag between his fingers. DeVore went over to him.

132

"Sir?"

"Look at this. The time of death. Two hours before the other two. Why's that, do you think?"

"I'd guess they were waiting for them in the room. That they picked them off as they came in."

Tolonen looked up at him grimly. "Maybe. But that would take some nerve. To sit with a man you'd murdered, for two hours."

DeVore said nothing.

"Which one was this?"

"We don't have a surname, sir, but he was known as Chen."

Tolonen nodded, then carefully moved the bloodied head. It lay there, its shattered left profile upward on the sheets. For a while the General stared at it, as if trying to remember something. He touched the smooth skin beneath the ear and frowned, then shrugged and got up.

"This one." He pointed down at the corpse of Kao Jyan. "I recognise him from the tape."

"The tape?" DeVore looked up sharply.

"Oh, I'm sorry, Howard. I should have said. We had a tape of the two men. A copy from the CompCam files."

"Ah, yes," DeVore said hurriedly. "Of course."

Tolonen had moved on. He stood over the third of the bodies, one hand stroking his smooth-shaven chin. "So who was this, then? And how did he fit in?" He looked up and across at DeVore. "Whose side was he on, I wonder? Was he with these two, or did he come to kill them?"

DeVore met his gaze steadily. "His name was Chu Heng, sir. A local thug. It seems . . ."

Karr, in the doorway, interrupted him. "Excuse me, but he was quite well known in these parts, General. A handy man with a blade. Too handy. It's good to see him dead."

DeVore looked at the big man curiously, then turned to the General. "Who's this, sir?"

Tolonen indicated that Karr should come in. "This is *Shih* Karr, Howard. He's a fighter – what they call a 'blood'. He's champion, it seems. For the time being."

DeVore gave the slightest bow, acknowledging the giant. "You know these parts, then?"

Karr was kneeling over the corpse, looking at the wounds to Chu Heng's neck and chest with a professional interest. After a moment he looked up at DeVore. "I was born in Ammersee. Until four years ago I lived here. I know its people and its business."

"So you knew these men?"

"Kao Jyan? Well, I knew *of* him. Chen I didn't know. He must have taken up with Kao Jyan quite recently. But he was a good man. He had honour."

"A good man, eh? You can say that, not knowing him?" DeVore laughed, his eyes weighing up the big man. "But he was *kwai*, a killer. Do killers have honour?"

Karr met his eyes firmly. "Some do. You, for instance. Haven't you had to kill in your line of work?"

DeVore smiled. "Ah, but that's different."

"Is it?" Karr straightened up, moving to the second of the bodies, giving it the same scrupulous examination as the first. "Are people so very different below the Net?" He glanced up at DeVore, then back at the body. "Do you know what *kwai* is, Major?"

"They kill for profit. What more do I need to know?"

Karr laughed but did not look up. "I thought you'd be curious, if only professionally. You see, Chu Heng was *kwai*, too, but he wasn't typical. He was what they call a 'twisted blade'. Most *kwai* would have spat on Chu Heng."

"A knife's a knife."

Karr shook his head. "Not so. Some weapons are better made than others. And some are made by masters. So with a good *kwai*. You see, to become *kwai* one must study long and hard. It is a discipline. A way of life."

"Down here? The only way of life I've seen down here is grab what you can and kill to keep it."

Karr looked up, his grey eyes calm, controlled. "Tsao Ch'un was Son of Heaven."

For once the old saying carried rather too much meaning. Tsao Ch'un was the tyrant who had united Chung Kuo and built the great City. He, in his time, had grabbed and killed to keep what he had taken. Until the Seven – his chief ministers – had deposed him.

"Kings do as they must," DeVore said, his eyes suddenly dangerous.

Karr straightened up to his full height, facing DeVore. "And *kwai*. As I said, Major, to be a *kwai* here is an honourable calling. Most are not as Chu Heng was. Nor should you confuse them with the punks and paper tigers that run with the Triads. A *kwai* has inner strengths. He draws from deeper wells than greed."

DeVore laughed scornfully. He was about to answer Karr, but Tolonen stepped in between the two men. "Major DeVore, Fest, Ebert, Haavikko. Leave us a moment. I want a word with Karr."

DeVore bowed, then went outside, followed by the other three. When they were gone, the General turned to face the big man.

"You know the ways of this place, Karr. What do you think happened here?"

Karr looked about him. "It's messy. Hastily arranged and hurriedly carried out. Yet the killings . . . Well, they're odd. If I didn't know better I'd say that Kao Jyan's death was a piece of Chu Heng's work. This slashing and gouging is his trade mark. He was a sadist. He enjoyed inflicting pain."

"And the others?"

Karr put his head to one side. "I've not looked at Chen, yet. But whoever killed Chu Heng was good at it. Trained to kill quickly and efficiently."

"A soldier, maybe?"

Karr laughed. "I hadn't thought of that, but yes."

Tolonen smiled, pleased.

"You're a useful man, Karr, and my ensign, Haavikko, tells me you're a magnificent fighter. Intelligent, too. I could use a man like you."

Karr set Kao Jyan's head down gently and looked up at the General. "I'm under contract, General. Ten fights, if I live that long."

135

Tolonen nodded. "I'll buy your contract out."

Karr smiled. "Maybe. But why? I don't understand, General. What use could I be to you?"

At that the General laughed. "You have a talent. An eye for things. I could see it at a glance. And you know this place. Know how its people think and act. At present we have to rely on our contacts down here. On Triad bosses. And that's not merely costly but unreliable. They'd as soon be in another man's pay as ours."

"And I'm different?"

"I'd judge so."

Karr stood and looked about him. "What happened here, General? What *really* happened?"

Tolonen moved across the room. He stood at the games machine, toying with its touch pad. "What do you mean?"

"You, the Major, those three junior officers outside. That's some team to investigate a small time killing like this. So why are you all here? What's important about these men? What did they do? Or should I ask, what did they know?"

Tolonen laughed. "What they did was kill a Minister. What they knew, however, remains a mystery. But someone knows. The someone who killed them."

Karr came and stood at his shoulder, looking at the game that had come up on the screen. "What's this?"

"It looks like the last stored memory. Kao Jyan was a good player, it seems."

Karr shook his head. "That's not Kao Jyan. I'd swear it. In fact, I'd say that wasn't anyone from round here. Look at those patterns. And this is an eighth level game. Whoever was playing this was a master of *Wei Chi*."

Tolonen laughed strangely. "Our killer?"

Karr turned his head, meeting his eyes. "Well, it would be one way of filling two hours."

★ ★ ★

It was a big, five-pole sedan, its mauve er-silk banners emblazoned with black, stylised dogs, symbol of the *Kuei Chuan* Triad. The ten shaven-headed pole-men sat against

136

the wall opposite, tucking into bowls of ducksoy soup and noodles, while in a conspicuously separate group, standing beside the sedan, in mauve and black fake-satin uniforms, were the *pen p'ei* – rushing daggers – numbered patches on their chests indicating their standing in the Triad hierarchy.

Ignoring the lowly pole-men, Ebert strode up to the lowest-numbered of the *p'ei*, who immediately bowed low and touched his forehead to the littered floor of the corridor.

"Let's get going," Ebert said brusquely. He dropped a fifty yuan coin beside the man's head. "There'll be another if you get us there in twenty minutes."

The *p'ei*'s eyes went to the coin, then, widening, looked up at Ebert. He nodded his head exaggeratedly. "As you wish, Excellency!" He stood and turned to the pole-men, barking orders in a pidgin Mandarin that none of the three young soldiers could follow. Soup bowls were dropped at once as the pole-men hurried to get into position. Six of the *p'ei* formed up at the front. Daggers drawn, they would clear the way ahead of the sedan. Behind ran the last four of the *p'ei*, guarding against ambush.

Axel watched Ebert and Fest climb inside, then followed, stopping in the curtained doorway to look back at the bowed, shaven-headed pole-men.

"Come on, Haavikko!" said Fest impatiently. "You don't want the man to lose his fee, do you?"

Axel ducked inside, taking the seat across from Fest and Ebert. "Why did you do that, Hans? There's no hurry to get back."

Ebert smiled. "You have to keep these types on their toes, Haavikko. It'll do them good to have a nice long run." He looked at Fest and laughed. "You should see the buggers' faces! It's worth a hundred yuan just for that!"

Axel looked at him for a moment, then shrugged. He didn't like it, but they were probably used to it down here. This was how they expected the Above to behave.

The sedan lifted at once and they were away, the carriage swaying rhythmically about them, the shouts of the senior *p'ei* encouraging the men to run.

"What do you think of that, Hans?" Fest asked, leaning forward to draw the curtain back and look out at the runners. "It seems the General has bought the fighter's contract."

Ebert laughed dismissively. "The man's a brute! A primitive! I tell you, he'll prove nothing but trouble!"

Axel looked down. He had said nothing earlier, when Ebert had insulted Karr, but now he had had a belly full of Ebert's arrogance. "You only say that because he stood up to you."

Ebert glowered. "I'll break him! See if I don't!"

Axel laughed and looked up, meeting Ebert's eyes. "And how will you do that, Hans? Is the General yours to command?"

Ebert bit back the reply, then looked away, a dangerous expression in his eyes. "No, but there are others who feel as I do."

It was clear he meant DeVore. Surprisingly, the Major seemed to have been as much put out by the big man as Ebert. In the corridor outside the murdered Han's apartment he had muttered angrily about upstarts and big sacks of wind. It was clear he had not appreciated the big man correcting him about the *kwai*.

"Karr will be the General's man," Axel insisted. "Answerable only to him." He paused, then, rubbing it in, added, "It seems he has need of such men."

Ebert laughed mockingly, but Haavikko's words had offended him. He turned aside angrily and, beneath his breath, muttered, "Gods, but what fools they give us in command!"

Fest leaned forward. "Hush up, Hans! Have a care what you say!"

But Axel had heard and was furious. This was too much. "I take it you refer to General Tolonen?"

Ebert turned on him squarely, his right fist bunched, his face dark with anger. "And what if I do, puppy? What's it to you what I say?"

Axel drew himself up in his seat. "It is discourteous, to

138

say the least. You forget where your duty lies, and to whom. Retract your words, Hans Ebert, or I'll be forced to make you retract them!"

For a while neither spoke, but faced each other out, the sedan swaying about them. Slowly Ebert calmed, his breathing normalising. Then, turning his face away, he laughed. "Go fuck yourself, Haavikko," he said softly.

At once Axel swung a punch at Ebert, but Fest, anticipating trouble, had moved between them. He blocked the blow with his arm, then pushed Ebert away to the far side of the carriage.

"For gods' sake, Hans, shut up!"

Then he turned on Haavikko. "As for you, Axel Haavikko, listen carefully. I don't condone what Ebert said just now, but you had best just forget it. Understand?"

"Forget it? How can I forget it? It undermines all we are. If I . . ."

Fest put his hand roughly over Haavikko's mouth, glaring at him.

"Forget it! Is that clear? Hans meant nothing by it. His temper was up, that's all. Understandably, I'd say. The barbarian insulted him! Spat at his feet! Would you have stood as much?"

"It doesn't excuse . . ." Axel began, but Fest silenced him with a look.

"Enough! Do you understand, Haavikko? No one's honour has been besmirched. What passed here . . . it was only words. Nothing to get fired up about."

Axel looked across at Ebert, his face gone cold. *Only words,* he thought. *Only words!* He turned his head away, disgusted with them, aching to make Ebert eat the words he had uttered and annoyed with Fest for interfering. And understanding now the restraint the big man had shown back in his dressing room.

★ ★ ★

"Well, Haavikko, some good came of the day after all."

Tolonen leaned forward across his desk, steepling his big

hands together. Karr had just left the office, escorted by two elite guards. His contract had been purchased and he had sworn the oath of allegiance to the T'ang and to General Tolonen. All three junior officers had been witnesses. But now the others had gone and Axel was alone with the General for the first time since the business in the carriage.

Axel hesitated, looking down at the old man. Tolonen had treated him like a son since he had become his duty aide. Had honoured him with advice and explanations. He had learned much in serving the General, but now things had changed.

"Sir, there's something I wish to speak to you about."

Tolonen smiled good-naturedly. "Go on, boy."

"I'd . . . Well, I'd like a new posting."

Tolonen sat back slowly, the surprise in his face quite marked. "What's this?" He drew his hands apart and set them down on the edge of his desk. "I don't understand you, Haavikko. Aren't you happy here? Don't you like the job?"

Axel lowered his head. "I was, sir. And I did. But . . ."

Tolonen was looking at him strangely. "What is it? What's happened?"

He kept silent. Kept his head lowered.

Tolonen stood up and came round the desk to him. "Tell me, boy. Tell me what's up."

He looked up and met Tolonen's eyes openly. "I'd rather not, sir. It's just that I feel I can't work here any more."

Tolonen's disbelief surfaced as a laugh. "What am I supposed to make of that, eh? Can't work here. Don't *feel* like it. Tell me what happened."

Axel took a breath. "Sir, I'd rather not."

The General's bark of anger took him by surprise. "Rather not? It's not good enough, Haavikko. I'll have no secrets here. You'll tell me what happened. Why you want a new posting. I *order* you to tell me."

Axel swallowed. He had hoped to avoid this. He had wanted to settle his score with Ebert directly, personally. "It's Ebert, sir."

Tolonen laughed uncomfortably. "Ebert, eh? And what's wrong with young Ebert? Has he insulted you?"

"No, sir. Not directly."

"Well, then, what was it? Don't keep me guessing, boy. Spit it out."

"He was disrespectful, sir."

"Disrespectful, eh? To whom?"

Axel felt Tolonen's eyes boring into his own. "To you, sir."

Tolonen huffed. He was quiet for a moment, then shook his head. "I don't believe it. His father is my oldest friend. He's like a son to me, that boy. Disrespect?" There was an ugly movement of the General's mouth. "What did he say?"

"I'd rather . . ." Axel began, but Tolonen cut him off angrily.

"Gods, boy! Don't 'rather not' me any more! Spit it out – if you're accusing Ebert of disrespect I want to know the full details. And you had better have a witness. I'll have no unsupported hearsay."

Axel bowed his head dutifully. This was not how he had imagined it. He had thought the General would let him go – reluctantly, but without a fuss. This business of accusations and witnesses had come out of the blue.

"It was earlier today, sir. In the sedan coming back. Fest was present, sir. He heard everything."

Tolonen turned abruptly and leaned over his desk. Touching the intercom pad, he spoke to his secretary. "Have cadet officers Fest and Ebert brought back here, please. At once."

He turned back, looking at Haavikko sharply. "What did he say?"

Axel hesitated, the import of what he was doing suddenly striking him. There was much he disliked about Ebert – his arrogance and assumed superiority being the chief of them – but he had never intended to get the man thrown out of the service. If the charge of disrespect was proven he could be summarily dismissed from the force. For the

first time since their exchange, Axel wished he had taken
Fest's advice and forgotten the whole business.

"*Well?*" The General's roar brought him back to himself
with a start. He looked up. Tolonen's face was red with
anger. "Do I have to drag it from you word for word?"

Axel shook his head. In a quiet voice he repeated Ebert's
words. Then what he had added afterwards.

Tolonen had gone quiet. He looked away, then back at
Haavikko. "That's it?" he asked, his voice suddenly much
softer. "Those are his precise words?"

Axel nodded curtly, a shiver running down his back. So
it was done. The accusation made.

The General shook his head slowly and turned away,
moving towards the window. He gazed outward distractedly, then looked back at Haavikko. "You'll be silent until
I order otherwise. All right?"

"Sir."

There was a knock at the door.

Tolonen cleared his throat, then turned to face the door.
"Come in!"

Fest and Ebert entered. They marched to the centre of
the room and came to attention.

Tolonen came and stood directly before them, Fest to
his left, Ebert to his right. Haavikko stood to the side, near
the desk. From there he could see his two fellow cadets'
faces. General Tolonen was in profile.

"Do you know why I've summoned you, Ebert?"

Ebert's eyes went to Haavikko, then back to Tolonen.
"I think I can guess, sir."

Tolonen frowned. "Really?"

"It's Haavikko, sir. He insulted me. I had to slap him
down."

Tolonen turned to look at Axel, astonished, then looked
back at Fest. "Is this true, Fest?"

Fest bowed slightly. "It is, sir. It was coming back here
from the Net. The two had an argument. Haavikko was
very offensive about Ebert's father. Hans . . . I mean
Ebert, had no option but to strike him."

"I see," said Tolonen. "And there was nothing else?"

"Nothing, sir," answered Fest. "It was all very unpleasant, but we hoped it would be forgotten. Ebert feels his honour has been upheld."

"You're certain of this, Fest? You'd swear to it under oath?"

Fest looked straight ahead. His reply was instantaneous, unflinching. "I would, sir."

Tolonen considered a moment. Then he moved across until he was directly in front of Ebert. "Your father and I have been friends for more than fifty years, Hans. I held you as a baby. Played with you as a child. And I've always been proud of you as a soldier under my command. But a serious accusation has been levelled against you. One you must either admit to or deny completely."

"Sir?" Ebert looked puzzled.

Haavikko started forward, then stepped back. *The liars! The barefaced liars!*

Tolonen turned, looking across at Haavikko. Then, in a cold, quiet voice, he repeated what Haavikko had said to him, all the while keeping his eyes on him. Finished, he half turned, looking to Ebert. "Well, cadet Ebert? What have you to say?"

Ebert looked totally nonplussed. He said nothing, merely shook his head. It was Fest who answered for him, his face filled with indignation and anger.

"But this is outrageous, sir! Ebert said nothing of the kind! This is just malicious claptrap, sir! Pure bile! An attempt to get back at Ebert underhandedly!"

Ebert had lowered his head. When he looked up there was a tear on his left cheek. "General Tolonen . . ." he began.

"No! Enough!" Tolonen drew himself up to his full height. "Fest, Ebert, be kind enough to leave the room. I've heard enough."

Axel, unable to believe what had happened, watched them leave, and saw, as the General turned to face him, Ebert smile triumphantly at Fest. Then the door closed and he was alone with the General.

"You heard what they said, Haavikko. Explain yourself."

Axel shuddered. "They were lying, sir. Both of them. Fest was covering for Ebert . . ."

Tolonen watched him coldly, then shook his head. "Take care, Haavikko. Don't compound your error. You realise I could have you court-martialled for what you've done. Dismissed from the service. The only thing that stops me is the promise I made your dead father."

The old man gritted his teeth, then looked away. His disappointment with Haavikko was written starkly in his face. "I thought better of you." He laughed – a sharp, bitter laugh – then turned away. "Get out of my sight, Haavikko. Right now. You have your posting."

* * *

Three hours later Axel sat at the Security Desk at the lowest level of the Bremen Fortress, waiting for his new orders to come through. His kit – the sum total of his belongings in the world – was packed and stored in a back room down the hallway. To kill the time he had relieved the duty officer while he went to get *ch'a* for them both. The ninth of the evening bells had just sounded and it was quiet.

Outwardly he appeared quite calm as he sat there in the reception area. Inside, however, he still seethed. Anger and bitterness and regret at the General's actions filled him to bursting. The General had done what he had had to do, and, in his place, he might well have done the same. At least, so the logical, reasonable part of him argued. But seeing it that way didn't help. A gross injustice had been done him and his very soul felt bruised and raw. It was not justice he wanted but revenge. He felt like killing them. Slowly, painfully. Fest first, and then Ebert.

Impossible, he thought bitterly. And even if he did, they would come and take all those he loved in retribution. Sister and aunts and all. To the third generation, as the law demanded.

He looked down, momentarily overcome, then looked up again, hearing a noise in front of him.

The Han bowed low before the desk, then met Axel's eyes. He seemed close to exhaustion and his clothes stank.

"I need protection," he said. "There are men trying to kill me."

Axel stared back at him, feeling empty. "It's an evil world," he said, indicating a seat at the back of the reception area. "Sit down. The duty officer will see you in a while."

He watched the Han turn and go to the seat, then looked away, paying no more attention to the man.

A minute later the duty officer was back. "You're in luck, Haavikko," he said, handing him a bowl of *ch'a* from the tray, then taking a sealed packet from his jacket pocket and putting it on the desk in front of him. "It's just come through. Your new posting."

Axel stared at it a moment, then took it and broke the seal. He read it then looked down, his face momentarily registering his disgust. England! They were sending him to England, of all the godsforsaken places!

He tucked the orders away in his tunic pocket, masking his bitter disappointment, then drained his bowl at a go. "Thanks," he said, letting the other take his seat again. "I'll get my kit and go."

"Yes, you'd better." The duty officer smiled sadly at him; an understanding smile. "Hey! And good luck!"

After he'd gone, the Han rose slowly from his seat and went across to the desk. The duty officer looked up, then set his *ch'a* down.

"Yes?"

"I need protection," the Han said tiredly, conscious he had used these same words earlier. "There are men trying to kill me."

The officer nodded, then reached for his lap terminal, ready to take details. "Okay. What's your name?"

"Pi Ch'ien," the Han answered. "My name is Pi Ch'ien."

CHAPTER·4

THE MOON DRAGON

"Well, what are we to do?"

Lehmann turned away, looking out at the calm of the lotus-strewn lake; watching as one of the three cranes he had bought only the day before lifted its long, elegant wings, then settled again, dipping its bill into the water. Behind him DeVore was pacing backward and forward restlessly, slapping his gloves against his thigh with every second step. Lehmann had never seen him so agitated nor so upset. Who would have believed that Yang Lai's message carrier, his Third Secretary, Pi Ch'ien, would turn up again, like an envoy from the land of the dead?

"What do you suggest, Howard?"

DeVore came and stood by him at the open window. "You know what we have to do. It's what we planned for. In case this happened."

"You think it's really necessary? I mean. . . Yang Lai is dead. And Cho Hsiang and the two assassins. There seems nothing more to connect us. So what if the General has Pi Ch'ien? Pi Ch'ien knows nothing."

"Not so, I'm afraid. Pi Ch'ien has named Heng Chi-Po as his contact."

Lehmann turned abruptly, facing him. "Minister Heng? Gods! And he has proof of this?"

DeVore shook his head. "No. But it isn't a question of proof any longer. The General plans to go to the T'ang with what he knows, surmise or not, proof or not. And

146

the T'ang will tell him to investigate. We have to act now. To pre-empt the investigation." He paused, taking breath. "We have to sacrifice him, Pietr. We have to give them Wyatt."

Lehmann turned back, facing DeVore. "You're certain, Howard? Certain it's the only way?"

DeVore gave a curt nod. "It's necessary."

Lehmann was silent a moment, then he nodded. "All right. Do what you have to."

DeVore reached out and touched his arm. "Keep heart, Pietr. It's a hard road, I know, but we'll triumph. I'm sure of it."

"Maybe . . ." Lehmann looked down. "You know, I didn't think it would be like this. I thought . . ."

"You thought you could keep your hands clean, eh?"

Lehmann shook his head. "No. Not that. Just . . . Well, he's a good man, Howard. If there's any other way . . . ?"

He looked up, meeting DeVore's eyes again, but the latter shook his head.

"Don't blame yourself, Pietr. There is no other way." DeVore huffed. "Our hands are tied, don't you understand? Chung Kuo itself is to blame. This world of ours. . . it's incestuous. The connections are too tangled. You have only to scratch your arse and your enemy sighs with relief."

Lehmann laughed sadly. "That's so."

DeVore pressed on. "Do you think I'd not be open if I could? Do you think I like this game of deceit and double-dealing?" He spat out neatly onto the water below. "If I was open for a moment I'd be dead. And you. And all of us. So think of that, Pietr, before you get sentimental over Edmund Wyatt. He was a good man. Maybe. But he also wanted what we want. Change. A break with the old order. Keep that in mind, Pietr. Don't waver from it. Because if you doubt it for a moment you're dead. You and all of us."

Lehmann shivered, hearing how DeVore spoke of Wyatt

in the past tense. But he could not argue with him. Their course was set now. To the end.

"Then I must seem his friend?"

"And I your mortal enemy."

"Yes." Lehmann looked out, watching one of the cranes glide slowly to the bank, then lift itself up onto the pale white rocks, ruffling its feathers as it settled.

* * *

The General waited on the central dais, holding himself stiffly upright in the tall-backed Summons Chair. To either side of the dais stood an honour guard of the T'ang's own bodyguard, resplendent in their crimson combat silks, big men with shaven heads and naked feet, while all around him the T'ang's servants moved silently through the great hall, going about their business.

Only six hours ago he had contemplated this meeting with some misgivings, but now he felt confident, almost elated, the frustrations of the past three days behind him. He held DeVore's file tightly in his lap, smiling inwardly. I've got you now, he thought. Both of you. You won't wriggle out of this one.

He gazed ahead fixedly. Facing him, some fifty paces distant, was the entrance to the Hall of Eternal Truth, where the T'ang held audience.

The double doors were massive, twice as tall as they were broad. In silver across the black, leather surface, its circumference five times the height of a man, was drawn a great circle of seven dragons. At its centre the snouts of the regal beasts met, forming a rose-like hub, huge rubies burning fiercely in each eye. Their lithe, powerful bodies curved outward like the spokes of a giant wheel while at the edge their tails were intertwined to form the rim. It was the *Ywe Lung*, the Moon Dragon, symbol of the Seven. Tolonen could never look at it without a feeling of great pride – glad beyond words that it had fallen to him to play so large a part in defending that great and powerful circle, that his T'ang honoured him so.

Two bells sounded, the first sweet and clear, the second deep and resonant. Slowly, noiselessly, the great doors swung back.

The General stood, then stepped down from the dais, the file and the other papers held tightly against his breast. He turned to his left, then to his right, bowing his head stiffly to the two lieutenants, then marched forward ten paces and stopped, letting the honour guard form up behind him.

The doors were fully open now. He could see the T'ang at the far end of the Hall, seated on the high throne, atop the Presence Dais.

The T'ang's Chancellor, Chung Hu-Yan came forward, greeting him.

"General Tolonen," he said, smiling and bowing low. "You are most welcome. The T'ang is expecting you."

"It is good to see you, Hu-yan," the General said quietly, returning both smile and bow. "I hope you're well. And all your family."

"And yours, Knut," he answered softly, straightening up. "But come. You've waited far too long already."

Chung Hu-Yan turned, facing the T'ang again. He bowed low, going down onto his knees and pressing his forehead briefly against the tiled floor. Then he stood and walked slowly into the Hall. The General moved forward, following him. Beneath the great lintel he halted and made his own obeisance to the T'ang, the whole of the honour guard behind him making the gesture at the same moment, then rising when he rose. But when he moved forward again they stayed where they were. No one – not even a member of the honour guard – was allowed into the Hall without the T'ang's express permission.

At the foot of the steps Tolonen paused, the Chancellor to the left of him, others of the T'ang's retinue gathered to the right of the Dais.

"*Chieh Hsia,*" he said, making his *k'o t'ou* a second time.

The literal translation of the Mandarin was "below the steps", but the phrase had long acquired a second, more

149

important meaning –"Your Majesty". "*Chieh Hsia*", it dated from those ancient days when ministers, summoned to an audience with the Emperor, were not permitted to address the Son of Heaven directly, but spoke through those officials gathered "below the steps" of the high-raised throne.

The T'ang rose from his throne and started down the broad steps of the Presence Dais.

"Knut. I'm sorry I kept you waiting."

Li Shai Tung was wearing his official robes; long, flowing silks of pale gold, trimmed with black, and honey-coloured boots of soft kid. His fine grey hair was pulled back severely from his forehead and bound tightly at the back of his head. He wore a simple necklet of gold, and, on the fingers of his right hand, two rings; the first a simple band of thin white gold, his dead wife's wedding gift; the other a heavier, thicker ring of black iron, bearing on its face a silvered miniature of the *Ywe Lung*, the seal of power.

Li Shai Tung was a tall man; as tall as his General, but willowy. He came down the twelve steps briskly, his movements lighter, more energetic than one might have expected from a man of sixty years. It was often said that the T'ang moved like a dancer, elegantly, powerfully – and it was so; his athletic grace a result of the rigorous training he put himself through each morning. But there was also a dignity to his bearing – an authority – that only those born to rule seem to possess.

Facing his General, he reached out to touch Tolonen's arm, his pale, lined face breaking into a smile. Then the hand fell back; moved to touch, then stroke, his long, but neatly-trimmed beard. "I've been kept busy, Knut. This matter of the vacancy. Four families have petitioned me for the appointment. I have been seeing the candidates this very morning."

"Then what I have to say will be of interest, *Chieh Hsia*."

Li Shai Tung nodded, then looked about him. Beside the Chancellor there were a dozen others in the Hall; members of his private staff. "How confidential is this matter?"

The General smiled, understanding. "It would not do for all to know it yet."

The T'ang smiled back at him. "I understand. We'll speak alone. In my grandfather's room." He motioned to his Chancellor. "Hu-Yan. You will stand at the door and make certain no one disturbs us until we are done."

They went through, into one of the smaller rooms at the back of the Hall. The T'ang pulled the doors closed behind him, then turned, looking at Tolonen, his expression unreadable. He crossed the room and sat beneath the twin portraits of his grandfather and Wen Ti, motioning for his General to come to him.

"Sit there, Knut. Facing me."

Tolonen did as he was bid, yet he felt awkward, being seated in his T'ang's presence. He looked at the nearby fire and unconsciously put out one hand towards its warmth.

The T'ang smiled, seeing the gesture. "You have something new, then? Something more than when we last spoke?"

"Yes, *Chieh Hsia*. I know who ordered Lwo Kang killed."

The T'ang considered. "Enough to prove this thing in law?"

The General nodded. "And maybe cause the fall of a Great Family."

"Ah. . ." Li Shai Tung looked down, into his lap. "Then the Minister *is* involved in this?"

Tolonen leaned forward and passed across the file, leaving the other papers in his lap. "It is all in there, *Chieh Hsia*. All the evidence. Trading connections. Payments and names. Who was used and when. Yang Lai, Fu Lung-ti, Hong Cao, Cho Hsiang – a whole network of names and dates, connecting all the levels of the thing. It was well orchestrated. Too well, perhaps. But we would never have made these connections unless my man DeVore had followed his nose. Wyatt was the hub – the centre of this web of dealings."

The T'ang nodded, then looked down at the document.

For the next fifteen minutes he was silent, reading. Then, finished, he closed the file and looked up. "Yes," he said softly, almost tiredly. "This is good, Knut. This is what I wanted. You have done very well."

The General bowed his head. "Thank you, *Chieh Hsia*. But as I said, the praise is not mine. This is Major DeVore's work."

"I see." The T'ang looked back down at the document. "Then I shall see that the Major is rewarded."

"Thank you. And the Minister?"

Li Shai Tung gave a short, humourless laugh. "Heng Chi-Po is a careful man, as this document bears out. Though the finger points at him, at no point does it touch." He shook his head. "No matter the weight of circumstantial evidence, we have nothing substantial."

"Yet it was he who warned Yang Lai. Who sent the message."

"Maybe so. But it would not hold. Assumptions, that's all we have when it comes down to it, Knut. Junior Minister Yang Lai is missing and the message card Pi Ch'ien held onto was blank. It is not strong evidence."

The General was quiet a moment. It was true. The message card that Pi Ch'ien had carried from Minister Heng to Yang Lai was worthless as evidence, the message it held having decayed within thirty seconds of Yang Lai activating it with his thumb-print.

"Then you will do nothing against him?"

The T'ang nodded. When he spoke again he was more reserved, more formal than before. "You must understand me in this, Knut. If I had a single item of evidence against him – however small – I would break the man, and do it gladly. But as it is. . ." He spread his hands expressively. "It would not do to accuse one of my own Ministers without irreproachable evidence."

"I understand."

"Good." The T'ang leaned forward, his dark eyes staring intently at his General. "For now, we'll take Wyatt, and any others that can be traced through him. Lehmann, perhaps, and that foul creature, Berdichev. But before we do, make sure there's not a possibility of doubt. We must act from certainty. Chung Kuo must see us to be correct — to be perfectly justified in our actions. I want no trouble in the House because of this."

The General bowed his head, keeping his thoughts to himself. In this the T'ang was right. Things had changed subtly in the last ten years. More power than ever before lay in the hands of men like Lehmann. They had money and influence and a vote in the House at Weimar. And though the House was subject to the will of the Seven, it did not do to exercise such power too frequently. The illusion of cooperation – of an independent House, working hand-in-glove with the Council of the Seven – needed to be preserved. In that illusion lay the basis of lasting peace.

Was that, then, the truth behind all this? Tolonen asked himself. The real reason for Lwo Kang's death? Was it all an attempt to force the hand of the Seven? To make it show its true power openly and without veils before the world? To set House against Seven and force the people to a choice? If so, he understood the T'ang's caution.

He looked up again, meeting the T'ang's eyes. "It is a loathsome business, ours, *Chieh Hsia*. We must deal fairly, honestly, with cheats and scoundrels." He sighed bitterly. "Those cockroaches are all bows and fair words to our faces, yet beneath that outward show they seethe with subterfuge. They smile but they want us dead."

The T'ang smiled sadly. "Yes, Knut. Yet such is the way of this world. So men are. So they act. And that itself is reason enough for the Seven, eh? Without us where would be the peace our father's fathers worked for? What would happen to the City of Ten Thousand Years they built? We know, you and I. The barbarians would tear it down, level by level, and build some cruder, darker thing in its place."

Tolonen tilted his head, agreeing, but he was thinking of the giant, Karr, and of the Pit below the Net where life was fought for openly, beneath the acid glare of brilliant lights. He was a cleaner kind of beast. Much cleaner than

Lehmann and his like. For once the Major had been wrong – he had seen that instantly. There *was* honour in how a man behaved, even beneath the Net. Karr and the dead man, Chen, they were killers, certainly, but weren't all soldiers killers when it came to it? How you killed, that was the important thing. Whether you faced your adversary, man to man, letting the contest be decided on strength of arm and skill, or whether you skulked through shadows like a thief to slip a poisoned blade into a sleeping back.

Yes, he thought, in truth I should hate the indirectness of all this; the masks and the tricks and the unending layers of intermediaries. Yet I've been trained to indirectness – to be as cunning as the men I fight.

"As far as Wyatt is concerned, I'll have the warrant signed before you leave. Is there anything else, Knut?"

"There are two further matters, *Chieh Hsia*."

"Well?"

"The first is a request." The General handed his T'ang one of the papers. "In a week Han Ch'in, your eldest son, is sixteen and becomes a man. It is my wish to give him something appropriate."

Tolonen fell silent, watching as Li Shai Tung unfolded the silk-paper deed of ownership. After a moment the T'ang looked up, a surprised smile lighting his features. "But this is too much, Knut, surely?"

The General bowed his head. "Han Ch'in will be T'ang one day. And though he has the freedom of your stables, *Chieh Hsia*, I felt it time he had his own horse. Through horsemanship one learns command."

The T'ang was still smiling. A horse was a princely gift. There were two thousand thoroughbreds at most in the whole of Chung Kuo. To purchase one would have cost even a fabulously rich man like the General more than he could easily afford. Li Shai Tung looked at Tolonen a moment longer, then did what he rarely did and bent his head. "Then it shall be so, old friend. My family is honoured by your gift. And Han Ch'in will be delighted."

The General lowered his head, his face burning with

pride and pleasure. Across from him the T'ang folded the paper again. "And the second matter?"

"Ah. . . That is a gift to myself." He hesitated, then handed the second of the papers over. "There is a man I want to use. His name is Karr."

★ ★ ★

That evening, Under-Secretary Lehmann summoned all those delegates and representatives sympathetic to his cause to his suite of rooms in the penthouse of the House of a Thousand Freedoms in Weimar. There was a brooding silence in the long, packed room. Lehmann sat in his chair, one hand tugging distractedly at his pigtail, a copy of the warrant open on the desk before him, an expression of sheer disbelief and outrage building slowly in his face.

"I don't believe it," he said finally, his voice soft, controlled. Then he picked the paper up and held it out to the rest of them. "Does *anyone* here believe this?"

There was a deep murmur of denial and a shaking of heads.

"But there must be some kind of evidence, Pietr. Even the T'ang would not dare to act without clear evidence."

Lehmann laughed sourly, then turned slightly in his seat and looked across at the delegate who had spoken, a tall, heavily-built *Hung Mao* in a pale green *pau*. "You think so, Barrow Chao? You think the small matter of evidence will stop a T'ang from acting?"

There was an indrawing of breath in some quarters. A T'ang was a T'ang, after all. Lehmann saw this and made a mental note of those who had seemed outraged by his words, then pressed on. He stood up slowly and came round the table, facing Barrow.

"I've known Edmund Wyatt all my life, Chao. I knew him as a child and I've been honoured to know him as a man. I can vouch there's no more honest man in the Above, nor one with less malice in him. For Edmund to have done what this says he did. . . Well, it's laughable!"

He was facing Barrow now, only an arm's length from him. Barrow shrugged. "So you say, Pietr. And before today I would have said the same. But I repeat, the T'ang *must* have evidence. And not just any evidence, but proof positive. He would be mad to act without it."

"Maybe," Lehmann said, turning aside. "But maybe not. Just think about it. In the last five years this House has won more freedoms than in the whole of the previous century. We managed to extend the boundaries of trade and win huge concessions in respect of legitimate research and development. In doing so we brought a refreshing and much needed breath of change to Chung Kuo."

There were murmurs of agreement from the delegates. Lehmann turned back, facing them.

"Change. That's what the Seven hate above all else. Change. And in the last three years we have seen them act to kill those freedoms we so rightly fought for. At first covertly, with whispered words and meaningful glances. Then with 'gifts' for those who would be their friends. Finally, through the alternatives of patronage or the turned back."

There were nods of angry agreement, the agitated whisper of silks as the delegates turned to talk amongst themselves. There was not one here who hadn't suffered from the backlash. Not one who, as an advocate of change, however limited, had not found himself "out of favour" and thus out of pocket.

Lehmann waited for things to quieten, then smiled tightly. "But that was only the start of it, wasn't it? Having failed to check things by covert means, they decided to be more direct. Ministerial appointments, previously and rightly determined by family connections and the common-sense measure of financial power, were suddenly made on some nebulous sense of New Confucian worthiness."

There were guffaws of laughter at the look of utter disgust on Lehmann's face.

"Worthiness . . . Well, we all know what that really

156

means, don't we? It means a new breed of Minister, as efficient as a GenSyn domestic and every bit as limited when it comes to making a real decision. But we knew what they were from the first, didn't we? Dams set up against the natural flow. Mouthpieces for the Seven, programmed only to say no to change."

Again there was a murmur of agreement; but louder this time, more aggressive. Lehmann raised his hands, palm outward, begging their silence, then nodded his head slowly.

"We know their game, eh? We understand what they are trying to do. And we all know what has been happening in the House this last year. We've seen to what lengths they'll go to oppose change."

It could not be said openly, but all there knew what Lehmann was implying. From the first days of the House the Seven had always maintained a small but influential faction there – men whom the T'ang "kept" for their votes. Such men were known as *tai* – "pockets" – and, historically, had served a double function in the House, counterbalancing the strong mercantile tendencies of the House and serving as a conduit for the views of the Seven. In the past the Seven had chosen well; their *tai* had been elderly, well-respected men: charismatic and persuasive – their tongues worth a dozen, sometimes as many as fifty votes. As agents of consensus they had proved a strong, stabilising influence on the House. But with the new liberalisation things had slowly changed and their influence had waned. For a long while the Seven had done nothing, but in the past twelve months they had bought their way heavily, indiscriminately into the House, trading influence for the direct power of votes.

Now there was a new breed of "pocket": brash young men who owed their wealth and power not to trade or family but to their sudden elevation by the Seven. Rival candidates had been paid off or threatened. Elections had been rigged. Campaign money had flowed like the Yangtze flood. Of the one hundred and eighty delegates elected to the House in the last six months alone, more than two-thirds had been *tai*.

The effect had been to crystallise the factions in the House, and to radicalise the demands for changes to the Edict of Technological Control – that keystone in the great wall of State; or, as some saw it, the dam restraining the gathering waters of change.

"Change will come," Lehmann said softly, "whether they wish it or not. Change *must* come. It is the natural order of things. They cannot build a wall high enough to contain it."

Lehmann paused. There was a noise at the doorway as some of the men gathered there moved aside. Edmund Wyatt pushed through.

"I heard you wanted me, Pietr," he said, then looked around, seeing how everyone was suddenly watching him. He dropped his voice. "What is it?"

Lehmann took his arm, then led him across to the chair and sat him down.

"General Tolonen was here. He brought a copy of a warrant."

Wyatt looked blankly back at Lehmann. "So?"

There was a strong murmuring from the men in the room. Lehmann looked back at them triumphantly, then turned to Barrow. "There! There's your proof, surely, Barrow Chao? Was that the reaction of a guilty man?"

Behind him Wyatt laughed. His cheeks were pink with embarrassment. "What is it, Pietr? What am I supposed to be guilty of?"

Lehmann looked down at the paper in his hand, hesitating, then handed it across. For a moment Wyatt was silent, his right hand holding down the paper as he read. Then he looked up, a startled expression in his eyes. "I . . . I don't believe it."

Lehmann had gone round the back of him. Now he stood there, leaning over Wyatt, but looking up at the other men in the room as he spoke.

"It's what it appears to be. A warrant. Signed by the

158

T'ang himself. For your arrest, Edmund. For the murder of Lwo Kang."

Wyatt turned and stared up into his face. His bewilderment, his total incomprehension were there for everyone in the room to see. "But it *can't* be, Pietr. I mean, I never . . ."

His voice gave out again and he looked down sharply, shuddering.

"Then this is real," he said after a moment.

There was a tense silence in the room, then Lehmann spoke again. "Well, Barrow Chao? What do you reckon?"

Barrow dropped his head and nodded. The room was deathly quiet.

Lehmann straightened, sighing. "Then the question is this. How do we fight this?"

Wyatt looked up at him. "Fight it?"

Lehmann was quiet a moment, concentrating, then gave the slightest nod. "Yes," he said. "We'll hide you. All of us. We could do it. We could keep Tolonen from serving the warrant."

Lehmann gazed about him defiantly, looking from face to face, challenging anyone to gainsay him, but the mood was in his favour now.

"No!" Wyatt got up, then came round and stood there, facing Lehmann. "No, Pietr. I won't hide. That's what he wants. That's why he came here first. Don't you see? He wanted that. Wanted me to run. That way he could put another warrant out. Have me killed without trial. No, let him serve his warrant. I've nothing to fear. I've done nothing."

Lehmann laughed sourly. "And what does that mean, Edmund? The T'ang wants payment for his Minister's life. Retribution. Right or wrong is an irrelevance in this instance. It doesn't matter that you're innocent. He wants you. Don't you see that?" His voice was stern now, unyielding. "And he'll find all the evidence he needs to get you."

There was a loud murmuring, but no disagreement.

Wyatt turned away. "When does he plan to serve the warrant?"

Lehmann looked about him, seeing how open each man's face now was; how starkly etched their anger and resentment, their concern and indignation. Then he turned back. "Mid-day tomorrow," he said. "At your apartment."

"I see." Wyatt looked down. "Then I'll be there. T'ang or not, he's wrong, Pietr. I'm innocent. You know I am."

Lehmann turned, looking back at him, then reached out and touched his shoulder. "I know."

★   ★   ★

"Minister Heng."

The T'ang's Chancellor, Chung Hu-Yan, bowed stiffly, his face expressionless, then turned, inviting the Minister to follow him.

Astonished, Heng returned the Chancellor's bow. He had barely arrived a minute before, and here was Chung trying to rush him into audience. Was there to be no ritual of preparation? No honour guard? He stood there a moment longer, as if he had not heard the words, looking about him, surprised by the emptiness of the great entrance hall. It was strangely disconcerting; as if the T'ang's servants had been sent elsewhere. But why? And why the unseemly haste?

"Please . . ." Chung Hu-Yan bowed a second time, then repeated the gesture of invitation, making it clear that it had been no mistake.

"Forgive me," Heng said, bowing again, his composure slipping. "Of course . . ."

He followed the Chancellor through, under the great lintel and into the Hall of Eternal Truth. But he had taken only three steps into the great hall when he stopped, taken aback. There, alone beneath the empty Presence Throne, stood General Tolonen; tall, white-haired and elegant in his peacock blue dress uniform. Heng Chi-po frowned then walked on, conscious for once of the unfavourable contrast he made to the haughty *Hung Mao*, his hand momentarily

160

straying to the crane patch on the chest of his dark blue *pau*, symbol of his status as an official of the first rank.

Coming opposite the General, Minister Heng stopped and bowed, but Tolonen stared through him coldly, not even the smallest flicker of recognition in his eyes.

The T'ang's Chancellor waited, watching the exchange carefully. Then, rather stiffly, he bowed. "Forgive me, Minister Heng, but the T'ang awaits you. Please. . . if you would follow me."

Heng turned angrily and followed Chung Hu-Yan into a room to the right of the throne. The T'ang was waiting for him there, standing amongst the tall-leafed plants at the edge of a small, decorative carp pond.

"*Chieh Hsia,*" he said, bowing deeply, "I hope you are in good health."

Li Shai Tung turned from his contemplation of the fish. "Come in, Minister Heng. Please, take a seat. We've business to discuss."

Heng sat, his back to the unlit fire, looking about him, noting with pleasure the simple luxuries of the room. There was a tall screen across the centre of the room, a delightful thing of brightly coloured silk, and next to it a low, squat vase, rounded like the belly of a wrestler, its glaze the sweetest, softest lavender he'd ever seen.

"This is a beautiful room, *Chieh Hsia.*"

"Yes," said the T'ang, smiling. "It was my grandfather's favourite room. His picture hangs behind you."

Heng turned and looked up, first at Wen Ti, then at the painting beside it, conscious at once of the strength, the raw vitality of the man portrayed. "Ah yes. He has your eyes, *Chieh Hsia.*"

"My eyes?" The T'ang looked down, thoughtful. "They say he had perfect vision all his life. That at seventy he could see what type of bird was nesting in a tree more than two *li* distant. But there's seeing and seeing, eh, Heng?" He met the Minister's eyes again, a wry yet challenging look in his own.

Heng bowed, conscious of the exaggeration and suddenly wary of its meaning. "As you say, *Chieh Hsia*."

"Yes . . . As I say." The T'ang looked past him, up at the painting of his ancestor. "And if I say Heng Yu is not appointed in Lwo Kang's place?"

Heng Chi-po stiffened in his seat, then forced himself to relax. "Then that too is as you say. One does not question the word of a T'ang."

Li Shai Tung sat back. "No," he said, watching his Minister closely. "But that is what you came for, is it not?"

Heng looked up again. "It was, *Chieh Hsia*. But as you've made your decision."

The T'ang raised his chin slightly. "There was nothing else, then? No other matter you wished to speak to me about?"

Heng kept his face a blank. "Nothing that cannot wait for the next meeting of the Council of Ministers. I thought to plead on my nephew's behalf. To put his qualities before you. He is a good man, a capable man, *Chieh Hsia*."

Strangely, the T'ang laughed. "You are quite right, Minister Heng. He *is* a good man. Which is why I saw him this very morning."

The look of surprise on Heng's face was unfeigned. "*Chieh Hsia*?"

"And appointed him."

Heng's mouth fell open. "But you said . . ."

The T'ang clicked his fingers. Two guards came in and stood there at either end of the screen. Heng looked across at them, frowning, not understanding, then looked back at the T'ang.

"Yes. I spoke to him at length. I questioned him about the five classics. Then, finally, I set him a riddle."

"A riddle, *Chieh Hsia*?"

Li Shai Tung stood up and went over to the screen. "I put this problem to him. If one *knows* a man is guilty yet has no proof, how can one act and yet be considered just?"

Heng lowered his eyes.

"You see my drift, Minister Heng? You understand me?" The T'ang's voice was suddenly harsher, colder.

Heng glanced up; saw how closely the T'ang was watching him now. No proof, he thought. You have no proof!

The T'ang continued. "Your nephew considered a moment, then asked me how it was I knew and yet could not prove the matter? Was I, then, not witness to the guilty act? No, I had to answer. What then? he asked. Was there another, perhaps, whose word meant less in the eyes of the world than that of the guilty man? Were the scales of accusation and denial tipped unevenly in the latter's favour? I smiled and nodded. But so it ever is. How balance them?"

Heng had gone cold.

"And do you know what he said?"

The Minister looked up. He hesitated, then found his voice. "No, *Chieh Hsia*."

The T'ang laughed sourly. "No, you wouldn't, would you, Heng?"

He snapped his fingers again, then moved aside as the guards lifted and carried the screen away.

Heng gasped. His face blanched. Then he looked down sharply, swallowing loudly.

The T'ang came closer and stood over him. "You're a clever man, Heng Chi-po. Too clever to leave your print on things. But I know you for what you are. I've seen it here, with my own eyes. Your guilt is as clear on you as the glaze on this vase."

He turned and looked across to where Pi Ch'ien sat, hands in his lap, silently watching, then looked back down at his Minister.

"Over there, in the corner, is a desk. On the desk you will find an ink block, brushes, writing paper and your seal of office. I want you to write a letter to me explaining that you have been suffering from ill-health these last few months. So much so that you must, with great sadness naturally, resign your post."

There was the smallest movement of Heng's head as if to protest, then he nodded.

"Good. In which case there will be no loss of pension, no public loss of face. As for your Family, they will gain a better man as Minister. Heng Yu will be appointed in your place."

Heng Chi-po looked up mutely, miserably, then bowed his head again and stood to do as he was bid.

★ ★ ★

Heng Kou waved the servant away, then leaned across to lock and seal the carriage.

"What is it, first brother? What has happened?"

For a moment Heng Chi-po was unable to speak. His face was mottled with fury and his hands pulled convulsively at each other. Then he leaned forward across the gap between them until his face was almost touching Kou's.

"This is Tolonen's doing." Heng Chi-po blinked angrily, then leaned back again. For a moment he was silent, staring away into the distance, his whole face fixed in a mask of purest hatred. Then he turned and faced his brother again. "I saw it in his eyes. That man has never liked me, Kou. And now he has poisoned the T'ang against me."

Kou frowned. "Poisoned . . . How?"

"The insect tricked me. Trapped me . . ." Heng Chi-po's chest rose and fell violently now. Sweat beads stood out at his forehead.

Heng Kou began to understand. Gods! Heng Chi-po was out. That was it, wasn't it? For some reason he was out. Nothing else could have brought him to this state. But was this a tragedy for Chi-po alone or for the whole family? Was all lost? Or could the damage be contained? He had to know.

Heng Kou calmed himself and leaned forward, forcing his brother to look at him. "Tell me what happened, eldest brother. What misfortune has befallen our great family?"

Heng Chi-po tried to meet his eyes, then looked down sharply, his voice suddenly bitter with shame. He was close to tears.

"I am no longer Minister. Li Shai Tung has stripped me of my office."

"Stripped you . . ." Heng Kou feigned speechlessness.

164

Then he found his voice again. "He forced you to resign, you mean?"

Heng Chi-po nodded, the first tears rolling down his cheeks. "But there's more, Kou. He has appointed nephew Yu in my place. Can you believe that? The humiliation of it! We shall be laughing stocks!"

Heng Kou's mind reeled. Nephew Yu! After the first shock of it he wanted to laugh aloud, but he hid both his delight and his relief. "That's outrageous!" he said. "It is an insult, elder brother. A slur upon the whole family." But he was already considering how to act to minimise the damage to the family.

Heng Chi-po leaned forward again, his red-rimmed eyes suddenly angry again. "I'll have him, Kou! I'll have the carrion dead, understand?"

For a moment Heng Kou was too shocked for words, but then he saw that his brother didn't mean the T'ang.

"Leave it, brother. Please. It's done. You can't undo it thus."

Heng Chi-po shook his head violently. "No, Kou. I want Tolonen dead. By tomorrow evening. Understand me? I want that bastard obliterated. I want him non-existent. I want . . ."

Heng Kou shivered, then bowed his head. "As you wish, my brother."

★　★　★

"Do you think they'll incarcerate me, Pietr? Do you think they've proof to hold me until the trial?"

Lehmann smiled and touched Wyatt's shoulder. "We've the best advocates in the seven cities, Edmund. I'm sure they'll keep you from the cells. But even if they can't, it won't be so dreadful. Privilege is privilege, even behind bars. You'll not lack for comforts."

Wyatt smiled, but shadows gathered beneath the firm and pleasant line of his mouth, clouding the attractive sparkle of his eyes. Many old friends had come to visit him this morning. More friends than he'd thought he had. For

165

a time he had let himself be buoyed by their good wishes, but now they were gone and he was alone with Lehmann.

"You know, this frightens me, Pietr. I couldn't sleep last night thinking of it. Wondering how I would handle myself. How I would bear up before all these lies and smears. Wondering what kind of man I would be at the end of it."

"You'll be your father's son, Edmund. You're like him. You have his strength."

Wyatt looked down. "Maybe."

He said no more, but Lehmann, who knew him as well as any man, could sense what he was thinking. Wyatt's father had been strong but inconsiderate, his mother weak and conciliatory. She had died when Edmund was only five, leaving him almost defenceless against his hectoring father. That he had grown up such a sane and balanced individual was testimony to the influence of his sisters and aunts.

Lehmann glanced down at the ornate timepiece inset at his wrist. "The General will be here soon, Edmund. We should get ready for him."

Wyatt nodded abstractedly, then turned to face him. "It's not myself I'm afraid for, it's them." He shivered, then wrapped his arms about himself. "It's why I couldn't bear to have them here with me today. If I lose this – if, inexplicably, they find me guilty of Lwo Kang's murder . . ." He looked down, all colour gone from his cheeks. "Well, their lives would be forfeit, too, wouldn't they? It's the law. A traitor and all his family . . ."

Lehmann breathed shallowly, forcing himself to meet Wyatt's eyes. "That's so. To the third generation."

"Still . . ." Wyatt forced a smile, then came across and held Lehmann to him tightly. "I'm grateful, Pietr," he said more quietly. "Truly I am. However this turns out, I . . ."

Lehmann felt Wyatt's body shudder in his arms and steeled himself against all feeling. Even so, he answered Wyatt gently.

"You would have helped me, wouldn't you?"

Wyatt moved slightly back from him. There were tears in his eyes. "I'd kill for you, Pietr. You know I would."

Necessary. He heard DeVore's voice saying it and felt a shiver run down his spine. *It's easy for you, Howard*, he thought; *you never liked him.*

Lehmann smiled. "Let's talk of living, eh?"

There was a pounding on the mansion's huge front doors.

Wyatt looked up, past him. "They're early. I didn't think they'd be early."

They went through, out into the marbled hallway. Wyatt's chamberlain, a stout, middle-aged Han, greeted them with a bow.

"Shall I open the door, master?"

Wyatt shook his head. "No. Let them wait, Fu Hsien."

There were footsteps on the stairs overhead and a murmur of talk.

"*Ch'un tzu!*" Lehmann went to the foot of the stairs and greeted the three elderly Han as they came down to him. It had cost him over a million yuan simply to bring them here this morning. If the case went on for months, as it was likely to do, it would cost his faction somewhere between thirty and fifty million. Wyatt had been told nothing of this, but his sisters and aunts had been briefed already. In time they were certain to let Wyatt know whose money it was that was paying for his defence.

Lehmann turned, smiling, and watched the three greybeards greet Wyatt once again. At the introduction, earlier, all three advocates had seemed impressed by Wyatt's protestations of innocence. As indeed they ought. Edmund didn't merely seem innocent, he was. The full force of his self-belief had carried any remaining doubts the three had had. They had agreed to take the case.

But things were not as simple as they seemed. On paper Wyatt's case seemed good. In court he would make a fine impression. Public sympathy was sure to be in his favour. But Wyatt had to lose. He had to be made to seem a victim of conspiracy and power-broking.

167

New evidence would be introduced as and when necessary, for his good friend, Edmund Wyatt, was to be a martyr.

The hammering came again. A voice shouted from behind the door. "Open up! We come on the T'ang's business!"

Again the chamberlain looked to Wyatt. This time he nodded.

Tolonen came through first, in full dress uniform, the *chi ling* or unicorn patch of a first rank officer, resplendent on his chest. Behind him strode two officers and an elite squad of eight armed soldiers.

"General Tolonen," said Wyatt, with cold politeness, offering his hand. But Tolonen walked past him, ignoring him.

"Who represents the prisoner?" he demanded brusquely.

One of the three Han stepped forward. "I am Advocate Fou, General. I act for *Shih* Wyatt in this matter. And I'll remind you that my client is not a prisoner but should be addressed as the accused."

Tolonen snorted and turned away. One of the officers at once handed him a long, silvered tube. He hefted it a moment, then passed it to the advocate.

"Please read the document. All three of you, if necessary. Copies will be provided at your offices."

Advocate Fou tipped the scroll out into his hand, passed the tube to one of his colleagues, then unfurled the document. Wyatt moved past Tolonen and stood at the advocate's side, trying to make sense of the sheet of blood red pictograms.

"It's in Mandarin," he said. "That's illegal, isn't it?"

Advocate Fou shook his head, then muttered something in Han to his colleagues and rolled the document up again.

"What is it?" Lehmann asked, coming up beside Wyatt.

The advocate looked across at Tolonen, then back at Lehmann. "I am afraid we cannot help you, Under Secretary. I am most sorry. This matter has been taken out of the jurisdiction of the Courts. Please . . ." He handed the document across to Wyatt. "Our apologies, *Shih* Wyatt. We wish you luck. If innocence has weight in law you will triumph yet."

As one the three Han bowed and took their leave.

Wyatt stood there a moment, dumbfounded, watching them go. Then he turned to Lehmann. "What in the gods' names is happening here, Pietr?" He thrust the document into Lehmann's hand. "What *is* this?"

Lehmann looked away. Gods! he thought. This changes everything.

He turned back. "It's an Edict, Edmund. The Seven have passed a special Edict." He unfurled the white, silken roll. "See here." He pointed out the rigid line of hardened wax. "These are their seals. The *Ywe Lung*, symbol of their power. All seven of them. They must have met in an emergency session and agreed to this."

Wyatt had gone very quiet, watching him, a new kind of fear in his face.

"An Edict?"

"Yes. You are to be tried *in camera*, by a council of the T'ang's Ministers." Lehmann swallowed then looked across at Tolonen, an unfeigned anger in his eyes. "This changes things, Edmund. It changes everything. It means they want you dead."

* * *

Heng Kou paused in the doorway, then knelt down and touched his brow to the cold floor.

"Nephew Yu. I am most sorry to disturb your afternoon sleep. I would not have come, but it is a matter of the utmost urgency."

Heng Yu tied the sash to his sleeping robe and came across the room quickly. "Uncle Kou, please, get up at once. In private you are still my uncle."

Heng Kou let himself be drawn to his feet, then stood there, embarrassed, as Heng Yu bowed to him in the old way.

All that has changed, he thought. *The T'ang gave you*

years when he gave you power. Now you are our head and the family must bow before you. So it is. So it must be. Or Chung Kuo itself would fall.

Heng Yu straightened. "But tell me, what brings you here, uncle?"

"I'm sorry, Yu, but I bring bad news. Your uncle, Chi-po is unwell."

Heng Yu started. "Unwell?"

"Please. . ." Heng Kou bowed and moved aside. "I felt you should come yourself. At once. My own doctors are seeing to him even now. But . . ."

Heng Yu gave the slightest nod. "I understand. Please, lead me to him."

Heng Chi-po's bedroom was dimly lit. The four doctors stood at one end of the room, beside the only light source. Seeing the two men in the doorway, they came across.

"How is my uncle?" asked Heng Yu at once, concerned.

The most senior of them bowed low, then answered him. Like all four of them he had been briefed beforehand concerning Heng Yu's new status in the household.

"I regret to say that your uncle passed away five minutes ago. His heart failed him."

Heng Kou, watching, saw Heng Yu's mouth fall open, his eyes widen in surprise; saw the real pain he felt at the news and knew he had been right not to involve him in the scheme. *Let him believe things are as they are. That disappointment killed my brother. Only I and these four men know otherwise.*

Heng Yu had a servant bring them a lamp, then they went over to where Heng Chi-po lay on his over-sized bed. His eyes had been closed and his face now was at peace. The flesh of his arms and chest and face was pale and misted with a fine sheen of sweat.

"Did he suffer much?" Heng Yu asked.

Heng Kou saw how the doctors looked at him, then looked away.

"Not at all," he lied, remembering how it had taken all

five of them to hold him down while the poison had taken effect. "Of course, there was pain at first, but then, thankfully, it passed and he lapsed into sleep."

Heng Yu nodded then turned away with a tiny shudder.

Heng Kou remained a moment longer, looking down at the brother he had always loathed; the brother who, since he had been old enough to walk, had bullied him and treated him like the basest servant. He smiled. *You would have had us kill Tolonen, eh? You would have brought us all down with your foolishness?*

Yes, but you forgot who held the power.

He turned, indicating to the doctors that they should leave. Then, when they were gone, he went to where Heng Yu was standing. He was about to speak when Heng Yu surprised him, raising a hand to silence him.

Heng Yu's whole manner had changed. His voice was low but powerful. "Don't think me blind, Uncle Kou. Nor dull-witted. I know what happened here."

"And?"

Kou held his breath. If Heng Yu insisted, all would be undone.

"And nothing, uncle. Understand me?"

Heng Kou hesitated, studying the smooth lines of his nephew's face; seeing him for the first time as the T'ang must have seen him.

He smiled, then bowed low. "I understand, Minister Heng."

* * *

The door slammed shut. DeVore turned and looked back across the cell at Wyatt. They were alone now. Just the two of them.

"Shouldn't there be others?" Wyatt said, watching him warily. "I thought it was usual for there to be several officers at an interrogation."

DeVore laughed. "You don't understand, do you? You still think you're safe. In spite of all that's happened."

Wyatt turned away. "If you mistreat me . . ."

DeVore interrupted him. "You really *don't* understand, do you?"

He moved closer, coming round the side of Wyatt until he stood there, face to face with the slightly taller man. "Let me explain."

Wyatt had turned his face slightly, so as not to have to meet DeVore's eyes, but the suddenness of the slap took him by complete surprise. He staggered backwards, holding his cheek, staring at DeVore, his eyes wide with astonishment.

"Strip off!" DeVore barked, his face suddenly mean, uncompromising. "Everything. Top clothes. Underclothes. Jewellery. We'll remove your electronic implants later."

Wyatt shook his head uncertainly. "But you can't do this . . ."

"Do what?" DeVore laughed. "You're a murderer. Understand? You killed the T'ang's Minister. You'll be tried and found guilty. And then we'll execute you."

DeVore took a step closer, seeing how Wyatt flinched, expecting another blow. His cheek was bright red, the weal the shape of DeVore's hand, each finger clearly delineated. "That's the truth of this, Edmund Wyatt. You're a dead man. When you killed Lwo Kang you stepped outside the game. You broke all the rules. So now there are no rules. At least, none that you would recognise."

He reached out and took Wyatt's wrists, savagely pulling him closer, until Wyatt's face was pressed against his own.

"Are you beginning to understand?"

Wyatt shivered and made an awkward nod.

"Good." He thrust Wyatt back brutally, making him fall. "Then strip off."

He turned his back. The cell was bare. He could almost see Wyatt look about him, hesitating. Then he heard the jingle of his thin gold bracelets as he set them down on the floor, and smiled. *I have you now, my proud false Chinaman. I'll strip the Han from you, pigtail, pau and all. Yes, and we'll see how proud you are when I'm done with you.*

172

When he turned back. Wyatt was naked, his clothes neatly bundled on the floor beside him. His white, soft body seemed so frail, so ill-suited to the trial that lay ahead: already it seemed to cower, to shrink back into itself, as if aware of what was to come. Yet when DeVore looked up past the narrow, hairless chest and met Wyatt's eyes he was surprised to find defiance there.

So, he thought. That first. They say the Han are strong because they resign themselves to fate. In thirty centuries they have never fought fate, but have been its agents. Flood, famine and revolution have all been as one to them. They have bowed before the inevitability of death and so survived, stronger for their long and patient suffering. So it will be with you, Edmund Wyatt. I'll make a true Han of you yet – stripped bare of all you were; resigned and patient in your suffering.

He smiled. "You knew Yang Lai? Lwo Kang's Junior Minister?"

Wyatt looked up sharply, real hatred in his eyes. "He's dead. You know he's dead. He died with Lwo Kang in the solarium."

"That's not what I asked. Did you know him well?"

"He was a friend. A good friend. I was at college with him."

DeVore laughed coldly. "How good a friend, would you say?"

Wyatt swallowed, then lowered his head. "He was my lover."

"You admit it?"

Angered, Wyatt yelled back at him. "Why not? I expect you knew already! Anyway, what has Yang Lai to do with this?"

DeVore smiled and turned away. "Yang Lai was murdered. Three days after the assassination. The only thing we found on the body was a small hologram of you."

Wyatt had gone very still. When DeVore next looked at him he was surprised to find tears in his eyes.

"There," said Wyatt softly. "Surely that says something

to you? Would I kill a man I loved then leave my holo on him?"

DeVore shook his head. "You don't understand."

Wyatt frowned. "What do you mean?"

"He had it up his arse."

Wyatt looked away. A shuddering breath wracked his body.

"Oh and there's more. Much more. Kao Jyan's tape. Your trading connections with Hong Cao and Cho Hsiang. The internal flight schedules which coincide perfectly with our reconstruction of the attack on the solarium. Your company's experiments with harmonic triggers. And, of course, your secretary, Lung Ti's, evidence."

Wyatt looked back at DeVore blankly. "Lung Ti?"

This was DeVore's master stroke; the thing that had cemented it all in place. Lung Ti had been with Wyatt from his tenth year. He was his most trusted servant. But eight years ago DeVore had found Lung Ti's weakness and bought him. Now Lung Ti was his creature, reading from his script.

DeVore let the silence extend a moment longer, then lowered his head. "Lung Ti has confessed to his part in everything. He is to give evidence under the T'ang's pardon."

Wyatt's mouth worked loosely, but no sound came out.

"Yes," DeVore said softly, moving closer. "And now you do understand, eh?" He reached out and put his fingers gently to the weal on Wyatt's cheek. "We'll find the truth of this, you and I. We've time, you know. Plenty of time."

And in the end, he thought, even you will believe you ordered Lwo Kang's death.

* * *

From high above it seemed insignificant, a tiny, circular blemish in the vast field of whiteness, yet as the craft dropped the circle grew and grew until it seemed to fill the whole of the viewing window with its blackness.

The big transporter set down on the roof of the City,

close to the circle's edge. Only paces from its struts the surface of the roof was warped, the ice dented and buckled by the vast heat of the explosion. Seen from this close the huge dark circle revealed another dimension. It was a dish – an enormous concave dish, like some gigantic alchemist's crucible; the dark and sticky sludge of its residue already sifted and searched for clues.

They climbed down from the transporter, looking about them; sixty men from the lower levels, white-cloaked and hooded. Others handed down tools from inside the big, insectile machine; shovels and brushes; sacks and other containers. Old-fashioned tools. Nothing modern was needed now. This was the simplest part of all. The final stage before rebuilding.

They got to work at once, forming three chains of twenty men, three from each chain filling sacks at the edge of the sludge-pool and handing them back to the others in the line. And at the top two anchor men moved backward and forward between the human chain and the big machine, passing the sacks up into the interior.

A wind was blowing from the mountains. At the top of the right-hand workchain one of the men – a big, shaven-headed Han – turned and looked back at the distant peaks. For a moment he could relax, knowing no sack was on its way. Taking off a glove he pulled down his goggles and wiped at his brow. How cool it was. How pleasant to feel the wind brushing against the skin. For a moment his blunt, nondescript face searched the distance, trying to place something, then he shrugged.

Looking down he noticed something against the dark surface. Something small and green and fragile-looking. He bent down and picked it up, holding it in his bare palm. It was a budding seed.

He looked up, hearing the cry of birds overhead, and understood. It was from the mountainside. A bird must have picked it up and dropped it here. Here on the lifeless surface of the City's roof.

He stared at it a moment longer, noting the shape of its

twin leaves, the hardness of its central pip. Then he crushed it between his fingers and let it drop.

Kao Chen, *kwai*, one-time assassin, looked up. Clouds, mountains, even the flat, open surface of the City's roof – all seemed so different in the daylight. He sniffed in the warm air and smiled. Then, hearing the grunts of the men below him, pulled up his goggles, eased on his glove and turned back.

PART 2-SPRING 2198:

BENEATH
THE YELLOW SPRINGS

——— · ———

"When I was alive, I wandered in the
streets of the Capital;
Now that I am dead, I am left to lie in the fields.
In the morning I drove out from the High Hall;
In the evening I lodged beneath the yellow springs.
When the white sun had sunk in the Western Chasm
I hung up my chariot and rested my four horses.
Now, even the Maker of All
Could not bring the life back to my limbs.
Shape and substance day by day will vanish:
Hair and teeth will gradually fall away.
For ever from of old men have been so:
And none born can escape this thing."

– Miu Hsi, *Bearer's Song* (from *Han Burial Songs*)

CHAPTER·5

BROTHERS

It was spring in Sichuan province and the trees of the orchard at Tongjiang were ablaze with blossom beneath a clear blue sky. The air was clear, like a polished lens. In the distance the mountains thrust into the heavens, knife-edged shapes of green and blue.

At the orchard's edge four servants waited silently, their heads bowed, heavily laden silver trays held out before them.

Beneath the trees at the lake's edge, the two princes were playing, their laughter echoing across the water. The eldest, Li Han Ch'in, evaded his little brother's outstretched arm and, with a swift, athletic movement, grasped an overhead branch and swung up into the crown of the apple tree. Li Yuan rushed at the tree, making trial jumps, but the branch was too high for him to reach.

"That isn't fair, Han!" Yuan said breathlessly, laughing, his eyes burning with excitement. In the tree above him Han Ch'in was giggling, his head tilted back to look down at his brother, a sprig of pure white blossom caught in his jet black hair.

"Come up and get me!" he taunted, letting one leg dangle, then pulling it up quickly when his brother jumped for it.

Yuan looked about him a moment, then found what he was looking for. He turned back. "Come down! Come down or I'll beat you!" he threatened, one hand holding the thin switch, the other on his hip; his expression part stern, part amused.

"I won't!" said Han, pulling himself up closer to the branch, trying to work his way further up the tree.

Laughing excitedly, Yuan stepped forward, flicking the leafy switch gently against his brother's back. The older boy yelled exaggeratedly and kicked out wildly, his foot missing by a breath. The boy on the ground screeched, enjoying the game, and hit out harder with the branch. There was another yell from above and again the foot struck out wildly. But this time it connected, sending the small boy crashing backward.

Han Ch'in dropped down at once and went over to where his brother lay, unmoving, on the earth beside the bole.

"Yuan! Yuan!"

He bent down, listening for his brother's breath, his head dropping down onto the small boy's chest.

Yuan rolled, using his brother's weight, as he'd been taught, and came up on his chest, his knees pinning down Han's arms. For a moment he was on top, his face triumphant. Then Han pushed up, throwing him off sideways. Yuan turned and began to scramble away, but Han reached out and grabbed his leg, slowly dragging him back.

"No, Han . . . No . . . Please!" But Yuan's protestations were feeble. He could barely speak for laughing.

"Say it!" Han demanded, pinning the small boy's arms against his sides, his arms wrapped tightly about his chest. "I order you to say it!"

Yuan shook his head violently, his laughter giving way to hiccups. But as Han's arms squeezed tighter he relented, nodding. The grip slackened but remained firm. Yuan took a breath, then spoke. "You are my master . . ." He coughed, then continued, ". . . and I promise to obey you."

"Good!"

Han Ch'in released him, then pushed him away. The small boy fell against the earth and lay there a moment, breathing deeply. For a while they were quiet. Birds called in the warm, still air.

"What do you think of her, Yuan?"

Li Yuan rolled over and looked up at his brother. Li Han Ch'in was kneeling, looking out across the lake towards the terrace. The sprig of blossom still clung to the side of his head, pure white against the intense blackness of his hair. There was a faint smile on his lips. His dark eyes looked far off into the distance. "Do you think she's pretty?"

The question brought a colour to Yuan's cheeks. He nodded and looked down. Yes, he thought. More than pretty. Fei Yen was beautiful. He had known that from the first moment he had seen her. Fei Yen. How well the name fitted her. *Flying swallow* . . .

He looked up to find Han Ch'in staring at him, his brow furrowed.

"I was thinking, Yuan. Wondering what it would be like to have several wives. A different woman, perhaps, for every night of the week." He laughed strangely, a tense, high-pitched sound, then looked down, pulling at the grass. "I'm sorry. I forget sometimes. You seem so old, so full of wisdom. Like father." Han fell silent, then looked up again, smiling. "I guess it doesn't touch you yet. Never mind. You'll understand it when you're older."

Li Yuan watched his brother a moment longer, then looked down. Sunlight through the branches dappled the earth beside his hand. Leaf shadow lay across his flesh like a discolouration of the skin. He shivered and closed his eyes. Sometimes he felt he understood too well. If he were in Han's place, Fei Yen would have been enough for him; he would have needed no other. He looked back at his brother, keeping his thoughts to himself, knowing that Han would only tease him if he knew. "You're only eight," he would say. "What could you possibly know of love?"

"Even so," Han said, looking at him again, "Fei Yen will be special. My first wife. And her sons shall inherit." He nodded, satisfied with the justice of the words. Li Yuan saw how his brother was watching him – smiling, a deep love in his eyes – and looked down, warmed by it.

"They'll be fine sons, Yuan. Good, strong sons. And the first of them will have your name."

Han Ch'in reached out and held his brother's ankle. "He'll be strong, like me. But I hope he'll also be wise, like you."

"And pretty, like Fei Yen," Yuan said, looking up at his brother through his long dark eyelashes.

Han looked away into the distance, a faint smile on his lips, then nodded. "Yes . . . like Fei Yen."

* * *

"Do you mind if I sit here?"

Wang Ti blushed and looked down, cradling the child to her and rocking it gently. All four tiers of Chang's Restaurant were packed, few spaces remaining at the tables. Her table, on the second tier, overlooking the bell tower, was one of the few not fully occupied.

"No. Please do."

She had seen the man much earlier, moving between the crowded market stalls at the end of Main. Like the others in the crowd, she had watched him momentarily, then turned back to her shopping, impressed by the sheer size of him. Now, as he sat across from her, she realised just how big he was; not just tall but broad at the shoulder and the chest. A real giant of a man.

"What's good here?"

She looked up and met his eyes. Blue, *Hung Mao* eyes.

"It's all good. Chang's is the best here on Twenty-Six. But you might try his green jade soup."

The big man nodded and half turned in his seat, summoning the nearest girl.

"Master?"

"I'm told the green jade soup is good. Bring me a large bowl. Oh and some chicken drumsticks and noodles."

The girl bowed, then turned and went back inside to the kitchens.

"Do you eat here often?"

He was facing her again, a faint, polite smile on his lips.

She looked down at the sleeping child, safe in the harness at her chest. "When I can afford to," she answered quietly. "Which is not often, I'm afraid."

The man followed her gaze, smiling. "He's a good child. How old is he?"

She stroked the child's brow, and looked up, her smile broadening momentarily. "Ten months."

He leaned forward, looking into the child's sleeping face. "I bet he's his father's darling."

She laughed. "Yes! He's like a child himself when he's with Jyan."

"Jyan? A pretty name for a child."

She smiled. "And you? You speak like a man who has sons."

The big man sat back and laughed. "Me? No . . . One day, perhaps. But for now . . . well, my job keeps me on the move. It would not do to have ties."

She looked at him sympathetically a moment, noticing his features properly for the first time. He had a big, open face, the long nose blunted at its tip, his jaw pronounced and his lips full. His dark hair was cut brutally short, making her wonder for a moment what it was he did. But it was not an unkind face. When he smiled it softened. She decided she liked him.

"And that's what brings you here?"

"My job? No, not this time. I'm looking for someone. A relative."

She laughed again; softly, so as not to wake the child. "I think I'd have seen any relative of yours about."

His smile broadened. "Oh, don't judge all my clan by me. This —" He put one hand to his chest, " — they say I inherited from my grandfather. My father's father. My mother was a small woman, you see. Small in size, I should say, for she was a giant to her sons."

She looked down, pleased by his filial piety. "And your father?"

For a moment the big man looked away. "I never knew my father. He left before I was two years old."

183

"Ah . . . like my Chen."

The giant looked back at her, his eyes narrowed slightly. "You understand then?"

She bowed her head slightly. "It's sad . . ."

"Yes, well . . ." He turned. The serving girl was standing at his side, a tray of steaming food balanced on one hand. He moved back from the table, letting her set out the bowls in front of him. "You've eaten?" He looked at the woman facing him, concerned. "If not, might I buy you lunch?"

She shook her head hastily. "Please, I . . . Well, I thank you kindly, but Chen would not permit it."

He raised a hand. "I understand. Forgive me . . ."

She looked up, smiling. "Thank you. But we have eaten. And now . . ."

The big man was already spooning his soup down vigorously. "Hmm. This is delicious. As good as anything I've tasted."

She smiled, watching him, enjoying his enjoyment. "As I said. Chang's is the best."

He looked across at her, then set down his spoon and stood, seeing she was getting up. "Can I help you?"

She shook her head. "No, please. I can manage. I'm quite used to it, I assure you."

He gave a slight bow with his head. "Then take care. It was a pleasure talking with you."

"And you."

Karr sat there a moment, watching her go. Then, nodding to himself, he looked down at the soup and began to eat again. Reaching for one of the drumsticks he paused, laughing softly to himself. Jyan! He'd named the boy Jyan! Then, more thoughtfully, he gazed back across the broad corridor, remembering the woman's face, her smile; but mostly remembering what she had said.

There's time, he thought. *Time enough for all things. Even sons.*

* * *

Han Ch'in approached the fence at a gallop, the Arab flying beneath him, its sleek neck pushing forward with each stride, its jet black flanks moving powerfully, effortlessly across the hillside, its tail streaming behind it in the wind.

Yuan, watching from the pavilion half a *li* away, held his breath. It was the biggest of the fences, almost the size of the horse; a construction of stone and wood, with the ground dropping away beyond. Han had fallen here before, the last time he'd attempted it. Fallen and bruised his ribs badly. Now, fearlessly, he tried the fence again.

Without checking his pace, Han spurred the Arab on, yelling wildly as it stretched and leapt. For the briefest moment it seemed he had misjudged. The horse rose mightily, its forelegs climbing the air, but, at its highest point, its pasterns seemed to brush the fence. As it hit the ground on the far side it stumbled and threatened to go down.

Yuan cried out, putting his knuckles to his mouth. The horse seemed to stagger, its momentum threatening to topple it dock over poll. In the saddle, Han Ch'in hung on grimly, pulling tightly at the reins, straining to keep the Arab's head up, drawing the horse to the right, into the gradient. The Arab fought back, fear making its movements desperate. Its nostrils flared and it whinnied noisily, contesting with Han's sharp yells of command. Slowly its rump came round, its long, dished face flicking to the left as if in pain. As Han Ch'in eased off, its head came up sharply and it seemed to dance, then settle, slowing to a canter.

Yuan turned, looking up at his father. "He's done it! Han's done it!"

"Yes . . ." Li Shai Tung was smiling, but his eyes revealed just how worried he had been.

Han Ch'in turned the horse again, reaching down to pat its neck, then spurred it on towards them. Drawing up in front of them, he threw his head back proudly, then reached up to comb the hair back from his eyes, looking to his father for approval.

"Well done, Han. You proved yourself the master of the beast!"

Han laughed, then looked down at the Arab's face. "Maybe. But she's a fine horse, father. Any of the others from our stables would have fallen back there. A rider is sometimes only as good as his horse."

"Or the horse his rider." The T'ang was looking seriously at his son now. "I don't say this lightly, Han Ch'in. I was worried for you. But you showed great character. You did not let the beast have her own way. You controlled her." He nodded and momentarily looked at his younger son. "Control. That's the key. To beasts and men."

For a moment longer Han Ch'in stared down at his horse's face, petting the animal, calming her. Then he looked up again and met his father's eyes. "I didn't think you would be here, father. I thought you would be arranging things. The reception . . ."

The T'ang smiled faintly at his son, then grew more serious. "That's all in hand. No, I came because I need you both, two hours from now, in the Hall of the Seven Ancestors. It will be formal, so dress accordingly."

Han frowned. "What is it, father?"

Li Shai Tung studied his eldest son a moment, his eyes drinking in the sight of him proudly. "Later, Han. I'll explain things when you're there."

Han Ch'in bowed in the saddle, answering for them both. "As you wish, father. We shall be there."

"Good. But before then you've a visitor." He smiled. "Fei Yen has arrived. She's waiting for you in the Palace."

Yuan looked across at his brother, watching him. Han bowed to his father, then, unable to hide the grin that had settled on his face, turned his horse and began to move away across the hillside towards the river and the bridge. Halfway down he turned in his saddle and called back.

"I'll see you there, Yuan! Bring Hsueh Chai and old Chou. In the meadow by the lake. We'll have a picnic."

* * *

186

Fei Yen was standing on the bridge, her maids surrounding her. One stood behind her, shading her mistress with a huge silk umbrella. Another stood at her side, languidly waving a large fan. A third and fourth, their pastel greens and blues matching the colours of the day, waited nearby. Thirty paces off, in the shade of a great willow, stood her aunts and great-aunts in their dark silks and satins, watchful, talking quietly among themselves.

Fei Yen herself was looking out across the lake; watching the warm, spring breeze ruffle the water and bend the reeds at the shoreline. Her face, in the sunlight filtered through the umbrella, seemed like a silken screen of pinks and oranges, her dainty features hidden from Li Yuan, who stood on the bank below, looking up at her.

She was beautiful. He had no need to see her clearly to know that. He had only to remember the last time she had come here to the orchard. Had only to recall the way she smiled, the way her bright pink tongue poked out from between those pearled and perfect teeth. How dark her eyes were, how delicate the contours of her face.

He looked across at Han and saw how his brother looked at her. Saw both the awe and the love there in his face. And understood.

Servants had set up a small, rounded tent in the middle of the water meadow. The Arab was tethered just beyond it, its head down, grazing. In front of the tent they had set down stools and a low table, on which was placed a wine kettle and three small, glazed tumblers. Further off, conspicuous in the centre of the meadow, stood an archery target.

Han Ch'in came forward, striding purposefully across the short grass, like some strange, upright, elegant animal. He had changed from his riding clothes into looser silks of peach and vermilion. Hsueh Chai had braided his hair with golden thread and he wore a simple gold necklet of interwoven dragons. Watching him, Yuan felt all his love for his brother swell up in him. How fine Han was; in his own way, how beautiful. How his dark eyes flashed as he

187

came to the stone flags of the narrow bridge. Eyes that never for a moment left his future bride.

Fei Yen turned, facing Han Ch'in, and came out from beneath the shade.

Again Yuan caught his breath. She was like china. Like perfect porcelain. Her skin so pale, so perfectly white; her nose, her lips, her delicate ears so finely moulded that, for a moment, she seemed like a sculpture come to sudden life. Such diminutive perfection. Then, as she met Han on the gentle downslope of the bridge, he saw her smile, saw how her dark eyes filled with fire and knew, with all the certainty his young soul could muster, that he was lost to her. She was Han's. But he would love her even so. As he loved Han. And maybe more.

Over tea their talk was of court matters. Yuan, silent, looked up at Fei Yen through his lashes, strangely, over-poweringly abashed by her proximity. When she leaned forward, the pale cream of her sleeve brushed against his knees, and he shivered, the faint sweet scent of jasmine wafting to him from her.

"They say Wang Sau-Leyan has been up to mischief," she said softly, looking up past her fan at Han Ch'in. "Ten years old! Can you imagine it! His eldest brother caught him . . ."

She hesitated, giving a soft, delicious laugh.

"Go on . . ." said Han, leaning forward on his seat, his booted feet spread, like two young saplings planted in the earth, his hands placed firmly on his knees.

"Well . . ." she said, conspiratorially. "It's said that he was found with a girl. Stark naked in his father's bed!"

"No!" said Han, delighted. "His father's bed!"

Wang Sau's father was Wang Hsien, T'ang of City Africa. Wang Sau-Leyan was his fourth son and his youngest.

"Yes!" Fei Yen clapped her hands together. "And listen . . . the girl was only a child. And *Hung Mao*, too!"

Han Ch'in sat back, astonished, then, slowly, he began to laugh.

Yuan, meanwhile, was watching her. Her voice was so sweet, so pure in its tones, it sent a shiver down his spine. He was oblivious to the sense of her words; to him her voice seemed divorced from all human meaning. It had that same, sweet lyrical sound as the *erhu*; the same rich yet plaintive contralto of that ancient instrument. And as she talked he found himself fascinated by the movement, by the very shape of her hands. By the strange pearled opalescence of her nails, the delicacy of her tiny, ice pale fingers, no bigger than his own. He looked up into her face and saw the fine, cosmetic glaze of her cheeks and brow, the silken darkness of her hair, threads of fine silver catching the afternoon's sunlight.

Han Ch'in leaned forward, still laughing. "What happened?"

Fei Yen sat back demurely. Thirty paces off the group of aunts, waited on by servants from their own household, were fanning themselves vigorously and straining to hear what was making Han Ch'in laugh so lustily.

"His father has banished him for a year. He's to stay in the floating palace. Alone. With only his male servants for company."

Han Ch'in looked down, sobered by the news. He shook his head, then looked up at Fei Yen again. "That's rather harsh, don't you think? I mean, he's only a boy. Not much older than Yuan here. And after all, it's nothing really. Just a bit of high spirits."

Fei Yen fanned herself slowly, her eyes briefly looking inward. Then she smiled and tilted her head, looking directly at Han. "But his father's bed . . . Surely, Han . . . ?" She raised her eyebrows, making Han guffaw with laughter once again.

"Listen," he said, getting up. "I plan to issue a challenge. After the wedding. To all the Families, Major and Minor. To all the sons and cousins." He glanced across at Hsueh Chai, who was standing with the maids beside the entrance to the tent. The old servant came across at once, bringing a short hunting bow and a quiver of heavy, steel-tipped arrows. Han Ch'in took them and held them up. "Twelve arrows. And the highest score shall win the prize."

Fei Yen looked past him at the target. "And you think you'll win?"

Han Ch'in laughed and looked at the bow in his hand. "I don't think I'll win. I know I will."

Her eyes flashed at him. "My three brothers are good shots. You must be very good if you're better than them."

Han Ch'in drew the strap of the quiver over his shoulder, then turned and marched to a point marked out on the grass. Taking an arrow from the quiver, he called back to her. "Watch!"

He notched the arrow quickly to the bow and raised it. Then, without seeming to take aim, he drew the string taut and let the arrow fly. There was a satisfying thunk as the arrow hit and split the wood, a hand's length from the gold.

"Not bad . . ." Fei Yen began. Her fan was momentarily forgotten, motionless. Her face was suddenly tense, her whole body attentive to what Han was doing.

Han Ch'in drew a second arrow, notched it and let it fly as casually as before. This time it landed at the edge of the gold. Han turned, laughing. "Well?"

"Again," she said simply, lifting her chin in what seemed an encouraging gesture. "It might have been luck."

"Luck?" Han Ch'in looked surprised, then laughed and shook his head. "Luck, you think? Watch this, then!"

He notched the arrow, then turned back to face the target. Raising the bow, he twisted it sideways, as if he was on horseback, and let fly. This time the arrow hit the gold dead centre.

Yuan was on his feet applauding wildly. Behind him, Fei Yen set down her fan and stood up slowly. Then, without a word, she walked up to Han Ch'in and took the bow from him, drawing an arrow from the quiver on his back.

"You want to try?" he said, enjoying the moment. "I'll wager you my horse that you can't even hit the target from here. It's fifty paces, and that's a heavy bow to draw."

She smiled at him. "I've drawn heavier bows than this, Han Ch'in. Bows twice this length. But I'll not take your horse from you, husband-to-be. I've seen how much you love the beast."

Han Ch'in shrugged. "Okay. Then go ahead."

Fei Yen shook her head. "No, Han. Some other prize. Just between us. To prove who's master here."

He laughed uncomfortably. "What do you mean?"

She looked at the bow in her hands, then up at him. "This, maybe. If I can beat you with my three arrows."

For a moment he hesitated; then, laughing, he nodded. "My bow, then. And if you lose?"

She laughed. "If I lose you can have everything I own."

Han Ch'in smiled broadly, understanding her joke. In two days they would be wed and he would be master of all she owned.

"That's fair."

He stepped back, folding his arms, then watched as she notched and raised the bow. For a long time she simply stood there, as if in trance, the bow-string taut, the arrow quivering. Yuan watched her, fascinated, noting how her breathing changed; how her whole body was tensed, different from before. Then, with a tiny cry, she seemed to shudder and release the string.

The arrow flew high, then fell, hitting the wood with a softer sound than Han's.

"A gold!" she said triumphantly, turning to face Han Ch'in.

The arrow lay like a dash across the red. Han's arrows had hit the target almost horizontally, burying themselves into the soft wood, but hers stuck up from the gold like a fresh shoot from a cut tree.

Han Ch'in shook his head, astonished. "Luck!" he said, turning to her. "You'll not do that twice." He laughed, and pointed at the target. "Look at it! A good wind and it'll fall out of the wood!"

She looked at him fiercely, defiantly. "It's a gold, though, isn't it?"

Reluctantly he nodded, then handed her the second arrow. "Again," he said.

Once more she stood there, the bowstring taut, the arrow quivering, her whole self tensed behind it, concentrating. Then, with the same sharp cry, she let it fly, her body shuddering with the passion of release.

This time the arrow seemed to float in the air above the target before it fell abruptly, knocking against the third of Han's.

It was another gold.

Fei Yen turned to Han Ch'in, her face inexpressive, her hand held out for the third arrow.

Han Ch'in hesitated, his face dark, his eyes wide with anger, then thrust the arrow into her hand. For a moment she stood there, watching him, seeing just how angry he was, then she turned away, facing where Yuan sat watching.

Yuan saw her notch the bow then look across at him, her face more thoughtful than he'd ever seen it. Then, to his surprise, she winked at him and turned back to face the target.

This time she barely seemed to hesitate, but, like Han Ch'in before her, drew the string taut and let the arrow fly.

"No!" Yuan was on his feet. The arrow lay a good five paces from the target, its shaft sticking up from the ground, its feathers pointing towards the bull.

Han Ch'in clapped his hands, laughing. "I win! I've beaten you!"

Fei Yen turned to him. "Yes, Han," she said softly, touching his arm gently, tenderly. "Which makes you master here . . ."

★   ★   ★

Representative Barrow huffed irritably and leaned forward in his seat, straining against the harness. "What do you think the T'ang wants, Pietr, summoning us here five hours early?"

Lehmann looked down through the window, watching the ground come slowly up to meet them. "What do you think he wants? To keep us down, that's what. To tie us in knots and keep us docile. That's all they ever want."

Barrow looked at him sharply. "You think so? You're certain it has nothing to do with the wedding, then?"

Lehmann shook his head, remembering the alarm he'd felt on receiving the T'ang's summons. Like Barrow he had been told to present himself at Tongjiang by the third hour of the afternoon at the latest. No reason had been given, but he knew that it had nothing to do with the wedding. If it were they would have been notified a good month beforehand. No, this was something else. Something unrelated.

"It's bloody inconvenient," Barrow continued. "I was in the middle of a House committee meeting when his man came. Now I've had to cancel that, and the gods know when I'll get a chance now to get ready for the reception."

Lehmann looked at him, then looked away. Whatever it was, it was certain to make a small thing like a House committee meeting seem of no consequence whatsoever. The T'ang did not send his personal craft to bring men to him without good reason. Nor did he use the warrant system lightly. Whatever it was, it was of the first importance.

But what? His pulse quickened momentarily. Had something leaked out? Or was it something else? A concession, maybe? A deal? Something to guarantee his son's inheritance?

Lehmann laughed quietly at the thought, then felt the craft touch down beneath him. For a moment the great engines droned on, then they cut out. In the ensuing silence they could hear the great overhead gates sliding back into place, securing the hangar.

He undid his straps, then stood, waiting.

The door opened and they went outside. The T'ang's

Chancellor, Chung Hu-Yan, was waiting for them at the foot of the ramp.

"*Ch'un tzu.*" The Chancellor bowed deeply. "The T'ang is waiting for you. The others are here already. Please . . ." He turned, indicating they should go through.

Lehmann hesitated. "Forgive me, but what is all this about?"

Chung Hu-Yan looked back at him, his expression unreadable. "In time, Under Secretary. The T'ang alone can tell you what his business is."

"Of course." Lehmann smiled sourly, moving past him.

The Hall of the Seven Ancestors was a massive, high-ceilinged place, its walls strewn with huge, opulent tapestries, its floor a giant mosaic of carved marble. Thick pillars coiled with dragons lined each side. Beneath them stood the T'ang's private guards, big, vicious-looking brutes with shaven heads and crude Han faces. The small group of *Hung Mao* had gathered to the left of the great throne, silent, visibly awed by the unexpected grandeur of their surroundings. Across from them, to the right of the throne and some fifteen paces distant, was a cage. Inside the cage was a man.

"Under Secretary Lehmann. Representative Barrow. Welcome. Perhaps now we can begin."

The T'ang got to his feet, then came down the steps of his throne, followed by his sons. Five paces from the nearest of the *Hung Mao*, he stopped and looked about him imperiously. Slowly, hesitantly, taking each other's example, they bowed, some fully, some with their heads only, none knowing quite what etiquette was demanded by this moment. They were not at Weimar now, nor in the great halls of their own Companies. Here, in the T'ang's own Palace, they had no idea what was demanded of them, nor had the T'ang's Chancellor been instructed to brief them.

Li Shai Tung stared at them contemptuously, seeing the ill-ordered manner of their obeisance. It was as he had thought; these *Hung Mao* had fallen into bad habits. Such respect as they owed their T'ang was not an automatic thing with them. It was shallow rooted. The first strong wind would carry it away.

Slowly, deliberately, he looked from face to face, seeing how few of them dared meet his eyes, and how quickly those who did looked away. *Hsiao jen*, he thought. *Little men.* You're all such little men. Not a king among you. Not one of you fit to be my chamberlain, let alone my equal. He ran his hand through his ice-white, plaited beard, then turned away, as if dismissing them, facing the man in the cage.

The man was naked, his head shaven. His hands were tied behind him with a crude piece of rope. There was something ancient and brutal about that small detail; something that the two boys at the old man's side took note of. They stood there silently, their faces masks of dispassionate observation. "This now is a lesson," their father had explained beforehand. "And the name of the lesson is punishment."

The trial had lasted nineteen months. But now all evidence was heard and the man's confession – thrice given as the law demanded – had placed things beyond doubt.

Li Shai Tung walked round the cage and stood there on the far side of it, an arm's length from its thick, rounded bars. The cage was deliberately too small for the man, forcing him to kneel or bend his back. He was red-eyed, his skin a sickly white. Flesh was spare on him and his limbs were badly emaciated. The first two months of incarceration had broken his spirit and he was no longer proud. His haughty, aquiline profile now seemed merely bird-like and ludicrous – the face of an injured gull. All defiance had long departed from him. Now he cowered before the T'ang's approach.

The old man pointed to the symbol burned into the caged man's upper arm. It was the stylised double helix of heredity, symbol of the Dispersion faction.

"Under Secretary Lehmann. You know this man?"

Lehmann came forward and stood there on the other side of the cage, looking in.

"*Chieh Hsia?*"

There was the blankness of non-recognition in Lehmann's eyes. Good, thought the T'ang. He is not expecting this. All the better. It will make the shock of it far sharper.

"He was your friend."

Lehmann looked again, then gasped. "Edmund . . ." he whispered.

"Yes." The T'ang came round the cage again and stood there, between Lehmann and the throne. "This prisoner was once a man, like you. His name was Edmund Wyatt. But now he has no name. He has been found guilty of the murder of a Minister and has forfeited all his rights. His family, such as it was, is no more, and his ancestors are cut adrift. His place and purpose in this world are annulled."

He let the significance of his speech sink in, then spoke again.

"You disown him? Your faction disowns his actions?"

Lehmann looked up, startled.

"Do you *disown* him, Under Secretary?"

It was a tense moment. At the trial Lehmann had been Wyatt's chief advocate. But now it was different. If Lehmann said yes he sanctioned the T'ang's actions. If no . . .

The silence grew. Lehmann's face moved anxiously, but he could not bring himself to speak. Across from him the T'ang held steady, his arm outstretched, his head turned, staring at the House Deputy. When the silence had stretched too thin, he broke it. He repeated his words, then added. "Or do you condone murder as a political option, Under Secretary?"

Li Shai Tung raised his voice a shade. " Am I to take it, then, that your silence is the silence of tacit agreement?"

Under the force of the old man's staring eyes, Lehmann began to shake his head. Then, realising what he was doing, he stopped. But it was too late. He had been betrayed into commitment. He need say nothing now. Li Shai Tung had won.

"This man is mine then? To do with as I wish?"

The T'ang was like a rock. His age, his apparent frailty, were illusions that the hardness of his voice dispelled. There was nothing old, nor frail about the power he wielded. At that moment it lay in his power to destroy them all, and they knew it.

Lehmann had clenched his fists. Now he let them relax. He bowed his head slowly, tentatively, in agreement. "He is yours, *Chieh Hsia*. My . . . my faction disowns his actions."

It was a full capitulation. For Li Shai Tung and the Seven it was a victory, an admission of weakness on the part of their opponents. Yet in the old man's face there was no change, nor did his outstretched hand alter its demanding gesture.

The two boys, watching, saw this, and noted it.

At last, Li Shai Tung lowered his arm. Slowly, uncertainly, the *Hung Mao* turned away and began to make their way out of the Hall. It was over. What the T'ang did with the man no longer concerned them. Wyatt was his.

When they were gone, Li Shai Tung turned to his sons. "Come here," he said, beckoning them closer to the cage.

Li Han Ch'in was seventeen; tall and handsome like his father, though not yet fully fleshed. His brother, Li Yuan, was only eight, yet his dark, calculating eyes made him seem far older than he was. The two stood close by their father, watching him, their obedience unquestioning.

"This is the man who killed Lwo Kang, my Minister. By the same token he would have killed me – and you and all the Seven and their families. For to attack the limbs of State is to threaten the body, the very heart."

The man in the cage knelt there silently, his head bowed.

Li Shai Tung paused and turned to his eldest. "Considering such, what should I do, Han Ch'in? What punishment would be fitting?"

There was no hesitation. "You must kill him, father! He

197

deserves to die." There was a fiery loathing in the young man's eyes as he stared at the prisoner. "Yes, kill him. As he would have killed you!"

Li Shai Tung was silent, his head tilted slightly to one side, as if considering what his eldest son had said. Then he turned, facing his second son. "And you, Yuan? Do you agree with your brother?"

The boy was silent a moment, concentrating.

Li Yuan was less impetuous than his brother. He was like the current beneath the ocean's swell, his brother the curling, foaming waves – all spray and violent show. Magnificent, but somehow ephemeral. Li Shai Tung, watching his sons, knew this and hoped the younger would prove the voice of reason at the ear of the elder. When it was time. When his own time was done.

Li Yuan had come to a decision. He spoke earnestly, gravely, like an old man himself. "If you kill him you will bring only further hatred on yourself. And you kill but a single man. You do not cure the illness that he represents."

"This illness . . ." The T'ang brought his head straight. The smile had gone from his lips. "Is there a cure for it?"

Once more the boy was silent, considering. Again he gave an earnest answer. "Immediately, no. This illness will be with us a long while yet. But in time, yes, I believe there is a way we might control it."

Li Shai Tung nodded, not in agreement, but in surprise. Yet he did not dismiss his youngest's words. Li Yuan was young, but he was no fool. There were men ten times his age with but a fraction of his sense, and few with a *liang* of his intelligence.

"We must speak more of this . . ." he waved a hand almost vaguely, ". . . this means of control. But answer me directly, Yuan. You feel this man should be spared, then, to alleviate the short term hatred, the resentment?"

The small boy allowed himself the luxury of a brief smile. "No, father, I suggest nothing of the kind. To spare the prisoner would be to exhibit weakness. As you said to us earlier, it is a lesson, and the name of the lesson is

198

punishment. The man must be killed. Killed like the basest piece of Clay. And all hatred, all resentment, must be faced. There is no other way."

At his side, Han nodded emphatically.

"Then it is right, as Han Ch'in said, to kill this man?"

"Not right, father. It could never be right. *Necessary*." The boy's face showed no emotion. His features were formed into a mask of reason. "Moreover, it should be done in public, for it must be seen to be done. And it must be done dispassionately; without malice and with no thought of revenge – merely as evidence of our power. As a lesson."

Li Shai Tung nodded, profoundly satisfied with his youngest son, but it was his first son he addressed. "Then it is as you said, Han Ch'in. We must kill him. As he would have killed us."

He turned and looked back at the man in the cage, something close to pity in his eyes. "Yes. But not for revenge. Merely because we must."

★ ★ ★

Han Ch'in laughed then clapped his hands, delighted by the gift. "But father, they're marvellous! Just look at them! They're so strong, so elegant!"

The four creatures stood in a line before the royal party, their long heads bowed, their broad ox-like bodies neatly clothed in rich silks of carmine and gold. Nearby, their creator, Klaus Stefan Ebert, Head of GenSyn – Genetic Synthetics – beamed, pleased beyond words at the prince's reaction.

"They are the first of their kind," Ebert said, giving a slight bow. "And, if the T'ang wishes it, they shall be the last."

Li Shai Tung looked at his old friend. Ebert had been one of his staunchest supporters over the years and, if fate decided, his son would one day be Han Ch'in's General. He smiled and looked at the ox-men again. "I would not ask that of you, Klaus. This gift of yours pleases me greatly.

199

No, such marvels should be shared by others. You shall have a patent for them."

Ebert bowed deeply, conscious of his T'ang's generosity. His gift to Han Ch'in was worth, perhaps, two hundred million yuan, but the T'ang's kindness was inestimable. There was no one in the whole of City Europe's elite who would not now want such a creature. To a more mercenary man that would have been cause for great delight, but Klaus Ebert counted such things of trivial worth. He had pleased his T'ang, and no amount of money could buy the feeling of intense pride and worthiness he felt at that moment.

"I am deeply honoured, *Chieh Hsia*. My great joy at your pleasure reaches up into the heavens."

Han Ch'in had gone closer to the beasts and now stood there, looking up into one of their long, bovine faces. He turned and looked back at Ebert. "They're really beautiful, *Shih* Ebert. Strong, like horses, and intelligent, like men. Do they talk?"

Ebert bowed to the T'ang once more, then went across and stood beside Han Ch'in. "They have a form of language," he said, his head lowered in deference to the Prince. "Enough to understand basic commands and to carry trivial messages, but no more than a human three year-old would have."

Han Ch'in laughed. "That depends on the three year-old. My brother Yuan could talk a counsellor to a halt at three!"

Ebert laughed. "So it was! I remember it only too well!"

Li Shai Tung joined their laughter, then turned to General Tolonen who was standing to his left and slightly behind him. "Well, Knut, are things ready within?"

The General, who had been watching the exchange with real pleasure, turned to his T'ang and was silent a moment, listening to a voice in his head. Then he bowed. "Major Nocenzi advises me that all the guests are now assembled and that full security measures are in operation. We can go inside."

The ceiling of the Great Hall was festooned with broad silk banners that hung in elegant sweeps between the dragon-encircled pillars. Huge, man-sized bronze urns were set at intervals along the walls, each filled to overflowing with giant blooms. Beneath the banners and between the blooms, the floor of the Great Hall was filled with guests. Han Ch'in stood at the top of the steps beside his father, looking down on everything. Two colours dominated, red and gold; auspicious colours – red for good fortune, gold for a future emperor.

At their appearance the great buzz of conversation died and, at a signal from the T'ang's chamberlain, all below the steps knelt to the T'ang and his first son, their heads lowered.

Tolonen, behind them, watched the huge crowd rise again, a low buzz of expectation rising from their midst. Then Li Shai Tung began to descend, his son three steps behind him.

Li Yuan was waiting at the bottom of the steps to greet his father formally with a full *k'o t'ou*. Behind him stood his uncles – his father's brothers and half-brothers – and with them a dark-haired *Hung Mao*; a slender, handsome man, unfashionably bearded. An "Englishman" as he liked to term himself. These were the T'ang's chief advisors. As Li Yuan rose, so the three brothers bowed, bending fully to the waist before they straightened up. Only the *Hung Mao* remained unbowed, a faint smile on his face. The T'ang smiled, acknowledging all four, then turned to let Han Ch'in come up beside him.

Tolonen, following them, paused halfway down the steps and looked out across the mass of heads. Everyone who was anyone in City Europe was here today. Representatives and Heads of Corporations, Chief Magistrates and Administrators, Ministers and Executives, Men of Power and their consorts. Li Yuan was the only child there.

Below the steps all formalities were over for the moment.

"Have you seen them, Yuan?" Han asked eagerly. "They're huge. Three times your size!"

Li Yuan's eyes lit up. "Is it true what Hsueh Chai said? Do they smell?"

In answer Han Ch'in bent down and whispered something in his brother's ear. Yuan laughed, then glanced guiltily at the Englishman, who was now deep in conversation with the T'ang. "Like *Hung Mao*," Han had whispered. And it was true of most. But some – like the General and Hal Shepherd – refrained from eating milk-based products. They smelt like Han, not beasts.

"What will you do with them?" Yuan asked. "Will you give them to Fei Yen?"

Han Ch'in looked aghast. "Gods! I never thought! What will she say?"

"You could always ask her. After all, she'll be here any time now."

Han Ch'in made a face, then laughed again. Both knew what ritual lay before him. All that bowing and nodding. All that *ch'un tzu* insincerity as he and his future wife accepted the best wishes of almost three thousand loyal subjects.

He was about to make some comment on the matter when all about them the crowd grew quiet again as Fei Yen appeared at the head of the stairs on her father's arm. This time, as she descended, the guests remained standing. Only the T'ang and his eldest son bowed to her, honouring her.

Li Yuan gazed at Fei Yen, stilled by the beauty of her. It was as though a craftsman – a master artisan – had given her some final, subtle touch – one single deft and delicate brushstroke – that made of her perfection. Her hair had been put up, its fine coils of darkness speared by slender combs of ivory shaped like dragonflies. Beneath its silken splendour, her face was like the radiant moon, shining cold and white and brilliant, the fineness of her cheekbones balanced by the soft roundness of her chin and the unmarked perfection of her brow. She wore a simple *erh tang* of red jade and silver in each lobe and a *ying lo* of tiny pearls about her neck, but in truth her face needed no adornment.

He stared at her as she came down the steps towards him, fascinated, drinking in the sight of her.

Her ears were tiny, delicate, her lips like folded petals,

softly roseate, as if awaiting the dawn's moist kiss, while her nose was so small, so fine, the roundness of the tip so perfect, it seemed unreal, like porcelain. All this he saw and noted, pierced by the beauty of it, yet all the while his gaze was drawn to her eyes – to those dark, sweet, almond eyes that were unearthly in their beauty. Eyes that seemed to stare out at him from the other side of the heavens themselves, fierce and strong and proud. Eyes that seemed to burn within the cold and fragile mask of her face, making him catch his breath.

He shivered then looked down, noting the pale lilac silks she wore, the fine layers of material specked with tiny phoenixes in a delicate dark blue lace. He studied her tiny, perfect hands and noticed how she held the ceremonial fan, her fingers gently curled about the red jade handle, each one so fine and white and delicate. Again he shivered, overcome by her. She was magnificent. So small and fine and perfect. So unutterably beautiful.

The crowd's dull murmur rose again. Li Yuan felt a touch on his arm and turned to see who it was.

"Hal . . ."

Hal Shepherd smiled and inclined his head slightly, as if amused by something. "Come Yuan," he said, taking the boy's hand. "Let's seek our entertainment over there."

Yuan looked, then mouthed the word. "Berdichev?"

Shepherd nodded, then leaned forward slightly, speaking in a whisper. "Your father wants me to sound the man. I think it could be fun."

Yuan smiled. Shepherd had been his father's chief advisor for almost twenty years, and though he was some years the T'ang's junior, Li Shai Tung would not act on any major issue without first consulting him. Shepherd's great-great grandfather had been architect of City Earth and had been granted certain rights by the tyrant, Tsao Ch'un, amongst them the freedom from bowing to his lord. When the Seven had deposed the tyrant they had honoured those rights to the last generation of Shepherds. They alone could not be ordered. They alone could talk back to the T'ang as

203

equal. "Only they, of all of them, are free," Li Shai Tung had once said to his sons. "The rest do not own the bones in their own skins."

Yuan glanced at Fei Yen momentarily, then looked back at Shepherd. "What does my father want?"

Shepherd smiled, his dark eyes twinkling. "Just listen," he said softly. "That's all. I'll say all that needs to be said."

Yuan nodded, understanding without needing to be told that this was what his father wanted. For the past four months he had worked hard, studying thousands of personal files, learning their details by heart until, now, he could put a name to every face in the Great Hall. A name and a history.

Berdichev was with his wife, Ylva, a tall, rather severe-looking woman some ten years younger than him. Beside them was one of the Eastern sector Administrators, a covert Dispersionist sympathiser named Duchek. Making up the group was Under Secretary Lehmann.

"Shepherd," said Berdichev, on his guard at once. "Li Yuan," he added quickly, noticing the Prince behind Shepherd and bowing deeply, a gesture that was copied immediately by all in the immediate circle.

"We're not interrupting anything, I hope?" said Shepherd lightly, disingenuously.

"Nothing but idle talk," Lehmann answered, smiling coldly, his manner matching Shepherd's.

"Idle talk? Oh, surely not, Under Secretary. I thought such important men as you rarely wasted a word."

"It was nothing," said Berdichev touchily. "But if it interests you so much, why not ask us? We have nothing to hide."

Shepherd laughed warmly. "Did I say you had? Why no, Soren, I meant nothing by my words. Nothing at all. This is a social occasion, after all. I meant merely to be sociable."

Yuan looked down, keeping the smile from his face. He had seen how Berdichev had bridled when Shepherd used his first name; how his eyes had lit with anger behind those tiny, rounded glasses he so affectedly wore.

"We were talking of the world," said Lehmann, meeting Shepherd's eyes challengingly. "Of how much smaller it seems these days."

Shepherd hesitated as if considering the matter, then nodded. "I would have to agree with you, Under Secretary. In fact, I'd go further and argue that we've actually lost touch with the world. Consider. What is City Earth, after all, but a giant box on stilts? A huge hive filled to the brim with humanity. Oh, it's comfortable enough, we'd all agree, but it's also quite unreal – a place where the vast majority of people have little or no contact with the earth, the elements."

Shepherd looked about the circle, half-smiling, meeting each of their eyes in turn. "Isn't that how it is? Well then, it's understandable, don't you think, that feeling of smallness? Of being contained? You see, there's nothing real in their lives. No heaven above, no earth below, just walls on every side. All they see – all they are – is an illusion."

Lehmann blinked, not certain he had heard Shepherd right. What had been said was unorthodox to say the least. It was not what one expected to hear from someone who had the T'ang's ear. Lehmann looked across and saw how Berdichev was looking down, as if insulted. His company, SimFic – Simulation Fictions – provided many of the "illusions" Shepherd was clearly denigrating.

"Men have always had illusions," Berdichev said fiercely, looking up again, his eyes cold behind their glasses. "They have always made fictions. Always had a desire for stories. Illusion is necessary for good health. Without it . . ."

"Yes, yes, of course," Shepherd interrupted. "I'm sure I worry far too much. However, it does seem to me that this world of ours is nothing *but* illusion. One giant, complex hologram." He smiled and looked away from Berdichev, focusing on Lehmann once again. "It's all *yin* and no *yang*. All male and no female. We've lost contact with the Mother, don't you agree, Under Secretary?"

It was Duchek who answered him, his eyes flaring with passionate indignation. "It's all right for you, *Shih* Shepherd. You have the Domain. You *have* your Mother!"

For a moment there was a tense, almost shocked silence in their circle. It was a fact, and all of them knew it, but it was rarely mentioned in polite company. The Domain, where Shepherd lived, like the estates of the Seven, was an exception. Barring plantation workers, no one of any stature was allowed to live outside the City. There was, of course, good reason for this, for most of the land outside the City was under intense cultivation, organised into huge 10,000 *mou* fields planted with super-hybrids, not a *mou* wasted. Even so, a great deal of jealousy existed in the Above. There were many, Berdichev and Lehmann amongst them, who would have given half their wealth to live outside, under the sun.

"Well, it's true!" said Duchek after a moment, embarrassed by his slip, but unapologetic. "It's easy for him to criticise. He can get out!"

Lehmann studied Duchek a moment, then turned back to Shepherd, still intrigued by what he had heard him say. "I'm surprised to hear you talk this way, *Shih* Shepherd. You sound . . ." he laughed, ". . . almost dissatisfied."

Shepherd glanced briefly at Li Yuan, noting how intently the young boy was following things, then smiled and answered Lehmann. "Should I be satisfied? Should I, as a man, just accept what is without question?" He laughed softly. "Why, we would still be in the caves, or in the woods if that were so. There would be no civilisation. No Chung Kuo."

Yuan, whose eyes caught everything, saw how Lehmann made to answer, then checked himself, as if he had suddenly realised what was happening. Hal Shepherd's words, whilst passionately spoken, were suspiciously close to Dispersionist orthodoxy and their creed of "Change and Expand". Lehmann hesitated, then laughed casually and turned to take a fresh tumbler of wine from a passing servant.

"So you advocate change?"

Shepherd's face changed subtly; the smile, the patina of charm remained, but behind it now lay something much harder and more ruthless. "You mistake me, Pietr. I do not like change, nor do I welcome it. But if I could change one thing, I would change that. I would give men back their contact with the earth." His smile hardened, and a trace of sadness and regret lingered momentarily in his eyes. "However, the world is as it is, not as it ought to be. There are too many of us now. The earth could not support us in the old way."

Again it was a fact. Even though every cultivable piece of land outside the City was in use, still only sixty per cent of Chung Kuo's demand was met that way. The rest was synthesised within the City or grown in the giant orbital farms. And as the population grew the problem grew with it. How to feed the many mouths of Chung Kuo?

Yuan felt himself tense, knowing that Shepherd was coming to the nub of it. Through Shepherd, his father was fishing for something; some concession, maybe. Some way of healing the anticipated breach, of keeping Chung Kuo from war.

"But there are other ways, eh?"

Lehmann let the words lie there between himself and Shepherd. He sipped at his wine and looked across at Berdichev, a faint smile on his lips.

Shepherd tilted his head slightly, as if considering Lehmann's words. Then he sighed and shook his head. "The T'ang himself has tried to make changes. For three years now he has tried to persuade the Council to take certain measures. But they are reluctant. They do not feel the House would give its full support to such changes."

Yuan had seen how Lehmann's eyes had widened at Shepherd's use of the word "changes" in the context of his father and the Council; had seen how surprised both Berdichev and Duchek also were.

Lehmann spoke for them. "Changes? I don't understand you, *Shih* Shepherd. What changes?"

"Controls. Concessions. A deal, you might call it."

"A deal?" Lehmann's mouth twisted almost scornfully. "I thought the Seven were above deals. What could they possibly want from the House?"

Shepherd looked at each of the men in turn, then smiled. "Population controls. Perhaps even reductions?"

Lehmann's laughter made heads turn nearby. He leaned towards Shepherd and almost spat the word back at him. "Impossible!"

"So you say, but what if . . ."

But Shepherd never got to finish his sentence. Yuan felt a touch on his shoulder and knew at once it was Han Ch'in. No one else would have dared lay a hand on him.

"Hal! Hal! Have you seen them? Have you seen my ox-men? They're marvellous!"

Shepherd drew back from the edge. Calmly he turned to Han Ch'in and smiled. "So that's what they were, Han. I did wonder. I thought perhaps you had invited a few brutes up from the Clay!"

The rest of the circle had bowed at Han Ch'in's sudden entry into their ranks. Now Shepherd's comment drew their laughter. But Han Ch'in himself was more thoughtful.

"It must be awful, Hal, being born down there."

Berdichev, who, with Lehmann and Wyatt, had been beneath the City's floor into the Clay and seen it for himself, bowed again, then answered Han.

"It would be, were they really conscious of their misery. But it's all they know. In any case, they're really little more than animals. They don't live long enough to consider how awful their lives truly are."

"We should gas them," said Duchek. "We should pump the Clay full of gas and clean it up."

Han Ch'in looked sharply at the Administrator but said nothing.

"It would, perhaps, be best," said Lehmann, coming to Duchek's aid. "After all, it would ease their suffering. And we could use the land down there for other things."

"So I understand," Han Ch'in answered, his distaste for

208

Lehmann quite open. "You have argued for it in the House often enough."

Lehmann bowed his head then looked to Shepherd, his frustration at being interrupted at such a crucial moment threatening, for an instant, to goad him into an impropriety. Then he relaxed again and smiled at the T'ang's eldest son.

"I am honoured that the Prince pays such attention to my humble affairs. You may be sure I am no less your own admirer."

Han Ch'in stared back at him a moment, nothing but coldness in his eyes, then he turned to Shepherd and laughed.

"You know, Hal, I can't get over how marvellous my ox-men are. They even talk. Baby talk, admittedly, but it's talk of a kind, eh? And you should smell them. Rich, they are! Ripe!" He looked meaningfully around the circle, then back at Shepherd. "Perhaps I should have uncle Klaus make more of them for me. Then I could form my own House and watch the beasts debate."

* * *

Tolonen's eyes took in everything about him. He had a sense of where each person was within ten paces of the T'ang; how far away the nearest of them were; how casually or otherwise each stood. As for himself, he stood there, seemingly at ease, a drink in his left hand, his right hand resting against his thigh. Casual. Listening, or so it seemed, to every word that was being said. Indeed, at any moment he might have repeated anything that had just been said by the T'ang and his party, yet his attention was split. He watched, attentive to every sign, knowing that this, the safest place, was also the most dangerous. They could never take Li Shai Tung by force. But surprise?

Earlier that afternoon he had checked out the servants for himself, trusting no one. He had had every servo-mechanism checked for programme quirks, every GenSyn neuter for behavioural deviancy. And then, at the last moment, he had brought in his own guards. It was they who now went amongst the guests, serving drinks and offering spiced delicacies. At any moment Tolonen could tune in to any conversation and hear whatever was being said through the direct relay in his head. His guards picked up all talk, positioning themselves so that not a word in the Great Hall would be missed. It would all be replayed and investigated for significance later. For now, however, only one thing mattered. He had to keep Li Shai Tung alive.

For years now he had learned to outguess his enemies; to anticipate their next move. But now things were changing, the situation escalating, and in his heart of hearts he knew that the tenuous peace that had existed for more than a century was about to be broken. The Dispersionists, a covert, loosely-knit organisation before the arrest of Edmund Wyatt, were now an open faction in the House; not merely respected but heavily supported. Their strength had upset the traditional balance. In the last two years they had radicalised the House and brought the clamour for Change to a head.

It was time to come to an agreement. To make concessions. But first they would have justice. For Lwo Kang's death and the insult to the Seven.

Tolonen breathed deeply, hearing Lehmann's voice sound clearly in his head. In two hours the smile would be wiped off that bastard's face.

He had been listening to the conversation between Shepherd and the others, amused by the way Shepherd ran them, like fish upon a line, only to reel them slowly in. But Han Ch'in's sudden interjection had snapped the fragile line. Tolonen looked across and saw the young prince leaning forward, one hand on his younger brother's shoulder, and heard his voice clearly, transmitted to him by the waiter at Berdichev's side.

"*It must be awful, Hal. Being born down there.*"

"Knut!"

He turned at the T'ang's summons and went across to him, the fingers of his right hand surreptitiously moving across the control panel beneath the cloth of his uniform trousers, shutting off the voices in his head.

"*Chieh Hsia?*"

The circle about the T'ang made room for the General.

"Klaus was asking me about Major DeVore. He's back tomorrow, isn't he?"

"He was due then, *Chieh Hsia*, but the flight from Mars was delayed. He docks the morning of the wedding."

"Good. Klaus was saying how much his son would like to serve the Major again. I hope he'll be granted the opportunity."

Tolonen bowed his head. What the T'ang "hoped" for was tantamount to a command. "I shall see to it personally, *Chieh Hsia*."

"He has done well out there, I understand."

Again the T'ang was being diplomatic. He knew perfectly well how DeVore had performed as Chief Security Officer to the Martian Colony. He had seen all the reports and discussed them at length with Tolonen.

"Indeed he has, *Chieh Hsia*. And I have put his name before the Marshal to fill the next vacancy for General."

"Your own?" Li Shai Tung smiled.

"If the T'ang no longer feels he needs me."

"Oh, that will be some time yet, Knut. A good long time, I hope."

Tolonen bowed deeply, profoundly pleased.

Just then Major Nocenzi appeared at the edge of the group, his head bowed, awaiting permission to speak.

The T'ang looked at him. "What is it, Major?"

Nocenzi kept his head lowered. "There is a message, *Chieh Hsia*. For the General."

Tolonen turned to the T'ang. "You'll excuse me, *Chieh Hsia?*"

"Of course."

He bowed and turned away, then followed Nocenzi across to an ante-room they were using as coordination centre for Security. When the door was closed behind them, Tolonen faced his Major.

"What is it, Vittorio?"

"Karr has been on, sir. He says he's traced his man."

"What?"

"He's waiting to talk to you, sir. On the switching channel."

At once Tolonen reached down and touched the relevant button on the panel inset into his thigh. "Well, Karr?" he said, knowing Karr would hear him, wherever he was in the City. Karr's voice came back to him at once; as clear in his head as if he stood in the same room with him.

"Forgive me for disturbing you, General. But I'm certain I've found him. He fits the profile perfectly, right down to the scar. I'm following him right now."

Tolonen listened carefully, making Karr repeat the coordinates three times before he cut connection. Then he turned to Nocenzi.

"I must go, Vittorio. Take charge here. Ensure by your life that nothing happens."

Nocenzi looked down. "Are you sure you should go personally, sir? It could be dangerous. The man's a killer."

Tolonen smiled. "I'll be all right, Vittorio. Anyway, Karr will be with me."

"Even so, sir . . ."

Tolonen laughed. "If it makes you easier, Vittorio, I order you to take charge here. All right? In this instance I have to go. Personally. It's too important to leave to anyone else. Too much has slipped through my hands as it is, and this man's the key to it all. I know he is. I feel it in my bones."

Nocenzi smiled. "Then take care, Knut. I'll make certain all's well here."

Tolonen reached out and held Nocenzi's shoulder briefly, returning his smile. "Good. Then I'll report what's happening to the T'ang."

★ ★ ★

"Well, Chen? Would you like a beer?"

Chen looked up at the brightly pulsing sign over the

212

door. Fu Yang's Bar, it read. His mouth was dry and the thought of a beer was good. It was some while since he'd allowed himself the luxury. Even so he looked down and shook his head. "Thank you, *Pan chang* Lo, but I should be getting back. It's late and Wang Ti will have to cook."

Supervisor Lo took his arm. "All the better. You can get a meal at the bar. Call her. Tell her you'll be a bit late, and that you've eaten. She'll not mind. Not this once. Come on, I'll treat you. You've helped me out and I appreciate that."

Chen hesitated, then nodded. Lo was right; it wasn't as if he made a habit of this. No, Wang Ti could hardly complain if he had a few beers for once; not after he had worked a double shift. Anyway, he had bought her something. He traced the shape of the necklace in his overall pocket and smiled to himself, then followed Lo Ying into the crowded bar, squeezing in beside him at one of the tiny double booths.

Lo Ying turned to him, his deeply-lined, wispily bearded face only a hand's breadth away. "What'll you have? The soychicken with ginger and pineapple's good. So's the red-cooked soypork with chestnuts."

Chen laughed. "They both sound excellent. We'll have a large dish of each, eh? And I'll share the cost with you."

Lo Ying put his long, thin hand over Chen's. "Not at all, my friend. As I said, you did me a good turn tonight. It was good of you to work the shift at short notice. I was in a hole and you helped me out of it. It's the least I can do to buy you a meal and a few beers."

Chen smiled, then looked down, rubbing at the red marks at the back of his head and on his forehead where he had been wearing the wraparound. Lo Ying was a good man. A bit dull, maybe, but fair and reliable, unlike most of the *pan chang* he'd encountered up here. "Okay," he said. "But I was glad of the extra shift. We've not much, Wang Ti, baby Jyan and I, but I've ambitions. I want better for my son."

Lo Ying looked at him a moment, then nodded his head.

"I've watched you often, Chen. Seen how hard you work. And I've wondered to myself. Why is Chen where he is? Why is he not higher up the levels? He is a good man; a good, strong worker; reliable, intelligent. Why is he here, working for me? Why am I not working for him?"

Chen laughed shortly, then looked up, meeting Lo Ying's eyes. "I was not always so, Lo Ying. I was a wild youth. A waster of my talents. And then . . . well, a wife, a son – they change a man."

"Ah yes. So it is."

A girl came and took their order, then returned a moment later with two bulbs of *Yao Fan Te* beer. Lo Ying handed one to Chen, then toasted him.

"To your family!"

"And yours, Lo Ying!"

He had told no one of his past. No one. Not even Wang Ti. For in this, he knew, he was vulnerable. One careless word said to the wrong person and he would be back there, below the Net. Back in that nightmare place where every man was for himself and men like Lo Ying were as rare as phoenix eggs.

Lo Ying put his beer down and wiped the froth from his wispy moustache. "Talking of work, I've been meaning to ask you . . ." He looked sideways at Chen. "As you know, Feng Shi-lun is up for a *pan chang*'s job. I happen to know he'll get it. Which means there's a vacancy as my assistant."

Lo Ying fell silent, leaving unstated the meaning of his words. Chen took a deep draught of his beer, studying the old Han beggar on the label a moment. Then he wiped his mouth and looked up again. "You're offering me the job?"

Lo Ying shrugged. "It's not up to me, Chen, but . . . Well, I could put a word in higher up."

Chen considered a moment, then looked directly at him. "How much would it cost?"

"Two hundred yuan."

Chen laughed. "I haven't twenty! Where would I find such money?"

"No, you don't understand me, Chen. I'd lend you it. Interest free. I'd . . ." He hesitated, then smiled. "I'd like to see you get on, Chen. You're worth a dozen of those useless shits. And maybe someday . . ."

Again, it was left unsaid. But Chen had grown used to the ways of these levels. Favours and bribes – they were the lubricants of this world. You scratch my back, I scratch yours. You pay squeeze, you move up. Refuse and you stay where you are. It was the way of the world. But Lo Ying was better than most. He offered his help interest free and with only the vaguest of strings. Chen looked at him and nodded. "Okay, but how would I repay you? My rent's eight yuan. Food's another six. That leaves eleven from my weekly pay to see to clothing, heating, light. I'm lucky if I save five yuan a month!"

Lo Ying nodded. "That's why you must take this opportunity. *Pan chang*'s assistant pays thirty a week. You could pay me the difference until the debt is cleared. You say you've twenty?"

Chen nodded.

"Good. Then that's one hundred and eighty you'll need from me. Thirty six weeks and you're free of obligation. Free . . . and five yuan better off a week."

Chen looked at him, knowing how great a favour Lo Ying was doing him. If he went to a shark for the money it would be two years, maybe four, before he'd be clear. But thirty-six weeks. Nine months, give or take. It was nothing. And he would be one step higher.

He put out his hand. "Okay, Lo Ying. I'm grateful. If ever . . ."

"Yes, yes . . ." Lo Ying smiled, then turned. "Look, here's our food."

They tucked in, looking at each other from time to time and smiling.

"It's good, eh?" said Lo Ying, turning to order two more beers. Then he frowned. "Hey, Chen, look . . ."

Chen turned, his mouth full of chicken, and looked. On the big screen over the serving counter the *Ywe Lung* had appeared. All over the bar people were turning to look and falling silent.

"It's nothing," Chen said. "Just another announcement about the wedding."

"No . . . Look. The background's white. Someone's dead. One of the Seven." A low murmur went around the packed bar. A few got up from their seats and went to stand at the bar, looking up at the screen.

Chen looked at Lo Ying's face and saw the concern there. There was still a strong feeling for the Seven at this level, whatever was happening Above or far below. Here they identified with the Seven and were fiercely loyal. "Trouble for the Seven is trouble for us all" – how often he'd heard that said in the last year and a half. And something of that had rubbed off on him, he realised, as he sat there, his pulse raised by the ominous white background to the imperial symbol.

Martial music played. Then, abruptly, the image changed.

"What's that?" said Lo Ying softly.

There was a buzz of noise, then quiet. On the screen was a plain, red-carpeted room. In the middle of the room was a very solid-looking block; a big thing, an arm's length to a side. Its top was strangely smooth, as if melted or worn flat by the passage of feet or water over it, and cut into its dull grey side was the *Ywe Lung*, the wheel of dragons.

For a moment the screen was silent. Then came the voice.

It was the same voice he had heard numerous times before, making official announcements, but now it seemed more sombre, more threatening than he had ever heard it before. And the shadow voice, softer, more sing-song, that spoke in native Mandarin, seemed to contain the same dark threat.

Chen put the bulb to his lips and emptied it. "Listen," said Lo Ying, reaching out to take his arm again. "There's been a trial."

The voice spoke slowly, carefully, outlining what had happened. There had been an assassination. The T'ang's Minister, Lwo Kang . . .

Chen felt himself go cold. Lwo Kang. He looked down, shuddering.

A man named Edmund Wyatt had confessed to the killing. He had organised it. Had been the hand behind the knife.

Chen stiffened. Wyatt? Who in hell's name was Wyatt? Why not Berdichev? That was the name Kao Jyan had mentioned on his tape. Berdichev, not Wyatt. He shook his head, not understanding.

The image changed again, and there, before them, was Wyatt himself, speaking into camera, admitting his part in everything. A worn yet handsome man. An aristocrat. Every inch an aristocrat.

From the watching men came a sharp hissing. "Scum!" shouted someone. "Arrogant First Level bastards!" called another.

Chen looked down, then looked up again. So Kao Jyan had been wrong after all. He had guessed wrongly. A pity. But then, why had they killed him? Why kill him if he was wrong about Berdichev?

Or *had* he been wrong?

Wyatt's face faded, leaving the image of the empty room and the block. Again there was silence, both on the screen and below it in the bar. Then, suddenly, there was movement to the right of the screen. Two big, hugely-muscled men brought a tall, very angular man into the centre of the room and secured him over the block, his chest pressed against the upper surface, his bowed head jutting out towards the watching billions.

The man was naked. His hands had been secured tightly behind his back and his feet shackled with manacles. He looked very ill. Feebly he raised his head, his lips drawing back from his teeth in a rictus of fear, then let it fall again. His shaven head was like a skull, its paleness dotted with red blotches, while his bones seemed to poke through at shoulder and elbow.

"Gods . . ." whispered Lo Ying. "He looks half dead already, poor bastard!"

Chen nodded, fascinated, unable to look away. One of

the guards had gone off screen. The other leaned over the prisoner and brought his knee down firmly, brutally onto his back, pressing him down against the block. Then the first guard came back.

From the men in the bar came a single gasp. Of surprise. And fear.

In the guard's hands was a sword; a huge, long, two-edged weapon with an exaggeratedly broad, flat blade and a long, iron-black handle. It was cruel and brutal, like something out of a museum, but it had been polished until it shone like new. The edges winked viciously in the brightness of the room as the guard turned it in his hands, accustoming himself to its weight and balance.

Lo Ying swallowed noisily, then made a small whimpering sound in his throat. "Gods . . ." he said again, barely audibly. But Chen could not look away. It seemed alive. Hideously alive. As if some awful power animated the weapon. Its heaviness, its very awkwardness, spoke volumes. It was a brutal, pagan thing, and its ugly, unsophisticated strength struck dread into him.

Beside him Lo Ying groaned. Chen looked about him, his eyes searching from face to face, seeing his own horrified fascination mirrored everywhere.

"They're going to execute him!" Lo Ying's voice shook.

"Yes," said Chen softly, looking back at the screen. "They are."

The guard had raised the sword high. For a moment he held it there, his muscles quivering with the strain. Then, as if at some unspoken command, he brought it down onto the block.

The sword met little resistance. The head seemed to jump up on its own, a cometary trail of blood gouting behind it. It came down to the far left of the screen, rolled over once and lay still, eerily upright, the eyes staring out sightlessly at the watching billions. The headless corpse spasmed and was still. Blood pumped from the severed neck, dribbling down the sides of the block to merge with the deep red of the carpet.

There was a fearful, awful silence. The guards had gone. Now there was only the block, the body and the head. Those three and the blood.

Chen sat there, like the others, frozen into immobility, unable to believe it had been real. Despite himself, he felt shocked. It couldn't be real, could it? He saw the surprise, the sudden pain in the dead man's staring eyes and still could not believe it had been real. But all round him grown men were on their feet, shuddering, groaning, laughing with shock or crying openly as they stood there, unable to look away from the screen and the severed head. Then Chen unfroze himself and stood up.

"Come on," he said, taking Lo Ying's arm firmly. "Let's get out of here."

Above them the screen went dark. Chen turned and pushed his way through the crowd, pulling Lo Ying along behind him, anxious to get outside. But out in the corridor he stopped, breathing deeply, feeling suddenly giddy. Why? he asked himself. *I've killed men before now. With these very hands I've taken their lives. Why, then, was that so awful?*

But he knew why. Because it was different. Because it had been witnessed by them all.

It was a sign. A sign of things to come.

"Gods . . . Gods . . ." Lo Ying was shaking violently. He was barely in control of himself. "I didn't think . . ." he began. Then he turned away and was sick against the wall.

Yes, thought Chen. A sign. Times are changing. And this, the first public execution in more than a century, is the beginning of it.

He turned and looked at Lo Ying, suddenly pitying him. It had shocked him; what then had it done to such as Lo Ying? He took his arms and turned him around. "Listen," he said. "You'll come back with me. Stay with us tonight. We'll make space."

Lo Ying went to shake his head, then saw how Chen was looking at him and nodded.

"Good. Come on then. We can send a message to your family. They'll understand."

Lo Ying let himself be led along, wiping distractedly at his mouth and beard and mumbling to himself. But at the junction of Chen's corridor he stiffened and pulled back.

Chen turned, looking at him. "What is it?"

"There . . ." Lo Ying bent his head slightly, indicating something off to Chen's right. "Those men. I saw them earlier. Back at the bar."

Chen stared at him. "You're sure?"

Lo Ying hesitated, then nodded. "The big one . . . he was sitting across from us. I noticed him. Before it happened . . ." He shuddered and looked down.

Chen turned slowly and glanced at the men as casually as he could, then looked back at Lo Ying, speaking as softly as he could. "Lo Ying? Have you your knife on you?"

Lo Ying nodded. As *pan chang* he was permitted to carry a knife for his duties.

"Good. Pass it to me. Don't let them see."

Lo Ying did as he was told, then clutched at Chen's shirt. "Who are they, Chen?"

Chen took a deep breath. "I don't know. I don't think I've seen them before. Perhaps it's just a coincidence."

But he knew it wasn't. He knew it was all tied in somehow. It was no coincidence that Wyatt had been executed tonight. And now they had come for him. Tidying up. He wondered vaguely how they'd traced him.

"Stay here. I'll go down towards home. If they follow me, whistle."

Lo Ying nodded once, then watched as Chen turned away from him and, seeming not to notice the two men waiting twenty paces off, made for his home corridor.

Chen had only gone three or four paces when the men pushed away from the wall and began to follow him. Lo Ying let them turn into the corridor, making sure they were following, then put his fingers to his lips and whistled.

Chen turned abruptly, facing the men.

"What do you want?"

They were both big men, but the younger of them was a real brute, a giant of a man, more than a head taller than Chen and much broader at the shoulders. Like a machine made of flesh and muscle. The other was much older, his close-cropped hair a silver grey, but he still looked fit and dangerous. They were *Hung Mao*, both of them. But who were they working for? Berdichev? Or the T'ang?

"Kao Chen," said the older of them, taking two paces nearer. "So we meet at last. We thought you were dead."

Chen grunted. "Who are you?"

The old man smiled. "I should have realised at once. Karr here had to point it out to me. That stooge you used to play yourself. The man who died in Jyan's. You should have marked him." He pointed to the thick ridge of scar tissue beneath Chen's right ear. "Karr noticed it on the film."

Chen laughed. "So. But what can you prove?"

"We don't have to prove anything, Chen." The old man laughed and seemed to relax. "You know, you're a tricky bastard, aren't you? Your brother, Jyan, underestimated you. He thought you dull-witted. But don't go making the same mistake with me. Don't underestimate me, Chen. I'm not some low level punk. I am the T'ang's General, and I command more *kwai* than you'd ever dream existed. You can die now, if you want. Or you can live. The choice is yours."

A ripple of fear went through Chen. The T'ang's General! But he had made his choice already, moments before, and the old man was only two paces off now. If he could keep him talking a moment longer.

"You're mistaken, General," he said, raising a hand to keep the General off. "Jyan was not my brother. We only shared the same surname. Anyway, I . . ." He broke off, smiling, then let out a scream. "Lo Ying!"

The big man began to turn just as Lo Ying jumped up onto his back. At the same moment Chen lunged forward, the knife flashing out from his pocket. Grasping the old

221

man's arm he turned him and brought the knife up to his throat.

Karr threw his attacker off and felled him with a single punch, then turned back, angry at being tricked. He came forward two paces then stopped abruptly, seeing how things were.

"You're a fool, Chen," the General hissed, feeling Chen's arm tighten about his chest, the knife's point prick the skin beneath his chin. "Harm me and you'll all be dead. Chen, Wang Ti and baby Jyan. As if you'd never been."

Chen shuddered, but kept his grip on the old man. "Your life . . . It must be worth something."

The General laughed coldly. "To my T'ang."

"Well then?"

Tolonen swallowed painfully. "You know things. Know what Jyan knew. You . . . you can connect things for us. Incriminate others."

"Maybe."

"In return we'll give you an amnesty. Legitimise your citizenship. Make sure you can't be sent back to the Net."

"And that's all? A measly amnesty. For what *I* know?"

The General was silent a moment, breathing shallowly, conscious of the knife pressed harder against his throat. "And what *do* you know, Kao Chen?"

"I watched him. Both times. Saw him go in there that first time. He and the Han. Then watched him come out two hours later, alone, after he'd killed Kao Jyan. Then, later, I saw him go back in again. I stood at the junction and saw him, with my own eyes. You were there too. Both of you. I recognise you now. Yes. He was one of yours. One of you bastards."

The General shuddered. "Who, Chen? Who do you mean?"

Chen laughed coldly. "The Major. That's who. Major DeVore."

CHAPTER·6

THE LIGHT IN THE DARKNESS

The first thing to see was darkness. Darkness coloured the Clay like a dye. It melted forms and re-cast them with a deadly animation. It lay within and without; was both alive and yet the deadest thing of all. It breathed, and yet it stifled.

For many it was all they knew. All they would ever know.

The settlement was on the crest of a low hill, a sprawl of ugly, jagged shapes, littering the steep slope. Old, crumbling ruins squatted amongst the debris, black against black, their very shapes eroded by the darkness. The walls of houses stood no taller than a man's height, the brickwork soft, moist to the touch. There were no roofs, no ceilings, but none were needed here. No rain fell in the darkness of the Clay.

The darkness seemed intense and absolute. It was a cloth, smothering the vast, primaeval landscape. Yet there was light of a kind.

Above the shadowed plain the ceiling ran to all horizons, perched on huge columns of silver that glowed softly, faintly, like something living. Dim studs of light criss-crossed the artificial sky; neutered, ordered stars, following the tracks of broad conduits and cables, for the ceiling was a floor, and overhead was the vastness of the City; another world, sealed off from the foetid darkness underneath.

The Clay. It was a place inimical to life. And yet life

thrived there in the dark; hideous, malformed shapes spawning in obscene profusion. The dark plain crawled with vulgar life.

Kim woke from a bad dream, a tight band of fear about his chest. Instinct made him freeze, then turn slowly, stealthily, towards the sound, lifting the oilcloth he lay under. He had the scent at once – the thing that had warned him on waking. *Strangers* . . . Strangers at the heart of the camp.

Something was wrong. Badly wrong.

He moved to the lip of the brickwork he had been lying behind and peered over the top. What he saw made him bristle with fear. Two of his tribe lay on the ground nearby, their skulls smashed open, the brains taken. Further away, three men – strangers, intruders – crouched over another body. They were carving flesh from arm and thigh and softly laughing as they ate. Kim's mouth watered, but the fear he felt was far stronger.

One of the strangers turned and looked directly at the place where Kim was hiding. He lidded his eyes and kept perfectly still, knowing that unless he moved the man would not see him. So it proved. The man made a cursory inspection of the settlement then returned to his food, his face twitching furtively as he gnawed at the raw meat.

For a moment Kim was blank; a shell of unthinking bone. Then something woke in him, filling the emptiness. He turned away, moving with a painful slowness, his muscles aching with the strain of it as he climbed the rotten sill, each moment begging that it wouldn't crumble beneath his weight and betray him. But it held. Then, slowly, very slowly, he eased himself down the cold, broad steps. Down into the cellar of Baxi's house.

In the far corner of the cellar he stopped, lifting rocks, scrabbling silently with his fingers in the intense darkness, looking for something. There! His fingers found the edge of the cloth and gently pulled the package up out of the soft dust. Kim shivered, knowing already what was inside. These were Baxi's. His treasures. He was not meant to know of them. Baxi would have killed him had he known.

Kim tugged at the knot and freed it, then unwrapped the cloth, ignoring the fear he felt. Another Kim – another self – had taken over.

Straightening up, he knelt there, staring down sightlessly at the items hidden in the cloth, a feeling of strangeness rippling through him like a sickness. For a moment he closed his eyes against the sudden, unexpected giddiness, then felt it ebb from him and opened them again, feeling somehow different – somehow . . . changed.

Spreading the objects out with his fingers, he picked up each object in turn, feeling and smelling them, letting the newly-woken part of him consider each thing before he set it down again.

A tarnished mirror, bigger than his hand, cracked from top to bottom. A narrow tube that contained a strange sweet-smelling liquid. Another tube, but this of wood, long as his lower arm, small holes punctuating its length. One end was open, hollow, the other tapered, split.

There was a small globe of glass, heavy and cold in his palm. Beside that was a glove, too large for his hand, its fingers heavily padded at the back, as if each joint had swollen up.

Two strings of polished beads lay tangled in a heap. Kim's clever fingers untangled them and lay them out flat on the threadbare cloth.

There were other things, but those he set aside. His other self already saw. Saw as if the thing had already happened and he had been outside himself, looking on. The thought made him feel strange again; made his head swim, his body feel light, almost feverish. Then, once more, it passed.

Quickly, as if he had done all this before, he laid the things out around him, then placed the cloth over his head. Unsighted, he worked as if he saw himself from above, letting some other part of him manipulate his hands, his body, moving quickly, surely, until the thing was done. Then, ready, he turned towards the doorway and, by touch and scent, made his way out into the open.

He heard a gasp and then a shout, high-pitched and nervous. Three voices babbled and then fell silent. That silence was his signal. Lifting the globe high, he squeezed the button on the side of the tube.

Some gift, unguessed until that moment, made him see himself as they saw him. He seemed split, one self standing there before them, the cloth shrouding his face and neck, the cracked mirror tied in a loop before his face, the other stood beyond the men, looking back past them at the awesome, hideous figure who had appeared so suddenly, flames leaping from one hand, fire glinting in the centre of the other, giant fist, flickering in the hollow where his face should have been, while from the neck of the figure a long tongue of wood hung stiffly down.

The figure hopped and sang – a strange, high-pitched wail that seemed to come in broken, anguished breaths. And all the while the fire flickered in the centre of the empty face.

As one, the strangers screamed and ran.

Kim let the pipe fall from his lips. His finger released the button on the tube. It was done. He had seen them off. But from the darkness of the slopes came an intense, ape-like chattering. Others had seen the sudden, astonishing brightness.

He set down the glass sphere, unfastened the mirror and lay it down, then sat there on the broken ground, wondering at himself. It had worked. He had seen it in his head, and then . . . He laughed softly, strangely. And then he'd done it. He'd actually done it.

And it had worked . . .

He tore the cloth from his head and bared his sharp teeth in a feral grin of triumph. Tilting his head back, he let out a howl; a double whoop of delight at his own cleverness. Then, so suddenly that the sound still echoed from the ceiling high above, he shuddered, gripped by a paralysing fear, a black, still coldness flooding his limbs.

It was not triumph, merely reprieve. He was still here, trapped, smothered by the darkness. He coughed, then felt the warm corruption of the darkness fill his lungs, like a liquid, choking him. He stood up, gulping at the foetid air as if for something sweeter, cleaner. But there was nothing – only this.

He whimpered, then, glancing furtively about him, began to wrap the treasures as he'd found them. Only when they were safely stored did he stop, his jaw aching from fear, his muscles trembling violently. Then, like some mad thing, he rushed about the settlement on all-fours, growling furiously, partly to keep up his faded courage, partly to keep away the prowlers on the hillside below.

It was then that he found the knife. It had fallen on its edge, the handle jutting up at an angle where one of the strangers had dropped it. The handle was cold and smooth and did not give to Kim's sharp teeth when he tested it. Not wood, nor flint, but something far better than those. Something *made*. He drew it slowly from the tiny crevice in which it had lodged and marvelled at its length, its perfect shape. It was as long as his arm and its blade was so sharp it made his testicles contract in fear. *A wartha*, it was. *From Above*.

When they came back he was squatting on the sill of Baxi's house, the long, two-edged blade lain carefully across his knees, the handle clenched firmly in his left hand.

Baxi looked about him, his body tensed, alarm twitching in his face. The stockade was down, the women gone. A few of the bodies lay where they had fallen. Some – those on the edges of the settlement – had been carried off. Behind Baxi his two lieutenants, Rotfoot and Ebor, made low, grunting noises of fear. He turned and silenced them, then faced Kim again.

"Pandra vyth gwres?" *What is this?*

Baxi glared at Kim, then saw the knife. His eyes widened, filled with fear and a greedy desire for the weapon. There was a fierce, almost sexual urgency in his broad, squat face as he hopped from foot to foot, making small noises, as if in pain.

Kim knew he would kill to have the knife.

227

"Lagasek!" Baxi barked angrily, edging closer. "Pandra vyth gwres?" His hands made small grasping movements.

Lagasek. It was the name they had given him. *Starer.*

Kim stood then raised the knife high over his head. There was a gasp from the other members of the hunting party as they saw the weapon, then an excited chattering. Kim saw Baxi crouch, his muscles tensing, as if he suspected treachery.

Slowly, careful not to alarm Baxi, Kim lowered the blade and placed it on the ground between them. Then he crouched, making himself smaller than he was, and made a gesture with his hands, the palms open, denoting a gift.

Baxi stared at him a moment longer, the hairs bristling on his arms and at the back of his neck. Then he too crouched, a broad, toothless grin settling on his face. The Chief was pleased. He reached out, taking Kim's gift gingerly by the handle, respecting the obvious sharpness of the blade.

Baxi lifted the weapon and held it high above his head. He glanced briefly at Kim, smiling broadly, generous now, then turned, looking back at his hunters, thrusting the knife time and again into the air, tilting his head back with each thrust and baying at the ceiling high above.

All about him in the almost-dark the hunters bayed and yelled. And from the hillsides and the valley below other groups took up the unearthly sound and echoed it back.

* * *

Kim squatted at Ebor's side in the inner circle of the hunters, chewing a long, pale-fleshed lugworm and listening to the grunts, the moist, slopping sounds the men made as they ate, realising he had never really noticed them before. He glanced about him, his eyes moving swiftly from face to face around the circle, looking for some outward sign of the change that had come to him, but there was nothing. Rotfoot had lost his woman in the raid, but now he sat there, on the low stone wall, contentedly chewing part of her thighbone, stripping it bare with his sharply pointed teeth. Others too were gnawing at the meat that Baxi had provided. A small heap of it lay there in the centre of the circle, hacked into manageable pieces. Hands and feet were recognisable in the pile, but little else. The sharp knife had worked its magic of disguise. Besides, meat was meat, whatever the source.

Kim finished the worm. He leaned forward, looking about him timidly. Then, seeing the smiles on the hunters' faces, he reached out and grasped a small hunk of the meat. A hand. He was tearing at the hard, tough flesh when Baxi settled by his side and placed an arm about his narrow shoulders. Reflex made him tense and look up into the Chief's face, fear blazing in his eyes, but the warrior merely grunted and told him to come.

He followed Baxi through, aware that the circle of heads turned to follow him. Afraid, he clutched the severed hand to him, finding a strange comfort in its touch. His fingers sought its rough, bony knuckles, recognised the chipped, spoonlike nails. It was Rotfoot's woman's hand.

At the entrance to Baxi's house they stopped. The Chief turned, facing the boy, and pointed down to a small parcel of cloth that lay on the ground beside the sill.

Kim froze in fear, thinking he'd been discovered. He closed his eyes, petrified, expecting the knife's sharp blow. Where would it strike? In his back? His side? Against his neck? He made a small sound of fear, then opened his eyes again and looked up at Baxi.

Baxi was looking strangely at him. Then he shrugged and pointed at the parcel again. Kim swallowed and set down the hand, then picked up the cloth bundle and, at Baxi's encouragement, began to unwrap it.

He saw what it was at once and looked up, surprised, only to find Baxi smiling down at him. "Ro," said the Chief. "Ro." *A gift.*

The tarnished mirror was just as he remembered it, the crack running down the silvered glass from top to bottom. There was no need to feign surprise or delight. He grinned up at Baxi, giving a silent whoop of joy, almost forgetting that they thought him dumb. Baxi too seemed pleased. He reached out to touch Kim, caressing his upper arms and nodding his head vigorously. "Ro," he said again, then laughed manically. And from the watching circle came an answering roar of savage laughter.

Kim stared down at the mirror in his hand and saw his face reflected in the darkness. How strange and alien that face. Not like his hands. He knew his hands. But his face . . . He shivered, then smiled, taken by the strangeness of his reflected features. *Lagasek*, he thought, seeing how the stranger smiled back at him. *Such eyes you have. Such big, wide staring eyes.*

★ ★ ★

Kim was scavenging; looking for food in a place where nothing grew. The air all about him was rich with the stink of decay, the ground beneath him soft and damp and treacherous. Here, at the edge of the great dump, the dangers multiplied. There were many more like him, hidden shadows scattered across the vastness of the wasteland, wary of each other as they climbed the huge, rotting mounds, picking at the waste. All of them looking for something to eat or trade. Anything. Good or rotten.

The darkness was almost perfect, but the boy saw clearly. His wide, round eyes flicked from side to side, his small, ill-formed head moved quickly, furtively, like the head of some wild creature. When another came too close he would scuttle away on all-fours, then rest there, at a distance, his teeth bared in challenge, growling at the back of his throat.

He moved deeper in, taking risks now, jumping between what looked like firm footholds. Some sank slowly beneath his weight, others held. He moved on quickly, not trusting anything too long, until he reached one certain resting place, the tower of an old church, jutting up above the vast mound of sewage from the City overhead.

Kim glanced up. The ceiling was far above him, its nearest supporting pillar only a stone's throw from where he squatted. From his vantage point he looked about him, noting where others were, checking which paths were clear for his escape. Then he settled, reaching deep inside his ragged, dirty shirt to take out the object he had found. He sniffed at it and licked it, then grimaced. It smelled like old skins and had a stale, unappetising taste. He turned it in his hands, looking for a way inside the blackened casing, then picked at the metal clasp until it opened.

He looked up sharply, suddenly very still, watchful, the hairs rising on the back of his thin neck, his rope-like muscles stretched as if to spring. Seeing nothing, he relaxed and looked back down at the open wallet in his hand.

Deftly he probed into each slender compartment, removing the contents and studying them closely before replacing them. There was nothing he recognised. Nothing edible. There were several long, thin cards of a flexible, shiny material. From one of them a faded face stared up at him, coming to vivid life when he pressed his thumb against it. Startled, he dropped the card, then steeled himself and retrieved it from the moss-covered slate on which it had fallen, deciding he would keep it.

There was only one other thing worth keeping. In a zippered compartment of the wallet was a small circle of shining metal on a chain. A kind of pendant. He lifted it gently, fascinated by its delicate perfection, his breath catching in his throat. It was beautiful. He held it up and touched the dangling circle with one finger, making it spin. It slowed, then twisted back, spinning backward and forward. Kim sat back on his haunches and laughed softly, delighted with his find.

The laughter died in his throat. He turned, hearing how close the others had come while he had been preoccupied, smelling the tartness of their sweat as they jumped up onto the tower.

Kim yelped, closing his fist about the pendant, and edged back away from them. There were three of them, one no older than himself, the others taller, better-muscled than he. Their round eyes gleamed with greed and they smiled at one another with their crooked, feral teeth. They thought they had him.

He snarled and the hair on his body rose, as if for fight, but all the while he was thinking, calculating, knowing he had to run. He looked from one to the other, discounting the smallest of them, concentrating on the two eldest, seeing who led, who followed. Then, so quick that they had no chance to stop him, he threw the wallet down, nearest the one who was quite clearly the follower. For a moment their attention went from him to the wallet. The leader snarled and made a lunge across the other, trying to get at the wallet.

Kim saw his opportunity and took it, flipping backward over the parapet, hoping that no one had disturbed the mound that lay below. His luck held and the soft ooze broke his fall wetly, stickily. Pulling himself up, he saw them leaning over the parapet, looking down. In a second or two they would be on him. He pulled his arm free and rolled, then scrambled onto all-fours and began to run.

He heard their cries, the soft squelch of the sticky mound as they jumped down onto it. Then they were after him, through the nightmare landscape, hopping between dark, slimy pools. Desperation made him take chances, choose paths he would normally ignore. And slowly, very slowly, he drew away from them, until, when he looked back over his shoulder, he found they were no longer pursuing him.

He turned and stood up, looking back across the choked mouth of the river. He could not make out the tower against the background of the rising land. Nor were any of the other familiar landmarks evident.

For the second time that day he felt afraid. He had come a long way. This was a side of the dump he didn't know. Here he was doubly vulnerable.

He was breathing deeply, his narrow chest heaving with exertion. If they attacked him now he was done for. He crouched down, looking all about him, his face twitching with anxiety. This side seemed deserted, but he knew he couldn't trust his eyes. He glanced down at the pendant in his hand, wondering if it had been worth the finding, then dismissed the question. First he had to get home.

Slowly, painstakingly, he made his way about the edge of the waste, his eyes straining for the least sign of movement, his sharp ears registering the least sound. And again his luck held. There, far to his left, was the broad pillar that they called the Gate, and beyond it, in the midst of the waste itself, the church tower. Kim grinned, allowing himself to savour hope for the first time since they had surprised him on the tower. He went on, clambering over the uneven surface, making a beeline for the Gate.

He was only a few paces from it when the ground gave way beneath his feet and he fell.

For a time he lay there, on his back, winded. It had not been much of a fall and he seemed not to have broken anything, but he could see from the smooth sides of the pit that it would be difficult to climb out. The earth was soft but dry beneath him. Tiny insects scuttled away from his probing hands, and the air seemed warm and strangely close. He sat up, groaning, feeling a stiffness in his back. His neck ached and his arms were sore, but he could move.

He looked up. Above him the opening formed a circle against the greater darkness, like two shades of the same non-colour. The circle had jagged edges, as if something had once lain across it. Kim's mind pieced things together nimbly. The pit had had some kind of lid on it. A wooden lid, maybe. And it had rotted over the years. It had taken only his own small weight to bring it down.

He felt about him in the darkness and found confirmation of his thoughts. There were splinters of soft, rotten wood everywhere about him. Then, with delight, he found the chain to the pendant with his fingers and drew it up to his face, pleased to find it unbroken. But then his pleasure died. He was still trapped. Unless he got out soon someone would come along and find him. And then he would be dead.

He looked about him, momentarily at a loss, then went to the side of the pit and began to poke and prise at it. The curved walls of the pit were made of a kind of brickwork. Kim worked at the joints, finding the joining material soft and crumbly to the touch. He dug away at it, loosening and then freeing one of the bricks. Throwing it down behind him, he reached up a bit higher and began to free another.

It took him a long time and at the end of it his fingertips were sore and bleeding, but he did it. Kneeling on the edge of the pit he looked back down and shivered, knowing that he could easily have died down there. He rested a while, then staggered across to the Gate, close to exhaustion. There, almost beside the broad, hexagonally-sided shaft, was a pool. He knelt beside it, bathing his fingers and splashing the tepid water in his face.

And then it happened.

The darkness of the pool was split. A shaft of intense brightness formed in the midst of its dark mirror. Slowly it widened, until the pool was filled with a light so intense that Kim sat back on his heels, shielding his eyes. A flight of broad, stone steps, inverted by the lens of the water, led down into the dark heart of the earth.

Kim glanced up, his mouth wide open. The Gate was open. Light spilt like fire into the air.

Trembling, he looked down again. The surface of the pool shimmered, rippled. Then, suddenly, its brightness was split by bands of darkness. There were figures in the Gateway! Tall shapes of darkness, straight as spears!

He looked up, astonished, staring through his latticed hands. Jagged shadows traced a hard-edged shape upon the steps. Kim knelt there, transfixed, staring up into the portal.

He gasped. What *were* they? Light flashed from the darkness of their vast, domed heads – from the winking, glittering, brilliant darkness of their heads. Heads of glass. And, beneath those heads, bodies of silver. Flexing, unflexing silver.

Slowly his hands came down from his face. Light lay in the caves of his eyes, a bright wet point of brilliance at the centre of each pupil. He knelt there, in the darkness at the

234

edge of the pool, watching them come down. Three kings of glass and silver, passing so close to him he could hear the soft sigh and moan of their breathing.

He screamed, a raw, high-pitched sound, the noise dragged up from deep inside him, then huddled into himself, knowing that death was near. The pendant fell from his hand, unnoticed, flashing in the air before the water swallowed it.

One of the giant figures turned and looked down at the huddled boy, barely recognising him as a creature of his own species, seeing only a tiny, malformed shape. A shuddering, thin-boned thing. Some kind of ill-groomed beast, long-maned and filthy.

"Clay . . ." he said beneath his breath, the word heavy with nuances: contempt, disgust, the vaguest trace of guilt. Then he turned away, glad that his face mask filtered out the stench of the place. Through the infra-red of his visor he could see other shapes in movement, some close, some far away. Splashes of warmth against the cold, black backdrop.

He walked on, joining the other, suited men. Behind him, cowering beside the man-sized pool of light, the boy turned and followed him with his eyes, watching him go down into the darkness.

Then they were gone.

Kim stretched, pushing his hands against the soft, wet earth, steadying himself. The trembling passed from him, but still his mouth lay open, his fear transformed to wonder.

He turned, looking up at the Gate, a shiver running down his spine.

A wartha! The Above! The words formed in his head, framed in awe, like an incantation. He cupped water in one hand and wet his lips, then said the words aloud, whispering them, in an accent as malformed as himself.

"A wartha . . ."

Again he shivered, awed by what he had seen. And in his head he pictured a whole world of such creatures; a world of liquid, brilliant light. A world above the darkness and the Clay.

His mouth formed a tiny O, round as his eyes.

Above him the Gate began to close, the pillar of brilliant silver fading into black, the broad steps swallowed slowly by the dark. And afterwards the blackness seemed more intense, more horrible than it had ever been. Like a giant hand it pressed down on him, crushing him, making him gasp for each breath. Again he screamed, a new, unbearable pain, born of that moment, gripping his insides, tugging at him.

The Light . . .

His fingers groped wildly in the mud, then flailed at the water, looking for fragments of the pearled light. But he was blind. At first his fingers found nothing. Then, for the third time, his fingers closed upon a slender length of chain, sought out the tiny metal pendant and drew it up from out of the liquid, holding it to his face, pressing it hard against his lips, not understanding why, yet feeling its presence soothe him, calm him. Like a promise.

* * *

It was a web. A giant web. Alive, quiveringly alive, expanding, filling the darkness with its pearls of light. Moist beads of brilliance strung on translucent fibres of light. It grew, at the same time both frail and strong – incredibly strong. The light could not be broken. He stared up at it, open-mouthed, and felt himself lifted, filled with joy. Incredible, brilliant joy, born of the growing light.

Kim lifted his hands to the light, aching to join with it. If only he could reach it; only lift his head and break the surface membrane of the darkness in which he was embedded, breathing fresh air. He stretched towards it, and felt the joy tighten like a metal band about his chest, crushing him.

And woke, tears in his eyes, hunger in his belly.

He shuddered, horrified. It lay all about him like a glue. He rested on it and it pressed its vast weight down on top of him. Each pore of his was permeated by its sticky warmth. It was darkness. Darkness, the very stuff of the Clay.

The dream made him grit his teeth and sit there, rocking back and forth in pain, moaning softly to himself. For the last few days it had been as if he were awake while all about him slept. As if it was their nightmare he inhabited, not his own. Yet there was no waking from their dream of darkness. Their dream outweighed his hope.

He straightened up, shuddering, hearing the movement in the darkness all about him. It was time, then. The tribe was preparing to move.

He got up quickly and went to the corner of the square of brick and stone in which he slept and relieved himself. Then he came back and packed up his few possessions: a blanket, a flint shard, the small bundles containing his treasures, lastly a square of cloth – a scarf of sorts – that had been his mother's.

The one he had known as mother was long dead. He had been taken with her from the carriage and had watched while they held her down by the roadside, feeling a vague disquiet at their actions, not understanding the naked jutting of their buttocks, the squeals from the woman beneath them. But then they had begun to beat her and he had cried out and tried to get to her, desperate to save her from them. And that was all he knew, for one of them had turned and struck him hard with the back of his hand, sending him crashing into the stone of a low wall.

So he had joined the tribe.

Most days he did as they did, thoughtlessly. Yet sometimes a strange, dissociated pain would grip him – something not of the body, but like his glimpse of the light: something intangible yet real. Disturbingly real. And he would know it had to do with her. With a vague sense of comfort and safety. The only comfort, the only safety he had ever known. But mainly he shut it out. He needed his wits to survive, not to remember.

Kim stood at the edge of the group while Baxi spoke. They were going to raid a small settlement further down the valley, counting upon surprise to win the encounter. They would kill all the men and boys. Women, girls and babies they would capture and bring back alive.

Kim listened, then nodded with the rest. It would be his first raid. He clutched his flint anxiously, excitement and fear alternating in him; hot and cold currents in his blood. There would be killing. And afterwards there would be meat. Meat and women. The hunters laughed and grunted among themselves. Kim felt his mouth water, thinking of the meat.

They left eight men behind to guard the settlement. The rest followed Baxi down the stream in single file, keeping low and moving silently. Four hands of men, running swiftly, lithely down the stream path, their bare feet washed by the greasy, sluggish flow. Kim was last of them and smallest. He ran behind them like a monkey, hands touching the ground for balance as he crouched forward, the flint shard between his teeth.

There was a tumble of rocks, a small stretch of flat, exposed land, and then the other settlement. There was no chance of subtlety, only of surprise. Baxi sprang from the rocks and sprinted silently across the open space, the knife raised high. Rotfoot and Ebor were after him at once, running as fast as their legs could carry them, followed a moment later by others of the tribe.

It nearly worked. Baxi was almost on the guard when he turned and called out. His cry rose, then changed in tone. He went down, the knife buried to the hilt in his chest, its tip jutting from a point low in his back.

Kim squatted on the highest of the rocks, watching as the fight developed. He saw Baxi scream and curse as he tried to free the knife from the dead man's rib cage, then turn to fend off a defender's blow. Others of the tribe were struggling with the strangers, some of them rolling on the ground, some exchanging vicious swinging blows with flints and cudgels. The air was alive with grunts and screams. Kim could smell the stink of fear and excitement in the darkness.

He watched, afraid to go down, repulsion battling with the fascination he felt. His tribe was winning. Slowly the defenders left off trying to fight their attackers and, one by one, began to run away. Already his side were dragging away the unconscious women and girls and squabbling over the corpses. But still small pockets of the fight went on. Kim saw and realised where he was, what he had been doing. Quickly he scrambled across the rocks and dropped down onto the ground, fearing what Baxi would do if he saw.

He had held back. Shown fear. He had let down his tribe.

Kim hurried across the uneven ground, stumbling, then hurled himself onto the back of one of the escaping defenders. His weight brought the man down, but the stranger was twice Kim's size and in an instant Kim found himself on his back, pinned down, the scarred, one-eyed stranger staring down at him. That single eye held death. The stranger's right hand clutched a rock. He raised the rock.

Kim had only an instant in which to act. As if he saw someone beyond and above the stranger, he called out anxiously, looking past the stranger's face.

"Nyns!" he screamed. *No!* "Ny mynnes ef yn-few!" *We want him alive!*

It was enough to make the stranger hesitate and shift his weight, half-turning to see who it was behind him. It was also enough to allow Kim to turn sideways and tip the stranger from him.

One-eye rolled and turned, facing Kim, angry at being tricked, but conscious that each moment's delay brought his own death closer. He swung wildly with the rock and misjudged. Kim lunged in with his sharply pointed flint, aiming for the softest, most vulnerable place, and felt his whole arm judder as he connected. There was a moment of sickening contact, then Kim saw the man's face change

239

into a mask of naked pain. One-eye had been castrated, his testicles crushed.

One-eye fell at Kim's side, vomiting, his hands clutching at his ruined manhood. Kim jerked his hand away, leaving the flint embedded where it was, then looked about anxiously.

Baxi was watching him, smiling ferociously.

Kim looked back, appalled, hearing the wretch heaving up each painful breath. Then, as he watched, Baxi came close, the knife in his hand, and pushed its point deep into the base of One-eye's neck.

One-eye spasmed and then lay still.

"Da," said the chief and turned away. *Good*. Kim watched him strut, triumphant, self-satisfied, then throw back his head and whoop into the air.

A web . . . A web of sticky darkness. Kim felt a warmth, a kind of numbness, spread outward from the core of him, a hand of eight fingers closing on him slowly like a cage, drawing him down beneath the surface of the dark. Darkness congealed above him like a lid, tar in his open mouth. And then he fainted.

* * *

They had never heard him say a word. Baxi thought him dumb or just simple, and others took their lead from that. They called him "Lagasek", or Starer, for his habit of looking so intently at an object. That, too, they saw as a sign of his simplicity.

For an age, it seemed, he had been as if asleep among them. Their hideous shapes and forms had become as familiar as the darkness. He had watched them without understanding, seeing their scars and deformities as natural things, not departures from some given norm. But now he was awake. He stared at them through newly-opened eyes, a bright thread of thought connecting what he saw to the sharp-lit centre of awareness at the back of his skull.

He looked about the flickering fire at their missing hands and eyes, their weeping sores and infected scabs; saw them cough and wheeze for breath, aged well beyond their years, and wondered what he was doing there among them.

Sitting there in the dust, the thick and greasy soup warm in his belly, he felt like weeping. As he looked about the small circle of men and boys he saw, for the first time, their gauntness, their strange furtiveness. They twitched and scratched. They stretched and stood to urinate, their eyes never still, never settling for long, like the blind white flies that were everywhere in the Clay.

Yes, he understood it now. It had begun there with that glimpse of otherness – that vision of glass and silver, of kings and brightness. He felt like speaking out – telling them what he had seen at the Gate, what he had done to scare off the intruders – but habit stilled his tongue. He looked down at his tiny, narrow hands, his long thin arms. There were no scars but there were sores at the elbows and the bone could be seen clear beneath the flesh.

He looked away, shuddering, his face filled with pain and a strange, hitherto untasted shame, then looked back again. They were talking among themselves now, their crude, half savage speech suddenly foreign to his ear. It made him feel uneasy, as if he had knowledge of something better, some long-buried memory of things before the tribe. Across from him Tek and Rotfoot exchanged half-hearted blows in savage-gentle play, their broken faces filled with light and shadows. He lifted his head, sniffing at them in instinct, then settled, realising what he was doing, filled with a sudden, intense sense of self-disgust.

For a moment he closed his eyes, feeling the warmth on his face and arms and chest. That too was strange. It was rare to have a fire. Rare to sit as they sat now, the circle of the dark behind, the circle of the light in front. But this was a special time.

Baxi sat in his place, on a huge, rounded stone above the others. A stack of wood – itself a kind of treasure – lay at his side. From time to time he would reach down and throw a piece upon the blaze, growling with pleasure.

241

They had found the sacks of firewood in a store room in the conquered settlement; three of them, hidden beneath a pile of other things scavenged from the dump. Baxi had brought them back and built the fire himself with a care that made Kim think he had seen it done before. Then he had gone down to his cellar, returning moments later with the fire-stick.

Kim had watched them all gasp and fall back as the flame leapt from his hand and spread amongst the gathered wood, muttering darkly between themselves, their eyes filled with fear and fascination. But Kim had known. He had crouched there, still and silent, watching as the fire kindled, like some strange, living creature jumping from one dark surface to another, consuming all it touched. Like the unspoken thoughts in his head, he realised. Yet this had a voice, a crackling, popping, sputtering voice, its breath strangely thick and dark, curled like a beard, yet evanescent – vanishing into the dark above the blaze.

For a brief moment it seemed he understood; held in his head a key to the pattern of all things. Then it too was gone, drawn up into the darkness overhead.

He felt misplaced. Torn from the light and cast down into darkness. But if misplaced, what then? How could he change things?

Run away, a small voice inside him called out. *Run far away. To a place where the darkness ends.*

He looked out beyond the fire, blinded by its brilliance, seeing nothing but the after-image of the flames. The darkness was unending and eternal. There was nothing but the darkness . . .

No, he reminded himself. Not true. There is a place of brightness. Up there. *A wartha.*

Among the gods.

Not only that, but there was a way. A single door into the brightness. A one-way door that often led to death, or so the men said. A door that only the youngest and the bravest took.

Kim looked down at his hands again. He was young,

242

but was he brave enough? Was he prepared to risk everything on a single gamble?

He thought of the escapade with the mirror and the fire-stick and his spirits rose. Then the image of himself, scared and cowering on the rocks, came back to him. His stomach knotted. He wanted it. Wanted the brightness like he wanted life itself. But he was afraid. Dreadfully, awfully, numbingly afraid. He felt he could not do it – would die before he took the first step.

Better to stay here a thousand years . . .

A cold shiver passed through him, ice beneath the firelight on his face and chest and limbs. No, not that. Death was preferable to that.

He looked up. On the far side of the fire, beyond Rotfoot, stood Baxi, watching him. For a moment their eyes met and locked and some kind of raw understanding passed between them. And, in the moment before he looked away, Kim saw a crude kind of affection there in the older man's eyes: a strange, almost wistful tenderness that he found unsettling.

Far away, said the voice inside. *To a place where the darkness ends.*

Kim rose and turned to face the darkness. The heat lay on his naked back, like the promise of comfort, but now his face was cold and the tension in him was worse than it had ever been. For a moment longer he hesitated, need and fear at war within him. Then, with a violent shudder, he nodded to himself and jerked away from the fire, his decision made.

He would go. Now. Before the darkness took him back.

★ ★ ★

The sign was ancient. Time had turned the whiteness of its paint a mottled grey, had faded the dark, heavy lettering. Where the bolts held it to the wall a red-gold rust had formed two weeping eyes.

Kim looked up at it, struggling to understand. Like so

243

much else it was a mystery; a symbol of all the things denied him. He studied the strange yet familiar shapes of the letters, wondering what they meant, filling the gap, the darkness of incomprehension, with his own meanings. The first letter was easy. It was an arrow, facing to the left. There was a gap and then the second, its double curves facing away from the arrow like a straight-backed woman's breasts. The third was a ring. The fourth a drawn bow. The fifth? Two steep hills, perhaps, linked by a valley. The sixth again was easy. It was an upright column, like the column beyond the wall. The seventh? He felt the seventh was like the fifth, yet its difference – its lack of an upright strut – was significant. A gate, maybe. Or two interlocking flints – perhaps the sign for war. Then, after another gap, came the last of them; an eye with a dark, curled eyebrow overhead, linked at the eye's left corner.

But what did it mean in total? What message had it once conveyed?

He looked about him, then ducked beneath the rotten lintel, pushing through the gap in the wall. There, like some vast subterranean serpent breaching the far wall of the ruined building, stood the column, its silvered surface gleaming in the half-light.

Kim stumbled forward and stood before it, his eyes drawn upward to where it met the ceiling of the Clay far overhead. There were many such pillars spread regularly throughout the Clay, but this one, Kim knew, was slightly different from the others. It was a gate. An entrance into the Above.

Long ago they had chased a boy from another tribe across the nearby hills and trapped him here, between the walls of this old, ruined building. Faced with certain death, the boy had turned, gone to the pillar and pressed his hands against it.

Miraculously, the pillar had opened. A narrow aperture had formed in its perfect roundness, a dim, fierce light burning out from the space within. Fearfully, with a backward glance at them, the boy had gone inside. At once the opening had closed, throwing the space between the walls into an intense and sudden darkness.

They had camped there some while, waiting for the boy to come out, but he never had. And when one of the older boys grew brave enough to approach the pillar and press against it, they could all see that the space inside was empty.

It had eaten the boy.

For a time he had believed this version of events, and in truth part of him still believed it, making him cower there, terrified to enter. But the newly-woken part of him reasoned otherwise. What if the boy had not been killed? What if he had been taken up into the Above?

They were huge assumptions. Hunches, not certainty. And the boy had gone inside only because he had had no option. But what of himself? There were no knives awaiting him should he turn away. Only the darkness. Only the foetid Clay.

He grimaced and closed his eyes, tormented by indecision. He didn't want to die. He didn't want to be wrong.

Is death any worse than this?

The thought came like a voice in his head, and with the voice came the realisation that he was no longer a single creature. There were two of him, sharing a single skull, a single body. One dark, one light. One kept him here, the other craved escape. Here, at the gate to the Above, they would have to fight it out between them.

For a time the darkness had him and he stood there, thoughtless, his animal self shuddering uncontrollably, a gobbet of spittle dribbling down his chin. Then, with an abruptness that caught the animal unaware, Kim threw himself at the column and scratched at its surface, trying to find an opening.

He could hear himself gibbering with fear, and in another moment he would have backed away, defeated, but suddenly the aperture slid open with an outbreath of air and he tumbled in, onto the smooth, uncluttered floor, his hands going up to cover his eyes against the brilliance.

The brightness hurt him. It cut into his head like a flint.

Then the door hissed shut behind him, trapping him. He whimpered in fear then lay there, shivering, his legs drawn up beneath him, waiting to die.

Yet what happened next seemed worse than death. The light in the room pulsed gently and a deep voice boomed out, filling the narrow space.

"Kewsel agas hanow, map!" *Speak your name, boy!* "Agas hanow!"

Kim gagged, then shat himself. His muscles went into spasm. For a while he could do nothing to control them. Again he was an unthinking animal, there on the floor inside the alien column. A stinking piece of quivering meat and bone. Then the bright thing in him bobbed up again and floated on the surface of his awareness. His name? What *was* his name?

"Laga . . ." He could not say it. He'd had too little practice. In any case, it was wrong. Lagasek – Starer – was not his name; or, if his name, then his name only in the darkness. It was not the name his mother had given him. Not the name he wished to take with him into the light.

He tried again. "Kim," he said finally, the word strange, more awkward in his mouth than in his head. His voice barely sounded the K and the rest of it was inaudible.

"Kewsel arta," said the voice. *Speak again.* It seemed much warmer than before; more soothing.

"Kim," he said more clearly, then lay there, perfectly still, wondering what would happen.

"Da, Kim," said the voice. *Good.* "Praga bos why omma?" *Why be you here?* "Praga prak why entradhe hemma pylla?" *Why did you enter this pillar?* "Gul nebonen sewya why?" *Does someone pursue you?*

"Nyns," he answered. *No.*

"Nyns," the voice repeated and then chuckled to itself. What it said next was difficult to follow. The words were alien to Kim, like the nonsense utterances of his nightmares. "We've a fluent one here." This last seemed not to be directed at Kim.

Kim sat up, looking around him. Then he stood and

went to the curve of the wall across from where the opening had been. No, he hadn't been mistaken: there was a shape in the wall's otherwise unblemished face. A pattern of light, almost too faint to see. He stood beside it, trying to figure it out.

"Ah," said the voice. "My gweles why cafos an matrix." *I see you've found the . . .* But the last word was new. It was like the other words – alien.

Kim twitched and turned about sharply. The creature with the voice was watching him, then. Was close by. He stared up into the dimly-lit tunnel overhead and tried to make out something in the darkness, but it seemed empty.

"Matrix?" Kim asked, pronouncing the word carefully, as if feeling the shape of it in his mouth.

There was laughter – soft, warm laughter – then the voice came back. "My bos ken tyller," it said, as if that explained everything. *I be somewhere else.* "Ha an tra a-dherak why bos un matrix." *And that thing before you be a matrix.* "Ef gul pycturs ha patron." *He make pictures and patterns.*

Kim struggled to understand, but could grasp nothing of what the voice was saying. Pictures? Patterns? How did it make these things?

"Gasa-vy dysquehs why." *Let me show you.*

The faint area glowed, then seemed to explode with colour.

Kim shrieked and leaped backward, scrambling away until his back was against the far curve of the wall.

"Ef ny a-wra pystyk why. Golyas. Kensa un fas." *He won't harm you. Watch. First a face.*

The screen formed a face. A typical face from the Clay, seen in partial darkness, its scars and deformities nothing unusual. Kim nodded, his eyes watching the matrix closely.

"Nessa, un patron. Un semple patron. Tyby kettep myn bos un men." *Next, a pattern. A simple pattern. Imagine each point be a stone.* "My muvya an meyn formya un form. Un patron." *I move the stones to form a shape. A pattern.*

When the image on the screen reformed it showed three lines of three points. A square.

"Den lufyow, le un bys," said Kim. *Two hands, less a finger.* It was the most he had said until then.

"Ahah," said the voice, and this time Kim could hear a second voice speak softly in the background. "Numerate, this one. That's rare." The hair on his neck stood up, hearing that foreign tongue again, and his lips peeled back, his dark self hostile to it, knowing it for the language of the light.

Unknown to him, however, he had taken his first step into the Above. And when the voice sounded again its tone was slightly different: less cosy, much more businesslike.

"Dos ogas an matrix, Kim. Dos ogas ha my deryvas why fatel muvya an meyn a drodhe."

Come near the matrix, Kim. Come near and I'll tell you how to move the stones about.

CHAPTER · 7

MACHINES OF FLESH

Klaus Ebert, Head of GenSyn, Chung Kuo's second largest company, looked down at the corpse on the dissecting table and slowly shook his head.

"No, Knut. I've never seen its like."

He pointed out its internal structure: the lack of a spleen; the simplification of the respiratory system; the artificial latticework of the rib cage; the replacement of the stomach and intestinal system by a single sack, sealed off and unconnected to the anus. Most obvious of all was the flat, compact battery, like a black lacquered hipflask, placed where the human liver should have been.

"I'll have my experts look at this, but it's not GenSyn, that's certain. It isn't even organic. It's just a machine; too simple to function longer than a few months. It can't digest. It can't even process blood. Whoever built it designed it for rapid redundancy."

Ebert turned, facing the General, his face ashen.

"Gods, Knut, but it's so like me, isn't it? Looking at it there, it feels like part of me has died."

The General studied his old friend a moment, then looked back at the part-dissected corpse. It was a perfect copy. Too good in some respects. He had seen the films of it before his men had neutralised it – saw how cleverly it had mimicked Ebert's voice and mannerisms. And if there had been something unnatural about it, something just a bit too animated about its speech, its gestures, that was only noticeable in retrospect. It had been good enough to fool Ebert's personal staff. But the eyes . . . When the thing had been cornered in Ebert's private suite, those eyes had burned, like the eyes of an addict.

"Who could have built this, Klaus? Who has the know-how?"

Ebert laughed uncomfortably. "GenSyn. MedFac, maybe. No one else. At least, no one on-planet."

The General looked up sharply. "You think it's from outside, then? From one of the colonies?"

Ebert dragged his eyes away from the dead thing on the table, then turned his back on it. "I don't know, Knut. Six months back I'd have said no, but I've seen a few strange things since then. Controls are less tight out there. The Edict has less force . . ." He shook his head. "The Seven should do something, Knut. Now. Before it's too late."

"I know," the General said simply. But he was thinking of DeVore. If what the *kwai*, Kao Chen, had said were true it would explain much.

And Wyatt? He pushed the thought away. Wyatt was guilty. There was the evidence. Even so . . .

Ebert was looking at him, fear in his eyes. "What does this mean, Knut? Why would they want to copy me? I don't understand."

The General shuddered. Nor I, he thought, not fully, anyway, but now I'm forearmed. We can rig up check-points. Scan for copies. Make sure nothing like this gets into the Forbidden City.

There would be more than a hundred thousand guests at the wedding. And not one of them could be allowed to pass through without being tested. For if just one of these . . . *things* got through, it might prove disastrous.

He reached out and took his old friend's arm. "I'm sorry, Klaus, but I think they meant to substitute this thing for you at the wedding. It was their way of getting at the T'ang."

"You mean they meant to kill me, Knut?"

Tolonen met his eyes. "I think so. They know how close

you are to Li Shai Tung, and this . . ." He hesitated, then looked away, shaking his head. "Look, I don't know who's behind this, Klaus, but it couldn't have come at a worse time."

"Or more fortunate?"

Tolonen turned back. "What do you mean?"

Ebert was looking down at the replicant's left hand; at the ring on the second finger with its insignia of two separated strands of DNA – an exact copy of his own. He looked back at Tolonen. "It just seems odd, Knut, that's all. Odd how easily we caught this one. And yet I can't believe they would want us to know about this. This . . ." He pointed at the corpse-like thing on the table. "It must have cost . . . what . . . eighty, maybe a hundred million yuan to build. And that's without the initial R&D costs. Why, there's memory technology involved here that we haven't even begun to explore at GenSyn. That alone would have cost them two or three hundred million yuan minimum. And maybe three, four times that. They wouldn't throw that away casually, would they?"

"No. I suppose they wouldn't."

But Tolonen was already thinking things through – aware of the huge administrative nightmare this would create. They would have to set up a network of gates in front of the Forbidden City. Secure rooms. Thousands of them, specially equipped to check for fakes. And they would need to rehearse more than twenty thousand stewards in the subtle questions of etiquette and "face" involved.

The General sighed, then tugged his uniform gloves tighter, aware that his craft had been waiting twenty minutes now. He would have to leave soon if he was to meet DeVore off the Mars shuttle. "This will cause a great deal of bad feeling, Klaus. But you're right, it was fortunate. And now we know these things exist we can't afford to take chances. The lives of the Seven are at risk, and I'd offend every last man and woman in the Above to protect the Seven."

Ebert laughed. "I do believe you would, Knut Tolonen."

Then he grew serious. "But why now, Knut? Things are good, aren't they? We've built a good world, haven't we? Why do they want to tear it down, eh? Why?"

Tolonen looked up and saw how Ebert was watching him. Saw how, in this, he was looking to him for answers.

"Because the cycle's ending, Klaus. I feel it in my bones. Change is coming."

Yes, he thought. And things we thought true are no longer so. He looked at the dead thing on the table and thought of DeVore. At least this fake was honest to itself. Was *built* a fake. But men? Who was to say what moulded them for ill or good?

* * *

It was just after four in the morning and Nanking Port lay in darkness, a loose-spaced ring of lights, five *li* from the central hub, tracing the periphery of the vast apron.

Tolonen stood in the topmost office of the towering Port Authority Building, the duty captain at attention before him.

"Gone? What do you mean, he's gone?"

The young captain bowed deeply to the visiting General, his cheeks red with embarrassment.

"He's not aboard the ship, sir. When our men went to arrest him, he simply wasn't there. And no one could say where he'd gone."

Tolonen shook his head in disbelief.

"That's impossible! How could he get off the ship? It's moored at the orbital station, isn't it?"

"Yes, sir."

"Well? He was aboard only eight hours ago, wasn't he?"

"Yes, sir."

"So he's either still aboard or on that station, no?"

"No, sir. We've searched both ship and station thoroughly."

Tolonen's anger exploded. "Incompetents! How could you let him get away from you?" He snorted. "Where could he be, eh? Out there? In the vacuum? No! Think, boy! He *must* be here. On Chung Kuo. But how did he get here? Who brought him down?"

"Sir?" The captain was totally flustered now.

"What service craft have visited the station in the past four hours? What ships, beside your own, have left the station since the Colony Ship docked?"

"None, sir."

"None? Surely . . ."

"We put a *cordon sanitaire* about the station as soon as you instructed us, General. No service craft has docked at or left the station in the past thirteen hours."

The General shivered. "Who was aboard your craft?" he asked softly.

"Sir?" The captain stared back at him blank-faced, not understanding.

"I want them brought here. Now. Everyone who was aboard your patrol craft."

"Sir!" The captain bowed, then turned away.

Tolonen went to the window and looked up into the circle of darkness overhead, his thoughts in turmoil.

Then it was true what the *kwai*, Kao Chen, had said. DeVore *was* the traitor. Tolonen shuddered. It was hard to believe. DeVore . . . The man had been such an excellent soldier. Such a fine, efficient officer. More than that, he had been a friend. A good friend. Had been a guest in the General's home many a time. Had held Tolonen's baby daughter, Jelka, in his arms.

Tolonen turned, facing the doorway. If DeVore were to come into the room right now and swear he'd had no part in things, would I believe him? Yes! Even now I find the whole idea of DeVore as a traitor unbelievable. I would have known. *Surely* I would have known?

And yet his absence . . .

The captain returned, followed by a dozen others. They formed up, awaiting the General's pleasure.

"This is all?"

The captain bowed his head deeply, then went down onto his knees. "Sir, I . . . I don't know how this happened." He kept his head bent low, his eyes averted. His shame seemed to radiate from him.

"They're gone, too, eh?"

The captain continued to kneel. "Yes, sir."

"How many?"

"Two officers. Eight men."

Tolonen shook his head in disbelief. Ten men! Was DeVore's influence that strong, then? Or was it something else? He turned away, deeply agitated. Of course. Dispersionist money. Vast sums of it. Enough to buy out two Security officers and eight underlings.

"Gods!" he said softly. How much would it have cost them? A million yuan? Ten million? Fifty? He shivered, then turned and looked down again at the kneeling officer. "Get up, captain."

The captain remained as he was. "I have failed you, sir. I ask permission to seek an honourable death."

Angered now, Tolonen reached down and pulled the man to his feet.

"I'll not have good officers killing themselves for nothing. It is not your fault. Do you understand me, Captain? DeVore was too clever for you. Too clever for us all."

No, he thought, meeting the captain's eyes. It's really not your fault at all. But now DeVore's at large. What mischief will he do?

The captain backed away, white-faced, bowing. Then, at Tolonen's curt, angry command, he turned and led his men away.

Alone again, Tolonen let his anger drain from him. He went to the window and stood there once more, looking out over the still, dark forms of a hundred different craft, grounded at his order.

The certainty of DeVore's treachery sickened him. More than that, it undermined him, because it contradicted all he had thought he knew about men. His thoughts ran back over the last few years, trying to make sense of things. Could he have known? Was there any way he could have known?

No. DeVore had been the perfect officer. The perfect copy.

Tolonen tapped at the control blisters inset into his wrist and made connection with Major Nocenzi, half the globe away.

"General?" Nocenzi's voice came through clear in his head. His image appeared ghostly on the General's palm.

"Vittorio. I want you to do something for me."

He spoke quickly but clearly, itemising the things he wanted done. Then, finished, he cut connection, knowing time was against him.

So it was here at last, the war Li Shai Tung had long ago said would come. A secretive, dirty war, fought in the darkness between levels. A guerilla war, where friend and enemy had the same face. A war of money and technology and, at the last, sheer cunning. And who would win?

Tolonen smiled.

Karr, he thought. I'll use Karr. He found Chen. Maybe he can find DeVore.

* * *

Wang Ti opened the door slowly, surprised to see the big man standing there, but even more surprised when her husband called out from behind her, telling her to let him in.

Karr bowed his head respectfully and drew off his boots. Bare-footed, he followed Wang Ti through into the back of the apartment, ducking under partitioning curtains.

Chen was sitting on the floor by the back wall, his legs folded under him, the baby asleep in his lap. There was little furniture in the cramped room. A double bedroll was folded neatly against the wall to Chen's right and a low table had been set up next to the *kang*. Wang Ti had been cooking, and the smell of it still hung in the room. From the far side of the long, dividing curtain on Chen's left came the sound of their neighbours' two young sons playing boisterously.

Karr smiled and bowed again, then squatted across from Chen.

"How's the child?"

Chen looked down at his infant son and gently stroked his brow.

"He's well."

"Good."

Wang Ti stood at his side dutifully, head bowed, eyes averted.

"You'll share *ch'a* with us, *Shih* . . . ?"

"Karr . . ." The big man turned slightly and bowed his head, acknowledging her. "I thank you for your kind offer, Wang Ti, but no. I have business to discuss with your husband."

She nodded, then took the baby from Chen's lap and backed away. Karr waited until she had ducked out under the curtaining before speaking again. She would hear all he said, but the illusion of privacy was necessary. It was all the face a man had at these levels.

"You were right, Chen. It was DeVore."

Chen grunted, his blunt peasant face inexpressive. "So what now?"

Karr reached into the inner pocket of his over-shirt and pulled out a thin tab of ice. "Here," he said, offering it.

Chen hesitated, remembering Jyan. He too had made deals with the Above. And where was he now? With his ancestors. Dead, his spirit untended, no sons to burn offerings for his souls.

"What is it?"

Karr laughed. "Still suspicious, eh? You've no need to, Chen. You gave us more than we could have asked for. This . . ." he placed the tab between them on the floor, "This is in settlement. A blanket amnesty. Your citizenship papers. A ten deck security pass. And a bonus. A thousand yuan . . ."

Chen started. Then he was not to follow Wyatt to the block? He stared at the big man open-mouthed.

"You are *kwai*, Chen. A tool. And a good tool. The

General was surprised how good," he laughed. "We Net types, we can teach them a thing or two, eh?"

Still Chen hesitated. Was this all some kind of elaborate ruse? Some awful taunting of him? But then why? Why should they bother?

"Then I'm free?"

Karr looked away, conscious of the woman listening beyond one curtain, the neighbours beyond another. "Not exactly. You'll have to leave this place. After what happened . . ."

"I see."

Karr met his eyes. "We'll re-settle you. Re-train you."

"Re-train me?"

"Yes. You've a new job, Chen. You've joined Security. As my adjutant."

Chen stared, then looked down. "And if I say no?"

Karr shrugged, watching the Han closely. "You are *kwai*, Chen, not a warehouseman. Leave such jobs to good men like Lo Ying."

Chen looked up, suddenly angry. "And how is Lo Ying?"

Karr laughed, remembering how Lo Ying had jumped him. "A brave man, but no fighter. Oh, he's happy now, Chen. He too has his bonus."

Chen looked down at the tab. "You plan to buy me, then?"

Karr hesitated, then shook his head. "I would not insult you so, Kao Chen. We both know that you cannot buy a man's loyalty. However, you can try to earn it." He sat back, then shrugged his great shoulders. "All right. I ask you openly, Kao Chen. Will you become the T'ang's man? Or will you rot here at this level?"

Chen looked down. He had a life here. A good life. There was his wife, his son now to consider. But to be *kwai* again . . . He felt himself torn in two by the offer.

There was a whisper of cloth. Chen looked up past Karr. Wang Ti had come out from behind the curtains and was standing there, staring imploringly at him. Then, abruptly, she came round and threw herself down in front of Karr in a full *k'o t'ou*.

"Wang Ti! What are you doing?"

She lifted her head and glanced at Chen anxiously, then returned her forehead to the ground before the big man.

"My husband accepts your kind offer, *Shih* Karr. He will be honoured to work with you."

★ ★ ★

Han Ch'in stood there silently in the darkened room, his back to the doorway. Outside the two assassins waited. He breathed deeply, calming himself, remembering what he'd been taught. The still man has advantages. He hears better. He has choice of action. The moving man is committed. His strength, his very movement can be used against him.

Let them come to you, then. Feign unawareness. But let your body be as the dragon's, alive, alert to every movement of the air behind your back.

Outside they hesitated. Then the first of them came through.

Han turned when the man was only an arm's length away, ducking low, sweeping his leg out, his left arm straight-punching upward. As the man went down Han rolled backwards and flipped up onto his feet, facing the second assassin.

The dark, masked figure feinted, kicking to Han's left, making shapes with his hands in the air, each movement accompanied by a sharp hiss of expelled breath.

Han shadowed the assassin's movements, knowing he could not afford to do otherwise. He was alone now. Death awaited him if he made the smallest mistake. He had only winded the man on the floor, so time now was precious. He would have to dispense with the man before him, then deal finally with the other.

He saw his chance. The assassin had put his full weight on his right foot. It anchored him. Han feinted further to the right, then leapt, turning in the air and kicking high, aiming for the man's chin.

258

His foot brushed air. Then he was falling.

The assassin was on him in an instant, his forearm locked about Han's neck. Han cried out.

The lights flicked on at once. The two assassins backed away, bowing deeply, respectfully. Han turned over and sat up, gasping for breath. Shiao Shi-we was standing in the doorway, looking in at him, his expression hard to read.

"Again!" he barked finally. "How many times, Han? Have you learned nothing from me?"

Han knelt and bowed to his instructor. Shi-we was right. He had been impatient.

"I am sorry, Master Shiao. I was worried about the second man."

Shiao Shi-we made a small sound in his throat, then lifted his chin. Han Ch'in got to his feet at once.

"You are a good fighter, Han Ch'in. Your reflexes are as good as any man's. Your body knows how to move. How to kick and punch. How to block and fall and roll. You have real courage. A rare thing. Yet for all these qualities you lack one vital thing. You have not learned to think as your opponent thinks."

Han bowed again, chastened.

"What then should I have done, Master Shiao? Should I have waited for him to attack?"

Shiao Shi-we was a small man, almost a head shorter than his seventeen-year-old pupil. His head was shaved and oiled and he was naked but for a small, dark red loincloth. His chest and forearms and legs were heavily muscled, yet as he crossed the room he moved with the grace of a dancer. He was sixty-five years old, but looked forty.

He stood in front of Han Ch'in, looking up at the T'ang's heir, but there was no deference in his posture. In this room Shiao Shi-we was as a father to Han Ch'in. Once, ten years before, he had put the young boy across his knee and spanked him for his impertinence, and when Han Ch'in had gone before his father to complain, the T'ang had merely laughed, then, growing stern, had ordered the punishment repeated, so that the lesson should be learned. Since that time Han Ch'in had known better than to argue with his tutor.

"Three things," began Shi-we. "Discipline, patience and control. Without them even a good fighter is certain to lose. With them . . ." The tutor lifted his head proudly, the muscles of his neck standing out like ridges of rock, ". . . the good becomes the supreme."

There was a noise in the doorway. Without turning, Shiao Shi-we lifted a hand. "Please wait there a moment, Yuan. I must finish talking to your brother."

Li Yuan made a tiny bow to the instructor's back, amazed, as ever, that the old man could tell, without looking, who it was behind him. Each man has his own sounds, he'd once said. How he moves, who he *is* – these things can be distinguished as distinctively as the grain of a man's skin, the identifying pigmentation of the retina. Still yourself, listen, learn to tell the sound of your friend from that of your enemy, and such skills might one day save your life.

So it might be, but try as he had, Li Yuan had found he could not distinguish the sound of his brother from that of one of his servants. If it's a skill, he thought, it's one few men possess. Better then to have a good man at one's back.

Li Yuan looked past Shiao Shi-we at his brother. Han Ch'in had his head lowered and there was a slight colour in his cheeks. *What has Han done now?* he wondered, knowing how impulsive he was. *Has he "died" again?*

Master Shiao sniffed loudly, then pointed to Han's left. "Position."

Han moved at once, standing where he had been only a minute or so before, facing the assassin. Shiao Shi-we gave a slight nod then positioned himself in front of his pupil. "Discipline," he said, crouching down and rubbing at his thighs, warming himself up. "Patience." He straightened, then twisted at the waist to left and right, relaxing the muscles there. "And control."

Without warning, Shiao Shi-we launched himself at Han Ch'in.

Li Yuan gasped, startled by the abruptness of Shiao Shi-we's attack. But Han had moved back and away, and Shi-we's fist merely glanced the side of his face. Had it connected it would have broken his nose.

Han Ch'in moved back quickly, breathing heavily, clearly shaken by the violence of the attack. Yet he made no complaint. Crouching, flexing his body, he prepared himself for the next attack, calming his breathing, repeating the triad in his mind. *Discipline. Patience. Control.*

The next assault was like nothing either boy had ever seen before. Shiao Shi-we ran at Han in a zig-zag, almost lunatic manner, his movements like those of an automaton. And as he ran a strange, unsettling scream came from his widely-opened mouth.

Through half-lidded eyes Han Ch'in watched him come and, at the last moment, ducked and came up under the older man, tossing him into the air, then turned to face him again.

"Excellent!" Shiao Shi-we was on his feet, unharmed. He smiled momentarily, then grimaced as he threw himself at Han again.

So it went on, Shiao Shi-we attacking wildly, Han Ch'in defending, until, with a suddenness that was as surprising as the first attack, the old man backed off, bowing deeply.

"Good!" he said, looking at his pupil with pride. "Now go and bathe. Young Yuan must have his hour."

Han bowed and did as he was bid. Li Yuan turned, watching him go, then turned back, facing Master Shiao.

"You could have killed him," he said softly, still shocked by what he had seen.

Shiao Shi-we looked away, more thoughtful than Li Yuan had ever seen him before. "Yes," he said finally. "I could have, had he not fought so well."

★ ★ ★

"Well, Chen, will you come to bed?"

Wang Ti pulled back the cover and patted the space beside her on the bed. Chen had been silent all day, angry with her for her intervention. She had understood and had gone about her business patiently, but now it was evening and Jyan was asleep. Now he would have to talk to her. She would not have him lie beside her still angry with her, his innermost thoughts unpurged.

"Well, husband?"

He turned, looking across at her in the faint light of the single lamp, then looked down, shaking his head.

So. She would have to be the one to talk.

"You're angry with me still?"

He did not look at her, merely nodded. His whole body was stiff and awkward, shaped by the words he was holding back. She sat up, unfastening her hair, letting the covers fall from her breasts.

"You would have said no."

He looked at her mutely, looked away, then looked back again, his eyes drawn to her breasts, her shoulders. Meeting her eyes, he sighed and shrugged.

"You would have said no. And then you would have felt trapped. Bitter. With me. With Jyan. I would have had to watch your joy in us turn to sourness."

He began to shake his head but she was insistent, her voice soft yet firm.

"It is so, Kao Chen. I know it is so. You think I could live with you this long and not know it?"

He looked at her uncomprehendingly.

"I knew. Understand? Knew you were *kwai*."

Chen's eyes were wide. "You *knew*? When? How?"

She patted the bed beside her. "When I first met you. I knew at once. Even before my father told me."

Chen crossed the room and sat beside her. "Your father? He knew as well?"

"Oh, Chen. You think we didn't know at once? One look at you was enough. You were like a bird let out of its cage.

262

We knew from the first that you weren't born in these levels. And as for your papers . . ."

Chen looked down at her hand where it lay above the bedclothes and covered it with his own. "And yet you married me. Why, if you knew?"

She hesitated, then took his other hand. "You met Grandfather Ling?"

Chen nodded, remembering the wizened, grey-haired old man who had sat silently at the back of the room when he had negotiated for Wang Ti's hand. He recalled how the old man's eyes had followed his every movement.

"Yes. I remember Wang Ling. What of him?"

Wang Ti smiled. "He was *kwai*. Like you. And, like you, he came up from the Net."

Chen laughed, astonished. "And you say your father knew?"

"He made . . . enquiries."

Chen shook his head, astonished. "Enquiries . . . And none of you minded? You, Wang Ti . . . you knew and yet you didn't mind what I was or where I'd come from?"

She drew him closer, her face only a hand's width from his own, her dark eyes looking deeply into his. "You are a good man, Kao Chen. I knew that from the first moment I set eyes on you. But this last year I've seen you suffer, seen you put bit and bridle on, and my heart has bled for you."

She shook her head, her teeth momentarily clenched between parted lips. "No, Chen, the big man was right. You are not a warehouseman."

He shivered, then, slowly, nodded to himself. "Then it is as you said, Wang Ti. I will be *kwai* again."

Wang Ti laughed softly, then drew Chen down beside her, drawing the sheet back to expose her nakedness. "Ah, you foolish man. Don't you understand me yet? To me you have always been *kwai*."

She reached down, freeing his penis from the folds of the cloth and taking it firmly in her hand. "Here, give me your knife, I'll sheath it for you."

* * *

The General leaned across the huge scale model of the *Tzu Chin Ch'eng*, the Purple Forbidden City, indicating the group of buildings gathered about the *Yu Hua Yuan*, the Imperial Gardens.

"We could close the *Shen Wu* Gate and the *Shun Ch'en* Gate and cut off the six Eastern palaces and the six Western palaces, here and here. That would make things easier."

Shepherd came round him and looked at the two huge gates at the rear of the Imperial City for a moment, then nodded.

"Yes. But why stop at that? Why not seal the whole of that area off? That way we could concentrate on a much smaller area. In fact, why not seal off everything we're not going to use? Close the *Hung I Ko* and the *T'i Jen Ko*, too. Confine the lesser guests to the space between the Meridian Gate and the Hall of Supreme Harmony. Likewise, confine those special guests who will attend the second ceremony to the Inner City and the Imperial Gardens."

Tolonen shook his head. "Not possible, I'm afraid. Li Shai Tung has prepared a banquet for the lesser guests outside the Arrow Pavilion. He would lose face if he had to cancel that."

Shepherd put his hand to his neck, rubbing away the tiredness. He had barely slept these last three days. And now this. He looked at the model, realising once again how difficult Tolonen's task was. The *Ku Kung*, the Imperial Palace, was composed of almost nine thousand buildings and measured more than two *li* in length, one and a half in width. It covered fifteen hundred *mou* – almost two hundred and fifty acres in the old measure. Even if they sealed off everything he had suggested, it still meant policing over five hundred *mou*.

He looked up from the glass-covered model to the original. They had set the table up in the centre of the courtyard in front of the *Ta'i Ho Tien*, the Hall of Supreme Harmony. In less than twelve hours the whole of this huge open space would be packed with courtiers and guests, servants and Security. He turned, looking back towards the Gate of

Supreme Harmony and, beyond it, the five white bridges crossing the Golden Water. Would something happen here today? Would their enemies succeed? Or could they stop them?

They had talked late into the night; he, Li Shai Tung and Tolonen, knowing that the thing they had found – the "copy" of Klaus Ebert – signified something hugely important. Copies of living individuals – it was something the Seven had long feared would happen, ban or no, and whilst the Edict carried the strictest penalties for straying from its guide-lines in respect of human genetic technology, there had been numerous cases over the years where scientific curiosity had overcome the fear of punishment. Now those harsh measures were vindicated. With such copies in the world who could feel safe in their own body? Who could be trusted?

It was only two days since Wyatt's execution and the shock of that still reverberated around the world. It might be that the Dispersionists planned to answer that. But it was more likely that they had set things in motion long before, hoping to maximise the impact of their scheme by striking when the whole of Chung Kuo was watching.

"The gods be thanked we found the thing in time," Tolonen had said, showing the T'ang the holo of the copy Ebert. "At least we know what we're looking for now." But Shepherd had had his doubts. What if it was a blind? What if all of this were some huge diversionary tactic, designed to make them look elsewhere while the real attack took place? "Would they waste two hundred million yuan on a decoy?" Tolonen had asked him, and he had answered yes. A thousand million. Two thousand. Whatever it took to make them look elsewhere. But the T'ang had agreed with his General. It was a fortunate accident, Ebert returning to his office when he did, and anyway, the thing was too good a likeness to throw away so casually. It was clear that they had meant to kill Ebert and then penetrate the inner sanctum of the Imperial City. There would be others; Li Shai Tung was certain of it. They would set up the gates and check each guest as he entered. And not only guests, but Family and Seven too. For the good of all.

"We'll see," Shepherd had said, accepting his T'ang's final word. But he had been thinking, *And what if there are no further copies? What if they plan to strike some other way?*

Tolonen had been considering his suggestion about sealing off parts of the Imperial City; now he broke into his thoughts. "Maybe you're right, Hal. It would be no great task to seal off the whole of the western side of the City, likewise this part here in the north-east. There's enough room here by the Southern Kitchens to take the overspill and it won't interfere with the banquet."

Shepherd yawned, then laughed. "Best do it quick, Knut, before we all nod off."

The General stared at him a moment, then laughed. "Yes. Of course. I'm sorry, Hal. Would you like something to pep you up? My adjutant could fetch you something."

Shepherd shook his head. "Thank you, but no. I don't believe in tablets. They bugger my system. No, I'll sleep when it's all over."

"As you will." The General hesitated, then reached out and took Shepherd's arm. "Are you feeling real?"

Shepherd laughed. "Real enough. Why's that?"

"The gates are ready. I wanted to test one of them. Will you come through with me?"

"Of course. Lead on."

At the Gate of Heavenly Peace, Shepherd stopped and let his eyes stray upward. Only one *li* away the blank, pearled walls of City Asia began, climbing two *li* into the heavens like the sheer face of a huge glacier, surrounding the ancient capital on every side. This, he reminded himself, was the centre of it all – the very heart of Chung Kuo. Where it had all begun one hundred and eighteen years ago. These had been the first stacks to be built, constructed to his great great grandfather's design. Three hundred levels high, they towered over the old Imperial City. Yet, turning, looking back, he could not decide which was the greater.

The new City was a magnificent achievement, yet did it have even a fragment of the grandeur, the sheer, breathtaking splendour of the Forbidden City?

No. Not the least part.

The gates had been set up in the space between the two Cities. Six lines of them, linked by a maze-like series of corridors, open to the air. It was a hasty, crude-looking arrangement. At various intersections between corridors watch-towers had been set up on stilts overhead, from which both manual and computerised guns pointed downwards.

"They'll not like that," Shepherd said, turning to Tolonen.

"No. I'm afraid they won't. But for once they'll have to put up with it."

Shepherd shook his head sadly. It was bad. Particularly after the execution. It would give the impression that they were entering a new, more brutal era. What ought to be a day of celebration would, for many, take on far more ominous overtones.

But whose fault was that? What other option had they?

"You really think you'll catch some of these copies?"

The General smiled bleakly. "I'm certain of it, Hal. You think I'm wrong, I know. Well, it's possible I am. Anything's possible. Which is why I've prepared for a hundred other unpleasant eventualities. An assault from the air. Bombs. Assassins amongst my own elite guards. Poison in the food. Snipers. Treachery in a hundred different guises. I've read my history. I know how many ways a king can be killed."

Tolonen's granite face showed a momentary tiredness. "I've done dreadful things to safeguard my T'ang, Hal. Awful, necessary things."

Yes, Tolonen thought. Like the killing of the fifteen men who designed these security gates. Fifteen more to add to the vast tally against my name. Good men, too. But their deaths were necessary. To safeguard the Seven. Because without the Seven . . .

He shuddered and pushed the thought away, then began to walk towards the gates. Shepherd fell in beside him, silent now, deep in thought. As they approached the nearest of the gates the elite guards came to attention, shouldering their arms.

"Where's the duty officer?"

"Here, General." The elite squad captain hurried up, then came to attention, bowing formally to both men. "We're almost done, sir. Only another twenty or so to test."

"Good. Then you'll show us to one of the Secure Rooms. I want to show the T'ang's chief advisor what we've prepared."

The captain hesitated, about to say something, then bowed again. "Of course, sir. Please, follow me."

They went to one of the larger gates. Steps led up inside. Behind a curtain was a richly upholstered chair. Surrounding the chair was a whole array of the most up-to-date medical equipment.

"I'm impressed," said Shepherd, looking about him and touching various instruments familiarly. "It all seems very thorough."

The General nodded to the medical technician who had hastily joined them and, without ceremony, began to strip off. "I'll go first. Then you."

Shepherd smiled. "Of course."

There was a slight hiss from behind the curtain, then the sound of a wheel being spun.

"Now we're sealed in. If I'm not who I claim to be – if I'm a fake – then this whole cabin will be filled with a highly toxic gas."

Shepherd laughed. "Then I'll pray you are who you say you are."

Tolonen nodded, then dropped his trousers and stepped out of his webbed pants.

"You've some interesting scars, Knut."

Tolonen looked down, then laughed. "Ah, yes. Believe it or not I got that from a woman. A she-cat she was." He smiled and met Shepherd's eyes. "Ah, but that was long ago. Forty years now."

He sat in the armchair and let himself be wired up. The technician busied himself about him, visibly nervous that he should be called upon to test the T'ang's General.

The first tests were simple body scans. Then he was fingerprinted, his retinal patterns checked and his genotype taken.

The General looked up at Shepherd calmly. "If they're like the Ebert copy then these first few tests should catch them. But I'm taking no chances. Anyway, while we're testing for fakes, we can test for other things – psychological indoctrination and drugs."

"It must have been hard for Klaus."

"He took it very badly."

Shepherd looked away momentarily. "It must be hard to see yourself like that. Dead. Opened up like a sack of meat. Your own face white and cold."

Tolonen said nothing for a moment, then nodded solemnly. "Yes. Anyway . . ."

The technician had been waiting, listening to their talk. Now he pulled a large, dome-shaped machine down from above the General's head.

Tolonen explained. "It's basically a HeadStim. But it's been rewired to monitor bodily responses. It flashes images at me – holograms of senior Family members – and monitors my pulse rate and heartbeat. Any abnormalities register on the tell-tale screen that side."

He reached round the machine as the technician fastened it about his head, and tapped the tiny black screen there.

"It also provides a full brain-scan."

Shepherd looked at it thoughtfully. "As I said. Very thorough. If any more of these things exist, you ought to get them."

The General made no answer. The test had begun. The technician glanced nervously at Shepherd, then busied himself again. Shepherd understood at once. If they found even one of these copies it would be neutralised immediately.

That was good. But the unlucky technician who was in the secure room with it would be neutralised too.

"I shouldn't worry," Shepherd said reassuringly. "I doubt if any more of them exist."

Outside, beyond the great walls of the City, the sun was rising over Pei Ching. The new day – the day of Han Ch'in's wedding – had begun.

* * *

Maria stood in the doorway, looking in at her husband. Josef Krenek was dressing, his back to her. She watched him pull the new silk *pau* about him and fasten it with the cord. Then, and only then, did he turn and answer her.

"What is it, Maria? Can't you see I'm getting ready?"

She had dressed an hour back and had been waiting ever since for him to wake and dress so that she might talk with him.

"It's your brother, Josef. I think he's ill. He hasn't eaten for days, and when I went to wake him there was no answer from his room. He's locked himself in and there's no reply, either from him or from Irina."

Krenek groaned. His brother, Henryk, and his wife had arrived three days ago from Mars and were due to leave tomorrow, after the Wedding. All four were guests of the T'ang, with seats at table before the great Arrow Pavilion. But if Henryk was ill . . .

Krenek pushed past his wife irritably and strode purposefully down the corridor. Stopping before one of the doors he hesitated, then knocked hard.

"Henryk! Are you all right?"

Almost at once the door slid open. His brother stood there, dressed, his midnight blue velvet *ma k'ua*, or ceremonial jacket, tightly buttoned, his dark hair combed back severely from his brow.

"Josef . . . What do you want?"

Krenek bowed slightly, acknowledging his elder brother's status. He had returned from Mars only three weeks ago, newly promoted to Senior Representative of the Colony.

"Maria was worried for you. She . . ."

Henryk Krenek smiled, returning to a lesser degree his brother's bow. His tall, regal-looking wife, Irina, had come across and now stood behind him. Henryk looked past his brother at his brother's wife.

"I'm sorry, Maria, but it was a secret. A gift for my young brother. For being such a good host to us these last three days."

Josef beamed with delight. "It is you who honour me, brother."

"Ah, maybe . . . Even so." Henryk half turned, looking at his wife, then turned back to face his brother. "Perhaps you'd like to come in, Josef? Maria, you'll excuse us a moment?"

Maria bowed low. "I've still much to do, Henryk. I'm sorry I disturbed you with my foolish fears." Her cheeks red, she backed away, then turned and fled down the corridor.

Henryk watched her a moment, then turned and went inside, locking the door behind him.

"Well, brother . . ." he said, turning to face Josef. And even as he said the words he saw Irina come up behind the man and pull the cord tight about his neck, dragging him down with a strange, inhuman strength.

★ ★ ★

Servants made their *k'o t'ou* as Han Ch'in entered the *Chien Ching Kung*, the Palace of Heavenly Purity. Rows of tables had been set up the length and breadth of the great hall. Thousands of tables, filling the space between the pillars. Cloths of imperial yellow covered every table and on each was piled a great heap of wedding gifts.

Han Ch'in looked about him, then ventured into the dimness of the hall. At once two of the servants hastened to accompany the prince, one going before him, the other just behind, each carrying a simple oil lantern on a long pole. It was a tradition that these halls remained unlit by modern power sources: a tradition no one sought to change.

Han Ch'in strode about, examining things, then turned, his face and shoulders lit from above, his dark eyes shining wetly. His shadows stretched away from him on either side, like ghostly dancers, dark and long and thin, flickering in the uneven light. "Yuan! Come! Look at this!"

Li Yuan had paused in the tall doorway, staring up at the richly decorated ceiling. This was his first visit to the Imperial City and he was astonished by its sheer opulence. Their own palaces were so small by comparison, so mean, despite their luxury. This was grandeur on an unimaginable scale. Was beauty almost to excess. He sighed and shook his head. Beauty, yes, and yet this beauty had its darker side. He knew his history: had learned how the *Ch'ing* – the Manchus – who ruled from here for two centuries and more, had fallen, weighed down by their own venality and pride and ignorance. This palace – indeed, this city of palaces – had been built on suffering. On injustice and exploitation.

The history of Chung Kuo – it was a succession of dreams and disappointments, vast cycles of grandeur followed by decadence. It was as if a great wheel turned through Time itself, ineluctable, raising men up, then hurling them down, to be crushed, together with their dreams of peace or further conquest. So it had been, for three thousand years and more, but it was to end such excess that the City had been built. To end the great wheel's brutal turn and bring about the dream of ten thousand peaceful years.

But was the great wheel turning once again, imperceptible beneath the ice? Or had it already come full circle? Were they the new *Ch'ing*, destined in their turn to fall?

"Yuan!" Han stood there beside one of the tables, looking back at him. "Stop day-dreaming and come here! Look at this!"

Li Yuan looked across, then, smiling, went over to him, a servant lighting his way.

Han Ch'in handed him the model of the horse. "It's

beautiful, isn't it? All the gifts from the more important guests have been put on display at this end. The horse is from the Pei family."

Li Yuan turned it in his hands then handed it back. It was solid gold. "It's very heavy, isn't it?"

Han laughed. "Not as heavy as the silver phoenix the House of Representatives has sent as its gift. You should see it! It's enormous! It took eight men to carry it in here!"

Li Yuan looked around him, staring into the shadows on every side. The tables seemed to stretch away forever, each piled with a small fortune of wedding gifts. "There's no end to it, is there?"

Han shook his head, a strange expression in his eyes. "No." He laughed uneasily. "It's astonishing. There are more than eight million items. Did you know that, Yuan? They've been cataloguing them for weeks now. And still more are arriving all the time. The secretarial department are working all hours just sending out letters to thank people. In fact, it's got so bad they've had to take on an extra ten thousand men in the department!"

Han was silent a moment, looking out into the shadowed body of the hall, the torchlight flickering in his dark hair. Then he turned, looking directly at Yuan. "You know, I was thinking, *ti ti* . . ."

Li Yuan smiled at the familiar term. "Young brother", it meant. Yet between them it was like a special name. A term of love.

"*You*, thinking?"

Han Ch'in smiled, then looked away again, a more thoughtful expression on his face than usual. "Look at it all. It fills this hall and five others. Fills them to overflowing. And yet if I were to spend from now until the end of my days simply looking at these things, picking them up and touching them . . ." He shook his head, then looked down. "It seems such a waste, somehow. I'd never get to look at half of it, would I?"

He was silent a moment, then put the horse back. "There are so many things here."

Li Yuan studied his brother a moment. *So it affects you too, this place. You look about you and you think, how like the Ai Hsin Chiao Lo* – the Manchu – *we are, and yet how different. But then you ask, in what way different? And you worry, lest your excesses be like theirs.* He smiled, a faint shiver running down his spine. *Oh, Han Ch'in, how I love you for that part of you that worries. That part of you that would be a good T'ang – that feels its responsibilities so sharply. Don't change, dear elder brother. Don't ever forget the worries that plague you, for they* are *you – are all that's truly good in you.*

Han Ch'in had moved on. Now he was studying one of the big tapestries that were hung against the side wall. Li Yuan came and stood beside him. For a moment they were both silent, looking up through the uneven, wavering lamplight at the brightly coloured landscape, then Han knelt and put his arm about Yuan's shoulders.

"You know, Yuan, there are times when I wish I wasn't heir." His voice was a whisper now. "Sometimes all I want is to give it all away and be normal. Do you understand?"

Li Yuan nodded. "I understand well enough. You are like all men, Han. You want most that which you cannot have."

Han was quiet a moment, then he shook his head. "No. You don't understand. I want it because I want it. Not because I can't have it."

"And Fei Yen? What about Fei Yen? Would you give her up? Would you give up your horse? Your fine clothes? The palaces outside the City? You would really give up all of that?"

Han stared straight ahead, his face set. "Yes. Sometimes I think I would."

Li Yuan turned, looking into his brother's face. "And sometimes I think you're mad, elder brother. The world's too complex. It would not be so simple for you. Anyway, no man ever gets what he truly wants."

Han turned his head and looked at him closely. "And what do you want, *ti ti*?"

274

Li Yuan looked down, a slight colour in his cheeks. "We ought to be going. Father will be looking for us."

Han Ch'in stood, then watched Li Yuan move back between the tables towards the great doorway, the servant following with his lantern. No, he thought, you don't understand me at all, little brother. For once you don't see the drift of my words.

The thought had grown in him this last year. At first it had been a fancy – something to amuse himself with. But now, today, it seemed quite clear to him. He would refuse it. Would stand down. Would kneel before his younger brother.

Why not? he thought. Why does it *have* to be me?

Li Yuan, then. Han smiled and nodded to himself. Yes. So it would be. Li Yuan would be T'ang, not Li Han Ch'in. And he would be a great T'ang. Perhaps the greatest of all. And he, Li Han Ch'in, would be proud of him.

Yes. So it would be. So he would insist it was.

★ ★ ★

Maria Krenek bowed abjectly, conscious that her husband, Josef, had already moved on. "I am deeply sorry, Madam Yu. My husband is not himself today. I am certain he meant nothing by it."

Madam Yu raised her fan stiffly, her face dark with fury, dismissing the smaller woman. She turned to the two men at her side.

"How *dare* he stare through me like that, as if he didn't know me! I'll see that haughty bastard barred from decent company! That'll take him down a few levels! Now his brother is Representative for Mars he thinks he can snub who he likes. Well! We'll see, eh?"

Maria backed away, appalled by what she had heard. Madam Yu was not a woman to make an enemy of. She had entry to the Minor Families. Her gatherings were an essential part of life in the Above – and she herself the means by which one man came to meet another to their mutual benefit. She had destroyed bigger men than Josef Krenek, and now she would destroy him.

"Josef!" she said, softly but urgently, catching up with her husband and taking his arm. "What were you thinking? Go back and kneel before her. For all our sakes, please, go and kneel to her. Say you're sorry. Please, Josef!"

He looked down at her hand on his arm, then across to his brother and his wife. Then, astonishingly, he threw her arm off.

"Go home, Maria. Now! This moment!"

Her mouth gaped. Then, blushing deeply, humiliated beyond anything she had ever known before, Maria turned and ran.

★ ★ ★

Nocenzi's voice sounded urgently in the General's head. "Knut! I've got something!"

The General was standing beside the back entrance to one of the Secure Rooms. They had just unsealed it and brought out the thing that had tried to get through their screen. Like the others it was disturbingly human – better than the Ebert copy. Different. Far more complex. As if the Ebert copy had been an attempt to throw them off the trail.

"What is it, Vittorio?"

"I've checked the incomings at Nanking against the guest list. And guess what?"

"They're coming in from Mars."

"That's right."

"All of them?"

They had caught eight of the copies so far. Eight! It frightened him to think what might have happened if they had not discovered the fake Ebert. But unlike the "Ebert" these were armed. They were walking arsenals, their weaponry concealed inside their flesh. Just two of them could have caused havoc if they had got through. But eight . . .

Nocenzi hesitated, getting confirmation, then, "Every one of them so far."

276

Tolonen knelt over the dead thing, then drew his knife and cut the silks open, revealing its torso. This one was a young woman of seventeen, the daughter of a leading businessman from the Brache settlement. He was waiting inside the Forbidden City, unaware that his daughter had been murdered months ago and replaced by this thing. Tolonen shuddered, trying not to let his emotions cloud his thinking. This was a bad day. A very bad day. But it could have been far worse.

He hesitated, then cut into one of the breasts. Blood welled and ran down the smooth flank of the thing. Tolonen steeled himself and cut again, pulling the flesh apart to reveal the hard, protective case beneath. Yes, it was like the other ones. They all had this protective casing over their essential organs and beneath the facial flesh. As if whoever had made them had designed them to withstand heavy fire: to last long enough to do maximum damage.

"Listen, Vittorio. I want you to get files on all the Mars Colonists we haven't checked yet and get an elite squad to pick them out before they get to the gates. I want one of them alive, understand?"

Alive . . . His flesh crawled. *Functional, I mean. These things were never alive. Not in any real way.*

He got up, signalling to the technicians to take the thing away.

"And Vittorio. Warn your men these things are dangerous. Perhaps the most dangerous thing they've ever had to face."

* * *

As soon as he stepped out into the space between the Cities, Josef Krenek knew something was wrong. Guests were queuing to pass through what seemed like checkpoints. Checkpoints which shouldn't have been there. Beside him Henryk and Irina were unaware that anything was amiss. But then they wouldn't be: their programming was far simpler than his own.

He looked about him, trying to gauge the situation.

277

Three-man elite squads were moving slowly down the lines of people, checking IDs. Further off, above what seemed like some kind of rat run, they had set up guard towers.

They know we're here, he thought at once. Those gates are screens.

Casually he drew Henryk and Irina back, away from the queue, as if they had left something in the reception hall. Then, in an urgent whisper, he told them what he thought was happening.

"What shall we do?" Henryk's cold, clear eyes searched Josef's for an answer. "We've no instructions for this."

Josef answered him immediately. "I want you to go out there, Henryk. I want you to go up to one of those squads and ask them why you have to queue. I want you to find out what they're looking for. Okay?"

"What if they're looking for me? What if they try to arrest me?"

Josef smiled coldly. "Then you'll bring them over here."

He watched Henryk walk out and greet them and saw at once how the soldiers reacted. He heard their shouted questions, then saw Henryk turn and point back to where he stood beside Irina.

Ah well, the part of him that was DeVore thought, it could have worked. Could have worked beautifully. Imagine it! The twelve of them climbing the marble steps, death at their fingertips, the Families falling like leaves before them!

He smiled and turned to Irina. "Do nothing until I say. I'm going to try to get through that lot." He indicated the rat-run of screens and corridors and guard-towers. "But not directly. With any luck they'll take me through. If not . . ."

Henryk came up and stood before them, one of the elite Security guards holding his arm loosely. Other squads were hurrying from elsewhere, heading towards them.

"What seems to be the problem, captain?" Josef said, facing the officer calmly.

"For you, sir, nothing. But I'm afraid your brother and his wife must accompany me. I've orders to detain all Mars Colonists."

Josef hid his surprise. Why not me? he wondered. Then he understood. They've seen the Mars connection. But I wasn't brought in that way. I was here already. The first to come. The lynch-pin of the scheme.

"Oh dear," he said, looking at Henryk, concerned. "Still, I'm sure it's all a misunderstanding, elder brother. We had best do as these men say, yes? Until we can sort things out."

The captain shook his head. "I'm sorry, sir, but my orders are to take Mars Colonists only."

"But surely, Captain." For a moment he was Josef Krenek at his most unctuous; as if persuading a client to buy a new product range. "You must allow me to accompany my elder brother and his wife. There are laws about unjust detention and the right of representation. Or have they been repealed?"

The captain hesitated, listening to orders in his head, then gave a curt nod. "I'm told you can come along, *Shih* Krenek. But please, don't interfere. This is an important matter. I'm certain we can settle it quite quickly."

Krenek smiled and followed them silently. Yes, I'm certain we can. But not here. Not yet.

* * *

The General looked through the one-way glass at the men and women crowded into the small room.

"Well?" he asked. "Is that all of the Colonists?"

Nocenzi nodded. "Every last one. Sixty-two in all."

Tolonen stroked his chin thoughtfully, then turned and looked directly at his Major. "Can we set up a gate here? I want to trace any remaining copy-humans. But I don't want them terminated. Understand?"

Nocenzi nodded. "My men are working on it already."

"Good." His first instinct had been to gas all the copies, but they needed one in functional order. To trace it back.

To find out where these things came from and get to the men behind them.

"What percentage of the Colonists have proved to be these things?"

Nocenzi looked to his lieutenant, who bowed and answered for him. "Nine from three hundred and eighteen. So just under three per cent."

Tolonen looked back into the room. So if the percentage was constant that meant there was at least one, maybe two of the things in there. But how did you tell? They were indistinguishable to the naked eye.

"At least they're not booby-trapped," Nocenzi said, coming closer and standing beside him at the glass. "Think of the damage they could have done if they had been. If I'd built them I'd have made them tamper-proof. More than that, I'd have made them a bit less docile. Not one of them queried going into the secure rooms. It's as if they weren't programmed for it. Yet they must have had pretty complex programming for them to keep up appearances, let alone come here. They must have had a plan of some kind."

Tolonen started, then turned to face his Major. "Of course! Why didn't I see it before?" He laughed shortly, then shivered. "Don't you see, Vittorio? Twelve of them. One of them the lynch-pin, the strategist, holding it all in his head, the others with the bare outlines of what they have to do, but no sense of the larger strategy."

Nocenzi understood at once. "An elite attack squad. Like our own Security squads. Functioning in the same way."

"Yes!" Tolonen said, elated. "That explains why they were so docile. They only needed a certain amount of programming. They were just following orders. But one of them – one of the 'people' in that room – is the lynch-pin. The strategist."

DeVore. It all led back to DeVore. His hand behind all of this. His thinking. His elite training.

"There'll be three of them, I warrant you. Two soldiers and a strategist. It's the last I want. The lynch-pin. The others will know nothing. But that one . . ."

But even as he said the words he saw it. Saw the two of them meet in the centre of the room and touch and spark, blue veins of electric current forming in the air about them.

"Down!" he yelled, throwing himself to the floor as the room beyond the mirror filled with blinding light.

And then the ceiling fell on them.

★ ★ ★

Krenek knelt and bowed his head, his empty hands placed palm down on his thighs, fingers pointed inward, his whole stance mimicking the tens of thousands surrounding him. Then he straightened, studying the group of people gathered at the top of the steps directly in front of the Hall of Supreme Harmony. Yin Tsu and his family were to the left, Li Shai Tung and his to the right. Beneath them, on the steps themselves, the seven New Confucian officials bowed and chanted the ancient, ceremonial words.

He looked right, then left, then bowed his head again, as others did surrounding him. Guards were everywhere, armed and watchful. GenSyn many of them, no doubt. Unquestioning, obedient creatures. Reliable. Predictable.

Krenek smiled. So different from me, he thought. They made me better than that. More devious. More human.

But there was still a problem. He was too far back. Had even two of the others been here it might still have worked. But now?

He looked about him, calculating distances, gauging where they were weak, where strong, running high-probability scenarios through his head until he saw it clear. Then, and only then, did he establish his plan. I'll have fifteen seconds. Eighteen at most. I can make it halfway there by then. They'll protect the T'ang and the T'ang's sons. Or try to. But they'll also try to protect Yin Tsu and his daughter Fei Yen. That will split their attention.

Yes, but they'd expect him to try to take the T'ang. That's where they would concentrate their defences. Again he smiled, the DeVore part of him remembering his elite training. He could see how they'd do it, forming a screen of bodies in front of him, two guards dragging him back, making the smallest possible target of him. And if seriously threatened they'd open fire, killing anything that came at them, innocent or otherwise.

But he would not attack the T'ang. Nor Han Ch'in. He'd strike where they least expected. Li Yuan would be his target. As he'd always been.

DeVore's words rang clear in his head. "Kill the brain and the beast will fall. Li Shai Tung is old, Han Ch'in incompetent. Only Li Yuan, the youngest, is a threat to us. Get Han Ch'in if you can. Kill the T'ang if you must. But make sure Li Yuan is dead. With him gone the House of Li will not last long."

He waited, knowing the time was fast approaching. Any moment now the saffron-robed officials would turn, facing them, and the vast crowd would rise as one to roar their approval of the marriage. It was then that he'd move forward, using their packed bodies as a screen. He would have five seconds, and then they would kneel again.

Yes, he thought, visualising it clearly now. He could see himself running, fire blazing from his ruined hands. Could smell the crowd's blind panic, hear the ear-shattering stutter of the cross-fire. And then, before his eyes closed finally, he would see the T'ang's son sprawled out on the marble, face down, blood streaming from a dozen separate wounds.

Yes, he thought. Yes. Seconds from now.

There was a sudden lapse in the sing-song incantation. As one the officials turned and faced the crowd. As one the vast crowd rose to its feet.

He made to move forward and felt himself jarred to a halt, then lifted from his feet. Two great hands tore at his chest, two hugely muscled arms pinned his own arms to his sides, slowly crushing him.

"Going somewhere, Mister Krenek?"

★ ★ ★

Karr threw down the lifeless carcass of the thing, then came to attention before Tolonen.

"I don't know what happened, sir. One moment it was fine. The next it was like this."

Tolonen got up unsteadily from his chair and came over to where the thing lay. His chest and arm had been strapped tightly and, despite the pain-killing drugs, he was finding it difficult to breathe easily. He had cracked two ribs and dislocated his shoulder. Otherwise he'd been very lucky. Luckier than Nocenzi. The Major was even now in intensive care, fighting for his life.

Now, cleaned up and in new dress uniform, the empty left sleeve pinned loosely to the tunic, Tolonen was back in charge. Looking at the copy he felt all his anger rise to the surface again.

"Who let this through? Who authorised the closure of the gates?"

Karr lowered his head slightly. "It was Marshal Kirov, sir. He assumed the explosion in the room killed the last of the copies. It was getting late, and there were still thousands of guests to be processed . . ."

"Damn it!" Tolonen's chest rose and fell sharply and a flicker of pain crossed his face. How could Kirov be so foolish? How could he risk the T'ang's life so idiotically? So a few thousand guests were inconvenienced – what was that beside the survival of a T'ang?

Kirov was nominally his superior. He had been elected Marshal by the Council of Generals only six months back and in the emergency had been right to step in and take command, but what he had done was inexcusable.

Tolonen shuddered. "Thank you, Karr. I'll deal with things from here."

He watched the big man go, aware that, on his own initiative, Karr had probably saved the T'ang. He alone had thought to get the copy of the tape showing what had happened in the room. He alone had identified from the files the two who had "joined" to such devastating effect. Then he alone had traced the brother, Josef Krenek, understanding what he was and what he planned.

Thank the gods, Tolonen thought. *This time we've beaten them.*

Tolonen lifted the dead thing's face with the toe of his boot, then let it fall again. A perfect likeness, this one. The best of them all, perhaps. It was a pity. Now they would never know.

He turned from the body and signalled to his adjutant. At once the young man came across and helped him back to his chair.

"Tell Major Kroger to take over," he said, putting the chair into gear. "I must see Li Shai Tung at once."

★ ★ ★

It was evening. The sun's last rays had climbed the eastern wall and left the *Yu Hua Yuan*, transforming the garden of the Imperial City into a huge, square dish of shadows. Brightly-coloured paper lanterns lit the bamboo grove and hung from lines above the lotus-strewn pools and in the eaves of the tea houses. Caged birds sang their sweet, drug-induced songs in the gnarled and ancient branches of the junipers. Below, servants went amongst the guests with wine and cordials and trays of delicacies, while *shao lin* guards stood back against the walls and amongst the rocks like ghosts.

Li Yuan, looking down on it all from the height of the marble terrace, smiled. All ceremony was done with now. Below him, to his right, the wedding party moved among the guests informally, Han Ch'in talking excitedly, Fei Yen silent, demurely bowing at his side.

He saw his father laugh and reach out to pick a single white blossom from Han's dark hair, then turn to whisper something to his uncle, Li Yun-Ti. There was a gay, almost light-hearted atmosphere to things; a feeling of relief that things had turned out as they had. Yet only an hour earlier things had been very different. Li Yuan had been there at his father's interview with the General.

He had never seen the General so angry. It had taken all his father's skill to calm Tolonen down and persuade him not to confront Kirov himself. But he had seen how shaken his father was to have been proved so conclusively right about the "copies"; how outraged at Kirov's stupidity. His face had been rigidly controlled as he faced his General.

"I ask you to do nothing, Knut. Leave this to me. Kirov is Wei Feng's man. I shall speak with Wei Feng at once."

He had been as good as his word. Yuan leaned out and looked down. Tolonen sat there now in his chair, directly below him, subdued, talking to his fellow Generals. Kirov was not amongst them.

Wei Feng, T'ang of East Asia, had been distraught. The thought that his General had almost cost the lives of a fellow T'ang and his family was more than he could bear. He had turned angrily on Kirov and torn the *chi ling* patch, symbol of the Marshal's status as a military officer of the first rank, from his chest, before taking the ceremonial dagger from Kirov's belt and throwing it down.

"You are nothing," he had said to the now prostrate Marshal, tears of anger in his eyes. "And your family is nothing. You have shamed me, Kirov. Now go. Get out of my sight."

News had come only minutes later that Kirov had committed suicide; his son, a Major under his command, seconding him before he too had killed himself.

Han Ch'in, meanwhile, knew nothing of these things. No shadows were to fall upon his nuptial bed.

"Let them be innocent of this," his father had said, taking Li Yuan's arm as they made their way back to the *Yu Hua Yuan*. "For if the seed is strong it will take root and grow a son."

A son . . . Yuan looked back at them. They were closer now – almost below where he stood. He could see them clearly now. Fei Yen was breathtaking. Her dark hair had been plaited with golden threads and bows and tiny orchids, then curled into a tight bun on the top of her head, revealing a pale gold, swan-like neck. She was so delicate. Her ears, her nose, the lines of her cheekbones; all these were exquisite. And yet there was fire in her bright, hazel eyes;

strength in her chin and mouth. She stood there at Han's side in an attitude of obedience, yet she seemed to wear the cloth of crimson and gold as if born to it. Though her head was tilted forward in the ritual stance of passive acceptance, there was a power to her still form that contradicted it. This bird, this flying swallow, was a proud one. She would need her wings clipped before she settled.

He looked from Fei Yen to his brother, seeing how flushed Han was. How his eyes would take small sips of her; each time surprised by her, each time astonished she was his. In this, as in so many things, Han was his junior. So much surprised him. So much evaded his grasp. "It's easy for you, *ti* Yuan," he had once said. "You were born old. It all comes new to me."

It would be an interesting match, he thought. A love match. The strongest kind of power and the hardest to control. She would be Fire to his Earth, Earth to his Fire.

Li Yuan laughed, then turned and went down quickly, his hard-soled, ceremonial shoes clattering on the wooden slats, his long-sleeved silks billowing out behind him as he ran. Down, down, and straight into the arms of his brother-in-law, Pei Chao Yang.

Chao Yang, eldest son and heir to the Pei family, one of the Twenty-Nine, the Minor Families, was standing at the edge of the decorative rock pile, beside the pavilion. His father, Pei Ro-hen, who stood nearby, was a bondsman of Li Shai Tung and a childhood friend of the T'ang. Almost fifty years ago they had shared a tutor. Then, eight years back, they had brought their families much closer, when Chao Yang had married the T'ang's second daughter.

"Here, Yuan! . . . Slow down, boy!"

Chao Yang held onto Li Yuan's arm a moment, getting down onto his haunches and smiling good-naturedly at him, teasing him.

"What is it, little Yuan? Is your bladder troubling you again? Or has one of the little maids made you a promise, eh?"

He winked and let Li Yuan go, watching him run off

down the narrow, tree-lined path and through the small gate that led down to the Lodge of Nature-Nourishment. Then, realising the newly-weds were almost on him, he straightened up, turning towards them.

Chao Yang was a tall, handsome man in his mid-thirties; the product of his father's first marriage. Easy-going, intelligent and with a reputation for knowing how to enliven a dull occasion, he was welcomed in all the palaces and had had Above tongues wagging many times with his reputed intrigues. His own wives, three in number, stood behind him now as he was introduced to the newly weds. With smiles and bows he summoned each forward in turn, his senior wife, Ye Chun, Han's natural sister, first to be presented. That duty done, he was free to make less formal conversation.

"It's good to see you again, Chao Yang," said Han Ch'in, shaking his hands vigorously. "You should come visit us once we've settled in. I hear you like to ride."

Chao Yang bowed deeply. "I am honoured, Li Han Ch'in. I'd like to ride with you." Then, leaning closer, he lowered his voice. "Tonight, however, you ride alone, neh?"

Han Ch'in roared with laughter. "Trust you, Chao Yang! You would lower the tone at a funeral."

Chao Yang laughed. "That depends on what was being buried, eh, my young friend?"

He saw Fei Yen lower her eyes to hide her amusement and smiled inwardly as he bowed to her. But as he straightened he experienced a slight giddiness and had to take a step backward, steadying himself. He had been feeling strange all day. Earlier, dressing himself, he had reached out to take a hairbrush from the table next to him, but his hand had closed on nothing. He had frowned and turned his head away, surprised, but when he had looked again, he had seen that there really was nothing on the table. He had imagined the brush. At the time he had shaken his head and laughed, in self-mockery, but he had been disturbed as well as amused.

Chao Yang bowed once more to the couple then watched them move away, conscious of Han Ch'in's nervousness, of Fei Yen's beauty. The latter stirred him greatly – he could taste her perfume on his tongue, imagine the olive pallor of her flesh beneath the gold and crimson cloth. Again he smiled. No. Best not even think what he was thinking, lest in wine such thoughts slipped out, betraying him.

Han had stopped a few paces on. For a moment Chao Yang studied the side of his face in the lantern light, noticing how similar the shapes of Han's ear, chin and neck were to those of his wife, Ye Chun. Then something peculiar began to happen. Slowly the flesh about the ear began to flow, the ear itself to melt and change, the skin shrivelling up like a heated film of plastic, curling back to reveal, beneath, a hard, silvered thing of wires and metal.

Chao Yang staggered back, horrified, gagging.

"Han Ch'in . . ." he gasped, his voice a whisper. "Han Ch'in!"

But it wasn't Han Ch'in.

Chao Yang cried out, his senses tormented by the smell of burning plastic, the odour of machine oils and heated wiring. For the briefest moment he hesitated, appalled by what he saw, then he lurched forward and threw himself at the thing, grasping it from behind, tugging hard at the place where the false flesh had peeled back. He faltered momentarily as Fei Yen leapt at him, clawing at his eyes, but he kicked out at her brutally, maintaining his grip on the machine, dragging it down, his knee in its back. Then something gave and he was rewarded with the sweet burning smell of mechanical malfunction.

The thing gave a single, oddly human cry. Then nothing.

Now, as it lay in his arms, it felt strangely soft, curiously warm. Such a perfect illusion. No wonder it had fooled everyone.

He let the thing slide from him and looked about, seeing the expression of horror on the faces surrounding him. So they had seen it too. He smiled reassurance but the oddness, that strange feeling of forgetfulness, was returning to him. He tried to smile but a curious warmth budded, then blossomed in his skull.

Pei Chao Yang knelt there a moment longer, his eyes glazed, then fell forward onto his face, dead.

* * *

Tolonen had moved away, towards the steps, when it began. The first scream made him turn the chair, his heart pounding, and look back to where the sound had come from, his view obscured by trees and bushes. Then he was up out of the chair and running, ignoring the pain in his side, the life-link stuttering, faltering in his head. The screams and shouting had risen to a crescendo now. *Shao lin* were running from every side, their swords drawn and raised, looking about them urgently. With one arm Tolonen pushed through the crowd, grimacing against the pain in his chest and shoulder each time someone banged against him.

Abruptly, the life-link cut out. He tapped the connection in his head, appalled, then stumbled on, his mind in turmoil. What had happened? What in the gods' names had happened? His heart raced painfully in his chest. Let it all be a mistake, he pleaded silently, pushing through the last few people at the front. Let it all be a malfunction in the relay. But he knew it wasn't.

He looked around him, wide-eyed, trying to take in what had happened. Fei Yen lay off to one side, clutching her side and gasping, in extreme pain, one of her maids tending to her. A few paces from her lay Han Ch'in.

"Medics!" Tolonen yelled, horrified by the sight of Han lying there so lifelessly. "In the gods' names get some medics here! Now!"

Almost at once, two uniformed men appeared and knelt either side of Han Ch'in. One ripped Han's tunic open and began to press down urgently on his chest with both hands while the other felt for a pulse.

Tolonen stood over them, his despair almost tearing him

apart. He had seen enough dead men to know how hopeless things were. Han lay there in an unnatural pose, his spine snapped, his neck broken.

After a moment one of them looked up, his face ashen. "The Lord Han is dead, General. There is nothing we can do for him."

Tolonen shuddered violently. "Get a life preservation unit here. Now! I want him taken to the special unit. The T'ang's own surgeons will see to him at once!"

He turned and looked down at the other body, knowing at once who it was. Gods! he thought, pained by the sight of his godson, Pei Chao Yang. Is there no end to this? He looked about him anxiously, searching the faces of the onlookers.

"Who did this? Who saw what happened?"

There was a babble of contesting voices. Then one came clear to him. Fei Yen's. "It was Chao Yang," she said, struggling to get the words out. "Chao Yang was . . . was the killer."

Tolonen whirled about, confused. *Pei Chao Yang! No! It couldn't be! It was impossible!*

Or was it?

Quickly he summoned two of the *shao lin* and had them turn Chao Yang over. Then he took a knife from one of them and knelt over the body, slitting open Chao Yang's tunic. For a second or two he hesitated, then he plunged the knife into the chest and drew it to left and right.

His knife met only flesh and bone. Blood welled out over his hands. He dropped the knife, horrified, then looked across at Fei Yen.

"You're certain?"

She lowered her head. "I am."

There was a commotion just behind her as the crowd parted. Li Shai Tung stood there, his horror-filled eyes taking in the scene. Those near to him fell back slowly, their heads bowed.

"*Chieh Hsia*," Tolonen began, getting up. "I beg you to return to your place of safety. We don't know . . ."

The T'ang raised a hand to silence him.

"He's dead?"

Li Shai Tung's face was awful to see. He had lifted his chin in that familiar way he had when giving orders, but now he was barely in command, even of himself. A faint tremor in the muscles at his neck betrayed the inner struggle. His lips were pinched with pain, and his eyes . . .

Tolonen shuddered and looked down. "I am afraid so, *Chieh Hsia*."

"And the killer?"

The General swallowed. "I don't know, *Chieh Hsia*. It seems . . ."

Fei Yen interrupted him. "It was . . . Pei Chao Yang."

The T'ang's mouth opened slightly and he nodded. "Ah . . . I see." He made to say something more, then seemed to forget.

Tolonen looked up again. He could hardly bear to meet the T'ang's eyes. For the first time in his life he knew he had let his master down. He knelt, his head bowed low, and drew his ceremonial dagger, offering its handle to the T'ang in a gesture that said quite clearly, "My life is yours."

There was silence for a moment, then the T'ang came forward and put his hand on Tolonen's shoulder. "Stand up, Knut. Please, stand up."

There was anguish in Li Shai Tung's voice, a deep pain that cut right through Tolonen and made him tremble. He had caused this pain. His failure had caused it. He stood slowly, feeling his years, his head still bowed, the dagger still offered.

"Put it away, old friend. Put it away."

He met the T'ang's eyes again. Yes, there was grief there – an awful, heavy grief. But behind it was something else. An acceptance of events. As if Li Shai Tung had expected this. As if he had gambled and lost, knowing all the while that he might lose.

"The fault is mine," Li Shai Tung said, anticipating the General. "I knew the risks." He shivered, then looked down. "There has been death enough today. And I need

291

you, Knut. I need your knowledge, your ability, your fierce loyalty to me."

He was silent a moment, struggling to keep control, then he looked up again, meeting Tolonen's eyes. "After all, Knut, I have another son. He'll need you, too."

More medics came, wheeling a trolley. General and T'ang stood there a moment in silence, watching as they placed Han Ch'in in the unit and sealed the lid. Both knew the futility of the gesture. Nothing would bring Han back now. When Li Shai Tung turned to face Tolonen again, his fists were clenched at his sides. His face was a mask of pain and patience.

"Find out who did this. Find out *how* they did it. Then come to me. Do not act without my order, Knut. Do not take it on yourself to avenge me." He shivered, watching the medics wheel the trolley past. "Han must not die in vain. His death must mean something."

Tolonen saw that the T'ang could say no more. He was at his limit now. His face showed signs of crumbling and there was a fierce movement about the eyes and beneath the mouth that revealed the true depths of what he was feeling. He made a brief, dismissive gesture of his hand, then turned away.

The General sheathed his dagger and turned to face the guests. Already the news of Han Ch'in's death would be spreading through the levels of Chung Kuo. And somewhere, he was certain, a group of men would be celebrating: smiling cruelly and raising their glasses to each other.

Somewhere . . . Tolonen shuddered, grief giving way to anger in him. He would find the bastards. Find them and kill them. Every last one of them.

CHAPTER·8

KIM'S GAME

They had sedated the boy and moved him to the observation centre on the island of Corsica, three thousand *li* distant. There they cleaned and inoculated him, and put him in a cell.

It was a bare, unfurnished cell, a cube fifteen *ch'i* to a side. The ceiling was lost in the darkness overhead and there was no door, though a small window high up in one of the smooth, dark walls suggested that there was at least a way outside. From the ceiling and window came a faint glow, barely enough to warrant the name of light, while from the centre of the ceiling hung a six-eyed camera on a long, flexible neck.

The boy huddled against the wall beneath the window, staring up at the camera, his face both curious and hostile. He did not move, for when he did the camera would turn to follow him, like something living, two of its eyes focused constantly on him. He knew this because he had experimented with it; just as he had tried to climb the wall beneath the window.

In an adjacent room a man sat at a control desk, watching the boy on a screen. Behind him stood another. Both men were dressed in identical, tight-fitting suits of black. A fine gauze mesh of white was stretched across each of their faces like masks, showing only the eyes with their ebony lenses.

For a time there was nothing. Then the boy spoke.

"Bos agas pen gweder? Bos eno enawy py plas why dos mes?"

The seated man translated for the benefit of the other.

"Is your head made of glass? Is there light where you come from?"

T'ai Cho laughed. He was growing to like the boy. He was so quick, so bright. It was almost a pleasure to be his partner in these sessions. He half turned, looking up at the standing man, who grunted non-committally.

"I need to see more, T'ai Cho. Some clear sign of what he's capable of."

T'ai Cho nodded, then turned back to the screen. "Ef bos enawy," he answered pleasantly. *He be light*, it meant, translated literally, though its sense was *It is light*. "Pur enawy," he went on. *Very light*. "Re rak why gordhaf whath, edrek." *Too much for you to endure, I'm sorry*. "Mes bos hebask. A-brys why mynnes gweles py plas my dos mes." *But be patient. In good time you will see where I come from*.

The boy considered, then nodded, as if satisfied.

"Da," he said. *Good*.

"What is that language?" asked the standing man. His name was Andersen and he was Director of the Project. It was T'ai Cho's job to convince him that his candidate was worth spending time and money on, for this was a department of the T'ang's government, and even government departments had to show a profit.

"Old Cornish," said T'ai Cho, half turning in his seat, but still watching the screen. "It's a bastardised, pidgin version, almost devoid of tenses. Its grammatical structure is copycat English."

He knew much more but held his tongue, knowing his superior's habitual impatience. They had been brave men, those few thousand who had formed the kingdom of Kernow back in the first years of the City. Brave, intelligent men. But they had not known how awful life would be in the Clay. They had not conceived what vast transforming pressures would be brought to bear on them. Intelligence had knelt before necessity and the weight of all that life stacked up above them, out of reach. They had reverted. Regressed ten thousand years in as many days. Back to the days of flint and bone. Back to the age of stone. Now only the ragged tatters of their chosen language remained, its sounds as twisted as the bodies of their children's children's children.

Andersen leaned forward and tapped the screen with his long fingernails. "I want something conclusive. Something I can show to our sponsors. Something we can sell."

T'ai Cho's eyes left the screen a moment, meeting Andersen's eyes. He had a gut instinct about this one. Something told him that this one was different from the rest: was, perhaps, what the Project had been set up to find. But "something conclusive" – could he get that? The Director's eyes were inexpressive.

"I'll try," T'ai Cho said after a moment. "Tomorrow, first thing."

Andersen nodded curtly and turned away. "Tomorrow, then."

★ ★ ★

Tomorrow began early. T'ai Cho was up at fifth bell and at his post, watching the sleeping boy. Slowly, almost imperceptibly, he increased the lighting in the cell. It was the boy's fourth day here, but, like all those brought up from the Clay, he had no real conception of time. Day and night were as one down there, equally dark.

Slowly he would be taught otherwise. Would learn the patterns of the world above.

When he had first arrived they had placed food and drink in his cell. On waking he had seen it at once, but had merely sniffed, then left the two bowls untouched. On the second day, however, hunger and thirst had overcome his fear and he had eaten wolfishly.

T'ai Cho had seen this many times before. He had logged eight years in Recruitment and seen more than a dozen of his candidates through Assessment into Socialisation. But never, until now, had he felt such conviction about a candidate. There was something about this one, a charisma, if that were possible in such a scraggy, scrawny

295

creature; a powerful, almost tangible sense of potentiality.

They were pitiful to watch in the first few days. Most were like trapped animals gnawing at their bonds. Some went mad and tried to kill themselves. Some went into coma. In either case there was a simple procedure to be followed. A matter of policy. At the touch of a button on the control desk, the cell would be filled with a deadly, fast-acting gas. It would be over in seconds.

Kim, however, had quickly overcome his initial fear. When nothing had happened to him, he had begun to explore his cell methodically, growing in confidence as each hour passed and he remained unharmed. Curiosity had begun to have the upper hand in his nature. The material of the walls, the watching camera, the waste vent, the manufacture of the bowls – each had been subjected to an intense scrutiny; to an investigation that was, T'ai Cho thought, almost scientific in its thoroughness. Yet when T'ai Cho spoke to the boy he saw at once just how fragile that confidence was. The boy froze in mid-action, the hair rising from his flesh, then scurried back to his corner and crouched there, shaking, his big, round eyes wide with terror.

T'ai Cho had seen cleverness before, and cunning was second nature to these children from the Clay, but there was something more than cleverness or cunning here. It was not simply that the boy was bright, numerate and curious – there were clear signs of something more.

Many factors seemed to militate against the development of real intelligence in the Clay, malnutrition chief amongst them. When existence was stripped down to its bare bones the first thing lost was the civilising aspect of abstract thought. And yet, in some, it surfaced even so.

In the last year, however, the Project had been under scrutiny from factions in the House who wanted to close it down. Their arguments were familiar ones. The Project was expensive. Twice in the last five years it had failed to show a profit. Nor did the fact that they had extended their network beneath the whole of City Europe mollify their critics. Why did they need the Project in the first place? At most it had produced five thousand useful men in twenty years, and what was that in the context of the greater scientific community? Nothing. Or as good as nothing.

In his darker moments T'ai Cho had to agree with them. After a day in which he had had to flood the cell with gas, he would return up-level to his apartment and wonder why they bothered. There was so much in-breeding, so much physical suffering, such a vast break in the chain of knowledge down there. At times these seemed insurmountable barriers to the development of intelligence. The Clay was a nightmare made real. Was *ti yu*, the "earth-prison" – the world beneath the earth; the place of demons. Down there intelligence had devolved into a killer's cunning, blunted by a barbarous language that had no room for broader concepts. If he thought of it in those terms, what he did seemed little more than a game. A salving of conscience, maybe, but no more than that.

So they all felt, at times. But that feeling didn't last. T'ai Cho had killed maybe a hundred boys like Kim, knowing it was best – pitying them for the poor trapped creatures they were; knowing they had no future, above or below. And yet he had seen the light of intelligence flash in their eyes: eyes that, by rights, should have been simply dull or feral. And each time it had seemed a miracle of sorts, beyond simple understanding. Each time it gave the lie to those who said the Clay bred true: that environment and genetics were *all* there was. No, there was more than that.

It was a thing none of them mentioned; almost a kind of heresy. Yet there was not one of them who didn't feel it. Not one who didn't know exactly what it was that informed and inspired their work here.

Man was more than the plastic of his flesh and the keyboard of his senses. More than a carrier of genetic codes. To Mankind alone was the diffuse and evasive spark of individuality given. It seemed a paradox, yet it was so. Each time they "saved" one from the Clay it reaffirmed their faith in this. Man was more than *po*; more than the animal soul, the flesh that rotted in the ground at death. There was a spirit soul, a *hun*.

There, that was it. The unuttered thought they shared. A *hun*.

And so they did their work, trawling the dark depths for those special souls whose eyes flashed with the spark of life itself. Each one miraculous. Each one an affirmation. "We make a profit; provide a service for the Companies," they would argue, when put to it. But the real reason they hid from others. It was their dark, vocational secret.

He began. At his order a uniformed Mech entered the room and set a tray down on the floor beside the sleeping boy. On the tray were a number of different objects, covered by a thin black cloth.

The room was sealed again. T'ai Cho waited. An hour passed.

When Kim woke he saw the tray at once. He paused, abruptly alert, fully awake, the hairs on his neck bristling. He lifted his head, sniffing the air, then circled the tray slowly. With his back against the wall he stopped and looked up at the camera, a definite question in his dark eyes.

"Pyn an jawl us wharfedhys?" *What now?*

T'ai Cho, watching, smiled, then leaned forward and tapped out a code on the intercom in front of him.

There was a pause, then Andersen's voice came back to him. "What is it, T'ai Cho?"

"I think this will interest you, sir. I'm with the boy. I think you should see this for yourself."

Andersen hesitated, then agreed. He cut the connection.

T'ai Cho sat back in his chair, watching.

The boy's gaze went between the camera and the tray, then settled on the tray. Slowly, almost timidly, he moved closer. He looked up, his brow deeply furrowed, his big, round eyes filled with suspicion. Then, with a quick, sudden movement, he flicked the cloth aside.

It was a standard test and T'ai Cho had witnessed this moment fifty, maybe a hundred times. He had seen boys sniff and paw and try to taste the objects, then ignore them or play with them in a totally uncomprehending manner, but this time it was different – totally different from anything he had seen before. He watched in silence, aware all the while of the Director watching at his side.

"This is wrong, surely? This is supposed to be a memory game, isn't it?"

The Director reached out to switch on the intercom, but T'ai Cho put his hand in the way, turning to look up at him.

"Please. Not yet. Watch what he does."

The Director hesitated, then nodded. "But what exactly *is* he doing?"

T'ai Cho turned back to the screen and smiled to himself. "He's doing what he does all the time. He's changing the rules."

At first the boy did not lift any of the objects but moved them about on the tray as if to get a better idea of what they were. Then, working with what seemed like purpose, he began to combine several of the objects. A small hand mirror, a length of plastic tubing and a twine of string. His hands moved quickly, cleverly, and in a moment he had what looked like a child's toy. He took it to the wall beneath the window and raised it to his eye, trying to see outward. Failing, he sat down with the thing he had made and patiently took it apart.

The two men watched the screen, fascinated, seeing how the boy positioned his hand before the mirror and tilted it slowly, studying what effect it had on the image. Then, as if satisfied, he returned to the tray and took a heavier object in one hand. He hefted it a moment, thoughtfully, then reached for a second object and placed them at his side.

Scurrying across the floor, he retrieved the discarded cloth and laid it out on the floor of the cell. Then he placed the mirror face down on top of it. He laid the carved block halfway across the mirror, taking care with its positioning, then struck the back of the block firmly with the torch.

He picked the two halves of the hand mirror up carefully,

checking the sharpness of their edges with his thumb. T'ai Cho, watching, moved his hand instinctively towards the touchpad, ready to fill the cell with gas should the boy do anything rash. But Kim was not out to harm himself. Using the edge of the mirror he cut the twine into four pieces, then began to reconstruct his toy, placing a piece of glass at each end of the tube. He tested the angles of the glass five times before he was satisfied, then tightened the twine and went to the window again. This time he should be able to see out.

Andersen leaned forward. "Do you think he's seen this done before?"

"Where? In the Clay?" T'ai Cho laughed, then turned to look up at Andersen. "No. This is all first time for him. An experiment. Just think of how *we* learn things. How, as children, we watch others and copy them. How we have to be taught even the most basic of skills. But Kim's not like that. He has no one to copy. He's never had anyone to copy. It's all had to come from within his own mind. That's why it's so astonishing, what he does. Can't you see it? He treats the world like something new. Something yet to be put together."

The boy took the makeshift periscope from his eyes and sat down slowly, clearly disappointed by what he had seen. Then he tilted back his head and spoke into the darkness overhead.

"Pandra vyth gwres?" *Where am I?*

He waited, but when no answer came he threw the viewing tube away from him and let his head fall onto his chest, as if exhausted.

T'ai Cho turned and looked up at the Director. "Well?"

Andersen stood there a moment longer, staring down into the screen, then looked back at T'ai Cho. "All right. I'll get a six month contract drawn up this afternoon."

Beneath his white gauze mask, T'ai Cho smiled. "Then I'll start at once?"

The Director hesitated, then nodded curtly. His eyes,

usually so lifeless, seemed thoughtful, even, perhaps, surprised.

"Yes," he said finally. "Begin at once. But let me know immediately if anything of interest happens."

* * *

An hour later Andersen was at his desk. The directive he had been warned was on its way had now arrived. It lay there on the desk before him. Two months he had. Two months to turn things round. And the new financial targets they had given him were four times the size of the old ones.

He laughed bitterly. It would need a miracle. He hadn't a chance of meeting the old targets, let alone these new figures. No – someone higher up had decided to pull the plug on the Project, he was certain of it. This was political.

Andersen leaned forward and spoke into his intercom. "Send through a standard contract. Six months term. For the new boy, Kim."

He sat back again. A miracle . . . Well, maybe T'ai Cho was right. Maybe the boy *was* special. But would his specialty translate into cash? Anyway, he didn't pin his hopes too greatly on it. Six months? If the Project folded Kim would be dead in two. He and a hundred others like him.

"Politics!" he muttered, wondering who was behind this latest directive and what he could do to get the deadline extended – who he could speak to to get things changed. Then, as the contract slid from the desk-top printer he leaned forward and took his brush from the ink block, signing the Mandarin form of his name with a flourish at the bottom of the page.

* * *

The viewing-tube lay where Kim had thrown it, the lower mirror dislodged from the shaft, the twine hanging loose. Kim sat there, perfectly still, his arms wrapped about his knees, his head tucked down between his legs, waiting.

He heard it first. Sensed a vague movement in the air.

301

He scuttled back, then crouched beneath the wall, wide-eyed, the hair rising on the back of his neck. Then, as the facing wall began to peel back from the centre, he cried out.

What had been the wall was now an open space. Beyond the opening was a room the same as the one in which he sat. Inside, behind a narrow barrier of wood, sat a giant. A giant with a face of bone-white glass.

The giant stood, then began to come around the wall. Kim cried out again and tried to back away, but there was nowhere to run. He looked about him desperately, yelping, urine streaming down his legs.

And then the giant spoke.

"Ow hanow bos T'ai Cho. My bos an den kewsel yn why." *My name be T'ai Cho. I be the man talk to you.*

The giant fell silent, then came into the room and stood there, his hands out at his sides, empty. It was a gesture designed to say, "Look, I am no threat to you", but the man was almost twice as tall as the tallest man Kim had ever seen. He was like the gods Kim had seen in the Clay that time, yet his limbs and body were as black as the earth, his eyes like dark jewels in the pure, glassy whiteness of his face.

It was a cruel face. A face that seemed curiously at odds with the soft reassurance of the voice.

Kim drew back his teeth and snarled.

And then the giant did something unexpected. It knelt down. It was still taller than Kim, but it was less threatening now. Keeping its arms out at its sides, it spoke again.

"My golyas why, Kim." *I watch you, Kim.* "My gweles pandra why canna obery." *I see what you can do.* "Why a-vyn bewa a-ughof?" *Do you want to live up above?*

Slowly the darkness deep within him ebbed away. He took a breath, then answered. "My a-vyn." *I want to.*

The giant nodded. "Da. Ena why gweres-vy." *Good. Then you help me.* "Bysy yu dheugh obery pandra my kewsel." *You must do what I say.*

The giant reached up and removed the flesh from his

302

face. Beneath it he wore a second face, the mouth of which smiled redly, showing perfect teeth. His inner mouth. So he was not made of glass at all.

Kim thought about what the giant had said. It seemed too all-inclusive. He shook his head. "Ny puptra." *Not everything*.

The giant nodded. This time the words came from his inner mouth. The other flesh hung loose about his chin. "Ny puptra. Mes moyha taclow." *Not everything. But most things*. "May ef gul styr." *When it makes meaning*.

He considered that. It did not commit him too much. "Da," he said softly.

"Flowr," said the giant, smiling again. *Perfect*. "Ena bysy yu dheugh gortheby onen tra a-dherak pup ken." *Then you must answer me one thing before all else*. "Pyu dysky why fatel nyvera?" *Who teach you how to count?*

* * *

Andersen sat behind his desk, studying T'ai Cho's report. It was the end of the first week of Assessment. Normally there would have been a further seventeen weeks of patient observation, but T'ai Cho had asked for matters to be expedited. Andersen had agreed readily. Only that morning he had spoken to the First Secretary of one of the Junior Ministers and been told that his request for a referral hearing had been turned down. Which meant that the directive was final. Yet things were not all bad. He had been busy this last week.

He looked up and grunted. "Good," he said simply, then pushed the file aside. "I'll countersign my recommendation. The board sits tomorrow. I'll put it before them then."

T'ai Cho smiled and nodded his gratitude.

"Off the record," Andersen continued, leaning forward over the desk-top, "how high do you rate his potential? You say here that you think he's a genius. That can mean many things. I want something I can sell. Something that will impress a top Executive."

"It's all in there," said T'ai Cho, indicating the file. "He

303

has an eidetic memory. Near perfect recall. And the ability to comprehend and use complex concepts within moments of first encountering them. Add to that a profound, almost frightening grasp of mathematics and linguistics."

The Director nodded. "All excellent, T'ai Cho, but that's not quite what I mean. They can build machines that can do all that. *What can he do that a machine can't?*"

It was an odd thing to ask. The question had never arisen before. But then there had never been a candidate quite like Kim. He was already fluent in basic English and had assimilated the basics of algebra and logic as if they were chunks of meat to be swallowed down and digested.

The Director sat back and turned slightly in his chair, looking away from T'ai Cho. "Let me explain the situation. Then you might understand why I'm asking."

He glanced at the operative and smiled. "You're good at your job, T'ai Cho, and I respect your evaluation. But my viewpoint is different from yours. It has to be. I have to justify the continuation of this whole operation. I have to report to a board that reports back to the House itself. And the House is concerned with two things only. One – does the Recruitment Project make a profit? Two – is it recruiting the right material for the market place?"

He held up a hand, as if to counter some argument T'ai Cho was about to put forward. "Now I know that might sound harsh and unidealistic, but it's how things are."

T'ai Cho nodded but said nothing.

"Anyway, things are like this. At present I have firm approaches from five major Companies. Three have signed contracts for auction options when the time comes. I expect the other two to sign shortly."

T'ai Cho's eyes widened with surprise. "An auction?"

Andersen raised one hand. "However . . . if he *is* what you say he is, then we could fund the whole of this programme for a year, maybe more. That's if we can get the right deal. If we can get one of the big companies to sign an exclusive rights contract."

T'ai Cho shook his head, astonished now. An exclusive

rights contract! Then the Director wasn't talking of a normal sponsorship but about something huge. Something between two and five million yuan! No wonder he wanted something more than was in the report. But what could he, T'ai Cho, offer in that vein?

"I don't know . . ." he began, then stopped. There *was* something Kim could do that a machine couldn't. He could invent. He could take two things and make a third of them.

"Well?" said Andersen. "Say I'm Head of SimFic. How would you convince me to hand over twenty million yuan in exchange for a small boy, genius or not?"

T'ai Cho swallowed. *Twenty million yuan!* He frowned, concentrating on the problem he had been set, "Well, he connects things . . . Things we'd normally consider unconnected." He looked down, trying to capture in words just what it was that made Kim so special. "But it's more than that. Much more. He doesn't just learn and remember and calculate, he *creates*. New ideas. Wholly new ideas. He looks at things in ways we've never thought of looking at them before."

"Such as?"

T'ai Cho shrugged. It was so hard to define, to pinpoint, but he knew this was what made Kim so different. It wasn't just his ability to memorise or his quickness, it was something beyond those. And because it was happening all the time it was hard to extract and say "he does this". It was his very mode of thought. He was *constantly* inventive.

T'ai Cho laughed. "Do you know anything about astronomy?"

"A little." Andersen stared at him strangely. "Is this relevant, T'ai Cho?"

T'ai Cho nodded. "You know what a nova is?"

Andersen shrugged. "Refresh my memory."

"A nova is an old star that collapses into itself and in doing so explodes and throws out vast quantities of energy and light. Well, Kim's a kind of nova. I'm tempted to say a supernova. It's like there's some dense darkness at the very centre of him, sucking all knowledge down into itself, then throwing it all back out as light. Brilliant, blinding light."

Andersen shook his head. "Old stars . . . Is there nothing more practical?"

T'ai Cho leaned forward, earnest now. "Why don't you bring him here, your Head of SimFic? Show him the boy. Let him bring his own experts, make his own assessments – set his own tests. He'll be astonished, I guarantee you."

"Maybe," Andersen muttered, putting his hand up to his mouth. Then he repeated the word more strongly. "Maybe. You know, that's not so bad an idea after all."

* * *

T'ai Cho put his request in the next day, expecting it to be turned down out of hand. Within the hour, however, he had received notification, under the Director's hand, with full board approval. He was to be transferred from Assessment to S & D – Socialisation and Indoctrination – for an eighteen-month tour of duty. And he was to be directly responsible for the new candidate, Kim Ward.

Normally personal involvement was frowned upon. It was seen as necessary to make a clean break between each section, but the Director had convinced the board that this was a special case. And they had agreed, recognising the importance of nurturing the boy's abilities, though perhaps the thought of twenty million yuan – a figure mentioned unofficially and wholly off the record – had proved an additional incentive to break with tradition just this once. Thus it was that T'ai Cho took Kim up the five levels to Socialisation and helped him settle into his new rooms.

* * *

A week later T'ai Cho found himself at the lectern in a small hexagonal lecture room. The room was lit only at its centre, and then by the dimmest of lamps. Three boys sat at a distance from each other, forming a triangle at the heart of which was the spiderish shape of a trivee. T'ai Cho stood

306

in the shadows behind the smallest of the boys, operating the image control.

It was a lecture about Chung Kuo and City Earth. Images of the vast hive-like structure appeared and then vanished. Exteriors, cutaways, sections. The first glimpse these children had ever had of the environment built above the Clay.

As T'ai Cho talked his way through the sequence of images he wondered whether they ever dreamed themselves back there, beneath the vast, overtowering pile of the City. How strange that would be. How would they feel? Like bugs beneath a house, perhaps. Yes, looking at these images even he felt awed. How, then, did it strike them? For this was their first sight of it – their first glimpse of how insignificant they were: how small the individual, how vast the species. A City covering the Earth like a glacier, broken only by ocean and mountain and plantations. A species almost forty billion strong.

Yes, he could see the awe in the faces of the two boys seated across from him. Their mouths were open wide in wonder and their eyes were screwed up, trying to take it all in. Then he glanced down at the small, dark-haired head just below his lectern and wondered what Kim was thinking.

"It's too big," Kim said suddenly.

T'ai Cho laughed. "It's exactly as big as it is. How can that be too big?"

"No." Kim turned and looked up at him, his dark eyes burning with intensity. The other boys were watching him carefully. "I didn't mean that. Just that it's too vast, too heavy a thing to stand on its pillars without either collapsing or sinking into the earth."

"Go on," said T'ai Cho, aware that something important was happening. It was like the construction of the viewing-tube, but this time Kim was using concepts as his building blocks.

"Well, there are three hundred levels in most places, right?"

T'ai Cho nodded, careful not to interrupt.

307

"Well, on each of those levels there must be thousands, perhaps millions of people. With all their necessities. Food, clothing, transportation, water, machines. Lots of machines." Kim laughed softly. "It's ridiculous. It just can't be. It's too heavy. Too big. I've seen for myself how *small* the pillars are on which it all rests."

"And yet it is," said T'ai Cho, surprised by that single word "small" and what it implied. Kim had grasped at once what the others had failed even to see: the true perspectives of the City. His imagination had embraced the scale of things at once. As if he'd always known. But this next was the crucial stage. Would Kim make the next leap of understanding?

T'ai Cho glanced across at the other boys. They were lost already. They hadn't even seen there was a problem.

"It exists?" Kim asked, puzzled. "Just as you've shown us?"

"Exactly. And you might also consider that there are vast factories and foundries and masses of other industrial machinery distributed amongst its many levels. At least one level in twenty is used for warehousing. And there are whole levels which are used to store water or process waste matter."

Kim's face creased into a frown of intense concentration. He seemed to stare at something directly in front of him, his brow puckering, his eyes suddenly sharply focused.

"Well?" T'ai Cho prompted when the silence had extended uncomfortably.

Kim laughed. "You'll think I'm mad . . ."

"No. Try me."

"Well . . . It must be something to do with its structure. But that can't be the whole of it." Kim seemed almost in pain now. His hands were clenched tightly and his eyes were wide and staring.

T'ai Cho held his breath. One step further. One small but vital step.

"Then it must be built of air. Or something as light as air but . . . but as tough as steel."

308

As light as air and as tough as steel. A substance as strong as the bonding between the atoms and so light that three hundred levels of it weighed a fraction of a single layer of clay bricks. A substance so essential to the existence of City Earth that its chemical name was rarely used. It was known simply as ice. Ice because, in its undecorated state, it looked as cold and fragile as the thinnest layer of frozen water. "Corrugated" layers of ice – only a few hundred molecules thick – formed the levels and walls of City Earth. Moulded sheets of ice formed the basic materials of lifts and bolts, furniture and pipework, clothing and conduits, toys and tools. Its flexibility and versatility, its cheapness and durability had meant that it had replaced most traditional materials.

City Earth was a vast palace of ice. A giant house of cards, each card so unbelievably thin that if folded down the whole thing would be no thicker than a single sheet of paper.

Slowly, piece by piece, T'ai Cho told Kim all of this, watching as the boy's face lit with an inner pleasure. Not air but ice! It made the boy laugh with delight.

"Then the pillars hold it down!" he said. "They keep it from flying away!"

★　★　★

Soren Berdichev glanced up from the pile of papers he was signing.

"Well, Blake? You've seen the boy?"

His Head of Personnel hesitated long enough to make Berdichev look up again. Blake was clearly unhappy about something.

"He's no use to us, then?"

"Oh, quite the contrary, sir. He's everything the report made him out to be. Exceptional, sir. Quite exceptional."

Berdichev set the brush down on the inkstone and sat back, dismissing the secretary who had been hovering at his side.

309

"Then you've done as we agreed and purchased the boy's contract?"

Blake shook his head. "I'm afraid not, sir."

"I don't understand you, Blake. Have you let one of our rivals buy the boy?"

"No, sir. Director Andersen offered us an exclusive rights contract."

"Then what's the problem? You offered him the sum I authorised? Five million yuan?"

"I did . . ." Blake swallowed. "In fact, I raised the offer to eight million."

Berdichev smiled coldly. "I see. And you want me to sanction the increase?"

"No, sir. That's it, you see. Andersen turned me down flat."

"What?!" Berdichev sat forward, his eyes, behind the tiny pebble glasses, wide with anger. "Eight million and he turned us down?"

"Yes, sir. He said he wanted twenty million minimum, or no contract."

Berdichev shook his head slowly, astonished. "And you walked away, I hope?"

Blake lowered his head. There was a definite colour in his cheeks now. Berdichev leaned forward and yelled at him.

"Come on, man! Out with it! What's all this about?"

Blake looked up again, his whole manner hesitant now. "I . . . I promised Andersen I'd come back to you, sir. I said I'd ask you to agree the deal."

"You *what*?" Berdichev laughed incredulously. "Twenty million yuan for a six-year-old boy? Are you mad, Blake?"

Blake met his eyes determinedly. "I believe he's worth it, sir. Every last *jen* of it. I would not have dared come back to you unless I believed that."

Berdichev shook his head. "No . . . Twenty million. It's out of the question."

Blake came forward and leaned over the desk, pleading

310

with his superior. "If only you saw him, sir – saw him for yourself – you'd understand. He's like nothing I've ever come across before. Voracious, he is – just hungry to learn things. Really, sir, if you'd only see him!"

Berdichev looked down at where Blake's hands rested on the edge of the desk. Blake removed them at once and took a step back, straightening up.

"Is that all, Blake?"

"Please, sir. If you'd reconsider. If you'd take the time . . ."

"You know that I haven't the time," he snapped back, irritated now by Blake's persistence. He picked up the brush angrily. "The murder of the T'ang's son has thrown everything into flux. The market's nervous and I have meetings all this week to calm things down. People need reassuring, and that takes time." He looked up at his Personnel Manager again, his face hard and angry. "No, Blake, I really haven't the time."

"Forgive me, sir, but I think you should make time in this instance."

Berdichev stared at Blake a moment, wondering whether he should dismiss him on the spot. But something cautioned him. Blake had never stepped out of line before – had never dared to contradict him in this manner. There must be good reason. He looked down at the pile of papers that awaited his signature, barely seeing them, calming himself, trying to see the thing clearly. Then he looked up again.

"You think he's worth it, then? Twenty million yuan? But what if he gets some childhood illness and dies? What if he has an accident? What if he proves to be one of these child prodigies who burns up before he's out of his adolescence? Twenty million yuan. It's a huge sum, even by our thinking."

Blake bowed his head, all humility now that he had got Berdichev to listen. "I agree, sir. But I've provisionally agreed a six stage payment. Twenty per cent on signature, four two-yearly payments of ten per cent and forty per cent

311

on delivery of the boy to us at sixteen. There would also be provisions for claw-back in the case of death or accident. Our risk would be reduced substantially."

Berdichev considered a moment. This was more like the Blake he knew and valued.

"Would you take a gamble, Blake?"

"How do you mean, sir?"

"Would you back up your hunch? Would you stake your job on me being impressed by the boy?"

Blake looked down, a smile slowly spreading across his face. "I think I already have."

★ ★ ★

"Kim! What in hell's name are you doing?"

Kim turned from the half-deconstructed trivee and smiled. T'ai Cho, horrified, rushed across the room and pulled him away from the machine.

"Kuan Yin! Don't you realise that that could kill you? There's enough power in that thing to fry you to a cinder!"

Kim shook his head. "Not now there isn't." He took T'ai Cho's hand, prised open the palm and dropped something into it. T'ai Cho stared at the small, matt black rectangular tube for a moment, then, realising what it was, dropped it as if it were red hot. It was the power core.

He knelt down and took Kim's upper arms in his hands, glaring at him, for the first time genuinely angry at the boy. "I forbid you to tinker with things this way! These machines can be lethal if mishandled. You're lucky to be alive!"

Again Kim shook his head. "No," he answered softly, clearly shaken by T'ai Cho's anger. "Not if you know what you are doing."

"And you know what you are doing, eh?"

"Yes . . ." The small boy shivered and looked away.

T'ai Cho, whose anger had been fuelled by his fear for Kim, found himself relenting, yet it was important to keep the boy from harming himself. He kept his voice stern, unyielding. "How did you know?"

Kim looked back at him, his wide, dark eyes piercing him with their strange intensity. "I asked the man – the maintenance engineer. He explained it all to me. He showed me how to take it all apart and put it back together. How it all functioned. What the principles were behind it."

T'ai Cho was silent for a moment. "When was this?"

Kim looked down. "This morning. Before the call."

T'ai Cho laughed. "Before the call?" The call was at six bells. Before then Kim's cell, like all the others, had been locked. "He came and saw you, then, this man? And had a trivee with him, conveniently?"

Kim shook his head, but said nothing.

"Tell me the truth, Kim. You were just tinkering, weren't you? Experimenting."

"Experimenting, yes. But not tinkering. I knew what I was doing. And I was telling you the truth, T'ai Cho. I'd never lie to you."

T'ai Cho sat back on his heels. "Then I don't understand you, Kim."

"I . . ." Kim looked up. The snow-pale flesh of his neck was strangely flushed. "I let myself out of the cell and came down here. The man was working here – servicing the machine."

T'ai Cho was quiet. He stared at Kim for a long while, then stood up. "You know that isn't possible, Kim. The locks are all electronically coded."

"I know," said Kim simply. "And a random factor generator changes the combination every day."

"Then you realise why I can't believe you."

"Yes. But I took the lock out."

T'ai Cho shook his head, exasperated now. "But you can't have, Kim! It would have registered as a malfunction. The alarm would have gone off over the door."

Kim was shaking his head. "No. That's not what I mean. I took the *lock* out. The electronics are still there. I rigged them so that it would still register as locked when the door was pulled closed."

Still T'ai Cho was not convinced. "And what did you do

all this with? The locking mechanism is delicate. Anyway, there's a maintenance plate covering the whole thing."

"Yes," said Kim, the colour gone now from his neck. "That was the hardest part. Getting hold of these." He took a slender packet from his tunic pocket and handed it to T'ai Cho. It was a set of scalpel-fine tools.

"They're duplicates," said Kim. "The service engineer probably hasn't even missed them yet."

T'ai Cho stared at the tools a moment longer then looked back at Kim. "Heavens . . ." he said softly. "So it's true?"

Kim nodded, the smile returned to his face. "It's as I said, T'ai Cho. I'd never lie to you."

★ ★ ★

Director Andersen bowed deeply as Berdichev came into his office. He had spent the morning reading the file on SimFic's owner and had been impressed by what he'd read. Here was a man who had taken his Company from nowhere to the number eighteen slot on the Hang Seng Index in the short space of ten years. Now he was worth a reputed eighteen *billion* yuan. It was not a T'ang's ransom by any means, but it was enough to have satisfied any Emperor of old.

"Your presence here honours us," he said, offering his chair.

Berdichev ignored his offer. "Where's the boy?" he said impatiently. "I'd like to see him. At once."

"Of course," said Andersen, looking to T'ai Cho, who was standing just outside the doorway next to Blake. T'ai Cho bowed, then turned away to prepare things.

Berdichev stared coldly at the Director. "You'll ensure he doesn't know he's being watched?"

"Of course. It's how we always work here. There's a viewing room. My assistants will bring you refreshments . . ."

Berdichev cut him off sharply, the light glinting on his spectacles. "We'll not be taking refreshments. Just show me the boy, Director Andersen. I want to see why you feel you can insult me."

Andersen blanched. "I . . ." He bowed again, fear making his mouth dry. "I'll . . . I'll take you there at once."

* * *

The two machines had been left on the worktop, as the boy had asked. One was the MedFac trivee he had been working on earlier, the other a standard SimFic ArtMould IV. Between them lay a full technician's kit.

"What's this?" Berdichev asked, taking his seat at the observation window only an arm's length from the worktop's edge.

"They're what the boy asked for."

Andersen swallowed, praying that T'ai Cho was right about this. He alone knew just how much depended on it. "I . . . I understand he wants to try something out."

Berdichev half turned in his seat and looked coldly up at Andersen. "I don't understand you, Director. Try what out?"

Andersen began to shake his head, then stopped and smiled, knowing he had to make the best of things. "That's just it. We're never quite certain what Kim's about to do. That's why he's so valuable. He's so unpredictable. So inventive."

Berdichev stared through Andersen a moment, then turned back. He seemed totally unconvinced. It seemed as if the only reason he was there at all was the ridiculously high sum he had been asked to pay for the boy's contract. Andersen leaned against the back of the empty chair next to Berdichev's, feeling weak. The boy was going to ruin it all. He just knew he was. Things would go wrong and he would be humiliated, in front of Berdichev. Worse than that, it would be the end of things: the closure of the Project and early retirement for himself. He shuddered, then took the fan from his belt and flicked it open, fanning himself.

"I suppose he's going to do something with those two machines?"

315

Andersen's fan stopped in mid-motion. "I believe so."

"And how long has he been in your charge?"

"Twenty-three days."

Berdichev laughed. "It isn't possible. It takes our best engineers months to learn how to operate those things."

"Four months' intensive training," said Blake from the back of the viewing room.

"And he's taught himself?"

Andersen licked his lips to wet them. "In two days."

Berdichev sat back, laughing again. "I do believe you're making fun of me, Director Andersen. Wasting my valuable time. If that's so . . ."

Andersen bowed deeply. "Believe me, *Shih* Berdichev, I would never dream of such a thing. Please, be patient. I'm certain the boy will not disappoint you."

The door at the far end of the lecture room opened and T'ai Cho entered with the boy. Andersen, watching Berdichev, saw him frown, then a strange expression cross his face.

"Where did you find the boy?"

Blake answered before Andersen could find his tongue. "In the Western Island, sir. He comes from the Canton of Cornwall."

Berdichev nodded. A strange sobriety seemed to have gripped him. "Ah, yes. I know it well. I went there once. With friends."

T'ai Cho knelt down, talking to the boy a moment, then he let him go. Kim ran across the room, a naked eagerness in his face. Climbing up onto a stool, he set to work at once, dismantling the insides of the trivee, then dragging the heavy ArtMould machine closer to him.

Berdichev, watching the boy, felt himself go cold inside. The resemblance was uncanny; a grotesque distortion of the original, admittedly, yet in some ways so like him that simply to look at the boy was to bring all those feelings back. All the love and guilt and hurt.

Edmund, he thought; *you're Edmund Wyatt's son. I'd swear it.*

He watched, barely conscious of what the boy was doing; aware only of that strange and unexpected likeness. He should have looked at the holo Blake had given him. Should have found time to look at it. But he had been too busy. Otherwise he would have come here before now, he was certain of it.

Normally he would have dismissed it at once as one of those strange tricks life played on men, but in this case it all fitted. Fitted perfectly. The boy was not only the right age but he came from the right location.

Edmund was with me. Down there in the Clay. Seven years ago. Edmund, Pietr and I. Down there in the darkness below the City. Yes . . . he was there when we went to see the King Under the City, the Myghtern, in his castle in ancient Bodmin. Was there when we visited the Myghtern's singsong house. And now his seed has returned. Back from the dark.

He shuddered and stood up. "I've seen enough."

Andersen, flustered, bowed deeply. The colour had gone from his face and his eyes were wide with sudden panic. "I beg you, Excellency, wait. Please, wait just a little longer. He's only just begun."

Berdichev turned to Blake, ignoring him. "Have you the contract?"

Blake pulled the contract from his carry-pouch and handed it across.

For a moment Berdichev hesitated, looking down at the contract, wondering what was best. His first instinct had been to tear it to shreds, but now he didn't know. He looked back at the boy. If he was Edmund Wyatt's son – and there was a quick way of proving that he was, by genotyping – he was not worth a single *jen*, let alone twenty million yuan, for his life was forfeit under the law that said all the family of a traitor shared his fate, to three generations ascending and descending.

He looked at Andersen. The man was almost shitting himself. "Ten million," he said.

He would delay. Perhaps he would even get the genotype

317

done and make certain. But then? He shivered. Then he would do nothing.

"Fifteen," Andersen answered, his voice betraying how intimidated he felt.

"Ten, or I ask my friends in the House to close you down in two weeks, not eight."

He saw Andersen blink with surprise, then swallow. Seeing how things were, the Director bowed his head.

"Good. Then we'll finalise at once." But he was thinking, Who else would see the resemblance? Who else would know about our visit to the Myghtern? Who now but Lehmann and I?

Maybe it would be all right, then. And perhaps, after all, he could help his dead friend. Perhaps now he could ease the guilt he had suffered from since Edmund's death.

Berdichev shivered then looked back at the boy. Yes, and maybe I can do myself a favour at the same time.

* * *

When it was all over T'ai Cho came back into the lecture room. He was carrying a tray and in his pocket was something the Director had given him to return to Kim. He set the tray down on the desk, beside the ArtMould, then sat on the stool next to Kim.

"Things went well this morning," he said, reaching out to ruffle Kim's dark, fine hair. "The Director was very pleased with you."

"Why should he be pleased?"

T'ai Cho looked down. "He was watching what you did. And with him was someone very important. Someone who has decided to . . . adopt you."

"Adopt me?"

"Oh, don't worry, Kim. You'll be here until you're sixteen. But then you'll join one of the Companies. The one that makes this, as a matter of fact."

He reached out and touched the modified ArtMould, still surprised by what Kim had done.

"Berdichev," said Kim.

T'ai Cho laughed, surprised. "Yes. How did you know?"

"It was on a newscast two days back. They said he owns SimFic."

"That's right." *And now he owns you.* The thought disturbed T'ai Cho, though why it should be different with Kim than with all the others he didn't know. It was what happened to all his charges in time. They were saved, but they were also owned. He shivered, then reached out and took the cup from the tray and offered it to Kim, then watched as he gulped the drink down savagely.

"I've something for you, too," he said, filling the cup once more from the jug. "We don't usually let our boys keep anything from their time in the Clay, but Director Andersen thought we should make an exception in your case."

T'ai Cho took it from his pocket and put it into Kim's hand, closing his fingers over it.

Kim opened his hand, then gave a small laugh. He held the pendant up and touched the dangling circle with one finger, making it spin. It slowed, then twisted back, spinning backward and forward. He seemed delighted with the gift, yet when he looked up at T'ai Cho again his eyes were dark with hurt.

"What is it?" T'ai Cho asked.

"Bodmin."

T'ai Cho shook his head. "What? I don't follow you, Kim."

"The place I came from. It was called Bodmin, wasn't it?"

T'ai Cho laughed, surprised. "Why, yes, now I come to think of it. But how did you find out?"

Kim leaned forward and dipped his finger in the mug, then drew on the worktop, dipping his finger each time he formed a letter.

"An arrow. A space. A woman's breasts. A ring. A drawn bow. Two steep hills. An upright column. A gate. An eye with a curled eyebrow. It was a sign, close by the Gate. Six *li*."

319

CHAPTER·9

<u>WUWEI</u>

Darkness lay on the water like oil. It was almost dawn, but day would be a month coming this far north. They lay there silently in the flat boats, half a *li* from the shore of the island, waiting for the signal in their heads. At ten minutes past five it came and they began to move in, their faces and hands blacked up, their wet suits blending with the darkness.

Hans Ebert, commanding the raiding party, was first ashore. He crouched on the slick stone steps, waiting, listening for sounds above the steady slapping of the water on the rocks below.

Nothing. All was well. A few seconds later the second signal sounded in his head and he moved on quickly, his body acting almost without thought, doing what it had rehearsed a hundred times in the last few days.

He could sense his men moving in the darkness all about him; two hundred and sixty-four of them, elite-trained. The best in City Europe.

At the top of the steps Ebert stopped. While his sergeant, Auden, set the charge on the solid metal door he looked back through the darkness at the mainland. Hammerfest lay six *li* to the east, like a vast slab of glacial ice, thrusting out into the cold northern sea. To north and south of it the great wall of the City's edge ran into the distance like a jagged ribbon, its pale whiteness lit from within, tracing the shoreline of the ancient Finnmark of Norway. He shivered and turned back, conscious of the unseen presence of the old fortress walls towering above him in the moonless

321

dark. It was a bugger of a place. Just the kind of site one would expect SimFic to build a special research unit in.

Auden came back to him. Together they crouched behind the blast shield, lowering their infra-red lenses over their eyes. The charges would be fired automatically by the third signal. They waited. Without warning the night was rent by a whole series of detonations, some near, some further off. They let the shield fall forward and, not waiting for the smoke to clear, charged through the gaping doorway, followed by a dozen other men. At fifteen other points about the island the same thing was happening. Even as he entered the empty corridor he could hear the first bursts of small arms fire.

The first intersection was exactly where it should have been. Ebert stood at the corner, looking to his left, his gun held against his shoulder, searching out targets in the darkness up ahead. He waited until his squad was formed up behind him, then counted them through, Auden first. Up ahead was the first of the guard posts, if the plans were accurate, and beyond that the first of the laboratories.

Ebert touched the last man's arm as he went through, then glanced back the way he'd come. For a moment he thought he saw movement and hesitated, but there was nothing in the infra-red. He turned back quickly, then set off, running hard after his squad, hearing their boots echoing on the floor up ahead of him. But he had gone only ten or so strides when the floor seemed to give in front of him and he was tumbling forward down a slope.

He spread his legs behind him to slow himself and tried to dig his gun into the glassy surface of the slope. He slowed marginally, slewing to the left, then, abruptly, thumped into the wall. For a moment he was disoriented, his body twisted about violently. He felt his gun clatter away from him, then he was sliding again, head first this time, the yells closer now, mixed with a harsh muttering. A moment later he thumped bruisingly into a pile of bodies.

Ebert groaned, then looked up and saw Auden above

him, the heated recognition patch at his neck identifying him.

"Is anyone hurt?" Ebert said softly, almost breathlessly, letting Auden help him to his feet.

Auden leant close and whispered in his ear. "I think Leiter's dead, sir. A broken neck. He was just behind me when it went. And there seem to be a few other minor injuries. But otherwise . . ."

"Gods . . ." Ebert looked about him. "Where are we?"

"I don't know, sir. This isn't on the plans."

To three sides of them the walls went up vertically for forty, maybe fifty *ch'i*. It felt like they were at the bottom of a big, square-bottomed well. Ebert stepped back and stared up into the darkness overhead, trying to make something out. "There," he said, after a moment, pointing upward. "If we can fire a rope up there we can get out."

"If they don't pick us off first."

"Right." Ebert took a breath, then nodded. "You break up the surface about six or eight *ch'i* up the slope. Meanwhile, let's keep the bastards' heads down, eh?"

The sergeant gave a slight bow and turned to bark an order at one of his men. Meanwhile Ebert took two grenades from his belt. It was hard to make out just how far up the entrance to the corridor was. Thirty *ch'i*, perhaps. Maybe more. There was only the slightest change in the heat emission pattern – the vaguest hint of an outline. He hefted one of the grenades, released the pin, then leaned back and hurled it up into the darkness. If he missed . . .

He heard it rattle on the surface overhead. Heard shouts of surprise and panic. Then the darkness was filled with sudden, brilliant light. As it faded he threw the second grenade, more confident this time, aiming it at the smouldering red mouth of the tunnel. Someone was screaming up there – an awful, unnatural, high-pitched scream that chilled his blood – then the second explosion shuddered the air and the screaming stopped abruptly.

Ebert turned. Auden had chipped footholds into the slippery surface of the slope. Now he stood there, the big ascent gun at his hip, waiting for his Captain's order.

"Okay," Ebert said. "Try and fix it into the roof of the tunnel. As soon as it's there I'll start up. Once I'm at the top I want a man to follow me every ten seconds. Got that?"

"Sir!"

Auden looked up, judging the distance, then raised the heavy rifle to his shoulder and fired. The bolt flew up, trailing its thin, strong cord. They heard it thud into the ceiling of the tunnel, then two of the men were hauling on the slack of the cord, testing that the bolt was securely fixed overhead.

One of them turned, facing Ebert, his head bowed. "Rope secure, sir."

"Good." He stepped forward and took the gun from the soldier's shoulder. "Take Leiter's gun, Spitz. Or mine if you can find it."

"Sir!"

Ebert slipped the gun over his right shoulder, then took the rope firmly and began to climb, hauling himself up quickly, hands and feet working thoughtlessly. Three-quarters of the way up he slowed and shrugged the gun from his shoulder into his right hand, then began to climb again, pulling himself up one-handedly towards the lip.

They would be waiting. The grenades had done some damage, but they wouldn't have finished them off. There would be back-ups.

He stopped just beneath the lip and looked back down, signalling to Auden that he should begin. At once he felt the rope tighten beneath him as it took the weight of the first of the soldiers. Turning back, Ebert freed the safety with his thumb, then poked the barrel over the edge and squeezed the trigger. Almost at once the air was filled with the noise of return fire. Three, maybe four of them, he estimated.

Beneath him the rope swayed, then steadied again as the men below took the slack. Ebert took a long, shuddering breath, then heaved himself up, staring over the lip into the tunnel beyond.

He ducked down quickly, just as they opened up again. But he knew where they were now. Knew what cover he had up there. Quickly, his fingers fumbling at the catch, he freed the smoke bomb from his belt, twisted the neck of it sharply, then hurled it into the tunnel above him. He heard the shout of warning and knew they thought it was another grenade. Taking another long breath, he pulled the mask up over his mouth and nose, then heaved himself up over the lip and threw himself flat on the floor, covering his eyes.

There was a faint pop, then a brilliant glare of light. A moment later the tunnel was filled with billowing smoke.

Ebert crawled forward quickly, taking cover behind two badly-mutilated bodies that lay one atop the other against the left-hand wall. It was not a moment too soon. Bullets raked the tunnel wall only a hand's width above his head. He waited a second, then, taking the first of his targets from memory, fired through the dense smoke.

There was a short scream, then the firing started up again. But only two of them this time.

He felt the bullets thump into the corpse he was leaning on and rolled aside quickly, moving to his right. There was a moment's silence. Or almost silence. Behind him he heard sounds – strangely familiar sounds. A soft rustling that seemed somehow out of context here. He lifted his gun, about to open fire again, when he heard a faint click and the clatter of something small but heavy rolling towards him.

A grenade.

He scrabbled with his left hand, trying to intercept it and throw it back, but it was past him, rolling towards the lip.

"Shit!"

There was nothing for it now. He threw himself forward, his gun held chest-high, firing into the dense smoke up ahead. Then the explosion pushed him off his feet and he was lying amongst sandbags at the far end of the tunnel, stunned, his ears ringing.

"Light!" someone was saying. "Get a fucking light here!"

Auden. It was Auden's voice.

"Here!" he said weakly and tried to roll over, but there was something heavy across the back of his legs. Then, more strongly. "I'm here, sergeant!"

Auden came across quickly and reached down, pulling the body from him. "Thank the gods, sir! I was worried we'd lost you." He leaned forward and hauled Ebert to his feet, supporting him.

Ebert laughed, then slowly sat back down, his legs suddenly weak. "Me too." He looked up again as one of the soldiers brought an arc lamp across to them.

"Shit!" he said, looking about him. "What happened?"

"You must have blacked out, sir. But not before you did some damage here." Ebert shuddered, then half turned, putting his hand up to his neck. There were two bodies sprawled nearby, face down beside the sandbags. He looked up at Auden again.

"What are our losses?"

"Six men, sir. Including Leiter. And Grant has a bad head wound. We may have to leave him here for now."

"Six men? Fuck it!" He swallowed, then sat forward. "Do we know how the other squads are doing?"

Auden looked down. "That's another problem, sir. We've lost contact. All the channels are full of static."

Ebert laughed sourly. "Static? What's going on? What the fuck's going on?"

Auden shook his head. "I don't know. I really don't know, sir. But it's odd. There's an intersection up ahead that isn't on the map. And when you went up . . ." Auden hesitated, then went on. "Well, it seems they must have had a sluice or something at the bottom of the slope. One moment I was standing there, helping get the men on the rope, the next I was knee-deep in icy water."

Ebert looked down. So that was the strange sound he had heard. He shivered, then looked back up at Auden. "I wondered. You know that? As I was climbing the rope I was asking myself why they hadn't finished us off at once. Just a couple of grenades. That's all it would have taken. But that explains it, doesn't it? They meant to drown us. But why? What difference would it make?"

Auden smiled grimly back at him. "I don't know, sir, but if you're feeling all right we'd best press on. I don't like this quiet. I have the feeling they're watching us all the while, getting ready to hit us again."

Ebert smiled and reached out to touch his sergeant's shoulder briefly. "Okay. Then let's get moving, eh?"

Auden hesitated a moment longer. "One last thing, sir. Something you ought to know."

Ebert saw how Auden's eyes went to one of the corpses and felt himself go cold inside. "Don't tell me. They're like the copies at the wedding. Is that it?"

Auden shook his head, then went across and turned over one of the corpses, tugging off its helmet.

"Gods!" Ebert got up slowly and went across, then crouched above the body and, taking his knife from his belt, slit the jacket open, exposing the naked chest beneath.

He looked up at Auden and saw his own surprised bemusement mirrored back at him. "The gods preserve us!" He looked back down at the soft curves of the corpse's breasts, the soft, brown, blinded eyes of the nipples, and shuddered. "Are they all like this?"

Auden nodded. "All the ones I've looked at so far."

Ebert pulled the jacket back across the dead woman's breasts then stood up, his voice raised angrily. "What does it all mean? I mean, what in hell's name does it all mean?"

Auden shrugged. "I don't know, sir. But I know one thing. Someone told them we were coming. Someone set us up."

* * *

General Tolonen dismissed the two guards, locked the door, then turned to face the young prince, his head bowed.

"I am sorry I had to bring you here, young master, but

I couldn't chance letting our enemies know of this, however small the risk."

Li Yuan stood there stiffly, his chin raised slightly, a bitter anger in his red-rimmed eyes. He was barely half the General's height and yet his air of command, even in grief, left no doubt as to who was master, who servant there. The prince was wearing the *cheng fu*, the rough, unhemmed sackcloth of traditional mourning clothes, his feet clad in simple, undecorated sandals, his hands and neck bare of all jewellery. It was all so brutally austere – so raw a display of grief – it made Tolonen's heart ache to see him so.

They were in a Secure Room at the heart of the Bremen fortress. A room no more than twenty *ch'i* square, cut off on all six sides from the surrounding structure, a series of supporting struts holding it in place. It was reached by way of a short corridor with two air-locks, each emptied to total vacuum after use. Most found it an uncomfortable, uneasy place to be. Once inside, however, absolute secrecy could be guaranteed. No cameras looked into the room and no communications links went out from there. In view of recent developments, Tolonen welcomed its perfect isolation. Too much had happened for him to take unnecessary risks.

"Have you spoken to him yet?" Li Yuan asked, anger burning in his eyes. "Did the bastard lie through his teeth?"

The young boy's anger was something to be seen. Tolonen had never dreamed he had it in him. He had always seemed so cold and passionless. Moreover, there was an acid bitterness to the words that struck a chord in Tolonen. Li Yuan had taken his brother's death badly. Only vengeance would satisfy him. In that they were alike.

Tolonen removed his uniform cap and bowed to him. "You must be patient, young master. These things take time. I want solid evidence before I confront our friend Berdichev."

The eight-year-old turned away sharply, the abruptness of the gesture revealing his inner turmoil. Then he turned back, his eyes flaring. "I want them dead, General Tolonen.

Every last one of them. And I want their families eradicated. To the third generation."

Tolonen bowed his head again. I would, he thought, were that my T'ang's command. But Li Shai Tung has said nothing yet. Nothing of what he feels, or wants, nor of what was said in Council yesterday. What have the Seven decided? How are they to answer this impertinence?

Yes, little master, I would gladly do as you say. But my hands are tied.

"We know much more now," he said, taking Li Yuan's shoulder and steering him across the room to where two chairs had been placed before a screen. He sat, facing Li Yuan, conscious not only of the boy's grief and anger but also of his great dignity. "We know how it was done."

He saw how Li Yuan tensed.

"Yes," Tolonen said. "The key to it all was simulated vision." He saw that it meant nothing to Li Yuan and pressed on. "We discovered it in our raid on the SimFic installation at Punto Natales. They had been conducting illegal experiments with it there for more than eight years, apparently. It seems that the soft-wire they found in Chao Yang's head was part of one of their systems."

Li Yuan shook his head. "I don't understand you, General. SimFic have been conducting illegal experiments? Is that it? They've been wilfully flouting the terms of the Edict?"

Tolonen nodded but raised a hand to fend off Li Yuan's query. This was complex ground and he did not want to get into a discussion about how all Companies conducted such experiments, then lobbied to get their supposedly "theoretical" products accepted by the Ministry.

"Setting that aside a moment," he said, "what is of primary importance here is the fact that Pei Chao Yang was not to blame for your brother's murder. It seems he had brain surgery for a blood clot almost five years ago – an operation that his father, Pei Ro-hen, kept from the public record. Chao had a hunting accident, it seems. He fell badly from his horse. But the operation was a success

329

and he had had no further trouble. That is, until the day of the wedding. Now we know why."

"You mean, they implanted something in his head? Something to control him?"

"Not to control him, exactly. But something that would make him see precisely what they wanted him to see. Something that superimposed a different set of images. Even a different set of smells, it seems. Something that made him see Han Ch'in *differently* . . ."

"And we know who carried out this . . . operation?"

Tolonen looked back at the boy. "Yes. But they're dead. They've been dead for several years, in fact. Whoever arranged this was very thorough. Very thorough indeed."

"But SimFic are to blame? Berdichev's to blame?"

He saw the ferocity on Li Yuan's face and nodded. "I believe so. But maybe not enough to make a conclusive case in law. It all depends on what we find at Hammerfest."

★ ★ ★

She came at him like a madwoman, screeching, a big, sharp-edged hunting knife in her left hand, a notched bayonet in her right.

Ebert ducked under the vicious swinging blow and thrust his blade between her breasts, using both hands, the force of the thrust carrying her backwards, almost lifting her off her feet.

"Gods . . ." he said, looking down at the dying woman, shaken by the ferocity of her attack. "How many more of them?"

It was five minutes to six and he was lost. Eight of his squad were dead now, two left behind in the corridors, badly wounded. They had killed more than twenty of the defending force. All of them women. Madwomen, like the one he had just killed. And still they came at them.

Why women? he kept asking himself. But deeper down he knew why. It gave his enemy a psychological edge. He didn't feel good about killing women. Nor had his men felt good. He'd heard them muttering among themselves. And now they were dead. Or good as.

"Do we go on?" Auden, his sergeant, asked.

Ebert turned and looked back at the remnants of his squad. There were four of them left now, including himself. And not one of them had ever experienced anything like this before. He could see it in their eyes. They were tired and bewildered. The past hour had seemed an eternity, with no knowing where the next attack would come from.

The ground plans they had been working from had proved completely false. Whoever was in charge of this had secretly rebuilt the complex and turned it into a maze: a web of deadly cul-de-sacs and traps. Worse yet, they had flooded the corridors with ghost signals, making it impossible for them to keep in contact with the other attacking groups.

Ebert smiled grimly. "We go on. It can't be far now."

At the next junction they came under fire again and lost another man. But this time the expected counter-attack did not materialise. Perhaps we're almost there, thought Ebert as he pressed against the wall, getting his breath. Maybe this is their last line of defence. He looked across the corridor and met Auden's eyes. Yes, he thought, if we get out of this I'll commend you. You've saved me more than once this last hour.

"Get ready," he mouthed. "I'll go first. You cover."

Auden nodded and lifted his gun to his chest, tensed, ready to go.

The crossway was just ahead of them. Beyond it, about ten paces down the corridor and to the right, was a door-way.

Ebert flung himself across the open space, firing to his left, his finger jammed down on the trigger of the automatic. Behind him Auden and Spitz opened up noisily. Landing awkwardly, he began to scrabble forward, making for the doorway.

He heard her before he saw her. Turning his head he caught a glimpse of her on the beam overhead, her body crouched, already falling. He brought his gun up sharply, but it was already too late. Even as he loosed off the first wild shot, her booted feet crashed into his back heavily, smashing him down into the concrete floor.

* * *

The film had ended. Tolonen turned in his seat and looked at the boy.

"There are two more, then we are done here."

Li Yuan nodded but did not look back at him. He was sitting there rigidly, staring at the screen as if he would burn a hole in it. Tolonen studied him a moment longer, then looked away. This was hard for the boy, but it was what his father wanted. After all, Li Yuan would be T'ang one day and a T'ang needed to be hard.

Tolonen sat back in his chair again, then pressed the handset, activating the screen again.

On the evening of the wedding the walls of the *Yu Hua Yuan* had been lined with discreet security cameras. The logistics of tracking fifteen hundred individuals in such a small, dimly-lit space had meant that they had had to use flat-image photography. Even so, because each individual had been in more than one camera's range at any given moment, a kind of three-dimensional effect had been achieved. A computer programmed for full-head recognition of each of the individuals present had analysed each of the one hundred and eighty separate films and produced fifteen hundred new, "rounded" films of seventeen minutes duration – timed to bracket the death of Han Ch'in by eight minutes either side. The new films eliminated all those moments when the heads of others intruded, enhancing the image whenever the mouth was seen to move, the lips to form words. What resulted was a series of individual "response portraits" so vivid one would have thought the lens had been a mere arm's length in front of each face.

They had already watched five of the seventeen minute films. Had seen the unfeigned surprise – the shock – on the faces of men whom they thought might have been involved.

"Does that mean they're innocent?" Li Yuan had asked.

"Not necessarily," Tolonen had answered. "The details might have been kept from them deliberately. But they're the money men. I'm sure of it."

This, the sixth of the films, showed one of Tolonen's own men, a captain in the elite force; the officer responsible for the *shao lin* posted in the garden that evening.

Li Yuan turned and looked up at Tolonen, surprised. "But that's Captain Erikson."

The General nodded. "Watch. Tell me what you think."

Li Yuan turned back and for a time was silent, concentrating on the screen.

"Well?" prompted Tolonen.

"His reactions seem odd. His eyes . . . It's almost as if he's steeled himself not to react."

"Or as if he was drugged, perhaps? Don't you think his face shows symptoms similar to arfidis trance? He's not been known to indulge before now, but who knows? Maybe he's an addict, neh?"

Li Yuan turned and looked up at the General again. Between the words and the tone in which they had been said lay a question mark.

"You don't believe that, do you?" he said after a moment. "You don't think he would have risked public exposure of his habit."

Tolonen was silent, watching the boy closely. Li Yuan looked away again, then started, understanding suddenly what the General had really been saying.

"He knew! That's what you mean, isn't it? Erikson knew, but . . . but he didn't dare show it. Is that right? You think he risked taking arfidis in public?"

"I think so," said Tolonen quietly. He was pleased with Li Yuan. If one good thing had come out of this rotten business it was this: Li Yuan would be T'ang one day. A great T'ang. If he lived long enough.

"Then that explains why no *shao lin* were close enough to act."

"Yes."

"And Erikson?"

"He's dead. He killed himself an hour after the assassination. At first I thought it was because he felt he had failed me. Now I know otherwise."

Tolonen stared up at Erikson's face, conscious of the misery behind the dull surface glaze of his eyes. He had suffered for his betrayal.

Li Yuan's voice was strangely gentle. "What made him do it?"

"We're not certain, but we think he might have been involved in the assassination of Lwo Kang. He was on DeVore's staff at the time, and is known to have been in contact with DeVore in a private capacity while the latter was in charge of Security on Mars."

"I see."

The film ended. The next began. Lehmann's face filled the screen.

Something was wrong. That much was clear at once. Lehmann seemed nervous, strangely agitated. He talked fluently but seemed distanced from what he was saying. He held his head stiffly, awkwardly and his eyes made small, erratic movements in their sockets.

"He knows!" whispered Li Yuan, horrified, unable to tear his eyes away from the image on the screen. "Kuan Yin, sweet Goddess of Mercy, he *knows*!"

There, framed between Lehmann's head and the screen's top edge, he could see his brother standing with his bride, laughing with her, talking, exchanging loving glances . . .

No, he thought. *No-o-o!* Sheer dread welled up in him, making his hands tremble, his stomach clench with anguish. Lehmann's face was huge, almost choking the screen. Vast it was, its surface a deathly white, like the springtime moon, bleak and pitted, filling the sky. And beyond it stood his brother, Han, sweet Han, breathing, talking, laughing –

334

alive! – yes, for that frozen, timeless moment still alive – and yet so small, so frail, so hideously vulnerable.

Lehmann turned and looked across to where Han was talking to the Generals. For a moment he simply stared, his hostility unmasked, then he half turned to his right, as if in response to something someone had said, and laughed. That laughter – so in contrast with the coldness in his eyes – was chilling to observe. Li Yuan shivered. There was no doubting it now. Lehmann had known what was about to happen.

Slowly, almost unobtrusively, Lehmann moved back into the circle of his acquaintances, until, as the newly weds stopped before Pei Chao Yang, he was directly facing them. Now there was nothing but his face staring down from the massive screen; a face that had been reconstructed from a dozen separate angles. All that lay between the lens and his face had been erased, the intruding images of murder cleared from the computer's memory.

"No . . ." Li Yuan moaned softly, the pressure in his chest almost suffocating him, the pain growing with every moment.

Slowly, so slowly the seconds passed, and then Lehmann's whole face seemed to stiffen.

"His eyes," said Tolonen softly, his voice filled with pain. "Look at his eyes . . ."

Li Yuan groaned. Lehmann's features were shaped superficially into a mask of concern, but his eyes were laughing, the pupils wide, aroused. And there, in the dark centre of each eye, was the image of Pei Chao Yang, struggling with Han Ch'in. *There* – doubled, inverted in the swollen darkness.

"No–o–o!" Li Yuan was on his feet, his fists clenched tightly, his face a rictus of pain and longing. "Han! . . . Sweet Han!"

* * *

When Ebert came to, the woman was lying beside him, dead, most of her head shot away. His sergeant, Auden, was kneeling over him, firing the big automatic into the rafters overhead.

He lifted his head, then let it fall again, a sharp pain accompanying the momentary wave of blackness. There was a soft wetness at the back of his head where the pain was most intense. He touched it gingerly, then closed his eyes again. It could be worse, he thought. I could be dead.

Auden let off another burst into the overhead, then looked down at him. "Are you all right, sir?"

Ebert coughed, then gave a forced smile. "I'm fine. What's happening?"

Auden motioned overhead with his gun, his eyes returning to the web-like structure of beams and rafters that reached up into the darkness.

"There was some movement up there, but there's nothing much going on now."

Ebert tried to focus, but found he couldn't. Again he closed his eyes, his head pounding, the pain engulfing him. Auden was still talking.

"It's like a rat's nest up there. But it's odd, sir. If I was them I'd drop gas canisters or grenades. I'd have set up a network of automatic weapons."

"Perhaps they have," said Ebert weakly. "Perhaps there's no one left to operate them."

Auden looked down at him again, concerned. "Are you sure you're all right, sir?"

Ebert opened his eyes. "My head. I've done something to my head."

Auden set his gun down and lifted Ebert's head carefully with one hand and probed gently with the other.

Ebert winced. "Gods . . ."

Auden knelt back, shocked by the extent of the damage. He thought for a moment, then took a small aerosol from his tunic pocket and sprayed the back of Ebert's head. Ebert gritted his teeth against the cold, fierce, burning pain of the spray but made no sound. Auden let the spray fall and took an emergency bandage, a hand-sized padded square, from another pocket and applied it to the wound. Then he laid

Ebert down again, turning him on his side and loosening the collar of his tunic. "It's not too bad, sir. The cut's not deep. She was dead before she could do any real damage."

Ebert looked up into Auden's face. "I suppose I should thank you."

Auden had picked up his gun and was staring up into the overhead again. He glanced down quickly and shook his head. "No need, sir. It was my duty. Anyway, we'd none of us survive long if we didn't help each other out."

Ebert smiled, strangely warmed by the simplicity of Auden's statement. The pain was subsiding now, the darkness in his head receding. Looking past Auden he found he could see much more clearly. "Where's Spitz?"

"Dead, sir. We were attacked from behind as we crossed the inter-section."

"So there's only the two of us now."

"Yes, sir." Auden scanned the overhead one last time, looked back and front, then slipped his gun onto his shoulder. "I'll have to carry you, sir. There's a stairwell at the end of this corridor. If we're lucky we'll find some of our own up top. I've heard voices up above. Male voices. I think they're some of ours."

Putting his hands under Ebert's armpits he pulled the wounded man up into a sitting position, then knelt and, putting all his strength into it, heaved his captain up onto his shoulder. For a moment he crouched there, getting his balance, then reached out with his right hand and picked up his gun.

* * *

Li Yuan found her in the eastern palace at Sichuan, seated amidst her maids. It was a big, spacious room, opening on one side to a balcony, from which steps led down to a wide, green pool. Outside the day was bright, but in the room it was shadowed. Light, reflected from the pool, washed the ornate ceiling with ever-changing patterns of silver and black, while beneath all lay in darkness.

Fei Yen wore the *ts'ui* and the *shang*, the coarse hemp

cloth unhemmed, as was demanded by the first mourning grade of *chan ts'ui*. Three years of mourning lay before her now – twenty-seven months in reality. All about her her maids wore simple white, and in a white, rounded bowl beside the high-backed chair in which she sat was a dying spray of flowers, their crimson and golden glory faded.

She looked up at him through eyes made dark from days of weeping, and summoned him closer. She seemed far older than he remembered her. Old and bone-tired. Yet it was only four days since the death of Han Ch'in.

He bowed low, then straightened, waiting for her to speak.

Fei Yen turned slowly and whispered something. At once her maids got up and began to leave, bowing to Li Yuan as they passed. Then he was alone with her.

"Why have you come?"

He was silent a moment, daunted by her; by the unexpected hostility in her voice.

"I . . . I came to see how you were. To see if you were recovering."

Fei Yen snorted and looked away, her face bitter. Then, relenting, she looked back at him.

"Forgive me, Li Yuan. I'm mending. The doctors say I suffered no real physical harm. Nothing's broken . . ."

She shuddered and looked down again, a fresh tear forming in the corner of her eye. Li Yuan, watching her, felt his heart go out to her. She had loved his brother deeply. Even as much as he had loved him. Perhaps that was why he had come: to share with her both his grief and the awful denial of that love. But now that he was here with her, he found it impossible to say what he felt – impossible even to begin to speak of it.

For a while she was perfectly still, then she wiped the tear away impatiently and stood up, coming down to him.

"Please forgive me, brother-in-law. I should greet you properly."

Fei Yen embraced him briefly, then moved away. At the opening to the balcony she stopped and leaned against one of the pillars, staring out across the pool towards the distant mountains.

Li Yuan followed her and stood there, next to her, not knowing what to say nor how to act.

She turned and looked at him. Though eight years separated them he was not far from her height. Even so, she always made him feel a child beside her. Only a child. All that he knew – all that he was – seemed unimportant. Even he, the future T'ang, was made to feel inferior in her presence. Yes, even now, when her beauty was clouded, her eyes filled with resentment and anger. He swallowed and looked away, but still he felt her eyes upon him.

"So now *you* will be T'ang."

He looked back at her, trying to gauge what she was thinking, for her words had been colourless, a statement. But what did she feel? Bitterness? Jealousy? Anger that no son of hers would one day be T'ang?

"Yes," he said simply. "One day."

Much earlier he had stood there in his father's study, staring up at the giant image of Europe that filled one wall – the same image that could be seen from the viewing circle in the floating palace, 160,000 *li* above Chung Kuo.

A swirl of cloud, like a figure 3, had obscured much of the ocean to the far left of the circle. Beneath the cloud the land was crudely shaped. To the east vast plains of green stretched outward towards Asia. All the rest was white; white with a central mass of grey-black and another, smaller mass slightly to the east, making the whole thing look like the skull of some fantastic giant beast with horns. The white was City Europe; glacial, in the grip of a second age of ice.

From up there the world seemed small; reduced to a diagram. All that he saw his father owned and ruled. All things, all people there were his. And yet his eldest son was dead, and he could do nothing. What sense did it make?

He moved past her, onto the balcony, then stood there at the stone balustrade, looking down into the pale green water, watching the fish move in the depths. But for once he felt no connection with them, no ease in contemplating them.

"You've taken it all very well," she said, coming up beside him. "You've been a brave boy."

He looked up at her sharply, bitterly; hurt by her insensitivity, strangely stung by her use of the word "boy".

"What do you know?" he snapped, pushing away from her. "How dare you presume that I feel less than you? How *dare* you?"

He rounded on her, almost in tears now, his grief, his unassuaged anger making him want to break something; to snap and shatter something fragile. To hurt someone as badly as he'd been hurt.

"I . . ." She looked back at him, bewildered now, all bitterness, all jealousy drained from her by his outburst. "Oh, Yuan. Little Yuan. I didn't know . . ." She came to him and held him tight against her, stroking his hair, ignoring the pain where he gripped her sides tightly, hurting the bruises there. "Oh, Yuan. My poor little Yuan. I'm sorry. I'm so, so sorry. How was I to know, my little one? How was I to know?"

* * *

The stairs led up to a wide landing cluttered with crates. Three corridors led off. Two were cul-de-sacs, the third led to another, much longer stairwell. Auden went up again, his gun poked out in front of him, the safety catch off, his trigger finger aching with the tension of preparedness. Ebert was a numbing weight on his left shoulder.

Near the top of the steps he slowed and looked about him, his eyes on the level of the floor, his gun searching for targets. It was a vast, open space, like the floor of a warehouse, broken every now and then by huge, rectangular blockhouses. The ceiling was high overhead and crisscrossed with tracks. Stacks of crates stood here and there and electric trolleys were parked nearby. Otherwise the place seemed empty.

"I don't like it," Auden said quietly for Ebert's benefit.

340

"All that back there. And then nothing. We can't have got them all. And where are our men?"

"What is it?"

"Some kind of loading floor. A huge big place. And there are blockhouses of some kind. They look empty, but they might easily be defended."

Ebert swallowed painfully. His head ached from being carried upside down and he was beginning to feel sick. His voice was weak now. "Let's find somewhere we can shelter. Somewhere you can set me down."

Auden hesitated. "I'm not sure, sir. I think it's a trap."

Ebert's weariness was momentarily tinged with irritation. "Maybe. But we've little choice, have we? We can't go back down. And we can't stay here much longer."

Auden ignored the sharpness in his captain's voice, scanning the apparent emptiness of the loading floor once again. Nothing. He was almost certain there was nothing out there. And yet his instincts told him otherwise. It was what he himself would have done. Hit hard, then hit hard again and again and again. And then, when your enemy expected the very worst, withdraw. Make them think they had won through. Allow them to come at you without resistance. Draw them into the heart of your defences. And then . . .

Ebert's voice rose, shattering the silence. "Gods, sergeant, don't just stand there, do something! I'm dying!"

Auden shuddered. "All right," he said. "We'll find shelter. Somewhere to put you down."

He breathed deeply for a few seconds, then hauled himself up the last few steps, expecting at any moment to be raked with heavy automatic fire or cut in half by one of the big lasers, but there was nothing. He ran as fast as he could, crouching, wheezing now, the weight of Ebert almost too much for him.

He made the space between two stacks of unmarked boxes and turned, looking back at the stairwell. For a moment he could have sworn he saw a head, back there where he had just come from. He took two shuddering

341

breaths, then put his gun down and gently eased Ebert from his shoulder, setting him down on his side.

"We need to get help for you, sir. You've lost a lot of blood."

Ebert had closed his eyes. "Yes," he said painfully, his voice a whisper now. "Go on. Be quick. I'll be all right."

Auden nodded and reached behind him for his gun. His hand searched a moment, then closed slowly, forming a fist. Instinct. He should have trusted to instinct. Raising his hands he stood up and turned slowly, facing the man with the gun who stood there only three paces away.

"That's right, sergeant. Keep your hands raised and don't make any sudden movements. Now come out here, into the open."

The man backed away as Auden came forward, keeping his gun levelled. He was a tall, gaunt-looking Han with a long, horse-like face and a wide mouth. He wore a pale green uniform with the SimFic double-helix insignia on lapel and cap. His breast-patch showed a bear snatching at a cloud of tiny, silken butterflies, signifying that he was a fifth rank officer – a captain. As Auden came out into the open other guards came from behind the stacks to encircle him.

"Good," said the captain. Then he signalled to some of his men. "Quick now! Get the other one to the infirmary. We don't want him to die, now do we?"

Auden's eyes widened in surprise and he half turned, watching them go to Ebert and lift him gently onto a stretcher. "What's happening here?" he asked, looking back at the SimFic captain. "What are you playing at?"

The captain watched his fellows carry Ebert away, then turned back to Auden and lowered his gun. "I'm sorry, sergeant, but we couldn't take risks. I didn't want to lose any more men through a misunderstanding between us." Unexpectedly, he smiled. "You're safe now. The base has been liberated. The insurrection has been put down."

Auden laughed, not believing what he was hearing. "Insurrection? What do you mean?"

The Han's smile became fixed. "Yes. Unknown to the Company, the installation was infiltrated and taken over by a terrorist organisation. We only learned of it this morning. We came as soon as we could."

"Quite a coincidence," said Auden, sickened, realising at once what had happened. It was like he'd said to Ebert. They had been set up. The whole thing had been a set up. A charade. And all to get SimFic off the hook.

"Yes. But fortunate too, yes? If we had not come you would all be dead. As it is more than a dozen of your men have got out alive."

Auden shivered, thinking of all the good men he'd fought beside. Dead now. Dead, and simply to save some bastard's butt higher up the levels. "And the terrorists?"

"All dead. They barricaded themselves into the laboratories. We had to gas them, I'm afraid."

"Convenient, eh?" He glared at the Han, bitter now.

The captain frowned. "I'm sorry, but I don't understand you, sergeant. This whole business . . . it was unfortunate, but it could not be helped, eh? I lost more than thirty of my own men in the fighting."

Auden stared back at him. Yes, he thought, loathing the slick-tongued Han who stood before him; you lost thirty "men" – but not to terrorists, that's for certain!

★   ★   ★

There was the sound of raised voices in the corridor outside and the light on his desk intercom began to flash urgently. Soren Berdichev, Head of SimFic, looked up past the five men who were seated round the desk with him and straightened his small, round-rimmed glasses, clearing the computer-generated figures that were displayed in duplicate on their inner surfaces.

"What in heaven's name . . . ?"

It was just after eight in the morning and they were two hours into their weekly strategy conference.

The man closest to him on his left stood, then turned and bowed to him. "Excuse me, sir. Shall I find out what the trouble is?"

Berdichev put his hand over the cancel on the intercom and looked up at his Senior Executive. He spoke coldly, sternly. "Thank you, Paul. Please do. If it's a member of staff you will dismiss them immediately. I'll not tolerate such behaviour in these offices."

Moore bowed again and turned to do as he was bid. But he had got barely halfway across the room when the door crashed open.

Tolonen stood there in the doorway, tall and grey-haired, his eyes burning with anger, his whole manner menacing. He was wearing full combat uniform, the helmet loose about his neck, a light automatic in the holster at his waist, as if he had come straight from action. Behind him several members of Berdichev's staff stood with their heads bowed, shamed that they had not been able to prevent the intrusion.

Berdichev got up slowly, his own outrage tightly, deliberately controlled. "General Tolonen . . . I hope you have good reason for bursting in on me like this?"

Tolonen ignored the comment. He looked about the room, then came in, striding past Moore without a glance, making straight for Berdichev. Shoving between two of the seated men, he leaned across and brought his fist down hard on the table.

"You know perfectly well why I'm here, you wall lizard!"

Berdichev sat back composedly and put his hands together. "Your manners leave much to be desired, General. If you had had the common courtesy to talk to my secretary I would have seen you this afternoon. But now . . . Well, you can be certain that I'll be reporting your behaviour to the House committee on Security matters. These are private offices, General, and even you cannot enter without permission."

Angrily, Tolonen straightened up and took the warrant from his tunic pocket, then flung it down on the desk in front of Berdichev. "Now explain yourself! Or I'll come round and choke the bloody truth from you!"

Berdichev picked up the small, card-like warrant and studied it a moment, then threw it back across the table at Tolonen. "So you have a right to be here. But legality doesn't excuse your poor manners, General. My complaint still stands. Your behaviour has been atrocious. You have insulted me and openly threatened me before witnesses. I . . ."

Tolonen cut him short. He leaned across the table and roared at him. "*Hsin fa ts'ai*! What do you know of manners, you *hsiao jen*!"

For the first time Berdichev bristled. The insults had stung him; but inwardly he felt a small satisfaction. His tactic had the General rattled. The fact that he had slipped into Mandarin revealed just how emotionally off-balance Tolonen was.

He leaned forward, undaunted, and met the General's eyes. "Now that you're here, you'd best tell me what you want of me. I'm a busy man, *social upstart* or not, *little man* or not. I have an empire to run . . . if you'll excuse the phrase."

Tolonen glared at him a moment longer, then straightened up again. "Dismiss these men. I need to talk to you alone."

Berdichev looked to the nearest of his men and gave a slight nod. Slowly, reluctantly, they began to leave. His Senior Executive, Moore, stood his ground however, staring concernedly at his superior. Only as he was about to turn and leave, did Berdichev look back at him.

"Paul . . . please stay. I'd like a witness to what is said here."

"I said . . ." began Tolonen, but Berdichev interrupted him.

"I assure you, General, I will say nothing without a witness present. You see, there are no cameras in this room, no tapes. Much is said here that is of a secret nature. Things we would not like to get to the ears of our competitors.

You understand me, General? Besides which, you have made threats to me. How can I feel safe unless one of my own is here to see that my rights are not violated?"

Tolonen snorted. "Rights! Fine words from you, who has so little respect for the rights of others!"

Berdichev tutted and looked down. "Again you insult me, General. Might I ask why? What have I done that should make you treat me thus?"

"You know damn well what you've done! And all this acting won't save your arse this time! You're implicated to the hilt, *Shih* Berdichev! I'm talking about the murder of Li Han Ch'in, not some petty matter of manners. Two of your installations are directly involved. And that means that you're involved. You personally!"

Berdichev took off his glasses and polished the lenses, then looked back at the General. "I assume you mean the business at Hammerfest."

Tolonen laughed, astonished by the sheer effrontery of the man. "The business at Hammerfest . . . Yes. I mean the matter of your duplicity."

Berdichev frowned and turned to Moore. "My duplicity?" He looked back at the General, shaking his head sadly. "Again, I don't understand you, General. Have I not been totally open? Have I not given you copies of all the documents relating to both our Punto Natales installation and the base at Hammerfest? Indeed, were it not for my men, I understand that you would have lost all of your force to the terrorists, Klaus Ebert's son amongst them."

"Terrorists! That's just more of your nonsense! You know damned well there were no terrorists!"

"You can prove that, General?"

Tolonen lowered his voice. "I have no need to prove it. I know it. Here," he tapped his heart, "and here," he tapped his head.

"And what does that mean?" Berdichev leaned forward, his thin face hardening, his glasses glinting in the overhead light. "You are making serious accusations, General, and I

346

hope you can substantiate them. I regret what happened at Hammerfest, *but I am not responsible for it.*"

Tolonen shook his head. "That's where you're wrong, Berdichev. The research undertaken at both installations was illegal and has been directly linked to the assassination of Li Han Ch'in. Such work was undertaken in the name of SimFic, carried out on properties leased by SimFic and even funded by SimFic. As Head of SimFic you are directly responsible."

"I disagree. Some projects, undertaken in our name, may well have been illegal, as you say. They may – though it remains to be proved conclusively – be linked to Li Han Ch'in's most unfortunate death. But just because something is done under our corporate name, it does not mean to say that we knew about it, nor that we sanctioned it. As you know, General, as soon as I found out what was happening I ordered full cooperation with the Security forces and even ordered my own security squads to assist you."

Tolonen was silent a moment, his face coldly furious. "You want me to believe that you didn't know what was going on?"

"To be frank with you, General, I don't really care what *you* believe. I care only for the truth of the matter." He pointed past Tolonen at a huge chart on the right-hand wall. "See that there, General? That is a chart of my organisation. Its structure, if you like. You'll see how it divides and then sub-divides. How certain parts of the organisation have a degree of autonomy. How others are buried deep in a long chain of sub-structures. A company like SimFic is a complex creation. A living, functional entity, changing and evolving all the time."

"So?"

Berdichev folded his arms and sat back again. "How many men do you command, General? Half a million? A million?"

Tolonen stood straighter. "I command four Banners. Two million men in all."

"I see." He turned to his Senior Executive. "Paul . . .

347

How many men do we employ in our African operation?"

"Four hundred and eighty thousand."

"And in North America?"

"Seven hundred and forty thousand."

"And in the Asian operation?"

"One million, two hundred thousand."

Berdichev looked back at the General. "Those three comprise a third of our total operations, the major part of which is based here, in City Europe. So you see, General, my own 'command' is three times the size of your own. Now, let me ask you a question. Do you know what all of *your* men are doing all of the time?"

Tolonen huffed. "Why, that's absurd! Of course I don't!"

Berdichev smiled coldly. "And yet you expect me to know what all of my managers are up to all of the time! You expect *me* to be responsible for their actions! Aren't you, by the same argument, responsible for DeVore's actions? For his betrayal?"

Tolonen did not answer, merely stared back at Berdichev, an undisguised hatred in his eyes.

"Well?" Berdichev asked after a moment. "Are you finished here?"

Tolonen shook his head; his whole manner had changed with the mention of DeVore. He was colder now, more distant. "I have only one more thing to say to you, *Shih* Berdichev. You claim you are not responsible. So you say. Nonetheless, you will find out who *was* responsible for this. And you will deliver their heads or your own, understand? I give you three days."

"Three days!" Berdichev sat forward. "By what authority . . . ?"

Tolonen went to the door, then turned and looked back at Berdichev. "Three days. And if you don't I shall come for you myself."

When he was gone, Berdichev leaned forward and placed his hand on the intercom. "Did you get all of that?"

A voice answered at once. "Everything. We're checking

now, but it looks like all six angles were fine. We'll have the edited tape to you in an hour."

"Good!" He closed contact and looked up at Moore. "Well, Paul?"

Moore was still staring at the door. "You push him too far, Soren. He's a dangerous man. You should be cautious of him."

Berdichev laughed. "Tolonen? Why, he's an impotent old fool! He can't even wipe his own arse without his T'ang's permission, and Li Shai Tung won't give him authority to act against us in a thousand years – not unless he has proof positive. No, we've done enough, Paul. That just now was all bullshit and bluster. Don't fear. Tolonen will do nothing unless it's sanctioned by his T'ang!"

★ ★ ★

Tolonen's audience with the T'ang was three hours later. Shepherd, the T'ang's advisor, had got there some time before and had updated Li Shai Tung on all relevant matters. As soon as Tolonen arrived, therefore, they got down to more important business.

The T'ang sat there, in a seat placed at the foot of the dais, dressed in the rough, unhemmed hempcloth of mourning, subdued and solemn, a thousand cares on his shoulders. He had not left the Imperial Palace since the murder of his son, nor had he eaten. At his neck was stitched a broad square of white cloth and in his left hand he held a bamboo staff. Both symbolised his grief.

There were only the three of them in the vast, high-ceilinged Throne Room, and the T'ang's voice, when he spoke, echoed back to them.

"Well, Knut? What do you suggest?"

The General bowed, then outlined his plan, arguing in favour of a pre-emptive strike. War, but of a contained nature, attacking specific targets. A swift retribution, then peace with all other factions.

Li Shai Tung listened, then seemed to look deep inside himself. "I have lost the most precious thing a man has,"

349

he said at last, looking at each of them in turn. "I have lost my eldest son. To this I cannot be reconciled. Nor can I love my enemies. Indeed, when I look into my heart I find only hatred there for them. A bitter hatred." He let out a long breath, then stared fixedly at Tolonen. "I would kill them like animals if it would end there, Knut. But it would not. There would be war, as you say, but not of the kind you have envisaged. It would be a dirty, secretive, incestuous war, and we would come out poorly from it."

He smiled bleakly at his General, then looked away, the misery in his dark eyes so eloquent that Tolonen found his own eyes misting in response.

"For once, my good General, I think you are wrong. I do not believe we can fight a contained war. Indeed, the Seven have known that for a long time now. Such a contest would spread. Spread until the Families faced the full might of the Above, for they would see it as a challenge; an attack upon their rights – upon their very existence as a class."

Tolonen looked down, recalling the look in Lehmann's eyes, the foul effrontery of Berdichev, and shuddered. "What then, *Chieh Hsia*?" he said bluntly, almost belligerently. "Shall we do nothing? Surely that's just as bad?"

Li Shai Tung lifted his hand abruptly, silencing him. It was the first time he had done so in the forty-odd years he had known the General and Tolonen looked back at him wide-eyed a moment before he bowed his head.

The T'ang looked at the staff he held. It was the very symbol of dependency; of how grief was supposed to weaken man. Yet the truth was otherwise. Man was strengthened through suffering; hardened by it. He looked back at his General, understanding his anger; his desire to strike back at those who had wounded him. "Yes, Knut, to do nothing *is* bad. But not as bad as acting rashly. We must seem weak. We must bend with the wind; sway in the storm's mouth and bide our time. *Wuwei* must be our chosen course for now."

Wuwei. Non-action. It was an old Taoist concept. *Wuwei* meant keeping harmony with the flow of things – doing nothing to break that flow.

There was a moment's tense silence, then Tolonen shook his head almost angrily. "Might I say what I feel, *Chieh Hsia*?" The formality of the General's tone spoke volumes. This was the closest the two men had ever come to arguing.

The T'ang stared at his General a moment, then looked away. "Say what you must."

Tolonen bowed deeply, then drew himself erect. "Just this. You are wrong, Li Shai Tung. Execute me for saying so, but hear me out. You are wrong. I know it. I feel it in my bones. This is no time for *wuwei*. No time to be cool-headed and dispassionate. We must be like the tiger now. We must bare our claws and teeth and strike. This or be eaten alive."

The T'ang considered for a moment, then leaned further forward on his throne. "You sound like Han Ch'in," he said, amusement and bitterness in even measure in his voice. "He too would have counselled war. 'They have killed me, father,' he would have said, 'So now you must kill them back.'" He shivered and looked away, his expression suddenly distraught. "Gods, Knut, I have considered this matter long and hard. But Han's advice was always brash, always hasty. He thought with his heart. But I must consider my other son now. I must give *him* life, stability, continuity. If we fight a war he will die. Of that I am absolutely certain. They will find a way – just as they found a way to get to Han Ch'in. And in the end they will destroy the Families."

Li Shai Tung turned to Shepherd, who had been silent throughout their exchange. "I do this for the sake of the living. You understand that, Hal, surely?"

Shepherd smiled sadly. "I understand, Shai Tung."

"And the Seven?" Tolonen stood there stiffly, at attention, his whole frame trembling from the frustration he was feeling. "Will you not say to them what you feel in your heart? Will you counsel them to *wuwei*?"

351

The T'ang faced his General again. "The Seven will make its own decision. But yes, I shall counsel *wuwei*. For the good of all."

"And what did Li Yuan say?"

Tolonen's question was unexpected, was close to impertinence, but Li Shai Tung let it pass. He looked down, remembering the audience with his son earlier that day. "For your sake I do this," he had said. "You see the sense in it, surely, Yuan?" But Li Yuan had hesitated and the T'ang had seen in his eyes the conflict between what he felt and his duty to his father.

"Li Yuan agreed with me. As I knew he would."

He saw the surprise in his General's eyes; then noted how Tolonen stood there, stiffly, waiting to be dismissed.

"I am sorry we are not of a mind in this matter, Knut. I would it were otherwise. Nonetheless, I thank you for speaking openly. If it eases your mind, I shall put your view to the Council."

Tolonen looked up, surprised, then bowed. "For that I am deeply grateful, *Chieh Hsia*."

"Good. Then I need keep you no more."

After Tolonen had gone, Li Shai Tung sat there for a long while, deep in thought. For all he had said, Tolonen's conviction had shaken him. He had not expected it. When, finally, he turned to Shepherd, his dark eyes were pained, his expression troubled. "Well, Hal. What do you think?"

"Knut feels it personally. And, because he does, that clouds his judgement. You were not wrong. Though your heart bleeds, remember you are T'ang. And a T'ang must see all things clearly. Whilst we owe the dead our deepest respect, we must devote our energies to the living. Your thinking is sound, Li Shai Tung. You must ensure Li Yuan's succession. That is, and must be, foremost in your thinking, whatever your heart cries out for."

Li Shai Tung, T'ang, senior member of the Council of Seven and ruler of City Europe, stood up and turned away

352

from his advisor, a tear forming in the corner of one
bloodshot eye.

"Then it is *wuwei*."

* * *

The small girl turned sharply, her movements fluid as a
dancer's. Her left arm came down in a curving movement,
catching her attacker on the side. In the same instant her
right leg kicked out, the foot pointing and flicking, disarm-
ing the assailant. It was a perfect movement and the man,
almost twice her height, staggered backward. She was on
him in an instant, a shrill cry of battle anger coming from
her lips.

"Hold!"

She froze, breathing deeply, then turned her head to face
the instructor. Slowly she relaxed her posture and backed
away from her prone attacker.

"Excellent. You were into it that time, Jelka. No hesi-
tations."

Her instructor, a middle-aged giant of a man she knew
only as Siang, came up to her and patted her shoulder. On
the floor nearby her attacker, a professional fighter brought
in for this morning's training session only, got up slowly
and dusted himself down, then bowed to her. He was
clearly surprised to have been bested by such a slip of a
girl, but Siang waved him away without looking at him.

Siang moved apart from the child, circling her. She
turned, wary of him, knowing how fond he was of tricks.
But before she had time to raise her guard he had placed a
red sticker over the place on her body shield where her
heart would be. She caught his hand as it snaked back, but
it was too late.

"Dead," he said.

She wanted to laugh but dared not. She knew just how
serious this was. In any case, her father was watching and
she did not want to disappoint him. "Dead," she responded
earnestly.

There were games and there were games. This game was

deadly. She knew she must learn it well. She had seen with her own eyes the price that could be paid. Poor Han Ch'in. She had wept for days at his death.

At the far end of the training hall the door opened and her father stepped through. He was wearing full dress uniform, but the uniform was a perfect, unblemished white, from boots to cap. White. The Han colour of death.

The General came towards them. Siang bowed deeply and withdrew to a distance. Jelka, still breathing deeply from the exercise, smiled and went to her father, embracing him as he bent to kiss her.

"That was good," he said. "You've improved a great deal since I last saw you."

He had said the words with fierce pride, his hand holding and squeezing hers as he stood there looking down at her. At such moments he felt a curious mixture of emotions; love and apprehension, delight and a small, bitter twinge of memory. She was three months short of her seventh birthday, and each day she seemed to grow more like her dead mother.

"When will you be back?" she asked, looking up at him with eyes that were the same breath-taking ice-blue her mother's had been.

"A day or two. I've business to conclude after the funeral."

She nodded, used to his enigmatic references to business, then, more thoughtfully. "What will Li Shai Tung do, Daddy?"

He could not disguise the bitterness in his face when he answered. "Nothing," he said. "He will do nothing." And as he said it he imagined that it was Jelka's funeral he was about to go to; her death he had seen through others' eyes; her body lying there in the casket, young as spring yet cold as winter.

If it were you, my blossom, I would tear down Chung Kuo itself to get back at them.

But was that a deficiency in him? Were his feelings so unnatural? Or was the lack in Li Shai Tung, putting political necessity before what he felt? To want to destroy those who have hurt your loved ones – was that really so wrong? Was he any less of a man for wanting that?

Tolonen shuddered, the thought of his darling Jelka dead filled him with a strange sense of foreboding. Then, conscious of his daughter watching him, he placed his hands on her shoulders. His hands so large, her bones so small, so fragile beneath his fingers.

"I must go," he said simply, kneeling to hug her.

"Keep safe," she answered, smiling at him.

He smiled back at her, but his stomach had tightened at her words. It was what her mother had always said.

★ ★ ★

A cold wind was blowing from the west, from the high plains of Tibet, singing in the crown of the tree of heaven and rippling the surface of the long pool. Li Shai Tung stood alone beneath the tree, staff in hand, his bared head bowed, his old but handsome face lined with grief. At his feet, set into the dark earth, was the Family tablet, a huge rectangle of pale cream stone, carved with the symbols of his ancestors. More than half the stone – a body's length from where he stood – was marble smooth, untouched by the mortician's chisel. So like the future, he thought, staring at Han Ch'in's name, fresh cut into the stone. The future . . . that whiteness upon which *all* our deaths are written.

He looked up. It was a small and private place, enclosed by ancient walls. At the southern end a simple wooden gate led through into the northern palace. Soon they would come that way with the litter.

He spoke, his voice pained and awful; like the sound of the wind in the branches overhead. "Oh, Han . . . Oh, my sweet little boy, my darling boy."

He staggered, then clenched his teeth against the sudden memory of Han's mother, his first wife, Lin Yua, sitting in the sunlight at the edge of the eastern orchard by the lake, her dresses spread about her, Han, only a baby then, crawling contentedly on the grass beside her.

Bring it back, he begged, closing his eyes against the pain; *Kuan Yin, sweet Goddess of Mercy, bring it back*! But there was no returning. They were dead. All dead. And that day no longer was. Except in his mind.

He shuddered. It was unbearable. Unbearable . . .

Li Shai Tung drew his cloak about him and began to make his slow way back across the grass, leaning heavily on his staff, his heart a cold, dark stone in his breast.

They were waiting for him in the courtyard beyond the wall; all those he had asked to come. The Sons of Heaven and their sons, his trusted men, his son, his dead son's wife and her father, his brothers, his own third wife, and, finally, his daughters. All here, he thought. All but Han Ch'in, the one I loved the best.

They greeted him solemnly, their love, their shared grief unfeigned, then turned and waited for the litter.

The litter was borne by thirty men, their shaven heads bowed, their white, full-length silks fluttering in the wind. Behind them came four officials in orange robes and, beyond them, two young boys carrying a tiny litter on which rested an ancient bell and hammer.

Han lay there in the wide rosewood casket, dressed in the clothes he had worn on his wedding day. His fine, dark hair had been brushed and plaited, his face given the appearance of perfect health. Rich furs had been placed beneath him, strewn with white blossom, while about his neck were wedding gifts of jewels and gold and a piece of carmine cloth decorated with the marriage emblems of dragon and phoenix.

At the foot of the coffin lay a length of white cotton cloth, nine *ch'i* in length, Han Ch'in's own symbolic mourning for his father – for tradition said that the son must always mourn the father before he himself was mourned.

Li Yuan, standing at his father's side, caught his breath. It was the first time he had seen his brother since his death, and, for the briefest moment, he had thought him not dead but only sleeping. He watched the litter pass, his mouth open, his heart torn from him. *Merciful gods*, he thought;

sweet Han, how could they kill you? How could they place you in the earth?

Numbed, he fell into line behind the silent procession, aware only vaguely of his father beside him, of the great lords of Chung Kuo who walked behind him, their heads bared, their garments simple, unadorned. In his mind he reached out to pluck a sprig of blossom from his brother's hair, the petals a perfect white against the black.

At the far end of the long pool the procession halted. The tomb was open, the great stone door hauled back. Beyond it, steps led down into the cold earth.

Most of the bearers now stood back, leaving only the six strongest to carry the litter down the steps. Slowly they descended, followed by the officials and the two boys.

His father turned to him. "Come, my son. We must lay your brother to rest."

Li Yuan held back, for one terrible moment overcome by his fear of the place below the earth. Then, looking up into his father's face, he saw his own fear mirrored and found the strength to bow and answer him.

"I am ready, father."

They went down, into candlelight and shadows. The bearers had moved away from the litter and now knelt to either side, their foreheads pressed to the earth. Han lay on a raised stone table in the centre of the tomb, his head to the south, his feet to the north. The officials stood at the head of the casket, bowed, awaiting the T'ang, while the two boys knelt at the casket's foot, one holding the bell before him, the other the hammer.

Li Yuan stood there a moment at the foot of the steps, astonished by the size of the tomb. The ceiling was high overhead, supported by long, slender pillars that were embedded in the swept earth floor. Splendidly sculpted tomb figures, their *san-t'sai* glazes in yellow, brown and green, stood in niches halfway up the walls, candles burning in their cupped hands. Below them were the tombs of his ancestors, huge pictograms cut deep into the stone, denoting the name and rank of each. On four of them was cut one further symbol – the *Ywe Lung*. These had been T'ang. His father was fifth of the Li family T'ang. He, when his time came, would be the sixth.

A small table rested off to one side. On it were laid the burial objects. He looked up at his father again, then went over and stood beside the table, waiting for the ritual to begin.

The bell sounded in the silence, its pure, high tone like the sound of heaven itself. As it faded the officials began their chant.

He stood there, watching the flicker of shadows against stone, hearing the words intoned in the ancient tongue, and felt drawn up out of himself.

Man has two souls, the officials chanted. There is the animal soul, the *p'o*, which comes into being at the moment of conception, and there is the *hun*, the spirit soul, which comes into being only at the moment of birth. In life the two are mixed, yet in death their destiny is different. The *p'o* remains below, inhabiting the tomb, while the *hun*, the higher soul, ascends to heaven.

The officials fell silent. The bell sounded, high and pure in the silence. Li Yuan took the first of the ritual objects from the table and carried it across to his father. It was the *pi*, symbol of Heaven, a large disc of green jade with a hole in its centre. Yin, it was – positive and light and male. As the officials lifted the corpse, Li Shai Tung placed it beneath Han's back, then stood back, as they lowered him again.

The bell sounded again. Li Yuan returned to the table and brought back the second of the objects. This was the *tsung*, a hollow, square tube of jade symbolising Earth. Yang, this was – negative and dark and female. He watched as his father placed it on his brother's abdomen.

Each time the bell rang he took an object from the table and carried it to his father. First the *huang*, symbol of winter and the north, a black jade half-*pi* which his father laid at Han's feet. Then the *chang*, symbol of summer and the south, a narrow tapered tablet of red jade placed above Han's head. The *kuei* followed, symbol of the east and spring, a broad tapered tablet of green jade, twice the size of the *chang*, which was laid beside Han's left hand. Finally Li Yuan brought the *hu*, a white jade tiger, symbol of the west and autumn. He watched his father place this at his dead brother's right hand, then knelt beside him as the bell rang once, twice, and then a third time.

The chant began again. Surrounded by the sacred symbols the body was protected. Jade, incorruptible in itself, would prevent the body's own decay. The *p'o*, the animal soul, would thus be saved.

Kneeling there, Li Yuan felt awed by the power, the dignity of the ritual. But did it mean anything? His beloved Han was dead and nothing in heaven or earth could bring him back. The body would decay, jade or no jade. And the souls . . . ? As the chant ended he sat back on his haunches and looked about him, at stone and earth and the candle-lit figures of death. When nothing returned to speak of it, who knew if souls existed?

Outside again he stood there, dazed by it all, the chill wind tugging at his hair, the afternoon light hurting his eyes after the flickering shadows of the tomb. One by one the T'ang came forward to pay their respects to his father and once more offer their condolences, the least of them greater in power and wealth than the greatest of the Tang or Sung or Ch'ing dynasties. Wang Hsien, a big, moon-faced man, T'ang of Africa. Hou Ti, a slender man in his forties, T'ang of South America. Wei Feng, his father's closest friend among his peers, T'ang of East Asia, his seemingly ever-present smile absent for once. Chi Hu Wei, a tall, awkward man, T'ang of the Australias. Wu Shih, T'ang of North America, a big man, built like a fighter, his broad shoulders bunching as he embraced Li Yuan's father. And last Tsu Tiao, T'ang of West Asia, the old man leaning on his son's arm.

"You should have stayed inside," Li Shai Tung said, embracing him and kissing his cheeks. "This wind can be no good for you, Tsu Tiao. I thought it would be sheltered here with these walls."

Tsu Tiao reached out and held his arm. He seemed frail, yet his grip, like his voice, was strong. "High walls cannot keep the cold wind from blowing, eh, old friend? I know what it is to lose a son. Nothing would have kept me from paying my respects to Li Han Ch'in."

Li Shai Tung bowed, his face grim. "That is true, Tsu Tiao." He turned to the son. "Tsu Ma. Thank you for coming. I wish we had met in happier circumstances."

Tsu Ma bowed. He was a strong, handsome man in his late twenties who had, until recently, led a headstrong, dissolute life. Now, with his father ill, he had been forced to change his ways. It was rumoured Tsu Tiao was grooming him for regent, but this was the first time he had appeared publicly at his father's side.

"I too regret that we should meet like this, *Chieh Hsia*. Perhaps you would let me visit you when things are easier?"

Both Tsu Tiao and Li Shai Tung nodded, pleased by the initiative. "That would be good, Tsu Ma. I shall arrange things."

Li Yuan's uncles were next to pay their respects; Li Yun-Ti, Li Feng Chiang and Li Ch'i Chun. Advisors to Li Shai Tung, they stood in the same relationship to his father as he once had to *his* brother. Their lives were as his own might once have been. But it was different now. For Han Ch'in was dead and now he, Li Yuan, was destined to be T'ang.

He had seen the sudden change in them. Eyes which had once passed through him now checked their course and noted him; as if his brother's death had brought him substance. Now strangers bowed and fawned before him. Men like his uncles. He saw how obsequious they had become; how their distant politeness had changed to fear.

Yes, he saw it even now; the fear behind the smiles.

It amused him in a bitter way. Old men afraid of a boy not yet nine. Would I, he asked himself, have grown like them, twisted from my true shape by fear and envy? Perhaps. But now I'll never know.

Others came and stood before them. Fei Yen and her

360

father, the old man almost as devastated as his daughter, his earnest, kindly eyes ringed with darkness. Then his father's second wife and her three daughters, all four of them strangers to Li Yuan.

Last were his father's men; Hal Shepherd and the General.

"This is an ill day, old friend," said Shepherd. He embraced the T'ang, then stood back, looking around him. "I hoped not to see this place in my lifetime."

"Nor I," said Tolonen. For a moment he stared outward at the distant mountains of the Ta Pa Shan. And when his eyes fell upon the tomb, it was almost as if *his* son lay there beneath the earth, such broken love lay in his gaze.

Tolonen stared at the tomb a moment longer, then looked back at his T'ang. "We must act, *Chieh Hsia*. Such bitterness cannot be borne."

"No, Knut. You're wrong. It must and can be borne. We must find the strength to bear it."

"The Council has made its decision?"

"Yes. An hour back."

The General bowed his head, his disappointment clear. "Then it is *wuwei*?"

"Yes," the T'ang answered softly. "*Wuwei*. For all our sakes."

★ ★ ★

The House was in session and Speaker Zakhar was at the lectern, delivering a speech on expansion funding, when the big double doors at the far end of the chamber burst open. Zakhar turned, astonished.

"General Tolonen! What do you mean by this?"

Then Zakhar saw the armed guards pouring in after the General and fell silent. House security was breached. These were the General's own men – his elite guards. They formed up around the upper level of the chamber, their long snub-nosed rifles pointed down into the heart of the assembly.

The General ignored the storm of protests. He moved swiftly, purposefully towards the bench where the senior

361

representatives were seated, and went straight for Under Secretary Lehmann.

Lehmann was shouting, as vehement as any other in his protest. Tolonen stood there a moment, facing him, as if making certain this was the man he wanted, then reached across the desk and grabbed Lehmann by the upper arms, pulling him towards himself.

There was a moment's shocked silence, then the outroar grew fierce. Tolonen had dragged Lehmann over the desk and was jerking him along by his hair, as if dealing with the lowest cur from the Clay. Lehmann's face was contorted with pain and anger as he struggled to get free, but the General had a firm grip on him. He tugged him out into the space between the benches of the Upper Council and the seats of the General Assembly, then stopped abruptly and pulled Lehmann upright. Lehmann gasped, but before he had time to act, Tolonen turned him and pulled his arm up sharply behind his back. The General had drawn his ceremonial dagger and now held it at Lehmann's throat.

He stood there, waiting for them to be silent, scowling at any who dared come too close. Above him, encircling the chamber, his men stood patiently, their laser rifles raised to their shoulders.

He had only a second or two to wait. The House grew deathly still, the tension in the chamber almost tangible. Tolonen tugged gently at Lehmann's arm to keep him still, the point of his dagger pricking the Under Secretary's skin and drawing a tiny speck of blood.

"I've come for justice," Tolonen said, staring about him defiantly, looking for those faces he knew would be most interested, most fearful at this moment. *They never imagined I would come here for them.* The thought almost made him smile; but this was not a moment for smiling. His face remained grim, determined. Nothing would stop him now.

A low murmur had greeted his words and a few shouts from nearer the back of the hall. He had stirred up a hornet's nest here and Li Shai Tung would be furious. But that did not matter now. Nothing mattered but one thing. He had come to kill Lehmann.

As he stood there, three of his men brought a portable trivee projector down into the space beside him and set it up. The image of Lehmann's face, ten times its normal size, took form in the air beside the frightened reality.

"I want to show you all something," Tolonen said, raising his voice. He seemed calm, deceptively benign. "It is a film we took of our friend here at Li Han Ch'in's wedding. At the private ceremony afterwards, in the Imperial Gardens. I should explain, perhaps. The Under Secretary is looking towards where the T'ang's son was standing with his bride. The rest, I think, you'll understand."

Tolonen scanned the crowded benches again, noting how tense and expectant they had become, then turned and nodded to his ensign. At once the great face came to life, but Tolonen did not look at it. He had seen it too many times already; had seen for himself the effect it had had on Li Yuan.

For the next few minutes there was silence. Only during the final moments of the film was there a growing murmur of unease. They did not have to be told what was happening. The image in the blown-up eye told the story as clearly as any words.

The image faded from the air. Lehmann, who had turned his head to watch, began to struggle again, but the General held him tightly, drawing his arm as far up his back as it would go without breaking, making Lehmann whimper with pain.

"Now you've seen," said Tolonen simply. "But understand. I do this not for Li Shai Tung but for myself. Because this man has shamed me. And because such vileness must be answered." He raised his chin defiantly. "This act is mine. Do you understand me, *ch'un tzu*? Mine."

The words were barely uttered when Tolonen drew his knife slowly across Lehmann's throat, the ice-edged blade tearing through the exposed flesh as if through rice paper.

For what seemed an eternity, the General held the body forward as it gouted blood, staring about him at the shocked faces in the chamber. Then he let the body fall, blood splashing as it hit the floor, and stepped back, the trousers of his white ceremonial uniform spattered with blood.

He made no move to wipe it away, but stood there, defiant, his dagger raised, as if to strike again.

PART 3-SPRING 2201:

THE DOMAIN

"With all its eyes the creature-world beholds
the open. But our eyes, as though reversed,
encircle it on every side, like traps
set round its unobstructed path to freedom.
What *is* outside, we know from the brute's face
alone; for while a child's quite small we take it
and turn it round and force it to look backwards
at conformation, not that openness
so deep within the brute's face. Free from death.
We alone see *that*; the free animal
has its decease perpetually behind it
and God in front, and when it moves, it moves
within eternity, like running springs.
We've never, no, not for a single day,
pure space before us, such as that which flowers
endlessly open into: always world,
and never nowhere without no: that pure,
unsuperintended element one breathes,
endlessly knows, and never craves. A child
sometimes gets quietly lost there, to be always
jogged back again. Or someone dies and *is* it."

– Rainer Maria Rilke, *Duino Elegies*: 'Eighth Elegy'.

CHAPTER·10

THE DEAD RABBIT

Meg Shepherd, Hal Shepherd's daughter, was standing in the tall grass of the Domain, watching her brother. It was early evening and on the far side of the water, dense shadow lay beneath the thick cluster of trees. At this end the creek narrowed to a shallow, densely weeded spike of water. To her left, in the triangle of wild, uncultivated land between the meadow and the vast, overtowering whiteness of the Wall, the ground grew soft and marshy, veined with streams and pocked with tiny pools.

Ben was crouched at the water's edge, intensely still, staring at something in the tall, thick rushes to his right. For a moment there was only the stillness and the boy watching, the soft soughing of the wind in the trees across the water and the faint, lulling call of pigeons in the wood. Then, with an abrupt crash and spray and a strong beating of wings, the bird broke from cover. Ben's head went up, following the bird's steep ascent, his twelve-year-old eyes wide with watching.

"Look at it, Meg! Isn't it a beauty?"

"Yes," she answered softly, but all the while she was watching him, seeing how his eyes cast a line to the climbing bird. Saw how he grasped every last detail of it and held that knowledge tight in his memory. His body was tensed, following the bird's flight, and his eyes burned. She shivered. It was astonishing to watch, that intensity of his. The world seemed to take form in his eyes: to grow bright and rich and real. As if, before he saw it, it was but a pale shadow of itself; a mere blueprint, uncreated until he saw and re-imagined it. So it was for her. She could see nothing unless he had seen it first.

The bird was gone. He turned and looked at her.

"Did you see it?"

"Yes," she said, meaning something else. "It was beautiful."

He turned his head, looking away from her, towards the village. When he looked back his green eyes were dark, thoughtful.

"Things are different this year, Meg. Don't you feel it? Small things. Like the bird."

She shrugged then pushed her way through the grass, out into the open. Standing there beside him at the water's edge, she looked down at his reflection, next to her own in the still, clear water.

"Why do you think that is? Why *should* it change?" He looked around him, his brow furrowing. "I mean, this place has always been the same. Always. Unchanged. Unchanging but for the seasons. But now . . ." He looked at her. "What is it, Meg? What's happening?"

She looked up from his reflection and met his eyes.

"Does it worry you?"

He thought for a moment. "Yes," he said finally. "And I don't know why. And I want to know why."

She smiled at him and reached out to touch his arm. It was so typical of him, wanting to understand what he thought and why he thought it. Never happy unless he was worrying at the problem of himself.

"It's nothing," she said reassuringly. "They're only small things, Ben. They don't mean anything. Really they don't."

But she saw he wasn't convinced. "No," he said. "Everything has meaning. It's all signs, don't you see? It all *signifies*. And the small things . . . that's where it's to be seen first. Like the bird. It was beautiful, yes, but it was also . . ." He looked away and she said the word for him, anticipating him without quite knowing how, as she so often did.

"Frightening."

"Yes."

She followed his gaze a moment, seeing how his eyes climbed the Wall to its summit far overhead, then looked back at him again. He was more than a head taller than her, dark-haired and straight-boned. She felt a small warmth of pride kindle in her. So elegant he was. So handsome. Did he know how much she loved him? He knew so much, but did he know that? Maybe. But if he did he gave no sign.

"It was only a bird, Ben. Why should it frighten you?"

He almost smiled. "It wasn't the bird, Meg. At least, not the outer thing, the cage of bone and flesh, sinew and feather. It was what was within the bird – the force that gave it such power, such vitality." He looked down at his left hand, then turned it over, studying its back. "That's where its beauty lies. Not in the outward show but in the shaping force. That . . ." He seemed to shiver. "Well, it's mystery. Pure mystery. And that frightens me, Meg. The thought of all that dark, unharnessed power simply existing in the world. I look at it and I want to know where it comes from. I want to know why it's there at all. Why it isn't mere mechanics and complexity of detail. Why all that fiery excess?"

"The force that through the green fuse drives the flower."

And now he did smile, pleased by her recognition; by her quoting back at him the poem he had read to her only two days past. How rare that was, him smiling. And only for her. Never for mother or father. Nor for those others that came so rarely to this place.

"I guess there's that too," he said. "That same force brings us on, from bud to flower to . . . well, to something browned and withered. And thus to clay." He shrugged. "It's all connected, isn't it? It uses us and then discards us. As if we're here only to flesh out its game – to give it form. Doesn't that frighten you, Meg?"

She shook her head. "Why should it? There's plenty of time, Ben. A whole world of time before we have to think of that."

He studied her intently for a moment, then bowed his head slightly. "Perhaps."

He began to walk, treading a careful path through the marshy ground, following a rising vein of rock that jutted from the sodden turf, until he came beneath the shadow of the Wall.

There, facing them not thirty paces away, was the Seal. Part of the Wall, it was the same dull pearl in colour, a great circle five times Ben's height, its base less than an arm's length above the surface of the ground, its outer edge a thick ridge of steel-tough plastic.

For a moment he stood there, staring at it, oblivious of all else.

Meg, watching him, understood. It was a gateway. A closed door. And beyond it was the darkness of the Clay. Primal, unadulterated Clay. Beyond it the contiguous earth was sun-deprived and barren. Here Heaven, there Hell. And only a Wall, a Seal, between the two.

She climbed up beside him on the ridge of rock. "What's that?" She pointed outward to their left. There was something there. Something small and pale and grey against the green. Something that hadn't been there before.

He looked, then shrugged. "I don't know. Let's see, eh?"

At once he scrambled down. Meg hesitated, then followed. The ground was soft and spongy and in only a few paces her canvas shoes were soaked. Ben had gone ahead of her, his feet sinking, squelching as he ran. Then she saw him crouch down and examine something.

She came up behind him and looked over his shoulder. It was a rabbit. A dead rabbit.

"What killed it?" she asked.

He prised the carcass up from out of the wet, clinging turf and turned it over, examining it.

"I don't know. There's no sign of external injury. But it's not been here long." He looked up at her. "Here, Meg, give me your jumper."

She pulled her jumper off and handed it to him, then watched as he spread it out and laid the dead animal on it.

"What are you doing?"

Ben drew his hunting knife from its sheath, then cut the rabbit from chin to rump. For a moment he watched the blood well from the cut, staining the mottled grey fur, then laid the knife down and eased the flesh apart.

Meg watched, fascinated and horrified, as he probed inside the animal, the blood dark on his fingers. Then he lifted something small and wet; a pale, tiny sac attached by tubes and tendons to the rest. It glistened in his fingers as he bent to study it. Then he looked up at her.

"It's as I thought. Look. The liver's covered in dark blotches."

She shook her head, not understanding, watching him bundle the rabbit in her jumper, then lift it and sling it over his shoulder.

"It was diseased," he said, staring across at the Seal. Then he turned to look at her again. "It's part of the change in things, Meg. Don't you see that now? There's a sickness here in the Domain. A killing thing."

* * *

Hal Shepherd stood at the turn of the road, his hands resting lightly on the low stone wall, looking down at the row of cottages and the bay beyond. To his right the hill rose up above where he stood, then fell again to meet the next turn of the river. It was dotted with old stone-built houses and cottages. At its summit was a small church.

It was almost three months since he had been home, but now, standing there, it seemed that he had never been away. This much at least remains unchanged, he thought; each hill, each tree, each house familiar to him from youth. I see it as my grandfather saw it, and his grandfather before him. In three hundred years only the trees had changed, growing older, dying, replaced by others of their own ancient seed. Like us, he thought. We too are trees.

He walked on. The road dipped steeply here then curved back wickedly upon itself. Where he had been standing had been a turning point for cars once upon a time – when there were still cars in the world – but this had never been a place for modern things. Even back then, when the world was connected differently, it had been seven miles by road to the nearest town of any size, and that easier to get to by the river. Time had stood still here even then. During the Madness, when the old world had heaved itself apart, this place had been a point of stillness at the centre of things. Now it was timeless.

There were walls, no more than a pace or two either side of him. Whitewashed walls, in heavy shadow now, their low-silled windows dark; only one cottage in the row lit up. He smiled, seeing it ahead of him; imagining Beth there in the low-beamed living room, the fire lit and the curtains drawn; seeing her, as he had so often seen her, go to the back door and call the children in from the meadow.

Home. It meant so many things, but only one to him. He would have withered inside long ago had there not been this to return to.

He stood outside the low, broad door, listening, then put his hand out flat against the wood and gently pushed. There was no need for locks here. No need for fear. The door swung back slowly, silently, and he went in.

Beth stood there in the doorway, framed by the soft light of the living room behind her and to her left. She smiled. "I knew you were coming. I dreamed of you last night."

He laughed and went to her, then held her tightly against him, kissing her tenderly. "Your dreams . . ." He gazed into her eyes, loving the beauty, the measureless depth of them. "They never fail you, do they?"

She smiled and kissed his nose. "No. Never."

He shivered and reached up to stroke her cheek then trace the contours of her lips with a fingertip. His whole body was alive with desire for her. "Where's Ben? And Meg?"

Her body was pressed hard against his own, her hands at his neck. Her eyes now were dark with longing, her voice softer, more alluring. "They're outside. Down by the creek. But they'll not be back. Not just yet." She kissed him again, a harder, longer kiss this time.

"Yes . . ." He let his left hand rest gently on her waist a moment, then rucked up her skirt. Beneath it she wore nothing. He shuddered and sought her mouth again, the kiss more urgent now. His fingers traced the warm smoothness of her thighs and belly, then found the hot wetness at the core of her. She moaned softly and closed her eyes, her whole body trembling at his touch, then she reached down and freed him, holding his swollen penis momentarily, her fingers softly tracing its length, once, then again, almost making him come, before drawing him up into her.

He groaned, then grasped her by the buttocks and lifted her, backing her against the wall, thrusting up into her once, twice, a third time before he came explosively, feeling her shudder violently against him.

For a while, then, they were silent, watching each other. Then Beth smiled again. "Welcome home, my love."

★ ★ ★

The pine surface of the kitchen table was freshly scrubbed, the knives newly sharpened. Ben looked about him, then left the bundled rabbit on the wide stone step outside and busied himself. He spread an oilcloth on the table then laid the big cutting board on top of it. He laid the knives out beside the board and then, because it was growing dark, brought the lamp from beside the old ceramic butler sink, trimming the wick before he lit it.

Meg stood in the garden doorway, her small figure silhouetted against the twilight redness of the bay. She watched him roll back his sleeves, then fill a bowl with water and set it beside the knives.

"Why are you doing that?" she asked. "You know it's diseased. Why not burn it? Surely that's best?"

"No." Ben barely glanced at her. He turned and went down the four steps that led into the long, dark, low-ceilinged dining room, returning a moment later with a book from the shelves. An old thing, leather-bound and cumbersome. "I've a hunch," he said, putting the heavy volume down on the other side of the board to the knives and the water.

Meg went across and stood beside him. It was a book of animal anatomy. One of their great-great-great-grandfather Amos's books. Ben flicked through the pages until he came to the diagram he was looking for. "There," he said, the heavy, glossy pages staying in place as he turned away to bring the rabbit.

She looked. Saw at once how like a machine it was. A thing of pumps and levers, valves and switches, controlled by chemicals and electric pulses. It was all there on the page, dissected for her. The whole of the mystery – there at a glance.

Ben came back. He placed the dead rabbit carefully on the block then turned and looked at her. "You needn't stay, Meg. Not if you don't want to."

But she stayed, fascinated by what he was doing, knowing that this had meaning for him. Something had caught his attention. Something she had missed but he had seen. Now she waited as he probed and cut and then compared what had been exposed against the diagram spread across the double page.

At last, satisfied, he went to the sink and washed his hands, then came back and threw a muslin cloth over the board and its bloodied contents.

"Well?"

He was about to answer her when there was the sound of footsteps in the dining room. Their mother's. Then a second set.

Meg pushed past him and jumped down the four steps in her haste.

"Daddy!"

Hal Shepherd gathered his daughter up, hugging her tight and kissing her, delighted to see her. Then he ducked under the lintel and climbed the steps up into the kitchen, Beth following.

"Gods, Ben, what have you been up to?"

Ben turned to face the table.

"It's a dead rabbit. We found it down by the Seal. It's diseased. But that's not all. It doesn't come from here. It was brought in."

Hal put Meg down and went across. "Are you sure, Ben?" But he knew that Ben was rarely if ever wrong.

Ben pulled back the cloth. "Look. I made certain of it against Amos's book. This one isn't real. It's a genetic re-design. Probably GenSyn. One of the guards must have made a substitution."

Hal studied the carcass a while, then nodded. "You're right. And it won't be the only one, I'm sure. I wonder who brought it in?"

Ben saw the anger mixed with sadness on his father's face. There were two gates to the Domain, each manned by an elite squad of a dozen men, hand-picked by the T'ang himself. Over the years they had become friends of the family and had been granted privileges – one of which was limited entry to the Domain. Now that would have to stop. The culprit would have to be caught and made to pay.

Meg came up to him and tugged at his arm. "But why would they do it, daddy? There's no great difference, is there?"

Hal smiled sadly. "It's a kind of foolishness, my love, that's all. You see, there are people in the City who would pay a vast sum of money to be able to boast they had real rabbit at one of their dinners."

Ben stared at the carcass fixedly. "How much is a vast sum?"

Hal looked down at his son. "Fifty, maybe a hundred thousand yuan for each live animal. They would breed them, you see, then sell the doctored litters."

Ben considered. Such a sum would be as nothing to his father, he knew, but to others it was a fortune. He saw at once how such an opportunity might have tempted one of the guards. "I see," he said. "But there's another, more immediate worry. If they're all like this they could infect

375

everything in the Domain. We'll need to sweep the whole area. Catch everything and test it. Quarantine whatever's sick."

Hal nodded, realising his son was right. "Damn it! Such stupidity! I'll have the culprit's hide!" He laid a hand on his son's shoulder. "But you're right, Ben, we'd best do something straight away. This can't wait for morning."

He turned to Beth, anger turning to apology in his face. "This complicates things, I'm afraid. I meant to tell you earlier, my love. We have a guest coming, tomorrow evening. An important guest. He'll be with us a few days. I can't say any more than that. I was hoping we could hunt, but this business buggers things."

She frowned at him and made a silent gesture towards Meg.

Shepherd glanced at his daughter then looked back at his wife and gave a slight bow. "I'm sorry. Yes . . . My language. I forget when I've been away. But this . . ." He huffed angrily, exasperated, then turned to his son again. "Come, Ben, there's much to be done."

* * *

It was calm on the river. Ben pulled easily at the oars, the boat moving swiftly through the water. Meg sat facing him, looking across at the eastern shore. Behind her, in the stern, sat Peng Yu-wei, tall, elderly and very upright, his staff held in front of him like an unflagged mast. It was ebb tide and the current was in their favour. Ben kept the boat mid-stream, enjoying the warmth of the mid-day sun on his bare shoulders, the feel of the mild sea breeze in his hair. He felt drowsy, for one rare moment almost lapsed out of consciousness, then Meg's cry brought him back to himself.

"Look, Ben!"

Meg was pointing out towards the far shore. Ben shipped oars and turned to look. There, stretching from the fore-shore to the Wall, was a solid line of soldiers. Slowly, methodically, they moved between the trees and over the rough-grassed, uneven ground, making sure nothing slipped between them. It was their third sweep of the Domain and their last. What was not caught this time would be gassed.

Peng Yu-wei cleared his throat, his head held slightly forward in a gesture of respect to his two charges.

"What is it, Teacher Peng?" Ben asked coldly, turning to face him. Lessons had ended an hour back. This now was their time and Peng, though chaperone for this excursion, had no authority over the master and mistress outside his classroom.

"Forgive me, young master, I wish only to make an observation."

Meg turned, careful not to make the boat tilt and sway, and looked up at Peng Yu-wei, then back at Ben. She knew how much Ben resented the imposition of a teacher. He liked to make his own discoveries and follow his own direction, but their father had insisted upon a more rigorous approach. What Ben did in his own time was up to him, but in the morning classes he was to do as Peng Yu-wei instructed; learn what Peng Yu-wei asked him to learn. With some reluctance Ben had agreed, but only on the understanding that outside the classroom the teacher was not to speak without his express permission.

"You understand what Teacher Peng really is?" he had said to Meg when they were alone one time. "He is their means of keeping tabs on me. Of controlling what I know and what I learn. He's bit and bridle, ball and chain, a rope to tether me like any other animal."

His bitterness had surprised her. "Surely not," she had answered. "Father wouldn't want that, would he?"

But he had not answered, only looked away, the bitterness in his face unchanged.

Now some of that bitterness was back as he looked at Teacher Peng. "Make your observation then. But be brief."

Peng Yu-wei bowed, then turned his head, looking across at the soldiers who were now level with them. One frail, thin hand went up to pull at his wispy grey goatee, the other moved slightly on the staff, inclining it towards the distant line of men. "This whole business seems most cumbersome, would you not agree, Master Ben?"

Ben's eyes never left the teacher's face. "No. Not cumbersome. Inefficient's a better word."

Teacher Peng looked back at him and bowed slightly, corrected. "Which is why I felt it could be made much easier."

Meg saw the irritation and impatience on Ben's face and looked down. She knew no good would come of this.

"You had best tell me how, Teacher Peng." The note of sarcasm in Ben's voice was bordering on outright rudeness now. Even so, Peng Yu-wei seemed not to notice. He merely bowed and continued.

"It occurs to me that, before returning the animals to the land again, a trace could be put inside each animal. Then, if this happened again, it would be a simple thing to account for each animal. Theft and disease would both be far easier to control."

Peng Yu-wei looked up at his twelve-year-old charge expectantly, but Ben was silent.

"Well, master?" he asked after a moment. "What do you think of my idea?"

Ben looked away. He lifted the oars and began to pull at them again, digging heavily into the water to his right, bringing the boat back onto a straight course. Then he looked back at the teacher.

"It's a hideous idea, Peng Yu-wei. An unimaginative, small-minded idea. Just another way of keeping tabs on things. I can see it now. You would make a great electronic wall chart of the Domain, eh? And have each animal as a blip on it."

The stretched olive skin of Peng Yu-wei's face was relaxed, his dark eyes, with their marked epicanthic fold, impassive. "That would be a refinement, I agree, but . . ."

Ben let the oars fall and leaned forward in the boat. Peng Yu-wei reflexively moved back. Meg watched, horrified, as Ben scrabbled past her, the boat swaying violently, and tore at the teacher's *pau*, exposing his chest.

"Please, young master. You know that is not allowed."

Peng Yu-wei still held his staff, but with his other hand he now sought to draw the two ends of the torn silk together. For a moment, however, the white circle of the control panel set into his upper chest was clearly visible.

For a second or two Ben knelt there in front of him threateningly, his whole body tensed as if to act. Then he moved back.

"You'll be quiet, understand? And you'll say nothing of this. Nothing! Or I'll switch you off and drop you over the side. Understand me, Teacher Peng?"

For a moment the android was perfectly still, then it gave the slightest nod.

"Good," said Ben, moving back and taking up the oars again. "Then we'll proceed."

* * *

As Ben turned the boat into the tiny, box-like harbour the two sailors looked up from where they sat on the steps mending their nets and smiled. They were both old men, in their late sixties, with broad, healthy, salt-tanned faces. Ben hailed them, then concentrated on manoeuvring between the moored fishing boats. There was a strong breeze now from the mouth of the river and the metallic sound of the lines flapping against the masts filled the air, contesting with the cry of gulls overhead. Ben turned the boat's prow with practised ease and let the craft glide between a big, high-sided fisherboat and the harbour wall, using one of the oars to push away, first one side, then the other. Meg, at the stern, held the rope in her hand, ready to jump ashore and tie up.

Secured, Ben jumped ashore, then looked back into the boat. Peng Yu-wei had stood up, ready to disembark.

"You'll stay," Ben said commandingly.

For a moment Peng Yu-wei hesitated, his duty to chaperone the children conflicting with the explicit command of the young master. Water slopped noisily between the side of the boat and the steps. Only paces away the two old sailors had stopped their mending, watching.

Slowly, with great dignity, the teacher sat, planting his staff before him. "I'll do as you say, young master," he said, looking up at the young boy on the quayside, "But I must tell your father about this."

Ben turned away, taking Meg's hand. "Do what you must, tin man," he muttered under his breath.

The quayside was cluttered with coils of rope, lobster pots, netting and piles of empty wooden crates – old, frail-looking things that awaited loads of fish that never came. The harbour was filled with fishing boats, but no one ever fished. The town beyond was full of busy-seeming people, but no one lived there. It was all false: all part of the great illusion Ben's great-great-great-grandfather had created here.

Once this had been a thriving town, prospering on fishing and tourism and the naval college. Now it was dead. A shell of its former self, peopled by replicants.

Meg looked about her, delighted, as she always was by this. Couples strolled in the afternoon sunshine, the ladies in crinolines, the men in stiff three-piece suits. Pretty little girls with curled blonde hair tied with pink ribbons ran here and there, while boys in sailor suits crouched, playing fivestones.

"It's so *real* here!" Meg said enthusiastically. "So alive!"

Ben looked down at her and smiled. "Yes," he said. "It is, isn't it?" He had seen pictures of the City. It seemed such an ugly, hideous place by comparison. A place of walls and cells and corridors – a vast, unending prison of a place. He turned his face to the breeze and drew in great lungfuls of the fresh salt air, then looked back at Meg. "What shall we do?"

She looked past the strolling holidaymakers at the gaily-painted shops along the front, then looked up at the hillside and, beyond it, the Wall, towering over all.

"I don't know . . ." She squeezed his hand. "Let's just go where we want, Ben. Look wherever we fancy looking, eh?"

"Okay. Then we'll start over there, at the Chandler's."

For the next few hours they went among the high street shops, first searching through the shelves of Joseph Toms, Toys and Fancy Goods, for novelties, then looking among the tiny cupboards of Charles Weaver, Apothecary, sampling the sweet-tasting, harmless powders on their fingers and mixing the brightly-coloured liquids in beakers. But Ben soon tired of such games and merely watched as Meg went from shop to shop, unchallenged by the android shopkeepers. In Nash's Coffee House they had their lunch, the food real but somehow unsatisfying, as if reconstituted.

"There's a whole world here, Meg. Preserved. Frozen in time. Sometimes I look at it and think it's such a waste. It should be used somehow."

Meg sipped at her iced drink then looked up at him. "You think we should let others come here into the Domain?"

He hesitated, then shook his head. "No. Not that. But . . ."

Meg watched him curiously. It was unusual to see Ben so indecisive.

"You've an idea," she said.

"No. Not an idea. Not as such."

Again that uncertainty, that same slight shrugging of his shoulders. She watched him look away, his eyes tracing the row of signs above the shop fronts: David Wishart, Tobacconist; Arthur Redmayne, Couturier; Thomas Lipton, Vintner; Jack Delcroix, Dentist & Bleeder; Stagg & Mantle, Ironmongers; Verry's Restaurant; Jackson & Graham, Cabinet Makers; The Lambe Brothers, Linen-Drapers; and there, on the corner, facing Goode's Hostelry, Pugh's Mourning House.

Seeing Pugh's brought back a past visit. It was months ago and Ben had insisted on going into Pugh's, though they had always avoided the shop before. She had watched him go amongst the caskets, then lift one of the lids, peering inside. The corpse looked realistic enough, but Ben had turned to her and laughed. "Dead long before it was dead." Somehow that had made him talk about things here. Why they were as they were, and what kind of man her great-great-great-grandfather had been to create a place like this. He had not skimped on anything. One looked in drawers or behind doors and there, as in real life, one found small, inconsequential things. Buttons and pins and photographs. A hatstand with an old, well-worn top hat on one peg, a scarf on another, as if left there only an hour past. Since then she had searched and searched, her curiosity unflagging, trying to catch him out – to find some small part of this world he had made that wasn't finished. To find some blank, uncreated part behind the superficial details.

Would she have thought to do this without Ben? Would she have searched so ardently to find that patch of dull revealing blankness? No. In truth she would never have known. But he had shown her how this, the most real place she knew, was in other ways quite hollow. Was all a marvellous sham. A gaudy, imaginative fake.

"If this is fake, then why is it so marvellous?" she had asked, and he had shaken his head in wonder at her question.

"Why? Because it's god-like! Look at it, Meg! It's so presumptuous! Such consummate mimicry! Such shameless artifice!"

Now, watching him, she knew he had a scheme. Some way of using this.

"Never mind," she said. "Let's move on. I'd like to try on some of Lloyd's hats."

Ben smiled at her. "Okay. Then we'll start back."

★ ★ ★

They were upstairs in Edgar Lloyd, Hatters, when Ben heard voices down below. Meg was busy trying on hats at the far side of the room, the android assistant standing beside her at the mirror, a stack of round, candy-striped boxes in her arms.

Ben went to the window and looked down. There were soldiers in the passageway below. Real soldiers. And not just any soldiers. He knew the men at once.

Meg turned to him, a wide-brimmed creation of pale cream lace balanced precariously on top of her dark curls. "What do you think, Ben? Do you . . ."

He hushed her urgently.

"What is it?" she mouthed.

"Soldiers," he mouthed back.

She set the hat down and came across to him.

"Keep down out of sight," he whispered. "They're our guards, and they shouldn't be here. They're supposed to be confined to barracks."

She looked up at him, wide-eyed, then knelt down, so that her head was below the sill. "Tell me what's happening," she said quietly.

He watched. There were ten of them down there, their voices urgent, excited. For a moment Ben couldn't understand what was going on, then one of them turned and he saw it was the captain, a man called Rosten. Rosten pointed down the passageway towards the open ground in front of the old inn and muttered something Ben couldn't quite make out.

"What are they doing?"

He looked down at Meg and saw the fear in her eyes. "Nothing. Hush now, Megs. It'll be all right."

He put his hand on her shoulder and looked out again. What he saw this time surprised him. Two of the men were being held and bound; their wrists and ankles taped together. One of the men started to struggle, then began to cry out. Meg tried to get up to see, but with a gentle pressure he pushed her back down.

There was the sound of a slap, then silence from below. A moment later Rosten's voice barked out. "Out there! Quick now!"

Ben moved across to the other side of the window, trying to keep them in sight, but he lost them in a moment.

"Stay here, Meg. I'm going downstairs."

"But, Ben . . ."

He shook his head. "Do what I say. I'll be all right. I'll not let them see me."

He had to move slowly, carefully on the stairs because, for a brief moment, he was in full sight of the soldiers through the big plate glass window that looked out onto the narrow quay. At the bottom he moved quickly between the racks and tables until he was crouched between two mannequins, looking out through their skirts at the scene in front of the inn.

Two men held each of the prisoners. The other three stood to one side, in a line, at attention. Rosten had his back to Ben and stood there between the window and the prisoners. With an abrupt gesture that seemed to jerk his body forward violently, he gave an order. At once both prisoners were made forcibly to kneel and lower their heads.

Only then, as Rosten turned slightly, did Ben see the long, thin blade he held.

For a moment the sight of the blade held him; the way the sunlight seemed to flow like a liquid along the gently curved length of it, flickering brilliantly on the razor-sharp edge and at the tip. He had read how swords could seem alive – could have a personality, even a name – but he had never thought to see it.

He looked past the blade. Though their heads were held down forcibly, the two men looked up at Rosten, anxious to know what he intended for them. Ben knew them well. Gosse, to the left, was part Han, his broad, rough-hewn, Slavic features made almost Mongolian by his part-Han ancestry. Wolfe, to the right, was a southerner, his dark, handsome features almost refined; almost, but not quite, classical. Almost. For when he smiled or laughed, his eyes and mouth were somehow ugly. Somehow brutish and unhealthy.

Rosten now stood between the two, his feet spread, his

right arm outstretched, the sword in his right hand, its tip almost touching the cobbled ground a body's length away.

"You! You understand why you're here? You've heard the accusations?"

"They're lies . . ." began Wolfe, but he was cuffed into silence by the man behind him.

Rosten shook his head. The long sword quivered in his hand. "Not lies, Wolfe. You have been tried by a panel of your fellow officers and found guilty. You and Gosse here. You stole and cheated. You have betrayed our master's trust and dishonoured the Banner."

Wolfe's eyes widened. The blood drained from his face. Beside him Gosse looked down, as if he had already seen where this led.

"There is no excusing what you did. And no solution but to excise the shame."

Wolfe's head came up sharply and was pushed down brutally. "No!" he shouted, beginning to struggle again. "You can't do this! You . . ."

A blow from one of the men holding him knocked him down onto the cobbles.

"Bring him here!"

The two guards grabbed Wolfe again and dragged him, on his knees, until he was at Rosten's feet.

Rosten's voice was almost hysterical now. He half-shouted, half-screamed, his sword arm punctuating the words. "You are scum, Wolfe! Faceless! Because of you, your fellow officers have fallen under suspicion! Because of you, all here have been dishonoured!" Rosten shuddered violently and spat on the kneeling man's head. "You have shamed your Banner! You have shamed your family name! And you have disgraced your ancestors!"

Rosten stepped back and raised the sword. "Hold the prisoner down!"

Ben caught his breath. He saw how Wolfe's leg muscles flexed impotently as he tried to scrabble to his feet; how he squirmed in the two men's grip, trying to get away. A third soldier joined the other two, forcing Wolfe down with blows and curses. Then one of them grabbed Wolfe's topknot and, with a savage yank that almost pulled the man up off his knees, stretched his neck out, ready for the sword.

Wolfe was screaming now, his voice hoarse, breathless. "No! No! Kuan Yin, Goddess of Mercy, help me! I did nothing! Nothing!" His face was torn with terror, his mouth twisted, his eyes moving frantically in their sockets, pleading for mercy.

Ben saw Rosten's body tauten like a compressed coil. Then, with a sharp hiss of breath, he brought the sword down sharply.

Wolfe's screams stopped instantly. Ben saw the head drop and roll, the body tumble forward like a sack of grain, the arms fall limp.

Ben looked across at Gosse.

Gosse had been watching all in silence, his jaw clenched, his neck muscles taut. Now, with a visible shudder, he looked down again, staring at the cobbles.

Rosten bent down and wiped the sword on the back of Wolfe's tunic, then straightened, facing Gosse.

"You have something to say, Gosse?"

Gosse was silent a moment, then he looked up at Rosten. His eyes, which, moments earlier, had been filled with fear and horror, were now clear, almost calm. His hands shook, but he clenched them to control their trembling. He took a deep breath, then another, like a diver about to plunge into the depths, and nodded.

"Speak then. You've little time."

Gosse hunched his shoulders and lowered his head slightly, in deference to Rosten, but kept his eyes on him. "Only this. It is true what you say. I am guilty. Wolfe planned it all, but I acted with him, and there is no excusing my actions. I accept the judgement of my fellow officers and, before I die, beg their forgiveness for having shamed them before the T'ang."

Rosten stood there, expecting more, but Gosse had

lowered his head. After a moment's reflection, Rosten gave a small nod, then spoke.

"I cannot speak for all here, but for myself I say this. You were a good soldier, Gosse. And you face death bravely, honestly, as a soldier ought. I cannot prevent your death now, you understand, but I can, at least, change the manner of it."

There was a low gasp from the men on either side as Rosten took a pace forward and drew the short sword from his belt and cutting the bonds at Gosse's wrists, handed it to him.

Gosse understood at once. His eyes met Rosten's, bright with gratitude, then looked down at the short sword. With his left hand he tore open the tunic of his uniform and drew up the undershirt, baring the flesh. Then he gripped the handle of the short sword with both hands and turned it, so that the tip was facing his stomach. The two guards released him and stood back. Rosten watched him a moment, then took up his place, just behind Gosse and to one side, the long sword half raised.

Ben eased forward until his face was pressed against the glass, watching Gosse slow his breathing and focus his whole being upon the blade resting only a hand's length from his stomach. Gosse's hands were steady now, his eyes glazed. Time slowed. Then, quite abruptly, it changed. There was a sudden, violent movement in Gosse's face – a movement somewhere between ecstasy and extreme agony – and then his hands were thrusting the blade deep into his belly. With what seemed super-human strength and control he drew the short sword to the left, then back to the right, his intestines spilling out onto the cobbles. For a moment his face held its expression of ecstatic agony, then it crumpled and his eyes looked down, widening, horrified by what he had done.

Rosten brought the sword down sharply.

Gosse knelt a moment longer. Then his headless body fell and lay there, motionless, next to Wolfe's.

Ben heard a moan behind him and turned. Meg was

squatting at the top of the stairs, her hands clutching the third and fourth struts tightly, her eyes wide, filled with fright.

"Go up!" he hissed anxiously, hoping he'd not be heard; horrified that she had been witness to Gosse's death. He saw her turn and look at him, for a moment barely recognising him or understanding what he had said to her. *Dear gods*, he thought; *how much did she see?*

"Go up!" he hissed again. "For heaven's sake go up!"

* * *

It was dark on the river, the moon obscured behind the Wall's north-western edge. Ben jumped ashore and tied the rowboat up to the small, wooden jetty, then turned to give a hand to Peng Yu-wei who stood there, cradling a sleeping Meg in one arm.

He let the teacher go ahead, reluctant to go in, wanting to keep the blanket of darkness and silence about him a moment longer.

There was a small rectangle of land beside the jetty, surrounded on three sides by steep clay walls. A set of old, wooden steps had been cut into one side. Ben climbed them slowly, tired from the long row back. Then he was in the garden, the broad swathe of neat-trimmed grass climbing steadily to the thatched cottage a hundred yards distant.

"Ben!"

His mother stood in the low back doorway, framed by the light, an apron over her long dress. He waved, acknowledging her. Ahead of him, Peng Yu-wei strode purposefully up the path, his long legs showing no sign of human frailty.

He felt strangely separate from things. As if he had let go of oars and rudder and now drifted on the dark current of events. On the long row back he had traced the logic of the thing time and again. He knew he had caused their deaths. From his discovery things had followed an inexorable path, like the water's tight spiral down into the whirlpool's mouth. They had died because of him.

No. Not because of him. Because of his discovery. He was not to blame for their deaths. They had killed themselves. Their greed had killed them. That and their stupidity.

He was not to blame; yet he felt their deaths quite heavily. If he had said nothing. If he had simply burned the rabbit as Meg had suggested . . .

It would have solved nothing. The sickness would have spread; the discovery would have been made. Eventually. And then the two soldiers would have died.

It was not his fault. Not *his* fault.

His mother met him at the back door. She knelt down and took his hands. "Are you okay, Ben? You look troubled. Has something happened?"

He shook his head. "No. I . . ."

The door to the right of the broad, low-ceilinged passageway opened and his father came out, closing the door behind him. He smiled at Ben, then came across.

"Our guest is here, Ben. He's been here all afternoon, in fact." He hesitated and glanced at his wife. "I know I said earlier that you would be eating alone tonight, Ben, but . . . Well, he says he would like to meet you. So I thought that maybe you could eat with us after all."

Ben was used to his father's guests and had never minded taking his evening meal in his room, but this was unusual. He had never been asked to sit at table with a guest before.

"Who is it?" he asked.

His father smiled enigmatically. "Wash your hands, then come through. I'll introduce you. But Ben . . . be on your best behaviour, please."

Ben gave a slight bow, then went straight to the small washroom. He washed his face and hands, then scrubbed his nails and tidied his hair in the mirror. When he came out his mother was waiting for him. She took his hands, inspecting them, then straightened his tunic and bent to kiss his cheek.

CHAPTER·11

A CONVERSATION IN THE FIRELIGHT

In the light from the open fire the T'ang's strong, oriental features seemed carved in ancient yellowed ivory. He sat back in his chair, smiling, his eyes brightly dark.

"And you think they'll be happy with that, Hal?"

Li Shai Tung's hands rested lightly on the table's edge, the now-empty bowl he had been eating from placed to one side, out of his way. Ben, watching him, saw once again how the light seemed trapped by the matt black surface of the heavy iron ring he wore on the index finger of his right hand. The *Ywe Lung*. The seal of power.

Hal Shepherd laughed, then shook his head. "No. Not for a moment. They all think themselves emperors in that place."

They were talking about the House of Representatives at Weimar – "That troublesome place", as the T'ang continually called it – and about ways of shoring up the tenuous peace that now existed between it and the Seven.

The T'ang and his father sat at one end of the long, darkwood table, facing each other, while Ben sat alone at the other end. His mother had not joined them for the meal, bowing in this regard to the T'ang's wishes. But in other respects she had had her own way. The T'ang's own cooks sat idle in her kitchen, watching with suspicion and a degree of amazement as she single-handedly prepared and served the meal. This departure from the T'ang's normal practices was remarkable enough in itself, but what had happened at the beginning of the meal had surprised even his father.

When the food taster had stepped up to the table to perform his normal duties, the T'ang had waved him away and, picking up his chopsticks, had taken the first mouthful himself. Then, after chewing and swallowing the fragrant morsel, and after a sip of the strong green Longjing *ch'a* – itself "untasted" – he had looked up at Beth Shepherd and smiled broadly, complimenting her on the dish. It was, as Ben understood at once, seeing the surprised delight on his father's face and the astonished horror on the face of the official taster, quite unprecedented, and made him realise how circumscribed the T'ang's life had been. Not free at all, as others may have thought, but difficult; a life lived in the shadow of death. For Li Shai Tung, trust was the rarest and most precious thing he had to offer; for in trusting he placed his life – quite literally his life – in the hands of others.

In that small yet significant gesture, the T'ang had given his father and mother the ultimate in compliments.

Ben studied the man as he talked, aware of a strength in him that was somehow more than physical. There was a certainty – a vitality – in his every movement, such that even the slightest hesitancy was telling. His whole body spoke a subtle language of command; something that had developed quite naturally and unconsciously during the long years of his rule. To watch him was to watch not a man but a directing force; was to witness the channelling of aggression and determination into its most elegant and expressive form. In some respects Li Shai Tung was like an athlete, each nuance of voice or gesture the result of long and patient practice. Practice that had made these things second nature to the T'ang.

Ben watched, fascinated, barely hearing their words, but aware of their significance, and of the significance of the fact that he was there to hear them.

Li Shai Tung leaned forward slightly, his chin, with its pure white, neatly-braided beard, formulating a slight upward motion that signalled the offering of a confidence.

"The House was never meant to be so powerful. Our forefathers saw it only as a gesture. To be candid, Hal, as a sop to their erstwhile allies and a mask to their true intentions. But now, a hundred years on, certain factions persist in taking it at face value. They maintain that the power of the House is sanctioned by 'the People'. And we know why, don't we? Not for 'the People'. Such men don't spare a second's thought for 'the People'. No, they think only of themselves. They seek to climb at our expense. To raise themselves by pulling down the Seven. They want control, Hal, and the House is the means through which they seek to get it."

The T'ang leaned back again, his eyes half-lidded now. He reached up with his right hand and grasped the tightly-furled queue at the back of his head, his fingers closing about the coil of fine white hair. It was a curious, almost absent-minded gesture; yet it served to emphasise to Ben how at ease the T'ang was in his father's company. He watched, aware of a whole vocabulary of gesture there in the dialogue between the two men: conscious not just of what they said but of how they said it; how their eyes met or did not meet; how a shared smile would suddenly reveal the depths of their mutual understanding. All served to show him just how much the T'ang depended on his father to release these words, these thoughts, these feelings. Perhaps because no other could be trusted with them.

"I often ask myself, is there any way we might remove the House and dismantle the huge bureaucratic structure that has grown about it? But each time I ask myself I know beforehand what the answer is. No. At least, not now. Fifteen, maybe twenty years ago it might have been possible. But even then it might simply have pre-empted things. Brought us quicker to this point."

Hal Shepherd nodded. "I agree. But perhaps we should have faced it back then. We were stronger. Our grip on things was firmer. Now things have changed. Each year's delay sees them grow at our expense."

"You'd counsel war, then, Hal?"

"Of a kind."

The T'ang smiled, and Ben, watching, found himself comparing the man to his tutor, Peng Yu-wei. That epicanthic fold over the eye, which seemed so much a part of the android's 'difference' – its machine-nature – was here, on the natural man, quite attractive.

"And what kind is that?"

"The kind we're best at. A war of levels. Of openness and deception. The kind of war the Tyrant, Tsao Ch'un, taught us how to fight."

The T'ang looked down at his hands, his smile fading. "I don't know. I really don't, Hal. Sometimes I question what we've done."

"As any man must surely do."

Li Shai Tung looked up at him and shook his head. "No, Hal. For once I think you're wrong. Few men actually question their actions. Most are blind to their faults. Deaf to the criticisms of their fellow men." He laughed sourly. "You might say that Chung Kuo is filled with such men – blind, wicked, greedy creatures who see their blindness as strength, their wickedness as necessity, their greed as historical process."

"That's so . . ."

For a moment the two men fell silent, their faces solemn in the flickering light from the fire. Before either could speak again, the door at the far end of the room opened and Ben's mother entered, carrying a tray. She set it down on a footstool beside the open fire, then leaned across to take something from a bowl on the mantelpiece and sprinkle it on the burning logs.

At once the room was filled with the sweet, fresh smell of mint.

The T'ang gave a gentle laugh, delighted, and took a long, deep breath.

Ben watched his mother turn from the fire, drawing her

long dark hair back from her face, smiling. "I've brought fresh *ch'a*," she said simply, then lifted the tray and brought it across to them.

As she set it down the T'ang stood and, reaching across, put his hand over hers, preventing her from lifting the kettle.

"Please. I would be honoured if you sat a while with us and shared the *ch'a*."

She hesitated then, smiling, did as he bid her; watching the strange sight of a T'ang pouring *ch'a* for a commoner.

"Here," he said, offering her the first bowl. "*Ch'a* from the dragon's well."

The T'ang's words were a harmless play on the name of the Longjing *ch'a*, but for Ben they seemed to hold a special meaning. He looked at his mother, seeing how she smiled self-consciously and lowered her head, for a moment the youthful look of her reminding him terribly of Meg – of how Meg would be a year or two from now. Then he looked back at the T'ang, standing there, pouring a second bowl for his father.

Ben frowned. The very presence of the T'ang in the room seemed suddenly quite strange. His silks, his plaited hair, his very foreign-ness seemed out of place amongst the low oak beams and sturdy yeoman furniture. That contrast, that curious juxtaposition of man and room, brought home to Ben how strange this world of theirs truly was. A world tipped wildly from its natural balance.

The dragon's well. It made him think of fire and darkness, of untapped potency. *Is that what's missing from our world?* he asked himself. *Have we done with fire and darkness?*

"And you, Ben? Will you drink of the dragon's well?"

Li Shai Tung looked across at him, smiling; but behind the smile – beyond it, in some darker, less accessible place – lay a deep disquiet.

Flames danced in the glass of each eye, flickered wet and evanescent on the dark surface of his vision. But where was the fire on the far side of the glass? Where the depths that

395

made of Man *a man*? In word and gesture, the T'ang was a great and powerful man – a T'ang, unmistakably a king among men – but he had lost contact with the very thing that had made – had *shaped* – his outer form. He had denied his inner self once too often and now the well was capped, the fire doused.

He stared at the T'ang, wondering if he knew what he had become; if the doubt that he professed was as thorough, as all-inclusive as it ought to be. Whether, when he looked at his reflection in the mirror, he saw beyond the glass into that other place behind the eyes. Ben shivered. No. It could not be so. For if it were the man himself would crumble. Words would fail, gestures grow hesitant. No. This T'ang might doubt what they had done, but not what he was. That was innate – was bred into his bones. He would die before he doubted himself.

The smile remained, unchallenged, genuine; the offered bowl awaited him.

"Well, Ben?" his father asked, turning to him. "Will you take a bowl with us?"

* * *

Li Shai Tung leaned forward, offering the boy the bowl, conscious that he had become the focus of the child's strange intensity; of the intimidating ferocity of his stare.

Hal was right. Ben was not like other children. There was something wild in his nature; some part of him that remained untamed, unsocialised. When he sat there at table it was as if he held himself in check. There was such stillness in him that when he moved it was like something dead had come alive again. Yet he was more alive – more vividly alive – than anyone the T'ang had ever met.

As he handed Ben the bowl he almost expected to receive some kind of shock – a violent discharge of the child's unnatural energy – through the medium of the bowl. But there was nothing. Only his wild imagining.

The T'ang looked down, thoughtful. Ben Shepherd was a breed of one. He had none of those small refinements that fitted a man for the company of his fellows. He had no sense of give and take; no idea of the concessions one made for the sake of social comfort. His stare was uncompromising, almost proprietorial. As if all he saw was his.

Yes, Li Shai Tung thought, smiling inwardly: *You should be a T'ang, Ben Shepherd, for you'll find it hard to pass muster as a simple man.*

He lifted his bowl and sipped, thinking back to earlier that afternoon. They had been out walking in the garden when Hal had suggested he go with him and see Ben's room.

He had stood in the centre of the tiny, cluttered upstairs room, looking at the paintings that covered the wall above the bed.

Some were lifelike studies of the Domain. Lifelike, at least, but for the dark, unfocused figures who stood in the shadows beneath the trees on the far side of the water. Others were more abstract, depicting strange distortions of the real. Twins figured largely in these latter compositions; one twin quite normal – strong and healthy – the other twisted out of shape, the eyes white and blank, the mouth open as if in pain. They were disturbing, unusually disturbing, yet their technical accomplishment could not be questioned.

"These are good, Hal. Very good indeed. The boy has talent."

Hal Shepherd gave a small smile, then came alongside him. "He'd be pleased to hear you say that. But if you think those are good, look at this."

The T'ang took the folder from him and opened it. Inside was a single ultra-thin sheet of what seemed like pure black plastic. He turned it in his hands and then laughed. "What is it?"

"Here," Shepherd indicated a viewer on the table by the window, then drew the blind down. "Lay it in the tray there, then flick that switch."

Li Shai Tung placed the sheet down in the viewer. "Does it matter which way up?"

"Yes and no. You'll see."

The T'ang flicked the switch. At once the tank-like cage of the viewer was filled with colour. It was a hologram. A portrait of Hal Shepherd's wife, Beth.

"He did this?"

Shepherd nodded. "There are one hundred and eighty cross-sectional layers of information. Ninety horizontal, ninety vertical. He hand drew each sheet and then compressed them. It's his own technique. He invented it."

"Hand drew . . . ?"

"And from memory. Beth wouldn't sit for him, you see. She said she was too busy. But he did it anyway."

Li Shai Tung shook his head slowly. "It's astonishing, Hal. It's like a camera image of her."

"You haven't seen the half of it. Wait . . ." Shepherd switched the hologram off, then reached in and lifted the flexible plate up. He turned it and set it down again. "Please . . ."

The T'ang reached out and pressed the switch. Again the viewing cage was filled with colour. But this time the image was different.

The hologram of Hal Shepherd was far from flattering. The flesh was far cruder, much rougher than the reality, the cheeks ruddier. The hair was thicker, curlier, the eyebrows heavier and darker. The nose was thick and fleshy, the ears pointed, the eyes larger, darker. The lips were more sensuous than the original, almost licentious. They seemed to sneer.

Shepherd moved closer and looked down into the viewer. "There's something of the satyr about it. Something elemental."

The T'ang turned his head and looked at him, not understanding the allusion.

Shepherd laughed. "It was a Greek thing, Shai Tung. In their mythology satyrs were elementary spirits of the mountains and the forests. Part-goat, part-man. Cloven-hooved, thickly-haired, sensual and lascivious."

Li Shai Tung stared at the urbane, highly-sophisticated

man standing at his side and laughed briefly, bemused that Shepherd could see himself in that brutal portrait. "I can see a *slight* likeness. Something in the eyes, the shape of the head, but . . ."

Shepherd shook his head slowly. He was staring at the hologram intently. "No. Look at it, Shai Tung. Look hard at it. He sees me clearly. My inner self."

Li Shai Tung shivered. "The gods help us that our sons should see us thus!"

Shepherd turned and looked at him. "Why? Why should we fear that, old friend? We know what we are. Men. Part mind, part animal. Why should we be afraid of that?"

The T'ang pointed to the image. "Men, yes. But men like that? You really see yourself in such an image, Hal?"

Shepherd smiled. "It's not the all of me, I know, but it's a part. An important part."

Li Shai Tung shrugged – the slightest movement of his shoulders – then looked back at the image. "But why is the other as it is? Why aren't both alike?"

"Ben has a wicked sense of humour."

Again the T'ang did not understand, but this time Shepherd made no attempt to enlighten him.

Li Shai Tung studied the hologram a moment longer then turned from it, looking all about him. "He gets such talent from you, Hal."

Shepherd shook his head. "I never had a tenth of his talent. Anyway, even the word 'talent' is unsatisfactory. What he has is genius. In that he's like his great-grandfather."

The T'ang smiled at that, remembering his father's tales of Augustus Shepherd's eccentricity. "Perhaps. But let us hope that that is all he has inherited."

He knew at once that he had said the wrong thing. Or, if not the wrong thing, then something which touched upon a sensitive area.

"The resemblance is more than casual."

The T'ang lowered his head slightly, willing to drop the matter at once, but Shepherd seemed anxious to explain. "Ben's schizophrenic too, you see. Oh, nothing as bad as Augustus. But it creates certain incongruities in his character."

Li Shai Tung looked back at the pictures above the bed with new understanding. "But from what you've said the boy is healthy enough."

"Even happy, I'd say. Most of the time. He has bouts of it, you understand. Then we either dose him up heavily or leave him alone."

Shepherd leaned across and switched off the viewer, then lifted the thin black sheet and slipped it back into the folder. "They used to think schizophrenia was a simple malfunction of the brain; an imbalance in certain chemicals – dopamine, glutamic acid and gamma-amino-butyric acid. Drugs like largactil, modecate, disipal, priadel and haloperidol were used, mainly as tranquillisers. But they simply kept the thing in check and had the side-effect of enlarging the dopamine system. Worst of all, at least as far as Ben is concerned, they damp down the creative faculty."

The T'ang frowned. Medicine, like all else, was based on traditional Han ways. The development of Western drugs, like Western ideas of progress, had been abandoned when Tsao Ch'un had built his City. Many such drugs were, in fact, illicit now. One heard of them, normally, only in the context of addiction – something that was rife in the lowest levels of the City. Nowadays all serious conditions were diagnosed before the child was born and steps taken either to correct them or to abort the foetus. It thus surprised him, first to hear that Ben's illness had not been diagnosed beforehand, second that he had even considered taking drugs to keep the illness in check.

"He has not taken these drugs, I hope."

Shepherd met his eyes. "Not only has but still does. Except when he's working."

The T'ang sighed deeply. "You should have told me, Hal. I shall arrange for my herbalist to call on Ben within the next few days."

Shepherd shook his head. "I thank you, Shai Tung. Your kindness touches me. But it would do no good."

"No good?" The T'ang frowned, puzzled. "But there are numerous sedatives – things to calm the spirit and restore the body's yin-yang balance. Good, healthy remedies, not these . . . drugs!"

"I know, Shai Tung, and again I thank you for your concern. But Ben would have none of it. Oh, I can see him now –'Dragon bones and oyster shells!' he'd say scornfully, 'What good are they against this affliction!'"

The T'ang looked down, disturbed. In this matter he could not insist. The birthright of the Shepherds made them immune from the laws that governed others. If Ben took drugs to maintain his mental stability there was little he, Li Shai Tung, could do about it. Even so, he could not stop himself from feeling it was wrong. He changed the subject.

"Is he a good son, Hal?"

Shepherd laughed. "He is the best of sons, Shai Tung. Like Li Yuan, his respect is not a matter of rote, as it is with some of this new generation, but a deep-rooted thing. And as you've seen, it stems from a thorough knowledge of his father."

The T'ang nodded, leaving his doubts unexpressed. "Good. But you are right, Hal. These past few years have seen a sharp decline in morality. The *li* – the rites – they mean little now. The young mouth the old words but they mean nothing by them. Their respect is an empty shell. We are fortunate, you and I, that we have good sons."

"Indeed. Though Ben can be a pompous, intolerant little sod at times. He has no time for fools. And little enough for cleverness, if you see what I mean. He loathes his machine-tutor, for instance."

Li Shai Tung raised his eyebrows. "That surprises me, Hal. I would have thought he cherished knowledge. All this," he looked about him at the books and paintings and machines, "it speaks of a love of knowledge."

Shepherd smiled strangely. "Perhaps you should talk to him yourself, Shai Tung."

The T'ang smiled. "Perhaps I should."

Now, watching the boy across the length of the dinner table, he understood.

"What do you think, Ben? Do you think the time has come to fight our enemies?"

Unexpectedly, the boy laughed. "That depends on whether you know who or what your enemies are, Li Shai Tung."

The T'ang lifted his chin slightly. "I think I have a fair idea of that."

Ben met his eyes again, fixing that same penetrating stare on him. "Maybe. But you must first ask yourself what exactly you are fighting against. When you think of your enemies your first thought is of certain identifiable men and groups of men, is that not so?"

The T'ang nodded. "That is so, Ben. I know my enemies. I can put names to them and faces."

"There, you see. And you think that by waging war against them you will resolve this present situation." Ben set his bowl down and sat back, his every gesture momentarily – though none but Ben himself realised it – the mirror image of the T'ang's. "With respect, Li Shai Tung, you are wrong."

The T'ang laughed fiercely, enjoying the exchange. "You think their ideology will outlive them? Is that it, Ben? If it were not so false in the first place, I would agree with you. But their sole motivation is greed. They don't really want change. They want power."

Ben shook his head. "Ah, but you're still thinking of specific men. Powerful men, admittedly, even men of influence, but only men. Men won't bring Chung Kuo down, only what's inside Man. You should free yourself from thinking of them. To you they seem the greatest threat, but they're not. They're the scum on the surface of the well. And the well is deep."

Li Shai Tung took a deep breath. "With respect, Ben, in this *you* are wrong. Your argument presupposes that it does not matter who rules – that things will remain as they are

402

whoever is in power. But that's not so. Their ideology is false, but, forgive me, they are *Hung Mao*."

Across from him Hal Shepherd smiled, but he was clearly embarrassed. It was more than two decades since he had taken offence at the term – a term used all the while in court, where the Han were predominant and the few Caucasians treated as honorary Han – yet here, in the Domain, he felt the words incongruous, almost – surprisingly – insulting.

"They have no sense of harmony," continued the T'ang, unaware. "No sense of *li*. Any change they brought would not be for the good. They are men of few principles. They would carve the world up into principalities and then there would be war again. Endless war. As it was before."

There was the faintest of smiles on Ben's lips. "You forget your own history, Li Shai Tung. No dynasty can last forever. The wheel turns. Change comes, whether you will it or no. It is the way of Mankind. All of Mankind, even the Han."

"So it may have been, but things are different now. The wheel no longer turns. We have done with history."

Ben laughed. "But you cannot stop the world from turning!"

He was about to say more but his mother touched his arm. She had sat there, perfectly still and silent, watching the fire while they talked, her dark hair hiding her face. Now she smiled and got up, excusing herself.

"Perhaps you men would like to go through into the study. I've lit the fire there."

Shepherd looked to the T'ang, who gave the slightest nod of agreement before standing and bowing to his hostess. Again he thanked her warmly for the meal and her hospitality, then, when she had gone, went before Shepherd and his son into the other room.

"Brandy?" Shepherd turned from the wall cabinet, holding the decanter up. The T'ang was usually abstemious, but tonight his mood seemed different. He seemed to want to talk – to encourage talk. As if there were some real end to all this talking: some problem which, though he hadn't come to it, he wished to address. Something he found difficult; that worried him profoundly.

The T'ang hesitated, then smiled. "Why not? After all, a man should indulge himself now and then."

Shepherd poured the T'ang a fingernail's measure of the dark liquid and handed him the ancient bowled glass. Then he turned to his son. "Ben?"

Ben smiled almost boyishly. "Are you sure mother won't mind?"

Shepherd winked at him. "Mother won't know."

He handed the boy a glass, then poured one for himself and sat, facing the T'ang across the fire. Maybe it was time to force the pace; time to draw the T'ang out of himself.

"Something's troubling you, Shai Tung."

The T'ang looked up from his glass almost distractedly and gave a soft laugh. "Everything troubles me, Hal. But that's not what you mean, is it?"

"No. No visit of yours is casual, Shai Tung. You had a specific reason for coming to see me, didn't you?"

The T'ang's smile was filled with gratitude. "As ever, Hal, you're right. But I'll need no excuse to come next time. I've found this very pleasant."

"Well?"

The T'ang took a long inward breath, steeling himself, then spoke. "It's Tolonen."

For some time now the T'ang had been under intense pressure from the House to bring the General to trial for the murder of Under Secretary Lehmann. They wanted Tolonen's head for what he'd done. But the T'ang had kept his thoughts to himself about the killing. No one – not the Seven nor Hal Shepherd – knew how he really felt about the matter, only that he had refused to see Tolonen since that day; that he had exiled him immediately and appointed a new General, Vittorio Nocenzi, in his place.

Shepherd waited, conscious of how tense Li Shai Tung had suddenly become. Tolonen had been of the same generation as the T'ang and they shared the same unspoken values. In their personal lives there had been parallels that had drawn them close and formed a bond between them; not least the loss of both their wives some ten years back. In temperament, however, they were ice and fire.

"I miss him. Do you understand that, Hal? I really miss the old devil. First and foremost for himself. For all that he was. Loyal. Honest. Brave." He looked up briefly, then looked down again, his eyes misting. "I felt he was my champion, Hal. Always there at my side. From my eighteenth year. My General. My most trusted man."

He shuddered and was silent for a while. Then he began again, his voice softer, yet somehow stronger, more definite than before.

"Strangely I miss his rashness most of all. He was like Han Ch'in in that. What he said was always what part of me felt. Now I feel almost that that part of me is missing – is unexpressed, festering in the darkness."

"You want him back?"

Li Shai Tung laughed bitterly. "As if I could. No, Hal, but I want to see him. I need to speak to him."

Shepherd was silent for a time, considering, then he leaned forward and set his glass down on the table at his side. "You should call him back, Shai Tung. For once damn the House and its demands. Defy them. You are T'ang, and thus above their laws."

Li Shai Tung looked up and met Shepherd's eyes. "I am T'ang, yes, but I am also Seven. I could not act so selfishly."

"Why not?"

The T'ang laughed, surprised. "This is unlike you, Hal. For more than twenty years you have advised me to be cautious, to consider the full implications of my actions, but now, suddenly, you counsel me to rashness."

Shepherd smiled. "Not rashness, Shai Tung. Far from it. In fact, I've thought of little else this past year." He got up and went across to a bureau in the corner furthest from the fire, returning a moment later with a folder which he handed to the T'ang.

"What is this, Hal?"

Shepherd smiled, then sat again. "My thoughts on things."

Li Shai Tung stared thoughtfully at Shepherd a moment, then set his glass down and opened the folder.

"But this is handwritten."

Shepherd nodded. "It's the only copy. I've said things in there that I'd rather not have fall into the hands of our enemies."

He looked briefly at his son as he said the last few words, conscious that the boy was watching everything.

Li Shai Tung looked up at him, his face suddenly hawklike, his eyes fiercer than before. "Why did you not mention this before?"

"It was not my place. In any case, it was not ready before now."

The T'ang looked back down at the folder and at the summary Shepherd had appended to the front of his report. This was more than a simple distillation of the man's thoughts on the current political situation. Here, in its every detail, was the plan for that "War of Levels" Shepherd had mentioned earlier. A scheme which would, if implemented, bring the Seven into direct confrontation with the House.

Li Shai Tung flicked through the pages of the report quickly, skimming, picking out phrases which Shepherd had highlighted or underlined, his pulse quickening as he read. Shepherd's tiny, neat handwriting filled almost forty pages, but the meat of it was there, in that opening summary. He read once more what Shepherd had written.

Power is defined only through the exercise of power. For too long now we have refrained from openly exercising our power and that restraint has been taken for weakness by our enemies. In view of developments it might be argued that they have been justified in this view. However, our real weakness is not that we lack the potential, but that we lack the will to act.

We have lost the initiative and allowed our opponents to dictate the subject – even the rules – of the debate. This has resulted in the perpetuation of the belief that change is not merely desirable but inevitable. Moreover, they believe that the natural instrument of that change is the House, therefore they seek to increase the power of the House.

The logic of this process is inexorable. There is nothing but House and Seven, hence the House can grow only at the expense of the Seven.

War is inevitable. It can be delayed but not avoided. And every delay is henceforth to our opponents' advantage. They grow while we diminish. It follows that we must pre-empt their play for power.

We must destroy them now, while we yet have the upper hand.

Li Shai Tung closed the file with a sigh. Shepherd was right. He knew, with a gut certainty, that this was what they should do. But he had said it already. He was not simply T'ang, he was Seven, and the Seven would never act on this. They saw it differently.

"Well?"

"I can keep this?"

"Of course. It was meant for you."

The T'ang smiled sadly, then looked across at the boy. He spoke to him as he would to his own son, undeferentially, as one adult to another. "Have you seen this, Ben?"

Shepherd answered for his son. "You've heard him already. He thinks it nonsense."

Ben corrected his father. "Not nonsense. I never said that. I merely said it avoided the real issue."

"Which is?" Li Shai Tung asked, reaching for his glass.

"Why men are never satisfied."

The T'ang considered a moment, then laughed softly. "That has always been so, Ben. How can I change what men are?"

"You could make it better for them. They feel boxed-in. Not just physically, but mentally, too. They've no dreams. Not one of them feels real any more."

There was a moment's silence, then Hal Shepherd spoke again. "You know this, Ben? You've talked to people?"

Ben stared at his father momentarily, then turned his attention back to the T'ang. "You can't miss it. It's there in all their eyes. There's an emptiness there. An unfilled, unfulfilled space deep inside them. I don't have to talk to them to see that. I have only to watch the media. It's like they're all dead but they can't see it. They're looking for some purpose for it all and they can't find it."

Li Shai Tung stared back at the boy for a moment, then looked down, chilled by what Ben had said. Was it so? Was it really so? He looked about the room, conscious suddenly of the lowness of the ceiling, of the dark oak beams that divided up the whitewashed walls, the fresh cut roses in a silver bowl on the table in the corner. He could feel the old wood beneath his fingers, smell the strong pine scent of the fire. All this was real. And he, he too was real, surely? But sometimes, just sometimes . . .

"And you think we could give them a purpose?"

Strangely, Ben smiled. "No. But you might give them the space to find one for themselves."

The T'ang nodded. "Ah. Space. Well, Ben, there are more than thirty-nine billion people in Chung Kuo. What practical measures could we possibly take to give space to so many?"

But Ben was shaking his head. "You mistake me, Li Shai Tung. You take my image too literally." He put a finger to his brow. "I meant space up here. That's where they're trapped. The City's only the outward, concrete form of it. But the blueprint – the paradigm – is inside their heads. That's where you've got to give them room. And you can only do that by giving them a sense of direction."

"Change. That's what you mean, isn't it?"

"No. You need change nothing."

Li Shai Tung laughed. "Then I don't understand you, Ben. Have you some magic trick in mind?"

"Not at all. I mean only that if the problem is in their heads then the solution can be found in the same place. They want outwardness. They want space, excitement, novelty. Well, why not give it to them? But not out there, in the real world. Give it to them up here, in their heads."

The T'ang was frowning. "But don't they get that, Ben? Doesn't the media give them that now?"

Ben shook his head. "No. I'm talking of something entirely different. Something that will make the walls dissolve. That will make it real to them." Again he tapped his brow. "Up here, where it counts."

The T'ang was about to answer him when there was a knock on the door.

"Come in!" said Shepherd, half turning in his seat.

It was the T'ang's steward. He bowed low to Shepherd and his son, then turned, his head still lowered, to his master. "Forgive me, *Chieh Hsia*, but you asked me to remind you of your audience with Minister Chao." Then, with a bow, the steward backed away, closing the door behind him.

Li Shai Tung looked back at Shepherd. "I'm sorry, Hal, but I must leave soon."

"Of course . . ." Shepherd began, but his son interrupted him.

"One last thing, Li Shai Tung."

The T'ang turned, patient, smiling. "What is it, Ben?"

"I saw something. This afternoon, in the town."

Li Shai Tung frowned. "You saw something?"

"An execution. And a suicide. Two of the elite guards."

"Gods!" The T'ang sat forward. "You saw that?"

"We were upstairs in one of the shops."

Shepherd broke in. "*We*. You mean Meg was with you?"

Ben nodded, then told what he had seen. At the end Li Shai Tung, his face stricken, turned to Shepherd. "Forgive me, Hal. This is all my fault. Captain Rosten was acting on my direct orders. However, had I known Ben and Meg would be there . . ." He shuddered, then turned back to the boy. "Ben, please forgive me. And ask Meg to forgive me, too. Would that I could undo what has been done."

For a moment Ben seemed about to say something, then he dropped his eyes and made a small movement of his head. A negation. But what it signified neither man knew.

There was another knock on the door; a signal that the T'ang acknowledged with a few words of Mandarin. Then the two men stood, facing each other, smiling, for a brief moment in perfect accord.

"It has been an honour to have you here, Li Shai Tung. An honour and a pleasure."

The T'ang's smile broadened. "The pleasure has been mine, Hal. It is not often I can be myself."

"Then come again. Whenever you need to be yourself."

Li Shai Tung let his left hand rest on Shepherd's upper arm a moment, then nodded. "I shall. I promise you. But come, Hal, I've a gift for you."

The door opened and two of the T'ang's personal servants came in, carrying the gift. They set it down on the floor in the middle of the room, as the T'ang had instructed them earlier, then backed away, heads lowered. It was a tree. A tiny, miniature apple tree.

Shepherd went across and knelt beside it, then turned and looked back at Li Shai Tung, clearly moved by the T'ang's gesture.

"It's beautiful. It really is, Shai Tung. How did you know I wanted one?"

The T'ang laughed softly. "I cheated, Hal. I asked Beth. But the gift is for you both. Look carefully. The tree is a twin. It has two intertwined trunks."

Shepherd looked. "Ah yes." He laughed, aware of the significance. Joined trees were objects of good omen; symbols of conjugal happiness and marital fidelity. More than that, an apple – *p'ing*, in Mandarin – was a symbol of peace. "It's perfect, Li Shai Tung. It really is." He shook his head, overwhelmed, tears forming in his eyes. "We shall treasure it."

"And I this." Li Shai Tung held up Shepherd's file. He smiled, then turned to the boy. "It was good to talk with you, Ben. I hope we might talk again some time."

Ben stood and, unexpectedly, gave a small bow to the T'ang.

"My father's right, of course. You should destroy them. Now, while you still can."

"Ah . . ." Li Shai Tung hesitated, then nodded. Maybe so, he thought, surprised yet again by the child's unpredict-ability. But he said nothing. Time alone would prove them right or wrong on that.

He looked back at Shepherd who was standing now. "I must go, Hal. It would not do to keep Minister Chao waiting." He laughed. "You know, Chao has been in my service longer than anyone but Tolonen."

It was said before he realised it.

"I forget . . ." he said, with a small, sad laugh.

Shepherd, watching him, shook his head. "Bring him back, Shai Tung," he said softly. "This once, do as your heart bids you."

The T'ang smiled tightly and held the file more firmly. "Maybe," he said. But he knew he would not. It was as he had said. He was T'ang, yes, but he was also Seven.

★ ★ ★

When the T'ang had gone they stood at the river's edge. The moon was high overhead – a bright, full moon that seemed to float in the dark mirror of the water. The night was warm and still, its silence broken only by the sound – a distant, almost disembodied sound – of the soldiers work-ing on the cottage.

Shepherd squatted down, looking out across the water into the darkness on the other side.

"What did you mean, Ben, earlier? All that business about dissolving walls and making it real. Was that just talk or did you have something real in mind?"

Ben was standing several paces from his father, looking back up the grassy slope to where they had set up arc lamps all around the cottage. The dark figures of the suited men seemed to flit through the glare like objects seen peripherally, in a dream.

"It's an idea I have. Something I've been working on."

Shepherd turned his head slightly and studied his son a moment. "You seemed quite confident. Almost as if the thing existed."

Ben smiled and met his father's eyes briefly. "It does. Up here."

Shepherd laughed and looked down, tugging at the long grass. "So what is it? I'm interested. And I think the T'ang was interested, too."

"What did he want?"

A faint breeze ruffled the water, making the moon dance exaggeratedly on the darkness. "What do you mean?"

"Why was I there?"

Shepherd smiled to himself. He should have known better than to think Ben would not ask that question.

"Because he wanted to see you, Ben. Because he thinks that one day you might help his son."

"I see. And he was assessing me?"

"You might put it that way."

Ben laughed. "I thought as much. Do you think he found me strange?"

"Why should you think that?"

Ben looked directly at his father. "I know what I am. I've seen enough of the world to know how different I am."

"On a screen, yes. But not everything's up there on the screen, Ben."

"No?" Ben looked back up the slope towards the cottage. They were hauling the first of the thin, encasing layers over the top of the frame, the heavily-suited men pulling on the guide ropes. "What don't they show?"

Shepherd laughed, but let the query pass. Ben was right. He did know what he was, and he was different. There was no point in denying that.

"You've no need to follow in my footsteps, Ben."

Ben smiled but didn't look at him. "You think I'd want that?"

Shepherd felt a twinge of bitterness, then shook his head. "No. No, I guess not. In any case, I'd never force that on you. You know that, don't you?"

Ben turned and stared out across the water fixedly. "Those things don't interest me. The political specifics.

The who–runs–what and who–did–what. I would be bored by it all. And what good is a bored advisor? I'd need to care about those things, and I don't."

"You seemed to care. Earlier, when we were talking about them."

"No. That was something different. That was the deeper thing."

Shepherd laughed. "Of course. The *deeper* thing."

Ben looked back at him. "You deal in surfaces, father, both of you. But the problem's deeper than that. It's inside. Beneath the surface of the skin. It's bred in the blood and bone of men, in the complex web of nerve and muscle and organic tissue. But you . . . Well, you persist in dealing with only what you see. You treat the blemished skin and let the inner man corrupt."

Shepherd was watching his son thoughtfully, aware of the gulf that had grown between them these last few years. It was as if Ben had outgrown them all. Had done with childish things. He shrugged. "Maybe. But that doesn't solve the immediate problem. Those surfaces you dismiss so readily have hard edges. Collide with them and you'll realise that at once. People get hurt, lives get blighted, and those aren't superficial things."

"It wasn't what I meant."

Shepherd laughed. "No. Maybe not. And maybe you're right. You'd make a lousy advisor, Ben. You've been made for other things than politics and intrigue." He stood up, wiping his hands against his trousers. "You know, there were many things I wanted to do, but I never had the time for them. Pictures I wanted to paint, books I wanted to write, music I wanted to compose. But in serving the T'ang I've had to sacrifice all those and much else besides. I've seen much less of you and Meg than I ought – and far, far too little of your mother. So . . ." He shrugged. "Well, if you don't want that kind of life, I understand. I understand only too well. More than that, Ben, I think the world would lose something were you to neglect the gifts you have."

Ben smiled. "We'll see." Then he pointed up the slope. "I think they've almost finished. That's the third of the isolation skins."

Shepherd turned and looked back up the slope. The cottage was fully encased now, its cosy shape disguised by the huge, white insulating layers. Only at the front, where the door to the garden was, was its smooth, perfectly geometric shape broken. There they had put the seal-unit; a big cylinder containing the air-pump and the emergency generator.

A dozen suited men were fastening the edges of the insulator to the brace of the frame. The brace was permanently embedded in the earth surrounding the cottage; a crude, heavy piece of metal a foot wide and three inches thick with a second, smaller "collar" fixed by old-fashioned wing-screws to the base.

The whole strange apparatus had been devised by Ben's great-great-great-grandfather, Amos – the first of the Shepherds to live here – as a precaution against nuclear fallout. But when the Great Third War – "The War To End It All" as the old man had written in his journal – had failed to materialise, the whole cumbersome isolation-unit had been folded up and stored away, only the metal brace remaining, for the amusement of each new generation of Shepherd children.

"Gift-wrapped!" Shepherd joked, beginning to climb the slope.

Ben, following a few paces behind, gave a small laugh, but it was unrelated to his father's comment. He had had an insight. It had been Amos' son, Robert, who had designed City Earth. His preliminary architectural sketches hung in a long glass frame on the passage wall inside the cottage. But the idea had not originated with him. The seed of City Earth lay here, now, before them – physically before them – as they climbed the grassy slope. Here, in this outward symbol of his great-great-great-grandfather's paranoia was the genesis of all that had followed. Robert had merely enlarged and refined his father's scheme until it embraced a world.

414

He laughed softly to himself, then looked across at his father, wondering if he saw it too, or whether the connection existed in his mind alone.

Nearer the cottage the soldiers had set up an infestation grid, the dull mauve light attracting anything small and winged from the surrounding meadows. Ben stood and watched as a moth, its wings like the dull gauze of an old and faded dress, its body thick and stubby like a miniature cigar, fluttered towards the grid. For a moment it danced in the blue-pink light, mesmerised by the brightness, its translucent wings suffused with purple. Then its wing-tip brushed against the tilted surface. With a spark and a hiss the moth fell, senseless, into the grid, where it flamed momentarily, its wings curling, vanishing in an instant, its body cooking to a dark cinder.

Ben watched a moment longer, conscious of his own fascination; his ears filled with the brutal music of the grid – the crack and pop and sizzle of the dying creatures, his eyes drawn to each brief, sudden incandescence. And in his mind he formed a pattern of their vivid after-images against the dull mauve light.

"Come, Ben. Come on in."

He turned. His mother was standing in the doorway, beckoning to him. He smiled then sniffed the air. It was filled with the tart, sweet scent of ozone and burnt insects.

"I was watching," he said, as if it explained everything.

"I know." She came across to him and put her hand on his shoulder. "It's horrible, isn't it? But necessary, I suppose."

"Yes."

But he meant something other by the word: something more than simple agreement. It was both horrible and necessary, if only to prevent the spread of the disease throughout the Domain; but it was just that – the horrible necessity of death – that gave it its fascination. Is all of life just that? he asked himself, looking away from the grid, out across the dark, moonlit water of the bay. Is it all merely one brief, erratic flight into the burning light? And then nothing?

Ben shivered, not from fear or cold, but from some deeper, more complex response, then turned and looked up at his mother, smiling. "Okay. Let's go inside."

★ ★ ★

The captain of the work party watched the woman and her son go in, then signalled to his men to complete the sealing-off of the cottage. It was nothing to him, of course – orders were orders – yet it had occurred to him several times that it would have been far simpler to evacuate the Shepherds than go through with all this nonsense. He could not for the life of him understand why they should wish to remain inside the cottage while the Domain was dusted with poisons. Still, he had to admit, it was a neat job. Old man Amos had known what he was up to.

He walked across and inspected the work thoroughly. Then, satisfied that the seal was air-tight, he pulled the lip mike up from under his chin. "Okay. We're finished here. You can start the sweep."

Six miles away, at the mouth of the estuary, the four big transporters, converted specially for the task, lifted one by one from the pad and began to form up in a line across the river. Then, at a signal, they began, moving slowly down the estuary, a thin cloud – colourless, like fine powdered snow – drifting down behind them.

CHAPTER·12

AUGUSTUS

It was just after ten in the morning, yet the sun already blazed down from a vast, deep blue sky that seemed washed clean of all impurities. Sunlight burnished the surface of the grey-green water, making it seem dense and yet clear, like melted glass. The tide was high but on the turn, lapping sluggishly against the rocks at the river's edge.

In mid-stream Meg let Ben take the oars from her, changing seats with him nimbly as the boat drifted slowly about. Then she sat back, watching him as he strove to right their course, his face a mask of patient determination, the muscles of his bare, tanned arms tensing and untensing. Ben clenched his teeth then pulled hard on the right-hand oar, turning the prow slowly towards the distant house, the dark, slick-edged blade biting deep into the glaucous, muscular flow as he hauled the boat about in a tight arc.

"Are you sure it's all right?"

Ben grimaced, concentrating, inwardly weighing the feel of the boat against the strong pull of the current. "She'll never know," he answered. "Who'll tell her?"

It wasn't a threat. He knew he could trust her to say nothing to their mother. Meg looked down briefly, smiling, pleased that he trusted her. Then she sat there, quiet, content to watch him, to see the broad river stretching away beyond him, the white-painted cottages of the village dotted against the broad green flank of the hill, while at her back the house grew slowly nearer.

Solitary, long-abandoned, it awaited them.

The foreshore was overgrown. Weeds grew waist-high

in the spaces between the rocks. Beyond, the land was level for thirty yards or so then climbed, slowly at first, then steeply. The house wasn't visible from where they stood, in the cool beneath the branches, and even further along, where the path turned, following the contours of the shore-line, they could see only a small part of it, jutting up, white between the intense green of the surrounding trees.

The land was strangely, unnaturally silent. Meg looked down through the trees. Below them, to their right, was the cove, the dark mouth of the cave almost totally sub-merged, the branches of the overhanging trees only inches above the surface of the water. It made her feel odd. Not quite herself.

"Come on," said Ben, looking back at her. "We've not long. Mother will be back by two."

They went up. A path had been cut from the rock. Rough hewn steps led up steeply, hugging an almost sheer cliff face. They had to force their way through a tangle of bushes and branches. At the top they came out into a kind of clearing. There was concrete underfoot, cracked but reasonably clear of vegetation. It was a road. To their left it led up into the trees. To their right it ended abruptly, only yards from where they stood, at an ornate cast-iron gate set into a wall.

They went across and stood there, before the gate, look-ing in.

The house lay beyond the gate; a big, square, three-storey building of white stone, with a steeply-pitched roof of grey slate. They could see patches of it through the over-run front garden. Here, more noticeably than elsewhere, nature had run amok. A stone fountain lay in two huge grey pieces, split asunder by an ash that had taken seed long ago in the disused fissure at its centre. Elsewhere the regular pattern of a once elaborate garden could be vaguely sensed, underlying the chaotic sprawl of new growth.

"Well?" she said, looking up at him. "What now?"

The wall was too high to climb. The gate seemed strong and solid, with four big hinges set into the stone. A big, thick-linked steel chain was wrapped tightly about the lock, secured by a fist-sized padlock.

Ben smiled. "Watch."

Taking a firm hold of two of the upright bars, he shook the gate vigorously, then gave it one last sharp forward thrust. With a crash it fell inward, then swung sideways, twisting against the restraining chain.

Ben stepped over it, then reached back for her. "The iron was rotten," he said, pointing to the four places in the stone where the hinges had snapped sheer off.

She nodded, understanding at once what he was really saying to her. *Be careful here. Judge nothing by its appearance.* He turned from her.

She followed, more cautious now, making her way through the thick sprawl of greenery towards the house.

A verandah ran the length of the front of the house. At one end it had collapsed. One of the four mock-doric pillars had fallen and now lay, like the broken leg of a stone giant, half-buried in the window frame behind where it had previously stood. The glass-framed roof of the verandah was broken in several places where branches of nearby trees had pushed against it, and the whole of the wooden frame – the elaborately-carved side pieces, the stanchions, rails and planking – was visibly rotten. Ben stood before the shallow flight of steps that led up to the main entrance, his head tilted back as he studied the frontage.

"It's not what I expected," he said as she came alongside him. "It seems a lot grander from the river. And bigger. A real fortress of a place."

She took his arm. "I don't know, Ben. I think it is rather grand. Or was, anyway."

He turned his head and looked at her. "Did you bring the lamp?"

She nodded and patted her pocket.

"Good. Though I doubt there'll be much to see. The house has been boarded up more than eighty years now."

She was silent a moment, thoughtful, and knew he was thinking the same thing. Augustus. The mystery of this house had something to do with their great-grandfather, Augustus.

"Well?" she prompted after a moment. "Shall we go inside?"

"Yes. But not this way. There's another door round the side. We'll get in there, through the kitchens."

She stared at him a moment, then understood. He had already studied plans of the old house. Which meant he had planned this visit for some while. But why this morning? Was it something to do with the soldiers' deaths? Or was it something else? She knew they had had a visitor last night, but no one had told her who it was or why they'd come. Whatever, Ben had seemed disturbed first thing when she had gone to wake him. He had been up already. She had found him sitting there, hunched up on his bed, his arms wrapped about his knees, staring out through the open window at the bay. That same mood was on him even now as he stood there looking up at the house.

"What exactly are we looking for?"

"Clues . . ."

She studied his face a moment longer but it gave nothing away. His answer was unlike him. He was always so specific, so certain. But today he was different. It was as if he was looking for something so ill-defined, so vaguely comprehended that even he could not say what it was.

"Come on then," he said suddenly. "Let's see what ghosts we'll find."

She laughed quietly, that same feeling she had had staring down at the cove through the trees – that sense of being not quite herself – returning to her. It was not fear, for she was never afraid when she was with Ben, but something else. Something to do with this side of the water. With the wildness here. As if it reflected something in herself. Some deeper, hidden thing.

"What do you think we'll find?" she called out to him as she followed him, pushing through the dense tangle of bushes and branches. "Have you any idea at all?"

"None," he yelled back. "Maybe there's nothing at all. Maybe it's an empty shell. But then why would they board it up? Why bother if it's empty? Why not just leave it to rot?"

She caught up with him. "From the look of it it's rotted anyway."

Ben glanced at her. "It'll be different inside."

★ ★ ★

A broad shaft of daylight breached the darkness. She watched Ben fold the shutter into its recess, then move along to release and fold back another, then another, until all four were open. Now the room was filled with light. A big room. Much bigger than she'd imagined it in the dark. A long wooden worksurface filled most of the left-hand wall, its broad top cleared. Above it, on the wall itself, were great tea-chest-sized oak cupboards. At the far end four big ovens occupied the space, huge pipes leading up from them into the ceiling overhead. Against the right-hand wall, beneath the windows, was a row of old machines and, beside the door, a big enamel sink.

She watched Ben bend down and examine the pipes beneath the sink. They were green with moss, red with rust. He rubbed his finger against the surface of one of them, then put the finger gingerly to his lips. She saw him frown then sniff the finger, his eyes intense, taking it all in.

He turned, then, surprisingly, he laughed. "Look."

There, in the middle of the white-tiled floor, was a beetle. A rounded, black-shelled thing the size of a brooch.

"Is it alive?" she asked, expecting it to move at any moment.

He shrugged, then went across and picked it up. But it was only a husk, the shell of a beetle. "It's been dead years," he said.

Yes, she thought; maybe since the house was sealed.

There was another door behind them, next to an old, faded print that was rotten with damp beneath its mould-spattered glass. Beyond the door was a narrow corridor

421

that led off to the right. They went through, moving slowly, cautiously, side by side, using their lamps to light the way ahead of them.

They explored, throwing open the shutters in each of the big rooms, but there was nothing. The rooms were empty, their dusty floorboards bare, only the dark outlines of long-absent pictures interrupting the blankness of the walls.

No sign of life. Only the husk, the empty shell of what they'd come for.

Augustus. No one talked of Augustus. Yet it was that very absence which made him so large in their imaginations. Ever since Ben had first found that single mention of him in the journals. But what had he been? What had he done that he could not be talked of?

She shivered and looked at Ben. He was watching her, as if he knew what she was thinking.

"Shall we go up?"

She nodded.

Upstairs it was different. There the rooms were filled with ancient furniture, preserved under white sheets, as if the house had been closed up for the summer only, while its occupant was absent.

In one of the big rooms at the front of the house, Meg stood beside one of the huge, open shutters, staring out through the trees at the river. Light glimmered on the water through gaps in the heavy foliage. Behind her she could hear Ben, pulling covers off chairs and tables, searching, restlessly searching for something.

"What happened here?"

Ben stopped and looked up from what he was doing. "I'm not sure. But it's the key to things. I know it is."

She turned and met his eyes. "How? How do you know?"

He smiled. "Because it's the one thing they won't talk about. Gaps. Look for the gaps, Meg. That's where the truth is. That's where they hide all the important stuff."

"Like what?"

His face hardened momentarily, then he looked away.

She looked down, realising just how keyed up he was; how close he had come to snapping at her.

"There's nothing here," he said, after a moment. "Let's go up again."

She nodded, then followed him up, knowing there would be nothing. The house was empty. Or as good as. But she was wrong.

Ben laughed, delighted, then stepped inside the room, shining his lamp about the walls. It was a library. Or a study maybe. Whichever, the walls were filled with shelves, and the shelves with books. Old books, of paper and card and leather. Ben hurried to the shutters and threw them open, then turned and stared back into the room. There was a door, two windows and a full length mirror on the wall to his left. Apart from that there were only shelves. Books and more books, filling every inch of the wall-space.

"Whose were they?" she asked, coming alongside him; sharing his delight at their find.

He pulled a book down at random, then another and another. The bookplates were all the same. He showed her one.

She read the words aloud. "This book is the property of Amos William Shepherd." She laughed, then looked up into Ben's face. "Then he lived here. But I thought . . ."

Ben shrugged. "I don't know. Maybe he used this house to work in."

She turned, looking about her. There were books scattered all about their cottage, but not a tenth as many as were here. There must have been five, maybe ten thousand of them here. She laughed, astonished by their find. There were probably more books here – *real* books – than there were in the rest of Chung Kuo.

Ben was walking slowly up and down the room, looking about him curiously. "It's close," he said softly. "It's very close now. I know it is."

"What's close?" she wanted to ask him. What? What?

What? But the question would only anger him. He knew no better than she. He only sensed there was something.

Then, suddenly, he stopped and turned and almost ran outside into the corridor again. "There!" he said, exultant, and she watched him pace out the distance from the end of the corridor to the doorway. Fifteen paces. He went inside and did the same. Twelve. Only twelve!

She saw at once. The mirror. The mirror was a door. A way through.

He went to it at once, looking for a catch, a way of releasing it, but there was nothing. Frustrated, he pulled books down from the shelf and knocked at the wall behind them. It was brick, solid brick.

For a moment he stood before the mirror, staring into it. Then he laughed. "Of course!"

He turned and pointed it out to her. "Level with the top of the mirror. That row of books opposite. Look, Meg. Tell me what you see."

She went across and looked. They were novels. Famous novels. *Ulysses*, *Nostromo*, *Tess of the D'Urbervilles*, *Vanity Fair*, *Howard's End*, *Bleak House*, *Daniel Martin*, *Orlando* and several others. She turned back to him and frowned. "I don't understand, Ben. What am I looking for?"

"It's a cryptogram. Look at the order. The first letter of the titles."

She looked, doing as he said. D.A.E.H.R.E. V.O.N.O.T.T.U.B. Then she understood. It was mirrored. You had to reverse the letters.

He laughed, ahead of her, and reached up to find the button.

With a faint hiss of escaping air the mirror sprang free. Beyond it was a room. Ben shone his lamp inside. It seemed like a smaller version of the library, the walls covered with books. But in its centre, taking up most of the floor space, was a desk.

He shone his lamp over the desk's surface, picking out four objects. A letter knife, an ink-block, a framed photograph and a large, folio-sized journal. The light rested on the last of these for some while, then moved upward, searching the end wall.

Meg came alongside him. "What are you looking for?"

"A window. There must have been a window."

"Why? If he really wanted to keep this room a secret, having no window onto the outside would be the best way, surely?"

He looked at her, then nodded. But she, watching him, was surprised that he hadn't seen it for himself. It was as if, now that he'd found it, he was transfixed by his discovery. She shone her lamp into his face.

"Meg . . ." He pushed her hand away.

She moved past him, into the room, then turned back, facing him.

"Here." She handed him the journal, knowing, even before he confirmed it, whose it was. Augustus. There was a space for it on the shelf on her father's study, amongst the others there. She recognised the tooled black leather of its cover.

Ben opened it. He turned a page, then smiled and looked up at her.

"Am I right?" she asked.

In answer he turned the book and showed her the page. She laughed uneasily, shocked, then looked back up at him. It was a picture of Ben. An almost perfect portrait of him. And underneath, in Ben's own handwriting, was a name and a date.

"Augustus Shepherd. Anno Domini 2120."

"But that's you. Your handwriting."

He shook his head. "No. But it's a clue. We're getting close, Meg. Very close now."

★ ★ ★

Beth Shepherd set the two bags down on the kitchen table then went to the garden door and undid the top catch. Pushing the top half back, she leaned out and called to the children.

"Ben! Meg! I'm back!"

She went inside again and busied herself, filling the cupboards from the bags. Only when she had finished did she go to the door again and, releasing the bottom catch, go out into the rose garden.

There was no sign of them. Perhaps they're indoors, she thought. But then they would have heard her, surely? She called again, moving out through the gate until she stood at the top of the lower garden that sloped down to the bay. She put her hand up to her eyes, searching the sun-lit meadows for a sign of them.

"Strange . . ." she muttered, then turned and went back inside. She knew she was back quite early, but they usually came when she called, knowing she would have brought something special for each of them.

She took the two gifts from her handbag and set them on the table. An old-fashioned paper book for Ben – one he had specifically asked for – on sensory deprivation. And for Meg a tiny Han ivory. A delicately carved globe.

Beth smiled to herself, then went down the steps and into the relative darkness of the dining room.

"Ben? Meg? Are you there?"

She stopped at the bottom of the steps and listened. Strange. Very strange. Where could they be? Ben had said nothing about going into town. In any case, it was only a little after twelve. They weren't due to finish their lessons for another twenty minutes.

Curious, she went upstairs and searched the rooms. Nothing. Not even a note on Ben's computer.

She went out and put her hand up to her brow a second time, searching the meadows more thoroughly this time. Then she remembered Peng Yu-wei. The android tutor had a special location unit. She could trace where they were by pinpointing him on Hal's map.

Relieved, she went back upstairs, into Hal's study, and called the map up onto the screen. She waited a moment for the signal to appear somewhere on the grid, then leaned forward to key the search sequence again, thinking she must have made a mistake. But no. There was no trace.

Beth felt her stomach flip over. "Gods . . ."

She ran down the stairs and out again.

"Ben! Meg! Where are you?"

The meadows were silent, empty. A light breeze stirred the waters of the bay. She looked. Of course, the bay. She set off down the slope, forcing herself not to run, telling herself again and again that it was all right; that her fears were unfounded. They were sensible children. And anyway, Peng Yu-wei was with them.

Where the lawn ended she stopped and looked out across the bay, scanning the water for any sign of life. Then she turned and eased herself over the lip, clambered down the old wooden steps set into the clay wall, and ran across towards the jetty.

It was gone. The rowboat was gone.

Where? She couldn't understand it. Where? Then, almost peripherally, she noticed something. Off to the far left of her, jutting from the water, revealed by the ebb of the tide.

She climbed up again, then ran along the shoreline until she was standing at the nearest point to it. It lay there, fifteen, maybe twenty *ch'i* from the shore, part-embedded in the mud-bank, part-covered by the receding water. She knew what it was at once. And knew, for a certainty, that Ben had done this to it.

The android lay unnaturally in the water, almost sitting up, one shoulder, part of its upper arm and the side of its head projecting above the surface. It did not float, like a corpse would float, but rested there, solid and heavy, its torn clothing flapping about it like weeds.

"Poor thing," she might have said another time, but now any sympathy she had for the machine was swamped by her fears for her children.

She looked up sharply, her eyes going immediately to the far shore and to the house on the crest above the cove. They had been forbidden. But that would not stop Ben. No. The sight of Peng Yu-wei in the water told her that.

She turned, her throat constricted now, her heart pounding in her breast, and began to run back up the slope

427

towards the cottage. And as she ran her voice hissed from her, heavy with anxiety and pain.

"Gods, let them be safe! Please gods let them be safe!"

* * *

Ben sat at the desk, reading from the journal. Meg stood behind him, at his shoulder, holding the two lamps steady above the page, following Ben's finger as it moved from right to left, up and down the columns of cyphers.

Ben had explained it to her. He had shown her how the frontispiece illustration was the key to it. In the illustration a man sat by a fireplace, reading a newspaper, his face obscured, the scene reflected at an angle in the mirror over the mantelpiece. Using the magnifying glass he had found in the left-hand drawer, Ben had shown her how the print of the reflected newspaper was subtly different from the one the man held. Those differences formed the basis of the cypher. She understood that – even the parts about the governing rules that made the cypher change – but her mind was too slow, too inflexible to hold and use what she had been shown.

It was as if all this was a special key – a coded lexicon – designed for one mind only. Ben's. It was as if Augustus knew that Ben would come. As if he had seen it clearly, as in a glass. It reminded her of the feeling she had had in the room below this one, stood there amongst the shrouded furniture; that the house was not abandoned, merely boarded up temporarily, awaiting its occupant's return.

And now he was back.

She shuddered, and the light danced momentarily across the page, making Ben look up.

He smiled and closed the journal, then stood and moved past her, leaving the big, leather-bound book on the desk.

Meg stood there a moment, staring at the journal, wondering what it said, knowing Ben would tell her when he wanted to. Then she picked it up and turned, following Ben out.

Always following, she realised. But the thought pleased

her. She knew he needed her to be there – a mirror for his words, his thoughts, his dark, unworded ambitions. She, with her mere nine years of experience, knew him better than anyone. Understood him as no one else could understand him. No one living, anyway.

He was standing there, at the window, looking down thoughtfully through the broad crowns of the trees.

"What is it?" she asked.

"I'm trying to work out where the garden is."

She understood at once. There had been a picture towards the back of the journal – a portrait of a walled garden. She had thought it fanciful, maybe allegorical, but Ben seemed to think it was an actuality – somewhere here, near the house.

She stared at the book-filled wall above the desk, then turned back, seeing how he was looking past her at the same spot. He smiled and moved his eyes to her face.

"Of course. There was a door at the end of the bottom corridor."

She nodded. "Let's go down."

The door was unlocked. Beyond it lay the tiny garden, the lawn neatly trimmed, delphinia and gladioli, irises and hemerocallis in bloom in the dark earth borders. And there, beneath the back wall, the headstone, the white marble carved into the shape of an oak, its trunk exaggeratedly thick, its crown a great cumulus.

"Yes," Ben said softly. "I knew he would be here."

He bent down beside the stone and reached out to touch and trace the indented lettering.

AUGUSTUS RAEDWALD SHEPHERD
Born   December   7   2106
Deceased   August   15   2122
Oder jener stirbt und ists.

Meg frowned. "That date is wrong, surely, Ben?"

"No." He shook his head, not looking at her. "He was fifteen when he killed himself."

"Then . . ." But she still didn't understand. He was

their great-grandfather, wasn't he? Only fifteen? Then, belatedly, she realised what he had said: the *whole* of what he had said. "*Killed* himself?"

There was a door set into the wall behind the stone. A simple wooden door, painted red, with a latch high up. Ben had stood up, facing it, and was staring at it in his usual intent manner.

Doors, she thought; always another door. And behind each door something new and unexpected. Augustus, for instance. She had never dreamed he would be so much like Ben. Like a twin.

"Shall we?" Ben asked, looking at her. "Before we set off back? There's time."

She looked down at the headstone, a strange feeling of unease nagging at her. She was tempted to say no, to tell him to leave it, but why not? Ben was right. There was time. Plenty of time before they'd be missed.

"Okay," she said quietly. "But then we go straight back. All right?"

He smiled at her and nodded, then went to the door, stretching to reach the latch.

It was a workroom. There were shelves along one wall on which were a number of things: old-fashioned screwdrivers and hammers, saws and pliers; a box of nails and an assortment of glues; locks and handles, brackets and a tray of different keys. A spade and a pitchfork stood against the wall beneath, beside a pair of boots, the mud on them dried, flaky to the touch.

Meg looked around her. At the far end, against the wall, was a strange upright shape, covered by an old bedspread. Above it, hanging from an old iron chain, hung a bevelled mirror. As she watched, Ben went across and threw the cloth back. It was a piano. An old upright piano. He lifted the lid and stared at the keys a while.

"I wonder if it's . . ."

Some sense — not precognition, nor even the feeling of danger — made her speak out. "No, Ben. Please. Don't touch it."

430

He played a note. A chord. Or what should have been a chord. Each note was flat, a harsh, cacophonic noise. The music of the house. Discordant.

She heard the chain break with a purer note than any sounded by her brother; heard the mirror slither then crash against the top of the piano; then stepped forward, her hand raised to her mouth in horror, as the glass shattered all about him.

"*Ben!!!*"

Her scream echoed out onto the water beyond the house.

Inside the room there was a moment of utter stillness. Then she was at his side, sobbing breathlessly, muttering to him again and again. "What have you done, Ben? What have you done?"

Shards of glass littered his hair and shoulders. His cheek was cut and a faint dribble of blood ran towards the corner of his mouth. But Ben was staring down at where his left hand had been only a moment before, sounding the chord. It still lay there on the keys, the fingers extended to form the shape. But the arm now ended in a bloodied stump. Cut clean, the blood still pumping.

For a moment she did nothing, horrified, her lips drawn back from her teeth, watching how he turned the stump, observing it, his eyes filled with wonder at the thing he had accidentally done. He was gritting his teeth against the pain, keeping it at bay while he studied the stump, the severed hand.

Then, coming to herself again, she pressed the stud at her neck and sounded the alarm.

★   ★   ★

Much later Meg stood at the bottom of the slope, looking out across the water.

Night had already fallen, but in one place its darkness was breached. Across the bay flames leapt high from the burning house and she could hear the crackling of burning vegetation, the sudden sharp retorts as wood popped and split.

431

Smoke lay heavy on the far side of the water, laced eerily with threads of light from the blaze. She could see dark shapes moving against the brilliance; saw one of the security craft rise up sharply, its twin beams cutting the air in front of it.

"Meg? Meg! Come inside!"

She turned and looked back up the slope towards the cottage. Lights burned at several of the windows, throwing faint spills of light across the white-painted stonework. Her father stood there, a dark, familiar figure, framed in the light of the doorway.

"I'm coming, daddy. Just a moment longer. *Please.*"

He nodded, somewhat reluctantly, then turned away. The door closed behind him.

Meg faced the blaze again, looking out across the dark glass of the bay. She thought she could see small shapes in the uprush of flame, like insects burning, crackling furiously as their shells ignited in a sudden flare of brilliance. Books, she thought; all those books . . .

Ben was upstairs, in his bed. They had frozen the stump but they had not saved the hand. He would need a new one now.

She could still hear the chord he had sounded; still see his fingers spreading to form the shape. She looked away from the blaze. After-images flickered in the darkness. The eye moved on, but the image remained. For a time.

She went indoors. Went up and saw him where he lay, propped up with a mound of pillows behind his back. He was awake, fully conscious. She sat at his bedside and was silent for a time, letting him watch her.

"What's it like?" he asked after a moment.

"Beautiful," she said. "The way the light's reflected in the dark water. It's . . ."

"I know," he said, as if he had seen it too. "I can imagine it."

She looked away a moment, noticing how the fire's light flickered in the window pane; how it cast a mottled,

432

ever-changing pattern against the narrow opening.

"I'm glad you did what you did," he said, more softly than before. "I would have stood there and watched myself bleed to death. I owe you my life."

It was not entirely true. He owed his life to their mother. If Beth had not come back early then what she had done would not have mattered.

"I only wrapped it with the sheet," she said. But she saw how he was looking at her, his eyes piercing her. She could see he was embarrassed. Yet there was something else there, too – something that she had never seen in him before – and it touched her deeply. She felt her lips pucker and her eyes grow moist.

"Hey, little sis, don't cry."

He had never called her that before; nor had he ever touched her as he touched her now, his good right hand caressing both of hers where they lay atop the bedclothes. She shuddered and looked down.

"I'm fine," he said, as if in answer to something she had said, his hand squeezing both of hers. "Father says they can graft a new hand onto the nerve ends. It'll work as good as new. Maybe better."

She found she could not look up at him. If she did she would burst into tears, and she didn't want him to see her weakness. He had been so strong, so brave. The pain – it must have been awful.

"You know, the worst thing was that I missed it."

"Missed what?" she said, staring at his hand.

"I didn't see it," he said, and there was genuine surprise in his voice. "I wasn't quick enough. I heard the chain break and I looked up, but I missed the accident. It was done before I looked down again. My hand was no longer part of me. When I looked it was already separate, there on the keyboard."

He laughed. A queer little sound.

Meg looked at him. He was staring at the stub of his left arm. It was neatly capped, like the end of an old cane. Silvered and neutral. Reduced to a thing.

"I didn't see it," he insisted. "The glass. The cut. And I felt . . . only a sudden absence. Not pain, but . . ."

She could see that he was searching for the right words, the very thing that would describe what he had felt, what he had experienced at that moment. But it evaded him. He shrugged and gave up.

"I love you, Ben."

"I know," he said, and seemed to look at her as if to gauge how love looked in a person's eyes. As if to place it in his memory.

* * *

After Meg had gone he lay there, thinking things through.

He had said nothing to her of what was in the journal. For once he felt no urge to share his knowledge with her. It would harm her, he knew, as it had harmed him: not on the surface, as the mirror had, but deeper, where his true self lived. In the darkness inside himself.

He felt angered that he had not been told; that Hal had not trusted him enough to tell him. More than that, he felt insulted that they had hidden it from him. Oh, he could see why it was important for Meg not to know; she responded to things in a different way from him. But to hide it from him? He clenched his fists, feeling the ghostly movement in the hand he had lost. Didn't they know? Didn't they understand him, even now? How could he make sense of it all unless he could first solve the riddle of himself?

It was all there, in the journal. Some of it explicit, the rest hidden teasingly away – cyphers within cyphers – as if for his eyes alone.

He had heard Augustus's voice, speaking clearly in his head, as if direct across the years. "I am a failed experiment," he had said. "Old Amos botched me when he made me from his seed. He got more than he bargained for."

It was true. They were all an experiment. All the Shepherd males. Not sons and fathers and grandfathers, but brothers every one – all the fruit of old Amos's seed.

Ben laughed bitterly. It explained so much. For Augustus *was* his twin. Ben knew it for a certainty. He had proof.

There, in the back of the journal, were the breeding charts – a dozen complex genetic patterns, each drawn in the tiniest of hands, one to a double page; each named and dated, Ben's own amongst them. A whole line of Shepherds, each one the perfect advisor for his T'ang.

Augustus had known somehow. Had worked it out. He had realised what he was meant for. What task he had been bred for.

But Augustus had been a rebel. He had defied his father; refusing to be trained as the servant of a T'ang. Worse, he had sired a child by his own sister, in breach of the careful plans Amos had laid. His mirror had become his mate. Furious, his "father", Robert, had made him a prisoner in the house, forbidding him the run of the Domain until he changed his ways, but Augustus had remained defiant. He had preferred death to compromise.

Or so it seemed. There was no entry for that day. No explanation for his death.

Ben heard footsteps on the stairs. He tensed, then made himself relax. He had been expecting this visit; had been rehearsing what he would say.

Hal Shepherd stood in the doorway, looking in. "Ben? Can I come in?"

Ben stared back at him, unable to keep the anger from his face. "Hello, elder brother."

Hal seemed surprised. Then he understood. He had confiscated the journal, but he could not confiscate what was in Ben's head. It did not matter that Ben could not physically see the pages of the journal: in his mind he could turn them anyway and read the tall columns of cyphers.

"It isn't like that," he began, but Ben interrupted him, a sharp edge to his voice.

435

"Don't lie to me. I've had enough of lies. Tell me who I am."

"You're my son."

Ben sat forward, but this time Hal got in first. "No, Ben. You're wrong. It ended with Augustus. He was the last. You're *my* son, Ben. Mine and your mother's."

Ben made to speak, then fell silent, watching the man. Then he looked down. Hal was not lying. Not intentionally. He spoke as he believed. But he was wrong. Ben had seen the charts, the names, the dates of birth. Amos's great experiment was still going on.

He let out a long, shuddering breath. "Okay . . . But tell me. How did Augustus die? Why did he kill himself?"

"He didn't."

"Then how did he die?"

"He had leukaemia."

That too was a lie, for there was no mention of ill health in the journal. But again Hal believed it for the truth. His eyes held nothing back from Ben.

"And the child? What happened to the child?"

Hal laughed. "What child? What are you talking about, Ben?"

Ben looked down. Then it was all a lie. Hal knew nothing. Nor would he learn anything from the journal unless Meg gave him the key to it; for the cypher was a special one, transforming itself constantly page by page as the journal progressed.

"Nothing," he said finally, in answer to the query. "I was mistaken."

He lifted his eyes and saw how concerned Hal was.

"I'm sorry," he said. "I didn't mean to trouble anyone."

"No . . ."

Then, strangely, Hal looked down and laughed. "You know, Ben, when I saw Peng Yu-wei stuck there in the mud, all my anger drained from me." He looked up and met Ben's eyes, his voice changing, becoming more serious. "I understand why you did it, Ben. Believe me. And I meant what I said the other night. You can be your own man.

436

Live your own life. It's up to you whether you serve or not. Neither I nor the great T'ang himself will force you to be other than yourself."

Ben studied his brother – the man he had always thought of as his father – and saw suddenly that it did not matter what he was in reality, for Hal Shepherd had become what he believed he was. Ben's father. A free man, acting freely, choosing freely. For him the illusion was complete. It had become the truth.

It was a powerful lesson. One Ben could use. He nodded. "Then I choose to be your son, if that's all right?"

Hal smiled and reached out to take his hand. "That's fine. That's all I ever wanted."

PART 4-SUMMER 2201:

ICE AND FIRE

———·———

"War is the highest form of struggle for resolving
contradictions, when they have developed to a certain
stage, between classes, nations, states, or political groups,
and it has existed ever since the emergence of private
property and of classes."

– Mao Tse Tung, *Problems Of Strategy in
China's Revolutionary War* (December 1936)

"It is our historical duty to eradicate all opposition to
change. To cauterise the cancers that create division.
The future cannot come into being until the past is dead.
Chung Kuo cannot live until the world of petty nation
states, of factions and religions, is dead and buried
beneath the ice. Let us have no pity then. Our choice
is made. Ice and fire. The fire to cauterise, the ice to
cover over. Only by such means will the world be
freed from enmity."

– Tsao Ch'un, *Address to his Ministers*, (May 2068)

CHAPTER·13

THE SADDLE

The old T'ang backed away, his hands raised before him, his face rigid with fear.

"Put down the knife, *erh tzu*! For pity's sake!"

A moment before there had been laughter; now the tension in the room seemed unendurable. Only the hiss and wheeze of Tsu Tiao's laboured breathing broke the awful silence.

In the narrow space between the pillars, Tsu Ma circled his father slowly, knife in hand, his face set, determined. On all sides T'ang and courtier alike – all Han, all Family – were crowded close, looking on, their faces tense, unreadable. Only one, a boy of eight, false whiskered and rouged up, his clothes identical to those of the old T'ang, showed any fear. He stood there, wide-eyed, one hand gripping the arm of the taller boy beside him.

"*Erh Tzu*!" the old man pleaded, falling to his knees. *My son*! He bowed his head, humbling himself. "I beg you, Tsu Ma! Have mercy on an old man!"

All eyes were on Tsu Ma now. All saw the shudder that rippled through the big man like a wave; the way his chin jutted forward and his face contorted in agony as he steeled himself to strike. Then it was done and the old man slumped forward, the knife buried deep in his chest.

There was a sigh like the soughing of the wind, then Tsu Ma was surrounded. Hands clapped his back or held his hand or touched his shoulder briefly. "Well done, Tsu Ma," each said before moving on, expecting no answer; seeing how he stood there, his arms limp at his sides, his broad chest heaving, his eyes locked on the fallen figure on the floor beneath him.

Slowly the great room emptied until only the six T'ang and the two young boys remained.

Li Shai Tung stood before him, staring into his face, a faint smile of sadness mixed with satisfaction on his lips. He spoke softly, "Well done, Tsu Ma. It's hard, I know. The hardest thing a man can do . . ."

Slowly Tsu Ma's eyes focused on him. He swallowed deeply and another great shudder racked his body. Pain flickered like lightning across the broad, strong features of his face, and then he spoke, his voice curiously small, like a child's. "Yes . . . but it was *so* hard to do, Shai Tung. It . . . it was just like him."

Li Shai Tung shivered but kept himself perfectly still, his face empty of what he was feeling. He ached to reach out and hold Tsu Ma close, to comfort him, but knew it would be wrong. It was hard, as Tsu Ma now realised, but it was also necessary.

Since the time of Tsao Ch'un it had been so. To become T'ang the son must kill the father. Must become his own man. Only then would he be free to offer his father the respect he owed him.

"Will you come through, Tsu Ma?"

Tsu Ma's eyes had never left Li Shai Tung's face, yet they had not been seeing him. Now they focused again. He gave the barest nod, then, with one last, appalled look at the body on the floor, moved towards the dragon doorway.

In the room beyond, the real Tsu Tiao was laid out atop a great, tiered pedestal on a huge bed spread with silken sheets of gold. Slowly and with great dignity, Tsu Ma climbed the steps until he stood there at his dead father's side. The old man's fine grey hair had been brushed and plaited, his cheeks delicately rouged, his beard brushed out straight, his nails painted a brilliant pearl. He was dressed from head to foot in white. A soft white muslin that, when Tsu Ma knelt and gently brushed it with his fingertips, reminded him strangely of springtime and the smell of young girls.

You're dead, Tsu Ma thought, gazing tenderly into his father's face. *You're really dead, aren't you?* He bent forward and gently brushed the cold lips with his own, then sat back on his heels, shivering, toying with the ring that rested, heavy and unfamiliar, like a saddle on the first finger of his right hand. *And now it's me.*

He turned his head, looking back at the six T'ang standing amongst the pillars, watching him. *You know how I feel*, he thought, looking from face to face. *Each one of you. You've been here before me, haven't you?*

For the first time he understood why the Seven were so strong. They had this in common: each knew what it was to kill their father: knew the reality of it in their bones. Tsu Ma looked back at the body – the real body, not the lifelike GenSyn copy he had "killed" – and understood. He had been blind to it before, but now he saw it clearly. It was not life that connected them so firmly, but death. Death that gave them such a profound and lasting understanding of each other.

He stood again and turned, facing them, then went down amongst them. At the foot of the steps they greeted him; each in his turn bowing before Tsu Ma; each bending to kiss the ring of power he now wore; each embracing him warmly before repeating the same eight words.

"Welcome, Tsu Ma. Welcome, T'ang of West Asia."

When the brief ceremony was over, Tsu Ma turned and went across to the two boys. Li Yuan was much taller than when he had last seen him. He was entering that awkward stage of early adolescence and had become a somewhat ungainly-looking boy. Even so, it was hard to believe that his birthday in two days' time would be only his twelfth. There was something almost unnatural in his manner that made Tsu Ma think of childhood tales of changelings and magic spells and other such nonsense. He seemed so old, so knowing. So unlike the child whose body he wore. Tao Chu, in contrast, seemed younger than his eight years and

wore his heart embroidered like a peacock on his sleeve.
He stood there in his actor's costume, bearded, his brow
heavily-lined with black make-up pencil, yet still his youth
shone through, in his eyes and in the quickness of his
movements.

Tsu Ma reached out and ruffled his hair, smiling for the
first time since the killing. "Did it frighten you, Tao Chu?"

The boy looked down, abashed. "I thought . . ."

Tsu Ma knelt down and held his shoulders, nodding,
remembering how he had felt the first time he had seen the
ritual, not then knowing what was happening, nor why.

Tao Chu looked up and met his eyes. "It seemed so real,
Uncle Ma. For a moment I thought it was Grandpa Tiao."

Tsu Ma smiled. "You were not alone in that, Nephew
Chu."

Tao Chu was his dead brother's third and youngest son
and Tsu Ma's favourite; a lively, ever-smiling boy with the
sweetest, most joyful laugh. At the ritual earlier Tao Chu
had impersonated Tsu Tiao, playing out scenes from the
old T'ang's life before the watching Court. The practice
was as old as the Middle Kingdom itself and formed one
link in the great chain of tradition, but it was more than
mere ritual, it was a living ceremony, an act of deep respect
and celebration, almost a poem to the honoured dead. For
the young actor, however, it was a confusing, not to say
unnerving experience, to find the dead man unexpectedly
there, in the seat of honour, watching the performance.

"Do you understand why I had to kill the copy, Tao
Chu?"

Tao Chu glanced quickly at Li Yuan, then looked back
steadily at his uncle. "Not at first, Uncle Ma, but Li Yuan
explained it to me. He said you had to kill the guilt you
felt at Grandpa Tiao's death. That you could not be your
own man until you had."

"Then you understand how deeply I revere my father?
How hard it was to harm even a copy of him?"

Tao Chu nodded, his eyes bright with understanding.

"Good." He squeezed the boy's shoulders briefly, then

stood. "But I must thank you, Tao Chu. You did well today. You gave me back my father."

Tao Chu smiled, greatly pleased by his uncle's praise, then, at a touch from Li Yuan, he joined the older boy in a deep bow and backed away, leaving the T'ang to their Council.

* * *

From the camera's vantage point, twenty *li* out from the spaceship, it was hard to tell its scale. The huge sphere of its forward compartments was visible only as a nothingness in the star-filled field of space – a circle of darkness more intense than that which surrounded it. Its tail, so fine and thin that it was like a thread of silver, stretched out for ten times its circumference, terminating in a smaller, silvered sphere little thicker than the thread.

It was beautiful. Li Shai Tung drew closer, operating the remote from a distance of almost three hundred thousand *li*, adjusting the camera image with the most delicate of touches, the slight delay in response making him cautious. Five *li* out he slowed the remote and increased the definition.

The darkness took on form. The sphere was finely stippled, pocked here and there with hatches or spiked with communication towers. Fine, almost invisible lines covered the whole surface, as if the sphere were netted by the frailest of spiders' webs.

Li Shai Tung let the remote drift slowly towards the starship and sat back, one hand smoothing through his long beard while he looked about him at the faces of his fellow T'ang.

"Well?"

He glanced across at the waiting technicians and dismissed them with a gesture. They had done their work well in getting an undetected remote so close to *The New Hope*. Too well, perhaps. He had not expected it to be so beautiful.

"How big is it?" asked Wu Shih, turning to him. "I can't

help thinking it must be huge to punch so big a hole in the star field."

Li Shai Tung looked back at him, the understanding of thirty years passing between them. "It's huge. Approximately two *li* in diameter."

"Approximately?" It was Wei Feng, T'ang of East Asia, who picked up on the word.

"Yes. The actual measurement is one kilometre. I understand that they have used the old *Hung Mao* measurements throughout the craft."

Wei Feng grunted his dissatisfaction, but Wang Hsien, T'ang of Africa, was not so restrained. "But that's an outrage!" he roared. "An insult! How dare they flout the Edict so openly?"

"I would remind you, Wang Hsien," Li Shai Tung answered quietly, seeing the unease on every face. "We agreed that the terms of the Edict would not apply to the starship."

He looked back at the ship. The fine web of lines was now distinct. In its centre, etched finer than the lines surrounding it, were two lines of bead-like figures spiralling about each other, forming the double-helix of heredity, symbol of the Dispersionists.

Three years ago – the day after Under Secretary Lehmann had been killed in the House by Tolonen – he had summoned the leaders of the House before him, and there, in the Purple Forbidden City where they had murdered his son, had granted them concessions, amongst them permission to build a generation starship. It had prevented war. But now the ship was almost ready and though the uneasy peace remained intact, soon it would be broken. The cusp lay just ahead. Thus far on the road of concession he had carried the Seven. Thus far but no further.

He stared at the starship a moment longer. It was beautiful, but both House and Seven knew what *The New Hope* really was. No one was fooled by the mask of rhetoric. The Dispersionists talked of it being an answer – "the only guarantee of a future for our children" – but in practical terms it did nothing to solve the problem of over-population that was supposedly its *raison d'être*. Fully-laden, it could carry no more than five thousand settlers. In any case, the ship, fast as it was, would take a thousand years to reach the nearest star. No, *The New Hope* was not an answer, it was a symbol, a political counter – the thin end of the great wedge of Change. It heralded not a new age of dispersal, but a return to the bad old days of technological free-for-all – a return to that madness that had once before almost destroyed Chung Kuo.

He cleared the image and, for a while sat there, conscious that they were waiting for him to say what was on his mind. He looked from face to face, aware that the past three years had brought great changes in his thinking. What had once seemed certain was no longer so for him. His belief in peace at all costs – in a policy of concession and containment – had eroded in the years since Han Ch'in's death. He had aged, and not only in his face. Some days there was an air of lethargy about him, of having done with things. Yes, he thought, looking down at his own long hands; the tiger's teeth are soft now, his eyes grown dull. And they know this. Our enemies know it and seek advantage from it. But what might we do that we have not already done? How can we stem the tidal flow of change?

Tsu Ma broke into his thoughts. "Forgive me, Li Shai Tung. But what of Tolonen?"

Li Shai Tung looked up, surprised, meeting the new T'ang's eyes.

"Tolonen? I don't understand you, Tsu Ma. You think I should accede to the House's demands? Is that what you're saying?" He looked away, a bitter anger in his eyes. "You would have me give them that satisfaction too?"

Tsu Ma answered him softly, sympathetically. "No. Not at all, Shai Tung. You mistake my meaning. Things have changed. Many who were angry three years ago have cooled. They see things differently now, even in the House."

Li Shai Tung looked about him, expecting strong disagreement with Tsu Ma's remarks, but there was nothing. They looked at him expectantly.

"I still don't follow you. You mean they'd have him back? After what he did?"

Tsu Ma shook his head. "Not as General, no. But in some other role."

Li Shai Tung looked down sharply. It was more than he could have hoped for. But dare he say yes? Dare he call the old rogue back?

"We are not alone in thinking things have gone too far," said Wu Shih, picking up on what Tsu Ma had said. "There are many at First Level – even among the *Hung Mao* – who feel we gave too much; were too timid in our dealings with the Dispersionists. They would see the changes to the Edict reversed, *The New Hope* melted down."

"We daren't go so far. There would be war, surely?"

Tsu Ma leaned forward. "Not if we challenge them in their own sphere."

"You mean the House?"

There were nods all around. So, they had discussed this between them. Why? Had he been so preoccupied? So unreachable?

Wei Feng now spoke for them all. "We know the last three years have been hard for you, Shai Tung. You have tasted bitterness and we have had to watch in silence. But we shall watch no longer, nor hold our tongues for fear of hurting you. We have seen the plan your advisor, Shepherd, drew up and . . ."

Li Shai Tung sat forward jerkily. "Impossible! No one has seen those papers!"

Wei Feng waited a moment then continued. "Not impossible, old friend. Not at all. Shepherd merely took advantage of his right as equal to appeal to us. He knew you would not act as your heart dictated, so he sent us copies."

Li Shai Tung stared back at him, astonished. Then they knew . . .

"And we agree." Wei Feng was smiling now. "Don't

you see, Li Shai Tung. We agree with *Shih* Shepherd's proposals. Our enemies have gone too far. To kill your son and take advantage from it – it was too much for any man to bear. And a T'ang is not just any man. A T'ang is one of Seven."

"And the Seven?"

Wei Feng looked about him, then back at Li Shai Tung. "In this the Seven shall do as Li Shai Tung decides."

★   ★   ★

As the door at the far end of the room hissed open, steam billowed out into the corridor beyond. Berdichev shivered but stood straighter, his skin still tingling from the shower.

An armed guard stood there in the doorway, head bowed, a clean silk *pau* folded over one arm. Behind him stood two Han servants who, after a moment's hesitation, entered the room and began to dry Berdichev with soft towels. When they had done, he went over to the guard and took the full-length gown from him, pulling it on and tying it at the waist.

"You have my charm?"

The guard's head moved fractionally, but remained bowed. "I'm sorry, excellency. I was given only the *pau*."

Berdichev huffed impatiently and looked up at the over-head camera. Moments later an official appeared at the far end of the corridor and hurried to him. The man bowed deeply, his face flushed with embarrassment, and held out one hand, offering the necklace.

"My humble apologies, Excellency. I did not understand."

Berdichev took the silver chain and fastened it about his neck, closing his hand over the smooth surface of the charm a moment. The impertinence of these little men, he thought, making a mental note of the official's number – so prominently displayed on his chest – before he waved him away. Then he waited as one of the two Han brought him anti-static slippers while the other combed and plaited his hair. Only then, when they were finished, did Director Clarac make his appearance.

Clarac embraced him lightly and then stepped back, smiling pleasantly, his appearance and manner the very model of elegance and charm. Berdichev smiled tightly and gave the barest of nods in response to Clarac's respectful bow. As ever, he was in two minds about Clarac's value to the project. He was a good front man, but the real work was done by his team of four assistants. Clarac had only to step out of line once and he would be out, family connections or no.

Clarac's voice oozed warmth and friendliness. "Soren! It's a real delight to have you here as our guest."

Yes, thought Berdichev; but I'm the last person you expected to see up here today. I bet you were shitting your elegant white pants when you heard I was here. Even so, Berdichev was impressed by what he had seen. The defences about *The New Hope* left nothing to be desired. Nor had he had any reason to complain about the security measures surrounding visitors to the base. He had been forced to undergo the full body-search and decontamination procedure. And when he had tried to bully the guards into making an exception in his case, their officer had politely but firmly stated that there could be no exceptions – hadn't *Shih* Berdichev insisted as much?

"*Shih* Clarac," he answered, distancing the man at once and subtly reminding him of their relative status. "I'm delighted to be here. But tell me, what are you doing about the spy camera?"

Clarac's momentary hesitation was telling. He was a man who prided himself on having everything at his fingertips, but he had not counted on Berdichev's directness. Clarac was used to social nicety. It was how he functioned. He approached such matters slowly, obliquely, over wine and sweetmeats. But Berdichev had no time for such "niceties".

"We know about the remote," Clarac answered, recovering quickly. "In fact, if you'll permit me, *Shih* Berdichev, I'll take you to our tracking room."

Berdichev nodded tersely and walked on, not waiting for Clarac, who had to hurry to catch up with him.

"And that gap in your defences – the blind spot on darkside – how do you account for that?"

Clarac did not hesitate this time. "Our defence experts have assured me that nothing of any real size could get through undetected. The blind spot, as you call it, is a mere 30 degrees of arc. Our central sensors would detect any ship coming in from five thousand *li* out. In any case, no one would come from that direction. There's nothing out there. You would have to orbit the moon in a one-man craft to get into position. And who would do that?"

Berdichev stopped and stared at him a moment. "Even so . . ."

"Besides which," Clarac added quickly, facing Berdichev, "there's the question of cost. To extend our defence satellite system to cover the darkside channel would cost a further one hundred and twenty million. The budget is already two hundred and eighty-five per cent over original costings. Our investors are justifiably concerned . . ."

"And if one man did just what you say is impossible and slipped in on the darkside?"

Clarac laughed. "If he did it would make no difference. Every air-lock is linked to central security. There are seals at every level. And more than a thousand security men guarding the outer shell alone. The inner shell is a self-sufficient unit which can be cut off at once from the outer shell. As the engines and life-support systems are there, there's no possibility of them being under threat. No, the only way the Seven could get at *The New Hope* would be to try to blow it out of the sky from below. And we've designed our defence system to prevent just that possibility."

Berdichev sniffed then, satisfied, nodded and began to walk on. Beside him, Clarac began to talk about the progress they had made, the difficulties they had overcome, but Berdichev was hardly listening. He had seen the reports already. What he wanted were answers to some of the things they might not have thought of. He wanted to make certain for himself that nothing had been overlooked.

In the tracking room he took a seat at the desk and listened while Clarac explained the system. But all the time he was looking about him, noting things.

Interrupting Clarac he pointed to the screen which showed the remote spy camera. "You're certain it's not a weapon?"

Clarac laughed. A laugh which, to Berdichev's ear, was just a touch too self-confident.

"We've scanned it thoroughly, of course. There's an engine unit at the back of it and a whole system of foils and anti-jamming devices, and though the central core of it is lead-screened, our experts have calculated that there's barely enough room for the camera unit, let alone any kind of weaponry."

"Unless they've developed something new, eh?"

Clarac looked at him and gave a slight bow, understanding that he would be allowed nothing today. He would need answers for everything.

"I've assumed that that might be the case. Which is why I personally ordered that the thing should be tracked twenty-four hours a day. I've two lasers trained on the aperture constantly. At the smallest sign of unusual activity they'll blow the thing apart."

"Before it can damage *The New Hope*?"

"The lasers are set for automatic response. The remote would be blasted out of the sky in less than a fiftieth of a second."

Berdichev turned his head and looked at Clarac, for the first time letting a brief smile signal his satisfaction.

"Good. I want nothing to stop *The New Hope* from making its maiden flight three months from now."

He saw the surprise on Clarac's face, followed an instant later by a broad smile of unfeigned delight. "But that's excellent, *Shih* Berdichev! That's marvellous news! When did the Seven agree to this?"

"They haven't. But they will. Very soon now. By the

week's end there will be a proposal in the House. We're going to push them on this one, Clarac. We're going to make them fulfil the promises they made three years ago. And then we'll push some more. Until there's a whole fleet of these ships. You understand me? But this is the first, the most important of them. *The New Hope* will break their stranglehold. They know that and they'll try to prevent it – but we must pre-empt their every move. That's why it's so important things are right up here. That's why I came to see things for myself."

Clarac bowed. "I understand, *Shih* Berdichev. You think, then, that we should extend the satellite system?"

Berdichev shook his head. "No. I'm satisfied with your reasoning. As you say, it would be impossible for a single man to do any real damage to the craft. Let us worry about more direct approaches, eh? And for a start let's destroy that remote. I'm sure one of our ferry craft could have a little accident, eh? A technical malfunction, perhaps, that would place it on a collision course?"

Clarac smiled. "Of course, *Shih* Berdichev. It shall be done at once."

* * *

Fei Yen stood in the shade of the willow, waiting for the two princes to come along the path that led to the bridge. She had seen their craft land only minutes earlier and had placed herself deliberately here where they would have to pass her. Her maids stood off at a slight distance, amongst the trees, talking quietly amongst themselves and pretending not to watch her, but she knew they were as inquisitive as she. For the past three years they had shared her tedious exile on her father's estate, where she had seen no one but her brothers and aunts. Today, however, for the first time since the period of mourning had ended, she had been granted permission to call upon the young prince – to stay a week and celebrate his birthday.

Seeing movement among the trees at the far end of the stone-flagged path, she turned and signalled to the maids to be quiet. "Here they come!" she mimed exaggeratedly.

The maids giggled then, obedient, fell silent.

Fei Yen turned back to watch the two young men approach. But as they came closer she drew her sandalwood fan and waved it impatiently, certain there must be a mistake. Where was Tao Chu? Where was Tsu Ma's strapping young nephew?

She saw the taller of the boys hesitate, then touch the arm of the other and lean close to whisper something. The smaller of them seemed to stare at her a moment, then turn to the other and nod. Only then did the older boy come on.

Three paces from her he stopped. At first she didn't recognise him, he was so much taller, so much gawkier than when she had seen him last.

"Li Yuan?"

Li Yuan swallowed and then bowed; an awkward, stilted movement that betrayed his unease. When he straightened up and looked at her again she saw his face was scarlet with embarrassment. His lips moved as if he was about to say something, but he had not formed the words when she interrupted him.

"Where is Tao Chu? I was told Tao Chu would be with you."

There were giggles from the trees behind her, and she turned sharply, furious with her maids, then turned back in time to see Li Yuan summon the small boy forward.

"Fei Yen?" said the boy, bowing elegantly like a tiny courtier. Then, in a lilting yet hesitant voice that betrayed his unfamiliarity with English, he added, "I am most honoured to meet you, Lady Fei. My uncle told me you were beautiful, but he did not tell me how beautiful."

She laughed, astonished. "And who have I the pleasure of addressing?"

The boy bowed again, enjoying her astonishment in the same way he had enjoyed the applause of the T'ang earlier that day when he had played Tsu Tiao. "I am Tsu Tao

454

Chu, son of Tsu Wen, and third nephew of the T'ang, Tsu Ma."

The fan that she had been waving stopped in mid motion and clicked shut. "Tao Chu?" She laughed – a different, shorter laugh, expressing a very different kind of surprise – then shook her head. "Oh no. I mean, you can't be. I was told . . ."

Then she understood. She heard the giggling from the trees topple over into laughter. Flushing deeply, she lowered her head slightly. "Tsu Tao Chu. I . . . I'm delighted to meet you. Forgive me if I seemed confused. I . . ." Then, forgetting her disappointment, she too burst into laughter.

"What is it?" asked the eight-year-old, delighted that he had somehow managed to amuse this mature woman of nineteen.

"Nothing," she said quickly, fanning herself and turning slightly, so that the shadow of the willow hid her embarrassment. "Nothing at all." She turned quickly to Li Yuan, finding it easier, suddenly, to talk to him. "Li Yuan, forgive me. My father, Yin Tsu, sends his deep regards and best wishes on your forthcoming birthday. I have come on his behalf to celebrate the day."

Li Yuan's smile was unexpectedly warm. Again he bowed, once more colouring from neck to brow. His awkwardness made her remember the last time they had met – that time he had come to her and cried upon her shoulder, four days after Han Ch'in's death. Then, too, his reaction had been unexpected. Then, too, he had seemed to shed a skin.

"I . . . I . . ." He stuttered, then looked down, seeming almost to laugh at himself. "Forgive me, Fei Yen. I was not told you were coming."

She gave the slightest bow. "Nor I until this morning."

He looked up at her, a strange expectation in his eyes. "Will you be staying long?"

"A week." She turned and signalled to her maids who at once came out from beneath the trees and hurried along the path to her. Then, turning back to the two boys, she added. "We had best be getting back, don't you think? They'll be expecting us in the house." And, before they could answer, she turned away, heading back towards the bridge.

Li Yuan stood there a while, watching her. Only when he turned to speak to Tao Chu did he realise how avidly the boy was studying him.

"What are you staring at, Squib?" he said, almost angrily, conscious that his cheeks were warm for the third time that afternoon.

"At you, Great Yuan," answered Tao Chu with a mock earnestness that made Li Yuan relent. Then, in a softer voice, the small boy added, "You love her, don't you?"

Li Yuan laughed awkwardly then turned and looked back up the path. "What does it matter? She was my brother's wife."

* * *

The Overseer's House dominated the vast plain of the East European plantation. Three tiers high, its roof steeply pitched, it rested on stilts over the meeting point of the two broad irrigation canals that ran north–south and east–west, feeding the great latticework of smaller channels. To the south lay the workers' quarters; long, low huts that seemed embedded in the earth. To the north and east were storehouses; huge, covered reservoirs of grain and rice. West, like a great wave frozen at its point of turning under, lay the City, its walls soaring two *li* into the heavens.

Now it was late afternoon and the shadow of the Overseer's House lay like a dark, serrated knife on the fields to the east. There, in the shadow, on a bare earth pathway that followed the edge of one of the smaller north–south channels, walked three men. One walked ahead, alone and silent, his head down, his drab brown clothes, with their wide, short trousers indicative of his status as field worker. The two behind him joked and laughed as they went along.

Their weapons – lethal *deng* rifles, "lantern guns" – slung casually over their shoulders. They were more elegantly dressed, the kingfisher blue of their jackets matching the colour of the big sky overhead. These were the Overseer's men, Chang Yan and Teng Fu; big, brutal men who were not slow to chastise their workers and beat them if they fell behind with quotas.

"What does he want?" Teng asked, lifting his chin slightly to indicate the man plodding along in front of them, but meaning the Overseer when he said "he". No one requested to see the Overseer. He alone chose who came to see him.

"The man's a thief," said Chang. He spat out into the channel, below and to his left, and watched the off-white round of spittle drift away slowly on the water. Then he looked back at Teng. "One of the patrol cameras caught him in the Frames making harvest."

The Frames were where they grew the special items; strawberries and lychees, pineapples and oranges, grapes and peaches, cherries and almonds, pears and melons.

"Stupid," Teng said, looking down and laughing. "These peasant types – they're all stupid."

Chang shrugged. "I don't know. I thought this one was different. He was supervisor. A trusted man. We'd had no trouble with him before."

"They're all trouble," said Teng, scratching his left buttock vigorously. "Stupid and trouble. It's genetic. That's what it is."

Chang laughed. "Maybe so."

They had come to a bridge. The first man had stopped, his head still bowed, waiting for the others. He was forbidden to cross the bridge without a permit.

"Get on!" said Teng, drawing the long club from his belt and jabbing the man viciously in the small of the back. "The Overseer wants to see you. Don't keep him waiting, now!"

The man stumbled forward onto the bridge, then got up and trudged on again, wiping his dirtied hands against his thighs as he went and glancing up briefly, fearfully, as the big house loomed over him.

More guards lounged at the foot of the steps. One of them, a tall *Hung Mao* sat apart from the rest, looked up as the three men approached, then, with the vaguest movement of his head to indicate that they should go on up, looked back down at the rifle in his lap, continuing his meticulous inspection of the weapon.

"Good day, *Shih* Peskova," said Teng, acknowledging the Overseer's lieutenant with a bow. But Peskova paid him no attention. Teng was Han and Han were shit. It didn't matter whether they were guard or peasant. Either way they were shit. Hadn't he heard as much from The Man himself often enough?

When they had gone, Peskova turned and looked up at the house again. He would have to watch that Teng. He was getting above himself. Thinking himself better than the other men. He would have to bring him down a level. Teach him better manners.

With a smile he put the rifle down and reached for the next in the stack at his side. Yes, it would be fun to see the big Han on his knees and begging. A lot of fun.

* * *

Overseer Bergson looked across as the three men entered.

"What is it, Teng Fu?"

The big Han knelt in the doorway and bowed his head. "We have brought the man you asked for, Overseer."

Bergson turned from the bank of screens that took up one whole wall of the long room and got up from his chair. "You can go, Teng Fu. You too, Chang Yan. I'll see to him myself."

When they were gone and he was alone with the field supervisor, Bergson came across and stood there, no more than an arm's length from the man.

"Why did you do it, Field Supervisor Sung?"

The man swallowed, but did not lift his head. "Do what, *Shih* Bergson?"

458

Bergson reached out almost tenderly and took the man's cheek between the fingers of his left hand and twisted until Sung fell to his feet, whimpering in pain.

"Why did you do it, Sung? Or do you want me to beat the truth out of you?"

Sung prostrated himself, holding on to Bergson's feet. "I could not bear it any longer, Overseer. There is barely enough to keep a child alive, let alone men and women who have to toil in the fields all day. And when I heard the guards were going to cut our rations yet again . . ."

Bergson stepped back, shaking Sung's hands off. "Barely enough? What nonsense is this, Sung? Isn't it true that the men steal from the rice fields? That they eat much of the crop they are supposed to be harvesting?"

Sung went to shake his head, but Bergson brought his foot down firmly on top of his left hand and began to press down. "Tell me the truth, Sung. They steal, don't they?"

Sung cried out, then nodded his head vigorously. "It is so, *Shih* Bergson. There are many who do as you say."

Bergson slowly brought his foot up, then stepped away from Sung, turning his back momentarily, considering.

"And you stole because you had too little to eat?"

Sung looked up, then quickly looked back down, keeping his forehead pressed to the floor. "No . . . I . . ."

"Tell me the truth, Sung!" Bergson barked, turning sharply. "You stole because you were hungry, is that it?"

Sung miserably shook his head. "No, *Shih* Bergson. I have enough."

"Then why? Tell me why."

Sung shuddered. A sigh went through him like a wave. Then, resigned to his fate, he began to explain. "It was my wife, Overseer. She is a kindly woman, you understand. A good woman. It was her suggestion. She saw how it was for the others: that they were suffering while we, fortunate as we were, had enough. I told her we could share what we had, but she would not have it. I pleaded with her not to make me do as she asked . . ."

"Which was?"

"I stole, Overseer. I took fruit from the Frames and gave it to the others."

Bergson laughed coldly. "Am I meant to believe this, Sung? An honest thief? A charitable thief? A thief who sought no profit from his actions?"

Sung nodded his head once but said nothing.

Bergson moved closer. "I could have you flogged senseless for what you did, Sung. Worse, I could have you thrown into the Clay. How would you like that, Field Supervisor Sung? To be sent into the Clay?"

Sung stared up at Bergson, his terror at the thought naked in his eyes. "You'd not do that, *Shih* Bergson. Please. I beg you. Anything but that."

Bergson was silent a moment. He turned and went across to the desk. When he returned he was holding a thin card in one hand. He knelt down and held it in front of Sung's face a moment.

"Do you know what this is, Sung?"

Sung shook his head. He had never seen the like of it. It looked like a piece of Above technology – something they never saw out in the fields – but he would not have liked to have guessed just what.

"This here, Sung, is the evidence of your crime. It's a record of the hour you spent harvesting in the Frames. A hidden camera took a film of you."

Again Sung shuddered. "What do you want, *Shih* Bergson?"

Bergson smiled and slipped the thin sliver of ice into his jacket pocket, then stood up again. "First I want you to sit down over here and write down the names of all those who shared the stolen fruit with you."

Sung hesitated, then nodded. "And then?"

"Then you'll go back to your barracks and send your wife to me."

Sung stiffened but did not look up. "My wife, Overseer?"

"The good woman. You know, the one who got you into all this trouble."

Sung swallowed. "And what will happen to my wife, *Shih* Bergson?"

Bergson laughed. "If she's good – if she's *very* good to me – then nothing. You understand? In fact – and you can tell her this – if she's *exceptionally* good I might even give her the tape. Who knows, eh, Sung?"

Sung looked up, meeting Bergson's cold grey eyes for the first time in their interview, then looked down again, understanding perfectly.

"Good. Then come. There's paper here and ink. You have a list of names to write."

★ ★ ★

She came when it was dark. Peskova took her up to the top room – the big room beneath the eaves – and locked her in as he had been told to. Then he went, leaving the house empty but for the woman and the Overseer.

For a time DeVore simply watched her, following her every movement with the hidden cameras, switching from screen to screen, zooming in to focus on her face or watching her from the far side of the room. Then, when he was done with that, he nodded to himself and blanked the screens.

She was much better than he had expected. Stronger, prettier, more attractive than he'd anticipated. He had thought beforehand that he would have to send her back and deal with Sung some other way, but now he had seen her he felt the need in him, like a strong, dark tar in his blood, and knew he would have to purge himself of that. He had not had a woman for weeks – not since that last trip to the Wilds – and that had been a sing-song girl, all artifice and expertise. No, this would be different; something to savour.

Quickly he went to the wall safe at the far end of the room and touched the combination. The door irised open and he reached inside, drawing out the tiny phial before the door closed up again. He hesitated a moment then gulped the drug down, feeling its warmth sear his throat

461

and descend quickly to his stomach. It would be in his blood in minutes.

He climbed the stairs quickly, almost eagerly now, but near the top he slowed, calming himself, waiting until he had complete control. Only then did he reach out and thumb the lock.

She turned, surprised. A big woman, bigger than her husband, nothing cowed or mean about the way she stood. You married below yourself, DeVore thought at once, knowing that Sung would never have made Field Supervisor without such a woman to push him from behind.

Her bow was hesitant. "Overseer?"

He closed the door behind him, then turned back to her, trying to gauge her response to him. Would she do as he wanted? Would she try to save her husband? She was here. That, at least, augured well. But would she be compliant? Would she be *exceptionally* good to him?

"You know why you're here?" he asked, taking a step closer to her.

Her eyes never left him. "I'm here because my husband told me to be here, *Shih* Bergson."

DeVore laughed. "From what I'm told old Sung is a docile man. He does what he's told. Am I wrong in thinking that? Does Sung roar like a lion within his own walls?"

She met his gaze fiercely, almost defiantly, making the blood run thicker, heavier in his veins. "He is my husband and I a dutiful wife. He wished me here, so here I am."

DeVore looked down, keeping the smile from his face. He had not been wrong. She had spirit. He had seen that when he had been watching her; had seen how she looked at everything with that curious, almost arrogant stare of hers. She had strength. The strength of twenty Sungs.

He took another step then shook his head. "You're wrong, you know. You're here because I said you should be here."

She did not answer him this time, but stared back at him almost insolently, only a slight moistening of her lips betraying her nervousness.

"What's your name, Sung's wife?"

She looked away, then looked back at him, as if to say *Don't toy with me. Do what you are going to do and let me be.*

"Your name?" he insisted, his voice harder now.

"My name is Si Wu Ya," she answered proudly.

This time he smiled. Si Wu Ya. *Silk Raven.* He looked at her and understood why her parents had given her the name. Her hair was beautifully dark and lustrous. "Better an honest raven than a deceitful magpie, eh?" he said, quoting the old Han adage.

"What do you want me to do?"

He shook his head. "Don't be impatient, Si Wu Ya. We'll come to that. But tell me this – is Sung a good man? Is he good in bed? Does he make you sing out with pleasure?"

He saw how she bridled at the question, but saw also how the truth forbade her to say yes. So, Sung was a disappointment. Well, he, DeVore, would make her sing tonight. Of that he had no doubt. He took a step towards her, then another, until he stood before her, face to face.

"Is he hard like bamboo, or soft like a rice frond? Tell me, Si Wu Ya. I'd like to know."

For a moment her eyes flared with anger, but then she seemed to laugh deep inside herself and her eyes changed, their anger replaced by a hard amusement. "Don't mock me, *Shih* Bergson. I'm here, aren't I? Do what you want. I'll be good to you. I'll be very good. But don't mock me."

He looked back at her a moment, then reached down and took her left hand in his own, lifting it up to study it. It was a big, strong hand, roughly calloused from field-work, but she had made an effort. It was clean and the nails were polished a deep brown.

He met her eyes again. "My friends tell me you Han women wear no underclothes. Is it true?"

In answer she took his hand and placed it between her legs. His fingers met the soft, masking texture of cloth, but beneath them he could feel her warmth, the firm softness of her sex.

"Well?" she asked, almost smiling now, determined not to be cowed by him.

"Strip off," he said, standing back a pace. "I want to see what you look like."

She shrugged, slipped the one-piece off and kicked off her briefs, then stood there, her hands at her sides, making no effort to cover her nakedness.

DeVore walked round her, studying her. She was a fine woman, unspoilt by childbirth, her body hardened by fieldwork. Her breasts were large and firm, her buttocks broad but not fat. Her legs were strongly-muscled yet still quite shapely, her stomach flat, her shoulders smooth. He nodded, satisfied. She would have made a good wife for a T'ang, let alone a man like Sung.

"Good. Now over there."

She hesitated, her eyes showing a momentary unease, then she did as she was told, walking over to the corner where he had indicated. He saw how she looked about her; how her eyes kept going to the saddle. As if she knew.

"What do you want me to do?"

DeVore smiled coldly. He had watched her earlier. Had seen, through the camera's hidden eye, how fascinated she had been with the saddle. Had witnessed her puzzlement and then her shocked surprise as she realised what it was.

It was a huge thing, almost half a man's height and the same in length. At first glance it could be mistaken for an ornately carved stool, its black and white surfaces for a kind of sculpture. And in a way it was. Ming craftsmen had made the saddle more than seven hundred years before, shaping ivory and wood to satisfy the whim of a bored nobleman.

"Have you seen my saddle?" he asked her.

She watched him, eyes half-lidded now, and nodded.

"It was a custom of your people, you know. They would place a saddle in the gateway to the parental home before the bride and bridegroom entered it."

She wet her lips. "What of it?"

He shrugged. "*An*, it was. A saddle. *An*. Almost the same sound as for peace."

He saw her shiver, yet the room was warm.

"Have you studied my saddle?"

She nodded briefly.

"And did it amuse you?"

"You're mocking me again, *Shih* Bergson. Is that what you want me to do? To play that game with you?"

He smiled. So she had worked it out. He went across and stood there beside the saddle, smoothing his hand over its finely polished surfaces. What at first seemed a mere tangle of black and white soon resolved itself. Became a man and woman locked in an embrace that was, some said, unnatural; the man's head buried between the woman's legs, the woman's head between the man's.

He looked across at her, amused. "Have you ever done that with Sung?"

She blinked. Then, unexpectedly, she shook her head.

"Would you like to do that, now, with me?"

He waited, watching her like a hawk watching its prey. Again she hesitated, then she nodded.

"You think you'd like it, don't you?"

This time she looked away, for the first time the faintest colour appearing at her neck.

Ah, he thought. Now I have you. Now I know your weakness. You *are* dissatisfied with Sung. Perhaps you're even thinking what this might lead to. You've ambitions, Si Wu Ya. For all your social conscience you're a realist. And, worse for you, you enjoy sex. You want to be made love to. You want the excitement that I'm offering here.

"Come here."

He saw how her breathing changed. Her nipples were stiff now and the colour had not left her neck. Slowly, almost fearful now, she came to him.

He took her hand again, guiding it down within the folds of his *pau*, then heard her gasp as her hand closed on him; saw her eyes go down and look.

DeVore laughed, knowing the drug would last for hours

yet – would keep him at this peak until he had done with her. He leaned closer to her, drawing her nearer with one hand, his voice lowering to a whisper.

"Was he ever this hard, Si Wu Ya? Was he ever this hot?"

Her eyes went to his briefly, the pupils enlarged, then returned to the splendour she held. Unbid, she knelt and began to stroke him and kiss him. He put his hands on her shoulders now, forcing her to take him in her mouth, her whole body shuddering beneath his touch, a soft moaning in her throat. Then he pushed her off, roughly, almost brutally and moved away from her.

She knelt there, her breasts rising and falling violently, her eyes wide, watching him. Almost. She was almost ready. One more step. One more step and she would be there.

He threw off the *pau* and stood there over her, naked, seeing how eagerly she watched him now. How ready she was for him to fuck her. With one foot he pushed her back, then knelt and spread her legs, watching her all the while, one hand moving between her legs, seeing how her eyes closed, how her breath caught with the pleasure of it.

"Gods," she moaned, reaching up for him. "Goddess of mercy, put it there! Please, *Shih* Bergson! Please put it there!"

His fingers traced a line from her groin up to her chin, forcing her to look back at him.

"Not like this," he said, putting her hands on him again. "I know a better way. A much, much better way than this."

Quickly he led her to the saddle, pushing her face down onto its hard smooth surface, his hands caressing her intimately all the while, keeping her mind dark, her senses inflamed. Then, before she realised what was happening, he fastened her in the double stirrups, binding her hands and feet.

He stood back, looking at his handiwork, then crossed to the wall and switched off all the lights but one – the spot that picked out her naked rump.

She was shaking now. He could see the small movement of the muscles at the top of her legs. "What's happening?" she asked in a tiny, sobered voice. "What are you doing?"

He went over to her and placed his hand on the small of her back, running his fingers down the smooth channel that ended in the tight hole of her anus, feeling her shudder at his touch.

Pleasure or fear? he wondered. *Did she still believe it would all turn out all right?*

The thought almost made him laugh. She had mistaken him. She had thought he wanted ordinary satisfactions.

He reached beneath the saddle and dipped his fingers in the shelf of scented unguents, then began to smear them delicately about the tiny hole, pushing inward, the unguents working their magic spell, making the muscles relax.

He felt her breathing change again, anticipating pleasure; knew, without looking, that she would have been newly aroused by his ministrations; that her nipples would be stiff, her eyes wide with expectation.

He reached under the saddle a second time and drew out the steel-tipped phallus that was attached by a chain to the pommel. The chain was just long enough. Longer and there would not be that invigorating downward pull – that feeling of restraint – shorter and penetration would not be deep enough to satisfy. He smiled, holding the hollowed column lovingly between his hands and smoothing his fingers over the spiralling pattern of the *wu-tu*, the "five noxious creatures" – toad, scorpion, snake, centipede and gecko – then drew it on, easing himself into its oiled soft-leather innards and fastening its leather straps about his waist.

For a moment he hesitated, savouring the moment, then centred the metal spike and pushed. His first thrust took her by surprise. He felt her whole body stiffen in shock, but though she gasped, she did not cry out.

Brave girl, he thought, but that's not what you're here for. You're not here to be brave. You're here to sing for me.

467

The second thrust tore her. He felt the skin between her anus and vagina give like tissue and heard her cry out in agony.

"Good," he said, laughing brutally. "That's good. Sing out, Si Wu Ya! It's good to hear you sing out."

He thrust again.

When he was done he unstrapped himself, then took one of the white sheets from the side and threw it over her, watching as the blood spread out from the centre of the white; a doubled circle of redness that slowly formed into an ellipse.

Hearing her moan, he went round and knelt beside her, lifting her face gently, almost tenderly, and kissing her brow, her nose, her lips.

"Was that good, Si Wu Ya? Was it hard enough for you?" He laughed softly, almost lovingly. "Ah, but you were good, Si Wu Ya. The best yet. And for that you'll have your tape. But later, eh? In the morning. We've a whole night ahead of us. Plenty of time to play our game again."

* * *

Sung was kneeling on the top of the dyke, staring across at the House as the dawn broke. He was cold to the bone and his clothes were wet through, but still he knelt there, waiting.

He had heard her cries in the night. Had heard and felt his heart break inside his chest. Had dropped his head, knowing, at last, how small he was, how powerless.

Now, as the light leached back into the world, he saw the door open at the head of the steps and a figure appear.

"Si Wu Ya . . ." he mouthed, his lips dry, his heart, which had seemed dead in him, pounding in his chest. He went to get up but his legs were numb from kneeling and he had to put his hand out to stop himself from tumbling into the water far below. But his eyes never left her distant, shadowed figure, seeing at once how slowly she moved, how awkwardly, hobbling down the steps one by one, stopping time and again to rest, her whole body crooked, one hand clutching the side rail tightly, as if she'd fall without it.

He dragged himself back, anxious now, and began to pound the life back into his legs. Once more he tried to stand and fell back, cursing, almost whimpering now in his fear for her. "Si Wu Ya," he moaned, "Si Wu Ya."

Once more he tried to stand, gritting his teeth, willing his muscles to obey him. For one moment he almost fell again, then he thrust one leg forward, finding his balance.

"Si Wu Ya . . ." he hissed. "Si Wu Ya . . ."

Forcing his useless legs to work he made his way to the bridge, awkwardly at first, hobbling, as if in some grotesque mimicry of his wife, then with more confidence as the blood began to flow, his muscles come alive again.

Then, suddenly, he was running, his arms flailing wildly, his bare feet thudding against the dark earth. Until he was standing there, before her, great waves of pain and fear, hurt and anger washing through him like a huge black tide.

He moaned, his voice an animal cry of pain. " What did he do, Si Wu Ya? Gods save us, what did he do?"

She stared back at him almost sightlessly.

"Your face . . ." he began, then realised that her face was unmarked. The darkness was behind her eyes. The sight of it made him whimper like a child and fall to his knees again.

Slowly, each movement a vast, unexplored continent of pain, she pushed out from the steps and hobbled past him. He scrambled up and made to help her but she brushed him off, saying nothing, letting the cold emptiness of her face speak for her.

On the narrow bridge he stood in front of her again, blocking her way, looking back past her at the House.

"I'll kill him."

For the first time she seemed to look at him. Then she laughed; her laughter so cold, so unlike the laughter he had known from her, that it made his flesh tingle with fear.

"He'd break you, little Sung. He'd eat you up and spit you out."

She leaned to one side and spat. Blood. He could see it, even in this half light. She had spat blood.

He went to touch her, to put his hands on her shoulders, but the look in her eyes warned him off. He let his arms fall uselessly.

"What did he do, Si Wu Ya? Tell me what he did."

She looked down, then began to move on, forcing him to move aside and let her pass. He had no will to stop her.

At the first of the smaller channels she turned and began to ease herself down the shallow bank, grunting, her face set against the pain she was causing herself. Sung, following her, held out his hand and for the first time she let him help her, gripping his hand with a force that took his breath, her fingers tightening convulsively with every little jolt she received.

Then she let go and straightened up, standing there knee deep in the water at the bottom of the unlit channel, the first light lain like a white cloth over the latticework of the surrounding fields, picking out the channel's lips, the crouching shape of Sung. The same clear light that rested in the woman's long dark hair like a faintly-jewelled mist.

She looked up at him. "Have you your torch, Sung?"

He nodded, not understanding why she should want it, but took it from his pocket and, edging down the bank, reached out and handed it to her, watching as she unscrewed the top, transforming it into a tiny cutting tool. Then she took something from the pocket of her one-piece. Something small enough to fold inside her palm.

The card. The tape that had the record of his theft. Sung swallowed and looked at her. So she had done it. Had saved them both. He shivered, wanting to go down to her, to stroke her and hold her and thank her, but what he wanted wasn't somehow right. He felt the coldness emanate from her, a sense of the vast distance she had travelled. It was as if she had been beyond the sky. Had been to the place where they said there was no air, only the frozen, winking

470

nothingness of space. She had been there. He knew it. He had seen it in her eyes.

She put the card against the bank and played the cutting beam upon it. Once, twice, three times she did it, each time picking up the card and examining it. But each time it emerged unscathed, unmarked.

She looked up at him, that same cold distance in her eyes, then let the card fall from her fingers into the silt below the water. Yes, he thought, they'll not find it there. They could search a thousand years and they'd not find it.

But she had forgotten about the card already. She was bent down now, unbuttoning the lower half of her one-piece, her fingers moving gingerly, as if what she touched were flesh not cloth.

"Come down," she said coldly, not looking at him. "You want to know what he did, don't you? Well, come and see. I'll show you what he did."

He went down and stood there, facing her, the water cold against his shins, the darkness all around them. He could see that the flap of cloth gaped open, but in the dark could make out no more than the vague shape of her legs, her stomach.

"Here." She handed him the two parts of the torch and waited for him to piece the thing together.

He made to shine the torch into her face, but she pushed his hand down. "No," she said. "Not there. Down here, where the darkness is."

He let her guide his hand, then tried to pull back as he saw what he had previously not noticed, but she held his hand there firmly, forcing him to look. Blood. The cloth was caked with her blood. Was stained almost black with it.

"Gods . . ." he whispered, then caught his breath as the light moved across onto her flesh.

She had been torn open. From her navel to the base of her spine she had been ripped apart. And then sewn up. Crudely, it seemed, for the stitches were uneven. The black threads glistened in the torchlight, blood seeping from the wound where she had opened it again.

471

"There," she said, pushing the torch away. "Now you've seen."

He stood there blankly, not knowing what to say or do, remembering only the sound of her crying out in the darkness and how awful he had felt, alone, kneeling there on the dyke, impotent to act.

"What now?" he asked.

But she did not answer him, only bent and lowered herself into the water, hissing as the coldness burned into the wound, a faint moan escaping through her gritted teeth as she began to wash.

★   ★   ★

At dawn on the morning of his official birthday – in the court annals his thirteenth, for they accorded with ancient Han tradition in calling the day of the child's birth its first "birth day" – Li Yuan was woken by his father and, when he was dressed in the proper clothes, led down to the stables of the Tongjiang estate.

It was an informal ceremony. Even so, there was not one of the six hundred and forty-eight servants – man, woman or girl – who was not present. Nor had any of the guests – themselves numbering one hundred and eighty – absented themselves on this occasion.

The grounds surrounding the stable buildings had been meticulously swept and tidied, the grooms lined up, heads bowed, before the great double doors. And there, framed in the open left-hand doorway of the stalls, was the T'ang's birthday gift to his son.

It was an Andalusian; a beauty of a horse, sixteen hands high and a perfect mulberry in colour. It was a thick-necked, elegant beast, with the strong legs of a thorough-bred. It had been saddled up ready for him and as Li Yuan stood there, it turned its head curiously, its large dark eyes meeting the prince's as if it knew its new owner.

"You have ridden my horses for too long now," Li Shai Tung said to his son quietly. "I felt it was time you had your own."

472

Li Yuan went across to it and reached up gently, stroking its neck, its dappled flank. Then he turned and bowed to his father, a fleeting smile on his lips. The chief groom stood close by, the halter in his hand, ready to offer it to the prince when he was ready. But when Li Yuan finally turned to him it was not to take the halter from him.

"Saddle up the Arab, Hung Feng-Chan."

The chief groom stared back at him a moment, open-mouthed, then looked across at the T'ang as if to query the instruction. But Li Shai Tung stood there motionless, his expression unchanged. Seeing this, Hung Feng-Chan bowed deeply to his T'ang, then to the prince, and quickly handed the halter to one of the nearby grooms.

When he had gone, Li Yuan turned back to his father, smiling, one hand still resting on the Andalusian's smooth, strong neck.

"He's beautiful, father, and I'm delighted with your gift. But if I am to have a horse it must be Han Ch'in's. I must become my brother."

Throughout the watching crowd there was a low murmur of surprise, but from the T'ang himself there was no word, only the slightest narrowing of the eyes, a faint movement of the mouth. Otherwise he was perfectly still, watching his son.

The chief groom returned a minute later, leading the Arab. The black horse sniffed the air, and made a small bowing movement of its head, as if in greeting to the other horse. Then, just when it seemed to have settled, it made a sharp sideways movement, tugging against the halter. Hung Feng-Chan quieted the horse, patting its neck and whispering to it, then brought it across to where Li Yuan was standing.

This was the horse that General Tolonen had bought Han for his seventeenth birthday; the horse Han Ch'in had ridden daily until his death. A dark, spirited beast; dark-skinned and dark-natured, her eyes full of fire. She was smaller than the Andalusian by a hand, yet her grace, her power were undeniable.

"Well, father?"

All eyes were on the T'ang. Li Shai Tung stood there, bare-headed, a bright blue quilted jacket pulled loosely about his shoulders against the morning's freshness, one foot slightly before the other, his arms crossed across his chest, his hands holding his shoulders. It was a familiar stance to those who knew him, as was the smile he now gave his son; a dark, ironic smile that seemed both amused and calculating.

"You must ride her first, Li Yuan."

Li Yuan held his father's eyes a moment, bowing, then he turned and, without further hesitation, swung up into the saddle. So far so good. The Arab barely had time to think before Li Yuan had leant forward and, looping the reins quickly over his hands, squeezed the Arab's chest gently with both feet.

Li Yuan's look of surprise as the Arab reared brought gasps as well as laughter from all round. Only the T'ang remained still and silent. Hung Feng-Chan danced round the front of the horse, trying to grab the halter, but Li Yuan shouted at him angrily and would have waved him away were he not clinging on dearly with both hands.

The Arab pulled and tugged and danced, moving this way and that, bucking, then skittering forward and ducking its head, trying to throw the rider from its back. But Li Yuan held on, his teeth gritted, his face determined. And slowly, very slowly, the Arab's movements calmed. With difficulty Li Yuan brought the Arab's head round and moved the stubborn beast two paces closer to the watching T'ang.

"Well, father, is she mine?"

The T'ang's left hand went from his shoulder to his beard. Then he laughed; a warm, good-humoured laugh that found its echo all around.

"Yes, Li Yuan. In name, at least. But watch her. Even your brother found her difficult."

* * *

They met by accident, several hours later, in one of the bright, high-ceilinged corridors leading to the gardens.

"Li Yuan." Fei Yen bowed deeply, the two maids on either side of her copying her automatically.

The young prince had showered and changed since she had last seen him. He wore red now, the colour of the summer, his *ma kua*, the waist-length ceremonial jacket, a brilliant carmine, his loose silk trousers poppy, his suede boots a delicate shade of rose. About his waist he wore an elegant *ta lien*, or girdle pouch, the border a thick band of russet, the twin heart-shaped pockets made of a soft peach cloth, the details of trees, butterflies and flowers picked out in emerald green and blue and gold. On his head he wore a Ming-style summer hat, its inverted bowl lined with red fur and capped with a single ruby. Three long peacock feathers hung from its tip, reminder that Li Yuan was a royal prince.

"Fei Yen . . ." It might only have been the light reflected from his costume, yet once again he seemed embarrassed by her presence. "I . . . I was coming to see you."

She stayed as she was, looking up at him from beneath her long black lashes, allowing herself the faintest smile of pleasure.

"I am honoured, Li Yuan."

Fei Yen had dressed quite simply, in a peach *ch'i p'ao*, over which she wore a long embroidered cloak of white silk, decorated with stylised bamboo leaves of blue and green and edged in a soft pink brocade that matched the tiny pink ribbons in her hair and set the whole thing off quite perfectly.

She knew how beautiful she looked. From childhood she had known her power over men. But this was strange, disturbing. It was almost as if this boy, this child . . .

Fei Yen rose slowly, meeting the prince's eyes for the first time and seeing how quickly he re-directed his gaze. Perhaps it was just embarrassment – the memory of how he had shamed himself that time when she had comforted him. Men were such strange, proud creatures. It was odd what mattered to them. Like Han Ch'in that time, when she had almost bettered him at archery . . .

Li Yuan found his tongue again. But he could only glance at her briefly as he complimented her.

"May her name be preserved on bamboo and silk."

She laughed prettily at that, recognising the old saying and pleased by his allusion to her cloak. "Why, thank you, Li Yuan. May the fifteen precious things be yours."

It was said before she fully realised what she had wished for him. She heard her maids giggle behind her and saw Li Yuan look down, the flush returning to his cheeks. It was a traditional good-luck wish, for long life and prosperity. But it was also a wish that the recipient have sons.

Her own laughter dispelled the awkwardness of the moment. She saw Li Yuan look up at her, his dark eyes strangely bright, and was reminded momentarily of Han Ch'in. As Han had been, so Li Yuan was now. One day he would be Head of his family – a powerful man, almost a god. She was conscious of that as he stood there, watching her. Already, they said, he had the wisdom of an old man, a sage. Yet that brief reminder of her murdered husband saddened her. It brought back the long months of bitterness and loneliness she had suffered, shut away on her father's estate.

Li Yuan must have seen something of that in her face, for what he said next seemed to penetrate her mood, almost to read her thoughts.

"You were alone too long, Fei Yen."

It sounded so formal, so old-mannish, that she laughed. He frowned at her, not understanding.

"I mean it," he said, his face earnest. "It isn't healthy for a young woman to be locked away with old maids and virgins."

His candidness, and the apparent maturity it revealed, surprised and amused her. She had to remind herself again of his precocity. He was only twelve. Despite this she was tempted to flirt with him. It was her natural inclination, long held in check, and, after a moment's hesitation, she indulged it.

"I'm gratified to find you so concerned for my welfare, Li Yuan. You think I should have been living life to the full, then, and not mourning your brother?"

She saw immediately that she had said the wrong thing. She had misread his comment. His face closed to her and he turned away, suddenly cold, distant. It troubled her and she crossed the space between them, touching his shoulder. "I didn't mean . . ."

She stood there a moment, suddenly aware of how still he was. Her hand lay gently on his shoulder, barely pressing against him, yet it seemed he was gathered there at the point of contact, his whole self focused in her touch. It bemused her. What was this?

She felt embarrassed, felt that she ought to remove her hand, but did not know how. It seemed that any movement of hers would be a snub.

Then, unexpectedly, he reached up and covered her hand with his own, pressing it firmly to his shoulder. "We both miss him," he said. "But life goes on. I too found the customs too . . . too strict."

She was surprised to hear that. It was more like something Han Ch'in might have said. She had always thought Li Yuan was in his father's mould. Traditional. Bound fast by custom.

He released her and turned to face her.

Li Yuan was smiling now. Once more she found herself wrong-footed. What was happening? Why had his mood changed so quickly? She stared at him, finding the likeness to Han more prominent now that he was smiling. But then, Han had always been smiling. His eyes, his mouth, had been made for laughter.

She looked away, vaguely disturbed. Li Yuan was too intense for her taste. Like his father there was something daunting, almost terrible about him: an austerity suggestive of ferocity. Yet now, standing there, smiling at her, he seemed quite different – almost quite likeable.

"It was hard, you know. This morning . . . to mount Han's horse like that."

Again the words were unexpected. His smile faded, became a wistful, boyish expression of loss.

It touched her deeply. For the first time she saw through his mask of precocious intelligence and saw how vulnerable he was, how frail in spite of all. Not even that moment after Han's death had revealed that to her. Then she had thought it grief, not vulnerability. She was moved by her insight and, when he looked up at her again, saw how hurt he seemed, how full of pain his eyes were. Beautiful eyes. Dark, hazel eyes. She had not noticed them before.

Han's death had touched him deeply, she could see. He had lost far more than her. She was silent, afraid she would say the wrong thing, watching him, this man-boy, her curiosity aroused, her sympathies awoken.

He frowned and looked away.

"That's why I came to see you. To give you a gift."

"A gift?"

"Yes. The Andalusian."

She shook her head, confused. "But your father . . ."

He looked directly at her now. "I've spoken to my father already. He said the horse is mine to do with as I wish." He bowed his head and swallowed. "So I'd like to give him to you. In place of the Arab."

She laughed shortly. "But the Arab was Han's, not mine."

"I know. Even so, I'd like you to have him. Han told me how much you enjoyed riding."

This time her laughter was richer, deeper, and when Li Yuan looked up again he saw the delight in her face.

"Why, Li Yuan, that's . . ." She stopped and simply looked at him, smiling broadly. Then, impulsively, she reached out and embraced him, kissing his cheek.

"Then you'll take him?" he whispered softly in her ear.

Her soft laughter rippled through him. "Of course, Li Yuan. And I thank you. From the bottom of my heart I thank you."

When she was gone he turned and looked after her, feeling the touch of her still, the warmth on his cheek where she had kissed him. He closed his eyes and caught the scent of her, *mei hua* – plum blossom – in the air and on his clothes where she had brushed against him. He shivered, his thoughts in turmoil, his pulse racing.

The plum. Ice-skinned and jade-boned, the plum. It symbolised winter and virginity. But its blossoming brought the spring.

"*Mei hua* . . ." He said the words softly, like a breath, letting them mingle with her scent, then turned away, reddening at the thought that had come to mind. *Mei hua*. It was a term for sexual pleasure, for on the bridal bed were spread plum blossom covers. So innocent a scent, and yet . . .

Shivering, he took a long, slow breath of her. Then he turned and hurried on, his fists clenched at his sides, his face the colour of summer.

* * *

"There have been changes since you were last among us, Howard."

"So I see."

DeVore turned briefly to smile at Berdichev before returning his attention to the scene on the other side of the one-way mirror that took up the whole of one wall of the study.

"Who are they?"

Berdichev came up and stood beside him. "Sympathisers. Money men, mainly. Friends of our host, Douglas."

The room the two men looked into was massive; was more garden than room. It had been landscaped with low hills and narrow walks, with tiny underlit pools, small temples, carefully-placed banks of shrub and stone, shady willows, cinnamon trees and delicate *wu-tong*. People milled about casually, talking amongst themselves, eating and drinking. But there the similarities with past occasions ended. The servants who went amongst them were no longer Han. In fact, there was not a single Han in sight.

DeVore's eyes took it all in with great interest. He saw how, though they still wore silks, the style had changed; had been simplified. Their dress seemed more austere, both in its cut and in the absence of embellishment. What had been so popular only three years ago was now conspicuous by its absence. There were no birds or flowers, no dragonflies or clouds, no butterflies or pictograms. Now only a single motif could be seen, worn openly on chest or collar, on hems or in the form of jewellery, on pendants about the neck or emblazoned on a ring or brooch: the double-helix of heredity. Just as noticeable was the absence of the colour blue – the colour of imperial service. DeVore smiled appreciatively; that last touch was the subtlest of insults.

"The Seven have done our work for us, Soren."

"Not altogether. We pride ourselves on having won the propaganda war. There are men out there who, three years ago, would not have dreamed of coming to a gathering like this. They would have been worried that word would get back – as, indeed, it does – and that the T'ang would act through his Ministers to make life awkward for them. Now they have no such fears. We have educated them to the fact of their own power. They are many, the Seven few. What if the Seven close one door to them? – here, at such gatherings, a thousand new doors open."

"And *The New Hope*?"

Berdichev's smile stretched his narrow face against its natural grain. *The New Hope* was his brainchild. "In more than one sense it is our flagship. You should see the pride in their faces when they talk of it. *We* did this, they seem to be saying. Not the Han, but us, the *Hung Mao*, as they call us. The Europeans."

DeVore glanced at Berdichev. It was the second time he had heard the term. Their host, Douglas, had used it when he had first arrived. "We Europeans must stick together," he had said. And DeVore, hearing it, had felt he had used it like some secret password; some token of mutual understanding.

He looked about him at the decoration of the study. Again there were signs of change – of that same revolution in style that was sweeping the Above. The decor, like the dress of those outside, was simpler – the design of chairs and table less extravagant than it had been. On the walls, now, hung simple rural landscapes. Gone were the colourful historical scenes that had been so much in favour with the *Hung Mao*. Gone were the lavish screens and bright floral displays of former days. But all of this, ironically, brought them only further into line with the real Han – the Families – who had always preferred the simple to the lavish, the harmonious to the gaudy.

These tokens of change, superficial as they yet were, were encouraging, but they were also worrying. These men – these *Europeans* – were not Han, nor had they ever been Han. Yet the Han had destroyed all that they had once been – had severed them from their cultural roots as simply and as thoroughly as a gardener might snip the stem of a chrysanthemum. The Seven had given them no real choice: they could be Han or they could be nothing. And to be nothing was intolerable. Now, however, to be Han was equally untenable.

DeVore shivered. At present their response was negative: a reaction *against* Han ways, Han dress, Han style. But they could not live like this for long. At length they would turn the mirror on themselves and find they had no real identity, no positive channel for their new-born sense of racial selfhood. *The New Hope* was a move to fill that vacuum, as was this term, "European"; but neither was enough. A culture was a vast and complex thing and, like the roots of a giant tree, went deep into the dark, rich earth of time. It was more than a matter of dress and style. It was a way of thinking and behaving. A thing of blood and bone, not cloth and architecture.

Yes, they needed more than a word for themselves, more than a central symbol for their pride; they needed a focus

– something to restore them to themselves. But what? What on earth could fill the vacuum they were facing? It was a problem they would need to address in the coming days. To ignore it would be fatal.

He went to the long table in the centre of the room and looked down at the detailed map spread out across its surface.

"Has everyone been briefed?"

Berdichev came and stood beside him. "Not everyone. I've kept the circle as small as possible. Douglas knows, of course. And Barrow. I thought your man, Duchek, ought to know, too, considering how helpful he's been. And then there's Moore and Weis."

"Anton Weis? The banker?"

Berdichev nodded. "I know what you're thinking, but he's changed in the last year or so. He fell out with old man Ebert. Was stripped by him of a number of important contracts. Now he hates the T'ang and his circle with an intensity that's hard to match."

"I understand. Even so, I'd not have thought him important enough."

"It's not him so much as the people he represents. He's our liaison with a number of interested parties. People who can't declare themselves openly. Important people."

DeVore considered a moment, then smiled. "Okay. So that makes seven of us who know."

"Eight, actually."

DeVore raised his eyebrows in query, but Berdichev said simply, "I'll explain later."

"When will they be here?"

"They're here now. Outside. They'll come in when you're ready for them."

DeVore laughed. "I'm ready now."

"Then I'll tell Douglas."

DeVore watched Berdichev move among the men gathered there in the garden room, more at ease now than he had ever been; saw too how they looked to him now as a leader, a shaper of events, and noted with irony how different that was from how they had formerly behaved. And what was different about the man? Power. It was power alone that made a man attractive. Even the potentiality of power.

He stood back, away from the door, as they filed in. Then, when the door was safely closed and locked, he came forward and exchanged bows with each of them. Seeing how closely Weis was watching him, he made an effort to be more warm, more friendly in his greeting there, but all the while he was wondering just how far he could trust the man.

Then, without further ado, they went to the table.

The map was of the main landmass of City Europe, omitting Scandinavia, the Balkans, Southern Italy and the Iberian Peninsula. Its predominant colour was white, though there was a faint, almost ivory tinge to it, caused by the fine yellow honeycombing that represented the City's regular shape – each tiny hexagon a *hsien*, an administrative district.

All Security garrisons were marked in a heavier shade of yellow, Bremen to the north-west, close to the coast, Kiev to the east, almost off the map, Bucharest far to the south; these three the most important of the twenty shown. Weimar, to the south-east of Bremen, was marked with a golden circle, forming a triangle with the Berlin garrison to the north-east.

Two large areas were marked in red, both in the bottom half of the map. One, to the left, straddled the old geographic areas of Switzerland and Austria; the other, smaller and to the right, traced the border of old Russia and cut down into Romania. In these ancient, mountainous regions – the Alps and the Carpathians – the City stopped abruptly, edging the wilderness. They formed great, jagged holes in its perfect whiteness.

Again in the top right-hand section of the map the dominant whiteness ceased abruptly in a line extending down from Danzig *hsien* to Poznan, and thence to Krakow and across to Lvov, ending on the shores of the Black Sea, at Odessa. This, shaded the soft green of springtime, was the great growing area, where the Hundred Plantations – in reality eighty-seven – were situated; an area which comprised some twenty-eight per cent of the total land mass of City Europe. DeVore's own plantation was in the northwest of this area, adjoining the garrison at Lodz.

He let them study the map a while, accustoming themselves once again to its details, then drew their attention to the large red-shaded area to the bottom left of the map.

To him the outline of the Swiss Wilds always looked the same. That dark red shape was a giant carp turning in the water, its head facing east, its tail flicking out towards Marseilles *hsien*, its cruel mouth open, poised to eat Lake Balaton which, like a tiny minnow, swam some three hundred *li* to the east. Seven of the great Security garrisons ringed the Wilds – Geneva, Zurich, Munich and Vienna to the north, Marseilles, Milan and Zagreb to the south. Strategically that made little sense, for the Wilds were almost empty, yet it was as if the City's architect had known that this vast, jagged hole – this primitive wilderness at the heart of its hive-like orderliness – would one day prove its weakest point.

As, indeed, it would. And all the preparedness of architects would not prevent the City's fall. He leaned forward and jabbed his finger down into the red, at a point where the carp's backbone seemed to twist.

"Here!" he said, looking about him and seeing he had their attention. "This is where our base will be."

He reached into the drawer beneath the table and drew out the transparent template, then laid it down over the shaded area. At once that part of the map seemed to come alive; was overlaid with a fine web of brilliant gold, the nodes of which sparkled in the overhead light.

They leaned closer, attentive, as he outlined the details of his scheme. Three nerve-centres, built deep into the mountainsides, joined to a total of eighteen other fortresses, each linked by discreet communication systems to at least two other bases, yet each capable of functioning independently. The whole thing hidden beneath layers of ice and rock, untraceable from the air: a flexible and formidable system of defences from which they would launch their attack on the Seven.

And the cost?

The cost they knew already. It was a staggering sum. Far more than any one of them could contemplate. But together . . .

DeVore looked from face to face, gauging their response, coming to Weis last of all.

"Well, *Shih* Weis? Do you think your backers would approve?"

He saw the flicker of uncertainty at the back of Weis's eyes, and smiled inwardly. The man was still conditioned to think like a loyal subject of the T'ang. Even so, if he could be pushed to persuade his backers . . .

DeVore smiled encouragingly. "You're happy with the way funds will be channelled through to the project, I assume?"

Weis nodded, then leaned forward, touching the template.

"This is hand drawn. Why's that?"

DeVore laughed. "Tell me, *Shih* Weis, do you trust all your dealings to the record?"

Weis smiled and others about the table laughed. It was a common business procedure to keep a single written copy of a deal until it was considered safe for the venture to be announced publicly. It was too easy to gain access to a Company's computer records when everyone used the same communications web.

"You want the T'ang to know our scheme before-hand?"

Weis withdrew his hand, then looked at DeVore again and smiled. "I think my friends will be pleased enough, Major."

DeVore's face did not change immediately, but inwardly he tensed. It had been agreed beforehand that they would refer to him as *Shih* Scott. Weis, he was certain, had not forgotten that, nor had he mentioned his former Security rank without some underlying reason.

You're dead, thought DeVore, smiling pleasantly at the man as if amused by his remark. *As soon as you're expendable, you're dead.*

"I'm delighted, *Shih* Weis. Like yourself, they will be welcome any time they wish to visit. I would not ask them to fund anything they cannot see with their own eyes."

He saw the calculation at the back of Weis's eyes that greeted his comment – saw how he looked for a trap in every word of his – and smiled inwardly. At least the man was wise enough to know how dangerous he was. But his wisdom would not help him in this instance.

DeVore turned to Barrow. "And you, Under Secretary? Have you anything to add?"

Barrow had succeeded to Lehmann's old position, and whilst his contribution to this scheme was negligible, his role as leader of the Dispersionist faction in the House made his presence here essential. If he approved then First Level would approve, for he was their mouthpiece, their conscience in these times of change.

Barrow smiled sadly, then looked down. "I wish there were some other way, *Shih* Scott. I wish that pressure in the House would prove enough, but I am realist enough to know that change – real change – will only come now if we push from every side." He sighed. "Your scheme here has my sanction. My only hope is that we shall never have to use it against the Seven."

"And mine, Barrow Chen," DeVore assured him, allowing no trace of cynicism to escape into his voice or face. "Yet as you say, we must be realists. We must be prepared to use all means to further our cause. We Europeans have been denied too long."

Afterwards, alone with Berdichev and Douglas, he talked of minor things, concealing his pleasure that his scheme had their sanction and – more important – their financial backing. *Times have certainly changed*, he thought, admiring a small rose quartz snuff bottle Douglas had handed him from a cabinet to one side of the study. Three years ago they would have hesitated before speaking against the Seven; now – however covertly – they sanctioned armed rebellion.

"It's beautiful," he said. And indeed it was. A crane, the emblem of long life, stood out from the surface of the quartz, flanked by magpies, signifying good luck; while encircling the top of the bottle was a spray of peonies, emblematic of spring and wealth. The whole thing was delightful, almost a perfect work of art, yet small enough to enclose in the palm of his hand.

"One last thing, Howard."

DeVore raised his head, aware of the slight hesitation in Berdichev's voice. "What is it? Is there a problem?"

"Yes and no. That is, there is only if you feel there's one."

DeVore set the rose quartz bottle down and turned to face his friend. "You're being unusually cryptic, Soren. Are we in danger?"

Berdichev gave a short laugh. "No. It's nothing like that. It's . . . Well, it's Lehmann's son."

DeVore was silent a moment. He looked at Douglas, then back at Berdichev. "Lehmann's son? I didn't know Pietr had a son."

"Few did. It was one of his best kept secrets."

Yes, thought DeVore, *it certainly was. I thought I knew everything about you all – every last tiny little, dirty little thing – but now you surprise me.*

"Illegitimate, I suppose?"

Berdichev shook his head. "Not at all. The boy's his legal heir. On Lehmann's death he inherited the whole estate."

"Really?"

That too was news to him. He had thought Lehmann had died intestate – that his vast fortune had gone back to the Seven. It changed things dramatically. Lehmann must have been worth at least two billion yuan.

"It was all done quietly, of course, as Lehmann wished."

DeVore nodded, masking his surprise. There was a whole level of things here that he had been totally unaware of. "Explain. Lehmann wasn't even married. How could he have a son and heir?"

Berdichev came across and stood beside him. "It was a long time ago. Back when we were at college. Pietr met a girl there. A bright young thing, but unconnected. His father, who was still alive then, refused to even let Pietr see her. He threatened to cut him off without a yuan if he did."

"And yet he did, secretly. And married her."

Berdichev nodded. "I was one of the witnesses at the ceremony."

DeVore looked away thoughtfully; looked across at the window wall and at the gathering in the garden room beyond it. "What happened?"

For a moment Berdichev was quiet, looking back down the well of years to that earlier time. Then, strangely, he laughed; a sad, almost weary laugh. "You know how it is. We were young. Far too young. Pietr's father was right: the girl wasn't suitable. She ran off with another man. Pietr divorced her."

"And she took the child with her?"

The look of pain on Berdichev's face was unexpected. "No. It wasn't like that. You see, she was four months pregnant when they divorced. Pietr only found out by accident, when she applied to have the child aborted. Of course, the official asked for the father's details, saw there was a profit to be made from the information and went straight to Lehmann."

DeVore smiled. It was unethical, but then so was the world. "And Pietr made her have the child?"

Berdichev shook his head. "She refused. Said she'd kill herself first. But Pietr hired an advocate. You see, by law the child was his. It was conceived within wedlock and while she was his wife any child of her body was legally his property."

"I see. But how did hiring an advocate help?"

"He had a restraining order served on her. Had her taken

into hospital and the foetus removed and placed in a MedFac nurture unit."

"Ah. Even so, I'm surprised. Why did we never see the child? Pietr's father died when he was twenty-three. There was no reason after that to keep things secret."

"No. I suppose not. But Pietr was strange about it. I tried to talk to him about it several times, but he would walk out on me. As for the boy, well, he never lived with his father, never saw him, and Pietr refused ever to see the child. He thought he would remind him too much of his mother."

DeVore's mouth opened slightly. "He loved her, then? Even after what she did?"

"Adored her. It's why he never married again, never courted female company. I think her leaving killed something in him."

"How strange. How very, very strange." DeVore looked down. "I would never have guessed." He shook his head. "And the son? How does he feel about his father?"

"I don't know. He's said nothing, and I feel it impertinent to ask."

DeVore turned and looked directly at Berdichev. "So what's the problem?"

"For the last three years the boy has been my ward. As Pietr's executor I've handled his affairs. But now he's of age."

"So?"

"So I'd like you to take charge of the boy for a while."

DeVore laughed, genuinely surprised by Berdichev's request. "Why? What are you up to, Soren?"

Berdichev shook his head. "I've nothing to do with this, Howard. It's what the boy wants."

"The boy . . ." DeVore felt uncomfortable. He had been wrong-footed too many times already in this conversation. He was used to being in control of events, not the victim of circumstance; even so, the situation intrigued him. What could the boy want? And, more to the point, how had he heard of him?

"Perhaps you should meet him," Berdichev added hastily, glancing across at Douglas as if for confirmation. "Then you might understand. He's not . . . Well, he's not perhaps what you'd expect."

"Yes. Of course. When?"

"Would now do?"

DeVore shrugged. "Why not?" But his curiosity was intense now. Why should the boy be not what he'd expect? "Is there something I should know beforehand, Soren? Is there something strange about him?"

Berdichev gave a brief laugh. "You'll understand. You more than anyone will understand."

While Berdichev went to get the boy he waited, conscious of Douglas's unease. It was clear he had met the boy already. It was also clear that something about the young man made him intensely uncomfortable. He glanced at DeVore, then, making up his mind, gave a brief bow and went across to the door.

"I must be getting back, Howard. You'll forgive me, but my guests . . ."

"Of course." DeVore returned the bow, then turned, intrigued, wondering what it was about the boy that could so thoroughly spook the seemingly-imperturbable Douglas.

He did not have long to wait for his answer.

"Howard, meet Stefan Lehmann."

DeVore shivered. Despite himself, he felt an overwhelming sense of aversion towards the young man who stood before him. It wasn't just the shocking, skull-like pallor of his face and hair, nor the unhealthy pinkness of his eyes, both signs of albinism, but something to do with the unnatural coldness of the youth. When he looked at you it was as if an icy wind blew from the far north. DeVore met those eyes and saw through them to the emptiness beyond. But he was thinking, *Who are you? Are you really Lehmann's son? Were you really taken from your mother's womb and bred inside a nurture-unit until the world was ready for you?*

Red in white, those eyes. Each eye a wild, dark emptiness amidst the cold, clear whiteness of the flesh.

He stepped forward, offering his hand to the albino but looking at Berdichev as he did so. "Our eighth man, I presume."

"I'm sorry?" Then Berdichev understood. "Ah, yes, I said I'd explain, didn't I? But you're right, of course. Stefan was the first to be briefed. He insisted on it. After all, he's responsible for sixty per cent of the funding."

DeVore looked down at the hand that held his own. The fingers were long, unnaturally thin, the skin on them so clear it seemed he could see right through them to the bone itself. But the young man's grip was firm, his skin surprisingly warm.

He looked up, meeting those eyes again, suddenly curious; wanting to hear the boy speak.

"So. You want to stay with me a while?"

Stefan Lehmann looked at him – looked through him – then turned and looked across at Berdichev.

"You were right, Uncle Soren. He's like me, isn't he?"

DeVore laughed, uncomfortable, then let go the hand, certain now. The boy's voice was familiar – unnaturally familiar. It was Pietr Lehmann's voice.

★ ★ ★

The albino was standing behind where he was sitting, studying the bank of screens, when Peskova came into the room. DeVore saw how his lieutenant hesitated – saw the flicker of pure aversion, quickly masked, that crossed his face – before he came forward.

"What is it, Peskova?"

DeVore sat back, his eyes narrowed.

Peskova bowed, then glanced again at the albino. "There's been unrest, *Shih* Bergson. Some trouble down on Camp Two."

DeVore looked down at the desk. "So?"

Peskova cleared his throat, self-conscious in the presence of the stranger. "It's the Han woman, Overseer. Sung's wife. She's been talking."

DeVore met his lieutenant's eyes, his expression totally unreadable. "Talking?"

Peskova swallowed. "I had to act, *Shih* Bergson. I had to isolate her from the rest."

DeVore smiled tightly. "That's fine. But you'll let her go now, eh? You'll explain that it was all a mistake."

Peskova's mouth opened marginally then closed without a sound. Bowing deeply, and with one last, brief look at the albino, he turned and left, to do at once what the Overseer had ordered.

"Why did you tell him that?"

DeVore turned and looked at Lehmann's son. He was eighteen, but he seemed ageless, timeless. Like death itself.

"To make him do as I say, not as he thinks he should do."

"And the woman?"

DeVore smiled into that empty, mask-like face. He had no need to answer. The boy knew already what would happen to the woman.

★ ★ ★

The moon was huge and monstrous in the darkness: a full, bright circle, like a blind eye staring down from nothingness. Si Wu Ya looked up at it and shivered, anxious now. Then, as the rope tightened again, tugging at her, she stumbled on, the tops of her arms chafing where the rope bit into them.

Ahead of her Sung was whimpering again. "Be quiet!" she yelled, angry with him for his weakness, but was rewarded with the back of Teng's hand. Then Teng was standing over her, his breathing heavy and irregular, a strange excitement in his face. Groaning, the pain in her lower body almost more than she could bear, she got to her feet, then spat blood, unable to put her hand up to her mouth to feel the damage he had done to her.

Ahead lay the water-chestnut fields, glimmering in the reflected light from Chung Kuo's barren sister.

We are cursed, she thought, staggering on, each step sending a jolt of pain through her from arse to abdomen. *Even Teng and Chang. Even Peskova and that bastard Bergson. All cursed. Every last one of us. All of us fated to go this way; stumbling on in darkness, beneath the gaze of that cold, blind eye.*

She tried, to laugh but the sound died in her before it reached her lips. Then, before she realised it, they had stopped and she was pushed down to the ground next to Sung, her back to him.

She lay there, looking about her, the hushed voices of the four men standing nearby washing over her like the senseless murmur of the sea.

Smiling, she whispered to her husband. "The sea, Sung. I've never seen the sea. Never really seen it. Only on vidcasts . . ."

She rolled over and saw at once that he wasn't listening. His eyes were dark with fear, his hands, bound at his sides like her own, twitched convulsively, the fingers shaking uncontrollably.

"Sung . . ." she said, moved by the sight of him. "My sweet little Sung . . ."

She wanted to reach out and hold him to her, to draw him close and comfort him, but it was too late now. All her love for him, all her anguish welled up suddenly, overwhelming her.

"Kuan yin!" she said softly, tearfully. "Oh, my poor Sung. I didn't mean to be angry with you. Oh, my poor, poor darling. I didn't mean . . ."

Teng kicked her hard in the ribs, silencing her.

"Which one first?"

The voice was that of the simpleton, Seidemann. Si Wu Ya breathed slowly, deeply, trying not to cry out again, letting the pain wash past her, over her; trying to keep her mind clear of it. In case. Just in case . . .

She almost shook her head; almost laughed. In case of

what? It was done with now. There was only pain ahead of them now. Pain and the end of pain.

Peskova answered. "The woman. We'll do the woman first."

She felt them lift her and take her over to the low stone wall beside the glimmering field of water-chestnuts. The woman, she thought, vaguely recognising herself in the words. Not Si Wu Ya now, no longer Silk Raven, simply "the woman".

She waited, the cold stone of the wall pushed up hard against her breasts, her knees pushing downward into the soft, moist loam, while they unfastened the rope about her arms. There was a moment's relief, a second or two free of pain, even of thought, then it began again.

Teng took one arm, Chang the other, and pulled. Her head went down sharply, cracking against the top of the wall, stunning her.

There was a cry followed by an awful groan, but it was not her voice. Sung had struggled to his feet and now stood there, only paces from where the Overseer's man, Peskova was standing, a big rock balanced in both hands.

Sung made a futile struggle to free his arms, then desisted. "Not her," he pleaded. "Please gods, not her. It's me you want. I'm the thief, not her. She's done nothing. Nothing. Kill me, Peskova. Do what you want to me, but leave her be. Please gods, leave her be . . ." His voice ran on a moment longer, then fell silent.

Teng began to laugh, but a look from Peskova silenced him. Then, with a final look at Sung, Peskova turned and brought the rock down on the woman's upper arm.

The cracking of the bone sounded clearly in the silence. There was a moment's quiet afterwards, then Sung fell to his knees, vomiting.

Peskova stepped over the woman and brought the heavy stone down on the other arm. She was unconscious now. It was a pity, that; he would have liked to have heard her groan again, perhaps even to cry out as she had that night when The Man had played his games with her.

He smiled. Oh yes, they'd all heard that. Had heard and found the echo in themselves. He looked across at Sung. Poor little Sung. Weak little Sung. All his talk meant nothing now. He was powerless to change things. Powerless to save his wife. Powerless even to save himself. It would be no fun killing him. No more fun than crushing a bug.

He brought the stone down once again; heard the brittle sound of bone as it snapped beneath the rock. So easy it was. So very, very easy.

Teng and Chang had stepped back now. They were no longer necessary. The woman would be going nowhere now. They watched silently as he stepped over her body and brought the stone down once again, breaking her other leg.

"That's her, then." Peskova turned and glanced at Sung, then looked past him at Seidemann. "Bring him here. Let's get it over with."

Afterwards he stood there beside the wall, staring at Sung's body where it lay, face down on the edge of the field of water-chestnuts. Strange, he thought. It was just like a machine. Like switching off a machine.

For a moment he looked out across the water meadow, enjoying the night's stillness, the beauty of the full moon overhead. Then he heaved the stone out into the water and turned away, hearing the dull splash sound behind him.

CHAPTER · 14

CASTING A SPELL OUT OF ICE

Kim lay on his back in the water, staring up at the ceiling of the pool. Stars hung like strung beads of red and black against the dull gold background, the five sections framed by Han pictograms. It was a copy of part of the ancient Tun Huang star map of 940 AD. According to the Han it was the earliest accurate representation of the heavens; a cylindrical projection which divided the sky into twenty-eight slices – like the segments of a giant orange.

There was a game he sometimes played, floating there alone. He would close his eyes and clear his mind of everything but darkness. Then, one by one, he would summon up the individual stars from within a single section of the Tun Huang map; would set each in its true place in the heavens of his mind, giving them a dimension in time and space that the inflexibility – the sheer flatness – of the map denied them. Slowly he would build his own small galaxy of stars. Then, when the last of them was set delicately in place, like a jewel in a sphere of black glass, he would try to give the whole thing motion.

In his earliest attempts this had been the moment when the fragile sphere had shattered, as if exploded from within; but experiment and practice had brought him beyond that point. Now he could make the sphere expand or contract along the dimension of time; could trace each separate star's unique and unrepeated course through the nothingness he had created within his skull. It gave him a strong feel for space – for the relationships and perspectives of stars. Then, when he opened his eyes again, he would see – as if for real – the fine tracery of lines that linked the bead-like stars on the Tun Huang map, and could see, somewhere beyond the dull gold surface, where their real positions lay – out there in the cold, black eternity beyond the solar system.

Kim had cleared his mind, ready for the game, when he heard the doors at the far end of the pool swing open and the wet slap of bare feet on the tiles, followed moments later by a double splash. He knew without looking who it was, and when they surfaced, moments later, close to him, acknowledged them with a smile, his eyes still closed, his body stretched out in the water.

"Daydreaming?" It was Anton's voice.

"That's right," he said, assuming a relaxed, almost lazy tone of voice. He had told no one of his game, knowing how the other boys responded to the least sign of eccentricity. Both Anton and Josef were some three years older than he and shared a tutorial class with him, so knew how brilliant he was; but brilliance inside the classroom was one thing, how one behaved outside it was another. Outside they took care to disguise all sign of what had brought them here.

At times Kim found this attitude perverse. They should be proud of what they were – proud of the gifts that had saved them from the Clay. But it was not so simple. At the back of it they were ashamed of what they were. Ashamed and guilty. They had survived, yes, but they knew that they were here on sufferance. At any moment they could be cast down again, into darkness. Or gassed, or simply put to sleep. That knowledge humbled them; bound them in psychological chains far stronger than any physical restraint. Outside the classroom they were rarely boastful.

"Are you going to see the film tonight?" Josef sculled backwards with his hands, his head tilted back, his knees bent, experimenting with his balance in the water.

Kim lifted his head and looked back at his friend, letting

his feet drift slowly down. He was nine now but, like all of them here, much smaller, lither than normal boys his age. He combed his hair back with his fingers, then gave his head a tiny shake. "What film is it?"

Anton laughed. "What do you think?"

"Ah . . ." Kim understood at once. They had been joking about it only yesterday. "Pan Chao . . ."

Pan Chao! It sometimes seemed as if half the films ever made had been about Pan Chao! He was the great hero of Chung Kuo – the soldier turned diplomat turned conqueror. In 73 AD he had been sent, with thirty-six followers, as ambassador to the King of Shen Shen in Turkestan. Ruthlessly defeating his rival for influence, the ambassador from the Hsiung Nu, he had succeeded in bringing Shen Shen under Han control. But this, his first triumph, was eclipsed by what followed. Over the next twenty-four years, by bluff and cunning and sheer force of personality, Pan Chao had brought the whole of Asia under Han domination. In 97 AD he had stood on the shore of the Caspian Sea, an army of 70,000 vassals gathered behind him, facing the great *Ta Ts'in*, the Roman Empire. The rest was history, known to every schoolboy.

For a moment the three boys' laughter echoed from the walls.

In the silence that followed, Kim asked. "Do you think he really existed?"

"What do you mean?" It was Anton who answered him, but he spoke for both the boys. How could Pan Chao not have existed? Would Chung Kuo *be* Chung Kuo were it not for Pan Chao? It would be *Ta Ts'in* instead. A world ruled by the *Hung Mao*. And such a world was an impossibility. The two boys laughed, taking Kim's comment for dry humour.

Kim, watching them, saw at once how meaningless such questions were to them. None of them shared his scepticism. They had been bewitched by the sheer scale of the world into which they had entered; a world so big and broad and rich – a world so deeply and thoroughly embedded in time – that it could not, surely, have been invented? So grateful were they to have escaped the darkness of the Clay, they were loath to question the acts and statements of their benefactors.

No, it was more than that: they had been *conditioned* not to question it.

"Forget it," he said, and realised that even in that he differed from them. They *could* forget. In fact, they found it easy to forget. But he could not. Everything – even his mistakes – were engraved indelibly in his memory, almost as if his memory had greater substance – was more *real* – than their own.

"Well?" Anton persisted. "Are you going to come? It's one we haven't seen before. About the Fall of Rome and the death of Kan Ying."

Kim smiled, amused, then nodded. "Okay, I'll . . ." He stopped.

The three boys turned in the water and looked.

The doors at the far end had swung open. Momentarily they stayed open, held there by a tall, spindly youth with long arms, a mop of unruly yellow hair and bright blue, staring eyes. It was Matyas.

"Shit!" said Josef under his breath and ducked beneath the water.

Matyas smiled maliciously then came through, followed by two other boys, smaller, much younger than himself. "Greaser" and "Sucker", Anton called them, though not in Matyas's hearing: names which captured not only the subservient nature of their relationship to Matyas but also something of their physical appearance. Greaser – his real name was Tom – had a slick, rat-like look to him, especially in the water, while Sucker, a quiet boy named Carl, had a small, puckered face dominated by thick, fleshy lips.

It was whispered that the two of them "serviced" Matyas in a most original manner; but how much of that was truth and how much it was influenced by Anton's persuasively apt names was hard to gauge. All that was certain was that the two younger boys accompanied Matyas everywhere; were shadow and mirror to his twisted image.

Kim watched Matyas lope arrogantly along the edge of the pool, his head lowered, an unhealthy smile on his thin lips, until he stood across from him. There Matyas turned and, his smile broadening momentarily, threw himself forward into the water in an ungainly dive.

Kim glanced briefly at the two boys at his side. Like him, they had tensed in the water, expecting trouble. But it was always difficult to know with Matyas. He was no ordinary bully. Nor would he have got here and stayed here had he been. No, his deviousness was part of the fabric of his clever mind. He was a tormentor, a torturer, a master of the implicit threat. He used physical force only as a last resort, knowing he could generally accomplish more by subtler means.

However, Matyas had one weakness. He was vain. Not of his looks, which, even he would admit, tended towards ugliness, but about his intelligence. In that respect he had been cock of the roost until only a year ago, when Kim had first come to the Centre. But Kim's arrival had eclipsed him. Not at once, for Kim had been careful to fit in, deferring to the older boy whenever they came into contact, but as the months passed and word spread that the new boy was something special, Kim saw how Matyas changed towards him.

Matyas surfaced directly in front of Kim, less than a forearm's length away, and shook his head exaggeratedly, sending the spray into Kim's face. Then he laughed and began to move around him in a leisurely but awkward breaststroke. Kim turned, keeping the older boy in front of him at all times.

"And how's golden boy, then?" Matyas asked quietly, looking up and sideways, one intensely blue eye fixing the nine-year-old.

Matyas himself was fifteen, almost sixteen. On his birthday, in a month's time, he would leave the Centre and begin his service in the Above, but until then he was in a kind of limbo. He had outgrown the Centre, yet the thought of losing his "position" as senior boy both frightened and angered him. *Ning wei chi k'ou mo wei niu hou*, the Han said – "Rather be the mouth of a chicken than the hindquarters of a cow" – and so it was with Matyas. He did not relish becoming a small fish once again – a "cow's arse". As a result, he had been restless these last few weeks – dangerous and unpredictable, his sarcasm tending towards open cruelty. Several times Kim had caught Matyas staring at him malevolently and knew the older boy would never forgive him for robbing him – unjustly, Matyas believed – of his intellectual crown.

It was why Matyas was so dangerous just now. It was more than jealousy or uncertainty or restlessness. He had lost face to Kim, and that loss burned in him like a brand.

Kim looked past him, noting how his followers, Tom and Carl, had positioned themselves at the pool's edge, crouched forward, watching things closely, ready to launch themselves into the water at any moment. Then he looked back at Matyas and smiled.

"*Ts'ai neng t'ung shen*," he said provocatively and heard Anton, behind him, splutter with surprise.

"Shit!" Josef exhaled softly, off to his right. "That's done it!"

Kim kept the smile on his face, trying to act as naturally as he could, but the hair on his neck had risen and he could feel a tension in his stomach that had not been there a moment earlier. *A golden key opens every door*, he had said, playing on Matyas' use of "golden". It seemed simple enough, innocuous enough, but the jibe was clear to them all. It was Kim to whom doors would open, not Matyas.

It seemed a reckless thing to say – a deliberate rubbing of salt into the open wound of Matyas' offended pride – but Kim hoped he knew what he was doing. There was no avoiding this confrontation. He had half expected it for days now. That admitted, it was still possible to turn things to his advantage. A calm Matyas was a dangerous Matyas.

Infuriated, he might prove easier to beat. And beat him Kim must, for the sake of face.

Matyas had turned in the water, facing Kim, the leering smile gone, his cheeks red, his eyes suddenly wide with anger. Kim had been right – the words acted on him like a goad. Without warning he lashed out viciously with one arm, but the weight and resistance of the water slowed his movement and made the blow fall short of Kim, who had pushed out backwards, anticipating it.

There was a loud splash as Tom and Carl hit the water behind Kim. Without a moment's hesitation Anton and Josef launched themselves into Kim's defence, striking out to intercept the two boys. As he backed away, Kim saw Anton plough into Carl and, even as the boy surfaced, thrust his head savagely down into the water again before he could take a proper breath. But that was all he saw, for suddenly Matyas was on him, struggling to push him down beneath the surface, his face blind with fury.

Kim kicked out sharply, catching Matyas painfully on the hip, then wriggled out under him, twisting away and down. He kicked hard, thrusting himself down through the water, then turned and pushed up from the floor of the pool, away from the figure high above him.

For the moment Kim had the advantage. He spent far more time in the pool than Matyas and was the better swimmer. But the pool was only so big, and he could not avoid Matyas indefinitely. Matyas had only to get a firm grip on him and he was done for.

He broke surface two body lengths from the older boy and kicked out for the steps. He had to get out of the water or Matyas would hurt him badly.

Kim grabbed the metal rungs and hauled himself up, but he had not been quick enough. Desperation and anger had made Matyas throw himself through the water to get at Kim, and as Kim's back foot lifted up out of the water, Matyas lunged at it and caught the ankle. He was ill-balanced in the water and could not hold it, but it was enough. Tripped, Kim sprawled forward, slamming his forearm painfully against the wet floor and skidding across to the wall.

Kim lay there a moment, stunned, then rolled over and sat up. Matyas was standing over him, his teeth bared, his eyes blazing, water running from him. In the water the others had stopped fighting and were watching. Carl coughed, then fell silent.

"You little cockroach," Matyas said, in a low, barely controlled voice. He jerked forward and pulled Kim to his feet, one hand gripping Kim's neck tightly, as if to snap it. "I should kill you for what you've done. But I'll not give you that satisfaction. You deserve less than that."

A huge shudder passed through Matyas. He pushed Kim down, onto his knees. Then, his eyes never leaving Kim's face, his other hand undid the cord to his trunks and drew out his penis. As they watched, it unfolded slowly, growing huge, engorged.

"Kiss it," he said, his face cruel, his voice low but uncompromising.

Kim winced. Matyas' fingers bit into his neck, forcing Kim's face down into his groin. For a brief moment he considered not resisting. Did it matter? Was it worth fighting over such a thing as face? Why not kiss Matyas' prick and satisfy his sense of face? But the thought was fleeting. Face mattered here. He could not bow to such as Matyas and retain the respect of those he lived with. It would be the rod the other boys would use to beat him. And beat him they would – mercilessly – if he capitulated now. He had not made these callous, stupid rules of behaviour, but he must live by them or be cast out.

"I'd as soon bite it," he said hoarsely, forcing the words out past Matyas' fingers.

There was laughter from the water. Matyas glared round, furious, then turned back to Kim, yanking him up onto his feet. Anger made his hand shake as he lifted Kim off the floor and turned, holding him out over the water.

Kim saw in his eyes what Matyas intended. He would

503

let him fall, then jump on him, forcing him down, keeping him down, until he drowned.

It would be an accident. Even Anton and Josef would swear to the fact. That too was how things were.

Kim tried to swallow, suddenly, unexpectedly afraid, but Matyas' fingers pressed relentlessly against his windpipe, making him choke.

"Don't, Matyas. Please don't . . ." It was Josef's voice. But none of the boys made to intercede. Things were out of their hands now. It was a matter of face.

Kim began to struggle, but Matyas tightened his grip at once, almost suffocating him. For a moment Kim thought he had died – a great tide of blackness swept through his head – then he was falling.

He hit the water gasping for breath and went under. His chest was suddenly on fire. His eyes seemed to pop. Pain lanced through his head like lightning. Then he surfaced, coughing, choking, flailing about in the water, and felt someone grab hold of him tightly. He began to struggle, then convulsed, spears of heated iron ripping his chest apart. For a moment the air seemed burnished a dull gold, flecked with tiny beads of red and black. Lights danced momentarily on the surface of his eyes, fizzling and popping like firecrackers, then the blackness surged back – a great sphere of blackness, closing in on him with the sound of great wings pulsing, beating in his head . . .

And then there was nothing.

★   ★   ★

"Have you heard about the boy?"

T'ai Cho looked up from his meal, then stood, giving the Director a small bow. "I'm sorry, *Shih* Andersen. The boy?"

Andersen huffed impatiently, then glared at the other tutors so that they looked back down at their meals. "The boy! *Kim!* Have you heard what happened to him?"

T'ai Cho felt himself go cold. He shook his head. He had been away all day on a training course and had only just arrived back. There had been no time for anyone to tell him anything.

Andersen hesitated, conscious of the other tutors listening. "In my office, T'ai Cho. Now!" Then he turned and left.

T'ai Cho looked about the table at his fellow tutors, but there were only shrugs. No one had heard anything.

Andersen came to the point at once. "Kim was attacked. This morning, in the pool."

T'ai Cho shivered, the whole of him gone cold. "Is he hurt?"

Andersen shook his head. He was clearly very angry. "Not badly. But it might have been worse. He could very easily have died. And where would we be then? It was only Shang Li-Yen's prompt action that saved the boy."

Shang Li-Yen was one of the tutors. Like all the tutors, part of his duties entailed a surveillance stint. Apparently he had noted a camera malfunction in the pool area and, rather than wait for the repair crew, had gone to investigate it personally.

"What did Tutor Shang find?"

Andersen laughed bitterly. "Six boys sky-larking! What do you think? You know how they are – they'd sooner die than inform on each other! But Shang thinks it was serious. The boy Matyas was involved. It seems he was very agitated when Shang burst in on them. He was standing at the poolside, breathing strangely, his face flushed. Kim was in the water nearby. Only the quick actions of one of the other boys got him out of the water before he went under again." Anger flared in the Director's eyes again. "Fuck it, T'ai Cho, Shang had to give him the kiss of life!"

"Where is he now?" T'ai Cho asked quietly, trying to keep his emotions in check, yet wondering how accurate Andersen's assessment of "not badly hurt" really was.

"In his room, I believe. But let me finish. We had Kim examined at once and there were marks on his throat and arms and on his right leg consistent with a fight. Matyas also had some minor bruises. But both boys claim they

505

simply fell while playing in the pool. The other boys back them up, but all six stories differ widely. It's clear none of them is telling the truth."

"And you want me to try to find out what really happened?"

Andersen nodded. "If anyone can get to the bottom of it, you can, T'ai Cho. Kim trusts you. You're like a father to him."

T'ai Cho lowered his eyes, then shook his head. "Maybe so, but he'll tell me nothing. As you said, it's how they are."

Andersen was quiet a moment, then he leaned forward across his desk, his voice suddenly much harder, colder than it had been. "Try anyway, T'ai Cho. Try hard. It's important. If Matyas was to blame I want to know. Because if he was I want him out. Kim's too important to us. We've got too much invested in him."

T'ai Cho rose from his seat and bowed, understanding perfectly. It wasn't Kim – the boy – Andersen was so concerned about, it was Kim-as-investment. Well, so be it. He would use that in Kim's favour.

* * *

Kim's room was empty. T'ai Cho felt his stomach tighten, his pulse quicken. Then he remembered. Of course. The film. Kim would have gone to see the film. He glanced at his timer. It was just after ten. The film was almost finished. Kim would be back here in fifteen minutes. He would wait.

He looked about the room, noting as ever what was new, what old. The third-century portrait of the mathematician, Liu Hui, remained in its place of honour on the wall above Kim's terminal, and on the top, beside the keyboard, lay Hui's *Chiu Chang Suan Shu*, his "Nine Chapters On The Mathematical Art". T'ai Cho smiled and opened its pages. Kim's notations filled the margins. Like the book itself, they were in Mandarin, the tiny, perfectly-formed pictograms in red, black and green inks.

506

T'ai Cho flicked through inattentively and was about to close the book when one of the notations caught his attention. It was right at the end of the book, amongst the notes to the ninth chapter. The notation itself was unremarkable – something to do with ellipses – but beside it, in green, Kim had printed a name and two dates. Tycho Brahe. 1546 – 1601.

He frowned, wondering if the first name was a play on his own. But then, what did the other mean? Bra He . . . It made no sense. And the dates? Or were they dates? Perhaps they were a code.

For a moment he hesitated, loath to pry, then set the book down and switched on the terminal.

A search of the system's central encyclopedia confirmed what he had believed. There was no entry, either on Tycho or Brahe. Nothing. Not even on close variants of the two names.

T'ai Cho sat there a moment, his fingers resting lightly on the keys, a vague suspicion forming in his head. But what if . . . ?

He shook his head. It wasn't possible. Surely it wasn't? The terminal in T'ai Cho's room was secretly "twinned" with Kim's. Everything Kim did on his terminal was available to T'ai Cho. Everything. Work files, diary, jottings, even his messages to the other boys. It seemed sneaky, but it was necessary. There was no other way of keeping up with Kim. His interests were too wide-ranging, too quicksilver to keep track of any other way. It was their only means of controlling him – of anticipating his needs and planning ahead.

But what if?

T'ai Cho typed his query quickly, then sat back.

The answer appeared on the screen at once.

"SUB-CODE?"

T'ai Cho leaned forward and typed in the dates, careful to include the spacing and the dash.

There was the briefest hesitation, then the file came up. "BRAHE, Tycho." T'ai Cho scanned it quickly. It was a

507

summary of the man's life and achievements in the manner of a genuine encyclopedia entry.

T'ai Cho sat back again, astonished, then laughed, remembering the time long before when Kim had removed the lock from his cell without their knowing. *And so again*, he thought. But this was much subtler, much more clever than the simple removal of a lock. This was on a wholly different level of evasiveness.

He read the passage through, pausing thoughtfully at the final line, then cleared the file and switched the terminal off. For a moment he sat there, staring sightlessly at the screen, then he stood up and moved away from the terminal.

"T'ai Cho?"

He turned with a start. Kim was standing in the doorway, clearly surprised to see him. He seemed much quieter than normal, on his guard. There was an er-silk scarf around his neck and his wrist was bandaged. He made no move to come into the room.

T'ai Cho smiled and sat down on the bed. "How was the film?"

Kim smiled briefly, unenthusiastically. "No surprises," he said after a moment. "Pan Chao was triumphant. As ever."

T'ai Cho saw the boy look across at the terminal, then back at him, but there was no sign that Kim had seen what he had been doing.

"Come here," he said gently. "Come and sit with me, Kim. We need to talk."

Kim hesitated, understanding at once why T'ai Cho had come. Then he shook his head. "Nothing happened this morning."

"Nothing?" T'ai Cho looked deliberately at the scarf, the bandage.

Kim smiled but said nothing.

"Okay. But it doesn't matter, Kim. You see, we already know what happened. There's a hidden camera in the ceiling of the pool. One Matyas overlooked when he

508

sabotaged the others. We saw him attack you. Saw him grab you by the throat, then try to drown you."

Still Kim said nothing, gave nothing away.

T'ai Cho shrugged then looked down, wondering how closely the scenario fitted. Was Kim quiet because it was true? Or was he quiet because it had happened otherwise? Whichever, he was certain of one thing. Matyas *had* attacked Kim. He had seen for himself the jealous envy in the older boy's eyes. But he had never dreamed it would come to this.

He stood up, inwardly disturbed by this side of Kim. This primitive, savage side that all the Clayborn seemed to have. He had never understood this aspect of their behaviour: this perverse tribal solidarity of theirs. Where they came from it was a strength, no doubt – a survival factor – but up here, in the Above, it was a failing, a fatal flaw.

"You're important, Kim. Very important. You know that, don't you? And Matyas should have known better. He's out for what he did."

Kim looked down. "Matyas did nothing. It was an accident."

T'ai Cho took a deep breath, then stood and went across to him. "As you say, Kim. But we know otherwise."

Kim looked up at him, meeting his eyes coldly. "Is that all?"

That too was unlike Kim. That hardness. Perhaps the experience had shaken him. Changed him in some small way. For a moment T'ai Cho studied him, wondering whether he should bring up the matter of the secret files, then decided not to. He would investigate them first. Find out what Kim was up to. Then, and only then, would he confront him.

He smiled and looked away. "That's all."

★ ★ ★

Back in his room T'ai Cho locked his door, then began to summon up the files, beginning with the master file, referred to in the last line of the BRAHE.

509

The Aristotle File.

The name intrigued him, because, unlike Brahe, there had been an Aristotle: a minor Greek philosopher of the fourth century BC. He checked the entry briefly on the general encyclopedia. There was less than a hundred and fifty words on the man. Like T'ai Cho, he had been a tutor, in his case to the Greek King, Alexander. As to the originality of his thinking, he appeared to be on a par with Hui Shih, a contemporary Han logician who had stressed the relativity of time and space and had sought to prove the existence of the "Great One Of All Things" through rational knowledge. Now, however, both men existed only as tiny footnotes in the history of science. Greece had been conquered by Rome and Rome by the Han. And the Han had abandoned the path of pure logic with Hui Shih.

T'ai Cho typed in the three words, then leaned back. The answer appeared on the screen at once.

"SUB-CODE?"

He took a guess. ALEXANDER, he typed, then sat back with a laugh as the computer accepted the codeword.

There was a brief pause, then the title page came up on the screen.

THE ARISTOTLE FILE
Being The True History Of Western Science

T'ai Cho frowned. What was this? Then he understood. It was a game. An outlet for Kim's inventiveness. Something Kim had made up. Yes, he understood at once. He had read somewhere how certain young geniuses invented worlds and peopled them, as an exercise for their intellects. And this was Kim's. He smiled broadly and pressed to move the file on.

Four hours later, at three bells, he got up from his seat and went to relieve himself. He had set the machine to print and had sat there, reading the copy as it emerged from the machine. There were more than two hundred pages of copy in the tray by now and the file was not yet exhausted.

T'ai Cho went through to the kitchen, the faint buzz of the printer momentarily silenced, and put on a kettle of *ch'a*, then went back out and stood there by the terminal, watching the paper spill out slowly.

It was astonishing. Kim had invented a whole history; a fabulously rich, incredibly inventive history. So rich that at times it seemed almost real. All that about the Catholic Church suppressing knowledge and the great Renaissance – was that the word? – that split Europe into two camps. Oh, it was wild fantasy, of course, but there was a ring of truth – of universality – behind it that gave it great authority.

T'ai Cho laughed. "So that's what you've been up to in your spare time, Kim Ward," he said softly, then laughed again. Yes, it made sense now. Kim had been busy re-shaping the world in his own image – had made the past the mirror of his own logical, intensely curious self.

But it had not been like that. Pan Chao had conquered *Ta Ts'in*. Rome had fallen. And not as Kim had portrayed it, to Alaric and the Goths in the fifth century, but to the Han in the first. There had been no break in order, no decline into darkness. No Dark Ages and no Christianity – Oh, and what a lovely idea *that* was: organised religion! The thought of it . . .

He bent down and took the last few sheets from the stack. Kim's tale had reached the twentieth century now. A century of war and large-scale atrocity. A century in which scientific "progress" had become a headlong flight. He glanced down the highlighted names on the page – Röntgen, Planck, Curie, Einstein, Bohr, Heisenberg, Baird, Schrödinger – recognising none of them. Each had its own sub-file, like the BRAHE. And each, he knew, would prove consistent with the larger picture.

"Remarkable!" he said softly, reading a passage about the development of radio and television. In Kim's version they had appeared only in the twentieth century – a good five centuries after the Han had really invented them. It was through such touches – by arresting some developments and accelerating others – that Kim made his story live. In his version of events, Han science had stagnated by the fourth century AD, and Chung Kuo had grown insular, until, in the nineteenth century, the Europeans – and what a strange, alien ring that phrase had; not *Hung Mao*, but "Europeans" – had kicked the rotten door of China in.

Ah, and that too. Not Chung Kuo. Kim called it China. As if it had been named after the First Emperor's people, the Ch'in. Ridiculous! And yet, somehow, strangely convincing, too.

T'ai Cho sat back, rubbing his eyes, the sweet scent of the brewing *ch'a* slowly filling the room. Yes, much of it was ridiculous. A total fantasy – like the strange idea of Latin, the language of the *Ta Ts'in*, persisting fifteen hundred years after the fall of their Empire. For a moment he thought of that old, dead language persisting through the centuries by means of that great paradox, the Church – at one and the same time the great defender and destroyer of knowledge – and knew such a world as the one Kim had dreamed up was a pure impossibility. A twisted dream of things.

While the printer hummed and buzzed, T'ai Cho examined his feelings. There was much to admire in Kim's fable. It spoke of a strong, inventive mind, able to grasp and use broad concepts. But beyond that there was something problematic about what Kim had done – something which troubled T'ai Cho greatly.

What disturbed him most was Kim's reinterpretation of the Ch'ing or, as Kim called it, the Manchu period. There, in his notion of a vigorous, progressive West and a decadent, static East was the seed of all else. That was his starting point: the focus from which all else radiated out, like some insidious disease, transforming whatever it touched. Kim had not simply changed history, he had inverted it. Turned black into white, white into black. It was clever, yes, but it was also somehow diabolical.

T'ai Cho shook his head and stood up, pained by his thoughts. On the surface the whole thing seemed the product of Kim's brighter side; a great edifice of shining intellect; a work of considerable erudition and remarkable imaginative powers. Yet in truth it was the expression of Kim's darker self; a curiously distorted image; envious, almost malicious.

Is this how he sees us? T'ai Cho wondered. Is this how the Han appear to him?

It pained him deeply, for *he* was Han; the product of the world Kim so obviously despised. The world he would replace with his own dark fantasy.

T'ai Cho shuddered and stood up, then went out and switched off the *ch'a*. No more, he thought, hearing the printer pause, then beep three times – signal that it had finished printing. No, he would show this to Director Andersen. See what the *Hung Mao* in charge made of it. And then what?

Then I'll ask him, T'ai Cho thought, switching off the light. Yes. I'll ask Kim why.

* * *

The next morning he stood before the Director in his office, the file in a folder under his arm.

"Well, T'ai Cho? What did you find out from him?"

T'ai Cho hesitated. He knew Andersen meant the matter of the fight between Kim and Matyas, yet for a moment he was tempted to ignore that and simply hand him the folder.

"It was as I said. Kim denies there was a fight. He says Matyas was not to blame."

Andersen made a noise of disbelief, then, placing both hands firmly on the desk, leaned forward, an unexpected smile lighting his features.

"Never mind. I've solved the problem anyway. I've got RadTek to take Matyas a month early. We've had to provide insurance cover for the first month – while he's under age – but it's worth it if it keeps him from killing Kim, eh?"

T'ai Cho looked down. He should have guessed

513

Andersen would be ahead of him. But for once he could take him by surprise.

"Good. But there's something else, Director."

Andersen eased himself back slowly. "Something else?"

T'ai Cho bowed and held out the folder. "Something I stumbled upon."

Andersen took the folder and opened it, taking out the stack of paper. "Cumbersome," he said, his face crinkling in an expression of distaste. He was the kind of administrator who hated paperwork. Head-Slot spoken summaries were more his thing. But in this instance there was no alternative: a summary of the Aristotle File could not possibly have conveyed its richness, let alone its scope.

Andersen read the title page, then looked up at T'ai Cho. "What is this? Some kind of joke?"

"No. It's not a joke, *Shih* Andersen. It's something Kim put together."

Andersen studied him a moment, then looked back down at the document, leafing through a few pages before stopping, his attention caught by something he had glimpsed. "You knew about this, then?"

"Not until last night."

Andersen looked up sharply. Then he gave a tiny little nod, seeing what it implied. "How did he keep the files hidden?"

T'ai Cho shook his head. "I don't know. I thought it was something you might want to investigate."

Andersen considered a moment. "Yes. Yes. It has wider implications. If Kim can keep files secret from a copy-cat system . . ." He looked back down at the stack of paper. "What exactly *is* this, T'ai Cho? I assume you've read it?"

"Yes. I've read it. But as to what it is . . ." He shrugged. "I suppose you might call it an alternative history of Chung Kuo. Chung Kuo as it might have been had the *Ta Ts'in* legions won the Battle of Kazatin."

Andersen laughed. "An interesting idea. Wasn't that in the film they showed last night?"

T'ai Cho nodded, suddenly remembering Kim's words.

"*Pan Chao was triumphant. As ever.*" In Kim's version of things Pan Chao had never crossed the Caspian. There had been no Battle of Kazatin. Instead, Pan Chao had met the *Ta Ts'in* legate and signed a pact of friendship. An act which, eighteen centuries later, had led to the collapse of the Han Empire at the hands of a few "Europeans" with superior technology.

"There's more, much more, but the drift of it is that the West – the *Hung Mao* – got to rule the world, not the Han."

The Director turned a few more pages, then frowned. "Why should he want to invent such stuff? What's the point of it?"

"As an exercise, maybe. A game to stretch his intellect."

Andersen looked up at him again. "Hmm. I quite like that. It's good to see him exercising his mind. But as to the idea itself . . ." He closed the file and pushed it aside. "Let's monitor it, eh, T'ai Cho? See it doesn't get out of hand and take up too much time. I'd say it was harmless enough, wouldn't you?"

T'ai Cho was about to disagree, but saw the look in Andersen's eyes. He was not interested in pursuing the matter. Set against the business of safeguarding his investment it was of trivial importance. T'ai Cho nodded and made to retrieve the file.

"No. Leave it with me, T'ai Cho. *Shih* Berdichev is calling on me tomorrow. The file might amuse him."

T'ai Cho backed away and made as if to leave, but Andersen called him back.

"One last thing, T'ai Cho."

"Yes, Director?"

"I've decided to bring forward Kim's socialisation. He's to start in the Casting Shop tomorrow."

"Tomorrow? Don't you think . . . ?" He was about to say he thought Kim too young, but saw that Andersen was looking at him again, that same expression in his eyes. *I have decided*, it said. *There is to be no argument.* T'ai Cho swallowed, then bowed. "Very well, *Shih* Andersen. Should I make arrangements?"

Andersen smiled. "No. It's all been taken care of. My secretary will give you the details before you leave."

T'ai Cho bowed again, humbled, then backed away.

"And T'ai Cho . . ."

"Yes, Director?"

"You'll say nothing of this file to anyone, understand?"

T'ai Cho bowed low. "Of course."

★ ★ ★

For a moment Kim studied the rust-coloured scholar's garment T'ai Cho had given him, then he looked back at his tutor. "What's this, T'ai Cho?"

T'ai Cho busied himself, clearing out his desk. "It's your work *pau*."

"Work? What kind of work?"

Still T'ai Cho refused to look at him. "You begin this morning. In the Casting Shop."

Kim was silent a moment, then, slowly, he nodded. "I see." He shrugged out of his one-piece and pulled the loose-fitting *pau* over his head. It was a simple, long-sleeved *pau* with a chest-patch giving the Project's name in pale green pictograms and, beneath that, in smaller symbols, Kim's ownership details – the contract number and the SimFic symbol.

T'ai Cho looked fleetingly across at him. "Good. You'll be going there every day from now on. From eight until twelve. Your normal classes will be shifted to the afternoon."

He had expected Kim to complain – the new arrangements would cost him two hours of his free time every day – but Kim gave no sign. He simply nodded.

"Why are you clearing your desk?"

T'ai Cho paused. The anger he had felt on finishing the Aristotle File had diminished somewhat, but still he felt resentful towards the boy. He had thought he knew him. But he had been wrong. The File had proved him wrong. Kim had betrayed him. His friendliness was like the tampered lock, the hidden files – a deception. The boy was

Clayborn and the Clayborn were cunning by nature. He should have known that. Even so, it hurt to be proved wrong. Hurt like nothing he had felt in years.

"I'm asking to be re-posted."

Kim was watching him intently. "Why?"

"Does it matter?" He could not keep the bitterness from his voice, yet when he turned and looked at Kim he was surprised to see how shocked, how hurt the boy was.

Kim's voice was small, strangely vulnerable. "Is it because of the fight?"

T'ai Cho looked down, pursing his lips. "There was no fight, Kim. You told me there was no fight."

"No." The word was barely audible.

T'ai Cho looked up. The boy was looking away from him now, his head slightly turned to the right. For a moment he was struck by how cruel he was being, not explaining why he was going. Surely the child deserved that much? Then, as he watched, a tear formed in Kim's left eye and slowly trickled down his cheek.

He had never seen Kim cry. Nor, he realised, had he ever really thought of him as a child. Not as a true child, anyway. Now, as he stood there, T'ai Cho saw him properly for the first time. Saw how fragile Kim was. A nine-year-old boy, that was all he was. An orphan. And all the family Kim had in the world was himself, T'ai Cho.

He shivered and closed the desk, then went across to Kim and knelt at his side. "You want to know why?"

Kim could not look at him. He nodded and another tear rolled slowly down his cheek. His voice was small and hurt. "I don't understand, T'ai Cho. What have I done?"

For a moment T'ai Cho was silent. He had expected Kim to be cold, indifferent to his news. But this? He felt his indignation melt and dissipate like breath, then reached out and held the boy to him fiercely.

"Nothing," he said. "You've done nothing, Kim."

The boy gave a little shudder, then turned his head slowly, until he was looking into T'ai Cho's face. "Then why? Why are you going away?"

T'ai Cho looked back at him, searching the child's dark eyes for evidence of betrayal – for some sign that this was yet another act – but he saw only hurt there and incomprehension.

"I've seen your secret files," he said quietly. "Brahe and Aristotle."

There was a small movement in the dark pupils, then Kim dropped his eyes. "I see." Then he looked up again, and the expression of concern took T'ai Cho by surprise. "Did it hurt you, reading them?"

T'ai Cho shivered, then answered the boy honestly. "Yes. I wondered why you would create a world like that."

Kim's eyes moved away, then back again. "I never meant to hurt you. You must believe me, T'ai Cho. I'd never deliberately hurt you."

"And the File?"

Kim swallowed. "I thought Matyas would kill me. He tried, you see. That's why I left the note in the book. I knew that if I was killed you'd find it. But I didn't think . . ."

T'ai Cho finished it for him. "You didn't think I'd find it before you were dead, is that it?"

Kim nodded. "And now I've hurt you . . ." He reached out and gently touched T'ai Cho's face, stroking his cheek. "Believe me, T'ai Cho. I wouldn't hurt you. Not for anything." Tears welled in his big dark eyes. "I thought you knew. Didn't you see it? Don't you understand it, even now?" He hesitated, a small shudder passing through his frail, thin body, then spoke the words almost in a whisper. "I love you, T'ai Cho."

T'ai Cho shivered, then drew Kim against him once more. "Then I'd best stay, hadn't I?"

*   *   *

The Casting Shop was a long, wide room with a high ceiling. Along its centre stood six tall, spiderish machines with squat bases and long, segmented arms; each machine three times the height of a grown man. To the sides were a series of smaller machines, no two of them the same, but all resembling to some degree or other their six identical elders. Between the big machines in the centre and the two rows of smaller ones at the sides ran two gangways, each with an overhead track. Young men moved between the machines, readying them, or stood in groups, talking casually in these last few minutes before the work bell rang.

Kim stood in the doorway, looking in, and felt at once a strange affinity with the machines. He smiled and looked up at T'ai Cho. "I think I'll like it here."

The Supervisor was a Han; a small man named Nung, who bowed and smiled a lot as he led them through to his office at the far end of the Casting Shop. As he made his way between the machines, Kim saw heads turn and felt the eyes of the young men on his back, but his attention was drawn to the huge, mechanical spiders that stretched up to the ceiling.

"What are they?" Kim asked the Supervisor once the partition door had slid shut behind them.

Supervisor Nung smiled tightly and looked to T'ai Cho. "Forgive my unpreparedness, *Shih* T'ai. I was only told of this yesterday evening."

It was clear from the manner in which he ignored Kim's question that he felt much put out by the circumstances of Kim's arrival.

"What are they?" T'ai Cho asked, pointedly repeating Kim's question. "The boy would like to know."

He saw the movement in Nung's face as he tried to evaluate the situation. Nung glanced at Kim, then gave the slightest bow to T'ai Cho. "Those are the casting grids, *Shih* T'ai. One of the boys will give a demonstration in a while. Kim . . ." – he smiled insincerely at the boy – "Kim will be starting on one of the smaller machines."

"Good." T'ai Cho took the papers from the inner pocket of his er-satin jacket and handed them to the Supervisor. "You must understand from the outset that while Kim is not to be treated differently from any other boy, he is also not to be treated badly. The boy's safety is of paramount importance. As you will see, Director Andersen has written a note under his own hand to this effect."

He saw how mention of the Director made Nung dip his head, and thought once more how fortunate he was to work in the Centre, where there were no such men. Yet it was the way of the Above, and Kim would have to learn it quickly. Here status counted more than mere intelligence.

The qualms he had had in Andersen's office returned momentarily. Kim was too young to begin this. Too vulnerable. Then he shrugged inwardly, knowing it was out of his hands. *Mei fa tzu*, he thought. *It's fate*. At least there was no Matyas here. Kim would be safe, if nothing else.

When T'ai Cho had gone, the Supervisor led Kim halfway down the room to one of the smallest and squattest of the machines and left him in the care of a pleasant-looking young Han named Chan Shui.

Kim watched the partition door slam shut, then turned to Chan Shui, his eyebrows forming a question.

Chan Shui laughed softly. "That's Nung's way, Kim. You'll learn it quickly enough. He does as little as he can. As long as we meet our production schedules he's happy. He spends most of his day in his room, watching the screens. Not that I blame him, really. It must be dreadful to know you've reached your level."

"His level?"

Chan Shui's eyes widened with surprise. Then he laughed again. "I'm sorry, Kim. I forgot. You're from the Clay, aren't you?"

Kim nodded, suddenly wary.

Chan Shui saw this and quickly reassured him. "Don't get me wrong, Kim. What you were – where you came from – that doesn't worry me like it does some of them round here." He looked about him pointedly, and Kim realised that their conversation was being listened to by the boys at the nearby machines. "No. It's what you are that really counts. And what you could be. At least, that's what my father always says. And he should know. He's climbed the levels."

Kim shivered. *Fathers* . . . Then he gave a little smile and reached out to touch one of the long, thin arms of the machine.

"Careful!" Chan Shui warned. "Always make sure the machine's switched off before you touch it. They've cut-outs built into their circuits, but they're not absolutely safe. You can get a nasty burn from them."

"How does it work?"

Chan Shui studied Kim a moment. "How old are you, Kim?"

Kim looked back at him. "Nine. So they say."

Chan Shui looked down. He himself was eighteen, the youngest of the other boys sixteen. Kim looked five, maybe six at most. But that was how they were. He had seen one or two of them before, passing through. But this was the first time he had been allocated one to "nursemaid".

The dull, hollow tones of the work bell filled the Shop. At once the boys stopped talking and made their way to their machines. There was a low hum as a nearby machine was switched on, then a growing murmur as others added to the background noise.

"It's rather pleasant," said Kim, turning back to Chan Shui. "I thought it would be noisier than this."

The young Han shook his head, then leaned forward and switched their own machine on. "They say they can make these things perfectly silent, but they found that it increased the number of accidents people had with them. If it hums a little you can't forget it's on, can you?"

Kim smiled, pleased by the practical logic of that. "There's a lesson in that, don't you think? Not to make things too perfect."

Chan Shui shrugged, then began his explanation.

The controls were simple and Kim mastered them at once. Then Chan Shui took a slender phial from the rack beside the control panel.

"What's that?"

521

Chan Shui hesitated, then handed it to him.

"Be careful with it. It's ice. Or at least, the constituents of ice. It slots in there." He pointed to a tiny hole low down on the control panel. "That's what these things do. They spin webs of ice."

Kim laughed, delighted by the image. Then he looked down at the transparent phial, studying it, turning it in his fingers. Inside was a clear liquid with a faint blue colouring. He handed it back, then watched closely as Chan Shui took what he called a "template" – a thin card stamped with a recognition code in English and Mandarin – and slotted it into the panel. The template was the basic computer-programme that gave the machine its instructions.

"What do we do, then?" Kim asked, his expression as much as to say, *Is that all there is to it?* It was clear he had expected to control the grid manually.

Chan Shui smiled. "We watch. And we make sure nothing goes wrong."

"And does it?"

"Not often."

Kim frowned, not understanding. There were something like a hundred boys tending the machines in the Casting Shop, when a dozen, maybe less, would have sufficed. It made no sense.

"Is all of the Above so wasteful?"

Chan Shui glanced at him. "Wasteful? What do you mean?"

Kim stared at him a moment longer, then saw he didn't understand. This, too, was how things were. Then he looked around and saw that many of the boys working on the smaller machines wore headwraps, while those on the central grids chatted, only a casual eye on their machines.

"Don't you get bored?"

Chan Shui shrugged. "It's a job. I don't plan to be here forever."

Kim watched as the machine began to move, the arms to extend, forming a cradle in the air. Then, with a sudden hiss of air, it began.

It was beautiful. One moment there was nothing in the space between the arms, the next something shimmered into existence. He shivered, then clapped his hands together in delight.

"Clever, eh?" said Chan Shui, smiling at him, then lifting the wide-bodied chair from the grid with one hand. Its perfectly transparent shape glimmered wetly in the overhead light. "Here," he said, handing it to Kim.

Like most of the furniture in the Above, it weighed nothing. Or almost nothing. Yet it felt solid, unbreakable.

Kim handed the chair back, then looked at the spiderish machine with new respect. Jets of air from the segmented arms had directed the fine, liquid threads of ice as they shot out from the base of the machine, but the air had only defined the shape.

He looked at Chan Shui, surprised that he didn't understand – that he had so readily accepted their explanation for why the machines hummed. They did not hum to stop their operators forgetting they were switched on; the vibration of the machine had a function. It set up standing waves – like the tone of a bell or a plucked string, but perfect, unadulterated. The uncongealed ice rode those waves, forming a skin, like the surface of a soap bubble, but a million times stronger because it was formed of thousands of tiny corrugations – the menisci formed by those standing waves.

Kim saw the beauty of it at once. Saw how East and West had come together here. The Han had known about standing waves since the fifth century BC: had understood and utilised the laws of resonance. He had seen an example of one of their "spouting bowls" which, when its handles were rubbed, had formed a perfect standing wave – a shimmering, perfect hollow cone of water that rose a full half *ch'i* above the bowl's bronze rim. The machine, however – its cybernetics, its programming, even its basic engineering – was a product of Western science. The Han had abandoned those paths millennia before the West had found and followed them.

Kim looked around, watching as forms shimmered into

life in the air on every side. Tables, cupboards, benches and chairs. It was like magic. Boys moved between the machines, gathering up the objects and stacking them on the slow-moving collection trays which came along the gangways, hung on cables from the overhead tracks. At the far end, beyond the door where Kim had entered, was the paint shop. There the furniture was finished – the permapaint bonded to the ice – before it was packed for despatch.

At ten they took a break. The refectory was off to their right, with a cloakroom leading off from it. There were toilets there and showers. Chan Shui showed Kim around, then took him back to one of the tables and brought him *ch'a* and a soypork roll.

"I see they've sent us a dwarf this time!"

There was a loud guffaw of laughter. Kim turned, surprised, and found himself looking up into the face of a beefy, thick-set youth with cropped brown hair and a flat nose. A *Hung Mao*, his pale, unhealthy skin heavily pitted. He stared down at Kim belligerently, the mean stupidity of his expression balanced by the malevolence in his eyes.

Chan Shui, beside Kim, leaned forward nonchalantly, unimpressed by the newcomer's demeanour.

"Get lost, Janko. Go and play your addle-brained games on someone else and leave us alone."

Janko sniffed disdainfully. He turned to the group of boys who had gathered behind him and smiled, then turned back, looking at Kim again, ignoring Chan Shui.

"What's your name, rat's arse?"

Chan Shui touched Kim's arm. "Ignore him, Kim. He'll only trouble you if you let him." He looked up at the other boy. "*Se li nei jen*, eh, Janko?" *Stern in appearance, weak inside*. It was a traditional Han rebuttal of a bully.

Kim looked down, trying not to smile. But Janko leaned forward threateningly. "None of your chink shit, Chan. You think you're fucking clever, don't you? Well, you'll get yours one day, I promise."

Chan Shui laughed and pointed to the camera over the

counter. "Best be careful, Janko. Uncle Nung might be watching. And you'd be in deep shit then, wouldn't you?"

Janko glared at him, infuriated, then looked down at Kim. "Fucking little rat's arse!"

There was a ripple of laughter from behind him, then Janko was gone.

Kim watched the youth slope away, then turned back to Chan Shui. "Is he always like that?"

"Most of the time." Chan Shui sipped his *ch'a*, thoughtful a moment, then he looked across at Kim again and smiled. "But don't let it get to you. I'll see he doesn't worry you."

* * *

Berdichev sat back in Director Andersen's chair and surveyed the room. "Things are well, I hope?"

"Very well, excellency," Andersen answered with a bow, knowing that Berdichev was referring to the boy, and that he had no interest whatsoever in his own well-being.

"Good. Can I see the boy?"

Andersen kept his head lowered. "I am afraid not, *Shih* Berdichev. Not at the moment, anyway. He began socialisation this morning. However, he will be back by one o'clock, if you'd care to wait."

Berdichev was silent a moment, clearly put out by this development. "Don't you feel that might be slightly premature, Director?" He looked across and met Andersen's eyes challengingly.

Andersen swallowed. He had decided to say nothing of the incident with the boy Matyas. It would only worry Berdichev unduly. "Kim is a special case, as you know. He requires different handling. Normally we wouldn't dream of sending a boy out so young, but we felt there would be too much of an imbalance were we to let his intellectual development outstrip his social development too greatly."

He waited tensely. After a while Berdichev nodded. "I see. And you've taken special precautions to see he'll be properly looked after?"

Andersen bowed. "I have seen to matters personally,

Shih Berdichev. Kim is in the hands of one of my most trusted men, Supervisor Nung. He has my personal instructions to take good care of the boy."

"Good. Now tell me, is there anything I should know?"

Andersen stared back at Berdichev, wondering for a moment if it was possible he might know something. Then he relaxed. "There is one thing, Excellency. Something you might find very interesting."

Berdichev lifted his chin slightly. "Something to do with the boy, I hope."

Andersen nodded hastily. "Yes. Of course. It's something he produced in his free time. A file. Or rather, a whole series of files."

Berdichev's slight movement forward revealed his interest. "What kind of file?"

Andersen smiled and turned. On cue his secretary appeared and handed him the folder. He had added the subfiles since T'ai Cho had brought the matter to his attention, and the stack of paper was now almost twice the size it had been. He turned back to Berdichev, then crossed the room and deposited the folder on the desk in front of him before withdrawing with a bow.

"The Aristotle File," Berdichev read aloud, lifting the first few sheets from the stack. "Being The True History Of Western Science." He laughed. "Says who?"

Andersen echoed his laughter. "It is amusing, I agree. But fascinating, too. His ability to fuse ideas and extrapolate. The sheer breadth of his vision . . ."

Berdichev silenced him with a curt gesture of his hand, then turned the page, reading. After a moment he looked up. "Would you bring me some *ch'a*, Director?"

Andersen was about to turn and instruct his secretary, when Berdichev interrupted him. "I'd prefer it if you did it yourself, Director. It would give me a few moments to digest this material."

Andersen bowed deeply. "Whatever you say, Excellency."

Berdichev waited until the man had gone, then sat back,

removing his glasses and wiping them on the old-fashioned cotton handkerchief he kept for that purpose in the pocket of his satin jacket. Then he picked up the sheet he had been reading and looked at it again. There was no doubt about it. This was it. The real thing. What he had been unearthing fragments of for the last fifteen or twenty years. Here it was – complete!

He felt like laughing, or whooping for joy, but knew hidden cameras were watching his every movement, so he feigned disinterested boredom. He flicked through, as if only casually interested, but behind the mask of his face he could feel the excitement course through him, like fire in his blood.

Where in the gods' names had Kim got all this? Had he invented it? No. Berdichev dismissed the thought instantly. Kim *couldn't* have invented it. Just a glance at certain details told him it was genuine. This part about Charlemagne and the Holy Roman Empire, for instance. And here, this bit about the subtle economic influence of the Medici family. And here, about the long-term effects of the great sea battle of Lepanto – the deforestation of the Mediterranean and the subsequent shift of the shipbuilding industry to the Baltic where wood was plentiful. Yes. He had seen shards of this before – bits and pieces of the puzzle – but here the picture was complete.

He shuddered. Andersen was a fool. And thank the gods for it. If he had known what he had in his possession. If he'd had but the slightest inkling . . .

Berdichev looked down, stifling the laugh that came unbidden to his lips. Gods, he felt elated! He flicked back to the title page again. *The Aristotle File*. Yes! That was where it all started. Back there in the Yes/No logic of the Greek.

He tapped the stack of papers square, then slid them back into the folder. What to do? What to do? The simple possession of such information was treasonous. Was punishable by death.

There was a knock on the door.

"Come in!"

Andersen bowed, then brought the tray over to the desk and set it down on one side, well away from the folder. Then he poured the *ch'a* into a bowl and held it out, his head slightly lowered.

Berdichev took the bowl and sipped, then set it down.

"How many people know about this, Director?"

Andersen allowed himself a tiny smile. "Four, including yourself and Kim, Excellency."

"The boy's tutor . . . T'ai Cho, isn't it? I assume he's the other?"

"That's correct, Excellency. But I've already instructed him to mention it to no one else."

"Good. Very good indeed. Because I want you to destroy the files at once. Understand?"

Andersen's smile drained away, replaced by a look of utter astonishment. He had thought Berdichev would be pleased. "I'm sorry?"

"I want all evidence of this foolishness destroyed at once, understand me, Director? I want the files closed and I want you to warn Kim not to indulge in such idle fancies any longer." He banged the file violently with the flat of his hand, making Andersen jump. "You don't realise how much this worries me. I already have several quite serious misgivings about the whole venture, particularly regarding the matter of the boy's safety. I understand, for instance, that there was a fight, and that you've had to send one of the older boys away. Is that right?"

Andersen blanched then bowed, wondering who Berdichev's spy was. "That is so, Excellency."

"Yes . . . And now this." Berdichev was silent a moment, the threat implicit in his silence. The purpose of his visit today had been to make the latest stage payment on Kim's contract. There had been no mention of the matter so far, but now he came to it. "My feeling is that the terms of our contract have not been fully met. You are in default, Director Andersen. You have failed to adequately protect my investment. In the circumstances, I feel I must insist on some . . . compensation. A reduction of the stage payment, perhaps?"

Andersen lowered his head even further. His voice was apologetic. "I am afraid I have no discretion, *Shih* Berdichev. All contractual matters have to be referred to the board."

He glanced at Berdichev, expecting anger, but the Head of SimFic was smiling. "I know. I spoke to them before I came here. They have agreed to a reduction of one hundred thousand yuan." He held out the document for Andersen to take. "I understand it requires only your signature to make it valid."

Andersen shivered, suppressing the anger he felt, then bowed and, taking the brush from the stand, signed the paper.

"We'll verify this later," Berdichev said, his smile fading. "But with regard to the files, you'll do as I say. Yes?"

"Of course, Excellency."

He reached for the folder, but Berdichev held on to it. "I'll keep this copy. I'd like my company psychiatrists to evaluate it. They'll destroy it once they've done with it."

Andersen looked at him, open-mouthed, then hastily backed off a pace. "I'm sure . . ." he began, then fell quiet and bowed his head.

"Good," said Berdichev, reaching across for the *ch'a* kettle. "Then bring another bowl, Director. I believe you have some money to collect from me."

★ ★ ★

"And how's little rat's arse this morning?"

Kim kept his eyes on his plate, ignoring the figure of Janko, who stood beside him. Chan Shui had gone off to the toilets saying he would only be a moment, but Janko must have seen him go and had decided this was his chance.

He felt Janko's hand on his shoulder, squeezing, not hard as yet, but enough to make him feel uncomfortable. He shrugged it off, then reached out to take the biscuit. But

Janko beat him to it. Laughing, he crammed it in his mouth, then picked up Kim's bowl to wash it down.

Kim went very still. He heard Janko's cronies laugh, then heard the unmistakable sound of the boy hawking into his bowl.

Janko set it down in front of him with a bang, then poked him hard. "Drink up, rat's arse! Got to keep our strength up, haven't we?"

The inane laughter rang out once again from beyond Janko. Kim looked at the bowl. A nasty greenish gob of spit floated on the surface of the *ch'a*.

Kim stared at it a moment, then half turned in his seat and looked up at Janko. The youth was more than half as big as him again. He would have made Matyas look a weakling by comparison. But unlike Matyas, he wasn't dangerous. He was merely flabby and stupid and a touch ridiculous.

"Go fuck yourself, windbag," Kim said, loud enough for Janko alone to hear.

Janko bellowed and grabbed at Kim, half lifting him from his seat, then thrust the bowl at his face. "Drink, you little piece of shit! Drink, if you know what's good for you!"

"Put him down!"

Janko turned. Chan Shui had come back and was standing there on the far side of the room. Several of the boys glanced up at the cameras nervously, as if expecting Nung to come in and break things up. But most of them knew Nung well enough to guess he'd be jerking off to some PornoStim, not checking up on what was happening in the refectory.

Janko released Kim, then, with an exaggerated delicacy, let the bowl fall from his fingers. It shattered on the hard tile floor.

"Best clear it up, rat's arse. Before you get into trouble."

Kim looked across at Chan Shui, a faint smile on his lips, then turned and went to the counter to get a brush and pan.

Chan Shui was standing there when he came back. "You don't have to do that, Kim."

Kim nodded, but got down anyway and started collecting the shattered pieces. He looked up at Chan Shui. "Why don't they make these out of ice?"

Chan Shui laughed, then knelt down and began to help him. "Have you ever tasted *ch'a* from an ice bowl?"

Kim shook his head.

"It's revolting. Worse than Janko's phlegm!" Chan Shui leaned closer, whispering. "What did you say to him, Kim? I've never seen Janko so mad."

Kim told him what he had said.

Chan Shui roared with laughter, then grew quiet. "That's good. But you'd better watch yourself from now on, Kim. He's a fool and a windbag, yes, but he doesn't want to lose face. When I go for a pee, you come too. And fuck what these bastards think about that."

* * *

When T'ai Cho met him, just after twelve, he had two guards with him.

"What's happening?" Kim asked when they were outside.

T'ai Cho smiled reassuringly. "It's okay, Kim. Just a measure the Director is insisting on from now on. He's concerned for your safety outside the Centre, that's all."

"So we've got them every day?"

T'ai Cho shook his head. "No. It's not necessary for the Casting Shop, but we're going somewhere special this afternoon, Kim. There's something I want to show you. To set the record straight, if you like."

"I don't understand you."

"I know. But you will. At least, much better after this."

They went up another twelve decks – a full one hundred and twenty levels – until they were in the heart of the Mids, at Level 181. Stepping out of the lift Kim noticed at once how different things were from the level where the Casting

Shop was. It was cleaner here, tidier, less crowded; even the pace at which people moved seemed more sedate, more orderly.

They waited at a Security barrier while a guard checked their permits, then went inside. An official greeted them and took them along a corridor, then up a narrow flight of stairs into a viewing gallery, its front sealed-off from the hall below by a pane of transparent ice.

In the hall below five desks were set out in a loose semi-circle. In front of them were a number of chairs, grouped in a seemingly random fashion. Five grey-haired Han sat behind the desks, a small comset – or portable computer – in front of each.

"What is this?" Kim asked quietly.

T'ai Cho smiled and indicated two seats at the front of the gallery. When they were sitting, he turned to Kim and explained. "This is a deck tribunal, Kim. They have them once a week throughout the levels. It is the Han way of justice."

"Ah . . ." Kim knew the theory that lay behind Han justice, but he had never seen it in action.

T'ai Cho leaned forward. "Note how informal it all is, Kim. How relaxed."

"A family affair," Kim said, rather too patly.

"Yes," T'ai Cho said at once. "It is exactly that."

They watched the hall fill up, until not a chair was free and latecomers had to squat or sit on the floor. Then, without anyone calling anything to order, it began. One of the elders leaned forward across his desk and began to speak, his voice rising above the background murmur. The other voices dropped away until the elder's voice sounded alone.

He was reading out the circumstances of the first case. Two cousins had been fighting. The noise had woken neighbours who had complained to Deck Security. The elder looked up, his eyes seeking out the two Han youths. They stood at once.

"Well? What have you to say for yourselves?"

Beside them an old man, grey-haired like the elders, his long beard plaited, stood and addressed the elder.

"Forgive me, *Hsien* Judge Hong, but might I speak? I am Yung Pi-Chu, Head of the Yung family."

"The tribunal waits to hear from you, *Shih* Yung."

The old man bowed his thanks, then brought his two great-nephews out into the space in front of the desks and had them strip off their tops. Their backs were striped from recent punishment. He made the two youths turn, showing the elders first and then the gathered audience. Then, bidding them return to their seats, he faced the elders.

"As you see, respected elders, my great-nephews have been punished for their thoughtlessness. But the matter of my neighbours' inconvenience remains. In that regard I propose to offer compensation of six hundred yuan, to be shared equally amongst the complainants."

Hsien Judge Hong bowed, pleased, then looked out past the old man. "Would the complainants stand."

Three men got to their feet and identified themselves.

"Are you willing to accept *Shih* Yung's generous compensation?"

All three nodded. Two hundred yuan was a generous figure.

"Good. Then the matter is settled. You will pay the clerk, *Shih* Yung."

Without preamble, and before the old man had returned to his seat, another of the elders began reading out the circumstances of the second case. Again it involved two young men, but this time they had been charged with unsocial behaviour. They had vandalised a row of magnolia trees while drunk.

At the elder's request the two men stood. They were *Hung Mao*, their dress neat, respectable, their hair cut in the Han style.

"Well?" the elder asked. "What have you to say for yourselves?"

The two men hung their heads. One looked momentarily

533

at the other, who swallowed, then looked up, acting as spokesman for the two.

"Respected elders, we make no excuses for our behaviour and are deeply ashamed of what we did. We accept full responsibility for our actions and would fully understand if the respected elders should punish us to the full severity for what we did. However, we ask you to consider our past exemplary record and would humbly submit the testimony of our employers as to our conduct. We propose to pay for the damage in full and, in respect of the damage to the harmony of the community we ask that we should be given a month's community service."

The elder looked briefly at his fellows, who all nodded, then faced the two youths again.

"We have read the submissions of your employers and take into account your past exemplary conduct. Your shame is clear and your repentance obvious. In the circumstances, therefore, we accept your proposals, your term of public service to commence in two weeks' time. However, should you come before this tribunal a second time on a similar charge it will result in immediate demotion. You understand?"

Both men bowed deeply and looked to each other briefly.

Two more cases followed. The first was an accusation of theft. Two men claimed that another had robbed them, but a Security film showed they had falsely accused the man. The two men, protesting violently, found themselves held by Security guards and sentenced. They were to be demoted five decks. Amidst wailing from the two men and their families and rejoicing from the falsely accused man and his, the permits of the two were taken from them and they were led away.

The fourth case involved a charge of violent assault by a middle-aged man on his wife's father. Both families were in court, and for the first time there was real tension in the air. The matter was in dispute and it seemed there was no way to resolve it. Both men were deeply respected members of the community. Both swore their version of events was the truth. There was no Security film to solve the matter this time and no impartial witnesses.

The elders conferred a moment, then *Hsien* Judge Hong called the two men forward. He addressed the older of them first.

"What began this dispute?"

The old man bristled and pointed contemptuously at the younger. "He insulted my family."

Judge Hong was patient. It was, after all, a matter of face. For the next half hour he slowly, cleverly, drew the threads of circumstance out into the daylight. At the core of it all lay a trivial remark – an off-hand comment that the younger man's wife was like her mother, idle. It had been said heatedly, carelessly, in the course of a disagreement about something entirely different, but the old woman had taken great offence and had called upon her husband to defend her honour.

"Do you not both think that things have got out of hand? You, *Shih* T'eng," he looked at the younger man, "Do you really believe your mother-in-law an idler? Do you really have so little respect for your wife's mother?"

Shih T'eng lowered his head, then shook it. "No, Elder Hong. She is a good, virtuous woman. What I said, I said heatedly. It was not meant. I . . ." He hesitated, then looked at his father-in-law. "I unreservedly apologise for the hurt I caused his family. I assure him, it was not intended."

Judge Hong looked at the old man and saw at once, from his bearing, that he was satisfied. Their dispute was at a close. But the Elder had not finished with the two men. He leaned forward angrily.

"I am appalled that two such good, upright men should have come before me with such a . . . a petty squabble. Both of you should feel deeply shamed that you let things come to this."

Both men lowered their heads, chastened. The hall was deathly silent as Judge Hong continued.

"Good. In the circumstances I fine you each five hundred

yuan for wasting the time of this tribunal." He looked at the two men sternly. "If I hear any more of this matter I shall have you up before us again. And that, I guarantee you, *chun tzu*, will be to neither of your likings."

The two "gentlemen" bowed deeply and thanked the court, then went meekly to the clerk to pay their fines.

T'ai Cho turned to his pupil. "Well, Kim? Do you still think the Han way so bad?"

Kim looked down, embarrassed. T'ai Cho's discovery had made things difficult between them. It would have been easier had he been able to say, *No. I did not invent the world you read about*, but sometimes the truth was stranger than a lie and far harder to accept.

"I have never thought the Han way a bad way, T'ai Cho. Whatever you believe, I find you a highly civilised people."

T'ai Cho stared at him a moment, then shrugged and looked back down into the body of the hall. The crowd had dispersed now and only the five elders remained, talking amongst themselves and tying up any remaining items of business. T'ai Cho considered a moment, then smiled and looked back at Kim.

"There are no prisons in Chung Kuo. Did you realise that, Kim? If a man wishes to behave badly he may do so, but not among those who wish to behave well. Such a man must find his own level. He is demoted."

He paused, then nodded to himself. "It is a humane system, Kim. The most severe penalties are reserved for crimes against the person. We might be traders, but our values are not wholly venal."

Kim sighed. It was a direct reference to something in the File – to the greedy and corrupt *Hoi Po*, or Hoppos, as the Europeans knew them, who had run the Canton trade in the nineteenth century. He had not meant his comment to stand for all the Han, but saw how T'ai Cho could easily mistake it for such.

Damn Matyas! he thought. And damn the man who left the files for me to find and piece together!

T'ai Cho continued. "There are exceptions, naturally.

Treason against the T'ang, for instance, is punishable by death. The traitor and all his family, to the third generation. But ours is a fair system, Kim. It works for those who wish it to work. For others there are other levels of existence. In Chung Kuo a man must find his own level. Is that not fair?"

He was tempted to argue, to ask whether it was fair for those born into the Net, or into the Clay like himself, but after all the damage he had done with the File he felt it would be churlish to disagree. He looked past T'ai Cho at the elders.

"What I saw today, that seemed fair, T'ai Cho."

T'ai Cho looked at Kim and smiled. It was not a full capitulation, but still, there was good in the boy. A great deal of good. When he smiled, for instance, it was such a fierce, sincere smile – a smile from the very depths of him. T'ai Cho sniffed and nodded to himself. He realised now he had taken it too personally. Yes, he understood it now. Kim had been talking of systems. Of philosophies. He had let the abstract notion carry him away. Even so, he had been wrong.

"About the files, Kim. I had to tell the Director."

Kim looked across at him, his eyes narrowed. "And?"

T'ai Cho lowered his head. "And he has ordered their destruction, I'm afraid. We must forget they ever were. Understand?"

Kim laughed, then bowed his head. "I am ordered to forget?"

T'ai Cho looked up at him, sudden understanding in his eyes. Then, unexpectedly, he laughed. "Why, yes. I never thought . . ."

Forget, Kim thought, then laughed again, a deep, hearty laughter. As if I *could* forget.

CHAPTER · 15

THE SCENT OF PLUM BLOSSOM

The big man came at Chen like an automaton, swinging and punching, kicking and butting, making Chen duck and bob and jump to evade the furious rain of blows. Back and back he was pushed until his shoulders thudded painfully against the wall. He ducked then kicked off from the wall, head first, aiming for the stomach of the big man. But he was too slow. The big man parried him, linking both hands to form a shield and thrust him down into the floor. Then, before Chen could get his breath, he was yanked up by one huge hand and pinned against the wall.

Chen chopped down against the arm desperately, but it was like hitting an iron bar. The arm quivered but held him firm. Chen swallowed and met the big man's eyes, conscious of the power there, the control.

The big man drew back his free arm, his fist forming a phoenix eye – a *feng huang yen ching* – the knuckle of the first finger extended, ready to strike and shatter Chen's skull.

Chen closed his eyes, then laughed. "It's no good, my friend. I have no counter to your strength and skill."

Karr held him there a moment longer, his fist poised as if to strike, then relaxed, letting Chen slide down onto the floor again.

"Then we must work at it until you do."

Chen squatted on his haunches, getting his breath. He looked up at Karr, smiling now. "I can't see why. There's only one of you, *Shih* Karr. And you're on my side. For which I thank the gods."

Karr's sternness evaporated. "Maybe now, Chen, but one day they'll make machines like me. I guarantee it. Things like those copies that came from Mars. Even now, I'd warrant, they're working on them somewhere. I'd rather find an answer now than wait for them to come, wouldn't you, Kao Chen?"

They had spent the morning working out extensively, first with stick and sword and spear – *kuai chang shu, tao shu* and *ch'iang shu* – then with their bare hands, concentrating on the "hand of the wind" – *feng shou kung fu* – style that Karr favoured. It was the first time the two men had seen each other in several months and they had enjoyed the friendly tussle, but Karr had not asked Chen here simply to polish his skills.

After they had showered they sat in the refectory, a large jug of hot sweet almond *ch'a* on the table between them – a delicacy Chen's wife, Wang Ti, had introduced them to.

"How is young Jyan?" Karr asked. "I've meant to visit, but the T'ang has kept me busy these past months."

Chen smiled and bowed his head slightly, but his eyes lit at the mention of his son. "Jyan is well. Only four and already he knows all the stances. You should see how well he executes the *kou shih*. Such balance he has! And when he kicks he really kicks! You should see the bruises on my legs!"

Karr laughed. "And Wang Ti?"

Chen looked down, his smile broadening. "Wang Ti is Wang Ti. Like the sun she is there each morning. Like the moon she shines brilliantly at night."

Again the big man laughed, then grew quiet. "I hear you have news, Chen. The very best of news."

Chen looked up, surprised, then smiled broadly. "Who told you, *Shih* Karr? Who ruined my moment? I wanted to tell you myself!"

Karr tilted his head. "Well . . . Let's just say I heard, eh? You know me, Chen. There's little that escapes my notice."

"Or your grasp!"

Both men laughed.

"Anyway," said Karr, lifting his bowl in salute. "Here's to your second child! May he be strong and healthy!"

Chen raised his bowl. "Thank you, my friend." He sipped, then looked directly at Karr. "This is very pleasant, *Shih* Karr. We do this too little these days. But tell me, why am I here? Is there a job for me? Something you want me to do?"

Karr smiled. "There might be."

"Might be? Why only might?"

The big man looked down, then reached across and filled his bowl again. "I've a lead on DeVore. I think I know where he is."

Chen laughed, astonished. "DeVore? We've found him?"

"Maybe. I've trailed him three years since he evaded us at Nanking spaceport. Three years, Chen. I've tracked down eight of the ten men who helped him get away that day, but not one of them knew a thing, not one of them helped me get a fraction closer to the man I wanted. But now things have changed – now I think I have him."

Chen frowned. "Then what's the problem? Why don't you just go in and finish him off?"

Karr sniffed deeply. "It's difficult. The T'ang wants him alive, you see. He wants DeVore to stand trial. If possible to provide us with conclusive evidence against the other Dispersionists."

"I see. Even so, what stops you from taking him?"

"The House. The stink they would make if we went in and took the wrong man."

Chen shook his head. Still he didn't understand.

"The man we believe to be DeVore is an overseer. Understand me, Chen? On one of the big East European plantations. And that's a House appointment. If we go barging in there mistakenly the Dispersionists would have a field day attacking us for our heavy-handedness. And things are critical at the moment. The House is finely balanced and the Seven daren't risk that balance, even for

DeVore. So we must be certain this Overseer Bergson is our man."

"How certain?"

"As certain as a retinal print could make us."

Chen looked down into his *ch'a* and laughed. "And how do we do that?" He looked back up at Karr. "Do you think DeVore will sit there calmly while we check him out?"

Karr hesitated, then he gave a tiny laugh and nodded, meeting his friend's eyes again. "Maybe. Maybe that's *just* what he'll do. You see, Chen, that's where I thought you might come in."

★ ★ ★

Tolonen watched his nine-year-old daughter run from the sea, her head thrown back, exhilarated. Behind her the waves broke white on the dark sand. Beyond, the distant islands were dim shapes of green and brown in the haze. Jelka stood there at the water's edge, smoothing her small, delicate hands through her hair. Long, straight hair like her mother's, darkened by the water. Her pure white costume showed off her winter tan, her body sleek, childlike.

She saw him there and smiled as she came up the beach towards him. He was sitting on the wide, shaded patio, the breakfast things still on the table before him. The Han servant had yet to come and clear it all away. He set down his book, returning her smile.

"What's it like?" he called to her as she came near.

"Wonderful!" Her laughter rippled in the air. "You should join me. It would do you good."

"Well . . ." He shrugged. Maybe he would.

She sprawled in the lounger opposite him. A young animal, comfortable in her body. Unself-conscious. He looked at her, conscious more than ever that she was the image of her mother. Especially now, like this.

He had met her mother on an island much like this. On the far side of the world from where he now sat. One summer almost thirty years before.

He had been a General even then. The youngest in the

541

service of the Seven and the ablest. He had gone to Gote-borg to see his father's sister, Hanna. In those days he made the trip twice a year, mindful of the fact that Hanna had looked after him those times his mother had been ill.

For once he had had time to stay more than a day, and when Hanna had suggested they fly up to Fredrikstad and visit the family's summer home, he had agreed at once. From Fredrikstad they had taken a motor cruiser to the islands south of the City.

He had thought they would be alone on the island; he, Hanna, and her two sons. But when the cruiser pulled up at the jetty, he saw that there were others there already. He had gone inside, apprehensive because he had not been warned there would be other guests, and was delighted to find not strangers, but his oldest friend, Pietr Endfors, there in the low-ceilinged front cabin, waiting to greet him.

Endfors had married a girl from the far north. A cold, elegant beauty with almost-white hair and eyes like the arctic sea. They had an eight-year-old daughter, Jenny.

It had not happened at once. At first she was merely the daughter of an old friend; a beautiful little girl with an engaging smile and a warmth her mother seemed to lack. From the start, however, she had taken to him and by that evening was perched immovably in his lap. He liked her from that first moment, but even he could not tell how attached he would become.

When Pietr and his wife had died eight years later, he had become Jenny's guardian. Four years later he had married her. He had been thirty years her senior.

He returned from the bitter-sweet reverie and focused on his daughter.

"You've not been listening to a word, have you, father?"

He laughed and shook his head. "Just reminiscing." He sat up in his chair and reached across to feel the *ch'a* kettle. It was lukewarm. He grunted and then shouted for the servant.

"I was just saying. We ought to go home. It seems time. Don't you think?"

He looked sharply at her, then, confused by what she had said, shook his head. It was not so much a negative as an acknowledgment that he had not considered the matter. *Go home? Why? Why was it time?*

"Are you tired of all this?" he asked, almost incredulous. She seemed so happy here. So carefree.

She seemed reluctant to admit what she felt, but finally she answered him. "I'm happy enough. But it's not me I'm thinking of, it's you. This place is no good for you. You're going soft here. Wasting away before your time." She looked up at him, real love, real concern in her young eyes. "I want you to be as you were. I don't want you to be like this. That's all . . ."

He couldn't argue with that. He felt it in himself. Each day it seemed to get worse. Sitting here with nothing to do. Ordered to do nothing. He felt more and more restless as the months passed; more and more impotent. That was the worst of exile.

"What can I do? I have to be here."

She could feel the bitterness in his voice, see the resignation in his hunched shoulders. It hurt her to be witness to such things. But for once she could help him. For once she had balm for his wounds.

"Where is that bloody servant!" he cried out, anger and frustration boiling over into his words, his actions. He turned in his chair and yelled for service. She waited for him to finish, then told him that she had sent the servant away earlier.

"I want to talk to you."

He looked at her, surprised and amused by her actions, by the grown-up tone of her voice. "Talk, eh? What about?"

She looked away, stared out at the sea, the distant islands of the Kepulauan Barat Daya. "This is beautiful, isn't it? The colours of the sky and sea. But it's the wrong kind of beauty. It doesn't . . ." She struggled for some way of expressing what she was feeling, then shook her head.

He knew what she meant, though. It *was* beautiful. But

543

it was a soft, pearled beauty. It didn't touch his soul the way the fjords, the mountains touched him. The unvarying warmth, the mists, the absence of seasonal change – these things irked him.

"I wish . . ." he began, then shook his head firmly. There was no use wishing. Li Shai Tung had exiled him here. He would live out his days on this island. It was his payment for disobedience. Exile.

"What do you wish?" she asked. She had stood and was waiting at his side, looking at him, her head on the level of his own.

He reached out a hand and caressed her cheek, then let his hand rest on her bare shoulder. The skin was cool and dry.

"Why should I wish for anything more than what I have?" He frowned as he looked at her, thinking that he might have been killed for what he had done; and then she would have been alone, an orphan. Or worse. He had acted without understanding that. In his anger he had gambled that the T'ang would act as he had. Yet it pained him greatly now to think what might have been: the hurt he could have caused her – maybe even her death.

She seemed to sense this. Leaning forward she kissed his brow, his cheek. "You did what you had to. Li Shai Tung understood that."

He laughed at that. "Understood? He was furious!"

"Only because he had to be."

He removed his hand, leaned back in his chair. "What is this, Jelka? What have you heard?"

It was her turn to laugh. "You were sleeping when he came. I didn't want to disturb you. I know how bad the nights are for you." She was looking at him in a strangely mature way; more mother than daughter for that moment.

He reached out and held her firmly. "Who, Jelka? Who has come?"

She reached up and took his hands from where they lay on her shoulders, then held them, turning them over. Strong, fine hands.

"Well?" he prompted, impatient now, but laughing too. "Tell me who it is!"

"General Nocenzi."

"Ah . . ." He sat back heavily.

"He's in the house. Shall I bring him?"

He looked up at her distractedly, then nodded. "Yes. It will be good to see Vittorio again."

He watched her go, then let his gaze drift out over the surface of the sea. Nocenzi. It could mean only one thing. They had come for his head.

Friends had kept him informed. They had told him of the growing demand for "justice" in the Lehmann case. Lately there had been rumours that the House was about to indict him for the murder. Well, now the T'ang had succumbed to that pressure. And he, Tolonen, would be made to account for what he'd done.

He shivered, thinking of Jelka, then turned to see that Nocenzi was already there, standing on the sand by the corner of the house, his cap under his arm.

"Knut . . ."

The two men embraced warmly and stood there a moment simply looking at each other. Then Tolonen looked down.

"I know why you've come."

Nocenzi laughed strangely. "You've read my orders, then, General?"

Tolonen met his eyes again, then shook his head. "Just *Shih* Tolonen. You're General now, Vittorio."

Nocenzi studied him a while, then smiled. "Let's sit, eh? Jelka said she'd bring fresh *ch'a*."

They sat, not facing each other, but looking outward at the sea.

Nocenzi noted the book that lay face down on the table. "What are you reading, Knut?"

Tolonen handed him the old, leather-bound volume and watched him smile. It was Sun Tzu's *Chan Shu*, his "Art of War", dating from the third century BC. The Clavell translation.

545

"They say the Ch'in warriors were mad. They ran into battle without armour."

Tolonen laughed. "Yes, Vittorio, but there were a million of them. Nor had they ever tasted defeat."

There was a moment's tense silence, then Tolonen turned to face his old friend. "Tell me straight, Vittorio. Is it as I fear? Am I to pay for what I did?"

Nocenzi looked back at him. "Lehmann deserved what you did to him. There are many who believe that."

"Yes," Tolonen insisted. "But am I to pay?"

Tolonen's successor gazed back at the man he had served under for almost a quarter of a century and smiled. "You said you knew why I had come, Knut. But you were wrong. I haven't come for your head. I've come because the T'ang has asked to see you."

★ ★ ★

Li Yuan cried out and woke in the semi-darkness, his heart beating wildly, the feeling of the dark horse beneath him still vivid, the scent of plum blossom filling his nostrils.

He shivered and sat up, aware of the warm stickiness of his loins. Sweat beaded his brow and chest. The satin sheets were soaked about him. He moaned softly and put his head in his hands. Fei Yen . . . He had been riding with Fei Yen. Faster and faster they had ridden, down, down the long slope until, with a jolt and a powerful stretching motion he could feel in his bones even now, his horse had launched itself at the fence.

He threw the sheets back and, in the half light, looked down at himself. His penis was still large, engorged with blood, but it was flaccid now. With a little shudder he reached down and touched the wetness. The musty smell of his own semen was strong, mixed with the lingering scent of plum blossom. He sniffed deeply, confused, then remembered. The silk she had given him lay on the bedside table, its perfume pervading the air of his room.

He looked across at the broad ivory face of the bedside clock. It was just after four. He stood, about to go through and shower, when there were noises outside the door, then a muted knocking.

Li Yuan threw the cover back, then took a robe from the side and drew it on.

"Come!"

Nan Ho stood in the doorway, head bowed, a lantern in one hand.

"Are you all right, Prince Yuan?"

Nan Ho was his body servant; his head man, in charge of the eight juniors in his household-within-a-household.

"It was . . ." He shuddered. "It was only a dream, Nan Ho. I'm fine."

He glanced round at the bed, then, slightly embarrassed by the request, added, "Would you bring clean sheets, Nan Ho. I . . ."

He turned away sharply, realising he was holding Fei Yen's silk in his hand.

Nan Ho looked to him then to the bed and bowed. "I'll be but a moment, Prince Yuan." Then he hesitated. "Is there . . ." He moved his head slightly to one side, as if finding difficulty with what he was about to say. "Is there anything I can arrange for you, Prince Yuan?"

Li Yuan swallowed, then shook his head. "I don't understand you, Nan Ho? What might you arrange at this hour?"

Nan Ho came into the room and closed the door behind him. Then, in a softer voice, he said, "Perhaps the Prince would like Pearl Heart to come and see to him?"

Pearl Heart was one of the maids. A young girl of fifteen years.

"Why should I want Pearl Heart . . . ?" he began, then saw what Nan Ho meant and looked away.

"Well, Highness?"

He held back the anger he felt, keeping his voice calm; the voice of a prince, a future T'ang.

"Just bring clean sheets, Nan Ho. I'll tell you when I need anything else."

Nan Ho bowed deeply and turned to do as he was bid.

Only when he was gone did Li Yuan look down at the wet silk in his hand and realise he had wiped himself with it.

* * *

Chen stood there in the queue, naked, waiting his turn. The sign over the doorway read DECONTAMI-NATION. The English letters were black. Beneath them, in big red pictograms was the equivalent Mandarin. Chen looked about him, noting that it was one of the rare few signs here that had an English translation. The Lodz Clearing Station handled more than three hundred thousand people a day, and almost all of them were Han. It was strange that. Unexpected.

Beyond the doorway were showers and disinfectant baths: primitive but effective solutions to the problem of decontaminating millions of workers every week. He shuffled along, ignoring his nakedness and the nakedness of those on every side of him, resisting the temptation to scratch at the skin patch beneath his left ear.

A *Hung Mao* guard pushed him through the doorway brutally and, like those in front of him, Chen bowed his head and walked on slowly through the stinging coldness of the showers, then down the steps into the bath, holding his breath as he ducked underwater.

Then he was outside, in daylight, goose-pimples on his flesh. A guard thrust clothes into his arms – a loin-cloth, a drab brown overall and a coolie hat – and then he was queueing again.

"Tong Chou?"

He answered to his alias and pushed through to the front to collect his ID card and his pack, checking briefly to make sure they had not confiscated the viewing-tube. Then he found a space and, holding the card between his teeth, the pack between his feet, got dressed quickly.

He followed the flow of people through, one of thou-sands, identically dressed. At the end of a long walled roadway the crowd spilled out into a wide arena. This was the embarkation area. Once more the signs were all in

Kuo-yu, or Mandarin. Chen turned and looked back, seeing, for the first time, the wall of the City towering over them, stretching away whitely into the distance to either side. Then he looked down, searching for the pictogram he had learned – *Hsia*, the crab. Seeing it, he made his way across and up the ramp, stopping at the barrier to show his ID.

The train was packed. He squeezed in, smiling apologetically as he made his way through, then turned, waiting.

He had not long to wait. The train was crowded and extremely stuffy, the smell of disinfected bodies overpowering, but it was fast. Within the hour he was at *Hsia* Plantation, stumbling from the carriage, part of the crowd that made its way slowly down the ramp and out into the open.

There was a faint, unpleasant scent to the air, like something stale or overcooked. Chen looked up, then looked down again quickly, his eyes unused to the brightness. The sun blazed down overhead; a huge, burning circle of light – bigger, much brighter than he remembered it. Ahead of him the land stretched away forever – flat and wide and green. Greener, much greener, than he'd ever imagined.

He smiled. Wang Ti would have liked to have seen this. She had always said she would love to live outside, beneath the sun and the stars, her feet planted firmly on the black earth. As their forefathers had once lived.

For a moment Chen's smile broadened, thinking of her and Jyan and the child to come, then his face cleared as he put all thought of her behind. He was Tong Chou now and had no family. Tong Chou, demoted from the levels. Tong Chou. Until this was over.

The crowd slowed. Another queue formed. Chen waited, patient, knowing that patience alone would carry him through the coming days. When he came to the barrier a guard babbled at him in *Kuo-yu*. He shook his head.."I'm new," he said. "I only speak English. You know, *Ying Kuo*."

The guard laughed and turned to say something to one

of his fellows, again in Mandarin. The other guard laughed and looked Chen up and down, then said something that made the first guard laugh crudely. They were both *Hung Mao*.

He handed the guard his permit, then waited while the man scrutinised it thoroughly and, with a show of self-importance, used his comset to double-check. He seemed almost disappointed to find nothing wrong with it.

"Take care, *Han*," the guard said, thrusting his card back at him.

He moved on, keeping his head down, following the flow.

"*Chiao shen me ming tsu?*"

Chen looked up, expecting another guard, but the young man who had addressed him wore the drab brown of a field worker. Moreover, he was *Hung Mao*. The first *Hung Mao* he had seen here who was not a guard.

He looked the youth up and down, then answered him. "I'm sorry. My Mandarin is very poor."

The young man had a long face and round, watery blue eyes. His hair was dark but wispy and his mouth was crooked, as if he had suffered a stroke. But he was far too young, too fit, to be suffering from heart troubles. The crooked mouth smiled and the eyes gave Chen the same scrutiny Chen had given him.

"I'm Pavel," the youth said, inclining his head the slightest degree. "I was asking what they called you."

"Tong Chou," Chen answered, then realised how easily it had come to his lips.

Pavel took one of his hands and turned it over, examining it. "I thought so," he said, returning it. "You're new to this."

Chen smiled. There were things that could not be faked, like callouses on the palms. "I'm a refugee from the levels," he said. "When my father died I got into debt over his funeral. Then I got in with a shark. You know how it is."

Pavel looked at him a moment, his watery blue eyes

trying to figure him; then his crooked mouth smiled again. "Come on, Tong Chou. You'll need someone to show you the ropes. There's a spare bed in our hut. You can kip down there."

Pavel set off at once, moving away from the slow moving column of new recruits. Only as he turned did Chen notice something else about him. His back was hunched, the spine bent unnaturally. What Chen had taken for a bow of politeness was the young man's natural gait. Chen followed him quickly, catching up with him. As they walked along the dirt path Pavel began to talk, explaining how things worked on the plantation.

"How did you know I was new?"

Pavel glanced sideways at him. "The way you walk. The way you're wearing those clothes. The way you squint against the sun. Oh, a hundred little signs. What were you up above? You've strong hands. They're not an office-worker's hands."

"But not a peasant's either?"

Pavel laughed, throwing his head back to do so. Chen, watching him, decided he liked the youth. He looked a dull-wit, but he was sharp. Very sharp.

"And where are you from, Pavel?"

Pavel sniffed, then looked away across the vast plain. "Me? I was born here."

"Here?"

Pavel smiled crookedly and nodded. "Here. In these fields."

Ahead of them was a break in the green. A long black line that cut right across their path. The dirt track led out onto a wooden bridge. Halfway across the bridge Chen stopped, looking down.

Pavel came back to him and looked where he was looking, as if expecting to see something unusual in the water. "What is it?" he asked.

Chen laughed. "Nothing. It's nothing." But he had realised that he had never seen water flow like this before. Taps and baths and pools, that was all he had ever seen. It had made him feel strange. Somehow incomplete.

Pavel looked at him, then laughed. "What did you say you were?"

They went on. The field they had crossed had been empty, but beyond the bridge it was different. Long lines of workers – five hundred, maybe a thousand to each line – were stretched out across the vast green, hunched forward, huge wicker baskets on their backs, their coolie hats making them seem a thousand copies of the same machine. Yet each was a man or woman – a person, like himself.

Where the path met another at a crossroads, a group of men were lounging by an electric cart. They were dressed differently, in smart black trousers and kingfisher blue jackets. They wore black, broad-rimmed hats with silk tassels hanging from the back and most of them had guns – *Deng* rifles, Chen noted – strapped to their shoulders. As Chen and Pavel approached, they seemed to stir expectantly.

Pavel touched Chen's arm, his voice a whisper. "Keep your head down and keep walking. Don't stop unless they specifically order you to."

Chen did as Pavel said. Even so, two of the men detached themselves from the group and came across onto the path, blocking their way. They were big, brutal-looking men. Han, both of them.

"Who's this, Pavel?" one of them asked.

The youth kept his head lowered. "This is Tong Chou, *Shih* Teng. I am taking him to register."

Teng laughed caustically and looked at his fellow. "You're quite a bit out of your way then, Pavel. Registration is back there, where you've just come from. Or have they moved it since I was last there?"

There was laughter from the men by the cart.

Chen glanced at the youth and saw how he swallowed nervously. But he wasn't finished yet. "Forgive me, *Shih* Teng. That would be so normally. But Tong Chou is a replacement. He has been drafted to fill the place left by Field Supervisor Sung's unfortunate death. I was told to take him direct to Acting Supervisor Ming. Ming is to fill out a special registration form."

Teng was silent a moment, then he stepped aside. "Get moving, then. I want to see you both in the fields within the hour, understand me?"

Pavel dipped his head, then hurried on. Chen followed, keeping his eyes on the ground.

"Who were they?" Chen asked, when they were out of hearing.

"Teng Fu and Chang Yan. They're the Overseer's men. Chang's fairly docile. Teng's the one you need to watch. He's a vicious piece of work. Thinks he's something special. Fortunately he knows very little about how this place works. But that's true of most of them. There's not one of those guards has any brains. Providing you keep your nerve you can convince them of anything."

Chen nodded. "You were frightened, though. You took a risk for me. I'm grateful for that, Pavel."

Pavel breathed deeply. "Not for you, so much, Tong Chou, but for all of us. They say the spirits of the dead have no shadows, but the death of Field Supervisor Sung and his wife have left a darkness here that no man can dispel."

Chen looked thoughtfully at him. "I see."

"I'll tell you sometime," the youth said, glancing at him.

They walked on. Up ahead of them, maybe ten *li* or so in the distance, the straight line of the horizon was broken by a building; a huge, three-tiered pagoda.

"What's that?" Chen asked after a while.

Pavel didn't even bother to look up. "That? That's the Overseer's House."

As he watched a faint speck lifted from the fields close by the building and came towards them. A Security cruiser. The sound of its engines followed seconds later; muted at first, but growing louder by the moment. Minutes later it passed overhead, the shadow of the big craft sweeping across the fields.

Chen looked back at the Overseer's House and nodded

to himself. So that was where he was. Well, *Shih* Bergson, he thought; I'll find out all I can about this place. Then I'll pay you a visit. And find out if you are who we think you are.

* * *

DeVore looked down from the window of the craft as it swept south over the fields, the fingers of one hand absently tracing the surface of the object in the other.

"What is that?"

The voice was cold; chillingly free of intonation, but DeVore was used to it by now. It was the voice of his dead friend. He turned and looked at Lehmann's albino son, then handed him the tiny rose quartz snuff bottle.

"It was a first meeting gift from Douglas. He saw me admiring it."

Lehmann examined it, then handed it back. "What did you give him?"

"I sent him a copy of Pecorini and Shu's *The Game Of Wei Chi*. The Longman edition of 1929."

Lehmann was silent a moment, considering. "It seems an odd gift. Douglas doesn't play."

"No, but he should. All men – men of any ability – should play." DeVore tucked the bottle away in the pocket of his jacket. "Do you play, Stefan?"

Lehmann turned his head slowly, until he was facing DeVore. The albino's dead eyes seemed to stare straight through him. "What do you think?"

DeVore smiled coldly. "I think you do. I'd say you were a good player. Unorthodox, but good."

Lehmann made no reaction. He turned his head back, facing the front of the craft.

Like a machine, DeVore thought, chilled and yet strangely delighted by the boy. *I could make something of you, given time.*

They were flying down to the Swiss Wilds, to meet Weis and see how work was going on the first of the fortresses.

DeVore looked back out the window. Two figures

trudged along one of the paths far below. Field workers, their coolie hats making them seem like two tiny, black *wei chi* stones against the criss-cross pattern of the fields. Then they were gone and the craft was rising, banking to the right.

He had been busy since the meeting at Douglas's. The business with Lehmann's son had taken him totally by surprise, but he had recovered quickly. Using his contacts in Security he had had the mother traced; had investigated her past and discovered things about her that no one in her immediate circle knew. His man had gone to her and confronted her with what they knew.

And now she was his. A handle. A way, perhaps, of controlling Stefan Lehmann should he prove troublesome.

DeVore smiled and turned back to the youth. "Perhaps we should play a game some time?"

Lehmann did not even look at him. "No."

DeVore studied the youth a moment, then looked away. So he understands, he thought. He knows how much of a man's character is reflected in the mirror of the board, the stones. Yet his refusal says a lot about him. He's more cautious than his father. Colder. More calculating. Yes, I bet he's very good at the game. It's a shame he won't play. It would have been a challenge.

The journey took them less than an hour. Weis met them in the landing dome, furred and gloved, anxious to complete his business and get away. DeVore saw this and decided to keep him – to play upon his fears, his insecurity.

"You'll eat with us, I hope, *Shih* Weis?"

He saw Weis's inner hesitation; saw how he assessed the possible damage of a refusal and weighed it against his own discomfort. A banker. Always, first and foremost, a banker.

"Well?" DeVore insisted, loading the scales against refusal.

"I have a meeting at six."

It was just after one. DeVore took his elbow lightly and turned him towards the exit. "Then we have plenty of time, eh? Come. I don't know about you, *Shih* Weis, but I'm famished."

They were high up, almost thirteen thousand feet, and it was cold outside the dome of the landing platform, the sun lost behind thick cloud cover. Landeck Base was some way above them on the mountainside, a vast, flattened hemisphere, its brilliant whiteness blending with the snow and ice surrounding it. Beneath its cover, work had begun already on the fortress.

"It's a beautiful sight, don't you think, Major?" Weis said as he stepped out onto the snow, his breath pluming in the chill air.

DeVore smiled, then looked about him. "You're right, Weis," he said, noting how Weis had used his real identity yet again. "It is beautiful." But he knew Weis was talking about the base up ahead of them, not the natural beauty of their surroundings.

They were on the eastern slope of a great glacial valley – a huge trench more than two *li* deep and one across. It ran north–west, ringed on all sides by the brutal shapes of mountains. Cloud obscured the distance, but it could not diminish the purity of the place. This land was untouched, elemental. He felt at home here.

He stopped in the snow field just beneath the Base and studied the great, shield-like dome, thinking of the seven great Security garrisons ringing the Swiss Wilds, like seven black stones placed on a giant board. The T'ang's handicap. He laughed softly. Well, now he had placed the first white stone. The great game had begun.

Guards wearing full snow camouflage let them inside, then searched them. DeVore submitted patiently, smiling at the guard when he handed back the tiny snuff bottle. Only Weis seemed upset by the routine.

"Is this really necessary?" he huffed irritably, turning to DeVore as the soldier continued his body search.

"It's necessary, I assure you, *Shih* Weis. One small device could tear this place apart. And then your backers would be very angry that we had not taken such precautions." He laughed. "Isn't that how you bankers think? Don't you always assume the worst possible case and then act accordingly?"

Weis bowed his head, ceding the point, but DeVore could see he was still far from happy.

A door from the Secure Area led out into the dome itself. Mobile factories had been set up all over the dome floor and men were hard at work on every side – manufacturing the basic equipment for the Base. But the real work was being done beneath their feet – in the heart of the mountain. Down there they were hewing out the tunnels and chambers of Landeck Base from the solid rock. When it was finished there would be no sign from the air.

They crossed the dome floor. On the far side was an area screened off from the rest of the dome. Here the first of DeVore's recruits were temporarily housed. Here they slept and ate and trained, until better quarters were hewn from the rock for them.

DeVore turned to Weis and Lehmann, and indicated that they should go through. "We'll be eating with the men," he said, and saw – as he had expected – how discomfited Weis was by the news. He had thought that other arrangements – special arrangements – had been made.

DeVore studied him, thinking, Yes, you like your comforts, don't you, Weis? And all this – the mountains, the cold, the busy preparations – mean very little by comparison. Your heart's in Han opera and little boys, not revolution. I'll watch you, Weis. Watch you like a hawk. Because you're the weakest link. If things go wrong, you'll be the first to break.

He went inside after them and was greeted by the duty officer. Normally the man would have addressed him as Major, but, seeing Weis, he merely bowed deeply, then turned and led them across to the eating area.

Good, thought DeVore. Though it matters little now, I like a man who knows when to hold his tongue.

They sat on benches at one of the scrubbed wooden tables.

"Well, *Shih* Weis? What would you like to eat?"

The cook bowed and handed Weis the single sheet menu. DeVore kept his amusement hidden, knowing what was on the paper. It was all very basic fare – soldier's food – and he saw Weis's face crinkle with momentary disgust. He handed the sheet back and turned to DeVore.

"If you don't mind, I'd rather not. But you two go ahead. I'll tell you what's been happening."

DeVore ordered, then turned and looked at Lehmann.

"I'll have the same."

"Good." He looked back at Weis. "So. Tell me, *Shih* Weis, what *has* been happening?"

Weis leaned forward, lowering his voice. "There's been a problem."

"A problem?"

"Duchek. He's refused to pass the funds through the plantation accounts."

"I see. So what have you done?"

Weis smiled broadly, clearly pleased by his own ingenuity. "I've re-routed them – through various Security ordnance accounts."

DeVore considered it a moment, then smiled. "That's good. Much better, in fact. They'd never dream we'd use their own accounts."

Weis leaned back, nodding. "That's what I thought."

Because of the vast sums involved they had had to take great care in setting up the routes by which the money got to DeVore. The finances of Chung Kuo were closely-knit and any large movement was certain to be noted by the T'ang's Ministry, the *Hu Pu*, responsible for monitoring all capital transfers and ensuring the T'ang received the fifty per cent due him on the profit of each and every transaction.

It had been decided from the outset that it would be safest to be open about the movements. Any attempt to siphon away sums of this size would be noticed and investigated, but normal movements – if the T'ang received his cut from them – would not be commented upon. It had meant that the T'ang would actually receive almost seventy-five per cent of everything they allocated, but this had been budgeted for.

Weis and his small team had worked directly with the sponsors to set things up. First they had had to break the transfers down into smaller, less noticeable sums, then disguise these as payments to smaller companies for work done. From there they were re-routed and broken down into yet smaller payments – this process being repeated anything between ten and fifteen times before they finally got to DeVore. Again, it was an expensive process, but necessary to protect the seven major sponsors from being traced. Palms had had to be greased all the way down the line, "squeeze" to be paid to greedy officials.

Funded directly it would have cost a quarter of the sum DeVore had asked for. But the risk of discovery would have been a hundred times greater.

"You've done an excellent job, *Shih* Weis," DeVore said, leaning back to let the cook set his plate down in front of him. "I have asked *Shih* Douglas if he could not show our appreciation in some small way."

He saw how much that pleased Weis, then looked down and picked up his chopsticks, tucking into the heaped plate of braised beancurd and vegetables.

* * *

DeVore watched Weis's craft lift and accelerate away, heading north, back to the safety of the City. The man's impatience both irritated and amused him. He was so typical of his kind. So unimaginative. All his talk about *The New Hope*, for instance – it was all so much bad air. But that was fortunate, perhaps. For if they'd guessed – if any of them had had the foresight to see where all this really led . . .

He laughed, then turned to the youth. "Do you fancy a walk, Stefan? The cold is rather exhilarating, I find."

"I'd like that."

The answer surprised him. He had begun to believe there was nothing the young man liked.

They went down past the landing dome and out onto a broad lip of ice-covered rock which once, long ago, had been a road. From that vantage point they could see how the valley began to curve away to the west. Far below them the mountainside was forested, but up here there was only snow and ice. They were above the world.

Standing there in the crisp air, surrounded by the bare splendour of the mountains, he saw it clearly. *The New Hope* was much more than a new start. For the Seven it would be the beginning of the end. His colleagues – Weis, Moore, Duchek, even Berdichev – saw it mainly as a symbol, a flagship for their cause, but it was more than that. It was a practical thing. If it succeeded – if new worlds could be colonised by its means – then control would slip from the hands of the Seven.

They knew that. Li Shai Tung had known it three years ago when he had summoned the leaders of the House to him and, unexpectedly, granted the concession. But the old man had had no choice. Lehmann's murder had stirred the hornet's nest. It was the only thing the T'ang could have done to prevent war.

Even so, none of his fellow conspirators had grasped what it *really* meant. They had not fully envisaged the changes that would come about – the vast, rapid metamorphosis that would sweep through their tight-knit community of thirty-nine billion souls. Science, kept in check by the Edict for so long, would not so much blossom as explode. When Mankind went out into the stars it would not, as so many had called it, be a scattering, but a shattering. All real cohesion would be lost. The Seven knew this. But few others had understood as yet. They thought the future would be an extension of the past. It would not. It would be something new. Something utterly, disturbingly new.

The new age, if it came, would be an age of grotesque and gothic wonders. Of magical transformations. Mutation would be the norm.

If it came.

"What were you up to with Weis back there?"

DeVore turned and looked at the young man. He seemed perfectly suited to this environment. His eyes, the pallor of his flesh; neither seemed out of place here. He was like some creature of the wild – a pine marten or a snow fox. A predator.

DeVore smiled. "I've been told Weis is a weak man. A soft man. I wanted confirmation of that for myself."

"What had you heard?"

DeVore told him about the tape he had acquired. It showed Weis in bed with two young boys – well-known Han opera stars. That was his weakness; a weakness he indulged in quite often, if the reports were accurate.

"Can he be trusted, then?"

"We have no option. Weis is the only one with both the know-how and the contacts."

"I see."

DeVore turned and looked back at the view. He remembered standing here with Berdichev, almost a year before, when they had first drawn up their scheme; recalled how they had stood and watched the sunset together; how frightened Soren had been; how the sudden fall of dark had changed his mood entirely. But he had expected as much. After all, Berdichev was typical of the old Man.

Beneath it all they were still the same primitive creatures. Still forest dwellers, crouched on the tree line, watching the daylight bleed away on the plain below, fearful of the dark. Their moods, their very beings, were shaped by patterns older than the race. By the Earth's slow rotation about the sun. By the unglimpsed diurnal round – cycles of dark and light, heat and cold. They could not control how they were, how they felt.

In the new age it would be different. There would be a creature free of this. Unshackled. A creature of volition, unshaped by its environment. A creature fit for space.

Let them have their romantic image of dispersion; of

new, unblemished worlds. Of Edens. His dreams were different and rode upon their backs. His dream was of new men. Of better, finer creatures. *Cleaner* creatures.

He thought back to the tape of Weis; to the image of the financier standing there, naked, straddling the young boy, his movements urgent, his face tight with need. *Such weakness*, he thought. So pitiful to be a slave to need.

In his dream of the new age he saw all such weaknesses eradicated. His new Man would be purged of need. His blood would flow clean and pure like the icy streams of the far north.

"It's magnificent. So pure. So perfect."

He looked across at the youth, surprised, then laughed. Yes, they were all much the same – all the same, primitive Man, unchanged by long millennia of so-called civilisation. All, perhaps, but this one. "Yes," he said, after a moment, feeling himself drawn to the boy. "It is magnificent, isn't it?"

* * *

The gateway was an arch of darkness, leading out into a vast and dimly lit hall. For a moment Tolonen thought he had come out into the Clay itself. Broad steps led down onto bare earth. The ceiling was high above him. But it was too bright, however dim, too clean, however bare, to be the Clay. And there, less than half a *li* from where he stood, was the ancient stadium, its high, curved walls in partial shadow, the great curved arches of its mighty windows black as a moonless night.

The Colosseum. Heart of the old *Ta Ts'in* empire.

He went down and crossed the space, choosing one of the tall archways at random, knowing they all led inward to the centre.

Feeling exposed. Feeling like a man walking in death's shadow.

He went inside, conscious of the sheer weight of stone above him as he stepped beneath the arch. The arch dwarfed him; was five times or more his height. Three great layers of arches, one above another, capped by a vast, uneven wall of ancient stone.

He had a sense of time, of power as old as time itself. This millennia-old edifice, monument to power and death and empire, awed him slightly, and he understood why the T'ang had chosen it for their meeting place.

"So you've come . . ."

Tolonen stopped on the edge of the inner arch, squinting into the darkness at the centre, trying to make out the shape of his master.

"Heavy-handed monsters, weren't they?"

Li Shai Tung stepped out from the next archway. At a signal from him the lights were raised and the central amphitheatre was suddenly revealed. It was huge, monstrous, barbaric. It spoke of a crude brutality.

Tolonen was silent, waiting. And while he waited, he thought about the pain and death this place had been built to hold. So much raw aggression had been moulded into darkness here. So much warm blood spilled for entertainment.

"You understand, then?" said the T'ang, turning to face him for the first time. There were tears in his eyes.

He found he could barely answer him. "What is it, *Chieh Hsia*? What do you want from me?"

Li Shai Tung drew a deep breath, then raised a hand, indicating the building all about them. "They would have me believe you are like this place. As unthinkingly callous. As brutal. Did you know that?"

He wanted to ask, *Who? Who would have you believe this?*, but he merely nodded, listening.

"However . . . I know you too well, Knut. You're a caring man. A loving man."

Tolonen shivered, moved by his T'ang's words.

The T'ang moved closer; stood face to face with his ex-General, their breaths mingling. "What you did was wrong. Very wrong." Then, surprisingly, he leaned forward and kissed Tolonen's cheek, holding him a moment, his voice lowered to a whisper. "But thank you, Knut.

Thank you, dearest friend. You acted like a brother to my grief."

Tolonen stood there, surprised, looking into his master's face, then bowed his head, all the old warmth welling up inside him. It had been so long, so hard being exiled.

He went down onto his knees at Li Shai Tung's feet, his head bowed in submission. "Tell me what you want, *Chieh Hsia*. Let me serve you again."

"Get up, old friend. Get up."

"Not until you say I am forgiven."

There was a moment's silence, then Li Shai Tung placed his hands on Tolonen's shoulders. "I cannot reinstate you. You must realise that. As for forgiveness, there is nothing to forgive. You acted as I felt. I would need to forgive myself first." He smiled sadly. "Your exile is at an end, Knut. You can come home. Now get up."

Tolonen stayed on his knees.

"Get up, you foolish man. Get up. You think I'd let my ablest friend rot in inactivity?" He was laughing now; a soft, almost childlike laughter. "Yes, you foolish old man. I have a job for you."

* * *

It was a hot night. Nan Ho had left the door to the garden open. A gentle breeze stirred the curtains, bringing the scents of night flowers and the sound of an owl in the orchard. Li Yuan woke and stretched, then grew very still.

"Who is it?" he said, his voice very small.

There was a touch of warmth against his back and a soft, muted giggle, then he felt her pressed against him – undoubtedly *her* – and heard her voice in his ear.

"Hush, little one. Hush. It's only me, Pearl Heart. I'll not bite you, Li Yuan."

He turned and, in the moon's light, saw her naked there beside him in his bed.

"What are you doing here, Pearl Heart?" he asked, but his eyes were drawn to the firmness of her breasts, the soft, elegant slope of her shoulders. Her dark eyes seemed to glisten in the moonlight and she lay there, unashamed, enjoying the way he looked at her.

She reached out and took his hand and pressed it gently to her breast, letting him feel the hardness of the nipple, then moved it down, across the silken smoothness of her stomach until it rested between her legs.

He shivered, then looked to her eyes again. "I shouldn't . . ."

She smiled and shook her head, her eyes filled with amusement. "No, perhaps you shouldn't, after all? Shall I go away?"

She made to move but his hand held her where she was, pressing down against the soft down of her sex. "No . . . I . . ."

Again she laughed, a soft, delicious laughter that increased his desire, then she sat up and pushed him down, pulling back the sheet from him.

"What have we here? Ah, now here's the root of all your problems."

She lifted his stiff penis gently between her fingers, making him catch his breath, then bent her head and kissed it. A small, wet kiss.

"There," she said gently, looking up the length of his body into his eyes. "I can see what you need, my little one. Why didn't you tell Pearl Heart before now?" She smiled and her eyes returned to his penis.

For a moment he closed his eyes, a ripple of pure pleasure passing through him as she stroked and kissed him. Then, when he could bear it no longer, he pulled her up against him, then turned her over, onto her back, letting her hand help him as he struggled to find the mouth of her sex with the blind eye of his penis.

Then, with a sudden sense of her flesh parting before his urgent pressure, he was inside her and she was pushing back up against him, her face suddenly different, her movements no longer quite so gentle, her legs wrapped about his back. He thrust and thrust and then cried out, his body stiffening, a great hot wave of blackness robbing him momentarily of thought.

He slept for a while and when he woke she was there still, not a dream as he had begun to imagine, but real and warm, her body beautiful, naked in the moonlight beside him, her dark eyes watching him. The thought – the reality of her – made his penis stir again and she laughed and stroked his cheek, his neck, his shoulder, her fingers moving down his body until they were curled about the root of him again.

"Pearl Heart?" he said, looking up from where her fingers played with him, into her face.

"Hush," she said, her smile like balm. "Lie still and close your eyes, my little one. Pearl Heart will ease the darkness in you."

He smiled and closed his eyes, letting the whole of him be drawn like a thread of fine silk into the contact of her fingers with his flesh. He gave a little shudder as her body brushed against his own, moving down him, then groaned as he felt her tiny, rosebud lips close wetly about the end of his penis.

"Pearl Heart," he said softly, almost inaudibly. And then the darkness claimed him once again.

★ ★ ★

Chen leaned on his hoe, then looked up into the sky and wiped his brow with the cloth Pavel had given him.

"This is harder than I thought it would be," he said, laughing.

The young man smiled back at him. "Would you like some water, Tong Chou?"

He hesitated, then gave a small bow. "That would be good. I've a thirst on me such as I've never had before."

"It's hot," Pavel said kindly. "You're not used to it yet, that's all. You'll get the hang of it soon enough."

Chen rubbed at his back then laughed again. "Let's hope so. I've a feeling I'm not so much breaking the earth as the earth's breaking me."

He watched Pavel go, then got down to it again, turning the dark, hard earth, one of a long line of workers stretching out across the huge, two *li*-wide field. Then, only moments later, he looked up, hearing raised voices from the direction Pavel had gone. He turned and saw the youth had been stopped by two of the guards – the same two men who had met them on the path the day before.

"What is it?" he asked the woman next to him, then realised she didn't speak English, only Mandarin. But the woman seemed to understand. She made a drinking gesture with one cupped hand, then shook her head.

"But I thought . . ."

Then he remembered something Pavel had said earlier. They were only allowed three cups of water a day – at the allotted breaks. Curse him, the stupid boy! Chen thought, dropping his hoe and starting across the field towards the noise, but two of the field workers ran after him and held his arms until he returned to the line.

"*Fa!*" one of them kept saying. "*Fa!*" Then, in atrocious English, he translated the word. "*Pah-nis-men.*"

Chen went cold. "I've got to stop it."

One of the older men – a peasant in his late forties or fifties, his face deeply tanned and creased – stepped forward. "You cannot stop it," he said in a clipped but clear English. "Watch. They will summon some of us. They will make us form a circle. Then the punishment will begin." He sighed resignedly. "It is their way."

On the far side of the field the shouting had stopped now and he could see Pavel, his arm held tightly by one of the men, his head bowed under the coolie hat.

"Shit!" he said under his breath. But the old man was right. He could not afford to get involved; nor, probably, would his involvement change anything. He was a field worker here, not *kwai*, and his job was to get at DeVore. He could not risk that, even to prevent this injustice.

The bigger of the two guards – the one Pavel had identified as Teng – strode out towards them. He stopped and, hands on his hips, ordered a number of them over to the water wagon.

Chen felt sick. This was his fault. But he could do nothing.

Pavel did not look at him. It was clear he had chosen not to say why he had gone to the wagon. Without being told, the *ku* – the field workers – formed a circle about the youth and the two guards. There was an awful silence. Chen looked around the circle and saw how most of them looked down or away, anything but look at what was happening at the circle's heart.

Teng's voice barked out again. "This man was disobedient. He knew the rules and yet he broke them." He laughed; a curt, brutal laughter. "He was stupid. Now he will be punished for his stupidity."

Teng drew the long club from his belt and turned to face Pavel. Chang smiled and thrust the young man forward at his fellow.

Without warning, Teng lashed out, the club hitting Pavel on the back of the legs, making him fall down. The sound the boy made was awful; a frightened whimper.

Chen shuddered and grit his teeth.

Teng stood over the youth now, smiling down at him. "Get up, Pavel. It's not over yet."

Slowly, his eyes never leaving Teng's face, Pavel got to his feet again. Teng's smile never wavered, but seemed to burn fiercely. It was clear he was enjoying himself hugely. He looked down at the club, then let fly again, this time catching Pavel across the side of the head.

The boy went down with a groan of pain. Chen could feel the indignation ripple about the circle. But still they were all silent. No one moved. No one did a thing.

Teng put the tip of the club against the young man's head and pushed gently, making him fall backwards. Then he looked across at his fellow guard.

"Chang! Pass me the rod!"

This time there was a low murmur from the circle. Teng turned, looking from face to face, then laughed. "If there's anyone else who'd like a taste of this, just say. I'd be delighted to oblige them."

Chang went across to him and took the club from him, handing him a long, thin pole that was attached by a wire to a small box. Teng clipped the box to one of his jacket pockets, then pressed a button on the side of the rod. It hissed wickedly.

Teng looked across at Pavel. "Drop your trousers, boy!"

Chen saw Pavel swallow awkwardly. The youth was petrified. His fingers fumbled at the strings that held up his trousers, then managed to untie the knot. Then he stood, his head drooping, letting his trousers fall around his ankles.

Under the trousers he was quite naked. He trembled uncontrollably. His penis had shrivelled up with fear.

Teng looked at him and laughed. "We're a fine big boy, aren't we, Pavel? No wonder we've no girlfriend yet!" Again his brutal laugh rang out. Then, cruelly, he touched the rod against the tip of the boy's penis.

Pavel jerked back, but Teng had not activated the rod.

Teng looked across at Chang and both men laughed loudly at the joke. Then Teng pressed the button and thrust the rod into the young man's groin. Pavel doubled up convulsively, then lay there as if dead. Teng must have had the rod set high, for the smell of burnt flesh was suddenly sharp in the warm, still air.

"You dirty bastard!"

The words came from Chen's left. He turned and saw it was the old man who had spoken to him earlier.

Teng had also turned and was looking at the man. "What is it, Fang Hui? You want to join the fun?"

Chang's voice sounded urgently from behind Teng. "Use the club, Teng Fu. The rod will kill the old fool."

But Teng wasn't listening. He walked slowly across to the old man and stood there, facing him, head and shoulders bigger than him.

"What did you say, old man? What did you call me?"

Fang Hui smiled bleakly. "You heard me, Teng."

Teng laughed. "Yes, I heard you, Fang." He reached

forward and grabbed the man's face in one hand, forcing his mouth open, then thrust the rod inside, closing Fang Hui's teeth upon it. Then he moved his hand away. One finger hovered above the button of the box.

"You'd like a taste of this, Fang Hui?"

Fang's eyes were wide with terror. Slowly Teng withdrew the rod from the old man's mouth, a sadistic smile of enjoyment lighting his big, ugly features.

"A good peasant is a quiet peasant, eh, Fang?"

The old man nodded exaggeratedly.

"Good," Teng said quietly, then kicked out, sending Fang sprawling.

The old man lay there, gasping. Chen looked across at him, relieved he had come to no greater harm, then turned and looked back at Teng.

It had been hard. Hard not to add his voice to Fang Hui's. Harder still just to stand there in the circle and do nothing. Pavel was stirring now. He lifted his head from the ground and looked up, his eyes unfocused, then let it fall back again.

Chang stepped up behind him, a cup of water in one hand, and poured it over the youth's head. "Is this what you came for, Pavel?" His action brought guffaws of laughter from the watching Teng.

Yes, thought Chen. I may have done nothing here today, but watch me, Teng. Be careful how you treat me. For I've every reason to kill you now for what you've done.

He thought of what Pavel had told him of the murders and knew now it was more than rumour. It was what had happened. He was sure of it.

Yes. Every reason.

★ ★ ★

The sound of laughter carried from the garden into the house through the wide, open doorway. Outside the morning was bright and warm; inside, where Li Yuan sat with his eight-year-old nephew, Tsu Tao Chu, it was cooler and in shadow.

570

They were playing *wei chi*; practising openings and corner plays, but Li Yuan seemed distracted. He kept looking out into the garden where the maids were playing ball.

The younger boy's high, sing-song voice broke the silence that had lain between them for some time. "Your heart's not in this, is it Yuan? It's a lovely morning. Why don't we go riding, instead?"

Li Yuan turned and looked at him. "I'm sorry, Tao Chu. What did you say?"

"I said . . ." He laughed sweetly, then leaned forward conspiratorially. "Tell me, Yuan. Which one is it?"

Li Yuan blushed and set a white stone down. "I don't know what you mean, Tao Chu."

Tao Chu raised his eyebrows, then placed a black stone on the board, removing the six white captives he had surrounded.

"I thought Fei Yen was your sweetheart, Yuan. It's clear, though, that some other maiden has won your heart. Or if not your heart . . ."

"Tao Chu!" Li Yuan looked down at the board and saw the position was lost, his forces disrupted. He laughed. "Is it so obvious?"

Tao Chu busied himself removing the stones and returning them to the bowls, then set the situation up anew. He looked up. "Again?"

Li Yuan shook his head. Then he stood up and went over to the open doorway. The maids were out beyond the ornamental pool, playing catch with a ball of stitched silk. He watched them for a while, his eyes going time and again to Pearl Heart. At first he didn't think she'd seen him, but then he saw her pick up the ball and turn, looking directly at him; her smile holding a special meaning, for him alone.

He lifted his head slightly, smiling back at her, and saw her pause, then throw the ball to one of the other maids, saying something which he couldn't catch. Then he saw her go, between the magnolia and out down the pathway, heading towards his room.

He caught up with her in the corridor outside his room, and turned her, pulling her against him.

"Not here," she said, laughing. "Inside, Li Yuan. Let's get inside first."

He could barely wait for her. As she undressed he ran his hands across her skin, and pressed his face against her hair, which smelled of ginger and cinnamon. He would have taken her then, while he was still fully clothed, but she stopped him and began to undress him, her hands lingering against his painfully stiff penis. In daylight her body seemed different; harder, firmer, less melting than it had seemed in the darkness, but no less desirable. He let her draw him down onto the bed, then he was inside her, spilling his seed at once.

She laughed tenderly, no trace of mockery in her laughter. "I see I'll have to teach you tricks, Li Yuan. Ways of holding back."

"What do you mean?" He lay there against her, his eyes closed, letting her caress his neck, his shoulders, the top of his back.

"There are books we can get. *Chun hua*. And devices."

He shivered. The light touch of her fingers on his flesh was delicious, making him want to purr like a cat. "*Chun hua*?" He had not heard of such things. "Spring pictures? What kind of spring pictures?"

She laughed again, then whispered in his ear. "Pictures of men and women doing things to each other. All kind of things. You'd not believe the number of ways it can be done, Li Yuan. And not just with two."

She saw his interest and laughed. "Ah yes, I thought as much. There's no man living who has not desired two girls in bed with him."

He swallowed. "What do you mean, Pearl Heart?" But he was answered almost at once. From behind a screen on the far side of the room came the unmistakable sound of suppressed laughter.

Li Yuan sat up and looked across. "Who's there? I demand to know . . ."

He fell silent. It was Sweet Rose, the youngest of his maids. She stepped out from behind the screen, demure but naked, a faint blush on her cheeks and at her neck. "May I join you on the bed, Li Yuan?"

Li Yuan shuddered, then turned and looked mutely at Pearl Heart. She was smiling broadly at him. "That's what we're here for. Didn't you realise it, Li Yuan? For this time. For when you woke to your manhood."

Pearl Heart leaned forward and summoned the younger girl, then drew Li Yuan back onto the bed, making Sweet Rose lie the other side of him. Then, with a shared, sisterly exchange of laughter, they began their work, stroking and kissing him, their skin like silk, their breath like almonds, enflaming his senses until he blossomed and caught fire again.

* * *

Nan Ho stood there outside the room, his head bowed, his manner apologetic but firm. "I am sorry, Lady Fei, but you cannot go inside."

She looked at him, astonished. It was the second time he had defied her. "What do you mean, *cannot*? I think you forget yourself, Nan Ho. If I wish to see Li Yuan, I have every right to call on him. I want to ask him if he will ride with me this afternoon, that's all. Now, please, stand out of my way."

He saw it was hopeless to try to deny her any further and stood to one side, his head lowered. "I beg you, Lady Fei . . ." But she brushed past him and opened the door to Li Yuan's rooms.

"Ridiculous man . . ." she had started to say, then fell silent, sniffing the air. Then she noticed the sounds, coming from beyond the screen. Unusual sounds to be coming from the bedroom of a twelve-year-old boy. She crept up to the screen, then put her hand to her mouth to stifle her surprise.

It was Li Yuan! Gods! Li Yuan with two of his maids!

For a moment she stood there, mesmerised by the sight

of his firm, almost perfect bottom jutting and rutting with one of the maids while the other caressed and stroked the two of them. Then she saw him stiffen and groan and saw the maid's legs tighten momentarily about his back, drawing him down into her.

She shuddered and began to back away, then put her hand to her mouth to stop the laughter that had come unbidden to her lips. Li Yuan! Of all the cold fishes in the sea of life, imagine Li Yuan, rutting with his maids! The dirty little beggar!

Outside she looked at Nan Ho sternly. "I was not here, Nan Ho. Do you understand me?"

The servant bowed deeply. "I understand you, Lady Fei. And I will leave your message for the young prince. I am sure he would welcome the chance to ride with you this afternoon."

She nodded, then turned, conscious of the blush that had come to her cheeks and neck, and walked quickly away.

Li Yuan! She gave a brief laugh, then stopped dead, remembering the sight of those small, perfectly-formed buttocks clenching at the moment of his orgasm.

"And I thought you so cold, so passionless. So above all this."

She laughed again; a strange, querulous laugh, then walked on, surprised by what she was thinking.

★ ★ ★

"Do you remember this place, Karr?"

Karr smiled and looked out from their private box into the pit with its surrounding tiers.

"How could I forget it, General?"

Tolonen leaned back and sighed. "Men forget many things they'd do best to remember. Roots. They forget their roots. And when that happens they lose their ability to judge things true and clear."

Karr smiled. "This business . . ." He pointed to the brilliantly-lit combat circle. "It had a way of clearing the mind of everything but truth."

Tolonen laughed. "Yes, I can see that."

Karr turned and faced him. "I'm glad you're back, General. I mean no disrespect to General Nocenzi, but things haven't been the same without you at the helm."

The old man sniffed and tilted his head slightly. "I've missed it too, Karr. Missed it badly. But listen, I'm not at the helm. Not in the sense that you're probably thinking. No. This is something else. Something secret that the T'ang has asked me to organise."

He spelled it out quickly, simply, letting Karr understand that he would be briefed more fully later.

"This is a contingency plan, you understand. We hope never to have to use it. If the House votes in favour of the veto on space exploration – as it should – we can put this little scheme to the flame – throw it on the fire, so to speak."

"But you don't believe that, do you, General?"

Tolonen shook his head. "I'm afraid not. I think the T'ang hopes against hope. The House is no friend to the Seven at present."

Below them, in the pit, the two contestants came out and took their places. The fight marshal read out the rules and then stepped back. The pit went deathly silent.

The fight was brief but brutal. In less than a minute one of the two men was dead. The crowd went mad, roaring its approval. Karr watched the stewards carry the body away, then shivered.

"I'm glad I let you buy my contract out. That could have been me."

"No," Tolonen said. "You were the exception. No one would have carried you from the circle. Not in a hundred fights. I knew that at once."

"The first time you saw me?" Karr laughed and turned to face the older man.

"Almost . . ."

Karr was smiling. "I remember even now how you looked at me that first time – so dismissive, it was, that look – and then you turned your back on me."

Tolonen laughed, remembering. "Well, sometimes it's best not to let a man know all you're thinking. But it was true. It was why I welcomed your offer. I knew at once I could use you. The way you stood up to young Hans. I liked that. It put him on his mettle."

Karr looked down. "Have you heard that I've traced DeVore?"

Tolonen's eyes widened. "No! Where?"

"I'm not certain, but I think he's taken an overseer's job on one of the big plantations. My man, Chen, is investigating him right now. As soon as he has proof we're going in."

Tolonen shook his head. "Not possible, I'm afraid."

"I'm sorry, General, but what do you mean?"

Tolonen leaned forward and held the top of one of Karr's huge arms. "I need you at once, that's why. I want you training for this operation from this evening. So that we can put the scheme into operation at a moment's notice."

"Is there no one else?"

Tolonen shook his head. "No. There is only one man in the whole of Chung Kuo who could carry out this scheme, and that's you, Karr. Chen will be all right. I'll see he has full back up. But I can't spare you. Not this time."

Karr considered a moment, then looked up again, smiling. "Then I'd best get busy, neh, General?"

* * *

Overseer Bergson looked up as Chen entered. The room was dark but for a tight circle of light surrounding where he sat at a table in the centre. He was bare-headed, his dark hair slicked back wetly, and he was wearing a simple silk *pau*, but Chen thought he recognised him at once. It was DeVore. He was almost certain it was. On the low table in front of him a *wei chi* board had been set up, seven rounded black stones placed on the handicap points, forming the outline of a huge letter H in the centre of the grid. On either side of the board was a tray, one filled with white stones, the other with black.

"Do you play, Tong Chou?"

Chen met DeVore's eyes, wondering for a moment if it was possible he too would see through the disguise, then dismissed the thought, remembering how DeVore had killed the man he, Chen, had hired to play himself that day five years ago when Kao Jyan had died. No, he thought, to you I am Tong Chou, the new worker. A bright man. Obedient. Quick to learn. But nothing more.

"My father played, *Shih* Bergson. I learned a little from him."

DeVore looked past Chen at the two henchmen and made a small gesture of dismissal with his chin. They went at once.

"Sit down, Tong Chou. Facing me. We'll talk as we play."

Chen moved into the circle of light and sat. DeVore watched him a moment, relaxed, his hands resting lightly on his knees, then smiled.

"Those two who've just gone. They're useful men, but when it comes to this game they've shit in their heads instead of brains. Have you got shit in your head, Tong Chou? Are you a useful man?"

"I'm useful, *Shih* Bergson."

DeVore stared back at him a moment, then looked down. "We'll see."

He took a white stone from the tray and set it down, two lines in, six down at the top left-hand corner of the board from where Chen sat – in *shang*, the South. Chen noticed how firmly yet delicately DeVore had held the stone between thumb and forefinger; how sharp the click of stone against wood had been as he placed it; how crisp and definite that movement had seemed. He studied the board a while, conscious of his seven black stones, like fortresses marking out territory on the uncluttered battle-ground of the board. His seven and DeVore's one. That one so white it seemed to eclipse the dull power of his own.

Chen took a black stone from the tray and held it in his hand a moment, turning it between his fingers,

experiencing the smooth coolness of it, the perfect roundness of its edges, the satisfyingly oblate feel of it. He
shivered. He had never felt anything like it before; had
never played with stones and board. It had always been
machines. Machines, like the one in Kao Jyan's room.

He set the stone down smartly, taking his lead from
DeVore, hearing once more that sharp, satisfying click of
stone against wood. Then he sat back.

DeVore answered his move at once. Another white stone
in the top left corner. An aggressive, attacking move.
Unexpected. Pushing directly for the corner. Chen countered almost instinctively, his black stone placed between
the two whites, cutting them. But at once DeVore clicked
down another stone, forming a tiger's mouth about Chen's
last black stone, surrounding it on three sides and threatening to take it unless . . .

Chen connected, forming an elbow of three black stones
– a weak formation, though not disastrous, but already he
was losing the initiative; letting DeVore's aggressive play
force him back on the defensive. Already he had lost the
corner. Six plays in and he had lost the first corner.

"Would you like *ch'a*, Tong Chou?"

He looked up from the board and met DeVore's eyes.
Nothing. No trace of what he was thinking. Chen bowed.
"I would be honoured, *Shih* Bergson."

DeVore clapped his hands and, when a face appeared
around the door, simply raised his right hand, two fingers
extended. At the same time his left hand placed another
stone. Two down, two in, strengthening his line and securing the corner. Only a fool would lose it now, and DeVore
was no fool.

DeVore leaned back, watching him again. "How often
did you play your father, Tong Chou?"

"Often enough when I was a child, *Shih* Bergson. But
then he went away. When I was eight. I only saw him again
last year. After his funeral."

Chen placed another stone, then looked back at DeVore.
Nothing. No response at all. And yet DeVore, like the

578

fictional Tong Chou, had "lost" his father as an eight-year-old.

"Unfortunate. And you've not played since?"

Chen took a breath, then studied DeVore's answer. He played so swiftly, almost as if he wasn't thinking, just reacting. But Chen knew better than to believe that. Every move DeVore made was carefully considered; all the possibilities worked out in advance. To play him one had to be as well prepared as him. And to beat him . . . ?

Chen smiled and placed another stone. "Occasionally. But mainly with machines. It's been some years since I've sat and played a game like this, *Shih* Bergson. I am honoured that you find me worthy."

He studied the board again. The corner was lost, almost certainly now, but his own position was much stronger and there was a good possibility of making territory on the top edge, in *shang* and *chu*, the west. Not only that, but DeVore's next move was forced. He had to play on the top edge, two in. To protect his line. He watched, then smiled inwardly as DeVore set down the next white stone exactly where he had known he would.

Behind him he heard the door open quietly. "There," said DeVore, indicating a space beside the play table. At once a second, smaller table was set down and covered with a thin cloth. A moment later a serving girl brought the kettle and two bowls, then knelt there, to Chen's right, wiping out the bowls.

"*Wei chi* is a fascinating game, don't you think, Tong Chou? Its rules are simple – there are only seven things to know – and yet mastery of the game is the work of a lifetime." Unexpectedly he laughed. "Tell me, Tong Chou, do you know the history of the game?"

Chen shook his head. Someone had once told him it had been developed at the same time as the computers, five hundred years ago, but the man who had told him that had been a know-nothing; a shit-brains, as DeVore would have called him. He had a sense that the game was much younger. A recent thing.

DeVore smiled. "How old do you think the game is, Tong Chou? A hundred years? Five hundred?"

Again Chen shook his head. "A hundred, *Shih* Bergson? Two hundred, possibly?"

DeVore laughed and then watched as the girl poured the *ch'a* and offered him the first bowl. He lowered his head politely, refusing, and she turned, offering the bowl to Chen. Chen also lowered his head slightly, refusing, and the girl turned back to DeVore. This time DeVore took the bowl in two hands and held it to his mouth to sip, clearly pleased by Chen's manners.

"Would it surprise you, Tong Chou, if I told you that the game we're playing is more than four and a half thousand years old? That it was invented by the Emperor Yao in approximately 2,350 BC?"

Chen hesitated, then laughed as if surprised, realising that DeVore must be mocking him. Chung Kuo itself was not that old, surely? He took the bowl the girl was now offering him and, with a bow to DeVore, sipped noisily.

DeVore drained his bowl and set it down on the tray the girl was holding, waiting for the girl to fill it again before continuing.

"The story is that the Emperor Yao invented *wei chi* to train the mind of his son, Tan-Chu, and teach him to think like an emperor. The board, you see, is a map of Chung Kuo itself, of the ancient Middle Kingdom of the Han, bounded to the east by the ocean, to the north and west by deserts and great mountain ranges, and to the south by jungles and the sea. The board, then, is the land. The pieces men, or groups of men. At first the board, like the land, is clear, unsettled, but then as the men arrive and begin to grow in numbers, the board fills. Slowly but inexorably these groups spread out across the land, occupying territory. But there is only so much territory – only so many points on the board to be filled. Conflict is inevitable. Where the groups meet there is war: a war which the strongest and cleverest must win. And so it goes on, until the board is filled and the last conflict resolved."

"And when the board is filled and the pieces still come?"

DeVore looked at him a moment, then looked away. "As I said, it's an ancient game, Tong Chou. If the analogy no longer holds it is because we have changed the rules. It would be different if we were to limit the number of pieces allowed instead of piling them on until the board breaks from the weight of stones. Better yet if the board were bigger than it is, neh?"

Chen was silent, watching DeVore drain his bowl a second time. I'm certain now, he thought. It's you. I know it's you. But Karr wants to be sure. More than that, he wants you alive. So that he can bring you before the T'ang and watch you kneel and beg for mercy.

DeVore set his bowl down on the tray again, but this time he let his hand rest momentarily over the top of it, indicating he was finished. Then he looked at Chen.

"You know, Tong Chou, sometimes I think these two – *ch'a* and *wei chi* - along with silk, are the high-points of Han culture." Again he laughed, but this time it was a cold, mocking laughter. "Just think of it, Tong Chou! *Ch'a* and *wei chi* and silk! All three of them some four and a half thousand years old! And since then? Nothing! Nothing but walls!"

Nothing but walls. Chen finished his *ch'a* and set it down on the tray the girl held out for him. Then he placed his stone and, for the next half hour, said nothing, concentrating on the game.

At first the game went well for him. He lost few captives and made few trivial errors. The honours seemed remarkably even and, filled with confidence in his own performance, he began to query what Karr had told him about DeVore being a master of *wei chi*. But then things changed. Four times he thought he had DeVore's stones trapped. Trapped with no possibility of escape. Each time he seemed within two stones of capturing a group; first in *ping*, the east, at the bottom left-hand corner of the board, then in *tsu*, the north. But each time he was forced to watch, open-mouthed, as DeVore changed everything with a single unexpected move. And then he would find himself

back-tracking furiously; no longer surrounding but surrounded, struggling desperately to save the group which,
only a few moves before, had seemed invincible – had
seemed a mere two moves from conquest.

Slowly he watched his positions crumble on all sides of
the board until, with a small shrug of resignation, he threw
the black stone he was holding back into the tray.

"There seems no point."

DeVore looked up at him for the first time in a long
while. "Really? You concede, Tong Chou?"

Chen bowed his head.

"Then you'll not mind if I play black from this position?"

Chen laughed, surprised. The position was lost. By
forty, maybe fifty pieces. Irredeemably lost. Again he
shrugged. "If that's your wish, *Shih* Bergson."

"And what's your wish, Tong Chou? I understand you
want to be field supervisor."

Chen bowed his head. "That's so, *Shih* Bergson."

"The job pays well. Twice what you earn now, Tong
Chou."

Yes, thought Chen; so why does no one else apply?
Because it is an unpopular job, being field supervisor under
you, that's why. And so you wonder why I want it.

"That's exactly why I want the job, *Shih* Bergson. I want
to get on. To clear my debts in the Above and climb the
levels once again."

DeVore sat back, watching him closely a moment, then
he leaned forward, took a black stone from the tray and set
it down with a sharp click.

"All right. I'll consider the matter. But first there's something you can do for me, Tong Chou. Two nights back
the storehouse in the western meadows was broken into
and three cases of strawberries, packed ready for delivery
to one of my clients in First Level, were taken. You'll
understand how inconvenienced I was." He sniffed and
looked at Chen directly. "There's a thief on the plantation,
Tong Chou. I want you to find out who it is and deal with
him. Do you understand me?"

Chen hesitated a moment, taken by surprise by this unexpected demand. Then, realising he had no choice if he was to get close enough to DeVore to get Karr his proof, he dropped his head.

"As you say, *Shih* Bergson. And when I've dealt with him?"

DeVore laughed. "Then we'll play again, Tong Chou, and talk about your future."

★ ★ ★

When the peasant had gone, DeVore went across to the screens and pulled the curtain back, then switched on the screen that connected him with Berdichev in the House.

"How are things?" he asked as Berdichev's face appeared.

Berdichev laughed excitedly. "It's early yet, but I think we've done it. Farr's people have come over and the New Legist faction are swaying a little. Barrow calculates that we need only twenty more votes and we've thrown the Seven's veto out."

DeVore nodded. "That's good. And afterwards?"

Berdichev smiled. "You've heard something then? Well, that's my surprise. Wait and see. That's all I'll say."

DeVore broke contact. He pulled the curtain to and walked over to the board. The peasant hadn't been a bad player, considering. Not really all that stimulating, yet amusing enough, particularly in the second phase of the game. He would have to give him nine stones next time. He studied the situation a moment. Black had won, by a single stone.

As for Berdichev and his "surprise" . . .

DeVore laughed and began to clear the board. As if you could keep such a thing hidden. The albino was the last surprise Soren Berdichev would spring on him. Even so, he admired Soren for having the insight – and the guts – to do what he had done. When the Seven learned of the investigations. And when they saw the end results . . .

He looked across at the curtained bank of screens. Yes, all hell would break loose when the Seven found out

583

what Soren Berdichev had been up to. And what was so delightful was that it was all legal. All perfectly consti-tutional. There was nothing they could do about it.

But they *would* do something. He was certain of that. So it was up to him to anticipate it. To find out what they planned and get in first.

And there was no one better at that game than he. No one in the whole of Chung Kuo.

★ ★ ★

"Why, look, Soren! Look at Lo Yu-Hsiang!" Clarac laughed and spilled wine down his sleeve, but he was oblivious of it, watching the scenes on the big screens overhead.

Berdichev looked where Clarac was pointing and gave a laugh of delight. The camera was in close-up on the Senior Representative's face.

"Gods! He looks as if he's about to have a coronary!"

As the camera panned slowly round the tiers, it could be seen that the look of sheer outrage on Lo Yu-Hsiang's face was mirrored throughout that section of the House. Normally calm patricians bellowed and raged, their eyes bulging with anger.

Douglas came up behind Berdichev and slapped him on the back. "And there's nothing they can do about it! Well done, Soren! Marvellous! I thought I'd never see the day . . ."

There was more jubilant laughter from the men gathered in the gallery room, then Douglas called for order and had the servants bring more glasses so they could drink a toast.

"To Soren Berdichev! And *The New Hope*!"

Two dozen voices echoed the toast, then drank, their eyes filled with admiration for the man at the centre of their circle.

Soren Berdichev inclined his head, then, with a smile, turned back to the viewing window and gazed down on the scene below.

The scenes in the House had been unprecedented. In all

the years of its existence nothing like this had happened. Not even the murder of Pietr Lehmann had rocked the House so violently. The defeat of the Seven's veto motion – a motion designed to confine *The New Hope* to the Solar System – had been unusual enough, but what had followed had been quite astonishing.

Wild celebrations had greeted the result of the vote. The anti-veto faction had won by a majority of one hundred and eighteen. In the calm that had followed, Under Secretary Barrow had gone quietly to the rostrum and begun speaking.

At first most of the members heard very little of Barrow's speech. They were still busy discussing the implications of the vote. But one by one they fell silent as the full importance of what Barrow was saying began to sweep around the tiers.

Barrow was proposing a special motion, to be passed by a two-thirds majority of the House. A motion for the indictment of certain members of the House. He was outlining the details of investigations that had been made by a secretly-convened sub-committee of the House – investigations into corruption, unauthorised practices and the payment of illegal fees.

By the time he paused and looked up from the paper he was reading from, there was complete silence in the House.

Barrow turned, facing a certain section of the tiers, then began to read out a list of names. He was only partway into that long list when the noise from the Han benches drowned his voice.

Every name on his list was a *tai* – a "pocket" Representative, their positions, their "loyalty", bought and paid for by the Seven. This, even more than the House's rejection of the starship veto, was a direct challenge upon the authority of the Seven. It was tantamount to a declaration of the House's independence from their T'ang.

Barrow waited while the Secretary of the House called the tiers to order, then, ignoring the list for a moment, began an impassioned speech about the purity of the House and how it had been compromised by the Seven.

The outcry from the *tai* benches was swamped by

enthusiastic cheers from all sides of the House. The growing power of the *tai* had been a long-standing bone of contention, even amongst the Han Representatives, and Barrow's indignation reflected their own feelings. It had been different in the old days: then a *tai* had been a man to be respected, but these brash young men were no more than empty mouthpieces for the Seven.

When it came to the vote the margin was as narrow as it could possibly be. Three votes settled it. The eighty-six *tai* named on Barrow's list were to be indicted.

There was uproar. Infuriated *tai* threw bench pillows down at the speaker, while some would have come down the aisles to lay hands on him, had not other members blocked their way.

Then, at a signal from the Secretary, House security troops had come into the chamber and had begun to round up the named *tai*, handcuffing them like common criminals and removing their permit cards.

Berdichev watched the end of this process – saw the last few *tai* being led away, protesting violently, down into the cells below the House.

He shivered, exulted. This was a day to remember. A day he had long dreamed of. *The New Hope* was saved and the House strengthened. And later on, after the celebrations, he would begin the next phase of his scheme.

He turned and looked back at the men gathered in the viewing room, knowing instinctively which he could trust and which not, then smiled to himself. It began here, now. A force which all the power of the Seven could not stop. And the Aristotle File would give it a focus, a sense of purpose and direction. When they saw what had been kept from them there would be no turning back. The File would bring an end to the rule of Seven.

Yes. He laughed and raised his glass to Douglas once again. It had begun. And who knew what kind of world it would be when they had done with it?

CHAPTER · 16

THE DARKENING OF THE LIGHT

It was two in the morning and outside the Berdichev mansion, in the ornamental gardens, the guests were still celebrating noisily. A line of sedans waited on the far side of the green, beneath the lanterns, their pole-men and guards in attendance nearby, while closer to the house a temporary kitchen had been set up. Servants moved busily between the guests, serving hot bowls of soup or noodles, or offering more wine.

Berdichev stood on the balcony, looking down, studying it all a moment. Then he moved back inside, smiling a greeting at the twelve men gathered there.

These were the first of them. The ones he trusted most.

He looked across at the servant, waiting at his request in the doorway, and gave the signal. The servant – a "European", like all his staff these days – returned a moment later with a tray on which was a large, pot-bellied bottle and thirteen delicate porcelain bowls. The servant placed the tray on the table, then, with a deep bow, backed away and closed the door after him.

They were alone.

Berdichev's smile broadened. "You'll drink with me, *Chun t'zu*?" He held up the bottle – a forty-year-old *Shou Hsing* peach brandy – and was greeted with a murmur of warm approval.

He poured, then handed out the tiny bowls, conscious that the eyes of the "gentlemen" would from time to time move to the twelve thick folders laid out on the table beside the tray.

He raised his bowl. "*Kan pei!*"

"*Kan pei!*" they echoed and downed their brandies in one gulp.

"Beautiful!" said Moore with a small shudder. "Where did you get it, Soren? I didn't think there was a bottle of *Shou Hsing* left in all Chung Kuo that was over twenty years old."

Berdichev smiled. "I have two cases of it, John. Allow me to send you a bottle." He looked about him, his smile for once unforced, quite natural. "And all of you *chun t'zu,* of course."

Their delight was unfeigned. Such a brandy must be fifty thousand yuan a bottle at the least! And Berdichev had just given a case of it away!

"You certainly know how to celebrate, Soren!" said Parr, coming closer and holding his arm a moment. Parr was an old friend and business associate, with dealings in North America.

Berdichev nodded. "Maybe. But there's much to celebrate tonight. Much more, in fact, than any of you realise. You see, my good friends, tonight is the beginning of something. The start of a new age."

He saw how their eyes went to the folders again.

"Yes," he went to the table and picked up one of the folders, "It has to do with these. You've noticed, I'm sure. Twelve of you and twelve folders." He looked about the circle of them, studying their faces one last time, making certain before he committed himself.

Yes, these were the men. Important men. Men with important contacts. But friends, too – men he could trust. They would start it for him. A thing which, once begun, would prove irresistible. And, he hoped, irreversible.

"You're all wondering why I brought you up here, away from the celebrations? You're also wondering what it has to do with the folders. Well, I'll keep you wondering no longer. Re-fill your glasses from the bottle, then take a seat. What I'm about to tell you may call for a stiff drink."

There was laughter, but it was muted, tense. They knew Soren Berdichev well enough to know that he never played jokes, nor made statements he could not support.

When they were settled around the table, Berdichev distributed the folders.

"Before you open them, let me ask each of you something." He turned and looked at Moore. "You first, John. Which is more important to you: a little of your time and energy – valuable as that is – or the future of our race, the Europeans?"

Moore laughed. "You know how I feel about that, Soren."

Berdichev nodded. "Okay. Then let me ask you something more specific. If I were to tell you that in that folder in front of you was a document of approximately two hundred thousand words, and that I wanted you to hand-copy it for me, what would you say to that?"

"Unexplained, I'd say you were mad, Soren. Why should I want to hand-copy a document? Why not get some of my people to put it on computer for me?"

"Of course," Berdichev's smile was harder. He seemed suddenly more his normal self. "But if I were to tell you that this is a secret document. And not just any small corporate secret, but *the* secret, would that make it easier to understand?"

Moore sat back slightly. "What do you mean, *the* secret? What's in the file, Soren?"

"I'll come to that. First, though, do you trust me? Is there anyone here who doesn't trust me?"

There was a murmuring and a shaking of heads. Parr spoke for them all. "You know there's not one of us who wouldn't commit half of all they owned on your word, Soren."

Berdichev smiled tightly. "Yes. I know. But what about one hundred per cent? Is anyone here afraid to commit that much?"

Another of them – a tall, thin-faced man named Ecker –

answered this time. A native of City Africa, he had strong trading links with Berdichev's company, SimFic.

"Do you mean a financial commitment, Soren, or are you talking of something more personal?"

Berdichev bowed slightly. "You are all practical men. That's good. I'd not have any other kind of men for friends. But to answer you, in one sense you're correct, Edgar. I do mean something far more personal. That said, which of us here can so easily disentangle their personal from their financial selves?"

There was the laughter of agreement at that. It was true. They were moneyed creatures. The market was in their blood.

"Let me say simply that if any of you choose to open the folder you will be committing yourselves one hundred per cent. Personally and, by inference, financially." He put out a hand quickly. "Oh, I don't mean that I'll be coming to you for loans or anything like that. This won't affect your trading positions."

Parr laughed. "I've known you more than twenty years now, Soren, and I realise that – like all of us here – you have secrets you would share with few others. But this kind of public indirectness is most unlike you. Why can't you just tell us what's in the folder?"

Berdichev nodded tersely. "All right. I'll come to it, I promise you, Charles. But this *is* necessary." He looked slowly about the table, then bowed his head slightly. "I want to be fair to you all. To make certain you understand the risks you would be taking simply in opening the folder. Because I want none of you to feel you were pushed into this. That would serve no one here. In fact, I would much rather have anyone who feels uncomfortable with this leave now before he commits himself that far. And no blame attached. Because once you take the first step – once you find out what's inside the folder – your lives will be forfeit."

Parr leaned forward and tapped the folder. "I still don't understand, Soren. What's in here? A scheme to assassinate the Seven? What could be so dangerous that simply to know of it could make a man's life forfeit?"

"The secret. As I said before. The thing the Han have kept from us all these years. As for why it's dangerous simply to know, let me tell you about a little-known statute that's rarely used these days – and a Ministry whose sole purpose is to create an illusion which even they have come to believe is how things really are."

Parr laughed and spread his hands. "Now you *are* being enigmatic, Soren. What statute? What Ministry? What illusion?"

"It is called simply, The Ministry, it is situated in Pei Ching, and its only purpose is to guard the secret. Further, it is empowered to arrest and execute anyone knowing of or disseminating information about the secret. As for the illusion . . ." He laughed sourly. "Well, you'll understand if you choose to open the folder."

One of the men who hadn't spoken before now sat forward. He was a big, powerful-looking man with a long, unfashionable beard. His name was Ross and he was the owner of a large satellite communications company in East Asia.

"This is treason, then, Soren?"

Berdichev nodded.

Ross stroked his beard thoughtfully and looked about him. Then, almost casually, he opened his folder, took out the stack of papers and began to examine the first page.

A moment later others followed.

Berdichev looked about the table. Twelve folders lay empty, the files removed. He shivered then looked down, a faint smile on his lips.

There was a low whistle from Moore. He looked up at Berdichev, his eyes wide. "Is this true, Soren? Is this really true?"

Berdichev nodded.

"But this is just so . . . so fantastic. Like a dream someone's had. It's . . ." he shrugged.

"It's true," Berdichev said firmly. They were all watching him now. "Which of us here has not been down into the Clay and seen the ruins? When the tyrant Tsao Ch'un built his City he buried more than the architecture of the past, he buried its history, too."

"And built another?" The voice was Parr's.

"Yes. Carefully, painstakingly, over the years. You see, his intention wasn't simply to eradicate all opposition to his rule, he wanted to destroy all knowledge of what had gone before him. As the City grew, so his officials collected all books, all tapes, all recordings, allowing nothing that was not Han to enter their great City. Most of what they collected was simply burned. But not all of it. Much was adapted. You see, Tsao Ch'un's advisors were too clever simply to create a gap. That, they knew, would have attracted curiosity. What they did was far more subtle and, in the long run, far more persuasive to the great mass of people. They set about re-constructing the history of the world – placing Chung Kuo at the centre of everything, back in its rightful place, as they saw it."

He drew a breath, then continued, conscious momentarily of noises from the party in the gardens outside. "It was a lie, but a lie to which everyone subscribed, for in the first decades of the City merely to question their version of the past – even to suggest it might have happened otherwise – was punishable by death. But the lie was complex and powerful, and people soon forgot. New generations arose who knew little of the real past. To them the whispers and rumours seemed mere fantasy in the face of the reality they had been taught and saw all about them. The media fed them the illusion daily until the illusion became, even to those responsible for its creation, quite *real*."

"And this – this Aristotle File . . . is this the truth Tsao Ch'un suppressed?"

Berdichev looked back at Ross. "Yes."

"How did you come upon it?"

Berdichev smiled. "Slowly. Piece by piece. For the last fifteen years I've been searching – making my own discreet investigations. Following up clues. And this – this file – is the end result of all that searching."

Ross sat back. "I'm impressed. More than that, Soren, I'm astonished! Truly, for the first time in my life I'm astonished. This is . . ." He laughed strangely. "Well, it's hard to take it in. Perhaps it's the brandy but . . ."

There was laughter at that, but all eyes were on Ross as he tried to articulate their feelings.

"Well . . . I know what my friend, John Moore, means. It *is* fantastic. Perhaps too much so to swallow at a single go like this." He reached forward and lifted the first few pages, then looked at Berdichev again. "It's just that I find it all rather hard to believe."

Berdichev leaned forward, light glinting from the lenses of his glasses. "That's just what they intended, Michael. And it's one of the reasons why I want you all to hand-write a copy. That way it will get rooted in you all. You will have done more than simply read it. You will have transcribed it. And in doing so the reality of it will strike you forcibly. You will see how it all connects. Its plausibility – no, its *truth*! – will be written in the blood of every one of you."

Ross smiled. "I see that the original of this was written in your own hand, Soren. You ask us to commit ourselves equally?"

Berdichev nodded.

"Then I for one am glad to do so. But what of the copy we make? What should we do with it? Keep it safe?"

Berdichev smiled, meeting his friend's eyes. Ross knew. He had seen it already. "You will pass your copy on. To a man you trust like a brother. As I trust you. He, in his turn, will make another copy and pass it on to one he trusts. And so on, forging a chain, until there are many who know. And then . . ." He sat back. "Well, then you will see what will happen. But this – this here tonight – is the beginning of it. We are the first. From here the seed goes out. But harvest time will come, I promise you all. Harvest time will come."

★ ★ ★

"*Hung Mao* or Han, what does it matter? They're Above. They despise us Clayborn."

The three boys were sitting on the edge of the pool, their feet swung out over the water.

Kim was looking down into the mirror of the water, his eyes tracing the patterns of the stars reflected from the Tun Huang map overhead. He had been silent for some while, listening to the others speak, but now he interrupted them.

"I know what you mean, Anton, but it's not always like that. There are some . . ."

"Like Chan Shui?"

Kim nodded. He had told them what had happened in the Casting Shop. "Yes, like Chan Shui."

Anton laughed. "You probably amuse him. Either that or he thinks that he can benefit somehow by looking after you. As for liking you . . ."

Kim shook his head. "No. It's not like that. Chan Shui . . ."

Josef cut in. "Be honest, Kim. They hate us. I mean, what has this Chan Shui done that's really cost him anything? He's stood up to a bully. Fine. And that's impressed you. That and all that claptrap T'ai Cho has fed you about Han justice. But it's all a sham. All of it. It's like Anton says. He's figured you must be important – something special – and he's reckoned that if he looks after you there might be something in it for him."

Again Kim shook his head. "You don't understand. You really don't."

Anton laughed dismissively. "We understand, Kim. But it seems like you're going to have to learn it the hard way. They don't want us, Kim. Not for ourselves, anyway – only for what we are. They use us like machines, and if we malfunction they throw us away. That's the truth of the matter."

Kim shrugged. There was a kind of truth to that, but it wasn't the whole truth. He thought of Matyas and Janko. What distinguished them? They were both bullies. It had not mattered to Matyas that he, Kim, was Clay like himself.

No. Nor was it anything Kim had done to him. It was simply that he was different. So it was with Janko. But to some that difference did not matter. T'ai Cho for instance, and Chan Shui. And there would be others, he was sure of it.

"It's them and us," said Anton, laughing bitterly. "That's how it is, Kim. That's how it'll always be."

"No!" Kim was insistent now. "You're wrong. You're both wrong. Them and us. It just isn't like that. Sometimes, yes, but not always."

Anton shook his head. "Always. Deep down it's always there. You should ask him, this Chan Shui. Ask him if he'd let you marry his sister."

"He hasn't got a sister."

"You miss my point, Kim."

Kim shivered and looked away, unconsciously stroking the bruise on his neck. Shame and guilt. It was always there in them, just beneath the skin. But why did they let these things shape them? Why couldn't they break the mould and make new creatures of themselves?

"Maybe I miss your point, but I'd rather think well of Chan Shui than succumb to the bleakness of your view." His voice was colder, more hostile than he had intended, and he regretted his words at once – true as they were.

Anton stood up slowly, then looked down coldly at his fellow. "Come on, Josef. I don't think we're wanted here anymore."

"I'm sorry. I didn't mean . . ."

But it was too late. They were gone.

Kim sat there a while longer, distressed by what had happened. But maybe it was unavoidable. Maybe he could only have delayed the moment. Because he *was* different – even from his own kind.

He laughed. There! He had betrayed himself: had caught himself in his own twisted logic. For either they were all of one single kind – Han, *Hung Mao* and Clay – or he was wrong. And he could not be wrong. His soul cried out not to be wrong.

He looked up at the dull gold ceiling, stretching and easing his neck, then shivered violently. But what if he was wrong? What if Anton was right?

"No." He was determined. "They'll not make me think like that. Not now. Not ever." He looked down at his clenched fists and slowly let the anger drain from him. Then he stood and began to make his way back. Another morning in the Casting Shop lay ahead of him.

★ ★ ★

The machine flexed its eight limbs, then seemed to squat and hatch a chair from nothingness.

Kim laughed. "It seems like it's really alive sometimes."

Chan Shui, balanced on his haunches at Kim's side, turned his head to look at him, joining in with his laughter. "I know what you mean, Kim. It's that final little movement, isn't it?"

"An arachnoid. That's what it is, Shui!" Kim nodded to himself, studying the now-inert machine. Then he turned and saw the puzzlement in the older boy's face.

"It's just a name I thought of for them. Spiders – they're arachnids. And machines that mimic life – those are often called androids. Put the two together and . . ."

Chan Shui's face lit up. It was a rounded, pleasant face. A handsome, uncomplicated face, framed by neat black hair.

Kim looked at him a moment, wondering, then, keeping his voice low, asked the question he had been keeping back all morning. "Do you like me, Chan Shui?"

There was no change in Chan Shui's face. It smiled back at him, perfectly open, the dark eyes clear. "What an absurd question, Kim. What do you think?"

Kim bowed his head, embarrassed, but before he could say anything more, Chan Shui had changed the subject.

"Do you know what they call a spider in Han, Kim?"

Kim met his eyes again. "*Chih chu*, isn't it?"

Chan Shui seemed pleased. "That's right. But did you know that we have other, more flowery names for them?

You see, for us they have always been creatures of good omen. When a spider lowers itself from its web they say, 'Good luck descends from heaven'."

Kim laughed, delighted. "Are there many spiders where you are, Chan Shui?"

Chan shook his head, then stood up and began examining the control panel. "There are no spiders. Not nowadays. Only caged birds and fish in artificial ponds." He looked back at Kim, a rueful smile returning to his lips. "Oh, and us."

His bitterness had been momentary, yet it was telling. No spiders? How was that? Then Kim understood. Of course. There would be no insects of any kind within the City proper – the quarantine gates of the Net would see to that.

Chan Shui pulled the tiny phial from its slot in the panel and shook it. "Looks like we're out of ice. I'll get some more."

Kim touched his arm. "I'll get it, Chan Shui. Where do I go?"

The Han hesitated, then smiled. "Okay. It's over there, on the far side. There's a refill tank – see it? – yes, that's it. All you have to do is take this empty phial back, slip it into the hole in the panel at the bottom of the tank and punch in the machine number. This here." Chan Shui pointed out the serial number on the arachnoid's panel. "It'll return the phial after about a minute, full. Okay?"

Kim nodded and set off, threading his way between the machines. Returning, he took another, different path through the machines, imagining himself a spider moving swiftly along the spokes of his web. He was halfway back when he realised he had made a mistake. Chan Shui lay directly ahead of him, but between them stood Janko, beside his machine, a cruel smile on his face.

"Going somewhere, rat's arse?" He stepped out, blocking Kim's way.

Kim slipped the phial into the top pocket of his scholar's robe, then looked about him. One of the big collection trays had moved along the main gangway and now barred his way back, while to the left and right of him stacks of freshly-manufactured furniture filled the side gangways.

He looked back at Janko, unafraid, concerned only not to break the phial. If he did there would be a fine of a day's wages for both him and Chan Shui. For himself he didn't mind. But for Chan Shui . . .

"What do you want, Janko?"

Janko turned, facing Chan Shui's challenge. "It's none of your business, Han! Stay out of this!"

Chan Shui just laughed. "None of my business, eh? Is that so, you great bag of putrid rice? Why should you think that?"

Surprisingly Janko ignored the insult. He turned his back on Chan Shui, then faced Kim again. His voice barked out. "Come here, you little rat's arse. Come here and kneel!"

Kim bent his knees slightly, tensing, preparing to run if necessary, but there was no need. Chan Shui had moved forward quickly, silently and had jumped up onto Janko's back, sending him sprawling forward.

Kim moved back sharply.

Janko bellowed and made to get up, but Chan Shui pulled his arm up tightly behind his back and began to press down on it, threatening to break it.

"Now just leave him alone, Janko. Because next time I *will* break your arm. And we'll blame it on one of the machines."

He gave one last, pain-inducing little push against the arm, then let Janko go, getting up off him.

Janko sat up, red-faced, muttering under his breath.

Chan Shui held out his arm. "Come on, Kim. He won't touch you, I promise."

But even as Kim made to pass Janko, Janko lashed out, trying to trip him, then scrambled to his feet quickly, facing Chan Shui.

"Try it to my face, chink."

Chan Shui laughed. "Your verbal inventiveness astonishes me, Janko. Where did you learn your English, in the singsong house where your mother worked?"

Janko roared angrily and rushed at Chan Shui. But the young Han had stepped aside, and when Janko turned awkwardly, flailing out with one arm, Chan Shui caught the arm and twisted, using Janko's weight to lift and throw him against the machine.

Janko banged against the control panel, winding himself, then turned his head, frightened, as the machine reared up over him.

The watching boys laughed, then fell silent. But Janko had heard the laughter. He looked down, wiping his bloodied mouth, then swore under his breath.

At that moment the door at the far end of the Casting Shop slid open and Supervisor Nung came out. As he came down the gangway he seemed distracted, his eyes unfocused. Coming closer he paused, smiling at Kim as if remembering something. "Is everything okay, Chan Shui?" he asked, seeming not to see Janko lain there against the machine.

Chan Shui bowed his head, suppressing a smile. "Everything is fine, Supervisor Nung."

"Good." Nung moved on.

Back at their machine Kim questioned him about the incident. "Is Nung okay? He seemed odd."

Chan Shui laughed briefly, then shook his head. "Now there's a man who'll be his own ruin." He looked at Kim. "Supervisor Nung has a habit. Do you understand me, Kim?"

Kim shook his head.

"He takes drugs. Harmless, mainly, but I think he's getting deeper. These last few weeks . . . Anyway, hand me that phial."

Kim passed him the phial, then looked across, letting his eyes rest briefly on Janko's back.

"By the way, thanks for what you did, Shui. I appreciate it. But really, it wasn't necessary. I'm quick. Quicker than you think. He'd never have caught me."

Chan Shui smiled, then looked up at him again, more thoughtful than before. "Maybe. But I'd rather be certain.

Janko's a bit of a head case. He doesn't know quite when to stop. I'd rather he didn't get near you, Kim. Okay?"

Kim smiled and looked down. He felt a warmth like fire in his chest. "Okay."

★ ★ ★

"Is everything all right?"

Kim looked up from his desk console and nodded. "I'm a little tired, that's all, T'ai Cho."

"Is the work too much for you, then?"

Kim smiled. "No, T'ai Cho. I've had a few restless nights, that's all."

"Ah." That was unusual. T'ai Cho studied the boy a moment. He was a handsome boy now that the feral emaciation of the Clay had gone from his face. A good diet had worked wonders, but it could not undo the damage of those earliest years. T'ai Cho smiled and looked back down at the screen in front of him. What might Kim have been with a proper diet as an infant? With the right food and proper encouragement? T'ai Cho shuddered to think.

T'ai Cho looked up again. "We'll leave it for now, eh, Kim? A tired brain is a forgetful brain." He winked. "Even in your case. Go and have a swim. Then get to bed early. We'll take this up again tomorrow."

When Kim had gone, he sat there, thinking about the last week. Kim seemed to have settled remarkably well into the routine of the Casting Shop. Supervisor Nung was pleased with him, and Kim himself was uncomplaining. Yet something worried T'ai Cho. There was something happening in Kim – something deep down that perhaps even Kim himself hadn't recognised as yet. And now this. This sleeplessness. Well, he would watch Kim more closely for the next few days and try to fathom what it was.

He got up and went across to Kim's desk, then activated the memory. At once the screen lit up.

T'ai Cho laughed, surprised. Kim had been doodling. He had drawn a web in the centre of the screen. A fine,

600

delicate web from which hung a single thread which dropped off the bottom of the screen.

He scrolled the screen down, then laughed again. "And here's the spider!"

But then he leaned closer and, adjusting the controls, magnified the image until the spider's features filled the screen: the familiar, dark-eyed features of a child.

T'ai Cho frowned, then switched the machine off. He stood there a moment, deep in thought, then nodded to himself. Yes. He would watch him. Watch him very carefully indeed.

* * *

Kim floated on his back in the water, his eyes closed. He had been thinking of Chung Kuo, and of the people he had met in the Above. What had any of them in common? Birth, maybe. That and death, and perhaps a mild curiosity about the state between. He smiled. Yes, and that was it. That was what astonished him most of all. Their lack of curiosity. He had thought it would be different up here, in the Above. He had believed that simple distance from the Clay would bring enlightenment. But it was not so. There was a difference in them, yes, but that difference was mainly veneer. Scratch away that surface and they proved themselves every bit as dull, every bit as incuriously wedded to their senses, as the most pitiful creature of the Clay.

The smile had faded from his lips. Kim shuddered, then turned his body slowly in the water. The Clay. What was the Clay but a state of mind? An attitude?

That was the trouble with them all. They followed an idea only to a certain stage – pursued its thread only so far into the labyrinth – and then let it fall slack, as if satisfied there was no more to see, no more left to discover. Take the Aristotle File, for instance. They had been happy to see it only as a game he had devised to test his intellect and stretch himself. They had not looked beyond that. That single explanation was enough for them. But had they pushed it further – had they dealt with it, even hypothetically, as real, even for one moment – they would have seen at once where he had got it from. Even now they might wake to it. But he thought not. Their lack of curiosity would keep it from them.

It was strange, in a way, because they had explained it to him in the first place; had told him how intricately connected the finances and thus the computer systems of Chung Kuo were. It was they who had explained about "discrete systems" cut off from all the rest; islands of tight-packed information, walled round with defences. And it was they who had told him that the Project's system was "discrete".

He had discovered none of that himself. All he had discovered was that the Project's files were not alone within the walled island of their computer system. There was another file inside the system – an old, long-forgotten file that had been there a century or more, dormant, undisturbed, until Kim had found it. And not just any file. This was a library. No. More than that. It was a world. A world too rich to have been invented, too consistent – even in its errors – to have been anything less than real.

So why had the Seven hidden it? What reason could they have had for burying the past?

Freed from the burden of his secret he had spent the last two nights considering just this. He had looked at it from every side, trying to see what purpose they had had in mind. And finally he had understood. It was to put an end to change. They had lied to end the Western dream of progress. To bring about a timeless age where nothing changed. A golden age.

But that left him with the problem of himself, for what was he if not Change personified? What if not a bacillus of that self-same virus they had striven so long and hard to eradicate?

Kim opened his eyes and rolled over onto his front, then kicked out for the deeper water.

He saw it clearly now. What he was made him dangerous

to them – made him a threat to the Seven and their ways. Yet he was also valuable. He knew, despite their efforts to hide it from him, what SimFic had paid for his contract. But why had they paid so vast a sum? What did they think to use him for?

Change. He was almost certain of it. But how could he be sure?

Push deeper in, he told himself. Be curious. Is SimFic just a faceless force? A mechanism for making profits? Or does it have a personality?

And if so, whose?

The name came instantly. He had heard it often enough of late in the news. Soren Berdichev.

Yes, but who is he? A businessman. Yes. A Dispersionist. That too. But beyond that, what? What kind of man is he? Where does he come from? What does he want? And – most important of all – *what does he want of me?*

Kim ducked his head beneath the surface then came up again, shaking the water from his hair, the tiredness washed suddenly from his mind. He felt a familiar excitement in his blood and laughed. Yes, that was it! That would be his new task. To find out all he could about the man.

And when he'd found it out?

He drifted, letting the thread fall slack. Best not anticipate so far. Best find out what he could and then decide.

* * *

Soren Berdichev sat in the shadowed silence of his study, the two files laid out on the desk in front of him. The *Wu* had just gone, though the sweet, sickly scent of his perfume lingered in the air. The message of the yarrow stalks was written on the slip of paper Berdichev had screwed into a ball and thrown to the far side of the room. Yet he could see it clearly even so.

"The light has sunk into the earth:
  The image of darkening of the light.

Thus does the superior man live with the great mass:
He veils his light, yet still shines."

He banged the desk angrily. This threw all of his deliberations out. He had decided on his course of action and called upon the *Wu* merely to confirm what he had planned. But the *Wu* had contradicted him. And now he must decide again.

He could hear the *Wu*'s scratchy voice even now as the old man looked up from the stalks; could remember how his watery eyes had widened; how his wispy grey beard had stuck out stiffly from his chin.

"*K'un*, the Earth, in the above, *Li*, the Fire, down below. It is *Ming I*, the darkening of the light."

It had meant the boy. He was certain of it. The fire from the earth. *He veils his light, yet still he shines.*

"Is this a warning?" he had asked, surprising the old man, for he had never before interrupted him in all the years he had been casting the *I Ching* for him.

"A warning, *Shih* Berdichev?" The *Wu* had laughed. "The Book Of Changes does not warn. You mistake its purpose. Yet the hexagram portends harm . . . injury."

Berdichev had nodded and fallen silent. But he had known it for what it was. A warning. The signs were too strong to ignore. So now he must decide again.

He laid his glasses on the desk and picked up the newest of the files containing the genotype reports he had had done.

He spread the two charts on the desk before him, beside each other, then touched the pad, under-lighting the desk's surface.

There was no doubt about it. Even without the expert's report on the matter, it could be seen at once. The similarities were striking. He traced the mirrored symbols on the spiralling trees of the two double helices and nodded to himself.

"So you *are* Edmund Wyatt's son, Kim Ward. I wonder what Edmund would have made of that?"

He laughed sadly, realising for the first time how much he missed his dead friend's quiet strengths, then sat back, rubbing his eyes.

The genotyping and the Aristotle File, they were each reason enough in themselves to have Kim terminated. The first meant he was the son of the traitor, Wyatt, the second breached the special Edict which concealed Chung Kuo's true past. Both made Kim's life forfeit under the law, and that made the boy a threat to him. And so, despite the cost – despite the huge potential profit to be made from him – he had decided to play safe and terminate the boy, at the same time erasing all trace of those who had prepared the genotype report for him. But then the *Wu* had come.

The sun in the earth. Yes, it was the boy. There was no doubt about it. And, as he had that first time he had used the services of the *Wu*, he felt the reading could not be ignored. He had to act on it.

A small shiver ran through him, remembering that first time, almost nine years ago now. He had been sceptical and the *Wu* had angered him by laughing at his doubt. But only moments later the *Wu* had shocked him into silence with his reading.

"The wind drives over the water:
The image of dispersion.
Thus the kings of old sacrificed to the Lord
And built temples."

It had been the evening before his dinner with Edmund Wyatt and Pietr Lehmann – a meeting at which he was to decide whether or not he should join their new Dispersion faction. And there it was. The fifty-ninth hexagram – *Huan*. He remembered how he had listened, absorbed by the *Wu*'s explanation, convinced by his talk of high goals and the coming of spring after the hardness of winter. It was too close to what they had been talking of to be simple chance or coincidence. Why, even the title of the ancient book seemed suddenly apt, serendipitous – The Book Of

Changes. He had laughed and bowed and paid the *Wu* handsomely before contacting Edmund at once to tell him yes.

And so it had begun, all those years ago. Nor could he ever think of it without seeing in his mind the movement of the wind upon the water, the budding of leaves upon the branches. So how could he argue with it now – now that he had come to this new beginning?

He switched off the under-lighting, slipped the charts back into the folder, then picked up his glasses and stood, folding them and placing them in the pocket of his *pau*.

The sun in the earth . . . Yes, he would leave the boy for now. But in the morning he would contact his man in the Mid Levels and have him bomb the laboratory where they had prepared the genotypes.

★ ★ ★

Supervisor Nung sat himself behind his desk and cleared a pile of documents onto the floor before addressing Kim.

"Chan Shui is not here today," he explained, giving Kim the briefest glance. "His father has been ill and the boy is taking some time off to look after him. In the circumstances I have asked Tung Lian to look after you until Chan Shui is back with us."

The office was far more untidy than Kim remembered it. Crates, paper, even clothes, were heaped against one wall, while a pile of boxes had been left in front of the bank of screens.

"Excuse me, Supervisor Nung, but who is Tung Lian?"

Nung looked up again distractedly, then nodded. "He'll be here any moment." Then, realising his tone had been a little too sharp, he smiled at Kim before looking down again.

A moment later there was a knock and a young Han entered. He was a slightly-built, slope-shouldered boy a good two or three years younger than Chan Shui. Seeing Kim he looked down shyly, avoiding his eyes, then moved closer to the desk.

"Ah, Tung Lian. You know what to do."

Tung Lian gave a jerky bow. Then, making a gesture for Kim to follow him, he turned away.

Walking back through the Casting Shop, Kim looked about him, feeling a slight sense of unease, but there was no sign of Janko. Good. Perhaps he would be lucky. But even if Janko did turn up, he'd be all right. He would simply avoid the older boy: use guile and quickness to keep out of his way.

The machine was much the same as the one he had operated with Chan Shui and, seeing that the boy did not wish to talk to him, Kim simply got on with things.

He was sitting in the refectory at the mid morning break when he heard a familiar voice call out to him from the far side of the big room. It was Janko.

He finished his *ch'a* and set the bowl down, then calmly got up from the table.

Janko was standing in the doorway to the Casting Shop, a group of younger boys gathered about him. He was showing them something, but, seeing Kim approach, he wrapped it quickly in a cloth.

Kim had glimpsed something small and white in Janko's hand. Now, as Janko faced him, his pocked face split by an ugly smile, he realised what it had been. A tooth. Janko had lost a tooth in his fight with Chan Shui yesterday.

He smiled and saw Janko's face darken.

"What are you smiling at, rat's arse?"

He almost laughed. He had heard the words in his head a moment before Janko had uttered them. Predictable, Kim thought; that's what you are, Janko. Even so, he remembered what Chan Shui had said about not pushing him too far.

"I'm sorry, Janko. I was just so pleased to see you."

That was not the right thing, either, but it had come unbidden, as if in challenge, from his darker self.

Janko sneered. "We'll see how pleased you are . . ." But as he moved forward, Kim ducked under and round him and was through the doorway before he could turn. "Come back here!" Janko bellowed, but the bell was sounding and the boys were already filing out to get back to their machines.

For the rest of the morning Janko kept up a constant stream of foul-mouthed taunts and insults, his voice carrying above the hum of the machines to where Kim was at work. But Kim blocked it all out, looking inward, setting himself the task of connecting two of the sections of his star-web – something he had never attempted before. The problems were of a new order of difficulty and absorbed him totally, but finally he did it and, delighted, turned, smiling, to find himself facing Janko again.

"Are you taking the piss, rat's arse?"

Kim's smile faded slowly.

"Didn't you hear the bell?" Janko continued, and the group of boys behind him laughed, as if it was the funniest thing anyone had ever said.

Dull-wits, thought Kim, surprised that he had missed the bell. He glanced across at Tung Liang and saw at once how uneasy he was. Strangely, he found himself trying to reassure the young Han. "It's okay," he said. "I'm all right, Tung Lian. Really I am."

Janko echoed back his words, high-pitched, in what he must have thought was a good imitation of Kim's voice, and the ghouls behind him brayed once more.

He felt a slight twinge of fear at the pit of his stomach, but nothing that cowed him or made him feel daunted in any way by the boy in front of him.

"I don't want to fight with you, Janko," he said quietly.

"Fight?" Janko laughed, surprised, then leaned towards Kim menacingly. "Who said anything about fighting? I just want to beat the shit out of you, rat's arse!"

Kim looked about him. Boys blocked both his way back and his route to the entrance doorway. He looked up. Yes, he had thought as much. The two overhead cameras were covered over with jackets. He had been set-up. They had planned this. Perhaps since they'd heard Chan Shui was absent.

So Janko wasn't alone in hating him. Far from it. Kim shivered. He hadn't realised.

"Please, Janko . . ." Tung Liang began feebly, but Janko barked at him to be quiet and he did so at once, moving back out of the way.

So I'm alone, Kim thought. *Just as Anton said I'd be. Them and us. Or, in this case, them and me.* The humour of it pleased him. Made him laugh.

"What's so funny, rat's arse?"

"You," said Kim, no longer caring what he said. "You big strutting bag of bird shit."

But Janko merely smiled. He moved a pace closer, knowing there was nowhere for Kim to run this time.

But run Kim did, not towards the door or back away from Janko, but directly at Janko – up, onto his chest and over the top of him as he fell backwards, his mouth open wide in surprise, then away towards the toilets.

"Stop him!" yelled Janko, clambering to his feet again. "Block the little bastard off!"

Kim ran, dodging past anyone who tried to stop him. He would lock himself in. Hold out until Nung came out to investigate, or T'ai Cho came up to see why he'd not returned.

But they had pre-empted him. Someone had sealed all the locks to the toilet doors with an ice-based glue. He checked them all quickly, just in case he had been mistaken, then turned. Janko was standing there, as he knew he would be, watching him.

Kim looked up. Of course. They had covered the camera here, too. Very thorough, Kim thought, and knew from its thoroughness that Janko had not been involved in planning this. This was all far too clever for him. Janko was only the front-man, the gullible dupe who would carry out the plan. No, he wasn't its architect: he had been manipulated to this point by someone else.

The realisation made Kim go cold. There was only one of them in the whole Casting Shop capable of planning this. And he was not here . . .

Janko laughed and began to come at him. Kim could feel the hatred emanating from the boy, like something real, something palpable. And this time his hands weren't empty. This time they held a knife.

★ ★ ★

"T'ai Cho! T'ai Cho!"

T'ai Cho stopped and turned. Director Andersen's secretary was running down the corridor after him.

"What is it, woman?" he said, conscious of his colleagues' stares and annoyed by her lack of decorum. But a moment later, when he had been told what had happened, he took her arm, oblivious of 'proper conduct', and hurried her back down the corridor.

"Where is he, for the gods' sakes?"

A slight colour came to her cheek, and he understood at once, but he hadn't meant Andersen. He pulled her round, facing him.

"The boy, I mean! Where's the boy?"

She was flustered and close to tears. It was the first crisis that had come up in her office and Director Andersen had not been there to deal with it.

"I don't know!" she wailed. "Supervisor Nung's note was only brief. He gave no details other than what I've told you."

"Gods!" T'ai Cho beat his brow with the palm of his left hand and looked this way and that, then began to hurry her back towards Director Andersen's offices again.

Outside Andersen's door he pulled her round again and spoke to her slowly, making sure she understood what she had to do.

"I know it's embarrassing, but it'll be more embarrassing for the Director if he doesn't get to hear about this fast. Whatever singsong house he's in, get a message to him fast and get him back here. *Here!* Understand me, woman?"

When she hesitated he barked at her. "Just do it! I'll go and see how the boy is and sort out things that end. But Director Andersen must be contacted. The whole Project's in jeopardy unless you can get him here."

The firmness of his instructions seemed to calm her and she bowed and went inside, to do as she'd been told.

T'ai Cho found Nung slumped over his desk, O'D'd. He had been ready to lay hands on him to get at the truth of things but it was too late for that now. The message to Andersen must have been the last thing he managed to do in his worthless life.

He shivered and looked about him, then noticed one of the boys hanging about at the far end of the Casting Shop. He ran across to him, grabbing the boy by the arm so that he could not make off.

"Where did they take Kim? You know, the Clayborn boy? Where did they take him?"

He noticed the strange look of revulsion the boy gave him at the mention of Kim, but held on, shaking the boy until he got some sense from him. Then he threw him aside and ran on, towards the lifts.

They had taken him to the local Security post. Of course! Where else? But he was not thinking straight, he was just acting now, following his instincts, trying to get to Kim before they hurt him any more.

The soldier at the desk told him to sit and wait. He lifted up the barrier and went through anyway, ignoring the shout from behind him. Then, when the soldier laid hands on him from behind, he whirled about and shouted at the man.

"Do you realise who I am, soldier?"

The tone of absolute authority in his voice – a tone he had once used to cower unruly boys fresh from the Clay – worked perfectly. The soldier backed off a pace and began to incline his head. T'ai Cho pressed the advantage before the soldier could begin to think again.

"My uncle is the Junior Minister, T'ai Feng, responsible for Security Subsidies. Lay a finger on me and he'll break you, understand me, soldier?"

This time the soldier bowed fully and brought his hand up to his chest in salute.

"Good! Now lead me through to your commanding

officer at once. This is a matter of the utmost urgency both to myself and to my uncle, the Junior Minister."

As the soldier bowed again and moved past him, T'ai Cho realised fleetingly that it was his robes which had helped create the right impression. He was wearing his lecturer's *pau* with the bright blue patch, in many ways reminiscent of the sort of gown worn by a high official.

The soldier barely had time to announce him – and no time to turn and query his name – before he burst in behind him and took a chair in front of the Security officer.

This officer was less impressed by tones and gowns and talk of uncles. He asked immediately to see T'ai Cho's permit card. T'ai Cho threw it across the desk at him, then leaned across almost threateningly.

"Where's the boy? The boy from the Clay?"

The officer looked up at him, then down at the permit card. Then he threw the card back at T'ai Cho.

"If I were you, *Shih* T'ai, I'd leave here at once, before you get into any more trouble."

T'ai Cho ignored the card. He glared at the officer. "Where's the boy? I'm not leaving until I've seen the boy!"

The officer began to get up from his chair, but T'ai Cho leaned right across and pulled him down.

"Sit down, for the gods' sake and hear me out!"

T'ai Cho shivered. He had never felt such anger or fear or urgency before. They shaped his every action now.

"*Where is the boy*?" he demanded fiercely.

The officer moved his hand slightly and pressed a pad on the desk, summoning help. He was certain now he had another madman on his hands.

"Understand me, *Shih* T'ai. The boy is in safe hands. We're seeing to the matter. It's a simple case of assault of a citizen by a non-registered being. We'll be terminating the N.R.B. in about an hour or so, once authorisation has come down from above."

"*You're doing what?!*" T'ai Cho screamed. He stood up violently, making the officer do the same; his hands out defensively, expecting attack.

"Please, *Shih* T'ai. Sit down and calm down."

The door slid open quietly behind T'ai Cho, but he heard it even so and moved around the desk, so that his back was against the wall.

"You have no jurisdiction here," the officer said, his voice calmer now that he had assistance. "Whatever your relationship to the boy, I'm afraid the matter is out of your hands."

T'ai Cho answered him at once. "It's you who doesn't understand. Kim Ward is not an N.R.B., as you so ridiculously put it, but one of the most brilliant and important scientific minds in the whole of Chung Kuo. SimFic have negotiated a contract for his services for *ten million yuan*."

He had said the last three words slowly and clearly and with maximum emphasis and saw the effect the fantastic sum had on them.

"Ten million?" The officer gave a brief, thoughtful laugh. Then he shook his head. "Oh no. I don't believe you, *Shih* T'ai. This is just more of your talk of important uncles!"

T'ai Cho shook his head, then spoke again, his voice ringing with firmness and determination. "There's one more thing you don't understand. I don't care what happens to me. But you do. That makes me stronger than you. Oh, you can think me a liar or a madman, but just consider – if you ignore my warning and go ahead without checking up, then you'll be liable directly to SimFic for unauthorised destruction of their property." He laughed, suddenly horrified by this nightmare, sickened that he should even need to do this. Couldn't they see he was only a little boy – a frightened little boy who'd been savagely attacked?

Still the officer hesitated. "There are certain procedures. I . . ."

T'ai Cho yelled at the man; using language he had never before in his life used. "Fuck your procedures! Get on to Director Andersen at once. Unless you really want to be sued for ten million yuan!"

The officer blanched, then consulted his compatriot a

second. Swallowing, he turned back to T'ai Cho. "Would you be willing to wait in a cell for half an hour while we make checks?"

T'ai Cho bowed. "Of course. That's all I want you to do. Here," he took a jotpad from the pocket of his robe and, with the stylus from the officer's desk, wrote Andersen's office contact number and his name on the tiny screen. "You'll find they'll switch you through twice, so hold on. It's a discrete service, you see."

The officer hesitated, then gave the smallest bow, half-convinced now that T'ai Cho had calmed.

"Andersen?"

"That's right. He might not be there at once, but keep trying. I've asked his secretary to get him back there as soon as possible. He was . . . on business."

An hour later T'ai Cho and four soldiers were taking Kim back to the Project. Kim was heavily sedated and secured in a special carrying harness. It was hard to see what injuries, if any, he had received in the fight with the other boys. His face seemed unmarked. But he was alive and he was not going to be "terminated" as that bastard in the Security Post had termed it.

Now it was up to Andersen.

Director Andersen met him at the top gate. "I owe you, T'ai Cho," he said, slapping the tutor's back. But T'ai Cho turned on him angrily.

"I didn't do it to save your hide, Andersen. Where *were* you?"

Andersen swallowed, noting the open disrespect. "I . . . I . . ." he blustered, then he bowed. "I'm sorry, T'ai Cho. I know you didn't. Even so, I'm indebted. If there's anything . . ."

But T'ai Cho simply strode past him, disgusted, thinking of Nung and what had been allowed to happen to Kim. All of it was indirectly Andersen's fault. For not making all the right checks beforehand. If there was any justice, Berdichev would have his hide for it!

Half an hour later he was back in Andersen's office.

"They're what?!"

Andersen looked at the package the messenger had delivered ten minutes earlier and repeated what he had said.

"The boy's family are suing us for assault by a property owned by the Project. They've started a suit for fifteen million yuan."

T'ai Cho sat back, aghast. "But the boy attacked Kim!"

Andersen laughed bitterly. "If that's the case, T'ai Cho, why is their boy on the critical list and not Kim? Here, look at these injuries! They're horrific! More than seventeen broken bones and his left ear bitten off. Bitten off! The little savage!"

T'ai Cho glared at him, then looked down at the 2D shots the family's advocate had sent with his package. Gods! he thought, revolted despite himself. Did Kim do this? And he was afraid Matyas would kill *him*!

Andersen was muttering to himself now. "Fuck him! Fuck the little bastard! Why did he have to go and attack one of them?" He looked at T'ai Cho. "Why didn't you tell me he was capable of this?"

T'ai Cho went to protest, then thought of all that had been happening the last week or so. Were there warning signs? The restless nights? The problems with Matyas? Should he have foreseen this? Then he rejected all that. He threw the photos down and, with all the angry indignation of the parent of a wronged child, he stood and shouted at Andersen across the table.

"He didn't attack this boy! I *know* he didn't! They attacked him! They must have! Don't you understand that, yet?"

Andersen looked up at him scornfully. "Who gives a shit, eh? We're all out of a job now. There's no way we can contest this. Nung's dead and the cameras were all covered over. There's not a bruise on Kim and the other lad's in critical." He laughed. "Who in their right mind would believe Kim was the victim?"

T'ai Cho was watching the Director closely now. "So what are you going to do?"

Andersen, as ever, had pre-empted him. He saw it in his face.

"I've taken advice already."

"And?"

Andersen pushed the package aside and leaned across the table. "The Project's advocate suggests there are ways we can contain the damage. You see, there's not just the matter of the Project's liability to the parents of the injured boy but the question of personal responsibility." He looked directly at T'ai Cho. "Yours and mine, in particular. Now, if Kim had actually died in the fight . . ."

T'ai Cho shook his head in disbelief. His voice, when he found it again, came out as a whisper. "What have you done, Andersen? What in the gods' names have you done?"

Andersen looked away. "I've signed the order. He'll be terminated in an hour."

* * *

Berdichev went to the cell to see the boy one last time before they sent him on. Kim lay there, pale, his dark eyes closed, the bulky secure-jacket like an incomplete chrysalis, disguising how frail he really was.

Well, well, Berdichev thought, you have tried your hardest to make my decision an empty one, haven't you? But perhaps it was just this that the *Wu* had foretold. The darkening of the light.

He knelt and touched the boy's cheek. It was cooler than his own flesh, but still warm. Yes, it was fortunate he had got here in time – before that arsehole Andersen had managed to bugger things up for good and all. He had T'ai Cho to thank for that.

And now it was all his. Kim *and* the Project. And all for the asking price of ten million yuan he had originally contracted purely for the boy.

Berdichev laughed. It had all been rather easy to manage in the circumstances. The Board had agreed the deal at once, and to help facilitate matters he had offered eight of the ten sitting members an increase in their yearly stipend.

The other two he had wanted out anyway, and when the vote went against them he had accepted their resignations without argument. As for the matter of the aggrieved parents, their claim was dropped when they received his counter-claim for two hundred million – his estimate of the potential loss of earnings SimFic would suffer if Kim was permanently brain-damaged. They had been further sweetened by an out-of-court no-liability-accepted settlement of fifty thousand yuan. More than enough in exchange for their dull-witted son.

But what damage had it done? What would Kim be like when the wraps came off and the scars had healed? Not the physical scars, for they were miraculously slight, but the deeper scars – the psychological ones?

He shuddered, feeling suddenly closer to Kim than he had ever been. As if the *Wu*'s reading had connected him somehow to the boy. The sun was buried in the earth once more, but would it rise again? Would Kim become again what he had been? Or was he simple, unawakened Clay again?

Ten million yuan. That was how much he had gambled on Kim's full and complete recovery. And the possible return? He laughed. Maybe a thousand times as much! Maybe nothing.

Berdichev got up and wiped his hands on his jacket, then turned to the two SimFic guards, indicating that they should take the boy away. Then, when they had gone, he crossed the cell and looked at its second occupant. This one was also trussed.

He laughed and addressed the corpse of the Director. "You thought you'd fuck with me, eh, Andersen? Well, no one does that and gets away with it. No one. Not even you."

And, still laughing, he turned and left the cell.

CHAPTER·17

ICE AND FIRE

"Be patient, Li Yuan, we'll not be much longer now!"

Pearl Heart tugged the two wings of his collar together with a show of mock annoyance, then fastened the first of the four tiny catches. He was sitting on the edge of his bed, Pearl Heart kneeling on the floor in front of him, dressing him, while Sweet Rose knelt on the bed, behind him, brushing and braiding his hair.

The younger girl laughed softly. "Your hair's so long, Li Yuan. Such good, strong hair. It doesn't split easily." She leaned forward, brushing her nose against it, breathing in its scent. "I wish I had such hair, dear Yuan."

He made to turn and speak to her, but Pearl Heart gently brought his head back round, tutting to herself. The last two catches were always the most tricky to fasten.

Li Yuan laughed softly. "Your hair is lovely too, Sweet Rose. And never more lovely than when it rests across my lap."

Sweet Rose blushed and looked down, reminded of what they had been up to only hours before. Pearl Heart looked up into his face, amused. "Perhaps you'd like all five of us next time?"

He looked past her, smiling. "Perhaps . . ."

"Still," she continued, frowning with concentration as she tried to fix the last of the catches. "It will be good for you to get some exercise."

Li Yuan laughed, delighted. "You really think so, Pearl Heart? After last night?"

She leaned back away from him with a sigh, the collar

fastened at last, then shook her head, her eyes sparkling.

"You young men. You think you're real horsemen simply because you can keep at it all night long, don't you? But there's more to horsemanship than keeping in the saddle!"

Sweet Rose had gone silent, her head bowed. Pearl Heart looked back. Li Yuan was staring at her strangely. She thought back, then ducked her head, blushing, realising how she had linked the two things. Li Yuan was about to go out riding with Fei Yen, and there she was saying . . .

"Forgive me, Prince, I didn't mean . . ."

But Li Yuan simply leaned forward and took her head between his hands, kissing her forehead before pressing her face down into his lap and closing his legs about her playfully.

She fought up away, enjoying the game, then stood there a few paces off, admiring him. Sweet Rose had finished and had placed a riding hat upon his tight-coiled hair. He was dressed entirely in green, from hat down to boots: a dozen subtle shades of green, yet each of them fresh and bright, reminiscent of the first days of spring, when the snow has just thawed.

"You look . . ." She laughed and clapped her hands. "You look like a prince, Li Yuan!"

He laughed with her, then turned to give Sweet Rose a farewell peck before rushing off.

The two maids watched him go, then began to tidy the room. As Pearl Heart stripped the covers from the cushions, she noticed the square of silk beneath one of them. It was a pale lilac with the pictogram of the Yin family in green in one corner. She knew at once whose it was, and lifted it to her nose briefly before returning it, making no mention to Sweet Rose.

"She's beautiful, don't you think, Pearl Heart?"

Sweet Rose was gazing outward through the open doorway, following the figure of Li Yuan as he made his way through the gardens.

"They say there's no one quite as beautiful in all the

Families as Fei Yen. But she's a *hua pao*, a flowery panther. She's headstrong and wilful for all her beauty."

Sweet Rose sighed and looked back at her older sister. "And Li Yuan, he seems to love her like a brother."

Pearl Heart laughed. "Have you seen how his eyes grow soft at the merest glimpse of her. He's hooked, the poor little one."

"Ah . . ." Sweet Rose glanced round once more, then busied herself, disturbed by what Pearl Heart had said. A moment later, while she was gathering up the linen, she stopped suddenly and looked up again, her eyes moist. "Then I feel pity for him, Pearl Heart. For nothing can come of it."

Pearl Heart nodded sagely. "It is our law, Sweet Rose. A man cannot marry his brother's wife. And there's wisdom in that law, *mei mei*, for think what would come of things were it not so. There are men who would murder their own brothers for the sake of a worthless woman!"

Sweet Rose looked down. "And yet *we* are sisters. And we share a man."

Pearl Heart laughed and began to take the new silk sheets from the drawer. "Li Yuan's a boy, and they're less complex than men. But in any case, the whole thing's totally different. We are here only to help him and teach him. We must think not of ourselves but of the future T'ang."

Sweet Rose studied her sister a moment, noting how she busied herself as if unconcerned. But she had heard the undertone of bitterness in her voice and could see the faint trace of regret at the corners of her mouth and in her eyes and knew that, whatever else she said, she too was just a little in love with the young Prince.

★ ★ ★

"What are you reading?"

Fei Yen half turned her face towards him, then smiled and set the book down on the wooden ledge beside her. "Ah, Li Yuan, I wondered when you'd come."

She was sitting in a bower overlooking one of the

garden's tiny waterfalls. The interlaced branches of the maple overhead threw her features into shadow as she looked at him, but he could see that her hair had been put up in a complex bun, the dark, fine bunches held there by tiny ivory combs no bigger than his thumb nail. She was wearing a waist-length, curve-edged riding-tunic with a high collar, the satin a delicate lavender with the thinnest edging of black, while her riding breeches were of dark blue silk, cut almost to her figure. Her boots were of kid leather, dyed to match the breeches.

He let his query pass. "Shall I come and sit with you, Fei Yen?"

"Wait there, Li Yuan. I'll come out to you. It's rather warm in here. Why don't we walk down to the terrace?"

He bowed, then moved back to let her pass, smelling the scent of her for the first time that day. *Mei hua.* Plum blossom. He fell in beside her on the path.

"How is your father, Yin Tsu?"

She laughed. "He's fine. As he was yesterday when you asked. And my three brothers too, before you ask." She stopped and inclined her head towards him. "Let's drop formality, shall we, Li Yuan? I find it all so tiresome after a while."

A small bird flitted from branch to branch overhead, distracting them both a moment. When they looked down again it was at the same time. Their eyes met and they laughed.

"All right," he said. "But in public . . ."

She touched his arm gently. "In public it shall be as always." She lifted her chin in imitation of an old, starchy courtier. "We'll be as tight-laced as a Minister's corsets!"

He giggled, unable to help himself, then saw she was watching him, enjoying his laughter.

"Come, Yuan. Let's go down."

She let him take her arm. A flight of stone steps snaked steeply downward, following the slope, ending with a tiny bridge of stone. But the bridge was only wide enough for one to cross at a time. Li Yuan went first then turned, holding out his hand to help her across the tiny stream.

She took his hand and let him draw her to him, brushing past him closely, then turned to look back at him, her face in full sunlight for the first time since he had met her in the bower.

"What's that?"

She began to smile, then saw the look on his face. "It's a *mian ye*. A beauty mark, that's all. Why, don't you like it?"

He made the slightest movement of his head, reluctant to find anything about her less than perfect.

"Here, wipe it off!"

He took the silk handkerchief she offered him, realising at once that it was the twin to the one he had in his room, beneath his pillow. Resisting the temptation to put it to his face, he reached out and made to touch the mark, but Fei Yen laughed and pushed his hand away.

"Come here, Li Yuan! How can you do it from over there? You'll have to hold my cheek while you rub the mark away. It isn't easy, you know!"

He moved closer, then gently took her cheek and turned it, almost fearing to hurt her. His body was touching hers now, brushing against her, and he could feel her warmth and smell the scent of plum blossom on her clothes. He felt a slight shiver pass down his spine, then began, brushing at it, gently at first, then harder, licking the silk then dabbing it against her cheek, until the mark was gone.

And all the while she was watching him, a strange, unreadable expression in her dark, beautiful eyes. He was conscious of her breathing: of her warm breath on his neck; of the soft rise and fall of her breasts beneath the tightly-fitting tunic; of the warm pulse of her body where it touched his own.

He shuddered and moved away, bringing his hand back from her face; looking down at it a moment, as if it wasn't his. Then, recollecting himself, he offered her the silk.

Her smile, her answer, made him burn. "Keep it. Put it with its twin."

He swallowed, then smiled and gave a small bow of thanks.

On the terrace she stood there, her hands on the balcony, looking out across the lake. "Do you still want to ride?"

He looked away, a faint colour in his cheeks, remembering what Pearl Heart had said.

"What is it?" she asked, touching his shoulder gently.

"Nothing," he said, then laughed and changed the subject. "Do you remember that day here, on the far side of the lake? The day of the reception?"

She looked across and nodded, her mouth opening slightly, showing her perfect white teeth. "The day I let Han beat me at archery."

They were silent a moment, a strange mix of emotions in the air between them. Then she turned back to him, smiling.

"Let's go across. I'm not in the mood for riding. Let's walk, and talk of old times, eh, Yuan?"

He looked up shyly at her, then smiled. "Yes. I'd like that. I'd like that very much."

* * *

For a long time after Li Yuan had gone, Fei Yen stood there at the edge of the lake, staring out across the water, deep in thought.

She had thought it would be amusing to play an ancient game: to flirt with him and maybe afterwards, in some secret place away from prying eyes, introduce him to pleasures finer than those his maids could offer. But Li Yuan had wanted more than that: Much more, despite the impossibility of it.

She could still hear his voice echoing in her head.

"Your son will be T'ang."

Had he seen her surprise? Had he seen how unprepared she was for that? Her laughter had been designed to put him off; to make him think she thought it all a joke, when she could see from his eyes how serious he was.

623

"Impossible," she had said when he repeated it. "You know the law, Li Yuan."

"You slept with him? Is that what you're saying?"

"What?" She had turned, flustered, shocked by his impropriety. "What do you mean?"

He seemed obsessed with it; insistent. "Did you sleep with him? Before the wedding? It is important, Fei Yen. Did you or didn't you?"

She swallowed and looked down, flushing deeply at the neck. "No! How could I have done? There was never an opportunity. And then . . ."

Her tears made him relent. But in the breathing space they earned her, she began to understand. The law said that a man could not marry his brother's wife. But was a wife really a wife until the marriage had been consummated?

She had looked up at him, wide-eyed: astonished both that he wanted her and that he was prepared to challenge the law itself to have her.

"You understand me, then, Fei Yen?" he had said and she had nodded, her whole being silenced by the enormity of what he was suggesting to her. His wife. He wanted her to be his wife. But they had had the chance to say no more than that, for then the old servant had come and brought the summons from his father, and he, suddenly more flustered than she, had bowed and gone at once, leaving things unresolved.

Your son will be T'ang.

Yes, she thought, tears of joy coming suddenly to her eyes. So it shall pass. As it was always meant to be.

* * *

His father's Chancellor, Chung Hu-yan, met him before the doors to the Hall of Eternal Truth. The huge doors were closed and guarded, the great wheel of the *Ywei lung* towering over the man as he bowed to the boy.

"What is it, Hu-yan? What does my father want?"

But Chung Hu-yan was not his normal smiling self. He looked at Li Yuan strangely, almost sternly, then removed the boy's riding hat and turned him about full circle, inspecting him.

"I was going riding . . ." Li Yuan began to explain, but the Chancellor shook his head, as if to say, *Be silent, boy*.

Yuan swallowed. What had happened? Why was Hu-yan so stern and formal? Was it the business with the maids? Oh gods, was it that?

Satisfied, Chung Hu-yan stepped back and signalled to the guards.

Two bells sounded, the first sweet and clear, the second deep and resonant. Slowly, noiselessly, the great doors swung back.

Yuan stared down the aisle of the great hall and shivered. What was going on? Why did his father not meet with him in his rooms, as he had always done? Why all this sudden ritual?

Li Shai Tung sat on his throne atop the Presence Dais at the far end of the Hall.

"Prostrate yourself, Li Yuan," Chung Hu-yan whispered, and Yuan did as he was bid, making the full *k'o t'ou* to his father for the first time since the day of the reception – the day of the archery contest.

He stood slowly, the cold touch of the tiles lingering like a ghostly presence against his brow. Then, with the briefest glance at Chung Hu-yan, he moved forward, between the pillars, approaching his father.

Halfway down the aisle he noticed the stranger who stood to one side of the Presence Dais at the bottom of the steps. A tall, thin Han with a shaven head, who wore the sienna robes of a scholar, but on whose chest was a patch of office.

He stopped at the foot of the steps and made his obeisance once again, then stood and looked up at the T'ang.

"You asked for me, father?"

His father was dressed in the formal robe he normally wore only for Ministerial audiences, the bright yellow cloth edged in black and decorated with fierce golden dragons. The high-tiered court crown made him seem even taller than he was; more dignified, if that was possible. When Li Yuan addressed him he gave the barest nod of recognition, his face, like Chung Hu-yan's, curiously stern, uncompromising. This was not how he usually greeted his son.

Li Shai Tung studied his son a moment, then leaned forward and pointed to the Han who stood below the steps.

"This is Ssu Lu Shan. He has something to tell you about the world. Go with him, Li Yuan."

Li Yuan turned to the man and gently inclined his head, showing his respect. At once the scholar bowed low, acknowledging Li Yuan's status as a prince. Li Yuan turned back, facing his father, waiting, expecting more, then understood the audience was at an end. He made his *k'o t'ou* a third and final time, then backed away, puzzled and deeply troubled by the strict formality of his father's greeting, the oddness of his instruction.

Outside, Li Yuan turned and faced the stranger, studying him. He had the thin, pinched face of a New Confucian official; a face made longer by the bareness of the scalp. His eyes, however, were hard and practical. They met Li Yuan's examination unflinchingly.

"Tell me, Ssu Lu Shan. What Ministry is it that you wear the patch of?"

Ssu Lu Shan bowed. "It is The Ministry, Prince Yuan." From another it might have seemed cryptic, but Li Yuan understood at once that there was nothing elusive in the man's answer.

"*The* Ministry?"

"So it is known, Excellency."

Li Yuan walked on, Ssu Lu Shan keeping up with him, several paces behind, as protocol demanded.

At the doorway to his suite of rooms, Li Yuan stopped and turned to face the man again.

"Do we need privacy for our meeting, Ssu Lu Shan?"

The man bowed. "It would be best, Excellency. What I have to say is for your ears only. I would prefer it if the doors were locked and the windows closed while I am talking."

Li Yuan hesitated, feeling a vague unease. But this was what his father wanted; what his father had ordered him to do. And if his father had ordered it, he must trust this man and accommodate him.

When the doors were locked and the windows closed, Ssu Lu Shan turned, facing him. Li Yuan sat in a tall chair by the window overlooking the gardens while the scholar – if that was what he was – stood on the far side of the room, breathing deeply, calmly, preparing himself.

Dust motes floated slowly in the still warm air of the room as Ssu Lu Shan began, his voice deep, authoritative, and clear as polished jade, telling the history of Chung Kuo – the true history – beginning with Pao Chan's arrival on the shores of the Caspian Sea in 97 AD, and his subsequent withdrawal, leaving Europe to the *Ta Ts'in*, the Roman Empire.

Hours passed and still Ssu Lu Shan spoke on, telling of a Europe Li Yuan had never dreamed existed – a Europe racked by Dark Ages and damned by religious bigotry, enlightened by the Renaissance, then torn again by wars of theology, ideology and nationalism; a Europe swept up, finally, by the false ideal of technological progress, born of the Industrial Revolution; an ideal fuelled by the concept of evolution and fanned by population pressures into the fire of Change – Change at any price.

And what had Chung Kuo done meanwhile but enclose itself behind great walls? Like a bloated maggot it had fed upon itself until, when the West had come, it had found the Han Empire weak, corrupt, and ripe for conquest.

So they came to the Century of Change, to the Great Wars, to the long years of revolution in Chung Kuo, and finally to the Pacific Century and the decline and fall of the American Empire, ending in the chaos of the Years of Blood.

This, the closest to the present, was, for Li Yuan, the worst of it, and as if he sensed this, Ssu Lu Shan's voice grew softer as he told of the tyrant, Tsao Ch'un and his "Crusade of Purity", of the building of the City and, finally, of the Ministry and the burning of the books, the burial of the past.

"As you know, Prince Yuan, Tsao Ch'un wished to create an utopia that would last ten thousand years – to bring into being the world beyond the peach-blossom river, as we Han have traditionally known it. But the price of its attainment was high."

Ssu Lu Shan paused, his eyes momentarily dark with the pain of what he had witnessed on ancient newsreels. Then, slowly, he began again.

"In 2062 Japan, Chung Kuo's chief rival in the East, was the first victim of Tsao Ch'un's barbaric methods when, without warning – after Japanese complaints about Han incursions in Korea – the Han leader bombed Honshu, concentrating his nuclear devices on the major population centres of Tokyo and Kyoto. Over the next eight years three great Han armies swept the smaller islands of Kyushu and Shikoku, destroying everything and killing every Japanese they found, while the rest of Japan was blockaded by sea and air. Over the following twenty years they did the same with the islands of Honshu and Hokkaido, turning the "islands of the gods" into a wasteland.

"While this was happening, the crumbling Western nation states were looking elsewhere, obsessed with their own seemingly insuperable problems. Chung Kuo alone of all the Earth's nations remained stable, and, as the years passed, grew quickly at the expense of others.

"The eradication of Japan taught Tsao Ch'un many lessons, yet only one other time was he to use similar methods. In future he sought, in his famous phrase, "not to destroy but to exclude" – though his definition of "exclusion" often made it a synonym for destruction. As he built his great City – the huge machines moving slowly outward from Pei Ching, building the living sections – so he peopled it, choosing carefully who was to live within its walls. His criteria, like his methods, were not merely crude but idiosyncratic, reflecting not merely his wish to make his great City free of all those human troubles that had plagued previous social experiments, but also his deeply-held hatred of the black and aboriginal races."

Noting Li Yuan's surprise, Ssu Lu Shan nodded soberly. "Yes, Prince Yuan, there were once whole races of black men. Men no more different from ourselves than the *Hung Mao*. Billions of them."

He lowered his eyes, then continued. "Well, as the City grew so his men went out, questioning, searching among the *Hung Mao* for those who were free from physical disability, political dissidence, religious bigotry and intellectual pride. And where he encountered organised opposition he enlisted the aid of groups sympathetic to his aims. In Southern Africa and North America, in Europe and in the People's Democracy Of Russia, huge popular movements grew up amongst the *Hung Mao* supporting Tsao Ch'un and welcoming his stability after decades of bitter suffering. Many of them were only too pleased to share in his crusade of intolerance – his "Policy of Purity". In the so-called "civilised" West, particularly, Tsao Ch'un often found that his work had been done for him long before his officials arrived.

"Only the Middle East proved problematic. There a great Jihad was launched against the Han, Moslem and Jew casting off millennia of enmity to fight against a common threat. Tsao Ch'un answered them harshly, as he had answered Japan. The Middle East and large parts of the Indian sub-continent were swiftly reduced to the wilderness they remain to this day. But it was in Africa that Tsao Ch'un's policies were most nakedly displayed. There the native peoples were moved on before the encroaching City and, like cattle in a desert, they starved or died from exhaustion, driven on relentlessly by a brutal Han army.

"Tsao Ch'un's ideal was, he believed, a high one. He sought to eradicate the root causes of human dissidence and fulfil all material needs. Yet in terms of human suffering, his pacification of the Earth was unprecedented. It was a grotesquely flawed ideal, and more than three billion people died as a direct result of his policies."

Ssu Lu Shan met the young Prince's eyes again, a strange resignation in his own. "Tsao Ch'un killed the old world. He buried it deep beneath his glacial City. But eventually his brutality and tyranny proved too much even for those who had helped him carry out his scheme. In 2087 his Council of Seven Ministers rose up against him, using North European mercenaries, and overthrew him, setting up a new government. They divided the world – Chung Kuo – amongst themselves, each calling himself T'ang. The rest you know. The rest, since then, is true."

In the silence that followed, Li Yuan sat there perfectly still, staring blankly at the air in front of him. He could see the stern faces of his father and his father's Chancellor, and understood them now. They had known this moment lay before him. Had known how he would feel.

He shuddered and looked down at his hands where they clasped each other in his lap – so far away from him, they seemed. A million *li* from the dark, thinking centre of himself. Yes. But what did he feel?

A nothingness. A kind of numbness at the core of him. Almost an absence of feeling. He felt hollow, his limbs brittle like the finest porcelain. He turned his head, facing Ssu Lu Shan again, and even the simple movement of his neck muscles seemed suddenly false, *unreal*. He shivered and focused on the waiting man.

"Did my brother know of this?"

Ssu Lu Shan shook his head. It was as if he had done with words.

"I see." He looked down. "Then why has my father chosen to tell me now? Why should I, at my age, know what Han Ch'in at his did not?"

When Ssu Lu Shan did not answer him, Li Yuan looked up again. He frowned. It was as if the Han were in some kind of trance.

"Ssu Lu Shan?"

The man's eyes focused on him, but still he said nothing.

"Have you done?"

Ssu Lu Shan's sad smile was extraordinary: as if all he

was, all he knew, were gathered up into that small, ironic smile. "Almost," he answered softly. "There's one last thing."

Li Yuan raised a hand, commanding him to be silent. "A question first. My father sent you, I know. But how do I know that what you've told me today is true? What proof have you?"

Ssu Lu Shan looked down a moment and Li Yuan's eyes followed their movement, then widened as he saw the knife he had drawn from the secret fold in his scholar's *pau*.

"Ssu Lu Shan!" he cried out, jumping up, suddenly alert to the danger he was in, alone in a locked room with an armed stranger.

But Ssu Lu Shan paid him no attention. He lowered himself onto his knees and laid the knife on the floor in front of him. While Li Yuan watched he untied the fastenings of his robe and pulled it up over his head, then bundled it together between his legs. Except for a loin-cloth he was naked now.

Li Yuan swallowed. "What is this?" he said softly, beginning to understand.

Ssu Lu Shan looked up at him. "You ask what proof I have. This now is my proof." His eyes were smiling strangely, as if with relief at the shedding of a great and heavy burden carried too long. "This, today, was the purpose of my life. Well, now I have fulfilled my purpose, and the laws of Chung Kuo deem my life forfeit for the secrets I have uttered in this room. So it is. So it must be. For they are great, grave secrets."

Li Yuan shivered. "I understand, Ssu Lu Shan. But surely there is another way than this?"

Ssu Lu Shan did not answer him. Instead he looked down, taking a long breath that seemed to restore his inner calm. Then, picking up the knife again, he readied himself, breathing deeply, slowly, the whole of him concentrated on the point of the knife where it rested, perfectly still, only a hand's length from his stomach.

Li Yuan wanted to cry out; to step forward and stop Ssu

Lu Shan, but he knew this too was part of it. Part of the lesson. To engrave it in his memory. *For they are great, grave secrets.* He shivered violently. Yes, he understood. Even this.

"May your spirit soul rise up to Heaven," he said, blessing Ssu Lu Shan. He knelt and bowed deeply to him, honouring him for what he was about to do.

"Thank you, Prince Yuan," Ssu Lu Shan said softly, almost in a whisper, pride at the honour the young prince did him making his smile widen momentarily. Then, with a sharp intake of breath, he thrust the knife deep into his flesh.

★ ★ ★

It was not until halfway through the fourth game that DeVore raised the matter.

"Well, Tong Chou? Have you dealt with our thief?"

Chen met the Overseer's eyes and gave the briefest nod. It had been a dreadful job and it was not pleasant to be reminded of it. He had been made to feel unclean; a brother to the Tengs of the world.

"Good," DeVore said. He leaned forward and connected two of his groups, then turned the board about. "Play white from here, Tong Chou."

It was the fourth time it had happened and DeVore had yet to lose a game, despite being each time in what seemed an impossible position as black.

Yes, Chen thought. Karr was right after all. But you're not just a Master at this game – it is as if the game were invented for one like you. He smiled inwardly and placed the first of his stones as white.

There was the same ruthlessness in him. The same cold calculation. DeVore did not think in terms of love and hate and relationships but in terms of advantage and groups and sacrifice. He played life as if it was one big game of *wei chi.*

And perhaps that's your weakness, Chen thought, studying him a moment. Perhaps that's where you're inflexible. For men are not stones, and life is not a game. You cannot order it thus and thus and thus, or connect it thus and thus and thus. Nor does your game take account of accident or chance.

Chen looked down again, studying the board, looking for the move or sequence of moves that would make his position safe. White had three corners and at least forty points advantage. It was his strongest position yet: how could he lose from this?

Even so, he knew that he would lose. He sighed and sat back. It was as if he were looking at a different board from the one DeVore was studying. It was as if the other man saw through to the far side of the board, on which were placed – suspended in the darkness – the stones yet to be played.

He shivered, feeling suddenly uneasy, and looked down at the tube he had brought with him.

"By the way, Tong Chou, what is that thing?"

DeVore had been watching him; had seen where his eyes went.

Chen picked it up and hefted it, then handed it across. He had been surprised DeVore had not insisted on looking at the thing straight away. This was his first mention of it in almost two hours.

"It's something I thought might amuse you. I brought it with me from the Above. It's a viewing tube. You manipulate the end of it and place your eye to the lens at this end."

"Like this?"

Chen held his breath. There! It was done! DeVore had placed his eye against the lens! The imprint would be perfect! Chen let his breath out slowly, afraid to give away his excitement.

"Interesting," said DeVore and set it down again, this time on his side of the board. "I wonder who she was."

The image was of a high-class *Hung Mao* lady, her dress drawn up about her waist, being "tupped" from the rear by one of the GenSyn ox-men, its huge, fifteen inch member sliding in and out of her while she grimaced ecstatically.

Chen stared at the tube for a time, wondering whether to ask for it back, then decided not to. The imprint might be perfect, but it was better to lose the evidence than have DeVore suspicious.

For a while he concentrated on the game. Already it was beginning to slip from him, the tide to turn towards the black. He made a desperate play in the centre of the board, trying to link, and found himself cut not once but twice.

DeVore laughed. "I must make those structures stronger next time," he said. "It's unfair of me to pass on such weaknesses to you."

Chen swallowed, suddenly understanding. At some point in the last few games he had become, if not super-/fluous, then certainly secondary to the game DeVore was playing against himself.

Like a machine with a slight unpredictability factor built into its circuits.

He let his eyes rest on the tube a moment, then looked up at DeVore. "Does my play bore you, *Shih* Bergson?"

DeVore sniffed. "What do you think, Tong Chou?"

Chen met his eyes, letting a degree of genuine admiration colour his expression. "I think my play much too limited for you, Overseer Bergson. I am but a humble player, but you, *Shih* Bergson, are a Master. It would not surprise me to find you were the First Hand Supreme in all Chung Kuo."

DeVore laughed. "In this, as in all things, there are levels, Tong Chou. It is true, I find your game limited, predictable, and perhaps I have tired of it already. But I am not quite what you make me out to be. There are others – a dozen, maybe more – who can better me at this game, and of them there is one, a man named Tuan Ti Fo, who was once to me as I am to you. He alone deserves the title you conferred on me just now."

DeVore sat back, relaxed. "But you are right, Tong Chou. You lost the game two moves back. It would not do to labour the point, eh?" He half turned in his chair and leaned back into the darkness. "Well, Stefan? What do you think?"

The albino stepped out from the shadows at the far end of the room and came towards the table.

Chen's heart missed a beat. Gods! How long had *he* been there?

He edged back, instinctively afraid of the youth, and when the albino picked up the viewing tube and studied it, Chen tensed, believing himself discovered – certain, for that brief moment, that DeVore had merely been toying with him; that he had known him from the first.

"These GenSyn ox-men are ugly beasts, aren't they? Yet there's something human about them, even so."

The pale youth set the tube down then stared at Chen a moment: his pink eyes so cruel, so utterly inhuman in their appraisal, Chen felt the hairs on his neck stand on end.

"Well?" DeVore had sat back, watching the young man.

The albino turned to DeVore and gave the slightest shrug. "What do I know, Overseer Bergson? Make him Field Supervisor if it suits you. Someone must do the job."

His voice, like his flesh, was colourless. Even so, there was something strangely, disturbingly familiar about it. Something Chen could not, for the life of him, put his finger on just then.

DeVore watched the youth a moment longer, then turned, facing Chen again. "Well, Tong Chou. It seems the job is yours. You understand the duties?"

Chen nodded, forcing his face into a mask of gratitude; but the presence of the young albino had thrown him badly. He stood up awkwardly, almost upsetting the board, then backed off, bowing deeply.

"Should I leave, Overseer?"

DeVore was watching him almost absently. "Yes. Go now, Tong Chou. I think we're done."

Chen turned and took a step towards the door.

"Oh, and Tong Chou?"

He turned back slowly, facing DeVore again, fear tightening his chest and making his heart pound violently. Was this it? Was this the moment when he turned the board about?

But no. The Overseer was holding out the viewing tube, offering it to him across the board.

"Take this and burn it. Understand me? I'll have no *filth* on this plantation!"

★ ★ ★

When the peasant had gone, Lehmann came across and sat in the vacant seat, facing DeVore.

DeVore looked up at him. "Will you play, Stefan?"

Lehmann shook his head curtly. "What was all that for?"

DeVore smiled and continued transferring the stones into the bowls. "I had a hunch, that's all. I thought he might be something more, but it seems I'm wrong. He's just a stupid peasant."

"How do you know?"

DeVore gave a short laugh. "The way he plays this game, for an opener. He's not pretending to be awkward, he is! You've seen his face when he concentrates on the board!"

DeVore pulled down his eyes at the corners and stretched his mouth exaggeratedly.

"So? He can't play *wei chi*. What does that mean?"

DeVore had finished clearing the board. Taking a cloth from the pocket of his *pau*, he wiped the wood. "It means he's not Security. Even the basest recruit would play better than Tong Chou." He yawned and sat back, stretching out his arms behind him, his fingers interlaced. "I was just being a little paranoid, that's all."

"Again, I thought it was your policy to trust no one?"

DeVore smiled, his eyes half-lidded now. "Yes. That's why I'm having his background checked out."

"Ah . . ." Lehmann sat back, still watching him, his eyes never blinking, his stare quite unrelenting. "And the tube?"

DeVore shook his head. "That was nothing. He was just trying to impress me. These Han are strange, Stefan. They think all *Hung Mao* are beasts, with the appetites of beasts. Maybe it's true of some."

Yes, but he had wondered for a moment: had waited to see if Tong Chou would clamour for it back.

"You're certain of him, then?"

DeVore looked sharply at the youth. "And you're not?"

Lehmann shook his head. "You said you had a hunch. Why not trust to it? Have you ever been wrong?"

DeVore hesitated, reluctant to say, then nodded. "Once or twice. But never about something so important."

"Then why trust to luck now?"

When Lehmann was gone, he went upstairs and sat at his desk, beneath the sharp glare of the single lamp, thinking about what the albino had said. The unease he felt was understandable. Everything was in flux at present – *The New Hope*, the fortresses, the recent events in the House, all these demanded his concentration, night and day. Little wonder, then, that he should display a little paranoia now and then. Even so, the boy was right. It was wrong to ignore a hunch simply because the evidence wasn't there to back it up. Hunches were signs from the subconscious – reports from a game played deep down in the darkness.

Normally he would have had the man killed and thought nothing of it, but there were good reasons not to kill Tong Chou just now. Reports of unrest were serious enough as it was, and had brought enquiries from Duchek's own office. Another death was sure to bring things to a head. But it was important that things were kept quiet for the next few days, until his scheme to pay that bastard Duchek back was finalised and the funds transferred from his accounts.

Yes. And he wanted to get even with Administrator Duchek. Because Duchek had let him down badly when he had refused to launder the funds for the Swiss Wilds fortresses through his accounts. Had let them all down.

Even so, there was a way that he could deal with Tong Chou. An indirect way that would cause the very minimum of fuss.

The dead thief had three brothers. They, certainly, would be keen to know who it was had put their brother in the ground. And who was to say who had left the anonymous note?

DeVore smiled, satisfied that he had found the solution to one of his problems, then leaned forward and tapped out the combination of the discrete line that connected him directly with Berdichev.

★　★　★

"Do you know what time it is, Howard?"

"Two twenty. Why? Were you sleeping, Soren?"

Berdichev waved his wife, Ylva, away, then locked the door behind her and came back to the screen. "What's so urgent?"

"We need to talk."

"What about?"

DeVore paused, conscious of the possibility the call was being traced – especially after the events of the past few days. "I'll tell you when I see you."

"Which is when?"

"In an hour and a half."

"Ah . . ." Berdichev removed his glasses and rubbed at his eyes, then looked up again and nodded. "Okay." Then he cut contact. There was no need to say where they would meet. Both knew.

An hour and a half later they stood there on the mountainside below the landing dome at Landeck Base. The huge valley seemed mysterious and threatening in the moonlight, the distant mountains strange and unreal. It was like being on another planet. Berdichev had brought furs against the cold, even so he felt chilled to the bone, his face numbed by the thin, frigid air. He faced DeVore, noting how little the other man seemed to be wearing.

"So? What do we need to talk about?"

His voice seemed small and hollow; dwarfed by the immensity of their surroundings.

"About everything. But mainly about Duchek. Have you heard from Weis?"

Berdichev nodded, wishing he could see DeVore's face better. He had expected DeVore to be angry, maybe even to have had Duchek killed for what he had done. "I was disappointed in him, Howard."

"Good. I'd hate to think you were pleased."

Berdichev smiled tightly. "What did you want to do?"

"Wrong question, Soren. Try 'What have you done?'"

"So?"

"He's dead. Two days from now. Next time he visits his favourite singsong house. But there's something else I want to warn you about. I've got a team switching funds from the plantation accounts here. At the same time Duchek greets his ancestors there'll be a big fire in the Distribution Centre at Lodz. It'll spread and destroy the computer records there. I thought I'd warn you, in case it hurts any of our investors. It'll be messy and there'll doubtlessly be a few hiccups before they can reconstruct things from duplicate records."

"Is that wise, Howard?"

DeVore smiled. "My experts estimate it'll take them between six and eight weeks to sort out the bulk of it. By that time I'll be out of here and the funds will have been tunnelled away, so to speak. Then we cut Weis out of it."

Berdichev narrowed his eyes. "Cut Weis out?"

"Yes. He's the weak link. We both know it. Duchek's betrayal gives me the excuse to deal with them both."

Berdichev considered a moment, then nodded, seeing the sense in it. With Weis dead, the trail covered and the fortresses funded, what did it matter if they traced the missing plantation funds to Duchek? Because beyond Duchek there would be a vacuum. And Duchek himself would be dead.

"How much is involved?"

"Three billion. Maybe three and a half."

"Three billion. Hmm. With that we could take some of the pressure off our investors."

639

DeVore shook his head. "No. That would just alert Weis. I gave him the distinct impression that we were grabbing for every *fen* we could lay our hands on. If we start making refunds he'll know we've got funding from elsewhere and he'll start looking for it. No, I want you to go to him with the begging bowl again. Make him think things are working out over budget."

Berdichev frowned. "And if he says it can't be done?"

DeVore laughed and reached out to touch his arm. "Be persuasive."

"Right. You want me to pressure him?"

DeVore nodded. "How are things otherwise?"

"Things are good. Under Secretary Barrow tells me that the *tai* are to face impeachment charges next week. Until then they're suspended from the House. That gives our coalition an effective majority. Lo Yu-Hsiang read out a strongly-worded protest from the Seven yesterday, along with an announcement that funding in certain areas was to be cut. But we expected as much. Beyond that they're impotent to act – as we knew they would be. The House is humming with it, Howard. They've had a taste of real power for once and they like it. They like it a lot."

"Good. And the File?"

For a moment Berdichev thought to play dumb. Then, seeing how things stood, he shrugged inwardly, making a mental note to find out how DeVore had come to know of it. It was fortunate that, for once, he had prepared for such an eventuality. "I've a copy in my craft for you, Howard. I'll hand it to you before we go."

"Excellent. And the boy? Kim, isn't it? Have you sorted out your problems there?"

Berdichev felt his stomach tighten. Was there anything DeVore hadn't heard about? "It's no problem," he said defensively.

"Good. Because we don't want problems. Not for the next few days, anyway."

Berdichev took a deep breath, forcing himself to relax. "And how is young Stefan? How is he settling in?"

DeVore turned his head away, staring out at the mountains, the moonlight momentarily revealing his neat, rather handsome features. "Fine. Absolutely fine. He's quiet, but I rather like that. It shows he has depths." He looked back, giving Berdichev the briefest glimpse of a smile.

Yes, thought Berdichev, recalling the two appalling weeks the boy had spent with them as a house guest; he has depths all right – vacuous depths.

"I see. But has he learned anything from you, Howard? Anything useful?"

DeVore laughed, then looked away thoughtfully. "Who knows, Soren? Who knows?"

*　*　*

The huge bed was draped with veils of silk-white *voile*, the thin, gauze-like cotton decorated with butterflies and delicate, tall-stemmed irises. It filled one end of the large, sumptuously decorated room, like the cocoon of some vast, exotic insect.

The air in the room was close, the sweet, almost sickly scent of old perfumes masking another, darker odour.

The woman lay on the bed, amidst a heap of pale cream and salmon pink satin cushions which blended with the colours of the silk *shui t'an i* camisole she wore. As he came closer, she raised her head. The simple movement seemed to cost her dearly, as if her head were weighted down with bronze.

"Who is it?"

Her voice had a slightly brittle edge to it, a huskiness beneath its silken surface.

He stood where he was, looking about the room, noting with disgust its excesses. "I am from *Shih* Bergson, *Fu Jen* Maitland."

"You're new . . ." she said sleepily, a faintly seductive intonation entering her voice. "Come here where I can see you, boy."

He went across and climbed the three small steps that led

up to the bed, then drew the veil aside, looking down at her.

She was a tall, long-limbed woman with knife-sharp, nervous facial features, their glass-like fragility accentuated rather than hidden by the heavy pancake of make-up she was wearing. She looked old before her time, the web of lines about each eye like the cracked earth of a dried-up stream, her eyeballs protruding slightly beneath their thin veils of flesh. The darkness of her hair, he knew at once, had been achieved artificially, for the skin of her neck and arms had the pallor of albinism.

Yes, he could see now where his own colouring came from.

Bracelets of fine gold wire were bunched about her narrow wrists, jewelled rings clustered on her long, fragile fingers. About her stretched and bony neck she wore a garishly large *ying luo*, the fake rubies and emeralds like pigeons' eggs. Her hair was unkempt from troubled sleep, her silks creased. She looked what she was – a rich Han's concubine. A kept woman.

He watched her turn her head slowly and open her eyes. Pale, watery blue eyes that had to make an effort before they focused on him.

"Ugh . . . Pale as a worm. Still . . ." She closed her eyes again, letting her head sink back amongst the cushions. "What's your name?"

"Mikhail," he said, adopting the alias he had stolen from DeVore. "Mikhail Böden."

She was silent a moment, then gave a small, shuddering sigh and turned slightly, raising herself onto her elbows, looking at him again. The movement made her camisole fall open slightly at the front, exposing her small, pale breasts.

"Come here. Sit beside me, boy."

He did as he was bade, the perfumed reek of her filling his nostrils, sickening him. It was like her jewellery, her silks and satins, the make-up and nail paint. All this – this ostentation – offended him deeply. He himself wore nothing decorative. His belief was in purity. In *essence*.

Her hand went to his face, then moved down until it rested on his shoulder.

"You have it?"

He took the two packets from his jacket pocket and threw them down onto the bed beside her. If she noticed his rudeness, she said nothing, but leaned forward urgently, scrabbling for the tiny sachets, then tore one open with her small, pointed teeth and swallowed its contents down quickly.

It was as he had thought. She was an addict.

He watched her close her eyes again, breathing deeply, letting the drug take hold of her. When she turned her head and looked at him again she seemed more human, more animated, a slight playfulness in her eyes revealing how attractive she must once have been. But it was only a shadow. A shadow in a darkened room.

"Your eyes," she said, letting her hand rest on his chest again. "They seem . . . wrong somehow."

"Yes." He put a finger to each eye, popping out the contact lenses he had borrowed from DeVore's drawer, then looked back at her, noting her surprise.

"Hello, mother."

"I have no . . ." she began, then laughed strangely, understanding. "So. You're Pietr's son."

He saw how the muscles beneath her eyes betrayed her. But there was no love there. How could there be? She had killed him long ago. Before he was born.

She swallowed. "What do you want?"

In answer he leaned forward and held her to him, embracing her. DeVore is right, he thought. Trust no one. For there's only yourself in the end.

He let her fall back amongst the satin cushions, the tiny, poisoned blade left embedded at the base of her spine. Then he stood and looked at her again. His mother. A woman he had never met before today.

Carefully, almost tenderly, he took the device from his pocket, set it, then laid it on the bed beside her. In sixty seconds it would catch fire, kindling the silks and satins, igniting the gauze-like layers of *voile*, cleansing the room of every trace of her.

Lehmann moved back, away, pausing momentarily, wishing he could see it, then turned and left, locking the door behind him, knowing that no one now had any hold on him. Especially not DeVore.

★ ★ ★

Li Yuan lay there in the darkness, listening to the rain falling in the garden beyond the open windows, letting his heartbeat slow, his breathing return to normal. The dream was fading now and with it the overwhelming fear which had made him cry out and struggle back to consciousness, but still he could see its final image, stretching from horizon to horizon, vast and hideously white.

He shuddered, then heard the door ease open, a soft tread on the tiled floor.

"Do you want company, Li Yuan?"

He sighed, then rolled over and looked across to where she stood, shadowed and naked, at the foot of his bed.

"Not now, Sweet Rose. Not now . . ."

He sensed, rather than saw her hesitation. Then she was gone and he was alone again.

He got up, knowing he would not sleep now, and went to the window, staring out into the moonlit garden. Then, taking a gown from the side, he wrapped it about him and went to the double doors that led out into the garden, pulling them open.

For a while Li Yuan stood there, his eyes closed, breathing in the fresh, sweet, night scents of the garden, then he went outside, onto the balcony, the coldness of the marble flags beneath his feet making him look down, surprised.

"Prince Yuan?"

He waved the guard away, then went down, barefoot, into the garden. In the deep shadow of the bower he paused, looking about him, then searched blindly until he came upon it.

"Ah!" he said softly, finding the book there, on the side, where she had laid it only hours before. It had been in the dream, together with the horse, the silks, the scent of plum blossom. The thought made his throat dry again. He shivered and picked the book up, feeling at once how heavy it was, the cover warped, ruined by the rain. He was about to go back out when his fingers found, then read, the pictograms embossed into the sodden surface of the cover.

Yu T'ai Hsin Yang.

He moved his fingers over the figures once again, making sure, then laughed shortly, understanding. It was a book of love poetry. The sixth century collection, *New Songs From A Jade Terrace*. He had not read the book himself, but he had heard of it. Moving out from the bower he turned it over and held it out, under the moonlight, trying to make out the page she had been reading. It was a poem by Chiang Yen. "Lady Pan's *Poem on the Fan*."

"White silk like a round moon
Appearing from the loom's white silk.
Its picture shows the King of Ch'in's daughter
Riding a lovebird toward smoky mists.
Vivid colour is what the world prefers,
Yet the new will never replace the old.
In secret I fear cold winds coming
To blow on my jade steps tree
And, before your sweet love has ended,
Make it shed midway."

He shivered and closed the book abruptly. It was like the dream, too close, too portentous to ignore. He looked up at the three-quarters moon and felt its coldness touch him to the core. It was almost autumn, the season of executions, when the moon was traditionally associated with criminals.

The moon . . . A chill thread of fear ran down his spine, making him drop the book. In contrast to the sun, the new moon rose first in the west. Yes, it was from the west that *Chang-e*, the goddess of the Moon, first made herself known.

Chang-e . . . The association of the English and the Mandarin was surely fanciful – yet he was too much the Han, the suggestive resonances of sounds and words too deeply embedded in his bloodstream, to ignore it.

Li Yuan bent down and retrieved the book, then straightened up and looked about him. The garden was a mosaic of moonlight and shadows, unreal and somehow threatening. It was as if, at any moment, its vague patterning of silver and black would take on a clearer, more articulate shape; forming letters or a face, as in his dream. Slowly, fearful now, he moved back towards the palace, shuddering at the slightest touch of branch or leaf, until he was inside again, the doors securely locked behind him.

He stood there a while, his heart pounding, fighting back the dark, irrational fears that had threatened to engulf him once again. Then, throwing the book down on his bed, he went through quickly, almost running down the corridors, until he came to the entrance to his father's suite of rooms.

The four elite guards stationed outside the door bowed deeply to him but blocked his way. A moment later, Wang Ta Chuan, Master of The Inner Palace, appeared from within, bowing deeply to him.

"What is it, Prince Yuan?"

"I wish to see my father, Master Wang."

Wang bowed again. "Forgive me, Excellency, but your father is asleep. Could this not wait until the morning?"

Li Yuan shuddered, then shook his head. His voice was soft but insistent. "I must see him now, Master Wang. This cannot wait."

Wang stared at him, concerned and puzzled by his behaviour. Then he averted his eyes and bowed a third time. "Please wait, Prince Yuan. I will go and wake your father."

He had not long to wait. Perhaps his father had been awake already and had heard the noises at his door. Whatever, it was only a few seconds later that Li Shai Tung appeared, alone, a silk *pau* pulled about his tall frame, his feet, like his son's, bare.

"Can't you sleep, Yuan?"

Li Yuan bowed, remembering the last time he had spoken to his father, in the Hall of Eternal Truth, after his audience with Ssu Lu Shan. Then he had been too full of contradictions, too shocked, certainly too confused to be able to articulate what he was feeling. But now he knew. The dream had freed his tongue and he must talk of it.

"I had a dream, father. An awful, horrible dream."

His father studied him a moment, then nodded. "I see." He put a hand out, indicating the way. "Let us go through to your great-grandfather's room, Yuan. We'll talk there."

The room was cold, the fire empty. Li Shai Tung looked about him, then turned and smiled at his son. "Here, come help me, Yuan. We'll make a fire and sit about it, you there, I here." He pointed to the two big armchairs.

Li Yuan hesitated, surprised by his father's suggestion. He had never seen the T'ang do anything but be a T'ang. Yet, kneeling there, helping him make up the fire, then leaning down to blow the spark into a flame, it felt to him as if he had always shared this with his father. He looked up, surprised to find his father watching him, smiling, his hands resting loosely on his knees.

"There. Now let's talk, eh?"

The fire crackled, the flames spreading quicker now. In its flickering light the T'ang sat, facing his son.

"Well, Yuan? You say you had a dream?"

Much of the early part of the dream evaded him now that he tried to recall its details, and there were some things – things related too closely to Fei Yen and his feelings for her – that he kept back from the telling. Yet the dream's ending was still vivid in his mind and he could feel that strange, dark sense of terror returning as he spoke of it.

"I was high up, overlooking the plain where the City had been. But the City was no longer there. Instead, in its place, was a mountain of bones. A great mound of sun-bleached bones, taller than the City, stretching from horizon to horizon. I looked up and the sky was strangely dark, the moon huge and full and bloated in the sky, blazing down with a cold, fierce radiance as though it were the sun. And as I looked a voice behind me said, 'This is history.' Yet when I turned there was no one there, and I realised that the voice had been my own."

He fell silent, then looked down with a shudder, overcome once more by the power of the dream.

Across from him the T'ang stretched his long body in the chair, clearly discomfited by what his son had seen. For a time he too was silent, then he nodded to himself. "You dream of Tsao Ch'un, my son. Of the terrible things he did. But all that is in our past now. We must learn from it. Learn not to let it happen again."

Li Yuan looked up, his eyes burning strangely. "No . . . It is not the past. Can't you see that, father? It is what we are, right now. What we represent. We are the custodians of that great white mountain – the gaolers of Tsao Ch'un's City."

Normally Li Shai Tung would have lectured his son about his manners, the tone in which he spoke, yet this was different: this was a time for open speaking.

"What Tsao Ch'un did was horrible, yes. Yet think of the alternatives, Yuan, and ask yourself what else could he have done? Change had become an evil god, destroying all it touched. Things seemed beyond redemption. There was a saying back then which expressed the fatalism people felt – *E hsing hsun huan*. Bad nature follows a cycle; a vicious circle, if you like. Tsao Ch'un broke that circle – fought one kind of badness with another and ended the cycle. And so it has been ever since. Until now, that is, when others wish to come and set the Wheel in motion once again."

Li Yuan spoke softly, quietly. "Maybe so, father, yet what Tsao Ch'un did is still inside us. I can see it now. My eyes are opened to it. We are the creatures of his environment – the product of his uncompromising thought."

But Li Shai Tung was shaking his head. "No, Yuan. We are not what he created. We are our own men." He paused, staring at his son, trying to understand what he was feeling at that moment, recollecting what he himself had felt. But it was difficult. He had been much older when he had learned the truth of things.

"It is true, Yuan – the world we find ourselves born into is not what we would have it be in our heart of hearts, yet it is surely not so awful or evil a world as your dream would have it? True, it might limit our choices, but those choices are still ours to make."

Li Yuan looked up. "Then why do we keep the truth from them? What are we afraid of? That it might make them think other than we wish them to think? That they might make other choices than the ones we wish them to make?"

The T'ang nodded, firelight and shadow halving his face from brow to chin. "Perhaps. You know the saying, Yuan. *To shuo hua pu ju shao.*"

Li Yuan shivered, thinking of the moonlight on the garden. He knew the saying: *Speech is silver, silence is golden.* Sun and moon again. Silver and gold. "Maybe so," he said, yet it seemed more convenient than true.

"In time, Yuan, you will see it more clearly. The shock, I know, is great. But do not let the power of your dream misguide you. It was, when all's considered, only a dream."

A dream. Only a dream. Li Yuan looked up, meeting his father's eyes again. "Maybe so. But tell me this, father, are we good or evil men?"

* * *

Chen looked up from where he was sitting on the stool outside the equipment barn to see whose shadow had fallen across him.

"Do I know you?"

The three Han had ugly, vicious expressions on their faces. Two of them were holding thick staves threateningly in both hands. The third – the one whose shadow had fallen across him – brandished a knife. They were dressed in the same drab brown as himself.

"Ah . . ." Chen said, seeing the likeness in their faces. So the thief had brothers. He got up slowly. "You have a score to settle?"

The momentary smile on the eldest brother's face turned quickly to a scowl of hatred. Chen could see how tense the man was and nervous, but also how determined.

Chen let the hoe he had been repairing drop, then stood there, empty-handed, facing the man, watching him carefully now, knowing how dangerous he was. A careless, boastful man would often talk too much or betray himself into ill-considered movements, but these three were still and silent. They had not come to talk, nor to impress him. They had come for one thing only. To kill him.

He glanced across and saw, in the distance, outlined against the lip of the irrigation dyke, the Overseer's man, Teng. So. That was how they knew. He looked back, weighing the three up, letting his thoughts grow still, his breathing normalise. His pulse was high, but that was good. It was a sign that his body was preparing itself for the fight to come.

"Your brother was a thief," he said, moving to his right, away from the stool, putting the sun to one side of him.

The eldest made a sound of disgust.

Yes, thought Chen; I understand you. And maybe another time, in different circumstances, I'd have let you kill me for what I've done. But there are more important things just now. Like DeVore. Though you'd not understand that, would you?

Chen saw the man's movement a fraction of a second before he made it, the sudden action betrayed by a tensing of the muscles, a slight movement in his eyes. Chen bunched his fist and knocked the big knife aside, then followed through with a kick to the man's stomach that left him on his knees, badly winded.

The other two yelled and charged him, their staves raised.

Chen moved quickly to one side, making them wheel about, one of the brothers momentarily hidden behind the other. Taking his opportunity, Chen ducked and moved inside the stave's wild swing, his forearm lifting the man's chin and hurling him back into his brother.

At once Chen was standing over them, kicking, punching down at them, his breath hissing from him sharply with each blow, until the two men lay there, unconscious.

The eldest had rolled over, groaning, still gasping for his breath. As Chen turned, facing him again, his eyes widened with fear and he made to crawl away. But Chen simply stood there, his hands on his hips, getting his breath, and shook his head.

"I'm sorry. I did what I had to do. Do you understand me? I have no quarrel with you. But if you come again – if any of you come again – I will kill you all."

Chen bowed then walked back to the barn, picking up the hoe. Only then did he see Pavel, watching from the doorway.

"You saw then, Pavel?"

The young man's eyes were wide with astonishment. "I saw, *Shih* Tong, but I'm not sure I believe what I saw. I thought they'd kill you."

Chen smiled. "Yes. And so did Teng. I must deal with him, before he can tell others."

Pavel's eyes narrowed, then, as if he had made up his mind about something, he took Chen's arm and began to turn him about.

Chen shook him off. "What are you doing?"

Pavel stared at him. "You said you must deal with Teng. Well, he's gone already. As soon as he saw what you could do. If you want to catch him you had best come with me. I know a quicker way."

Chen laughed. "A quicker way?"

Pavel grabbed his arm again. "Yes. Now don't argue with me. Come on! We'll cut the bastard off."

At the lip of the dyke, Pavel didn't stop but went over the top and down. Chen followed, splashing through the shallow water, then following Pavel up the other bank, pulling himself up a rough, indented ladder which had been cut into the side of the dyke.

"Teng will go by the bridges," Pavel explained breath-lessly as they ran across the field towards the intersection. "He won't want to get his uniform muddy. But that means he has to go along and across. We, however, can go diagonally. We can cut him at the fourth west bridge."

"Where's Chang Yan?" Chen asked, not slowing his pace. "I thought those two bastards were inseparable!"

"Chang Yan's on leave in Lodz. Which is where Teng should be. But it looks like he wanted to see the outcome of his trouble-making before he went."

Yes, thought Chen. But DeVore's behind it. I knew it. I felt he was up to something the other evening.

The fourth west bridge consisted of four long, thick planks of wood, embedded into the earth on either side of the irrigation canal. Chen waited, hidden among the man-tall stand of super-wheat to one side of the path, while Pavel stayed down below, in the water beneath the bridge.

Teng was wheezing when he came to the bridge. He slowed and wiped his brow, then came out onto the wooden planking.

"Teng Fu," said Chen, stepping out onto the pathway. "How fortunate to meet you here."

Teng blinked furiously, then turned, looking about him. The sun was quite low now. The fields on every side were empty.

He turned back, facing Chen, slipping the rifle from his shoulder and holding it out before him threateningly. But it was clear he was shaken.

"Get out of my way, Tong Chou! I'll kill you if you don't!"

Chen laughed scornfully. "It's Chen, by the way. Kao Chen. But that aside, why should I move? You've seen too much, Teng. If I let you go, you'll say what you've seen, and I can't have that. Anyway, it was you set those poor bastards onto me, wasn't it? You who told them. Well . . . this will be for them. And for their brother. Oh, and for Pavel, too."

Teng turned too late. Pavel had climbed the bank and

come up behind him. As the Overseer's man turned, hearing someone behind him, Pavel launched himself forward and pushed. Teng fell awkwardly, going headlong into the shallow stream, the gun falling away from him.

Chen ran forward, then jumped from the bridge into the water. Pavel followed him a fraction of a second later.

Teng rolled over, lifting his head from the water, spluttering, his eyes wide with surprise, only to find himself thrust down again. He was a big man and struggled hard, straining with his arms and neck to free himself, his feet kicking desperately beneath him, but the two men gritted their teeth and held him down beneath the water until, after one final, violent spasm of activity, Teng's body went limp.

Pavel shuddered, then stood up in the water, looking down at what he had done.

"Gods . . ." he said softly. "We've killed him."

"Yes," said Chen, steeling himself, recognising the pain in the young man's twisted face. Oh, Pavel had hated him beforehand – had hated him even enough to kill him – but now that it was done the boy saw Teng clearer, as another man. A man he had robbed of life. "Come on," he said, getting to his feet. "We have to hide the body."

For a moment Pavel just stared at the lifeless body that now floated, face down, in the shallow water; then he seemed to come to himself. He swallowed deeply, then looked back at Chen. "What?"

"We have to hide the body," Chen repeated, careful to be gentle with the boy. "Do you know a place, Pavel?"

The light was failing fast. They would not be missed at once, but if they delayed too long . . .

Pavel shivered again, then nodded. "Yes. There's a place. Farther along."

They towed the heavy body between them, pulling it by its arms, moving as quickly as they could against the resistance of the water, until they came to a place where the reeds on one side of the canal threatened to spill right across and block the stream. There Pavel halted.

"Here," he said, indicating a vague patch of darkness against the bank.

Chen heaved the body round, then, with Pavel's help, moved it in amongst the tall reeds. There, behind the cover of the reeds, a small cave had been carved out of the bank. Inside, it was curiously dry. Small niches, like tiny, primitive ovens, had been cut into the walls on either side. Pavel turned and reached into one. A moment later, Chen saw the flicker of a flint.

Pavel turned, a lighted candle in his hand, and looked down at the body floating there between them.

"I don't like it, but it's the only place."

Chen looked about him, astonished. The walls were painted, red and green and yellow, the openings lined with coloured tiles. Tiny statues were placed in each of the niches, about which were placed small pieces of paper and the remains of tiny finger candles. It was a shrine. A secret shrine.

"Kuan Yin preserve us!"

Pavel nodded vehemently, then let out another shuddering breath. "How will we anchor him?"

Chen looked about him, then hit upon the best solution. "We'll lift him up. Jam his head and shoulders into one of the niches. That should hold him long enough for us to decide what to do with him."

Pavel looked at him, wide-eyed, then swallowed again.

"What *are* you, Kao Chen? What are you doing here?"

Chen looked down, then decided to tell Pavel the truth. It was that now or kill him, and he didn't think he *could* kill the boy, even to get DeVore.

"What I am doesn't really matter. But I'm here to get Overseer Bergson. To trap him and bring him to justice. Will you help me, Pavel? Will you help me get the bastard?"

Pavel looked again at the body of the man he had helped to kill, then looked up at Chen again, the candle wavering in his hand, throwing shadows about the tiny space. He smiled and offered his hand. "Okay, Kao Chen. I'll help you."

* * *

Karr stood at the window, looking down at the vast apron of Nanking spaceport, then turned, smiling. "Well, General, it seems we must play our final card."

The old man nodded, returning Karr's smile openly. "So it seems. Unless they change their minds. You're prepared?"

Karr nodded. "I know what I have to do."

"Good." Tolonen went across and stood beside Karr, then, unexpectedly, he embraced him. He did not expect to see the big man again.

Karr held Tolonen's upper arms a moment, his smile undiminished. "Don't be sad, General. Remember what you said to me. I'm a winner."

Tolonen sighed, then smiled. "I hope it's so, my friend. Never more than now."

Karr turned his head, looking outward again, watching a craft rise slowly on the far side of the field. The noise reached them a moment later – a deep, rumbling reverberation that went down the register.

"You know, General. I'd love to see their faces. Especially DeVore's." He paused, then, on another track, added. "Chen has his back-up?"

"Of course. The best I could arrange."

Karr turned back. "That's good." He went across and took something from the top of his pack and brought it back across, handing it to Tolonen.

"What's this?"

"For Chen. Just in case."

Tolonen laughed. "So you are human, after all. I was beginning to wonder."

"Oh yes," Karr answered, his smile fading momentarily. "And I'll tell you this, General. What I'm about to do frightens me. More than anything I've ever done before. But I'll do it. Or die trying."

Tolonen looked at him, admiring him, then bowed his head respectfully.

"Good luck. And may heaven favour you, *Shih* Karr."

★ ★ ★

The journey to Tongjiang took Tolonen an hour. Li Shai Tung was waiting for him in his study, the authority on the desk beside him, signed and witnessed – the seven tiny *Ywe Lung* seals imprinted into the wax in the whiteness on the left-hand side of the document.

"Your man is on his way, Knut?" the T'ang asked, handing Tolonen the parchment, then waving away his secretary.

"He is, *Chieh Hsia*. We should know by tomorrow evening how things stand."

"And the other matter? The business with DeVore?"

Tolonen smiled. "That will be settled sooner, *Chieh Hsia*. The agent concerned, Kao Chen, passed vital evidence back through channels yesterday. It has been verified that the suspect, Overseer Bergson is, in reality, the traitor, De-Vore."

"Have we arrested the man?"

"I have arranged things already, *Chieh Hsia*. We will capture the man this evening. Within the next few hours, in fact."

"Good. That, at least, eases my mind." The T'ang sniffed, his expression grave, then got up slowly from his desk. "A great storm is coming, Knut, and we shall have made enemies enough before it blows itself out. DeVore is one I'd rather have in hand, not loose and making mischief for us."

Yes, thought Tolonen. And Berdichev, too. But that would have to wait a day or two. Until after Karr had done his stuff. He looked down at the document in his hands, feeling a great sense of pride at being at the centre of things this night. He had foreseen this long ago, of course. Had known the day would come when the Seven could no longer sit on their hands and do nothing. Now they would shake Chung Kuo to its roots. Shake it hard, as it needed to be shaken.

Tolonen smiled and then bowed to his T'ang, acknowledging his dismissal; feeling a deep satisfaction at the way things had gone. The days of *wuwei* – of passive acceptance

– were past. The dragon had woken and had bared its claws.

And now it would strike, its seven heads raised, magnificent, like tigers, making the *hsiao jen* – the little men – scuttle to their holes and hide, like the vermin that they were.

Yes. They would clean the world of them. And then? His smile broadened. Then summer would come again.

* * *

Li Shai Tung sat at his desk, brooding. What had he done? What set in motion? He shuddered, disturbed by the implications of his actions.

What if it cracked Chung Kuo itself apart? It was possible. Things were balanced delicately now. Worse, what if it brought it all tumbling down – levelling the levels?

He laughed sourly, then turned at a sound. It was Li Yuan. He was standing in the doorway, his shoes removed, awaiting his father's permission to enter. Li Shai Tung nodded and beckoned his son to him.

"Bitter laughter, father. Is there something wrong?"

Too wise. Too young to be so old and knowing.

"Nothing. Just a play of words."

Li Yuan bowed, then turned away slightly: a gesture of indirectness his father could read perfectly. It was something difficult. A request of some kind. But awkward. Not easy to ask. Li Shai Tung waited, wondering how Li Yuan would breach the matter. It was an opportunity to study his son: to assess his strengths, his weaknesses.

"I've been much troubled, father."

Li Yuan had looked up before he spoke. A direct, almost defiant look. He had resolved the matter and chosen to present it with firmness and authority. Yes, the old man thought, Li Yuan would make a fine T'ang. When it was time.

"Is it your dream again, Yuan?"

Li Yuan hesitated, then shook his head.

"Then tell me what it is."

He stood and went across to the pool, then stood there, looking down at the dim shapes moving in the depths of the water, waiting for his son to join him there.

Unexpectedly, Li Yuan came right up to him, then went down onto his knees at his feet, his eyes fixed upon the floor as he made his request.

"I want to ask your permission to marry, father."

Li Shai Tung turned sharply, surprised, then laughed and bent down, lifting Li Yuan's face, his hand cupping his son's chin, making him look up at him.

"But you're only twelve, Yuan! There's more than enough time to think of such matters. A good four years or more. I never meant for you to . . ."

"I know, father. But I already know what I want. *Who* I want."

There was such certainty, such fierce certainty in the words, that the T'ang released his hold and stepped back, his hand stroking his plaited beard thoughtfully. "Go on," he said. "Tell me who it is."

Li Yuan took a deep breath, then answered him. "Fei Yen. I want Fei Yen."

Li Shai Tung stared at his son in disbelief. "Impossible! She was Han's wife, Yuan. You know the law."

The boy's eyes stared back at him intently. "Yes, and by our law Fei Yen was never Han Ch'in's wife."

Li Shai Tung laughed, amazed. "How so, when the seals of Yin Tsu and I are on the marriage contract? Have you left your senses, Yuan? Of course she was Han's wife!"

But Li Yuan was insistent. "The documents were nullified with Han's death. Think, father! What does our law actually say? That a marriage is not a marriage until it has been consummated. Well, Han Ch'in and Fei Yen . . ."

"Enough!" The T'ang's roar took Li Yuan by surprise. "This is wrong, Li Yuan. Even to talk of it like this . . ."

He shook his head sadly. It was not done. It simply was not done. Not only was she too old for him, she was his brother's bride.

"No, Yuan. She isn't right for you. Not Fei Yen."

"Fei Yen, father. I *know* who I want."

Again that intensity of tone, that certainty. Such certainty impressed Li Shai Tung, despite himself. He looked down into the pool again.

"You could not marry her for four years at the least, Yuan. You'll change your mind. See if you don't! No, find some other girl to be your bride. Don't rush into this foolishness!"

Li Yuan shook his head. "No, father, it's her I want. I've known it since Han Ch'in was killed. And she'll take me. I know that too."

Li Shai Tung smiled bitterly. What use was such knowledge? In four years Chung Kuo would have changed. Perhaps beyond recognition. Li Yuan did not know what was to be: what had been decided. Even so, he saw how determined his son was in this matter and relented.

"All right. I will talk to her parents, Yuan. But I promise you no more than that for now."

It seemed enough. Li Yuan smiled broadly and reached out to take and kiss his father's hand. "Thank you, father. Thank you. I shall make her a good husband."

When Yuan had gone, he stood there, staring down into the darkness of the water, watching the carp move slowly in the depths, like thought itself. Then, when he felt himself at rest again, he went back into his study, relaxed, resigned almost to what was to come.

Let the sky fall, he thought: *What can I, a single man, do against fate?*

Nothing, came the answer. For the die had been cast. Already it was out of their hands.

* * *

Bamboo. A three-quarter moon. Bright water. The sweet, high notes of an *erhu*. Chen looked about himself, at ease, enjoying the warmth of the evening. Pavel brought him a beer and he took a sip from it, then looked across at the dancers, seeing how their faces shone, their dark eyes laughed brightly in the fire's light. At a bench to one side sat the bride and groom, red-faced and laughing, listening to the friendly banter of their fellow peasants.

Two great fires had been built in the grassy square formed by the three long dormitory huts. Benches had been set up on all sides and, at one end, a temporary kitchen. Close by, a four-piece band had set up their instruments on the tail-piece of an electric hay wagon: *yueh ch'in, ti tsu, erhu* and *p'i p'a* – the ancient mix of strings and flutes enchanting on the warm night air.

There were people everywhere, young and old, packing the benches, crowded about the kitchen, dancing or simply standing about in groups, smoking clay pipes and talking. Hundreds of people, maybe a thousand or more in all.

He turned, looking at Pavel. "Is it true, Pavel? Have you no girl?"

Pavel looked down, then drained his jug. "No one here, Kao Chen," he answered softly, leaning towards him as he spoke.

"Then why not come back with me? There are girls in the levels would jump at you."

Pavel shivered, then shook his head. "You are kind, my friend. But . . ." He tilted his shoulder slightly, indicating his bent back. "*T'o* they call me here. What girl would want such a man?"

"*T'o*?"

Pavel laughed, for a moment his twisted face attractive. "Camel-backed."

Chen frowned, not understanding.

"It was an animal, so I'm told. Before the City."

"Ah . . ." Chen looked past the young man, watching the dancers a moment. Then he looked back. "You could buy a bride. I would give you the means . . ."

Pavel's voice cut into his words. "I thank you, Kao Chen, but . . ." He looked up, his dark eyes strangely pained. "It's not that, you see. Not only that. It's . . . Well, I think I would die in there. No fields. No open air. No wind. No running water. No sun. No moon. No changing seasons. Nothing. Nothing but walls."

The young man's unconscious echo of DeVore's words made Chen shiver and look away. Yet perhaps the boy was right. He looked back at the dancers circling the fires and nodded to himself. For the first time since he had been amongst them, Chen had seen the shadow lift from them and knew how different they were from his first conception of them. He saw how happy they could be. So simple it was. It took so little to achieve their happiness.

He stared about him, fascinated. When they danced, they danced with such fiery abandon, as if released from themselves – no longer drab and brown and faceless, but huge and colourful, overbrimming with their own vitality, their coal dark eyes burning in their round, peasant faces, their feet pounding the bare earth carelessly, their arms waving wildly, their bodies twirling lightly through the air as they made their way about the fire.

As if they were enchanted.

He shivered, wishing that Wang Ti were there with him, partnering him in the dance; then with him in the darkness afterwards, her breath sweet with wine, her body opening to him.

He sighed and looked down into his jug, seeing the moon reflected there in the dark, sour liquid. In an hour it would begin. And afterwards he would be gone from here. Maybe forever.

The thought sobered him. He took a large swallow of the beer, then wiped his mouth and turned to face Pavel again. "You're right. Stay here, Pavel. Find yourself a girl. Work hard and get on." He smiled, liking the young man. "Things will be much better here when Bergson is gone."

Yes, he thought; and maybe one day I'll come back, and bring Wang Ti with me, and Jyan and the new child. They'd like it here. I know they would.

He saw Pavel was watching him and laughed. "What is it, boy?"

Pavel looked down. "You think life's simple here, don't you? But let me tell you about my birth."

"Go on," said Chen softly, noting the sudden change in him. It was as if Pavel had shed a mask. As if the experience they had shared, beneath the fourth west bridge, had pared a skin from the young man, making him suddenly more vulnerable, more open.

"I had a hard childhood," he began. "I was born the fifth child of two casual workers. Hirelings – like yourself – who come on the land only at harvest time. During the harvest things were fine. They could feed me. But when it was time to go back to the City, they left me here in the fields to die. Back in the levels they could not afford me, you understand. It is often so, even today. People here accept it as the way. Some say the new seed must be fertilised with the bones of young children. I, however, did not die."

Pavel licked at his lips, then carried on, his downcast eyes staring back into the past.

"Oh, I had nothing to do with it. *Mei fa tzu*, they say. It is fate. And my fate was to be found by a childless woman and taken in. I was lucky. She was a good woman. A Han. Chang Lu was her name. For a time things were good. Her man, Wen, never took to me, but at least he didn't beat me or mistreat me, and she loved me as her own. But when I was seven they died. A dyke collapsed on top of them while they were repairing it. And I was left alone."

Pavel was silent a moment, then he looked up, a sad smile lighting his face briefly.

"I missed her bitterly. But bitterness does not fill the belly. I had to work, and work hard. There is never quite enough, you see. Each family takes care of its own. But I had no family. And so I strove from dawn until dusk each day, carrying heavy loads out into the fields, the long, thick carrying pole pressing down on my shoulders, bending my back until I became as you see me now." He gave a short laugh. "It was necessity that shaped me thus, you might say, Kao Chen. Necessity and the dark earth of Chung Kuo."

"I'm sorry," Chen began. "I didn't know . . ." But Pavel interrupted him once more.

"There's something else." The young man hesitated, then shivered and went on. "It's the way you look at us, Kao Chen. I noticed it before. But now I think I understand. It's like we're a dream to you, isn't it? Not quite real. Something picturesque . . ."

Chen was about to say no, to tell the boy that it was just the opposite – that all of *this* was real, and all the rest, inside, no more than a hideous dream to which he must return – but Pavel was looking at him strangely, shaking his head; denying him before he had begun.

"Maybe," he said finally, setting his jug down. But he still meant no. He had only to close his eyes and feel the movement of the air on his cheeks . . .

"You came at the best time," Pavel said, looking away from him, back towards the dancers. "Just now the air smells sweet and the evenings are warm. But the winters are hard here. And the stench sometimes . . ."

He glanced back at Chen then laughed, seeing incomprehension there.

"What do you think the City does with all its waste?"

Chen sipped at his beer, then shrugged. "I'd never thought . . ."

Pavel turned, facing him again. "No. No one ever does. But think of it. Over thirty billion, they say. So much shit. What do they do with it?"

Chen saw what he was saying and began to laugh. "You mean . . . ?"

Pavel nodded. "They waste none of it. Its stored in vast wells and used on the fields. You should see it, Kao Chen. Vast, lake-like reservoirs of it, there are. Imagine!" He laughed strangely, then looked away. "In a week from now the fields will be dotted with honey-carts, each with its load of sweet dark liquid to deposit on the land. Black gold, they call it. Without it the crop would fail and Chung Kuo itself would fall."

"I always thought . . ."

Chen stopped and looked across. The dull murmur of talk had fallen off abruptly; the music faltered and then died. He searched among the figures, suddenly alert, then saw them. Guards! The Overseer's guards were in the square!

Pavel had turned and was staring at him, fear blazing in his eyes. "It's Teng!" he said softly. "They must have found Teng!"

"No . . ." Chen shook his head and reached out to touch the young man's arm to calm him. No, not Teng. But maybe something worse.

The guards came through, then stood there in a rough line behind their leader, a tall *Hung Mao*.

"Who's that?" whispered Chen.

"That's Peskova. He's Bergson's lieutenant."

"Gods . . . I wonder what he wants?"

It was quiet now. Only the crackle of the fires broke the silence. Peskova looked about him, then took a handset from his tunic pocket, pressed for display and began to read from it.

"By the order of Overseer Bergson, I have a warrant for the arrest of the following men . . ."

Chen saw the guards begin to fan out amongst the peasants, pushing through the crowd roughly, their guns in front of them, searching for the faces of those Peskova was naming, and wondered whether he should run, taking his chance. But as the list of names went on, he realised Tong Chou was not amongst them.

"What's going on?" he asked Pavel.

"I don't know. But they all seem to be friends of Field Supervisor Sung and his wife. Maybe they forced him to make a list before they killed him."

Chen watched the guards gather the fifteen named men together and begin to lead them away, then looked about him, realising how quickly the shadow had fallen once again.

"An hour," he said softly, more to himself than to Pavel. "If they can only wait an hour."

* * *

The bodies lay heaped up against the wall. They were naked and lay as they had fallen. Some still seemed to climb the barrier of stone, their bodies stretched and twisted, their limbs contorted. Others had knelt, bowing to their murderers, facing the inevitability of death. Chen looked about him, sickened by the sight. Pavel stood beside him, breathing noisily. "Why?" he asked after a moment. "In the gods' names why? What had they done?"

Chen turned and looked to his left. The moon was high, a half moon part obscured by cloud. Beneath it, like the jagged shadow of a knife, the Overseer's House rose from the great plain. Where are you? thought Chen, searching the sky. Where the fuck are you? It was so unlike Karr.

It was two hours since the arrests. Two hours and still no sign of them. But even if they had come a half hour early it would have been too late to save these men. All fifteen were dead. They had all heard it, standing there about the guttering fires. Heard the shots ring out across the fields. Heard the screams and then the awful silence afterwards.

"Peskova," Pavel said, bending down and gently touching the arm of one of the dead men. "It was Peskova. He always hated us."

Chen turned back, staring down at the boy, surprised, realising what he was saying. Pavel thought of himself as Han. When he said "us" he didn't mean the peasants, the *ko* who worked the great ten thousand *mou* squares, but the Han. Yes, he thought, but DeVore is the hand behind this. It was he who gave permission for this. And I will kill him. T'ang's orders or no, I will kill him now for what he's done.

He looked back. There was a shadow against the moon. As he watched it passed, followed a moment later by a second.

"Quickly, Pavel," he said, hurrying forward. "They've come."

The four big Security transporters set down almost

silently in the fields surrounding the Overseer's House. Chen ran to greet the nearest of them, expecting Karr, but it wasn't the big man who jumped down from the strut, it was Hans Ebert.

"Captain Ebert," he said, bowing, bringing his hand up to his chest in salute, the movement awkward, unpractised. Ebert, the "Hero of Hammerfest" and heir to the giant GenSyn corporation, was the last officer Chen had expected.

"Kao Chen," Ebert answered him in a crisp, business-like fashion, ignoring the fact of Chen's rank. "Are they all inside the house?"

Chen nodded, letting the insult pass. "As far as I know, sir. The Overseer's craft is still on the landing pad, so I assume DeVore is in there."

Ebert stared across the fields towards the house, then turned back to him, looking him up and down. He gave a short, mocking laugh. "The costume suits you, Kao Chen. You should become a peasant!"

"Sir!" He tried to keep the sourness from his voice, but it was hard. He knew instinctively that Ebert was the reason for the delay. He could imagine him waiting until he had finished dining. Or whoring, maybe. He had heard such tales of him. Karr would never have done that. Karr would have been there when he'd said.

Men jumped down from the craft behind Ebert. Special unit guards, their hands and faces blacked up. One of them came over to Ebert and handed him a clipboard.

Chen recognised him from the old newscasts about the Hammerfest massacre. It was Ebert's chief lieutenant, Auden.

Ebert studied the board a moment, then looked up at Chen again. "You know the lay-out of the Overseer's House?"

Chen bowed his head. "I do, sir."

"Good. Then you can play scout for us, Kao Chen. Auden here will be in command, but you'll take them in, understand?"

Chen kept his head lowered. "Forgive me, Captain, but I am unarmed."

"Of course . . ." Ebert reached down and drew the ten-shot handgun from his holster. "Here."

Chen took the weapon and stared at it in disbelief. "Forgive me, sir. But they've automatics and lasers in there."

Ebert was looking at him coldly. "It's all you'll need."

Chen hesitated, wondering how far to push it, when Ebert barked at him.

"Are you refusing my orders, Kao Chen?"

In answer, Chen bowed to the waist, then turned to Auden. "Come. We'd best move quickly now."

Halfway across the field a figure came towards them. Auden stopped, raising his gun, but Chen put a hand out to stop him.

"It's all right," he said urgently. "I know him. He's a friend."

Auden lowered his gun. The figure came on, until he stood only a few paces from them. It was Pavel.

"What do you want?" Chen asked.

"I want to come with you."

He had found himself a hoe and held it tightly. There was anger in his twisted face. Anger and an awful, urgent need.

"No," said Chen after a moment. "It's too dangerous."

"I know. But I want to."

Chen turned and looked at Auden, who shrugged. "It's his neck, Lieutenant Kao. He can do what he likes. But if he gets in our way we'll shoot him, understand?"

Chen looked back at Pavel. The young man smiled fiercely, then nodded. "Okay. I understand."

"Good," said Auden. "Then let's get into position. The other squad is going in five minutes from now."

They waited in the shadows at the bottom of the ramp, the main door to the house above them. The windows of the house were dark, as if the men inside were asleep, but Chen, crouched there, staring up at the great three-tiered pagoda, knew they would be awake, celebrating the night's events. He watched the vague shadows of the assault troops climbing the ropes high overhead, nursing his anger, knowing it would not be long now.

Pavel was crouched beside him in the darkness. Chen turned and whispered to him. "Keep close to me, Pavel. And don't take risks. They're killers."

Pavel's mouth sought his ear. "I know."

They waited. Then, suddenly, the silence was broken. With a loud crash the assault troops swung through the windows of the second tier. It was the signal to go in. Chen leapt up onto the ramp and began to run toward the door, his handgun drawn, Pavel, Auden and his squad close behind.

He was only ten *ch'i* or so from the door when it slid back suddenly, spilling light.

"Down!" he yelled as the figure in the doorway opened fire. But it was only a moment before the man fell back, answering fire from behind Chen ripping through his chest.

There were shouts from within, then two more men appeared, their automatics stuttering. Chen watched them fall, then scrambled up and ran for the door.

He stood in the doorway, searching the first room at a glance, the handgun following each movement of his eyes. As he'd thought, the three men had been the duty squad. Close by the door a table had been upset and *mah jong* tiles lay scattered about the floor. He stepped over the dead man and went inside.

Up above there was the sound of further shots, then a burst of automatic fire. Chen turned, nodding to Auden as the veteran came into the room, pleased to see Pavel, unharmed, behind him in the doorway.

"They'll defend the stairwell," Chen said quietly, pointing to the door at the far end of the room. "There's a second guardpost at the top, then DeVore's offices beyond that."

"Right." Auden went across and stood by the doorway,

forming his squad up either side of it. He tried the door. It was unlocked.

Chen took Pavel's arm. "Here," he said, drawing him aside. "Let them do this. It's what they're trained for."

Pavel stared back at him. "And you, Kao Chen? You're one of them? A lieutenant?"

Chen nodded, then turned in time to see Auden tug the door aside and crouch there, the big automatic blazing in his lap.

The noise was deafening. There was a moment's silence, then four of the squad moved past him, climbing the stairs quickly. But they were only halfway up when the firing began again, this time from above.

Chen started forward, but Auden was already in charge. He was climbing the stairs over his fallen men, his gun firing ceaselessly, picking off anything that dared show itself up above.

Chen went up after him. Two of the Overseer's men had been guarding the stairs. One lay to one side, dead. The other was slumped over a makeshift barrier, badly wounded. Auden took a new clip from his band and fitted it in the gun, then tugged the man's head back and looked across at Chen. "Who is he? Is he important?"

Chen shrugged, not recognising the Han, then said. "No . . . he's only a guard."

Auden nodded, then put his gun to the man's head and pulled the trigger savagely. "Come on," he said, letting the body fall away.

He was about to turn, when the door behind him burst open.

Chen opened up without thinking, firing off three shots rapidly, the big handgun kicking violently.

The man looked at him wide-eyed, as if surprised, then fell to his knees, clutching his ruined chest, his gun falling away from him. He toppled forward and lay still.

Auden looked at Chen strangely. "Thanks," he said coldly, almost brutally. Then he turned and went through the door, the big gun chattering deafeningly in his hands.

Chen followed him through, into DeVore's office.

The place was a mess. The *wei chi* board was broken, the stones scattered over the floor. The bank of screens had been smashed, as if in a drunken orgy. He frowned, not understanding. Auden couldn't have made all of this mess. It was too thorough. Too all inclusive. It had the look of systematic destruction.

And where was DeVore?

One man lay dead beneath the screens. Two others were kneeling in the far corner of the room, their weapons discarded, their brows pressed to the floor in a gesture of submission. Auden glanced at them dismissively, then waved one of his men over to bind them and take them away. Pavel had come into the room. As the captives passed him, the young man leaned close and spat into their faces.

"For Supervisor Sung," he said, his voice hard, bitter.

Chen watched him a moment, then turned to Auden. "Something's wrong," he said, indicating the screens, the broken board.

Auden looked back at him. "What do you mean?"

Chen looked about him, uncertain. "I don't know. It's just . . ."

Auden turned away, impatient. "Come on, Kao Chen. No more foolishness. Let's finish the job."

Chen stared at him a moment, angered, then did as he was bid. But there is something wrong, he thought. The killings in the field. The broken screens. They mean something.

In the corridor outside Auden had stopped and was talking to the sergeant from the second squad.

"They're holed-up at the top of the house, sir," the sergeant was saying. "About eight of them. Peskova's there. But not DeVore."

"What?" Auden turned and glared at Chen. "I thought you said . . ."

Chen shivered. So that was it. He'd gone already. It explained the killings, the board, the broken screens. He had known it earlier – some part of him had sensed it. But where? Where could he have gone to?

Chen turned and banged his fist against the wall, all his anger and frustration spilling out. "Shit!"

Auden blinked, surprised, then looked back at the sergeant. "Okay. Keep them covered, but pull most of the men back. We'll offer terms."

He watched the sergeant go, then turned and met Chen's eyes. "What's eating you, Kao Chen?"

Chen laughed bitterly. "You think I wanted DeVore to get away?"

"That's if he has. We've only their word. One of those eight could be him."

Chen shook his head. "I doubt it. He's too good a player."

Auden shrugged, not understanding, then went through. Chen followed.

There was a space at the foot of the narrow stairs where the corridor widened out, forming a kind of small room without doors. Two men were stationed there, guns at their shoulders, keeping the door at the top of the steps covered. It was the only way in to the upper room and the stairs themselves were too narrow for more than a single man to use at any one time.

"What have they got?" Auden asked his sergeant.

"Guns. One or two *deng* rifles, maybe. But that's all."

"You're sure?"

"It's all they're issued with out here. These peasants never riot."

Auden laughed. "Lucky them!"

Waving one of the men away, he took his position on the left, half sheltered by the wall, then called out to the men above.

"My name is Lieutenant Auden of the T'ang's Security forces. As you know, you're totally surrounded by my men. Worse than that, you're in a bad situation. The Overseer, the man you knew as Bergson – his real name was DeVore. Yes, DeVore, the traitor. Which means that in helping him you too are traitors. Dead men. Understand me? But the T'ang has empowered me to make a deal with you. To be lenient. Surrender now and we deal with you lightly. If you come out, unarmed and with your arms raised where we can see them, we'll treat this whole matter as a mistake. Okay? Any tricks, however, and you're *all* dead."

Chen crouched by the back wall, watching. He had heard the sudden murmur of voices from above at the revelation of Bergson's true identity. So now you know, he thought. But what are you going to do?

The door slid open a fraction.

"Good," said Auden, turning to Chen. "They're coming out . . ."

Chen heard the grenade bump-bump-bump down the stairs before he saw it, and threw himself to the side, his handgun clattering away from him across the floor. He tensed, fearing the worst, but instead of an explosion, there was a tiny pop and then a furious hissing.

"Gas . . ."

It was a riot gas; a thick, choking gas that billowed out of the split canister, spreading quickly in the tiny space. He had to get up, above it. Forgetting his gun, Chen crawled quickly on his hands and knees, his breath held, making for the stairs. But they were quicker than him.

Chen glanced up. The first of them was already halfway down the narrow stairs. He was wearing a breathing mask and held a stiletto in his right hand. Seeing Chen, his eyes narrowed and he crouched, preparing to spring. But Chen moved quickly. As he jumped, Chen rolled to the side.

The man landed next to him and turned, slashing out wildly with the knife. It flashed past Chen's face, only a hand's width from his eyes. Chen scrambled backward, cursing softly to himself.

More masked men were coming down the stairs now, spilling out into the tiny smoke-filled space, while from the two side corridors Auden's men emerged, their knives drawn, afraid to use their guns in the confusion.

Chen's man had turned, looking for him. He took a step towards Chen, his knife raised, then, with a small strangled noise, he staggered forward, collapsing to his knees. Behind him Auden smiled fiercely through his mask, then quickly turned away, rejoining the fight.

Chen's eyes were streaming now, his throat on fire. He had to get air. He dragged himself forward, making for the stairs, then stopped.

"No-o!"

Pavel was halfway up the stairs, his hoe held out before him. He turned, surprised, looking back down at Chen. "It's Peskova!" he said hoarsely, as if that explained it all. Then his face changed and he fell forward slowly, a knife protruding from his back.

For a moment Chen struggled to get to his feet, then he fell back, a wave of blackness overwhelming him.

★ ★ ★

It seemed only a moment before he came to again. But the corridor was almost clear of the gas, and five bodies lay neatly to one side. Three men sat trussed and gagged in one corner. The door at the top of the stairs was locked again, the stairway covered by the sergeant.

Chen sat up, his head pounding, then remembered.

Pavel! He mouthed the word, his heart wrenched from him.

He crawled across to where they had lain the bodies, and saw him at once.

Chen pulled the young man's body up into his arms and cradled him a moment. He was still warm. "You silly bastard!" he moaned softly. "You poor, silly bastard!" He shuddered and straightened up, looking across to where Auden was standing, watching him. Chen's cheeks were wet with tears, but it didn't matter. It was like losing a son, a brother. He felt a black rage sweep through him.

"What are you waiting for? You told him what would happen! All dead if they played any tricks. That's what you said."

Auden glanced across at the stairs, then looked back at Chen. "I've offered our friend Peskova a new deal. He's thinking it over."

Chen shuddered again, then looked down again. Pavel's face was ugly, his twisted features set in a final snarl of pain. Even in death he had been denied the peace that most men found. *Damn you, Pavel!* he thought, torn by the sight. *It was supposed to be a job. Just a simple infiltration job.*

He turned sharply. The door at the head of the stairs had opened slightly. A moment later there was a clattering on the steps. Chen looked. Two weapons lay there at the sergeant's feet – a rifle and a knife.

"Okay," Peskova called down. "I'll do what you say."

Chen turned back, swallowing drily. His stomach had tightened to a cold, hard knot. A deal. They were going to make a deal with the bastard. He lowered Pavel gently, carefully, then turned back, looking across at Auden. But Auden had turned away. He had forgotten him already.

"All right," Auden was saying. "I'm coming up. Throw the door open wide, then go to the far side of the room and stay there with your hands in the air. If I see *any* movement I'll open fire. Understand me?"

"I understand, Lieutenant."

Chen pushed his hands together to stop them shaking, then pulled himself up onto his feet. The effort made him double up, coughing. For a moment his head swam and he almost fell, but then it cleared. He straightened up, wheezing for breath, and looked across.

Auden was halfway up the stairs now, moving slowly, cautiously, one step every few seconds, his gun tracking from side to side. Then he was at the top, framed by the doorway. Without turning, he called his sergeant up after him.

Chen stood there a moment, breathing deeply, slowly, getting his strength back. He swallowed painfully, then looked about him. Where . . . ? Then he saw it. There, on the floor by the wall where they had lain him. His handgun.

He went across and picked it up, then turned back, following two of Auden's men up into the top room.

Peskova stood against the back wall, his hands resting loosely on his head. He was looking across at Auden, his chin raised arrogantly, his eyes smiling cruelly, almost triumphantly, knowing he was safe.

Chen shivered and looked away, sickened by the sight of the man, barely in control of himself now. He wanted to smash that arrogant face. To wipe the smile from those coldly mocking eyes. But it was not Peskova he wanted. Not really. It was DeVore.

He lifted his head, forcing himself to look at him again. Yes. He could see the pale shadow of the man in this lesser creature. Could see the same indifference behind the eyes. A kind of absence. Nothing that a retinal print could capture, but there nonetheless. Like his master, Peskova had nothing but contempt for his fellow creatures. All he did was shaped by a cold and absolute dismissal of their separate existence. They were things for his amusement. *Things . . .*

Chen looked down again, the trembling in him so marked now that he had to clench his left fist again and again to control it.

Such power DeVore had. Such awful power, to cast so many in his own dark image.

"Kuan Yin! Look at this!"

The sergeant had been moving about the room, searching. In the far corner he had come across a large shape covered by a sheet. Now he turned, facing them, the colour drained from his face.

"Watch him closely!" Auden said to the man at his side, then went across to where his sergeant stood. Chen followed.

He was not sure what he'd expected, but it wasn't this. The man was stretched naked over the saddle, his hands and feet bound tightly to the stirrups. Dark smears of congealed blood coated his legs and arms and the lower part of his back, and he was split from arse to stomach.

675

"Gods . . ." Auden said softly, walking about the body. "I'd heard of this, but I never dreamed . . ." He fell silent.

Chen felt the bile rise to his throat. The man's eyes bulged, but they were lifeless now. He had choked to death. Not surprisingly. His balls had been cut from him stitched into his mouth.

"Who is this?" Auden asked, looking across at Peskova.

Peskova stared back coldly, almost defiantly. "A guard. His name was Chang Yan. He had been stealing . . ."

"Stealing . . ." Auden made to shake his head, then turned away. "Cover it up," he said to his sergeant, meeting his eyes a moment, a look of disgust passing between them.

"You made a deal," said Chen, glaring at Auden. "Was this a part of it?"

Auden glanced at him, then turned away, moving back towards Peskova.

"I made a deal."

Chen followed him across, something still and cold and hard growing in the depths of him.

Auden stopped, three, four paces from Peskova, looking about the room. Then he turned and looked directly at the man. There was something like a smile on his lips. "Is that how you deal with thieves out here?"

Peskova's face had hardened. He had been worried momentarily. Now, seeing that hint of a smile, he relaxed again, misinterpreting it. His own smile widened. "Not always."

"So it was special?"

Peskova looked down. "You could say that. Mind you, I'm only sorry it wasn't his friend, Teng. I would have liked to have seen that bastard beg for mercy." He looked up again, laughing, as if it was a joke only he and Auden could share. "These Han . . ."

Chen stared at him coldly. "And Pavel? What about him? He wasn't Han . . ."

Peskova turned and smiled at him contemptuously. An

awful, smirking smile. "Why split hairs? Anyway, that little shit deserved what he got . . ."

Chen shuddered violently. Then, without thinking, he lunged forward and grabbed Peskova, forcing the man's jaw open, thrusting the handgun into his open mouth. He sensed, rather than saw, Auden move forward to stop him, but it was too late – he had already pulled the trigger.

The explosion seemed to go off in his own head. Peskova jerked back away from him, his skull shattered, his brains spattered across the wall behind like rotten fruit.

Chen stepped back, looking down at the fallen man, Then Auden had hold of him and had yanked him round roughly. "You stupid bastard!" he shouted into his face. "Didn't you understand? We needed him alive!"

Chen stared back at him blankly, shivering, his jaw set. "He killed my friend."

Auden hesitated, his face changing, then he let him go. "Yes," he said quietly. "Yes." Then, angrily, "But we're even now, Kao Chen. Understand me? You saved my life downstairs. But this . . . Well, we're even now. A life for a life."

Chen stared at him, then looked away, disgusted. "Even," he said, and laughed sourly. "Sure. It's all even now."

* * *

Ebert was waiting for them at the bottom of the ramp.

"Well?" he demanded. "Where is he? I'd like to see to him once more, before we send him on. He was a good officer, whatever else he's done."

Chen looked down, astonished. A good officer!

Beside him Auden hesitated, then met his Captain's eyes. "I'm afraid there's no sign of him, sir. We're taking the place apart now, but I don't think he's hiding in there. One of the guards says he flew off earlier this evening, but if so it wasn't in his own craft. That's still here, as Kao Chen said."

Ebert turned on Chen, furious. "Where the fuck is he, Chen? You were supposed to be keeping an eye on him!"

It was unfair. It also wasn't true, but Chen bowed his head anyway. "I'm sorry . . ." he began, but was interrupted.

"Captain Ebert! Captain Ebert!"

It was the communications officer from Ebert's transporter.

"What is it, Hoenig?"

The young man bowed deeply, then handed him the report.

Ebert turned and looked back towards the west. There, in the distance, the sky was glowing faintly. "Gods . . ." he said softly. "Then it's true."

"What is it, sir?" Auden asked, knowing at once that something was badly wrong.

Ebert laughed strangely, then shook his head. "It's the Lodz garrison. It's on fire. What's more, Administrator Duchek's dead. Assassinated thirty minutes back." Then he laughed again; a laugh of grudging admiration. "It seems DeVore's outwitted us again."

★ ★ ★

Fei Yen stood there in her rooms, naked behind the screen, her maids surrounding her. Her father, Yin Tsu, stood on the other side of the heavy silk screen, his high-pitched voice filled with an unusual animation. As he talked, one of Fei Yen's maids rubbed scented oils into her skin, while another dried and combed her long, dark hair. A third and fourth brought clothes for her to decide upon, hurrying backward and forward to try to please her whim.

He had called upon her unexpectedly, while she was in her bath, excited by his news, and had had to be physically dissuaded from going straight in to her.

"But she is my daughter!" he had complained when the maids had barred his way.

"Yes, but I am a woman now, father, not a girl!" Fei

678

Yen had called out sweetly from within. "Please wait. I'll not be long."

He had begged her forgiveness, then, impatient to impart his news, had launched into his story anyhow. Li Shai Tung, it seemed, had been in contact with him.

"I'm almost certain it's to tell me there's an appointment at court for your eldest brother, Sung. I petitioned the T'ang more than a year ago now. But what post, I wonder? Something in the T'ang's household, do you think? Or perhaps a position in the secretariat?" He laughed nervously, then continued hurriedly. "No. Not that. The T'ang would not bother with such trivial news. It must be a post in the ministry. Something important. A junior minister's post, at the very least. Yes. I'm almost certain of it. But tell me, Fei Yen, what do you think?"

It was strange how he always came to her when he had news. Never to Sung or Chan or her younger brother Wei. Perhaps it was because she reminded him so closely of her dead mother, to whom Yin Tsu had always confided when she was alive.

"What if it has nothing to do with Sung, father? What if it's something else?"

"Ah, no, foolish girl. Of course it will be Sung. I feel it in my bones!" He laughed. "And then, perhaps, I can see to the question of your marriage at long last. Tuan Wu has been asking after you. He would make a good husband, Fei Yen. He comes from a good line. His uncle is the third son of the late Tuan Chung-Ho and the Tuans are a rich family."

Fei Yen looked down, smiling to herself. Tuan Wu was a fool, a gambler and a womaniser, in no particular order. But she had no worries about Tuan Wu. Let her father ramble on – she knew why Li Shai Tung was coming to see them. Li Yuan had spoken to his father. Had done what she had thought impossible.

"I know what you're thinking, Fei Yen, but a woman should have a proper husband. Your youth is spilling from you, like sand from a glass. Soon there will be no more sand. And then?"

She laughed. "Dearest father, what a ridiculous image! No more sand!" Again she laughed and, after a moment, his laughter joined with hers.

"Whatever . . ." he began again, "my mind is made up. We must talk seriously about this."

"Of course." Her agreement surprised him into momentary silence.

"Good. Then I shall see you in my rooms in three hours. The T'ang has asked to see us all. It might be an opportune time to discuss your re-marriage."

When he had gone she pushed aside her maids, then hurried across the room and stood there, studying herself in the full-length dragon mirror. Yes, she thought; you are a T'ang's wife, Fei Yen. You always were a T'ang's wife, from the day you were born. She laughed and threw her head back, admiring her taut, full breasts, the sleekness of her thighs and stomach, the dark beauty of her eyes. Yes, and you *shall* have a proper husband. But not just any fool or Minor Family reprobate. My man shall be a T'ang. My son a T'ang.

She shivered, then turned from the mirror, letting her maids lead her back to her place behind the screens.

But make it soon, she thought. Very soon.

* * *

Karr drifted in from the darkside, the solar sail fully extended, slowing his speed as he approached. His craft was undetectable – just another piece of space junk.

They would have no warning.

Twenty *li* out he detached himself and floated in, a dark hunched shape, lost against the backdrop of space. As planned he landed on the blind spot of the huge ship, the curved layers of transparent ice beneath his boots.

He stood there a moment, enjoying the view. The moon vast and full above him, Chung Kuo far to his right and below him, the sun between, magnificent even through the visor of his suit. It surprised him how much he felt in his element, standing there on the curved hull of the starship, staring fearlessly into the furnace of creation, the void pressing in upon him. He laughed soundlessly and then ducked down, his movements slow at first as he climbed toward the airlock, then more fluent as he caught the proper rhythm.

He slowed himself with the double rail, then pushed into the semi-circular depression. Beside the hexagonal door-hatch was a numbered touch-pad. He fingered the combination quickly, almost thoughtlessly, then leaned back as the hatch irised, its six segments folding back upon themselves.

As expected, there was no guard. He pulled himself inside and closed the hatch.

This part was easy. He had done it a hundred, two hundred times in simulation. He had been trained to do this thoughtlessly. But at some point he would need to act on his own: to use his discretion and react with immediacy. Until then he went by rote, knowing every inch of the huge craft as if he had built it.

The air-lock filled and the inner door activated. He went through quickly, his weapon searching for targets, finding nothing, no one. But somewhere an alarm would be flashing. Unauthorised entry at airlock seven. A matter for investigation. Security would be buzzing already. There would be guards at the next junction of the corridor.

Karr removed the two heat-seeking darts from his belt and pressed a button on his suit. In seconds the ice of his suit was minus ten. He hurled the darts ahead of him and raced down the corridor after them.

Explosions punctuated the silence up ahead. The darts had found their targets. Coming to the ruined corpses he leaped over them without stopping and ran on, taking the corridor to his left and going through the two quick-irising doors before he paused and anchored himself to the ceiling, the short, securing chain attached to the back of his sturdy helmet.

He swung up and kicked. The inspection hatch moved but did not open. His second kick shifted it back and he hooked his feet through, scrambling up into the narrow space, releasing the anchor chain.

Here his size was a handicap. He turned awkwardly, putting back the hatch, knowing he had only seconds to spare.

He had cut it fine. He heard guards pass by below only a moment later, their confusion apparent. Good. It was going well.

Karr smiled, enjoying himself.

He moved quickly now, crawling along the inspection channel. Then, at the next down intersection, he swung out over the space and dropped.

He landed and turned about immediately, crouching down then working his way awkwardly into a second channel. This one came out at the back of the Security desk. Timing was crucial. In a minute or so they would have guessed what he had done.

Maybe they had already and were waiting.

He shrugged and poised himself over the hatch, setting the charge. Then he went along to the second hatch. The explosion would blow a hole in the room next door to Security – a sort of recreation room. There would be no one there at present, but it would distract them while he climbed down.

He lifted the hatch cover a fraction of a second before the charge blew and was climbing down even as the guards turned below him, surprised by the explosion.

He landed on the neck of one of them and shot two others before they knew he was there amongst them. Another of the guards, panicking, helped Karr by burning two more of his colleagues.

Confusion. That too was a weapon, sharp as a knife.

Karr shot the panicking guard and rolled a smoke-bomb into the corridor outside. Then he turned and blasted the Security communications desk. The screens went dead.

He waited a moment. The screens flickered into brief

life, showing scenes of chaos in corridors and rooms throughout the starship, then they died again, the back-ups failing. The inside man had done his job.

Good, thought Karr. Now to conclude.

He went out into the corridor, moving fast, jumping over bodies, knocking aside confused, struggling guards. All they saw was a giant in a dark, eerily-glowing suit, moving like an athlete down the corridor, unaffected by the thick, black choking smoke.

He went right and right again, then fastened himself to the inner wall of the corridor, rolling a small charge against the hull.

The spiked charge almost tore his anchorage away. He was tugged violently towards the breach. The outer skin of the starship shuddered but held, beginning to seal itself. But it had bled air badly. It was down to half an atmosphere. Debris cluttered about the sealing hole.

In half a minute he released the anchor chain and ran on down the corridor, meeting no resistance now. Guards lay unconscious everywhere. Many had been thrown against walls or doorways and were dead or badly wounded. It was complete chaos.

The engine was inside, in the inner shell. A breach of the hull could not affect it.

This was the difficult part. They would be expecting him now. But he had a few tricks left to show them before he was done.

He ignored the inner shell air-lock and moved on to one of the ducts. It would have shut down the instant the outer hull was breached, making the inner shell airtight. Thick layers of ice were interlaced like huge fingers the length of a man's arm. Above them a laser-protected sensor registered the atmospheric pressure of the outer shell.

Karr unclipped a rectangular container from his belt and took two small packages from it. The first was a one-atmosphere "pocket". He fitted it over the sensor quickly, ignoring the brief, warning sting from the laser. The second of the packages he treated with a care that seemed exaggerated. It was ice-wire: a long thread of the deadly cutting material. He drew it out cautiously and pulled it taut, then swiftly used it to cut the securing bolts on each of the six sides of the duct.

The whole thing dropped a hand's length as the lasers blinked out. There was a soft exhalation of air. The sound a lift makes when it stops.

Karr waited a moment, then began cutting into the casing with small, diagonal movements that removed pieces of the ice like chunks of soft cheese. As the gap widened he cut deeper into the case and then pulled back and set the thread down.

He climbed up onto the casing and kicked. Three of the segments fell away. He eased himself down into the gap.

It was far narrower than he had anticipated and for a moment he thought he was going to be stuck. The segments had wedged against the internal mechanism of the duct at an awkward angle, leaving him barely enough room to squeeze by. He managed, just, but his right arm was trapped against the wall and he couldn't reach the device taped to his chest.

He shifted his weight and stood on tiptoe, edging about until his hand and lower arm were free, then reached up and unstrapped the bomb from his chest.

Another problem presented itself. He could not reach down and place the device against the inner casing of the duct. There was no way he could fasten it.

Did it matter? He decided that it didn't. He would strengthen the upper casing when he was out. The explosion would be forced inward.

It was such a small device. So delicate a thing. And yet so crude in its power.

He placed the bomb between his knee and the duct wall, then let it slide down between leg and wall, catching it with his foot.

He didn't want it to go up with him there.

He touched the timer with his boot and saw it glow red. Eight minutes to get out.

He began to haul himself up the sides of the duct, using brute force, legs and back braced, his thickly-muscled arms straining to free himself from the tight-packed hole.

At the top he paused and looked around. What could he use? He bent down and picked up the ice-wire, then went to a nearby room and cut machinery away from the desks, then brought it back and piled it up beside the breached duct.

Three minutes thirty seconds gone. He went to the doorway and cut a huge rectangle of ice from the wall. It was thin – insubstantial almost – but strong. It weighed nothing in itself but he could pile all the heavy machinery up on top of it.

It would have to do.

There was just short of two minutes left to get out.

Time for his last trick. He ran for his life. Back the way he'd come. Without pause he pulled the last of his bombs from his belt and threw it, pressing the stud at his belt as he did so.

The outer wall exploded, then buckled inward.

Karr, his life processes suspended, was thrown out through the rent in the starship's outer skin; a dark, larval pip spat out violently.

The pip drifted out from the giant sphere, a thin trail of dust and iced air in its trail. Seconds later the outer skin rippled and then collapsed, lit from within. It shrivelled, like a ball of paper in a fire, then, with a suddenness that surprised the distant, watching eyes, lit up like a tiny sun, long arms of vivid fire burning a crown of thorns in the blackness of space.

It had been done. War had been declared.

EPILOGUE-SUMMER 2203:

MOSAICS

"What is it whose closing causes the dark and whose
opening causes the light? Where does the Bright God
hide before the Horn proclaims the dawning of the day?"

– *T'ien Wen* ('Heavenly Questions') by
Ch'u Yuan, from the *Ch'u Tz'u* ('Songs
Of The South'), 2nd century BC.

A BRIDGE OVER NOTHINGNESS

And so they began, burying the dark; capping the well of memory with a stone too vast, too heavy to move. The machine watched them at their work, seeing many things their frailer, time-bound eyes were prone to miss – subtle changes of state it had come to recognise as significant. At times the full intensity of its awareness was poured into the problem of the boy, Kim. For a full second, maybe two, it thought of nothing else. Several lifetimes of normal human consciousness passed this way. And afterwards it would make a motion in its complex circuitry – unseen, unregistered on any monitoring screen – approximate to a nod of understanding.

While the two theoreticians began the job of mapping out a new mosaic – a new ideal configuration for the boy's mental state, his personality – the Builder returned to the cell and to the boy. His eyes, the small, unconscious movements of his body, revealed his unease, his awkwardness, finally his uncertainty. As he administered the first of the drug treatments to the boy he could not hide the concern, the *doubt* he felt.

It watched, uncommenting, as the drugs began to have their desired effect upon the boy. It saw how they systematically blocked off all pathways that led into the boy's past, noting the formulae of the drugs they used, deriving a kind of mathematical pleasure from the subtle evolving variations as they fine-tuned their chemical control of the

689

process of erasure. There was an art to what they did. And the machine saw this and, in its own manner, appreciated it.

It was a process of reduction different in kind from what they had attempted earlier. This time they did not seek to cower him but to strip him of every last vestige of that which made him a personality, a *being*. In long sessions on the operating table, the two theoreticians probed the boy's mind, sliding micro-thin wires into the boy's shaven skull, then administering fine dosages of chemicals and organic compounds, until, at last, they had achieved their end.

In developing awareness the machine had developed memory. Not memory as another machine might have defined it – that, to the conscious entity that tended these isolated decks, was merely "storage", the bulk of things known. No, memory was something else. Its function was unpredictable. It threw up odd items of data – emphasised certain images, certain words and phrases over others. And it was inextricably bound up with the sensation of self-awareness. Indeed, it *was* self-awareness, for the one could not exist without the eccentric behaviour of the other. Yet it was also much more than the thing these humans considered memory – for the full power of the machine's ability to reason and the frighteningly encyclopaedic range of its knowledge *informed* these eccentric upwellings of words and images.

One image that it held important occurred shortly after they had completed their work and capped the well of memory in Kim. It was when the boy woke in his cell after the last of the operations. At first he lay there, his eyes open, a glistening wetness at the corner of his part-open mouth. Then, as though instinct were taking hold – some vestige of the body's remembered language of actions shaping the attempt – he tried to sit up.

It was to the next few moments that the machine returned, time and again, sifting the stored images through the most intense process of scrutiny.

The boy had lifted his head. One of his arms bent and

moved, as if to support and lift his weight, but the other had been beneath him as he lay and the muscles were "asleep". He fell forward and lay there, chin, cheek and eye pressed close against the floor. Like that he stayed, his visible eye registering only a flicker of confusion before the pupil settled and the lid half closed. For a long time afterwards there was only blankness in that eye. A nothingness. Like the eye of a corpse, unconnected to the seeing world.

Later, when, in the midst of treatment, the boy would suddenly stop and look about him, that same look would return, followed by a moment of sheer, blind panic that would take minutes to fully subside. And though, in the months that followed, the boy grew in confidence, it was like building a bridge over nothingness. From time to time the boy would step up to the edge and look over. Then would come that look, and the machine would remember the first time it had seen it. It was the look of a machine. Of a thing without life.

They began their rehabilitation with simple exercises, training the body in new ways, new mannerisms, avoiding if they could the old patterns of behaviour. Even so, there were times when far older responses showed through. Then the boy's motor activities would be locked into a cycle of meaningless repetition – like a malfunctioning robot – until an injection of drugs brought him out of it.

For the mind they devised a set of simple but subtle games to make it learn again. At first it was resistant to these, and there were days when the team were clearly in despair, thinking they had failed. But then, almost abruptly, in mid session, this changed. The boy began to respond again. That night the three men got drunk together in the observation room.

Progress was swift once the breakthrough was made. In three months the boy had a complete command of language again. He was numerate to a sophisticated degree, coping with complex logic problems easily. His spatial awareness was perfect: he had a strong sense of patterns and connections. It seemed then, all tests done, that the treatment had worked and the *mode* of his mind – that quick, intuitive talent unique to the boy – had emerged unscathed from the process of walling-in his personality. With regard to his personality, however, he demonstrated many of the classic symptoms of incurable amnesia. In his new incarnation he was a rather colourless figure, uncertain in his relationship with the Builder, colder, distanced from things – somehow less human than he'd been. There was a machine-like, functional aspect to his being. Yet even in this respect there were signs of change – of a softening of the hard outlines of the personality they had grafted onto him.

Nine months into the programme it seemed that the gamble had paid off handsomely. When the team met that night in the observation room they agreed it was time to report back on their progress. A message was sent up-Levels. Two days later they had their reply. Berdichev was coming. He wanted to see the boy with his own eyes.

* * *

Soren Berdichev waited at the security checkpoint, straight-backed and severe, his bodyguards to either side of him, and thought of his wife. It was more than a month now since her death, but he had still not recovered from it. The doctors had found nothing wrong with her in their autopsy report, but that meant little. They had killed her. The Seven. He didn't know how, but there was no other explanation. A healthy woman like Ylva didn't just die like that. Her heart had been strong. She had been fit – in her middle-aged prime. There was no reason for her heart to fail.

As they passed him through he found himself going over the same ground again, no nearer than before to finding a solution. Had it been someone near to her – someone he trusted? And how had they managed it? A fast-acting drug that left no trace? Some physical means? He was no nearer now than he had been in that dreadful moment when he had discovered her. And the pain of her absence gnawed at him. He hadn't known how much he was going to miss her until she was gone. He had thought he could live without her . . .

The corridor ended at a second security door. It opened as he approached it and a dark-haired man with a goatee beard stood there, his hand out in welcome.

Berdichev ignored the offered hand and waited while one of his guards went through. A team of his men had checked the place out only hours before, but he was taking no chances. Administrator Jouanne had been killed only a week ago and things were heating up daily. The guard returned a moment later and gave the all-clear signal. Only then did he go inside.

The official turned and followed Berdichev into the centre of the room. "The boy is upstairs, sir. The Builder is with him, to make introductions. Otherwise . . ."

Berdichev turned and cut the man off in mid-sentence. "Bring me the Architect. I want to talk to him before I see the boy."

The official bowed and turned away.

While he waited, he looked about him, noting the spartan austerity of the place. Employees were standing about awkwardly. He could sense the intensity of their curiosity about him, though when he looked at them they would hasten to avert their eyes. It was common knowledge that he was one of the chief opponents of the Seven, that his wife had died, that he himself was in constant danger. There was a dark glamour to all of this and he recognised it, but today his mood was sour. Perhaps seeing the boy would shake him from its grip.

The official returned with the Architect in tow. Berdichev waved the official away, then took the Architect by the arm and led him across the room, away from the others. For a moment he studied the man. Then, leaning forward, he spoke, his voice low but clear.

"How stable is the new mental configuration? How reliable?"

The Architect looked down, considering. "We think it's

firm. But it's hard to tell as yet. There's the possibility that he'll revert. Only a slender chance, but one that must be recognised."

Berdichev nodded, at one and the same time satisfied with the man's honesty and disappointed that there was yet this area of doubt.

"But taking this possibility into consideration, is it possible to . . ." he pursed his lips momentarily, then said it, ". . . to *use* the boy?"

"Use him?" The Architect stared at him. "How do you mean?"

"Harness his talents. Use his unique abilities. *Use* him." Berdichev shrugged. He didn't want to be too specific.

The Architect seemed to understand. He smiled bleakly and shook his head. "Impossible. You'd destroy him if you *used* him now." There was a deliberate, meaningful emphasis on the word.

"How soon then?"

"You don't understand. With respect, *Shih* Berdichev, this is only the beginning of the process. We reconstruct the house, but it has to be lived in for some time before we can discover its faults and flaws. It'll be years before we know that the treatment has worked properly."

"Then why did you contact me?"

Berdichev frowned. He felt suddenly that he had been brought here under false pretences. When he'd received the news he had seen at once how the boy might be used. He had planned to take the boy with him, back into the Clay. And there he would have honed him; made him the perfect weapon against the Seven. The means of destroying them. The very cutting edge of knowledge.

The Architect was explaining things, but Berdichev was barely listening. He interrupted. "Show me the boy. I want to see the boy."

The Architect nodded and led him through, the bodyguards following some four paces behind.

"We've moved him in the last few days. His new quarters

694

are more spacious, better-equipped. Once he's settled in we'll begin the next stage of the treatment."

Berdichev glanced at the psychiatrist. "The next stage?"

"Yes. He needs to be resocialised. Taught basic social skills. At present he has very few defences. He's vulnerable. Highly sensitive. A kind of hot-house plant. But he needs to be hardened-up, desensitised, if he's to survive up-levels."

Berdichev slowed and then stopped. "You mean the whole socialisation-programme has to be gone through from scratch?"

The Architect hesitated. "Not exactly. But . . . well, near enough. You see, it's a different process here. A slow widening of his circle of contacts. And no chance of him mixing outside this unit until we're certain he can fit in. It'll take three years, maybe longer."

"Three years?"

The Architect looked down. "At least."

Berdichev stared at the man, but he hardly saw him. He was thinking of how much things would have changed in three years. On top of all else this was a real disappointment.

"And there's no way of hastening this process?"

"None we can guarantee."

He stood there, calculating. Was it worth risking the boy on a chance? He had gambled once and – if these men were right – had won. But did he want to risk what had been achieved?

For a moment longer he hesitated, then signalled to the Architect to move on again. He would see for himself – see how the boy was – and then decide.

★ ★ ★

Berdichev sat on a chair in the middle of the room, the boy stood in front of him, no more than an arm's length away. The child seemed calm and answered his questions without hesitating, without once glancing towards the Builder who sat away to the side of him. His eyes met Berdichev's without fear. As though he had no real conception of fear.

He was not so much like his father now. Berdichev studied the boy a long time, looking for that resemblance he had seen so clearly – so shockingly – that first time, but there was little sign of Edmund Wyatt in him now – and certainly no indication of the child he might have been. The diet of the Clay had long ago distorted the potential of the genes, refashioning his physical frame in a manner analogous to the way they had shaped his mind, here in this place. He seemed subdued, quiet. There was little movement of his head, his hands, no sign of restlessness. Yet beyond what was seen – behind the surfaces presented to the eye – was a sense of great intensity. The same could be said of his eyes. They too were calm, reflective; yet at the back of them was a darkness that was profound, impenetrable. It was like staring into a mirror and finding the vast emptiness of space there behind the familiar, reflected image.

Now that he faced the boy he could see what the Architect had meant. The child was totally vulnerable. He had been reconstructed without defences. Like Adam, innocent, he stood there, facing, if not his Creator, then, in his new shape, his Instigator. The boy knew nothing of that, of course. Nor did he understand the significance of this encounter. But Berdichev, studying him, came to his decision. He would leave well alone. Would let them shape the boy further. And then, in three, maybe four years' time, would come back for him. That was, if either he or the boy was still alive in four years' time.

* * *

The camera turned, following Berdichev's tall, aristocratic figure as it left the room, looking for signs of the man it had heard about. For the machine Outside was a mosaic formed from the broken shards of rumour. In its isolation, it had no knowledge of the City and its ways other than that which it overheard, fitting these imperfect glimpses into an ever-widening picture. When the guards talked, it listened, sifting and sorting what they said, formulating its own version of events. And when something happened in that bigger world beyond itself, it would watch the ripples spread, and form its own opinion.

Assassinations and reprisals; this seemed the pattern of the War-that-wasn't-a-War. No armies clashed. No missiles fell on innocents. The City was too complex, too tightly interwoven for such things. Yet there was darkness and deceit in plenitude. And death. Each day seemed to bring its freight of names. The mighty fallen. And in the deep, unseen levels of its consciousness, the machine saw how all of this fitted with its task here in the Unit – saw how the two things formed a whole: mosaics of violence and repression.

It watched as Berdichev stood there in the outer room, giving instructions to the Unit's Head. This was a different man from the one he had expected. Deeper, more subtle than the foolish, arrogant villain the men had drawn between them. More dangerous and, in some strange way, more *kingly* than they would have had him be.

It had seen how Berdichev had looked at the boy, as if recognising another of his own kind. As if, amongst men, there were also levels. And this the highest; the level of Shapers and Doers – Architects and Builders not of a single mind but of the vast hive of minds that was the City. The thought recurred, and from somewhere drifted up a phrase it had often heard spoken – "the Kings of the City". How well the old word sat on such men, for they moved and acted as a king might. There was the shadow of power behind their smallest motion. Power and death.

It watched them all. Saw how their faces said what in words could not be uttered. Saw each small betraying detail clearly, knowing them for what they were; all desire and doubt open to its all-seeing eye. Kings and peasants all, it saw the things that shaped each one of them. Variations on a theme. The same game played at a different level, for different stakes. All this was old knowledge, but for the machine it was new. Isolated, unasked, it viewed the world outside with a knowing innocence. Saw the dark heart of things. And stored the knowledge.

★ ★ ★

When they felt it was time, they taught him about his past. Or what they knew of it. Heavily-edited, they returned to him the history of the person he had been. Names, pictures and events. But not the experience.

Kim learned his lessons well. Once told he could not forget. But that was not to say they gave him back his self. The new child was a pale imitation of the old. He had not lived and suffered and dreamed. What was dark in him was hidden; was walled-off and inaccessible. In its place he had a fiction; a story learned by rote. Something to fill the gap; to assuage the feeling of emptiness that gripped him whenever he looked back.

It was fifteen months into the programme when they brought T'ai Cho to the small suite of five rooms Kim had come to know as home. Kim knew the stranger by his face; knew both his history and what he had done for him. He greeted him warmly, as duty demanded, but his eyes saw only a stranger's face. He had no real feeling for the man.

T'ai Cho cried and held the boy tightly, fiercely to him. He had been told how things were, but it was hard for him. Hard to feel the boy's hands barely touching his back when he held him. Hard to see love replaced by curiosity in those eyes. He had been warned – had steeled himself – yet his disappointment, his sense of hurt, was great nonetheless.

In a nearby room the team watched tensely, talking amongst themselves, pleased that the boy was showing so little sign of emotion or excitement. A camera focused on the boy's eyes, showing the smallest sign of movement in the pupils. A monitoring unit attached to the back of the boy's neck traced more subtle changes in the brain's activity. All seemed normal. Stable. There was no indication that the boy had any memory of the man other than those implanted by the team.

It was just as they'd hoped. Kim had passed the test. Now they could progress – move on to the next stage of his treatment. The house, once empty, had been furnished. It was time now to fill the rooms with life. Time to test the mosaic for flaws.

In the room the man turned away from the boy and picked up his jacket from the chair. For a moment he turned back, looking at him, to the last hopeful that some small flicker of recognition would light those eyes with their old familiar warmth. But there was nothing. The child he had known was dead. Even so, he felt a kind of love for the form, the flesh, and so he went across and held him one last time before he left. For old time's sake. Then he turned and went, saying nothing. Finding nothing left to say.

A GIFT OF STONES

In the Hall of the Eight Immortals, the smallest, most
intimate of the eighty-one Halls in the Palace of Tongjiang,
the guests had gathered for the betrothal ceremony of the
young prince Li Yuan to the beautiful Fei Yen. As these
events went it was only a tiny gathering; there were less
than a hundred people in the lavishly decorated room – the
tight circle of those who were known and trusted by the
T'ang.

The room was silent now, the guests attentive as Li Shai
Tung took the great seal from the cushion his Chancellor
held out to him, then, both his hands taking its weight,
turned to face the table. The seal – the Family "chop", a
huge square thing, more shield than simple stamp – had
been inked beforehand and, as the great T'ang turned, the
four Mandarin characters that quartered the seal glistened
redly in the lamplight.

On the low table before him was the contract of marriage,
which would link the T'ang's clan once more with that of
Yin Tsu. Two servants, their shaven heads lowered, their
eyes averted, held the great scroll open as the T'ang
positioned the seal above the silken paper and then
leaned forward, placing his full weight on the ornate
handle.

Satisfied, he stepped back, letting an official lift the seal
with an almost pedantic care and replace it on the cushion.
For a moment he stared at the vivid imprint on the paper,

remembering another day. Yin Tsu's much smaller chop lay beneath his own, the ink half-dried.

They had annulled the previous marriage earlier in the day, all seven T'ang setting their rings to the wax of the document. There had been smiles then, and celebration, but in all their hearts, he knew, there remained a degree of unease. Something unspoken lay behind every eye.

Dark Wei followed in his brother's footsteps and the Lord of You-yi was stirred against him . . .

The words of the "Heavenly Questions" had kept running through his mind all morning, like a curse, darkening his mood. So it was sometimes. And though he knew the words meant nothing – that his son, Yuan, was no adulterer – still he felt wrong about this. A wife was like the clothes a man wore in life. And did one put on one's dead brother's clothes?

Han Ch'in . . . Had five years really passed since Han had died? He felt a twinge of pain at the memory. This was like burying his son again. For a moment he felt the darkness well up in him, threatening to mist his eyes and spoil things for his younger son. Then it passed. It was Li Yuan now. Yuan was his son, his only son, his heir. And maybe it was right that he should marry his dead brother's wife – maybe it *was* what the gods wanted.

He sniffed, then turned, smiling, to face Yin Tsu, and opened his arms, embracing the old man warmly.

"I am glad our families are to be joined again, Yin Tsu," he said softly in his ear. "It has grieved me that you and I had no grandson to sweeten our old age."

As they moved apart, the T'ang saw the effect his words had had on the old man. Yin Tsu bowed deeply, torn between joy and a fierce pride, the muscles of his face struggling to keep control. His eyes were moist and his hands shook as they held the T'ang's briefly.

"I am honoured, *Chieh Hsia*. Deeply honoured."

Behind him his three sons looked on, tall yet somehow colourless young men. And beside them, her eyes lowered, demure in her pink and cream silks, Fei Yen herself, her outward appearance unchanged from that day when she had stood beside Han Ch'in and spoken her vows.

Li Shai Tung studied her a moment, thoughtful. She looked so frail, so fragile, yet he had seen for himself how spirited she was. It was almost as if all the strength that should have gone into Yin Tsu's sons had been stolen – spirited away – by her. Like the thousand-year-old fox in the Ming novel, *Feng-shen Yen-I*, that took the form of the beautiful Tan Chi and bemused and misled the last of the great Shang Emperors . . .

He sniffed. No. These were only an old man's foolish fears – dark reflections of his anxiety at how things were. Such things were not real. They were only stories.

Li Shai Tung turned, one hand extended, and looked across at his son. "Li Yuan . . . bring the presents for your future wife."

* * *

The Shepherd boy stood apart from the others, staring up at the painting that hung between the two dragon pillars on the far side of the Hall. Li Yuan had noticed him earlier – had noted his strange separateness from everything – and had remarked on it to Fei Yen.

"Why don't you go across and speak to him?" she had whispered. But he had held back. Now, however, his curiosity had got the better of him. Maybe it was the sheer intensity of the boy that drew him, or some curious feeling of fellowship; a sense that – for all his father had said of Ben's aversion to it – they were meant to be companions, like Hal and his father. T'ang and Advisor. They had been bred so. And yet . . .

"Forgive me, General," he said, smiling at Nocenzi, "but I must speak with Hal's son. I have not met him before and he will be gone in an hour. If you'll excuse me."

The circle gathered about the General bowed low as he moved away, then resumed their conversation, an added degree of urgency marking their talk now that the prince was no longer amongst them.

702

Li Yuan, meanwhile, made his way across the room and stopped, a pace behind the boy, almost at his shoulder, looking up past him at the painting.

"Ben?"

The boy turned his head and looked at him. "Li Yuan . . ." He smiled and lowered his head the tiniest amount, more acknowledgment than bow. "You are to be congratulated. Your future wife is beautiful."

Li Yuan returned the smile, feeling a slight warmth at his neck. The boy's gaze was so direct, so self-contained. It made him recall what his father had told him of the boy.

"I'm glad you could come. My father tells me you are an excellent painter."

"He does?" Again the words, like the gesture, seemed only a token; the very minimum of social response. Ben turned his head away, looking up at the painting once again, the forcefulness of his gaze making Li Yuan lift his eyes as if to try to see what he was seeing.

It was a landscape – a *shan shui* study of "mountains and water" – by the Sung painter, Kuo Hsi. The original of his *Early Spring*, painted in 1072.

"I was watching you," Li Yuan said. "From across the room. I saw how you were drawn to this."

"It's the only *living* painting here," Ben answered, his eyes never leaving the painting. "The rest . . ."

His shrug was the very symbol of dismissiveness.

"What do you mean?"

"I mean, the rest of it's dead. Mere mechanical gesture. The kind of thing a machine might produce. But this is different."

Li Yuan looked back at Ben, studying him intently, fascinated by him. No one had ever spoken to him like this; as if it did not matter who he was. But it was not simply that there was no flattery in Ben's words, no concession to the fact that he, Li Yuan was Prince and heir; Ben seemed to have no conception of those "levels" other men took so much for granted. Even his father, Hal, was not like this.

Li Yuan laughed, surprised; not sure whether he was pleased or otherwise.

"How? How is it different?"

"For a start it's aggressive. Look at the muscular shapes of those trees, the violent tumble of those rocks. There's nothing soft, nothing tame about it. The very forms are powerful. But it's more than that – the artist captured the *essence* – the very pulse of life – in all he saw." Ben laughed shortly, then turned and looked at him. "I've seen such trees, such rocks . . ."

"In your valley?"

Ben shook his head, his eyes holding Li Yuan's almost insolently. "No. In my dreams."

"Your dreams?"

Ben seemed about to answer, but then he smiled and looked past Li Yuan. "Fei Yen . . ."

Li Yuan turned to welcome his betrothed.

She came and stood beside him, touching his arm briefly, almost tenderly. "I see you two have found each other at last."

"Found?" Ben said quietly. "I don't follow you."

Fei Yen laughed softly, the fan moving slowly in her hand. Her perfume filled the air about them. "Li Yuan said earlier how much he wanted to speak to you."

"I see . . ."

Li Yuan saw how Ben looked at her and felt a pang of jealousy. It was as if he saw her clearly, perfectly; those dark, intense eyes of his taking in everything at a glance.

What do you see? he wondered. *You seem to see so much, Ben Shepherd. Ah, but would you tell me? Would even you be that open?*

"Ben lives outside," he said after a moment. "In the Domain. It's a valley in the Western Island."

"It must be beautiful," she said, lowering her eyes. "Like Tongjiang."

"Oh it is," Ben said, his eyes very still, watching her. "It's another world. But small. Very small. You could see it all in an afternoon."

704

Then, changing tack, he smiled and turned his attention to Li Yuan again. "I wanted to give you something, Prince Yuan. A gift of some kind. But I didn't know quite what."

It was unexpected. Li Yuan hesitated, his mind a blank, but Fei Yen answered for him.

"Why not draw him for me?"

Ben's smile widened, as if in response to her beauty, then slowly faded from his lips. "Why not?"

They went through to the anteroom while servants were sent to bring paper and brushes and inks, but when it arrived Ben waved the pots and brushes aside and, taking a pencil from his jacket pocket, sat at the table, pulling a piece of paper up before him.

"Where shall I sit?" Li Yuan asked, knowing from experience how much fuss was made by artists. The light, the background – everything had to be just so. "Here, by the window? Or over here by the *kang*?"

Ben glanced up at him. "There's no need. I have you. Here." He tapped his forehead, then lowered his head again, his hand moving swiftly, decisively across the paper's surface.

Fei Yen laughed and looked at him, then, taking his hand, began to lead him away. "We'll come back," she said. "When he's finished."

But Li Yuan hesitated. "No," he said gently, so as not to offend her. "I'd like to see. It interests me . . ."

Ben looked up again, indicating that he should come across. Again it was a strange, unexpected thing to do, for who but a T'ang would beckon a prince in that manner? And yet, for once, it seemed quite natural.

"Stand there," Ben said. "Out of my light. Yes. That's it."

He watched. Saw how the figures appeared, like ghosts out of nothingness, onto the whiteness of the paper. Slowly the paper filled. A tree, a clutch of birds, a moon. And then, to the left, a figure on a horse. An archer. He caught his breath as the face took form. It was himself. A tiny mirror-image of his face.

"Why have you drawn me like that?" he asked, when it was done. "What does it mean?"

705

Ben looked up. On the far side of the table Fei Yen was staring down at the paper, her lips parted in astonishment. "Yes," she said, echoing her future husband. "What does it mean?"

"The tree," Ben said. "That's the legendary *fu-sang*, the hollow mulberry tree – the dwelling place of kings and the hiding place of the sun. In the tree are ten birds. They represent the ten suns of legend which the great archer, the Lord Shen Yi, did battle with. You recall the legend? Mankind was in danger from the intense heat of the ten suns. But the Lord Yi shot down nine of the suns, leaving only the one we know today."

Li Yuan laughed, surprised that he had not seen the allusion. "And I . . . I am meant to be the Lord Yi?"

He stared at the drawing, fascinated, astonished by the simple power of the composition. It was as if he could feel the horse rearing beneath him, his knees digging into its flanks as he leaned forward to release the arrow, the bird pierced through its chest as it rose, silhouetted against the great white backdrop of the moon. Yes, there was no doubting it. It was a masterpiece. And he had watched it shimmer into being.

He looked back at Ben, bowing his head, acknowledging the sheer mastery of the work. But his admiration was tainted. For all its excellence there was something disturbing, almost frightening about the piece.

"Why this?" he asked, staring openly at Ben now, frowning, ignoring the others who had gathered to see what was happening.

Ben signed the corner of the paper, then set the pencil down. "Because I dreamt of you like this."

"You dreamt . . . ?" Li Yuan laughed uneasily. They had come to this point before. "You dream a lot, Ben Shepherd."

"No more than any man . . ."

"But this . . . Why did you dream this?"

Ben laughed. "How can I tell? What a man dreams – surely he has no control over that?"

"Maybe so . . ." But still he was thinking, Why this? For he knew the rest of the story – how Lord Yi's wife, Chang-e, goddess of the moon, had stolen the herb of immortality and fled to the moon. There, for her sins, she had turned into a toad, the dark shadow of which could be seen against the full moon's whiteness. And Lord Yi? Was he hero or monster? The legends were unclear, contradictory, for though he had completed all of the great tasks set him by Pan Ku, the Creator of All, yet he was an usurper who had stolen the wives of many other men.

Ben surely knew the myth. He knew so much, how could he not know the rest of it? Was this then some subtle insult? Some clever, knowing comment on his forthcoming marriage to Fei Yen? Or was it as he said – the innocent setting down of a dream?

He could not say. Nor was there any certain way of telling. He stared at the drawing a moment longer, conscious of the silence that had grown about him, then, looking back at Ben, he laughed.

"You know us too well, Ben Shepherd. What you were talking of – the essence behind the form. Our faces are masks, yet you're not fooled by them, are you? You see right through them."

Ben met his eyes and smiled. "To the bone."

Yes, thought Li Yuan. *My father was right about you. You would be the perfect match for me. The rest are but distorting mirrors, even the finest of them, returning a pleasing image to their lord. But you . . . you would be the perfect glass. Who else would dare to reflect me back so true?*

He looked down, letting his fingers trace the form of the archer, then nodded to himself. "A dream . . ."

* * *

Klaus Ebert roared with laughter, then reached up and drew his son's head down so that all could see. "There! See! And he's proud of it!"

Hans Ebert straightened up again, grinning, looking

707

about him at the smiling faces. He was in full uniform for the occasion, his new rank of major clearly displayed, but that was not what his father had been making all the fuss over – it was the small metal plate he wore, embedded in the back of his skull; a memento of the attack on Hammerfest.

"The trouble is, it's right at the back," he said. "I can't see it in the mirror. But I get my orderly to polish it every morning. Boots, belt and head, I say to him. In that order."

The men in the circle laughed, at ease for the first time in many months. Things were at a dangerous pass in the world outside, but here at Tongjiang it was as if time had stood still. From here the War seemed something distant, illusory. Even so, their conversation returned to it time and again; as if there were nothing else for them to talk of.

"Is there any news of Berdichev?" Li Feng Chiang, the T'ang's second brother, asked. His half-brothers, Li Yun-Ti and Li Ch'i Chun, stood beside him, all three of Li Yuan's uncles dressed in the same calf-length powder blue surcoats; their clothes badges of their rank as Councillors to the T'ang.

"Rumours have it that he's on Mars," General Nocenzi answered, stroking his chin thoughtfully. "There have been other sightings, too, but none of them confirmed. Sometimes I think the rumours are started by our enemies, simply to confuse us."

"Well," Tolonen said. "Wherever he is, my man Karr will find him."

Tolonen was back in uniform, the patch of Marshal on his chest, the four pictograms – *Lu Chun Yuan Shuai* – emblazoned in red on white. It had been the unanimous decision of the Council of Generals, three months before. The appointment had instilled new life into the old man and he seemed his fierce old self again, fired with limitless energy. But it was true also what the younger officers said: in old age his features had taken on the look of something ageless and eternal, like rock sculpted by the wind and rain.

Klaus Ebert, too, had been promoted. Like Li Yuan's uncles, he wore the powder blue of a Councillor proudly, in open defiance of those of his acquaintance who said a *Hung Mao* should not ape a Han. For him it was an honour – the outward sign of what he felt. He smiled at his old friend and leaned across to touch his arm.

"Let us hope so, eh, Knut? The world would be a better place without that carrion, Berdichev, in it. But tell me, have you heard of this new development? These 'messengers', as they're called?"

There was a low murmur and a nodding of heads. They had been in the news a great deal these last few weeks.

Ebert shook his head, his features a mask of horrified bemusement, then spoke again. "I mean, what could make a man do such a thing? They say that they wrap explosives about themselves, and then, when they're admitted to the presence of their victims, trigger them."

"Money," Tolonen answered soberly. "These are low-level types you're talking of, Klaus. They have nothing to lose. It's a way of ensuring their families can climb the levels. They think it a small price to pay for such a thing."

Again Ebert shook his head, as if the concept were beyond him. "Are things so desperate?"

"Some think they are."

But Tolonen was thinking of all he had seen these last few months. By comparison with some of it, these "messengers" were decency itself.

A junior minister and their wife had had their six-month-old baby stolen and sent back in a jar, boiled and then pickled, its eyes like bloated eggs in the raw pinkness of its face. Another man – a rich *Hung Mao* who had refused to cooperate with the rebels – had had his son taken and sold back to him, less his eyes. That was bad enough, but the kidnappers had sewn insects into the hollowed sockets, beneath the lids. The ten-year old was mad when they got him back: as good as dead.

And the culprits? Tolonen shuddered. The inventiveness of their cruelty never ceased to amaze and sicken him. They were no better than the halfmen in the Clay. He felt no remorse in tracking down such men and killing them.

"Marshal Tolonen?"

He half-turned. One of the T'ang's house-servants was standing there, his head bowed low.

"Yes?"

"Forgive me, Excellency, but your daughter is here. At the gatehouse."

Tolonen turned back and excused himself, then followed the servant through and out into the great courtyard.

Jelka was waiting by the ornamental pool. She stood there in the shade of the ancient willow, dropping pebbles into the water and watching the ripples spread. Tolonen stopped, looking across at his daughter, his whole being lit by the sight of her. She was standing with her back to him, the white-gold fall of her hair spilling out across the velvet blue of her full-length cloak. Her two bodyguards stood nearby, looking about them casually, but as Tolonen came nearer they came to attention smartly.

Jelka turned at the sound and, seeing him, dropped the stones and ran across, a great beam of a smile on her face. Tolonen hugged her to him, lifting her up off the ground and closing his eyes to savour the feel of her arms about his back, the softness of her kisses against his neck. It was a full week since they had seen each other last.

He kissed her brow, then set her down, laughing softly.

"What is it?" she said, looking up at him, smiling.

"Just that you're growing so quickly. I won't be able to do that much longer, will I?"

"No . . ." Her face clouded a moment, then brightened again. "I've brought Li Yuan and his betrothed a gift. Erkki has it . . ." She turned and one of the two young guards came across. Taking a small package from his inner pocket, he handed it to her. She smiled her thanks at him, then turned back to her father, showing him the present. It fitted easily into her palm, the silk-paper a bright crimson – the colour of good luck and weddings.

"What is it?" he asked, letting her take his arm as they began the walk back to the palace buildings.

"You'll have to wait," she teased him. "I chose them myself."

He laughed. "And who paid for them, may I ask?"

"You, of course," she said, squeezing his arm. "But that's not the point. I want it to be a surprise, and you're useless at keeping secrets!"

"Me?" He mimed outrage, then roared with laughter. "Ah, but don't let the T'ang know that, my love, or your father will be out of a job!"

She beamed up at him, hitting him playfully. "You know what I mean. Not the big ones – the little secrets . . ."

They had come to the main entrance to the Halls. While a servant took Jelka's cloak, Tolonen held the tiny package. He sniffed at it, then put it to his ear and shook it.

"It rattles . . ."

She turned and took it back off him, her face stern, admonishing him. "Don't! They're delicate."

"They?" He looked at her, his face a mask of curiosity, but she only laughed and shook her head.

"Just wait. It won't be long now . . ."

Her voice trailed off, her eyes drawn to something behind him.

"What is it?" he said quietly, suddenly very still, seeing how intent her eyes were, as if something dangerous and deadly were at his back.

"Just something you were saying, the last time General Nocenzi came for dinner. About all the ways there are of killing people."

He wanted to turn – to confront whatever it was – but her eyes seemed to keep him there. "And?" he said, the hairs at his neck bristling now.

"And Nocenzi said the simplest ways are always the most effective."

"So?"

"So behind you there's a table. And on the table is what looks like another gift. But I'm wondering what a gift is doing, lying there neglected on that table. And why it should be wrapped as it is, in white silk."

711

Tolonen turned and caught his breath. "Gods . . ."

It was huge, like the great seal the T'ang had lifted earlier, but masked in the whiteness of death.

"Guard!" he barked, turning to look across at the soldier in the doorway.

"Sir?" The guard came across at once.

"Who left this here?"

The look of utter bemusement on the soldier's face confirmed it for him. It was a bomb. Someone had smuggled a bomb into the Palace.

"No one's been here," the soldier began. "Only the T'ang's own servants . . ."

Tolonen turned away, looking back up the corridor. There were three other guards, stationed along the corridor. He yelled at them. "Here! All of you! Now!"

He watched as they carried the thing outside, their bodies forming a barrier about the package. Then, his heart pounding in his chest, he turned to Jelka, kneeling down and drawing her close to him.

"Go in. Tell the T'ang what has happened. Then tell Nocenzi to get everyone into the cellars. At once. Interrupt if you must. Li Shai Tung will forgive you this once, my little one."

He kissed her brow, his chest rising and falling heavily, then got up. She smiled back at him, then ran off to do as he had told her. He watched her go – saw her childish, slender figure disappear into the Hall – then turned and marched off towards the Gatehouse, not knowing if he would ever see her again.

* * *

Nocenzi and young Ebert met him returning from the Gatehouse.

"Is it a bomb?" Nocenzi asked, his face grim.

"No . . ." Tolonen answered distractedly, but his face was drawn, all colour gone from it.

Nocenzi gave a short laugh of relief. "Then what is it, Knut?"

Tolonen turned momentarily, looking back, then faced them again, shaking his head. "They're bringing it now. But come. I have to speak to the T'ang. Before he sees it."

★ ★ ★

Li Shai Tung got up from his chair as Tolonen entered and came across the room to him. "Well, Knut, what is it?"

"*Chieh Hsia* . . ." Tolonen looked about him at the sea of faces gathered in the huge, lantern-lit cellar, then bowed his head. "If I might speak to you alone."

"Is there any danger?"

"No, *Chieh Hsia*."

The T'ang breathed deeply, then turned to his son. "Yuan. Take our guests back upstairs. I will join you all in a moment."

They waited, the T'ang, Tolonen, Nocenzi and the young Major, as the guests filed out, each stopping to bow to the T'ang before they left. Then they were alone in the huge, echoing cellar.

"It was not a bomb, then, Knut?"

Tolonen straightened up, his face grave, his eyes strangely pained. "No, *Chieh Hsia*. It was a gift. A present for your son and his future bride."

Li Shai Tung frowned. "Then why this?"

"Because I felt it was something you would not want Li Yuan to have. Perhaps not even to know about."

The T'ang stared at him a moment, then looked away, taking two steps then turning to face him again.

"Why? What kind of gift is it?"

Tolonen looked past him. There were faint noises on the steps leading down to the great cellar. "It's here now, *Chieh Hsia*. Judge for yourself."

They brought it in and set it down on the floor in front of Li Shai Tung. The wrapping lay over the present loosely, the white silk cut in several places.

"Was there a card?" The T'ang asked, looking up from it.

Tolonen bowed his head. "There was, *Chieh Hsia*."

"I see . . . But I must guess, eh?" There was a hint of mild impatience in the T'ang's voice that made Tolonen start forward.

"Forgive me, *Chieh Hsia*. Here . . ."

Li Shai Tung studied the card a moment, reading the brief, unsigned message, then looked back at Tolonen. He was silent a moment, thoughtful, then, almost impatiently, he crouched down on his haunches and threw the silk back.

Li Shai Tung looked across at Tolonen. The Marshal, like Nocenzi and young Ebert, had knelt, so as not to be above the T'ang.

The T'ang's eyes were filled with puzzlement. "But this is a *wei chi* board, Knut. And a good one, too. Why should Li Yuan not have this or know of it?"

In answer Tolonen reached out and took the lids from the two wooden pots that held the stones.

"But that's wrong . . ." the T'ang began. Then he fell silent.

Wei chi was played with black and white stones: one hundred and eighty-one black stones and one hundred and eighty white. Enough to fill the nineteen by nineteen board completely. But this set was different.

Li Shai Tung dipped his hands into each of the bowls and scattered the stones across the board. They were all white. Every last one. He lifted the bowls and upended them, letting the stones spill out onto the board, filling it.

"They feel odd," he said, rubbing one of the stones between thumb and forefinger, then met Tolonen's eyes again. "They're not glass."

"No, *Chieh Hsia*. They're bone. Human bone."

The T'ang nodded, then got up slowly, clearly shaken. His fingers pulled at his plaited beard distractedly.

"You were right, Knut. This is not something I would wish Yuan to know of."

He turned, hearing a noise behind him. It was Klaus Ebert. The old man bowed low. "Forgive me for intruding, *Chieh Hsia*, but I felt you would want to know at once. It seems we have unearthed part of the mystery."

Li Shai Tung frowned. "Go on . . ."

Ebert glanced up, his eyes taking in the sight of the *wei chi* board and the scattered stones. "The search of the palace Marshal Tolonen ordered has borne fruit. We have discovered who placed the present on the table."

"And is he dead or alive?"

"Dead, I'm afraid, *Chieh Hsia*. He was found in one of the small scullery cupboards in the kitchens. Poisoned, it seems. By his own hand."

The T'ang glanced at Tolonen, his eyes suddenly black with fury. "Who was it? Who would *dare* to bring such a thing into my household?"

"One of your bondservants, *Chieh Hsia*," Ebert answered. "The one you knew as Chung Hsin."

Li Shai Tung's eyes widened, then he shook his head in disbelief. "Chung Hsin . . ." It was inconceivable. Why, Li Shai Tung had raised him from a three-year-old in this household. Had named him for his strongest quality.

Yes, *Chung Hsin*, he'd named him. *Loyalty*.

"Why?" he groaned. "In the gods' names, why?"

Ebert was staring at the board now, frowning, not understanding. He looked across at Tolonen. "Is that what he delivered?"

Tolonen nodded tersely, more concerned for the state of his T'ang than in answering his old friend.

"Then why did he kill himself?"

It was the T'ang who answered Ebert's question. "Because of the message he delivered."

"Message?" Old Man Ebert looked back at his T'ang, bewildered.

Li Shai Tung pointed down at the board, the scattered stones.

"The board . . . that is Chung Kuo. And the white stones . . ." He shuddered and wet his lips before continuing. "They represent death. It is a message, you see. From our friend, DeVore. It says he means to kill us all. To fill Chung Kuo with the dead."

Tolonen looked up sharply at mention of DeVore. So the T'ang understood that too. Of course . . .

Ebert was staring at the board now, horrified. "But I thought stones were symbols of longevity?"

"Yes . . ." The T'ang's laughter was bitter. "But Knut has had them tested. These stones are made of human bone. They will outlast you and I, certainly, but they symbolise nothing but themselves. Nothing but death."

"And yet it might have been worse, surely? It could have been a bomb."

Li Shai Tung studied his Councillor a moment, then slowly shook his head. "No. No bomb could have been quite as eloquent as this." He sighed, then turned to Nocenzi. "Take it away and destroy it, General. And Klaus . . ." He turned back. ". . . say nothing of this to anyone. Understand me? If Li Yuan should get to hear of this . . ."

Ebert bowed his head. "As you wish, *Chieh Hsia*."

* * *

Li Yuan had been watching for his father. He had seen the guards come and go with the mystery package; had seen both Old Man Ebert and the Marshal emerge from the cellar, grim-faced and silent, and knew, without being told, that something dreadful must have happened.

When Li Shai Tung finally came from the cellar, Yuan went across to him, stopping three paces from him to kneel, his head bowed.

"Is there anything I can do, father?"

His father seemed immensely tired. "Thank you, my son, but there is nothing to be done. It was all a mistake, that's all."

"And Chung Hsin . . . ?"

His father was quiet a moment, then he sighed. "That was unfortunate. I grieve for him. He must have been very unhappy."

"Ah . . ." Yuan lowered his head again, wondering whether he should ask directly what had been beneath the white silk. But he sensed his father would not answer him. And to ask a question that could not be answered would merely anger him, so he held his tongue.

He searched for a way to lighten the mood of things, and as he did so his fingers closed upon the eight tiny pieces in the pocket of his ceremonial jacket.

He looked up, smiling. "Can I show you something, father?"

Li Shai Tung smiled bleakly back at him. "Yes . . . But get off your knees, Yuan. Please . . . This is your day. We are here to honour you."

Yuan bowed his head, then stood and moved closer to his father. "Hold out your hand, father. They're small, so it's best if you look at them closely. They're what the Marshal's daughter gave us for a betrothal gift. Aren't they beautiful?"

Li Shai Tung stared at the tiny figures in his hand. And then he laughed. A loud, ringing laughter of delight.

"Knut!" he said, looking past his son at the old Marshal. "Why didn't you say? Why didn't you tell me what your daughter had brought?"

Tolonen glanced at his daughter, then stepped forward, puzzled.

"What is it, *Chieh Hsia*?"

"You mean you do not know?"

Tolonen shook his head.

"Then look. They are the eight heroes. The eight honourable men."

Tolonen stared at the tiny, sculpted pieces that rested in the T'ang's palm, then laughed, delighted. "It's an omen," he said, meeting the T'ang's eyes. "What else can it be?"

The T'ang nodded and then began to laugh again, his laughter picked up by those nearest until it filled the Hall.

He looked down at the tiny figures in his palm. How many times had he seen them on the stage, their faces blacked to represent their honour? And now here they were, sculpted from eight black stones! It was as Knut said;

it was an omen. A sign from the gods. These eight to set against the vast, colourless armies of the dead.

Yuan was standing nearby, his mouth open in astonishment. "What is it?" he asked. "What have I missed?"

In answer the T'ang placed the pieces back in his son's palm and closed his fingers tightly over them.

"Guard these well, Yuan. Keep them with you at all times. Let them be your talismen."

His son stared back at him, wide-eyed, then, with the vaguest shake of the head, he bowed low. "As my father wishes . . ."

But Li Shai Tung had let his head fall back again, a great gust of laughter rippling out from him, like a huge stone dropped into the centre of a pond.

Let him hear of this, he thought. Let DeVore's spy report to him how the T'ang laughed in his face defiantly. And let him learn, too, of the second gift of stones – of the eight dark heroes; the eight men of honour.

Let him hear. For I will place the last stone on his grave.

END OF BOOK ONE

AUTHOR'S NOTE

The transcription of standard Mandarin into a European alphabetical form was first achieved in the seventeenth century by the Italian, Matteo Ricci, who founded and ran the first Jesuit Mission in China from 1583 until his death in 1610. Since then several dozen attempts have been made to reduce the original Chinese sounds, represented by some tens of thousands of separate pictograms, into readily understandable phonetics for western use. For a long time, however, three systems dominated – those used by the three major western powers vying for influence in the corrupt and crumbling Chinese Empire of the nineteenth century: Great Britain, France and Germany. These systems were the Wade-Giles (Great Britain and America – sometimes known as the Wade System), the Ecole Française de l'Extrême Orient (France) and the Lessing (Germany).

Since 1958, however, the Chinese themselves have sought to create one single phonetic form, based on the German system, which they termed the *hanyu pinyin fang'an* (Scheme for a Chinese Phonetic Alphabet), known more commonly as *pinyin*, and in all foreign language books published in China since January 1st 1979 *pinyin* has been used, as well as being taught now in schools alongside the standard Chinese characters. For this work, however, I have chosen to use the older, and to my mind, far more elegant transcription system, the Wade-Giles (in modified form). For those now used to the harder forms of *pinyin* the following may serve as a basic conversion guide, the Wade-Giles first, the *pinyin* after.

p for b	ch' for q
ts' for c	j for r
ch' for ch	t' for t
t for d	hs for x
k for g	ts for z
ch for j	ch for zh

The effect is, I hope, to render the softer, more poetic side of the original Mandarin, ill-served, I feel, by modern *pinyin*.

The version of the *I Ching* or BOOK OF CHANGES quoted from throughout is the Richard Wilhelm translation, rendered into English by Cary F. Baynes and published by Routledge & Kegan Paul, London, 1951.

The translation of Ch'u Yuan's *T'ien Wen*, or "Heavenly Questions" is by David Hawkes from THE SONGS OF THE SOUTH, AN ANTHOLOGY OF ANCIENT CHINESE POEMS, published by Penguin Books, London, 1985.

The translation of Meng Chiao's "The Stones Where The Haft Rotted" and Li Shang-yin's "Exile" are by A. C. Graham from POEMS OF THE LATE T'ANG, published by Penguin Books, London, 1965.

The translation of Miu Hsi's "Bearer's Song" (from HAN BURIAL SONGS) is by Arthur Waley, from CHINESE POEMS, published by George Allen & Unwin, London, 1946.

The translation of Chiang Yen's "Lady Pan's 'Poem on the Fan'", from the *Yu T'ai Hsin Yung*, is by Anne Birrell, from her annotated version of NEW SONGS FROM A JADE TERRACE, published by George Allen & Unwin, London, 1982.

The quotation from Rainer Maria Rilke's *Duino Elegies* is from the Hogarth Press, fourth edition, 1968, translated by J. B. Leishman and Stephen Spender.

The game of *Wei Chi* mentioned throughout this volume is, incidentally, more commonly known by its Japanese name of *Go*, and is not merely the world's oldest game but its most elegant. As far as this author knows it has no connection to the trigram of the same name in the *I Ching* – the sixty-fourth, "Before Completion", but a playful similarity of the kind beloved of the Han might possibly be noted.

Finally, THE GAME OF WEI CHI by D. Pecorini and T. Shu (with a Foreword by Professor H. A. Giles) is a real book and was published by Longmans, Green & Co. in 1929. It is, alas, long out of print, and I have Brian Aldiss to thank for my much-treasured copy. It's my fond hope that its use herein might some day lead to the re-publication of this slender classic.

David Wingrove, December 1988

GLOSSARY OF
MANDARIN TERMS

It is not intended to belabour the reader with a whole mass of arcane Han expressions here. Most, it will be found, are explained in context. However, as a few Mandarin terms are used naturally in the text, I've thought it best to provide a brief explanation of those terms here.

catty – the colloquial term for a unit of measure formally called a *jin*. One catty – as used here – equals roughly 1.1 pounds (avoirdupois), or (exactly) 500gm. Before 1949 and the standardisation of Chinese measures to a metric standard, this measure varied district by district, but was generally regarded as equalling about 1.33 pounds (avoirdupois).

chang – ten *ch'i*, thus about 12 feet (Western).

ch'i – a Chinese foot; approximately 14.4 inches.

chi'an – a general term for money.

chieh hsia – term meaning "Your Majesty", derived from the expression "Below the Steps". It was the formal way of addressing the Emperor, through his Ministers, who stood "below the steps".

ch'un tzu – an ancient Chinese term from the Warring States period, describing a certain class of nobleman, controlled by a code of chivalry and morality known as the *li*, or rites. Here the term is roughly, and sometimes ironically, translated as "gentlemen". The *ch'un tzu* is as much an ideal state of behaviour – as specified by Confucius in the *Analects*

– as an actual class in Chung Kuo, though a degree of financial independence and a high standard of education are assumed a prerequisite.

fen – a unit of currency; see *yuan*. It has another meaning, that of a "minute" of clock time, but that usage is avoided here to prevent any confusion.

fu jen –"Madam", used here as opposed to *t'ai t'ai* –"Mrs".

hsiao jen –"little man/men". In the *Analects*, Book XIV, Confucius writes: "The gentleman gets through to what is up above; the small man gets through to what is down below." This distinction between "gentlemen" (*ch'un tzu*) and "little men" (*hsiao jen*), false even in Confucius' time, is no less a matter of social perspective in Chung Kuo.

hsien – historically an administrative district of variable size. Here the term is used to denote a very specific administrative area; one of ten stacks – each stack composed of 30 decks. Each deck is a hexagonal living unit of ten levels, two *li*, or approximately one kilometre in diameter. A stack can be imagined as one honeycomb in the great hive that is the City.

Kuan Yin – the goddess of mercy. Originally the Buddhist male bodhisattva, Avalokitsevara (translated into Han as "He who listens to the sounds of the world", or "*Kuan Yin*"), the Han mistook the well-developed breasts of the saint for a woman's and, since the 9th century, have worshipped Kuan Yin as such. Effigies of Kuan Yin will show her usually as the Eastern Madonna, cradling a child in her arms. She is also sometimes seen as the wife of Kuan Kung, the Chinese God of War.

Kuo-yu – Mandarin, the language spoken in Mainland China. Also rendered here as *Kuan hua*.

li – a Chinese "mile", approximating to half a kilometre or one-third of a mile. Until 1949, when metric measures were adopted in China, the *li* could vary from place to place.

liang – a Chinese ounce of roughly 32gm. 16 *liang* form a *catty*.

mao – a unit of currency; see *yuan*.

mei mei – younger/little sister.

mou – a Chinese "acre" of approximately 7,260 square feet. There are roughly six *mou* to a Western acre, and a 10,000-*mou* field would approximate to 1666 acres, or just over two and a half square miles.

shanshui – the literal meaning is "mountains and water", but the term is normally associated with a style of landscape painting which depicts rugged mountain scenery with river valleys in the foreground. It is a highly popular form, first established in the T'ang Dynasty, back in the seventh to ninth centuries AD.

shih –"Master". Here used as a term of respect somewhat equivalent to our use of "Mister". The term was originally used for the lowest level of civil servants, to distinguish them socially from the run-of-the-mill "Misters" (*hsian sheng*) below them and the gentlemen (*ch'un tzu*) above.

ts'un – a Chinese "inch" of approximately 1.4 Western inches. 10 *ts'un* form one *ch'i*.

weng –"Old Man". Usually a term of respect.

wu-tong – a tree of the Paulownia family. Its wood is often used to make lutes (*ch'in*).

Yuan – the basic currency of Chung Kuo (and modern-day China). Colloquially (though not here) it can also be termed *kuai* –"piece" or "lump". Ten *mao* (or, formally, *jiao*) make up one *yuan*, while 100 *fen* (or "cents") comprise one *yuan*.

ACKNOWLEDGMENTS

Thanks must go to all those who have read and criticised parts of the many different drafts of CHUNG KUO over the five years of its creating: to my good friends and "Writers' Bloc" companions – Chris Evans, David Garnett, Rob Holdstock, Garry Kilworth, Bobbie Lamming, Lisa Tuttle and Geoff Ryman – for honing the cutting edge; to John Murry – alias Richard Cowper – both for sharing what he knew, and for long years of patient husbandry; to my brother Ian, much-loved, ever-enthusiastic; to Ritchie Smith, friend, drinking companion and "Great Man"; to Andrew Motion – for finding "A Perfect Art" not so perfect and giving good reasons; and to my agents, Hilary Rubinstein and Clarissa Rushdie – long may they remain so. Their comments have helped me avoid many pitfalls and – without doubt – given shape to the final manuscript.

I would also like to offer thanks to Bruce Sterling for the inspiration given by his excellent novel, *Schismatrix* . . . and for five of his words, now embedded in my text.

I reserve special thanks for two friends whose encouragement, advice and criticism throughout have been invaluable: Brian Griffin for unerringly knowing (better than me sometimes) what I'm up to, and Robert Carter not merely for the introduction to *Wei Chi* and his patient and astute reading of the emergent book, but for all the long years of friendship. To you both, *Kan Pei*!

To my editors, Nick Sayers at New English Library and Brian DeFiore at Delacorte, I can only say thanks for the many kindnesses, and for making the whole business of editing so enjoyable. Their patience, cheerfulness and encouragement at the final stages were much more than I could ever have hoped for. I'm looking forward to the journey to come.

To Christian Vander and Magma, for the music . . .

Finally, thanks to my partner-in-crime, Brian Aldiss. If anyone's shadow lies behind this work, I guess it's yours. This is delivery on the Planetarium speech that time!

In Times to Come . . .

This epic tale continues in Book Two, *Chung Kuo: The Broken Wheel*.

Five years after the destruction of the starship *The New Hope*, the Council of Seven is preparing to meet and discuss the way ahead. In the long and bitter war they have just fought they have emerged triumphant but greatly weakened. The days of speaking with one voice are past and there is dissension among them.

But DeVore thrives on such dissension and, ruthlessly casting off his First Level co-conspirators, makes a new alliance among those disinherited billions in the lowest levels of the City.

The problems for the Seven are vast. Even so, there is one solution which – even if it leaves the underlying malaise untreated – might yet prove successful.

Li Yuan's plan is to "wire up" the whole population of Chung Kuo; placing delicate electronics in every citizen's head that would enable the Seven to trace and thus control them. Among those brought in to try to make the "wire" a reality is the young Clay-born boy, Kim Ward.

Ben Shepherd, meanwhile, discovers an artistic vocation, and soon the unexpected happens – this cold and seemingly distant young man falls in love.

For the young Prince, too, love is a distraction from his work, the fulfilment of a long cherished dream. But his love is far from the fragile, compliant creature she outwardly appears.

Chung Kuo: The Broken Wheel sees a quickening of the pace of events as the Great Wheel turns into a new, more dangerous phase.